MURDER MOST
MOST

CONFEDERATE

CELTIC

MERRY

Other Titles in Random House Value's
Murder Most Series

Murder Most Romantic
Murder Most Medieval
Murder Most Divine
Murder Most Postal
Murder Most Delectable
Murder Most Feline

MURDER MOST CONFEDERATE

EDITED BY MARTIN H. GREENBERG

MURDER MOST CELTIC

EDITED BY MARTIN H. GREENBERG

MURDER MOST MERRY

EDITED BY ABIGAIL BROWNING

GRAMERCY BOOKS
NEW YORK

This 2005 edition published by Gramercy Books,
an imprint of Random House Value Publishing, a division of
Random House, Inc., New York, by arrangement with
Cumberland House Publishing, Nashville, TN, for *Murder Most Confederate*,
edited by Martin H. Greenberg and *Murder Most Celtic*, edited by
Martin H. Greenberg and by arrangement with Dell Magazines, New York,
for *Murder Most Merry*, edited by Abigail Browning.

Pages 273, 575, and 961-962 constitute an extension of this copyright page.

Gramercy is a registered trademark and the colophon
is a trademark of Random House, Inc.

Random House
New York • Toronto • London • Sydney • Auckland
www.randomhouse.com

Printed in the United States of America

Catalog records for these titles are available from the Library of Congress.

ISBN 0-307-29022-0

CONTENTS

Murder Most Confederate

Tales of Crimes Quite Uncivil

Contents

Introduction

The War Between the States. The War of the Rebellion. The War of Northern Aggression. The North versus the South. A conflict fought by one-half of a nation against the other more than a century ago, and a conflict that inspires close examination and deep passion even today.

With a higher casualty rate than any other war involving our nation, the Civil War threatened to tear a relatively young United States apart just when it was on the cusp of becoming a powerful nineteenth-century force. Divided by economic, political, and social issues such as individual states' sovereign rights, industrial vs. agrarian economies, and slavery, the nation was a powder keg of dissent waiting for a fateful match. On December 20, 1860, South Carolina voted to repeal the U.S. Constitution. They were followed by Mississippi, Florida, Alabama, Georgia, Louisiana, Texas, Virginia, Arkansas, Tennessee, and North Carolina. Thousands of men flocked together to rally behind their respective banners. In the South the conflict was seen as a call to arms to preserve their continued way of life and states' rights. For the North this, too, was a war of great importance, as they saw themselves battling to hold a young nation together.

Actual hostilities didn't commence until April 12, 1861, when General P. G. T. Beauregard exercised orders to fire upon Fort Sumter in South Carolina, then held by Union troops. The Confederates unleashed a firestorm that would rage from the Pennsylvania valleys of Gettysburg to the twisted wreckage of Georgia in the wake of General Sherman's infamous march to the sea. More than three million men donned either Union blue or Rebel gray and marched into a war that lasted four and a half years. When the cannons finally fell silent, almost half a million men lay dead, and America was still one nation, but at a terrible price.

The South began the war seemingly outmanned, outsupplied, and outgunned, but what they lacked in men, materials, and equipment they made up for in the brilliance of their military leaders—men like Robert E. Lee, Thomas "Stonewall" Jackson, and Nathan Bedford Forrest—and the tenacity and spirit of the men they commanded. The courage and honor of the men who fought for the Confederacy still exist in the men and women of the region, and the ideals the South fought for, especially the sovereign rights of the state, are still upheld, although now more as a tribute to what had been lost after the war.

Of course, when a nation's attention is turned toward something as significant as war, opportunities for other crimes present themselves. Against the backdrop of brother fighting brother and cities and states under siege, civilians and soldiers alike could use the cover of conflict to steal, cheat, spy, and even murder, for whatever reason, whether it be for the honor of their cause or pure personal gain. Sometimes, the crimes committed because of war can be the most terrible of all.

With that in mind, we've assembled this all-new anthology of crime and mystery stories set in the Confederacy. From the war-torn city of Richmond, Virginia, where a husband and wife run an unusual boarding house, to the story of two brothers fighting on opposite sides of the war, and of the terrible price one of them pays for happiness. From men and women doing their duty for their country to rogues and criminals committing crimes obscured by the ongoing horrors of the Civil War, the savage side of war is revealed is these stories of murder most Confederate.

—John Helfers

Murder Most Confederate

The Hessian

Doug Allyn

Horsemen drifted out of the dawn mist like wolves, strung out loosely across the hillside in a ragged line. Two outriders on the flanks, seven more in the main body. Polly guessed they'd already put riflemen in position at the stone fence beyond her barn, ready to cut down anyone who tried to run.

Her son was sitting on the corner of the porch, whetting the scythe, daydreaming.

"Jason," Polly said quietly. "Riders are coming. Get to the barn. And walk! All the way."

Without a word the ten-year-old rose and sauntered across the yard as he'd been taught, toting a hay blade longer than he was tall. He disappeared inside. A moment later the upper loading loft door opened a crack.

Picking up a besom broom, Polly casually swept her way across the porch to the front door of the farmhouse. She opened it to sweep off the sill, leaving it ajar as she turned to face the riders coming across the stubbled fields to the house.

Federals. Of a sort. Only one rider was in full uniform—a Union cavalry captain; tall, hollow-eyed, and gaunt as a vulture, with a thin mustache and goatee. His men were

3

irregulars, dressed in a mix of work clothes and uniform coats or pants. Farmers and tradesmen from the look of them. Definitely Union, though. Their mounts were sleek and well fed. She'd heard Forrest's men were slaughtering their horses for food.

The riders sized her up as they filed into the yard. A farm wife, square as a stump in a man's flannel shirt, canvas trousers, and pebble-leg boots; handsome once, but care-worn now, auburn hair awry in the November wind, her hands reddened and rough from field work.

Polly scanned their faces, desperately hoping to recognize someone—damn. Aaron Meachum was with them, slouch hat down over his eyes, stubbled cheek distorted by a plug of chaw. Trouble. Casually, she sidled half a step closer to the door.

"Good day to you, ma'am," their leader said softly. "I am Captain Charles Gilliaume, of the Eighth Missouri. My men and I—"

"These men aren't Eighth Missouri," Polly said coldly. "They're militia. Hessians, most likely."

"Hessians?"

"It's what these Rebs call the kraut-heads," Meachum said. "Like them German mercenaries back in the revolution? Most of Sigel's troops was Germans from Saint Louis when they raided through here in '62."

"I see," The captain nodded. "You're quite right, ma'am. My men are a militia unit from Jefferson City, and many of them are of German heritage. But they're as American as you or I now. May we step down?"

"Captain, there is a creek on the far side of my garden. You're welcome to water your animals. I have nothing more to offer you. We've been picked clean by both sides. Hospitality in southern Missouri is runnin' a little thin these days, hard to come by as seed corn."

"She'd find grain quick enough if we were wearin' butternut brown," Aaron Meachum said, spitting a stream of tobacco juice onto her porch. "The whole damn McKee family's secesh; everybody 'round here knows it."

"Is that true, ma'am?" the captain asked. "I see no men about. Are they with the rebels?"

"My husband is in Springfield trying to earn a few dollars. His eldest son is with Bedford Forrest up Tennessee way; his second boy's with the Union blockade at Charleston. The two youngest went off with Sterling Price after he whipped y'all at Wilson's Creek in '61."

"Rebels," Meachum spat.

"Three Confederates," Polly corrected, "and one Federal. At least they're *real* soldiers, Captain."

"As we are, ma'am."

"Real soldiers don't ride with trash. This fella, Aaron Meachum, is a jayhawker who was murdering and burning in Kansas long before the war. He runs easier with coyotes than with men."

"Mr. Meachum isn't actually a member of our unit, ma'am; he was retained as a guide."

"Well, he doubtless knows the trails through these hills. He's used most of them running from the law. If he's your guide, Captain, you're on the road to perdition."

"Armies are like families, ma'am; you can't choose your kin. We're seeking slaves and deserters, Miz McKee. I'm told you have slaves here."

"Who told you that? Meachum? Captain, this ain't no plantation. We raise saddle horses and draft animals, and we're only three days from the Illinois line. Even if we held with slavery, and we don't, it's tough enough to keep animals from runnin' off to say nothin' of men. Our stock's been stolen, our crops burned. We had no slaves before the war and we've surely no need of them now. There's only me and my boy here, you have my word."

"In that case a search won't take long," Gilliaume said. At his nod, the troopers and Meachum began to dismount.

"No!" Polly's voice cracked like a whip, freezing them as she snaked the scattergun from inside the open door, leveling it at Gilliaume, cocking back both hammers.

"Ma'am, be reasonable, you can't possibly prevail against us."

"It won't matter to you, Captain. Or to Meachum. Or to one or two near you. My boy is covering you from the barn with a ten-gauge goose gun loaded with double-ought buckshot. If I fire, so will he."

"You'll still die. As will your son."

"No matter. We've only a little flour and some corn meal. My boy's legs are bowing 'cause Rebs butchered our milk cow. Soldier boys have taken all but the gleanings of the fields. For God's sake, sir, your animals are better fed than most folks around here. We have nothing for you. Unless Old Sam Curtis is passing out medals for murdering women and boys."

Gilliaume stared coolly down at Polly, ignoring the shotgun muzzle, taking her measure. She knew that look. Death had pushed past him to kill his friends so often that he was weary of waiting, impatient for his turn.

But not today. "Gentlemen, the lady says she has no slaves and I believe her. And since there's obviously no forage for us here, we'll move on."

"You're lettin' her run us off?" Meachum said, outraged. "Our orders say deserters, slaves, and arms. She's armed, ain't she?"

"So she is," Gilliaume said wryly. "Personally, I interpret our orders to mean military arms, not rusty shotguns, but you have my permission to disarm her if you wish, Mr. Meachum. But kindly give me a moment to back my mount away. This is my best coat and bloodstains are damned bothersome to remove."

Clucking to his gelding, Gilliaume backed off a few paces, touched his hat brim to Polly, then turned away. The other riders followed. Leaving her to face Meachum alone. She shifted the shotgun, centering it on his chest.

"You got the edge today, Polly McKee." Meachum spat. "But this ain't over. I'll be back."

"But not by daylight I'll wager, you jayhawk son of a bitch. If you ever set foot on my land again, Aaron Meachum, I'll blow you out of your raggedy-ass boots. Now git! *Git!*" she roared into the face of his mount, spooking the beast. It shied away, kicking. Meachum sawed at the reins but the brute's manners were no better than its owner's. Bucking and snorting, it sprinted off to rejoin the others, with Meachum clinging to the saddle horn, cursing his animal and Polly all the way.

The laughter and catcalls that greeted him echoed off the hills. It wasn't much comfort, but it was something.

She waited on the porch, her old scattergun in the crook of her arm, watching the troop splash through the creek and vanish into the woods beyond. And then she waited a bit longer, until she was dead certain they were gone.

Stepping into the house, she carefully stood the shotgun in its customary place by the door. And then, in the sweet-scented silence of her parlor, she released a long, ragged breath. And hugged herself, fiercely, trying to control the trembling.

IT WAS A DAY for visitors. A little before noon, working in the barn, Polly heard the *tlot, tlot* of approaching hoofbeats. Meachum? Not likely, not openly. She peeked out through the crack of the door.

A single-seat Stanhope buggy was coming up the road from the west, a lone woman at the reins. Turning the rig in at the gate, she guided her animal down the long lane, slowing it to a walk as she approached the farmhouse.

Polly stepped out, shading her eyes, waiting. Her visitor was dressed warmly for travel, a fine, seal plush cape over a tailored woolen suit, the first new clothes Polly'd seen since . . . she couldn't remember how long.

"Afternoon, ma'am. Can I help you?"

"Pleasse, I'm becomp lost," the woman replied, her accent harsh. Hessian. Polly's eyes narrowed. "I left Corridon this mornink—"

"Just wheel that buggy around and head out the gate, miss. A mile farther on, the road splits. The north fork will take you to Centerville."

"I'm not going to Centerville."

"Look, ma'am, I haven't got all day—"

"Pleasse, I'm seeking the McKee place," the Hessian woman said desperately. "Is it far from here?"

Polly stepped closer to the buggy, frowning up at the woman. Younger than she thought, face as pale as buttermilk, nearly invisible eyelashes. A bruise and some swelling along her jaw. Still, all in all, a handsome girl, Hessian or not.

"What do you want with the McKees? Who are you?"

"My name is Birgit Randolph. My hussband is Tyler Randolph. He iss a cousin to Angus McKee. He—"

"I'm Polly McKee, Gus's wife. I've known Tyler since he was a sprout, but I still don't know who the hell you are. Tyler ain't married."

"We married earlier this year. We met when he was with the state militia in Saint Louis and became friends. He was very . . . dashing. After the riots he joined General Price. We wrote back and fort' when he was in Arkansas. This past April he came for me and we were married."

"What do you mean he came for you? Came where?"

"To Saint Louis. Tyler iss not a soldier anymore. He was wounded at Pea Ridge. He is discharged now."

"Wounded how? How bad?"

"His leg. Shot. It is mostly healed, but he limps. It causes him pain, I think. He never says. He's very . . . stubborn."

"That sounds like Tyler. Where have y'all been stayin'?"

"At his farm near Mountain Grove."

"I'll be damned," Polly said, shaking her head. It was too much; first, Meachum and his jayhawks, now a half-daft Hessian woman claiming to be kin. The damned war was making the world a madhouse.

"Well, you might as well step in out of the wind, miss—I mean—Mrs. Randolph. I'm afraid we're out of coffee—"

"I haff tea and some sugar," Birgit said, offering Polly a three-pound sack. "Tyler said the plundering hass been bad here."

"We get hit by both sides," Polly conceded grimly, leading the way. "Come into the kitchen, I'll make us some tea."

Birgit hesitated just inside the door. Though the walls hadn't seen paint in years, the small farmhouse was immaculate.

"You have a nice home. Very clean. Even it smells nice."

"What did you expect? A pig pen?"

"No, I—please. I know I don't always say things right but I don't mean to make you angry. I think I've come at a bad time."

"There aren't any good times nowadays. And exactly why have you come, ma'am? What do you want here?"

"Tyler—told me to come to you. He hoped you can drive me to Saint Louis, then bring the buggy back here. He will send for it later."

"Send for the buggy? But not for you? Why? Farm life too rough for your taste?"

"No. I grew up on farm in Bavaria. I'm not afraid of work."

"What then? Ah, the lame dirt farmer isn't a dashing rebel lieutenant anymore? So you go runnin' home to Mama. Sweet Jesus, serves Tyler right for marryin' a Hessian in the first place."

"I'm not Hessian."

"Don't lie to me, I know damned well what you are!"

"I'm not!" Birgit glared, flushing, not backing off an inch. "My family is German, but we are come from Freystadt in Bavaria! Hessians come from *Hesse*! I'm not Hessian! And I didn't leaf Tyler. He drove me out!"

"What are you talking about?"

"It's true! I tell him our child is growing in me, and he got terrible angry. He says I must go back to my family. And I say no, and he says I must obey him. Still I say no. And he . . . struck me!" Her hand strayed to her bruised mouth, her eyes brimming. "And now I am come here, and you are angry with me, too—I don't know why—but I don't anymore know what to do. I don't know what to do!"

Polly knew. Wordlessly, she wrapped the younger woman in her massive arms, holding her while she sobbed like a lost child. Which she was, in a way. Good lord, the girl couldn't be more than seventeen or eighteen. Polly was barely forty, but Birgit's age seemed like a fever dream, dimly remembered now. The low moan of the blue enameled teapot broke the spell.

"I'm sorry," Birgit said, pulling away. "This is my own trouble. I shouldn't burden you."

"Don't talk foolish," Polly said, lifting the kettle off the stove lid, filling two vitreous china mugs. "God help you, girl, we're family now. Sit yourself down at the kitchen table, we'll work something out."

"But how?" Birgit asked numbly, sipping the steaming brew. "Tyler doesn't want me. He doesn't want my child."

"That can't be true. He had to snake through half the damned Union army to marry you. Discharge papers or no, he could have been lynched or thrown in prison any step of the way. Tyler's a stubborn boy; all the Randolphs are, and the McKees, too. There's no quit in any of 'em. If he was willing to risk dyin' to marry you in April, he hasn't changed his mind. There must be more to this. How are things between you two? Has he hit you before?"

"No, never, never. It's been good with us. The best. But this last month, he's . . . dark. Far off. He stays up nights, watching. There are fires in the hills near the farm. Deserters, he says. Or jayhawkers. Then a few days ago, men took our plowhorse. Five of them. Came up on Tyler in the field and just took it. He doesn't speak to me since. I thought telling him of the baby would cheer him but . . ." She swallowed, shaking her head.

Polly sipped her tea, mulling it over. "He's afraid," she said simply.

"Afraid? Tyler?"

"Oh, not of dyin'. After all the warrin' that boy's seen, death's less troublesome than a drunken uncle. It's you he's afraid for. Afraid he can't protect you. Or your child. That's a terrible fear for a man to face, especially a soldier like Tyler. He's seen the killing, knows what can happen. And in his heart, he's afraid of failing you, though I doubt he realizes it."

"So he drives me away?"

"Looks like it."

"What do I do?"

"Depends. Maybe he's right. God knows there's trouble in the wind around here."

"You stay."

"This place is all we've got. You'll be safer in Saint Louis, Birgit. Maybe you should go home."

"No. Tyler is my home."

"You sure about that? You seem awful young to me."

"It's true, I am, maybe. But I know. When I met Tyler, Saint Louis is full of young soldiers. Thousands. And I am at a cotillion, and Tyler is laughing with friends when he sees me. And he walks over and we talk a minute. No more. And I already know."

"Know what?"

Birgit eyed Polly's wind-weathered face a moment, then shrugged. "Laugh if you want, but I look at Tyler and I see . . . our children. I see my life. With him. But maybe you're right, maybe I am just . . . Hessian."

"No. I was wrong about that. And about you. I'm sorry for that. And Tyler was dead wrong to treat you like he done, though I can't fault his reasons."

"I don't care about his reasons. He's wrong to push me away. And I was wrong to leaf. I want to go back."

"It's not that simple. These are dangerous times, he's got good cause to fear for you."

"I know. I am afraid, too. But I'm more afraid to lose him, to lose what we have together."

"Havin' a stout heart's all well and good, darlin', but it ain't hardly enough. There are men in these hills who'd kill you for your horse or a dollar. Or no reason at all. And the truth is, Tyler can't always be there to protect you. You'll have to protect one another. Do you know about guns?"

"A little. Tyler bought me a pocket pistol. He tried to teach me but I'm terrible with it."

"Just like a man," Polly said dryly. "Give the little lady a little gun. Know the trouble with pistols? Men won't believe women can shoot. You have to kill 'em to prove it. Or die tryin'. That there's a woman's gun," she said, indicating a coach shotgun beside the back door. "No skill required, only sand enough to touch it off. You still have to watch out for border trash, but they'd better watch out, too. I can teach all you need to know in twenty minutes. If you'd like."

"Yes, I would. Thank you."

"We'll finish our tea first, talk a little. These days I seldom see other women. I work like a man, dress like one. Sometimes I think I'm turning into one."

"I think you are very much woman, Mrs. McKee. And your home—now don't be mad with me—*is* very clean. It even smells clean. What is that scent?"

"*Eau de Lilac.* Lilac water. Before the war, with the boys home and their clothes and boots and such, sometimes it'd get to smellin' like a horse barn in here. Lilac water helps. I'm surprised you can smell it at all; I've watered it down somethin' fierce tryin' to make it last. The boys each promised to bring me a fresh bottle when they went off soldierin'. "

"You say *boys.* How many?"

"Angus had the four older boys by his first wife, Sarah. She died of the consumption, quite young. It wasn't like you and Tyler with us, me and Gus didn't meet at no dance. I was orphaned, livin' with kin, and Angus needed a mother for his boys. I was only fifteen when we married. We've got a boy of our own now, Jason, and I lost a girl at childbirth. It ain't always been easy, but we've built ourselves a life here. It was a good place before the war. We'll make it so again."

"But you . . . care for him? Your husband?"

"Oh, surely. But Gus is . . . a bit older, set in his ways. But we're a good match, mostly we pull together like a yoked team. But I can't say I've ever had a moment like you talked about, no . . . special feeling like that. We just make the best we can of whatever comes. To be honest, he's been gone so long I wonder sometimes if things will be the same with us . . . afterward."

"Gone to where?"

"The hills. I tell folks he's in Springfield, but he's not. After Price's troops got drove down to Arkansas, both sides were raidin' the border, runnin' off our stock. So Angus took the last of our horses up into the hills. Been movin' around with 'em since, hidin' 'em away so us and the boys can start over when the war ends. If it ever does. When he left we thought it'd be few months, a year at most. Seems like forever now."

"Maybe not much longer. Tyler says it will end soon."

"Darlin', I've been hearin' that ol' song since '61."

"No, it is true. Tyler saw a paper. The Federals have all the Shenandoah Valley. Price's men are scattered. Hood is retreating from Atlanta and the city is burning."

"Atlanta burning? But why?"

Birgit shrugged helplessly. Even in faultless English, no words could explain the madness on the land.

"Dear God," Polly said, slumping back in her chair. "This war may stop someday, but it won't be finished for a hundred years. No wonder the hills are fillin' with deserters and the jayhawkers are on the prowl. Both sides smell blood. You need to get home, girl, if that's what you mean to do. But first I'm gonna teach you a little about killin'. In a lady-like fashion, of course."

In half an hour, Polly instructed Birgit in the basics of the short-barreled coach gun. Pointed and fired at close range, the stunted scattergun would erase anything in its path from a poplar stump to three men standing abreast.

The girl took to the gun as a practical matter, learning to dispense death in defense of herself and her own with no more compunction than killing a coyote after chickens. Or a child.

Neither woman derived the pleasure men take from slaughter. It was a chore to be done, perhaps more dangerous than some, but also more necessary. At the lesson's end Birgit could manage the coach gun competently. And as she seated herself in the buggy to leave, Polly placed the stubby weapon on her lap.

"You take this with you, I've got another. And if there's trouble on the road, don't hesitate. These boys been killin' each other regular for a long time, they're damned quick at it. Surprise and that gun are all you have."

"I'll manage. If nothing else, I think Tyler will hear me out when I explain how things will be with us now."

"I expect he will at that," Polly grinned. "You can make Corridon before dusk. Stay the night there, move on in the morning. You'll be home before supper."

"And in spring, when my time comes for the baby, can I send for you?"

"Of course, darlin', surely. I'll come runnin' and we'll haul that child into this world together. I'll see you then, Mrs. Randolph, maybe sooner if this madness ends and our boys come home. Meantime, you take care, hear?"

Jason brought in a load of kindling he had gathered in the woods and after feeding him, Polly sent him down the valley to stay over with a cousin, as was customary during the nights of a new moon.

But instead of finishing her work in the barn, Polly spent the last of the afternoon cleaning the house, absurdly pleased that Birgit noted how well she kept it. Only women's opinions matter. Men wouldn't notice a slaughtered hog on the sofa unless they had to shift it to sit down.

With the house immaculate, Polly hauled the copper bathtub into the kitchen and put water on to boil. And for a moment, she glimpsed herself in the hall mirror. And couldn't help thinking how fresh and young Birgit looked. Her own face was growing leathery, weathered by the wind and the work. She wondered how Angus saw her now, and wondered if she'd ever truly feel like a woman again . . .

Gunshot. A single blast, echoing down the valley like distant thunder. Polly froze, listening for another. Nothing. Which might be good. Because she was sure she'd recognized the bark of a coach gun. And not many used them. Banking the fire in the kitchen stove, she took her own gun and eased out onto the shaded porch. To wait.

An hour crept by. Half of another. Dusk settled over the hills and still she waited, standing in the shadows. A sliver of silver moon was inching above the trees when she heard the distant drum of hoofbeats nearing, then the clatter of a wagon as the Stanhope buggy burst over the crest of a hill, hurtling madly down the moonlit road toward the farm.

Polly was up and running as the buggy skidded through the gate into the yard. Birgit sawed on the reins, yanking her lathered, gasping animal to a halt. Her face and clothing were mud-smeared and filthy, hair awry, eyes wild.

"What happened?"

"A man came out of the woods, grabbed the horse. I warned him off but he won't let go. I struck him with the buggy whip and he rushed at me, grabbed me, tried to drag me down and"—she swallowed—"and I shot him!

"He pulled me from the buggy as he fell and I ran into the woods. Lost. Couldn't find my way. After a while I came out on the road. And I see the buggy. He's laying by it."

"Dead?"

"I—think so," Birgit said, gulping down a sob. "I'm pretty sure. His head—oh, God. Yes, he's dead. He must be."

"It's all right, girl. You did right. But we're not out of this. Is the body in the road?"

"By the side, yes."

"And the gun? Where is it?"

"I—lost it when I fell. I don't know what happened to it."

"All right, now listen here to me," Polly said, seizing the girl's shoulders. "We have to go back. Now."

"I can't!"

"We *have* to! Don't matter if he was Federal or Reb, if his friends find him kilt they'll come after us, 'specially if that gun's nearby. Too many people know it. I'd go alone, but I might go past him in the dark. Can you find that place again?"

Birgit nodded mutely.

"Good. Wait here. I'll get a shovel."

THEY NEARLY MISSED HIM. Moonlit, dappled with shadows, the road was a slender ribbon threading through the darkness of the hills. Birgit wasn't sure how far she'd traveled or how long she'd been lost. But she recognized the spot. And the crumpled form beside the road.

"Wait here," Polly hissed, stepping down from the buggy, her shotgun leveled. No need. The blast had shredded his upper body. She could smell the reek of death from ten feet away. Not just the stench of blood and voided bowels, but the sickly sweet odor of gangrene as well. Couldn't tell if he was Reb or Federal. Linsey-woolsey shirt drenched with blood, canvas pants, broken-down boots. The strays of both sides had been living off the land so long they much resembled each other. Especially in death.

"Is he . . . ?" Birgit whispered.

"Oh, yes. Dead as a stone. He was dyin' anyway. Got a bandaged wound on his thigh and it was mortifyin'. Gangrene. You probably did the poor bastard a favor, girl. Let's get him underground."

Straining, stumbling, the two women tried to drag the reeking corpse into the trees, but he kept snagging on the underbrush. In the end, Polly lifted him by the shoulders while Birgit took his legs, and they carried him bodily into the forest.

Spotting a natural trench at the base of a fallen sycamore, Polly widened it with her shovel, then they rolled the corpse in and covered it over with dirt and forest debris.

"Leaves are already fallin'," Polly panted, straightening. "A day or two, it'll be like we was never here."

"We should say words for him," Birgit said.

"Pray? For a damn road agent?"

"We can't just leave him like this. It's wrong." Her voice was shaking.

"All right, girl, all right. Do you know what to say?"

"Not—in English."

"Then say it in Hessian. Or whatever that place is you're from."

"Bavaria. But the language is the same."

"Well, I expect the good lord understands 'em all, and this poor devil's beyond carin'. Go ahead."

Kneeling silently in the moist forest mold beside Birgit while she prayed, Polly didn't understand a word of it. Yet somehow she felt better as they made their way back to the road. The girl was right. A proper buryin' was the decent thing to do, even for no-account border trash.

They found the gun in the brush beside the road where Birgit had dropped it. After reloading, Polly handed it up to the girl in the buggy.

"You drive on now. Corridon's less than an hour away and you'll be safer travelin' this time of night than in daylight. You shouldn't have no more trouble, but if you do, well, God help 'em."

"But what will you do?"

"Walk home. I been in these hills my whole life; moonlight's as bright as a lantern for me. Don't worry. You just take care of yourself and that baby. I'll see you come spring, girl. I promise."

Polly watched until the buggy disappeared, then set off for home, a long, weary march. It was well after midnight when she finally trudged up the lane to her home.

She'd thought Angus might be waiting. He usually came down from the hills for provisions on the first night of the new moon. But he wasn't there, at least not yet.

Exhausted, she relit the kitchen woodstove to warm the water, then stumbled into her bedroom. By the light of a lone candle, she filled the basin from the pitcher on the washstand, then stripped off her shirt, hanging it carefully on the doorknob to avoid getting bloodstains on the bedspread.

But as she plunged her arms in the basin to rinse off the gore, the scent of it came roiling up, suffusing the air, a powerful sweet-sour blend of gangrene and . . .

Lilacs. Stunned, Polly stared down at the basin, already reddening with blood. Leaning down, her face just above the water, she drew a long, ragged breath. Dear God. It was *Eau de Lilac.* Full strength, undiluted.

Her throat closed so tightly she could hardly breathe. Still, she forced herself to take her shirt from the doorknob to sniff a bloodstained sleeve. It was drenched with lilac water. No doubt about it.

The—person—Birgit killed must have been carrying the bottle in his shirt pocket. The shotgun blast splattered it all over his chest.

With a low moan, Polly sank to the bed, burying her face in her hands, rocking. No tears, her agony was soundless and soul deep, a pain so savage she thought she might die. And wished she could.

Which boy had they buried? She'd never looked into his face, hadn't wanted to. He was just another lost scarecrow of war, another starving, walking corpse, looking for a place to die.

Or to kill. Why had he attacked Birgit on the road? Too sick to walk any farther? Or had the war bled the pity from him, made him into another Meachum? Taken his soul?

Wasn't sure how long she sat there. Must have fallen asleep. Because she woke with a start. Someone was moving in the kitchen. And for a wild moment she thought she'd been mistaken, the boy hadn't been dead, somehow he'd clawed his way out of the earth . . . but no.

In the kitchen Angus was fumbling with a lantern.

"Don't light that," Polly said, carrying her candle to the table. "Cavalry was here today. They might be watching the house."

"Whose cavalry?"

"Federals, out of Jefferson City."

"Oh." In the flickering shadows, her husband's seamed face was hewn from granite, his beard unkempt, his graying hair wild. She wanted to hold him, to feel his strength. But it wasn't their custom. And she wanted no questions.

"You're late," she said, her voice quiet, controlled. "It's nearly three."

"I walked in. Took longer than I figured."

"You walked? Why?"

He avoided her eyes, almost sheepishly. "I loaned out my horse."

"The mare? Loaned it to who?"

"Some boy. Union deserter from Curtis's outfit. Came stumblin' into my camp yesterday. Nice boy. Family's got a farm up near Cairo, Illinois. He needed to get home. So I put him on my horse and set him on an old jayhawk trail. Figured I'd be better off with him gone than hangin' around the hills tellin' his pals about the crazy old man hidin' in the pineywoods with his raggedy-ass horses. Told him I'd send one of the boys for the animal after the war."

"Might not be too much longer. Had a visitor today, Tyler Randolph's new wife. She said the Federals burned Atlanta. Hood's retreating."

"Might be," he nodded. "I've been seein' a lot of strays in the hills, mostly Rebs but some Union. Federals are shootin' deserters now. Huntin' 'em down like coyotes. Is that why the cavalry came?"

"That, and to steal anything that wasn't nailed down. Aaron Meachum was with them. Gave me some mouth, nothing I couldn't handle."

"Meachum," Angus rasped, his eyes narrowing. "That bloodsuckin' scum's ridin' high now, got the Hessians around him, thinks he's safe. But when this is over and the boys are home, we'll be payin' a visit to that jayhawker sonofabitch—"

Polly slapped him, hard! Snapping his head around! He stared at her in stunned disbelief.

"No! By God, Angus, when this is over, it's truly gonna be over for us. We've given enough, bled enough. Let the dead bury the dead. No more killing, no more burning, not for revenge nor anything else!"

"What the hell's got into you, Pol?"

"I met Tyler Randolph's wife! And she's Hessian, except she's not—she's from some other place in Germany. But she's a fine girl! And God willing, she and Tyler will have children. I can midwife for her, and they can come visit on a Sunday, stay at Christmas, maybe. But so help me God, Angus, if you ever say any more about killin' or use that word *Hessian* to me again, I'll leave you! I'll take our boy and go! Do you understand?"

Tears were streaming now, she couldn't stop them and didn't care. Angus eyed her like a stranger, utterly baffled. He touched his lip and his fingertip came away bloody.

"No," he said slowly, "I don't understand. But I think it's a damn sight more than we can talk through tonight. I better go. Need to be in the hills before sunup anyhow."

"No! Not yet. You came in for warm food and a bath, and you're damned well gonna have 'em!"

"I came in for a kind word, too. But I guess I'll settle for a bath."

"Good!" Polly carried the steaming buckets from the woodstove to the tub, filling it with practiced ease as Angus warily unbuttoned his shirt, watching her all the while.

When the tub was full, he turned his back and so did she, giving him privacy, as was their habit.

But not tonight. Instead, she turned and watched him strip off his frayed shirt and the tattered union suit beneath. Saw his pale, scrawny frame, the lump on his shoulder where a horse had broken his collarbone years ago, his flat butt, the hipbones showing through.

My God. He'd been up in those hills for nearly three years, living with their animals, living *like* an animal. Freezing and going hungry. For her. For their boys. With no complaints.

As he turned to climb in the bath, he saw her watching and colored with embarrassment. But he said nothing. Just eased his aching bones down in the steaming water with a groan.

But in that briefest of moments, when their eyes met, she'd seen her life. With him. And nothing else mattered. Nothing. Not the hunger, not the war, not even the boy lost in the forest. Somehow they'd get through this. They would.

Ordinarily she left him alone to bathe. Instead she knelt behind the tub and wrapped her arms around his narrow shoulders, holding him. "I'm sorry," she said, after a time.

"No need. Up in them hills I forget how hard it must be for you holdin' on here alone. Comin' home feels so good to me that . . . well, I forget, that's all. Are you all right?"

"I will be. When all this is over."

"Soon, maybe. And you're right. When it's finished we'll get back to some kind of life. Make up for these sorry times. All of us. I miss you, Polly, miss our boys, our home. Even miss the way it smells, like now. What's that stuff again?"

"*Eau de Lilac,*" she said. "Lilac water."

The Price of Coal

Edward D. Hoch

I n September of 1864, at the age of nineteen, I left home in Liverpool and signed on as an ordinary seaman aboard the newly launched schooner *Night Owl*, bound for Halifax. It was not until I was on board and sailing into the open sea that I learned the true nature of the ship.

"She's a blockade runner," my new friend Robinson told me, gazing out at the wake we were leaving in the Irish Sea. "We'll be lucky if we aren't blown out of the water by a Union gunboat."

"Go on! You're trying to scare me! The captain's as English as we are."

Robinson was a jovial lad, not much older than me, who was always kidding about something. We bunked together belowdecks and the hot, crowded conditions made us companions at once. "The captain's only a front until we reach Confederate waters. That's so the ship won't lose her mercantile register. But the other officers are all Confederates. Couldn't you tell by their Southern accents?"

He went on to explain that several small, fast ships had been built for the Confederacy in England and Scotland, with more on the way. The *Night Owl* was a two-funneled side-wheeler, long and low with a molded steel hull, perfect for the tasks it would be called upon to perform. I felt rather foolish listening to him instruct me in such things that I should have known. "What cargo are we carrying?" I asked finally.

"Tea, on this run. But we'll be picking up the real cargo somewhere below the Mason-Dixon Line."

"I thought we were bound for Halifax."

"That's just the first stop, to make it look good. Block-ade-running was quite successful in the war's early days, but each year it grows more dangerous as the Union builds up its navy. Some say the South should be building more cruis-ers to break the blockade."

The journey across the North Atlantic seemed placid enough to me, though it was my first taste of the ocean and every day brought new discoveries. I marveled at the way gulls followed the ship, waiting for each day's garbage to be thrown off the stern. It was my first voyage on a side-wheeler, and the ship moved with remarkable speed. She was painted white, which had surprised me from the moment I first saw her, but Robinson explained that was to make her elusive when pursued by Union vessels in the North Atlantic Blockading Squadron.

In less than a week's time we were sailing into Halifax Harbor. Two days later, on the first of October, we entered the harbor at Wilmington, North Carolina, without incident, under the watchful guns of Fort Fisher. I was anxious to get ashore in this new country, but our superior, a boatswain's mate named Roger Frye, ordered us to stay on board. "We'll be loading a new cargo and leaving port within forty-eight hours," he told us. "Captain Morguane will be speaking to you directly."

Once we'd left Halifax and sailed down the Atlantic coast into Confederate waters, I'd become aware that our British captain was no longer in charge. An American, one of the Confederate officers on board, had assumed com-mand of the ship and was taking her into port. Morguane was a Southern gentleman with coal-black hair and mustache, and when he spoke to us he came right to the point.

"Gentlemen, this ship is now under the command of the Confederate States of America. We will be transporting cargo to and from the islands of Bermuda, Cuba, the Bahamas, and elsewhere. At times we may be in some peril, but my job will be to bring both crew and cargo home safely. I promise you I will do that. If any of the English seamen who joined us in Liverpool wish to leave the ship now, they may do so and we will attempt to arrange safe passage back home. For those of you who stay, there will be a bonus paid after the successful completion of our first voyage."

The other crewmen and I exchanged glances. Most of them had known what they were getting into, and there was no quitting now. The promised bonus, like a pot of gold at the end of some illusionary rainbow, was enough to hold us in thrall.

"Good!" Captain Morguane exclaimed. "A united crew is a happy crew. Now a word about our ship. The *Night Owl* and its sister ship the *Night Hawk* were built to specific dimensions. The cargo hold has a capacity of 850 bales of cotton, and that is what we will leave with in two days' time. The cotton is the currency with which the Confederacy purchases what it needs from other countries. Over the past year I have made thirty-three successful runs on various ships, bringing in meat, lead, saltpeter for explosives, shoes, blankets, coffee, rifles, cannon, and medicines. Occasionally, there are passengers who must reach the Confederate States on important business. When we leave here with our cargo we will sail due east to Bermuda, where we will trade the cotton for shoe machinery and two hundred tons of coal."

Later, when we were in our bunks, I wondered aloud about our chances of trouble. "Are the Northern ships heavily armed, Robinson?"

"That they are, but we are faster with our light arms. Even with a heavy cargo we should outrun them easily."

On the morning of our arrival at Bermuda, Roger Frye had us scrubbing down three of the ship's passenger cabins in preparation for two women and a man who would be joining us on the return trip.

"What a waste of time," I grumbled to Robinson, scrubbing the floor on my hands and knees. "No one has used these cabins since the ship was launched. How could they be dirty?"

"The salt air gets into everything," he said. "You'll learn that soon enough, lad."

I resented being called a lad by someone only a couple of years older than I was, but I let it pass. "Two women and a man. Are they traveling together?"

"Don't know. Probably not, if they need three cabins."

As with our other stops so far, the crew was not allowed ashore at Bermuda. The bales of cotton were quickly unloaded, but it was already growing dark, and the captain decided to wait until morning for the new cargo. In the fading light I could see that the mid-Atlantic harbor was a port for other ships as well as ours. Some were low-slung blockade runners, easy to identify now that I recognized their sleek lines and iron-hulled sides. Most were side-wheelers like the *Night Owl.*

"See that one?" Frye asked, coming up from the hold to join me at the railing. "It's our sister ship, the *Night Hawk.* She's just pulling out. I served on her for a couple of runs. That's why they put me on this one."

"Where's she headed?" I asked.

"Who knows? Maybe the same place we are."

"How does all this cargo arrive in Bermuda?"

"It comes from countries like England that are sympathetic to the Confederate cause."

"Why England? Slavery was abolished in the entire British Empire more than thirty years ago." At least I'd learned that much during my school days.

Roger Frye laughed. "Maybe I should have said countries like England that are unsympathetic to the Union cause. Anyway, their ships can't sail into the blockaded area, so they leave their cargoes here, or in Havana or Nassau, for the blockade runners to pick up in exchange for cotton."

It was a world I'd never known in all of my nineteen years, but I was learning about it quickly.

IN THE MORNING I was awakened by the first glimmers of the rising sun through our porthole. "Time to go to work," Robinson muttered, turning over in his narrow bunk.

What passed for breakfast was served in the ship's galley, and when we finished we went out on deck. A line of horse-drawn wagons had come onto the dock, filled with loads of coal. I recognized Captain Morguane on the bridge of the *Night Owl*, observing the entire operation with a stout red-faced man by his side. Even at that distance I could see that both men were counting the loads as they were hoisted on board. "Who would that be?" I asked Robinson.

"Beats me."

Before long, a carriage arrived carrying a stout woman who appeared to be about my mother's age. She had her belongings in two carpetbags, and Frye immediately ordered us down to carry them on board for her. "You've booked passage with us?" Robinson asked her, though there was no other reason for her presence on the dock at this hour of the morning.

"I have," she told him. "Please inform your captain that Selma Quiggin has arrived."

"The captain is checking the cargo right now," Robinson told her politely. "Let us escort you to your cabin, and I will see that Captain Morguane is informed of your arrival, ma'am." It always amazed me that he could speak like a gentleman when the occasion called for it. He picked up her bags and led the way up the gangplank.

Because two other passengers were expected, I asked Frye if I should remain on the dock to assist them. "They've already arrived," he told me, gesturing up toward the ship's bridge. "That's Simon Kostner, and his niece is traveling with him. He's the agent handling the coal sale, and they're counting the loads to make sure he delivers the full shipment."

I didn't see Kostner's niece until I passed her with her uncle, making their way to an early dinner in the officers' mess. She was an attractive young lady, about my age or a bit older, with ringlets of brown hair framing a soft and attractive face. Her long white gown might have been more suitable for a ballroom than an officers' mess. I heard her uncle address her as Mignon. Robinson and I ate early, too, because the *Night Owl* was sailing with the tide, and we had to be at our stations to cast off.

As we moved out of Bermuda Harbor into the open sea, I returned to the deck near the officer's mess, hoping to catch another glimpse of the young lady. She appeared within ten minutes, accompanied not by her uncle but by the older woman, Selma Quiggin. "Have you never been to America, dear?" the woman was asking.

"Yes, but not to the Confederate States," Mignon responded. They passed without seeming to notice me at the rail.

A few minutes later I'd taken out my tobacco pouch and was rolling a cigarette when Mignon returned alone, walking directly up to me. "What is your name, boy?" she inquired.

I was momentarily at a loss for words. When she repeated the question, I managed to stammer out, "Phillips, miss."

"Are you allowed to smoke cigarettes on deck, Phillips?"

"We're not carrying any combustible cargo, miss."

She stared into my eyes, not quite smiling. "Isn't coal a combustible cargo?"

"I—" I felt she was trying to trick me or mock me, but at that moment I couldn't come up with a good answer.

"I've seen you watching me, Phillips. You have been watching me, haven't you?"

"I may have noticed you on the way to dinner."

"Do you find me attractive? Am I as pretty as your English girls?"

"Oh yes, ma'am."

"Perhaps we should inspect the ship's hold together, to make certain the coal has not caught on fire."

"I don't think I should—"

She cut off my words with a wave of her hand. "Or should I tell my uncle you were rude to me?"

She opened a hatch door and disappeared quickly down a flight of steps. I had no choice but to follow her. "You shouldn't be here," I told her.

"Why not? It's my uncle's coal."

"Not anymore. He traded it for that cotton we unloaded."

She reached the deck of the cargo hold and waited for me. "You're not so smart. The cotton paid for the shoe machinery. The coal was paid for in gold by your captain."

"Gold?"

"Gold coins from the San Francisco mint. No one is foolish enough to accept Confederate money in payment. Uncle Simon has a bag of them in his cabin that must weigh thirty pounds."

We'd reached the forward hold, and she opened the bulkhead door without trouble. The choking odor of coal dust assaulted my nostrils. "We can't go in there," I told her.

"Have you ever made love on a pile of coal, Phillips?"

I grabbed her arm and yanked her out of there. "No, and I'm not going to start now! That dress is much too pretty to be smeared with coal dust." I closed the bulkhead door and pulled her up the steps behind me. "It's no wonder they say women are bad luck aboard ship."

"What about Selma Quiggin? Is she bad luck, or just the pretty ones?"

"You're impossible! I don't even know what either of you are doing on this ship."

"Running the blockade, like everyone else. Selma Quiggin is carrying vital dispatches for President Jefferson Davis. My uncle is returning home with his profits from the sale of the coal."

We reached the open air of the deck, and I was relieved to breathe fresh air again. "And why are you traveling with him?" I asked.

At first she didn't answer, and I expected another of her attempts to shock me. But after a moment she said, "My father was killed in the war last year. Uncle Simon thought the trip with him might help take my mind off it."

"I understand many good men have died fighting for the Confederate cause."

She averted her face and shook her head. "He fought on the Union side. He was a captain, killed at Gettysburg."

"And his brother sells coal to the South?"

"There are many brothers on opposite sides in this war. It has torn families apart. But Uncle Simon is in it more for the money than anything else."

Before she could say more, we were interrupted by Selma Quiggin, strolling the deck in the moonlight. She had a colorful shawl wrapped around her dress, though the evening was mild. "Lovely night, Mignon," the stout woman said. "Perhaps too lovely, if we wish to slip safely through the blockade."

"I have confidence in Captain Morguane," the young woman answered. "Miss Quiggin, this is Mr. Phillips, one of the *Night Owl*'s able seamen."

I blushed a bit as I bowed to the woman. "Only an ordinary seaman so far, Miss Quiggin. It's a pleasure to meet you."

"If you'll excuse me," Mignon said, "I think I'll retire to my cabin."

"Are you on duty, Mr. Phillips?" the woman asked when we were alone.

"We're always on duty, ma'am. Would you like me to escort you to your room?"

"That would be kind of you. I don't quite have my sea legs yet."

I offered my arm and guided her down to the cabin deck. Her room was just across the passage from those of Kostner and his niece, and adjoined Captain Morguane's quarters. As I remembered from scrubbing their floors, none of these cabins were very large. The *Night Owl* had not been built for pleasure cruising.

Selma Quiggin handed me the key to her cabin, and I was about to unlock the door for her when Mignon suddenly burst forth from the cabin across the way, her face white as chalk. "My God, someone has killed my uncle!"

I ran to the door, fearing she would swoon at any moment. Selma followed, and she helped Mignon across the passage to her cabin while I ventured inside. Simon Kostner's cabin was dark, and I had to relight the oil lamp before I could make out the terrible sight that had greeted Mignon. Kostner was propped up on the bed, holding his bloody stomach with both hands. His eyes were open but there was no doubt that he was dead.

I HURRIED ACROSS TO the captain's cabin and knocked on the door. There was no answer and I was wondering what to do next when Roger Frye happened along the passage. "Is that you, Phillips? What are you doing at Captain Morguane's door?"

"There's been a terrible accident! Simon Kostner is dead."

Frye quickly followed me into Kostner's cabin and closed the door. "This is terrible," he said after a quick examination of the body. "He's been stabbed several times. Do you see a knife around anywhere?"

"No, but the porthole is open. It could have been thrown into the sea."

"Captain Morguane is on the bridge. Go summon him while I stay with the body," Frye instructed me. "Say nothing to anyone else."

As I started down the passageway, Selma came out of her cabin. "Mignon is still unconscious, but I think she'll be all right. It's just the shock of the thing. I want to see if they have any smelling salts on board."

"Come along," I told her. "I'm on my way to inform the captain now."

"She had his blood on the front of her dress," she told me, trying to wipe a spot away with her handkerchief. "This is a terrible thing. Why would anyone want to kill him?"

"I understand he received payment in gold coins for the coal. Someone might have wanted them."

I led the way up the stairs to the bridge, with Selma puffing behind me. Captain Morguane was startled at our sudden intrusion into his private realm "What is the meaning of this?" he demanded.

"There's been a killing," I managed.

Selma chimed in with the details. "Someone has stabbed Simon Kostner!"

Morguane's head jerked at the news. "Kostner? Dead?"

"In his cabin," I hurried on. "Mr. Frye sent me to summon you."

"And do you have any smelling salts on board?" Selma added. "Finding the body was quite a shock for Kostner's niece."

The captain surrendered the wheel to his first mate and opened a small medicine cabinet. "Here's your smelling salts. Now let's get down there."

Selma returned to her cabin to minister to Mignon, while I entered Kostner's cabin where Frye stood guard. Captain Morguane took one look at the dead man on the bed and averted his eyes. "Are we to believe that some member of our crew killed him?" he asked Frye.

"It appears so, sir, unless it was one of the ladies."

"They were both in my company on deck shortly before the body was discovered," I said, but from the look the captain gave me, I realized immediately that I should not have admitted to conversation with the passengers.

"Know your place, lad, if you wish to get ahead in this man's navy."

I was about to apologize when Selma Quiggin appeared at the door supporting Mignon. "I must see him again," the poor girl managed between her tears. "I could not believe my eyes when I entered the cabin earlier."

Morguane moved quickly to block her view of the body. "Stay back, miss. It is not a pleasant sight."

"I tried to keep her away," Selma assured the captain.

He stepped over to Mignon and said in a kindly voice, "I know this has been a terrible experience for you, Miss Kostner. If you could tell me exactly what happened . . . "

She took a deep breath and began to speak. "I was returning to my cabin when I noticed that my uncle's door was slightly ajar. I knocked and pushed the door open. When I went in, I saw all this blood and I panicked."

"You saw this in the dark?" I asked, remembering how I'd found the cabin.

She shook her head. "The lamp was on. I must have blown it out in my confusion. I wanted to blot out what I'd seen."

"Take her out, please," Captain Morguane requested. "We have work to do here."

Mignon wished to rest in her own cabin, and I accompanied them there. While Selma turned up the lamp, I sat on the edge of the bunk and tried to comfort the dead man's niece. "I'll be all right," she assured me. "It was just the shock of seeing him. I fainted right away."

Selma left us the smelling salts and returned to her cabin. Frye stuck his head in the door to say, "I'll need you in five minutes, in Kostner's cabin. The captain has sent me to find Robinson, too."

When they were alone Mignon took my hand. "Forgive me for how I acted earlier, belowdecks. I was only playing with you. I'm not that sort of girl." The color was beginning to return to her face.

"I'm glad. I want you as unspotted as your gown. That coal would have ruined it."

She smiled. "You're nice. Perhaps I can make an able seaman of you yet."

"Tell me about your uncle. Who could have killed him?"

"Anyone after that gold, I suppose. It's a great deal of money in these desperate times."

I remembered Frye's summons. "I must return to work. I'll try to see you later."

When I reached the dead man's cabin I found Frye and Robinson already at work. The body had been placed in a canvas bag. "Will he be buried at sea?" I inquired.

Frye shook his head. "We must take him back to establish the cause of death, in the event there is an arrest and a trial. Help us carry him below, Phillips, and then we'll return here."

We placed the body in a large locker and came back up to the cabin deck. "What happened?" Robinson asked me, and I quickly filled him in, omitting my aborted escapade with Mignon.

Back in the cabin Frye said, "We're to search everywhere for the gold coins Captain Morguane paid Kostner for the coal. The captain is convinced they were the motive for the crime. If we don't find them here, we're to search the women passengers' cabins and then the crew quarters."

"Surely he doesn't think Mignon would have killed her own uncle," I protested.

Frye looked at me and muttered, "You've a lot to learn, lad."

"What does that mean?"

He didn't answer but Robinson told me later, while we searched. "Middle-aged uncles sometimes travel with young nieces who are not really their nieces."

"What? What are you saying?"

"It's the way of the world, lad."

"I don't believe it. You can't say that about a girl like Mignon."

We searched her cabin along with Selma's but found nothing. Then we moved on to the crew's quarters, and storage facilities belowdecks. We found nothing. Finally, toward daybreak, Frye reported our failure to the captain. "Did you search my cabin?" he asked the boatswain's mate.

"No sir."

He handed Frye the key. "Do so, now!"

But there was nothing. Robinson and I were finally allowed to sleep as the sun rose in the eastern sky.

THE WINDS WERE WITH us as we made our way due west through the breaking waves toward Cape Fear. The captain said we should make port in two days' time. Simon Kostner's death had been announced to all, but the manner of his dying was spread only in whispers. Robinson and I spent our working hours in more unsuccessful searching for the missing gold, and I saw nothing of Mignon.

"You know what I think?" Robinson asked me on our last day at sea. "I think the killer dropped the gold out that porthole to a waiting boat."

"That would be risky at night. What if he missed?"

"Maybe he dropped it into the water with a rope attached, so he could haul it up later."

That made more sense to me, but a tour of the railings around the decks revealed no mysterious ropes hanging into the water.

The captain had estimated we would be within sight of Cape Fear by dark, and everyone knew that was the most dangerous time. If we were sighted by the North Atlantic

Blockading Squadron, they would surely try to board us or even sink us.

"Will we be able to make it into port in the dark?" I asked Frye.

"There are treacherous waters, but the lighthouse will guide us."

Wind-driven clouds had been building up all afternoon, and as we came in sight of land a heavy fog began to settle in. It was just then that the ship's whistle sounded, alerting the crew that an enemy ship had been sighted. Robinson grabbed up a spyglass and scanned the horizon. "There she is," he announced grimly, passing the glass to me.

The ship's guns seemed monstrous to me, even at that distance, easily capable of blowing us out of the water. They were signaling us to heave to for boarding, but the captain ignored them and stayed on course for Cape Fear. Suddenly, as the Union ironclad closed the gap between us, I saw a puff of smoke and heard the cough of a cannon. Almost at once we were hit on our upper deck near the bridge, and we heard a scream of agony.

As the ironclad moved into position to fire again, Captain Morguane changed course. "He's trying to reach that fog bank," Robinson shouted. "It's our only hope!"

Frye joined us from the upper deck, his face ashen. "That was a thirty-pounder. It took off Match Madick's leg. He's probably a goner. They were aiming at our front stack."

The Union warship fired again, but this time the ball passed across our bow. Then we slipped into the fog bank and were safe for the moment. "Will they find us?" Robinson asked.

"Not in here, but we have to emerge sooner or later. And then we have to make it into port somehow."

Our two women passengers, terrified by the cannon fire, had appeared on deck. "Are we going to sink?" Mignon asked.

"No fear of that," Frye reassured her. "Captain Morguane will get us out of this, with a little help from the fog."

Selma Quiggin, holding her sizable waist, had gone to the railing to peer through the fog. At that moment the cannon's roar reached us again, but the ball came nowhere near. "Will they keep on until they hit us?" she asked.

Robinson shook his head. "Not likely. They'll save their ammunition until they have a visible target."

Mignon suddenly gasped, and I saw that the front of her frock had a spot of blood on it. I hurried to pull her out of the way as blood continued dripping from the upper deck where the crewman named Madick lay dying. "Stay away from there," I cautioned, but I could not take my eyes from the blood on her dress.

"Is everyone here safe?" Captain Morguane asked, climbing down from the bridge. "We've suffered one serious casualty, but the ship seems secure. If we can sail out of this fog bank, I think we can make it into Wilmington."

"Captain—," I managed to say, catching his attention.

"What is it, lad?"

"I think I know what happened to Mr. Kostner."

"There'll be time for that later. I have to get back to the bridge now."

Robinson was staring at me. "What do you mean, Phillips?"

"The blood on Mignon's dress."

All eyes were on her then, as she tried to wipe it away. "It reminded you of her uncle's blood?" Frye asked.

I shook my head. "It reminded me that there was no blood on her dress after Kostner's body was found. I even remarked to her how unspotted it was. And yet Selma here explained away the blood on her own dress by saying it had come off Mignon's when she helped the girl. That couldn't be true."

Selma Quiggin laughed harshly. "Are you saying I killed that man?"

"Yes, and hid the blood with that colorful shawl you wrapped around yourself, even in this mild air."

The ship was free of the fog bank now, with the Cape Fear lighthouse within sight. The captain was distracted from the conversation by something he saw in the channel. "Hand me that spyglass," he told Frye.

"You did kill him," I told the woman. "How else could you know he'd been stabbed when the cabin was in darkness and you only stood at the door for an instant."

"I never said—"

"Yes, you did. When we went up on the bridge you told the captain he'd been stabbed."

Frye was at the captain's side. "What are you seeing, sir?"

"It's our sister ship, the *Night Hawk*. The Union raiders have sunk her in the channel. I don't know if we can get around her. The sea is quite rough."

The next hour was a nightmare, with Selma Quiggin and Kostner's murder forgotten for the moment. Captain Morguane took control of the wheel and tried to guide us into the channel past Fort Fisher. But darkness was falling fast, and the smoldering wreckage of the *Night Hawk* left us too little room to maneuver. Just after sunset we ran aground on a sandbar. The captain gave the order for the passengers and most of the crew to abandon ship, which meant wading through the rough surf to the shore. With less weight Morguane hoped to free his grounded ship.

We went down the gangway to the water, and I held tight to Mignon all the way in. No one noticed what happened to Selma Quiggin and perhaps no one cared. At daybreak, with the *Night Owl* still stuck fast to the sandbar, we found her body washed up on shore. Simon Kostner's stolen gold coins, the sale price of the coal, were found in a money belt around her ample waist. It was one place we hadn't searched, and the weight of them had pulled her down beneath the foaming surf.

WHEN MORGUANE WAS UNABLE to free his ship from the sandbar after a week of trying, Robinson and I were given passage back to Bermuda aboard another blockade runner. From there we would return to England. I wanted no more of the war at sea.

I told Mignon I would write to her, and I did, but so far our paths have not crossed. It's a big world, and a big ocean between us.

Last Hours in Richmond

Brendan DuBois

In the fourth year of the War of Secession, Mary Stuart-son of Richmond, Virginia, was in the rear of Colling-wood's Grocers, thinking sourly of a time not so long ago when she and her husband could have purchased this entire store and its belongings with as much effort as it took to prepare a bank draft. Now, in this cold winter, when each day seemed to last forever, along with the cold and mud, with her family shattered and her family fortune nearly gone, she found herself dickering over the price of a shrunken ham.

"Come now, Mister Collingwood," she protested. "Tell me again what price you're asking for this sorry piece of meat?"

Collingwood smirked, wiping both hands on his dull gray store apron. In this part of the store, the windows were smeared and dark, not allowing hardly any light inside. The shelves themselves were empty, having been empty for

months. Like most shopkeepers in this embattled Confederate capital, what few goods that existed were kept securely in
rear rooms.

The shopkeeper said, "Madam, truly I'm grieved by
what you say. The fact that I am offering this ham to you at
this price shows the high esteem in which I hold you as a customer. The price is fair. You cannot do better at any other
establishment, if even they have any hams left."

"But three hundred dollars!" she said, hardly even
believing the words as they left her mouth. "Three hundred
dollars for a ham!"

Collingwood shrugged. "If you don't take it at that
price, madam, then some other lady shall come in and purchase it for four hundred. Supply and demand, Missus Stuartson. Supply and demand. With you at your boarding
house, you should know better than anyone."

She looked at the smug face and freshly washed beard,
the plump cheeks. She wished she could shoot the man,
shoot him right here in his store, but the damnable
scoundrel was right. Supply and demand, and with Richmond being strangled each day by the damn Federals, everything was in short supply. Save for cold, hunger, and despair.

Mary went through her cloth bag, pulled out a rolled-
up piece of cloth. "I don't have that kind of money with me,
Mister Collingwood. But what I do have is this."

She unrolled the piece of cloth on the wooden counter,
revealing a heavy gold watch and chain, and a man's gold
ring. She saw the look in the shopkeeper's eyes as he picked
them up and examined them. He looked over at her and
said, "Deal, Missus Stuartson."

She shook her head. "Not so fast. I want some coffee, as
well. Mister Stuartson so enjoys a cup of coffee."

"Coffee!" he exclaimed. "Why, I don't think—"

She made to take back the jewelry. "I know for a fact
you have coffee, Mister Collingwood. You sold some here
yesterday. That's the arrangement I desire. Ham and coffee
for this jewelry. Or I go elsewhere."

The grocer finally nodded and went back into a rear storage area, and when he returned, he wrapped up both the ham and a small bag of coffee in an old copy of the *Richmond Examiner*. Mary didn't bother reading the headlines as the old newspaper was used as wrapping paper. All of the headlines these past months had been filled with bad news. It was horrible enough to read them once. She need not read them again.

As he passed over the small bundle, the well-fed grocer seemed almost apologetic. "It's the terrible times we live through, Missus Stuartson. These terrible times make all of us do what we can to survive."

"Yes, you're right, Mister Collingwood," she said, putting the package into her cloth purse. "We do what we can to survive."

OUTSIDE, THE COLD FEBRUARY wind seemed to cut through her as she navigated along the muddy streets, holding up her skirts with one hand. With her other hand, she kept it inside her bag, holding on to the revolver that belonged to her husband. In the four short years since this city had become the capital of a new nation, the population had almost tripled and what little police were here could not handle the increase in forgers, robbers, and deserters that crowded these muddy avenues. It seemed each week that besides the war news, the newspapers had breathless stories of murders most foul, and men and women gone missing in the dark alleys and streets of Richmond after dark.

Wagons went by, horses with their ribs showing through, carrying whatever goods still dribbled into Richmond. They were followed by a line of colored men, walking slowly, most of them barefoot, carrying shovels and picks over their shoulders, heading out to strengthen the city's defenses. She kept her eyes about her, knowing that some desperate men—and even desperate women!—were not above robbing women as they left shops, trying to steal what little they had. She remembered a time earlier, when Mister Collingwood had been more cheerful and open with his store, and how he always had a sweet for her son, Tom, and her daughter, Lucinda. Now Tom and Lucinda were dead, he on a battlefield in Pennsylvania, and she in a common grave here in Richmond after a long illness, and no sweets were to be had, ever again.

As she turned a corner, only a few blocks away from her home, she heard the distant rumble of cannon fire, as the damn Federals kept pressing on. *What this war has done to us*, she thought, *all of us*. There had been a time when she wouldn't have gone out even for such a short distance without a matched pair and carriage, and her clothes would have been clean and crisp. Now, like most of the women passing her by, she wore black, in perpetual mourning for her family and her nation, and the horses had been taken into service for the army. And these poor women in this city, nearly two years ago exactly, they had finally had enough and a food riot had erupted. Stores had been robbed and burnt, and they had stopped only when President Jefferson Davis himself, the mighty Sphinx, had arrived to plead the women to disperse, before the militia would fire upon them. Oh, the horror, of seeing good men of Virginia preparing to fire upon their own mothers, wives, sisters, and daughters.

Mary paused at the small gate to her house, tears suddenly filling her eyes at what she saw. Once her house had been the envy of the neighborhood, as her husband's business thrived with all of the shipping traffic coming and going on the James River. But now the house looked old and tired, with broken panes of glass being filled in by newspaper. The white picket fence around the house had long been broken up and burnt for fuel, leaving only the granite posts for the main gate. And her husband's business had collapsed—as so many others had—when the Union Navy's blockade had put its foot upon the throat of so many Southern ports.

She gathered herself up and went up to the house, forcing the tears to stop. Their house had been taking in guests now for nearly two years, ever since her husband had returned wounded from Pennsylvania, at a place called Gettysburg. Henry had not said much for months, grieving for their lost victory and their lost son, Tom. But as she had said to the grocer, they did what they had to do to survive, and turning their comfortable home into a boarding house for strangers had been that first, dramatic, and dark step into their new lives.

INSIDE THE HOUSE IT was damp and cold, and she went past the parlor and to the kitchen, where the cabinets were firmly locked. She took a ring of keys and unlocked the cabinets, tried to come up with a decent dinner for her three guests. They paid in many ways—from notes from other Southern cities to foreign money to even Union greenbacks—but even then, coming up with a meal was always a struggle. She looked through her meager possessions, trying to think of what she had down below, in the root cellar, also firmly locked and chained. Before the war, house breaking was almost unheard of in these neighborhoods of Richmond, but with each passing month of the war, more and more houses were entered by the hungry and the cold.

There was a noise and she turned. The door leading to the cellar opened and Henry came up, wearing heavy cotton pants and a well-patched shirt. His face was lined and his beard had turned white, ever since coming back from Gettysburg, and his eyes always had the look of being so very tired. She ached at seeing him there, the once-strong and confident man who had wooed her heart and soul. Now he was strong no more, and the firm arms which had held her tight over the years had been shattered as much as their family. His right arm was withered and his left arm—struck by a Union ball—had been amputated just below the elbow.

He bowed slightly. "Good day, wife."

She came up to him, kissed him on the cheek. "And good day to you, husband. Is there any news?"

He shook his head, reached into the doorway of the stairway and pulled out a dirt-encrusted shovel. "We have another guest. A Major Tomlison. A dandy officer, he is, with nice long sword and bright shiny boots. Officers." He spat the word out like an epithet. "The kind who knows every-thing about men and war from some damn Prussian drill manual. Officers. He looks as stupid as the officers who sent us up to that ridge in Gettysburg, right into the face of all that cannon . . ."

"Henry," she said simply, seeing how his expression had changed, how he was reliving those horrid moments. "Henry, it will be fine. Will you fetch me wood for dinner?"

He looked up, gave her a weak smile. "It will be my honor."

Honor, she thought, looking up again to the cabinets. One of the words that was on the lips of many a noble South-erner who fought his way to battle. But would honor help her now feed an unexpected fourth guest?

THE EVENING MEAL WAS simple, fried mush and day-old bread, smeared with molasses, and boiled turnip greens that she had canned last fall. As she served her guests—all men—she looked at all of them in turn. There was a Mister Cloutier from Louisiana, a representative to the Congress who no longer represented his voters, since they were all now under Union occupation. A Mister Puddleton, a quiet man who wrote for the Richmond Examiner and who sat next to Mister Gray, who worked in one of the struggling banks. These three had been here for months, and while they all had their foibles and difficulties, she had gotten used to them. In a way, they had almost become family to her.

But now this evening, there was the new guest, Major Tomlison, and she recognized what Henry had said: the man was certainly a dandy. The other three men's clothes were worn and ill-repaired, but the Major's uniform was shiny and freshly cleaned. He had a thick mustache and his eyes seemed merry, and he wore heavy gold rings on both index fingers.

As she served the simple meal, she listened to the bits of conversation from the men, wondering how long this could last, how long all of them could last in this besieged city.

". . . Grant's getting more troops, that's what we've heard . . ."

". . . more prisoners tried to escape from the warehouses last night, but all of those poor wretches were recaptured . . ."

". . . another murder was reported down by Rockett's Landing, a man with his throat slit and tossed into the river . . ."

". . . colored troops, fighting for Virginia. Can you imagine that, colored men with guns? We should just surrender to Lincoln if that ever happens . . ."

Then, a strong voice, booming over the others: "I hear the war will be over within a month, and on terms favorable to the Confederacy."

She stopped serving, looked at the confident officer who had just uttered those remarks. Major Tomlison looked about, nodded again. Mister Puddleton, the newspaper man, quietly spoke up. "And what brings that opinion to the fore, Major?"

The major spooned up some of the fried mush. "No matter how many troops and cannon and ships the Yankees have, we have something they don't. General Lee. You mark my words. The Yankees are tired after so many years of war. A couple of more sharp victories against the Yanks, and then they'll sue for peace, and Britain will finally come around to help us. Just you wait and see."

Her husband, sitting at the end of the table, kept quiet, but his face glowered and his lips were pursed. Mister

Cloutier coughed into a handkerchief and said, "Begging the Major's pardon, but after our setbacks at Vicksburg and New Orleans and Atlanta . . ."

The major turned on him. "Are you a defeatist? Sir? Is that what you're saying?"

Mister Gray, the bank man, took off his spectacles and rubbed at the glass with his napkin. "My brother is a captain, serving in the lines near Petersburg. His men are nearly starving. They have no shoes, no coats, and damn little powder or shot. They may have General Lee and other fine generals, sir, but the Federals are well-fed and well-armed and well-rested."

Major Tomlison swallowed another spoonful of mush. "The odds have been against us, right from the start. Just you see. General Lee is the best general this continent has ever seen. And he'll achieve another series of noble victories, just you see. Then old Abe will have to give us what we want and leave us alone."

Her husband spoke up. "Like Gettysburg, do you mean? Another noble victory like Gettysburg?"

Mary stepped in, raising her voice. "Now, now, gentlemen. Let us have no more talk of war at this table. We talk so much about it, day in and out. Let us have at least a few minutes of peace."

The major's face was reddened and she saw how her husband stared at him, hatred in his eyes. She sat down and began eating, the food nearly tasteless.

AFTER THE WASHING AND the cleaning, the men retired to the parlor, where Mister Cloutier, the congressman, passed around a pouch of tobacco, and soon all four of her guests were sitting on her fine chairs, smoking pipes and talking in low voices. She lit a small fire in the fireplace, which was enough for a little heat and hardly any light. She trusted these men not to go through her meager supply of firewood, and as she finished cleaning in the kitchen, her husband Henry came in.

"Did you hear that arrogant officer, that stupid young pup?" Henry demanded. "A few more victories and all will be won. Bah! Such stupidity! Did you hear what he said?"

"Yes, yes, I did," she said, putting away her dishes, suddenly tired of it all. She missed everything so much, from the voices and touches of her son and daughter, from a time when the house was snug and warm and oil lamps kept everything well lit, to feasts and meals that went on for hours. And laughter. She could not remember the last time she had laughed long and loud.

Henry stepped closer. "I'm sorry, Mary," he said, his voice low. "I'm sorry I raised my voice back there, at dinner. Just seeing that officer, full of himself and nonsense . . ."

She wiped her cold hands. "It's all right, Mister Stuartson. It is quite all right."

He shook his head, and his eyes glistened in the dim light. "No, it's not all right. I should have never let Tom out of my sight. Not once. But the smoke and the cannon fire . . . That's when I missed him, Mary. Just for a moment. And when the smoke cleared away, I managed to find him, Mary. Our only son. Dead in a field. I tried to drag him back to our lines but by then, I was wounded. I tried, oh Lord, I tried . . ."

She reached over and stroked his lined cheek. "I know you tried, dear sir. I know you did. You did what you could."

Her husband only nodded. She went on. "I am about to retire. And you, dear husband?"

"I . . . I have a little work to do. Then I shall join you."

"Very well."

LATER THAT EVENING SHE was in their bedroom, and at a small writing desk, lit by a single candle, she wrote a letter to her sister Carol, who lived in Charleston, South Carolina. She had not heard from her sister in over a month, which was not unusual, considering the state of the mail service. Yet she refused to give up, and she wrote Carol once a week. She tried to keep her letter as bright and as cheerful as possible, knowing that Charleston was under a worse siege than Richmond, with Union navy forces shelling almost every day. Poor Carol had no need to know of her own sister's difficulties.

As she wrote, she often looked up to the wall, where a framed sampler hung, outlining the alphabet and the first nine numerals. Her daughter, Lucinda, had done this sampler almost seven years ago, and she remembered with pride how nimble and quick those fingers had been, bringing everything together. *My poor dear*, she thought. *Never again to sit at my side in the parlor, to laugh and gossip and to sew, never again.* Two winters ago she had caught ill, and what few doctors remained in Richmond had been no help. She had done what she could as her daughter burned with fever, and her husband had stood there as well, still gaunt and pained from his wounds.

In the end, she had simply expired in her sleep, her poor little girl's heart finally giving out. Oh, how did she survive those dark days, knowing she and Henry were now childless, their son and daughter taken away in this damnable war . . .

She looked down at her desk, finished the letter, and then folded it over. It was late. Where could Henry be?

IT WAS DARK. SHE awoke at the sound of her husband, entering the room, carrying a small oil lamp. She sat up. "Husband, are you all right?"

He put the lamp down on a nearby table. "Yes, I am . . . I am just so tired, that's all."

"Then come to bed."

He cupped the lamp with his sole hand and blew out the wick. She noted how stained and dirty his fingers were, dirt encrusted under his fingernails. She remembered a time when he would have never even allowed himself to be seen in such a condition, never mind retiring to bed with dirty fingers. *But we've all changed,* she thought. *This war is much more than a war of brother against brother. It's a war against our entire way of life, the way we think and eat and act, and we're losing so desperately.*

The bed shifted as he slowly climbed under the covers. She moved over and rested her head against his shoulder. She could feel his heart beating wildly, and she wondered how he was feeling.

"Henry, is everything all right?"

"Yes, yes, Mary. Everything is fine. Nothing to worry about. It's just that I'm . . . I'm so very tired. I feel like I could sleep for a month, my dear. I really do."

She reached up in the dark and gently stroked his face. "One of these days, husband, one of these days it will be warm and sunny and the war will be over, and we will have enough to eat and we will be warm. Never again to be cold and hungry. One of these days."

He breathed out. "Yes, one of these days."

She cuddled closer to him, the only man she had ever loved. "I have lost my son and my daughter. All I have now is you. And I will do everything in my power to keep you, husband, forever."

She rested on his shoulder for long minutes, until he finally drifted off to sleep.

In the morning she prepared breakfast, some of the ham she had purchased the day before from Mister Collingwood, served with a single fried egg and a thin slice of toasted bread. It was served with coffee made from chicory; the real coffee she had purchased yesterday would be saved only for her husband.

When she had set the table, she looked and noted an empty chair. "Has anyone seen the good major?" she asked, after placing down the food platter. Mister Cloutier said, "I recall hearing his door open up during the night. But if he ever came back, I was asleep."

Henry said, "Perhaps the young officer is sleeping off after a night of carousing down by the docks."

Mister Gray said, "If that's the case, then he'll be lucky to be alive. There are rough gangs down there, gangs who will even take on well-dressed officers."

Henry made to leave the table. "I'll go upstairs and see if I can't wake him."

Mary shook her head and left the dining room. "No, you men eat before it gets cold. I'll see if he's awake or not."

She gathered up her skirt as she went up the stairs, to the first room on the left. It had been a room for her sewing and needlepoint, and it was rather small, but with a bed and washstand, it was much better than some of the other rooms being rented out in this crowded city. Mary rapped twice on the door. "Major Tomlison? Are you awake? Major Tomlison?"

There was no answer. Well, that was that, then. She tried one more time and then went back to the dining room. Henry said, "What, then? Will he be joining us?"

She sat down, placed a napkin in her lap. "I knocked on the door three times, and raised my voice as well. There was no answer, and I shan't delay breakfast any more."

As she picked up her knife and fork, she noted the looks of the men around her, staring self-consciously at the empty chair and the plate in front of it. Mary noted the looks and then reached over and retrieved the plate. "And if he can't bestir himself to join us for a meal, then I won't waste the food."

Carefully, she cut the fried egg and ham slice and bread into five pieces, and then passed the plate towards Mister Cloutier, who smiled as he placed the extra food onto his plate. Then he passed the plate towards Mister Gray.

"If we're fortunate tonight, then perhaps the good major will sleep through the evening meal as well," Mister Cloutier said, and the other men laughed.

But not Henry. He bent down to his plate and resumed eating.

LATER IN THE MORNING, as she was preparing the daily wash of the sheets and linens, there came a knock at the front door. She went to the foyer, wiping her reddened hands on a towel. When she opened the door to the cold February air, two officers were standing there, hats in hand, bowing in her direction.

"I'm sorry, gentlemen," she said. "I've no more rooms to rent. Perhaps you could try Missus Green, four houses down."

Both officers looked alike, tired eyes and chest-length beards. The one on the left spoke up. "Begging your pardon, madam, but we're not here to rent rooms. We are making an inquiry concerning one of your guests. A Major Tomlison."

"And how can I assist you?" she asked, holding herself tight against the February wind.

The officer on the right said, "I am Captain Slater, and this is Captain Abrams. We are on the staff at the War Department. Major Tomlison was supposed to meet with us there at nine this morning. As you can note, it is nearly eleven."

"I'm afraid I've not seen the major since last evening's meal," Mary said, looking into the tired eyes of both officers.

"So he is staying here?" Captain Abrams asked, hat still in his hand.

She shrugged. "He paid up for two nights. Where he goes is his business."

Captain Slater asked, "Did he join you for breakfast?"

"No, he did not."

A team of horses went by, spraying mud up from their hooves, hauling a gun carriage. The men riding the horses looked so tired that they could fall asleep on the backs of the animals. For some reason Mary watched them until they turned the corner.

Captain Abrams cleared his throat. "If we may, madam
. . . I mean, with your permission. Could we see his room?
Please?"

She hesitated, looking at them, wondering why they
were here. This dandy of a major, her husband had noted.
What possible use could he be to the War Department? Or
to the Confederacy? She sighed, opened the door wider.

"Do come in, gentlemen, but mind your boots. I've
swept and cleaned this doorway this morning. I have no
urge to do it again."

She went up the stairs and the two officers followed her,
keeping quiet. She could sense their embarrassment and difficulty, but she had no sympathy for either of them. At the
War Department, they were out of the way of Union cannon
or Union riflemen, and she was sure they both ate better
than the men in the lines.

At the bedroom door she knocked, twice. "Major Tomlison? Sir, are you ill? There are men here to see you."

There was no answer.

Mary turned to the two officers. "That's the response I
received earlier this morning, gentlemen."

"And you did not enter?" Captain Slater asked suspiciously. "To see if anything was amiss?"

"Sir," she said, trying to sound shocked. "If the major
did not want to come down for breakfast, what business is
that of mine?"

Captain Abrams moved closer. "Madam, if you will . . .
could you please open the door for us?"

She looked at them both again, these well-fed and well-
bred officers who thought they were fighting for honor and
nobility and everything that was grand about the Confederacy. Mary felt cold again and lonely and wished for nothing
more right then than for enough fuel to fill the fireplace, to
empty this house of its cold and dampness.

"Of course, Captain," she said. "At your request."

Mary unlocked the door and opened it up. A small
window on the far wall gave enough light to show a small bed,

nightstand with white jug and basin, and a wooden chair. The wallpaper was beginning to peel away. The two captains entered the room, followed by Mary. The officers looked at each other. The bed was made and did not appear slept in, which made sense, for Major Tomlison was not there.

CAPTAIN ABRAMS SPOKE UP. "His luggage. Did he leave it here in this room, or someplace else in the house?"

Mary said, "All guests here are responsible for their own belongings. I know not where they may be."

Captain Slater looked about the room and out the window. He turned and said, "Madam, earlier you mentioned something about a guest hearing something. Again, what was said?"

"One of the guests, a Mister Cloutier," she said. "A representative to the Congress. He said the door opened during the night, and that Major Tomlison left. But he also said he fell asleep before noticing whether the major had returned."

Captain Slater did not look happy. "Is it possible somebody entered the house at night, to spirit away the major?"

"For what reason?" Mary asked.

"I do not know, madam," Captain Slater said, again looking out the window. "This city is full with Union sympathizers and spies. Major Tomlison had a sensitive position at the War Department. If he had been captured and made to talk . . ."

Mary shook her head. "My husband promptly locks the door at eleven. We have a rule for our guests, that they must be back in our home by then. And I assure you, Captain Slater, that our door was not broken into last night."

The two captains looked at each other, and then Captain Abrams said, "Madam, you have been of service. If Major Tomlison returns, or if you hear any news of where he might have gone, please let either of us know. We can be contacted at the War Department."

"Certainly," she said, leaving the room, and the two captains followed her. As she led them out to the entrance way, Captain Slater turned and said, "This is quite a lovely house, madam."

She smiled. "You do me a service, sir. At one time this house was grand, quite grand. Until . . . well, until circumstances forced my husband and me to open our home to boarders. My husband is an invalid veteran, gentlemen, and we had to do what we could to survive."

Captain Abrams nodded and Captain Slater, the one with the suspicious look about him, touched the brim of his hat in a salute. "Madam, so many of us now do that. In order to survive. Good day, madam."

"And good day to you both," she said.

WHEN THE DOOR CLOSED, she looked out the small door window, until she saw that they had made their way out of sight. Then she went back to the kitchen, splashed some cold water on her face, and then stood before the cold stove, shivering. She looked out the rear window, to the tiny garden where she raised potatoes and turnips these past three summers. Henry was nowhere to be seen. She shivered again, took a lamp down from a shelf, and lit it with a sulfur match.

Mary went over to the cellar door and opened it up. There were noises down there, and she made out the flickering light of a lantern. She called down, "Henry?"

There was silence for a bit, until she called down again. "Henry? It is I, your wife, Mary."

A weak voice. "What do you want, wife?"

She kept her voice steady. "I'm coming down. I must talk with you."

"Mary," came the voice. "Please don't come down. I insist."

"I am sorry," she said. "I have no choice."

She gathered up her skirt and went down the narrow wooden steps, holding the lamp out before her. The air was cold and dank, and when she reached the bottom of the stairs, she turned left. The cellar was made up of arched brickways, with a dirt floor, and in the distance, she saw her husband, head down, staring at his feet.

Mary went closer to him, lamp still held high, and then everything was illuminated as she got closer. Henry was standing there, shovel held in the crook of his half-arm, as he looked down upon the partially filled long hole at his feet. Mary came closer, feeling so cold she could shiver, and she lifted up the lamp and looked down at the hole. She felt like she couldn't breathe. Looking up at her from the bottom of the squared-off hole were the unseeing eyes of one Major Tomlison of the Confederate Army.

"HENRY . . ." SHE SAID, HER voice filled with sadness. "What is the meaning of this?"

"I'm . . . I'm sorry, Mary," he said. "It won't happen again."

She looked up at him, her voice now filled with anger. "You fool! I just had two officers from the War Department upstairs, trooping around this man's room, asking me questions. What would have happened if they had pressed me further, had asked me to come into the cellar?"

He said nothing, staring down at the shovel, his withered arm quivering, and tears came to his eyes. She reached over and hugged him. "I'm sorry, Mister Stuartson. So sorry to raise my voice."

"It's just hard, that's all," he said. "Trying to shovel such a hole with less than two arms. I didn't expect it to take so long."

"No, of course not," she said, looking around the cellar. "And we must be running out of room by now. This is the sixth one, is it not?"

"Yes, it is," he said, his voice filled with pride. "And we did well. Two rings, a watch, the sword and good leather boots. We did well."

She nodded in satisfaction, remembering the first time this had occurred. It had been an accident, that's all. An officer—whose name she could not remember—had gotten drunk at one of the port bars and had come back, and had assaulted her in her own room. Henry had been outdoors in the privy and when he had come back, his voice roaring with rage, he had split the officer's head in with a shovel.

There had never been talk of reporting the matter. Her honor was at stake . . . how could she face anyone in the society circles of Richmond, knowing what had almost happened? And there had been no witnesses, none at all, and so the man had been buried in the cellar. But not before being stripped of his money and valuables, and that one drunk officer had helped pay for food that late fall.

Now, five more men—all of them rich, arrogant officers—had followed the first one, and Mary had been surprised at how easy it had all been. Other officers had come to stay with them at their house, and so many had been fine, courteous men. But those who had been rich, who had been arrogant, who had the type of manner who would order a young boy like her son Tom into lines of Union cannon . . . well, that had been easy enough. Henry would bring them down into the cellar on some promise or another—usually the offer of a strong drink—and they would not suspect a thing. Why would they, with a man before them with only one arm?

Then, there was room in the cellar, and it being so cool, nothing untoward would ever happen. Henry took care of the digging and the disposal, and Mary would quietly exchange whatever goods they secured from the dead officers for food, for clothes, for fuel. And it being wartime, with so many troops moving in and out of Richmond, with desertions rising each month, no one had been missed.

Until this morning, with that stupid officer who had to be connected with the War Department. That had been a narrow escape. But now Mary looked around the cellar, knowing they were running out of room, running out of time.

"Henry," she said simply.

"Madam?" he said, resting wearily on the shovel.

"We must talk, of what is to happen next."

He looked puzzled. "What do you mean?"

Her chest felt heavy at what she was about to say. "The war is lost. You know that. We all know it. In a matter of weeks or months, the Federals will press through and Richmond will be occupied. When that happens, we cannot stay."

"Mary . . . This is our home . . ."

Her eyes filled with tears. "No, it is not. These are our last hours in Richmond. Your business is gone. Our children are gone. Many of our friends and relatives are no longer alive. There is no point in staying here. All I know now is how to run a boarding house, and with the war over, I will not stay in this city and continue to do such work. In wartime, yes. But not here, not in peacetime. And you and I know that the only way we have lived here these years has been because of them."

With that, she moved her hand with the oil lamp, motioning to the mounds of dirt that marked the guests who had come here and who had never left. Mary said, "When the Federals take control of Richmond, the chaos and disorder will eventually disappear. There will be martial law of a sort. And missing guests from a boarding house will be noticed, with the Union Army in charge. No, my dear husband, we must move from Richmond, as quickly as possible, when the time comes."

"To where?" he said, his voice weak. "Where could we possibly go?"

"North. To a large city. Perhaps Baltimore. Perhaps New York."

"New York!" Henry exclaimed. "Among those Yankees and bankers? New York?"

She gently touched his face. "You've told me several times, about how sometimes you have guilt about what you have done. In striking down officers of the Confederate Army. Even if they are sour men who deserve their fate, you've told me that it has troubled you. Am I correct, sir?"

"Yes . . ."

She moved closer, kissed his lined cheek. "Then think of what we can do in New York City," she whispered. "All of those rich Yankees. All of those smug, arrogant Yankees who supported the troops and raised the money to pay for their cannon and uniforms, and who voted for Lincoln twice, all so that you would be wounded and Tom killed and Lucinda made ill and me brought to the class of a boarding house owner. Won't that make you feel better? To strike against them, at their den in New York? Won't it, Henry?"

Finally he smiled, and then bent over to kiss her. "Yes, that is true. That would make me happy indeed. To set our efforts against Yankees, even if there is a peace. Now, if you will excuse me, madam, I must finish."

And then she was going to kiss him again, when the voice came down from upstairs: "Missus Stuartson? Missus Stuartson?"

Henry froze, his eyes wide, but Mary moved away and went to the bottom of the stairs. Up in the kitchen, Mister Gray was looking down at her. "Yes, what is it?" she asked.

"There's an officer here to see you," he said. "He says it is urgent. His name is Captain Slater, and he says it concerns Major Tomlison. The missing officer."

From behind her, she thought she heard Henry make a noise, but she moved forward, going up the stairs.

"Tell him I shall see him momentarily."

IN THE KITCHEN HER hands were shaking, and she washed her face again. To be brought to this . . . to face arrest and ruin and no doubt death . . . both she and Henry, hung by their neck or shot by a firing squad. She took a deep breath, went into the parlor, where Captain Slater, the suspicious-looking officer, was standing by himself by the cold fireplace. She remembered all of the fine parties and receptions that had been held in this very room . . . this room, which was now cold and whose curtains had been torn down and made into sheets for the guests' beds.

Captain Slater turned as she entered the parlor. He bowed to her and removed his hat. "Madam, if I may . . . please excuse this intrusion, but I must speak to you. Alone. Which is why Captain Abrams is not with me."

She stood still in the parlor, looking at him, glad that her skirts were hiding her quivering knees. "Go on, sir."

"It involves Major Tomlison. I believe you know why I am here."

By now her hands were shaking and she brought them behind her, holding them tight. She would not let this officer see her afraid. She would not let this young man think he had gotten the best of her. "Perhaps I do. But perhaps you will tell me."

His face took on a frown. "This is rather delicate, and I apologize in advance for any discomfort I may bring to you. But my station and my responsibilities force me to ask you the question."

Oh, husband, how I wish you were here with me right now. She cleared her throat and tried to keep her voice strong. "Then ask me the question, Captain. Do not be shy."

Here it comes, she thought. *Here it comes. The accusation, the questions, the demand of having her home searched . . . what would she do, oh, what would she say to him when the questions started.*

Captain Slater coughed and said, "Major Tomlison. His room."

"Yes? Would you care to search it again?"

"No, madam, I do not care to search it again. I was going to ask you . . . is his room available? To rent?"

It felt like the foundations of her home had turned to mud and that the house was swaying underneath her, for she felt seconds away from fainting dead away. "To rent?" she asked weakly. "You would care to rent his room?"

The officer nodded. "I am currently living in a loft over a horse barn, near the warehouse district. There are no amenities, no fireplace, and the meals are intolerable. Which is why I came back here by myself, and so quickly. This appears to be a very respectable house, in a very respectable neighborhood. So I ask you again, madam, may I rent that room?"

She then looked at him, at the polished boots and fine sword, and the heavy gold ring on his left hand, and the watch chain about his waist. An officer, true, but an officer assigned to the War Department, one who makes the plans and issues the orders and sends the troops into battle, especially one's husband and one's son . . .

"Of course," she said, bowing to him slightly. "We would be honored."

For the first time she saw him smile. "Madam, I am at your service."

And she smiled in return. "I am sure you will be, Captain. I am sure you will."

Veterans

John Lutz

I t began because Confederate Major General Henry Heth's troops needed boots.

In search of a new supply in a town called Gettysburg, Heth's men marched unknowingly toward death and history. They were noticed by Union soldiers serving under Brigadier General John Buford, who were bivouacked on a nearby hill. Buford sent for Union reinforcements. The ensuing Union troop movements were observed by Heth, who attacked. The newly arrived First Corps, led by Major General John Reynolds, took the brunt of the assault on McPherson's Ridge. Casualties were high, the Union's crack Iron Brigade lost more than half its men, and Reynolds was killed.

Corporal Will Faver, born in Oak River, Missouri, and a Union volunteer, survived. Grape shot had grazed his head, leaving a nasty gash, and a minie ball had taken a bite out of his left arm, but he was alive and still full of fight. Bandaged and determined, he rejoined Union forces on Cemetery Ridge, where they'd been driven backward to hold after fierce fighting.

The Rebs decided not to press the attack in the evening's waning light, so during that night the Yanks regrouped and waited. Reb troops were moving in from the north and west. Pickets were needed to take up position in those directions, well away from the main body of troops, to act as isolated lookouts and give warning of approaching Confederate forces. Dangerous assignments. Which was why Will Faver, wounded but not seriously, and mostly unknown by the men around him, was given picket duty. With a youth named Elliott Nance, a lean and sad-faced Pennsylvanian, Will was sent about half a mile north to take up position in a peach orchard.

There was a moon that night, and the two men were spotted near the orchard and had to break into a run when Confederate light artillery opened fire on them.

Will, who'd won many a picnic foot race in Oak River, simply put his head down and sprinted for the trees. Nance decided to weave to avoid the Rebel fire. Entering the cover of the orchard, Will heard the young trooper's shrill scream.

Will found himself alone in the orchard.

He moved farther into the shelter of the trees. It was June and they'd borne early fruit. The sweet scent of peaches rotting on the ground spooked him, reminding him of decay and death. His lost comrades in the First Corps . . . young Nance. Morose and afraid, he stumbled through the darkness beneath the tree cover, waiting for the artillery to be trained on the orchard. Will had seen wooded areas assaulted by artillery, leafless, blackened skeletal ruins where no life could survive. He hadn't much hope.

The ground dropped out from beneath him, and with a gasp of surprise he slid on his back into a dry creek bed. It would provide him some cover if the artillery decided to open up on the entire orchard. He scooted around to sit with his back braced against the slope of the hard dirt bank. And there he sat listening to his harsh, ragged breathing, living his fear, knowing his duty.

As he had so many times in danger, he slid his hand beneath his shirt and caressed the silver locket with

Sharleen's curl of blonde hair tucked beneath its oval lid. The metal warmed to his touch and calmed him. His faith returned. He would survive this night, this war, and get back to Oak River and live out his life with his wife and the children they planned on having. He knew at that moment that Will and Sharleen Faver would grow old together.

Then his brother said, "Move a muscle, Yank, and I shoot you dead as a stump."

Terror froze Will so he couldn't have moved if he tried. Then through his cold panic seeped warm realization. *The Reb's voice! He couldn't mistake that voice!*

"Luther?"

Luther Faver, Will's older brother, had taken sides in the war first, and joined the Tennessee Volunteers. He'd been in the tobacco business with partners in Memphis, and that was where his loyalties lay. Will was the brother who took over the family farm rather than let it lie fallow, married Sharleen, and sank his own roots deep and forever in Oak River.

"Luther? That you, Luther?"

The dark form of the Reb aiming his musket down at Will didn't move. Then slowly the long barrel of the gun dropped low and to the side.

"My God, it *is* you," Luther said, and scampered down into the gouge of the creek bed with Will. "How in the hell you been, boy?"

"Stayin' alive, I guess."

"Good thing we had orders to bring back prisoners if we could find 'em, or I'da surely opened fire on you when I saw you here." Luther, a tall man with a lean face and darker hair than his brother's, wiped the back of a hand across his forehead and took a swig from a canteen. He recapped the canteen and tossed it over to Will. "Seen Ma lately?"

And Will remembered that Luther wouldn't know their mother had died six months ago. Will had managed to return briefly to Oak River for her funeral. "Gone . . . ," he said, and took a long pull of water from the canteen.

Luther didn't say anything, just stared up at the night sky beyond the peach tree branches. "How 'bout Sharleen?" he asked at last.

"Good. Seen her last six months ago. Me an' her been workin' the farm. She's keepin' it goin' till I come back for good."

"Why'd you ever leave her, Will. You didn't have to fight in this war."

"Neither did you," Will said.

Luther looked surprised. "Me? Why, I had financial considerations."

Will nodded, understanding. "I plumb forgot you were a businessman." He capped the canteen and tossed it back to his brother. "Thing is, Luther, what are we gonna do now."

"Now?"

"I mean, about this here situation."

"I still don't understand why you ever left Sharleen," Luther said.

Will was trying to think of a good answer when Luther shot him between the eyes.

LUTHER SURVIVED THE REST of the war, sustaining only a slight gunshot wound in the Battle of Kennesaw Mountain the following year.

He returned to Oak River a hero. The Mason-Dixon Line ran close to the town, and veterans of both armies were welcomed home. People were eager for healing.

The second day home, Luther rode the aging horse he'd been allowed to keep the three miles out of town to the farm. It was where he'd grown up none too happily. He'd always been jealous of Will, who was the favorite and had gotten everything, from their parents' attention to . . . Sharleen.

Sharleen must have seen him from a window. She came out onto the porch as he approached the log house. The house itself didn't look bad, though it could use a little upkeep, some chinking between the logs and some paint on the shutters. And the porch roof sagged some.

Sharleen had aged better than the house. Though she looked older, she was still trim and beautiful, with her calm blue eyes, and her wonderful blonde hair pulled back now and tied in a swirl atop her head. She was wearing a faded flower-print skirt and a white blouse molded to her by the prairie breeze.

Luther reined in the horse a few feet in front of the porch and gave her back her smile. Then he stopped smiling. "I sure am sorry about Will."

Her smile left her face as if caught by the breeze. "So'm I, Luther. More'n you can know."

He dismounted and walked to stand at the base of the three wooden steps to the plank porch. "Place looks good, except for the fields for this time of summer."

"Frank Ames helps out some. Did some mending and painting last month."

Luther looked at her, fingering the brim of his hat held in front of him. "Ames survived the war?"

"He come back to Oak River six months ago. Lost him a leg at Gettysburg."

"Then he's lucky to be alive."

"He 'peers to think so," Sharleen said. She seemed to shake off her sadness and managed a bright smile that brought back memories to Luther. The smile had been there the night Sharleen had taken the walk with him among the cottonwoods in the moonlight, the times at the local dances when she whirled gaily to the music. The smile that was so uniquely hers was there when she'd won the turkey shoot one cold Thanksgiving, and when she filled in teaching at the schoolhouse, and when she and Will surprised everyone by saying they were getting married. The smile had been there on her wedding day. And no doubt on her wedding night . . .

". . . my manners."

Luther realized she was speaking.

"Do come on into the house," she was saying. "Luther?"

"Sorry," he told her. "My mind was wandering."

"It's no wonder," she said solemnly, "after what all you been through." Over her shoulder, as she led him into the house, she said, "Least it was over and final for Will after Gettysburg. Some small comfort in that."

The inside of the house was neat and clean if sparsely furnished. Will sat in a wooden chair at a square oak table in the kitchen. Sharleen had been cooking. The scent of baked bread was in the air, along with that of brewed coffee.

He watched the sway of her hips beneath her skirt as she moved to the wood stove and poured coffee into a tin cup. She set the cup in front of him, then sat down across from him at the table.

"Gotta be a rough life here for a woman alone," Luther remarked.

"Oh, I'm not alone." Her glance slid to an open doorway.

Luther didn't understand at first. Then he stood up, walked over, and peered into the room. A small child was sleeping in a wooden crib.

"That's Samuel," Sharleen said, when Luther had sat down again at the table.

"Will's son," he said with a forced smile.

"The precious thing he left me," Sharleen said. "I got Samuel. And I got Frank Ames."

Luther took a deep breath. "Sharleen, is Ames . . . ? I mean, are you and him . . . ?"

She appeared surprised, touching the side of her neck lightly in a way he remembered she'd done long ago when she was embarrassed. "Oh, no! It's nothing like that, Luther."

"Maybe not to you, but what about to him?"

She seemed to think on the question. "I don't believe so, and a woman oughta know. I think it's just he's a kind man and he runs the bank and's in a position to help out now and again. I know I'm not the only one he's helped."

Luther raised his eyebrows. "Runs the bank, does he?"

"Surely does. You remember he worked there before leaving to fight. Well, old man Scopes retired and sold his interest to Frank. There's partners and a board, but Frank's president and makes the decisions."

"I'll talk to him," Luther said, and took a sip of coffee.

" 'bout what?"

"Getting a loan to run some irrigation to the fields, turn the soil, and put in some good seed for spring planting. That horse I got out there ain't worth much, but he surely can pull a plow."

He couldn't read the expression on Sharleen's face.

"Luther . . ."

"Remember," he said, "I was raised here on this land. It ain't that I see it as mine, but you and Samuel are family, and nothing can change that." He gave her a reassuring smile. "With what happened to Will and all . . . I mean, I feel duty bound to help."

She studied his face, then nodded, stood up, and poured him some more hot coffee. "It ain't as if we don't need it," she said.

"You done all right," Luther said.

"The Lord knows I tried." She lowered her head, almost as if she were going to pray, but she began to cry quietly.

Luther got up, strode around the table, and hugged her to him until her back stopped heaving and she wiped her nose and was calm.

He caressed her cheek with the backs of his knuckles and she turned her face away. He walked back to his chair and sat down.

"Coffee was something we could never get enough of during the war," he told her. "Towards the end, we'd make it outta most anything we could grind between two stones." He shook his head glumly. "There was lots of things we couldn't get enough of."

"I just bet there was," Sharleen said.

Luther went to see Frank Ames the next morning at the Oak River Bank. Ames was a small man with a jutting chin and bushy dark mustache. He looked startled to see Luther, then stood up behind his desk and shook hands with him. That he'd stood up surprised Luther, as Sharleen had said Ames lost a leg to the Yanks.

"I'm real glad to see you made it back here safe and sound," Luther said.

Ames smiled. Though his angular face hadn't changed much, his gray eyes were a lot older than when he and Luther had competed in the county games five years ago. "Safe, maybe. But I'm not exactly sound, Luther. Lost a leg."

"Wouldn't guess it."

"Got a wood one, foot and all," Ames said, and limped out from behind the desk. "Don't have to work my boot off and on it, anyway. Silver lining." He motioned for Luther to sit in a nearby chair, then went back to sit behind the desk. He ducked his head and looked strangely at Luther. "I heard you were dead, killed at Chickamauga."

Luther raised his eyebrows in surprise, then smiled. "Don't look that way, does it?"

"Nope. Don't have to touch you to know you're real and still among the living."

"War was hell," Luther said.

Ames nodded. "Damned Sherman." He made a pink steeple with the fingers of both hands. "This visit about business, Luther?"

"It is. I understand you been helping my sister-in-law Sharleen. We appreciate that, but now that I'm back, I want to do my duty to her. After all, she's my brother's widow. Family's all that's left after this war, and for lots of folks not even that."

"It was a shame about Will. He was a good boy."

"He was that."

"His widow deserves better than what she's got," Ames said. "What do you have in mind, Luther?"

"A loan for a decent plow my horse can pull, for some irrigation work, a new barn and chicken coop, a well that ain't run dry, and good seed come the spring."

"That's a lot," Ames said.

"Sharleen needs a lot."

"Gettysburg was hell worse than Sherman," Ames said. "Made a lot of Southern widows."

"Northern ones, too."

Ames nodded. "Carpetbaggers are gonna come in here from the North, change this country. Oak River is gonna grow. Guess Sharleen's farm can grow with it."

"You'll help, then?"

"I'll loan you the money, Luther. The work's up to you."

"And I'm up to it," Luther said.

"Just figure out what you need."

Luther drew a sheet of paper from his pocket and unfolded it. "I got it right here."

OAK RIVER GREW JUST as Frank Ames had predicted. And Sharleen's farm prospered. Luther worked hard and became a substitute father for young Samuel, and stayed in the old barn while he built a new one. By late fall the farm had new or repaired outbuildings, but the harvest was meager.

Winter was cold and with more than the usual snow, but Luther kept at his work. Before spring planting, he located water with a divining rod fashioned from a forked branch from a peach tree, a talent that had always been his, and with help from town dug a new well. The spring planting produced a rich harvest that late summer and fall, and Luther and Sharleen began to repay Frank Ames's bank.

At the beginning of their second winter together Luther and Sharleen were married. By that time, nobody was much surprised, and the wedding was a joyful event. The farm became known to the townspeople as the Faver Place.

Both Luther and Sharleen continued to work hard, and when Samuel got old enough he took to farm work. Besides farming, Luther gained a reputation with his dowsing, and the carpetbaggers moving into Oak River paid him handsomely to locate water with his divining rod so they'd not waste time and money digging dry wells.

Frank Ames was soon paid off, and with profits no longer going toward the loan, Luther and Sharleen began to grow rich by Oak River's standards. They replaced the log farmhouse with a fine two-story frame home with a green marble fireplace and a wide front porch.

At the turn of the century Luther had lived longer than he imagined was possible, almost to sixty. But he was healthy and saw more good years ahead for him and for Sharleen.

Samuel had become a tall, handsome man who looked more like Luther than Will, and moved with his young bride to Joplin where they managed a dry goods emporium. One day he appeared at the farm with a fancy carriage pulled by two fine horses, and in his wife's arms was Luther's grandson.

Will's grandson.

"We named him Will!" Samuel said proudly. Then he asked how they liked the carriage and said, "I seen 'em with motors in Kansas City. Nothin' else pullin' 'em!"

"Horseless carriages?" Sharleen asked in amazement. Though graying and thicker through the middle, she was still a beautiful woman, and her eyes widened with the enthusiasm of a youthfulness that would always be hers. The past lived with her and in her.

"So they're called," Samuel told his mother. "I'm gonna talk to a man about a dealership. The carriages might be horseless, but they ain't without profit." He grinned at Luther. "And Dad taught me the value of plannin' ahead."

That evening, sitting before the warm blaze in his marble fireplace, Luther Faver considered that he was one of the luckiest men alive.

The next morning his illness introduced itself, and it never left him. His stomach was never right, and he lost weight until his elbows and knees made sharp angles. Then his hair began to fall out.

Doc Newsner in town didn't know what to make of it. He tried different medications on Luther and bled him with leeches. Nothing seemed to help.

Only Sharleen could comfort him. She stayed awake through the night with him at times, holding his hand while the pain wracked him and caused him to moan and draw up his knees. The nights were the worst time. She would place a folded damp cloth on his forehead and croon softly to him. But the pain persisted.

When Sharleen suddenly came down ill, Doc Newsner figured maybe it was something in the well water.

It wasn't, though. Two days later she died from a burst appendix.

Luther was too ill to attend the funeral. He lay bedridden and alone in the big farmhouse on the Faver Place. Samuel was coming in from Joplin to take him back there to die. Nobody had any illusions about that. They would travel by train to Joplin so Luther could pass while among family.

The night before Samuel was to arrive, Frank Ames paid Luther a visit.

Ames hadn't aged well. He was bent at the waist, walking with the aid of a walnut cane, and his face was deeply lined. His mustache had become gray and scraggly above bloodless lips. As he limped into the bedroom, Luther thought Ames probably wouldn't live much longer than he would.

"Some whiskey in the kitchen," Luther offered.

"Can't drink the stuff anymore," Ames said. His voice had become older than he was, hoarse and so soft you had to listen hard to whatever he was saying.

Luther weakly waved an arm toward the easy chair alongside the bed, and Ames settled into it with a long sigh, his wooden leg extended straight out in front of him.

"Sharleen was buried well," he told Luther. "She was a good woman."

"Always," Luther said. "I hope I did right by her."

Ames drew a briar pipe from his pocket and gave his wooden leg a sharp rap with it. "We came a long ways from Gettysburg," he said, and began packing the pipe's bowl with tobacco from a leather pouch.

"War's a long time ago now," Luther agreed.

"To some it is." Ames struck a wooden match to flame with his thumbnail and held fire to tobacco. He puffed until he got the pipe burning well, then he shook out the match and put the blackened remains of it in the vest pocket of his banker's suit. The room filled with the acrid-sweet scent of the smoldering tobacco leaf.

"Long time ago for everyone," Luther told him. "Time buries everything."

"Sometimes it takes a while, though," Frank Ames said. He reached into the pocket where he'd slipped the burnt match, withdrew an object and laid it on the nightstand alongside the bed where Luther could see it.

Luther raised his head and peered to the side at the glittering object.

"I shined it up for you," Ames said.

"What is it?"

"A locket. Silver. Pretty old now. There's a lock of Sharleen's hair in it."

Something dark and immortal stirred in Luther.

"Your brother Will wore it for good luck in the war. Had it on him when he died."

"Did they send his personal effects to Sharleen?"

"Nope." Ames settled back in his chair and spoke around the pipe stem clamped in his teeth. "I was with Longstreet's troops at Gettysburg, camped near Cemetery Ridge and waiting for morning and the hell it'd bring, when we spotted a couple of Yanks headed for picket duty. The moonlight made them good targets, and some artillery pieces opened fire on them. Killed one of them. The other made it to cover in a peach orchard. I was one of three men sent to capture that lone picket so he wouldn't give information to the Yanks. We didn't know another patrol was sent from Heth's First Corps to capture him. You were in that patrol." The burning pipe tobacco made a soft whispering sound in the quiet room. "I was in the peach orchard and saw what happened that night, Luther. I saw you shoot your brother."

Luther's heart seemed to shrivel. He was having even more difficulty than usual breathing. Possession of the locket was proof of Ames's story. Proof that he was in the peach orchard that night and proof enough of murder. Luther knew that he'd come close to being hanged long ago.

"Why didn't you tell someone?" he heard his own rasping voice ask. "Why didn't you tell Sharleen what happened?"

"I never told her nor anyone else because I knew she needed you," Ames said. "And Samuel needed a father. Me with my missing leg, there was no way in hell I could help her enough, no way I could farm crops and build and be a father to a son not my own. But I loved Sharleen and wanted to do something for her. I couldn't bear to sit and watch her live such a hard life and fall ill and die, or bend beneath her load and become an old woman before her time. You were the answer, Luther. The solution to the problem you created."

"I killed Will so I could have Sharleen," Luther said feebly. There were tears in his eyes. He hadn't cried in decades, not even when Sharleen died.

"That was easy to figure," Ames said. "You always loved her, and you were always jealous of your brother."

"I was a good husband to Sharleen," Luther said. "A good provider, and a good father to her son. Maybe I made it up to her, in a way. Maybe I made amends for what I did."

Ames drew on his pipe and exhaled a cloud of smoke. "I don't think so. I don't think that was enough."

"At least she never found out."

"I didn't say that, Luther."

Luther couldn't lift his head, but he craned his neck painfully so he could see Ames. He didn't like what he saw in Ames's face.

"I told her 'bout a year ago," Ames said. "Showed her the locket."

Luther felt himself go cold from the inside. "She never said anything to me."

"She decided to poison you instead."

Now Luther did manage to raise his head. "Wha . . . ?" The back of his head sank back into his sweat-soaked pillow.

"She's been feeding you arsenic, Luther. Exacting her revenge little by little for what you did to her young husband. Exacting justice. Nothing you can do about it now. It's too late to fix the damage that's been done to you or reverse the process. The poison'll soon have its way."

Luther struggled to speak but could only croak weakly and gasp.

"I thought you oughta know," Ames said, bracing himself with his cane and standing up from his chair with difficulty. "Maybe because I'm a banker and I believe there needs to be an accounting. It's only right. You haven't got much longer and things oughta be settled."

Ames made to leave, then paused and turned. "We were on the losing side, Luther, but you thought you won your own personal war. It took a long time, but you lost just like the rest of us."

Ames limped toward the door. His cane clattered like dry bones as he clumped down the stairs.

Then there was complete silence.

Luther lay with ghosts in the darkening room.

The Cobblestones of Saratoga Street

Avram Davidson

"Cobblestones to Go" said the headline. Miss Louisa lifted her eyebrows, lifted her quizzing-glass (probably the last one in actual use anywhere in the world), read the article, passed it to her sister. Miss Augusta read it without eyeglass or change of countenance, and handed it back.

"They shan't," she said.

They glanced at a faded photograph in a silver frame on the mantelpiece, then at each other. Miss Louisa placed the newspaper next to the pewter chocolate-pot, tinkled a tiny bell. After a moment a white-haired colored man entered the room.

"Carruthers," said Miss Augusta, "you may clear away breakfast."

"WELL. I THINK IT is outrageous," Betty Linkhorn snapped.

"My dear," her grandfather said mildly, "you can't stop progress." He sipped his tea.

"Progress my eye! This is the only decently paved street in the whole town—you know that, don't you, Papa? Just because it's cobblestone and not concrete—or macadamor—"

"My dear," said Edward Linkhorn, "*I* remember when several of the streets were still paved with wood. I remember it quite particularly because, in defiance of my father's orders, I went barefoot one fine summer's day and got a splinter in my heel. My mother took it out with a needle and my father thrashed me . . . Besides, don't you find the cobblestones difficult to manage in high-heeled shoes?"

Betty smiled—not sweetly. "I don't find them difficult at all. Mrs. Harris does—but, then, if *she'd* been thrashed for going barefoot . . . Come on, Papa," she said, while her grandfather maintained a diplomatic silence, "admit it—if Mrs. Harris hadn't sprained her ankle, if her husband wasn't a paving contractor, if his partner wasn't C. B. Smith, the state chairman of the party that's had the city, country, *and* state sewn up for twenty years—"

Mr. Linkhorn spread honey on a small piece of toast, "'If wishes were horses, beggars would ride.'"

"Well, what's wrong with that?"

"'. . . and all mankind be consumed with pride.' My dear, I will see what I can do."

HIS HONOR WAS INTERVIEWING the press. "Awright, what's next? New terlets in the jail, right? Awright, if them bums and smokies wouldn't of committed no crimes they wouldn't be in no jail, right? Awright, what's next? Cobblestones? *Cob*blestones? Damn it, again this business with the cobblestones! You'd think they were diamonds or sumpthin'. Awright. Well, um, look, except for Saratoga Street, the last cobblestones inna city were tore up when I was a boy, for Pete's sake. Allathem people there, they're living inna past, yaknowwhatimean? Allathem gas lamps in frunna the houses, huh? Hitching posts and carriage blocks, for Pete sakes! Whadda they think we're living inna horse-and-buggy age? Awright, they got that park with a fence around it, private property, okay. But the streets belong to the City, see? Somebody breaks a leg on wunna them cobblestones, they can sue the City, right? So—cobblestones? Up they come, anats all there is to it. Awright, what's next?"

His comments appeared in the newspaper (the publisher of which knew what side his Legal Advertisements were buttered on) in highly polished form. *I yield to no one in my respect for tradition and history, but the cobblestoned paving of Saratoga Street is simply too dangerous to be endured. The cobblestones will be replaced by a smooth, efficient surface more in keeping with the needs of the times.*

As the Mayor put it, "What's next?"

Next was a series of protests by the local, county, and state historical societies, all of which protests were buried in two-or-three-line items in the back of the newspaper. But (as the publisher put it, "After all, C. B., business is business. And, besides, it won't make any difference in the long run, anyway.") the Saratoga Street Association reprinted them in a full-page advertisement headed "Protect Our Heritage," and public interest began to pick up.

It was stimulated by the interest shown in the metropolitan papers, all of which circulated locally, "Bluebloods Man the Barricades," said one. "20th Century Catches Up with Saratoga Street," said another. "Beloved Cobblestones Doomed, Historical Saratoga Street Prepares to Say Farewell" lamented a third. And so it went.

And it also went like this: *To the Editor: Sir, I wish to point out an error in the letter which claimed that the cobblestones were laid down in 1836. True, the houses on Saratoga Street were mostly built in that year, but like many local streets it was not paved at all until late in the '90s. So the cobblestones are not so old as some people think.*

And it went like this, too:

Mr. Edward Linkhorn: Would you gentlemen care for anything else to drink?

Reporter: Very good whiskey.

Photographer: Very good.

Linkhorn: We are very gratified that a national picture magazine is giving us so much attention.

Reporter: Well, *you* know—human interest story. Not so much soda, Sam.

Photographer: Say, Mr. Linkhorn, can I ask you a question?

Linkhorn: Certainly.

Photographer: Well, I notice that on all the houses—in all the windows, I mean—they got these signs, *Save Saratoga Street Cobblestones.* All but one house. How come? They *against* the stones?

Reporter: Say, that's right, Mr. Linkhorn. How come—?

Linkhorn: Well, gentlemen, that house, number 25, belongs to the Misses de Gray.

Reporter: de Gray? de Gray?

Linkhorn: Their father was General de Gray of Civil War fame. His statue is in de Gray Square. We also have a de Gray Avenue.

Reporter: His *daughters* are still living? What are they like?

Linkhorn: I have never had the privilege of meeting them.

MISS ADELAIDE TALLMAN'S FAMILY was every bit as good as any of those who lived on Saratoga Street; the Tallmans had simply never *cared* to live on Saratoga Street, that was all. The Tallman estate had been one of the sights of the city, but nothing remained of it now except the name *Jabez Tallman* on real estate maps used in searching land titles, and the old mansion itself—much modified now, and converted into a funeral parlor. Miss Tallman herself lived in a nursing home. Excitement was rare in her life, and she had no intention of passing up any bit of attention which came her way.

"I knew the de Gray girls well," she told the lady from the news syndicate. This was a big fib; she had never laid eyes on them in her life—but who was to know? She had *heard* enough about them to talk as if she had, and if the de Gray girls didn't like it, let them come and tell her so. Snobby people, the de Grays, always were. What if her father, Mr. Tallman, *had* hired a substitute during the Rebellion? *Hmph.*

"Oh, they were the most beautiful things! Louisa was the older, she was blonde. Augusta's hair was brown. They always had plenty of beaux—not that I didn't have my share of them, too, mind you," she added, looking sharply at the newspaper lady, as if daring her to deny it. "But nobody was ever good enough for *them.* There was one young man, his name was Horace White, and—oh, he was the *hand*somest thing! I danced with him myself," she said complacently, "at the Victory Ball after the Spanish War. He had gone away to be an officer in the Navy, and he was just the most handsome thing in his uniform that you ever saw. But *he* wasn't good enough for them, either. He went away after that— went out west to Chicago or some such place—and no one ever heard from him again. Jimmy Taylor courted Augusta, and William Snow and Rupert Roberts—no, Rupert was sweet on Louisa, yes, but—"

The newspaper lady asked when Miss Tallman had last seen the de Gray sisters.

Oh, said Miss Tallman vaguely, many years ago. *Many* years ago . . . (Had she really danced with anybody at the Victory Ball? Was she still wearing her hair down then? Perhaps she was thinking of the Junior Cotillion. Oh, well, who was to know?)

"About 1905," she said firmly, crossing her fingers under her blanket. "But, you see, nobody was *good* enough for them. And so, by and by, they stopped seeing *anybody.* And that's the way it was."

THAT WAS NOT QUITE the way it was. They saw Carruthers.

Carruthers left the house on Sunday mornings only—to attend at the A.M.E. Zion Church. Sunday evenings he played the harmonium while Miss Louisa and Miss Augusta sang hymns. All food was delivered and Carruthers received it either at the basement door or the rear door. The Saratoga Street Association took care of the maintenance of the outside of the house, of course; all Carruthers had to do there was sweep the walk and polish the brass.

It must not be thought that because his employers were recluses, Carruthers was one, too; or because they did not choose to communicate with the outside world, he did not choose to do so, either. If, while engaged in his chores, he saw people he knew, he would greet them. He was, in fact, the first person to greet Mrs. Henry Harris when she moved into Saratoga Street.

"Why, hel-lo, Henrietta," he said. "What in the world are *you* doing here?"

Mrs. Harris did not seem to appreciate this attention.

Carruthers read the papers, too.

"What do they want to bother them old stones for?" he asked himself. "They been here long as I can remember."

The question continued to pose itself. One morning he went so far as to tap the Cobblestones story in the newspaper with his finger and raise his eyebrows inquiringly.

Miss Augusta answered him. "They won't," she said.

Miss Louisa frowned. "Is all this conversation necessary?"

Carruthers went back downstairs. "That sure relieves my mind," he said to himself.

"THE NEWSPAPERS SEEM TO be paying more attention to the de Gray sisters than to the cobblestones," Betty Linkhorn said.

"Well," her grandfather observed, "people *are* more important than cobblestones. Still," he went on, "*House of*

Mystery seems to be pitching it a little stronger than is necessary. They just want to be left alone, that's all. And I rather incline to doubt that General M. M. de Gray won the Civil War all by himself, as these articles imply."

Betty, reading further, said, "*Hmmm*. Papa, except for that poor old Miss Tallman, there doesn't seem to be anyone alive—outside of their butler—who has ever *seen* them, even." She giggled. "Do you suppose that maybe they could be *dead*? For years and *years*? And old Carruthers has them covered with wax and just dusts them every day with a feather mop?"

Mr. Linkhorn said he doubted it.

COMPARISONS WITH THE COLLIER brothers were inevitable, and newsreel and television cameras were standing by in readiness for—well, no one knew just what. And the time for the repaving of Saratoga Street grew steadily nearer. An injunction was obtained; it expired. And then there seemed nothing more that could be done.

"It is claimed that removal would greatly upset and disturb the residents of Saratoga Street, many of whom are said to be elderly," observed the judge, denying an order of further stay, "but it is significant that the two oldest inhabitants, the daughters of General M. M. de Gray, the Hero of Chickasaw Bend, have expressed no objection whatsoever."

Betty wept. "Well, why *haven't* they?" she demanded. "Don't they realize that this is the beginning of the end for Saratoga Street? First the cobblestones, then the flagstone sidewalks, then the hitching posts and carriage blocks—then they'll tear up the common for a parking lot and knock down the three houses at the end to make it a through street. Can't you *ask* them—?"

Her grandfather spread his hands. "They never had a telephone," he said. "And to the best of my knowledge—

although I've written—they haven't answered a letter for more than forty years. No, my dear, I'm afraid it's hopeless."

Said His Honor: "Nope, no change in plans. T'morra morning at eight A.M. sharp, the cobblestones *go*. Awright, what's next?"

AT EIGHT THAT MORNING a light snow was falling. At eight that morning a crowd had gathered. Saratoga Street was only one block long. At its closed end it was only the width of three houses set in their little gardens; then it widened so as to embrace the small park—"common"—then narrowed again.

The newsreel and television cameras were at work, and several announcers described, into their microphones, the arrival of the Department of Public Works trucks at the corner of Saratoga and Trenton Streets, loaded with workmen and air hammers and pickaxes, at exactly eight o'clock.

At exactly one minute after eight the front door of number 25 Saratoga Street, at the northwest corner, swung open. The interviewers and cameramen were, for a moment, intent on the rather embarrassed crew foreman, and did not at first observe the opening of the door. Then someone shouted, *"Look!"* And then everyone noticed.

First came Carruthers, very erect, carrying a number of items which were at first not identifiable. The crowd parted for him as if he had been Moses, and the crowd, the Red Sea. First he unrolled an old, but still noticeably red, carpet. Next he unfolded and set up two campstools. Then he waited.

Out the door came Miss Louisa de Gray, followed by Miss Augusta. They moved into the now absolutely silent crowd without a word; and without a word they seated themselves on the campstools—Miss Louisa facing south, Miss Augusta facing north.

Carruthers proceeded to unfurl two banners and stood at parade rest, so to speak—with one in each hand. The snowy wind blew out their folds, revealing them to be a United States flag with thirty-six stars and the banner of the Army of the Tennessee.

And while at least fifty million people watched raptly at their television sets, Miss Louisa drew her father's saber from its scabbard and placed it across her knees; and Miss Augusta, taking up her father's musket, proceeded to load it with powder and ball and drove the charge down with a ramrod.

After a while the workmen debated what they ought to do. Failing to have specific instructions suitable to the new situation, they built a fire in an ashcan, and stood around it, warming their hands.

THE FIRST TELEGRAM CAME from the Ladies of the G.A.R.; the second, from the United Daughters of the Confederacy. Both, curiously enough, without mutual consultation, threatened a protest march on the City Hall. In short and rapid succession followed indignant messages from the Senior Citizens' Congress, the Sons of Union Veterans, the American Legion, the B'nai Brith, the Ancient Order of Hibernians, the D.A.R., the N.A.A.C.P., the Society of the War of 1812, the V.F.W., the Ancient and Accepted Scottish Rite, and the Blue Star Mothers. After that it became difficult to keep track.

The snow drifted down upon them, but neither lady, nor Carruthers, moved a thirty-second of an inch.

At twenty-seven minutes after nine the Mayor's personal representative arrived on the scene—his ability to speak publicly without a script had long been regarded by the Mayor himself as something akin to sorcery.

"I have here," the personal representative declared loudly, holding up a paper, "a statement from His Honor announcing his intention to summon a special meeting of the Council for the sole purpose of turning Saratoga Street into a private street, title to be vested in the Saratoga Street

Association. *Then*—" The crowd cheered, and the personal representative held up his hands for silence. "*Then*, in the event of anyone sustaining injuries because of cobblestones, the City won't be responsible."

There were scattered boos and hisses. The representative smiled broadly, expressed the Municipality's respect for Tradition, and urged the Misses de Gray to get back into their house, please, before they both caught cold.

Neither moved. The Mayor's personal representative had not reached his position of eminence for nothing. He turned to the D.P.W. crew. "Okay, boys—no work for you here. Back to the garage. In fact," he added, "take the day off!"

The crew cheered, the crowd cheered, the trucks rolled away. Miss Louisa sheathed her sword, Miss Augusta unloaded her musket by the simple expedient of firing it into the air, the Mayor's representative ducked (and was immortalized in that act by twenty cameras). The Misses de Gray then stood up. Reporters crowded in and were ignored as if they had never been born.

Miss Louisa, carrying her sword like an admiral as the two sisters made their way back to the house, observed Betty and her grandfather in the throng. "Your features look familiar," she said. "Do they not, Augusta?"

"Indeed," said Miss Augusta. "I think he must be Willie Linkhorn's little boy—are you?" Mr. Linkhorn, who was seventy, nodded; for the moment he could think of nothing to say. "Then you had better come inside. The girl may come, too. Go home, good people," she said, pausing at the door and addressing the crowd, "and be sure to drink a quantity of hot rum and tea with nutmeg on it."

The door closed on ringing cheers from the populace.

"Carruthers, please mull us all some port," Miss Louisa directed. "I would have advised the same outside, but I am not sure the common people would *care* to drink port. Boy," she said, to the gray-haired Mr. Linkhorn, "would you care to know why we have broken a seclusion of sixty years and engaged in a public demonstration so foreign to our natures?"

He blinked. "Why . . . I suppose it was your attachment to the traditions of Saratoga Street, exemplified by the cobble—"

"Stuff!" said Miss Augusta. "We don't give a hoot for the traditions of Saratoga Street. And as for the cobblestones, those dreadful noisy things, I could wish them all at the bottom of the sea!"

"Then—"

The sisters waved to a faded photograph in a silver frame on the mantelpiece. It showed a young man with a curling mustache, clad in an old-fashioned uniform. "Horace White," they said, in unison.

"He courted us," the elder said. "He never would say which he preferred. I refused Rupert Roberts for him, I gave up Morey Stone. My sister sent Jimmy Taylor away, and William Snow as well. When Horace went off to the Spanish War, he gave us that picture. He said he would make his choice when he returned. We waited."

Carruthers returned with the hot wine, and withdrew.

The younger sister took up the tale. "When he returned," she said, "we asked him whom his choice had fallen on. He smiled and said he'd changed his mind. He no longer wished to wed either of us, he said. The street had been prepared for cobblestone paving, the earth was still tolerably soft. We buried him there, ten paces from the gas lamp and fifteen from the water hydrant. And there he lies to this day, underneath those dreadful noisy cobblestones. I could forgive, perhaps, on my deathbed, his insult to myself—but his insult to my dear sister, that I can *never* forgive."

Miss Louisa echoed, "His insult to *me* I could perhaps forgive, on my deathbed, but his insult to my dear sister that I could *never* forgive."

She poured four glasses of the steaming wine.

"Then—" said Mr. Linkhorn, "you mean—"

"I do, I pinioned him by the arms and my sister Louisa shot him through his black and faithless heart with Father's musket. Father was a heavy sleeper, and never heard a thing."

Betty swallowed. "Gol-*ly*."

"I trust no word of this will ever reach other ears. The embarrassment would be severe . . . A scoundrel, yes, was Horace White," said Miss Augusta, "but—and I confess it to you—I fear I love him still."

Miss Louisa said, "And I. And I."

They raised their glasses. "To Horace White!"

Mr. Linkhorn, much as he felt the need, barely touched his drink; but the ladies drained theirs to the stem, all three of them.

A House Divided

Marc Bilgrey

It was a sunny afternoon in late March 1865. My company had been on its way to Richmond, when we were ambushed. I ran for cover in the nearby woods, hoping to circle around the Rebs and take them from the opposite direction. I thought I might bring down an officer or two in the process. But no sooner had I entered the dense foliage, when I was met by a gray who butted me in the head with his rifle. I dropped to the ground like a marble statue. After that everything went black.

When I awoke hours later, I clutched my aching head and looked up to discover a full moon shining in a dark sky. Around me were the bodies of both Union and Confederate men. I can only suppose that both sides had left me for dead.

As I gazed upon this macabre sight I thought about what a grim business it all was. I had agreed to serve my government to the best of my abilities, for I am not a coward. But, just the same, I took no particular joy in it either.

Staggering to my feet I discovered that my Colt .32 caliber revolver, Enfield .57 caliber rifle, knapsack, haversack, belt, and cartridge box were gone. Looted no doubt. After looking in vain for a canteen amongst the corpses I made my way through the trees till I came to a clearing. There I hoped to find a drink of water.

"Good evening, Billy Yank," said a voice.

Instinctively, I reached for my gun but found nothing, not even a holster. I spun around to see a Reb staring me in the face. His gray uniform was ripped in the right arm, and he had dried blood on his upper lip. He looked to be even younger than me, which was twenty. The tiny bugle insignia on his kepi told me he was infantry, same as me. I saw him aim his Smoothbore musket straight at my chest.

"Good evening, Johnny Reb," I said. Without my gun I knew my options were extremely limited.

He came closer. As he did, I heard a cannon blast in the far distance. For a split second he turned toward it. This brief lapse of attention allowed me the time to leap upon him.

He fought fiercely as we wrestled about in the dirt like two dogs fighting over a bone. He was able to land a blow to my stomach. Recovering quickly, I sent an uppercut to his chin, dazing him enough so that I was able to pry the musket out of his hands. I turned the barrel to his head as my finger found the trigger.

"Drop your gun, Yankee!" yelled a voice behind me. "Drop it or I kill you!"

I let the musket fall from my hands to the ground.

"Stand up now!" said the man's voice. "The both of you, and I ain't got all day."

The Reb and I stood up. As we did we looked at the man who was giving us the orders. He was wearing a pair of brown trousers, boots, and a green shirt. He had a long white beard and in his right hand was a C. S. Spiller and Burr .36 caliber revolver.

"Now," he said, addressing us, "step away from the musket."

When we had taken a few steps back, the old man came over, still holding the revolver and staring us down, reached over and picked up the Reb's musket. Then to my amazement, he smashed the musket against some rocks and threw the pieces off into the woods.

"I don't understand," said the Reb, "why are you doing this? We're on Confederate soil. You ought to be helping me take this here Yankee to his just reward, not—"

"I'll thank you to not be giving me any advice, soldier," said the old man, moving his gun just slightly toward the Reb.

"Didn't anyone ever tell you to show a little respect 'round your elders?" The old man pursed his lips and said, "Okay, boys, here's how it's gonna be. You listen to me and do exactly as I say, or I will put some very large holes in you. Nod if you understand me."

I nodded. I was too scared to even look toward the Reb. Being taken prisoner by the enemy was one thing, but what this man had in mind, only the fates knew for certain.

"All right, fellas," said the old man, "now y'all gonna turn around and start walking. You will walk up to that there ridge, and then you will continue to walk till I tell you to stop. And keep in mind that I have the firearm and I ain't afraid to use it. In point of fact, I would be more than glad to use it. It don't matter to me which one of you boys tries anything in the way of an escape attempt. I will kill you where you stand same as I would kill a squirrel for my dinner. Or if you both give it a try, so much the better. I could use the target practice. Not that I need it. I been known to bag a songbird at one hundred paces. Now then, let's start marching."

We began walking. The Reb was next to me. Neither of us said a word. Behind us I heard the old man's footfalls in the twigs. We passed trees and bushes and not much else. I wondered where this old man was taking us. Was it some kind of Rebel trick? Perhaps they were working together and planned to torture me for the purpose of extracting information. I hoped not, since I didn't know a blessed thing. I was a private, not a general.

Here I was, six months into my conscription and thus far luck or providence had prevailed. Though I had seen battle, other than a few minor cuts, I had emerged unscathed. But now I was convinced all was lost.

I was suddenly seized by a severe bout of homesickness. It occurred to me that I would never again witness a sunrise over the Hudson River nor picnic in the bucolic hills of the Bronx with my parents and sisters. The thought of no longer being able to stop in front of Van Horn's Dry Goods Shop, look in the window, and see my father working behind the counter, conversing with the owner or a customer, filled me with a great sadness. How I longed to walk the noisy, crowded streets of Broadway one last time. Odd, the thoughts of a condemned man.

Approximately five minutes later, by the light of a bright moon, I saw a small cabin appear amidst some trees. When we reached the structure (which had boarded-up windows with a few bullet holes in them) the old man told us to stop.

"All right, boys," said the old man, as we turned to look at him, "I want you both to walk inside and each of you to sit down on one of my chairs. And, once again, if you got any ideas of trying to get away from me, give them up now. If a man can't shoot two intruders in his own cabin, ain't no place on this here earth that he *can* do any shootin'. Now, get inside. Get!"

The Reb went in first and then I followed behind him. Inside the cabin we found hardback chairs and each sat down on one. In one corner was a stone fireplace where crackling flames cast a pale yellow glow throughout the room. An oil lamp flickered on a table. The walls were unadorned except for one shelf which held a few books. In the dim light I could not read the titles. Across the room was a door which might have led to another room or a closet. In another corner was a coat rack.

"Move them chairs close together," said the old man. "I want them right next to each other."

We did as we were told.

The old man sat down on a chair opposite us and held the gun pointed in our direction. "How rude of me," he said. "I don't know your names. Mine's Samuel."

The Reb sat up stiffly and said, "I am Private—"

"Stop!" said the man. "Ain't no ranks in my home. I just want your Christian name."

"Owen," said the Reb, reluctantly.

"And you?" he said, looking at me.

"It's Andrew," I said.

"Just like the vice president," he said.

"He ain't no vice president of mine," said Owen, with disdain.

"Oh, no?" said Samuel. "And why is that?"

"Come on, man. You live not twenty-five miles from Richmond and have to ask that question? Are you a traitor? Or just a Northern spy?"

I had to admit he had a valid question, one I had thought of myself.

"I am neither a traitor nor a spy. I am neutral," said the old man.

"Ain't no one neutral in this war," said Owen. "You are either Union or Confederate, and that's a fact."

"You seem to know a lot, boy, how old are you?" said Samuel.

"I'm nineteen," he said, holding up his chin.

"Yup," said Samuel, smirking, "nineteen's about the age when one knows everything."

Now it was my turn to speak. "Sir, I mean you no disrespect, but what do you intend to do with us? Did you bring us to your home simply to have a discussion?"

"You ain't any more polite than your brother, here," said Samuel.

"He ain't no brother of mine," said Owen.

"All men are brothers," said Samuel. "Andrew?"

"New York," I said, "born and bred."

"Dirty Yankee," said Owen.

"I'll thank you not to speak unless spoken to, Owen," said Samuel, tilting his gun at the Rebel. "Now then, would anyone like a drink of water?"

My mouth was parched and so apparently was Owen's. After Samuel gave each of us some water from a tin cup, he sat back down on the chair in front of us and, still holding the revolver, looked us over. I tried to figure out what he would do next. Would he kill me first or Owen? And why bring us to the cabin at all? Why not simply do the deed outside amidst the lost souls I had encountered only moments earlier? Unless he first meant to see if we possessed any knowledge of our superior's plans.

I put aside speculating upon my captor's motives long enough to think about my sweet Bessie. How I longed to see her beautiful brown eyes, her long chestnut hair and feel the touch of her hand again. Why had I delayed in asking for her father's blessing, and postponed my proposal of marriage? The idea that I had wanted to wait till I became a journeyman in order to receive a higher salary seemed so unimportant now.

"Owen, you never told us where you were from," said Samuel.

"I'm from Georgia," he said, "Two days' ride from Atlanta. Or what's left of it after that devil, Sherman, got finished turning it to rubble." Owen looked at me and sneered.

"I suppose Sherman had a hand in Harper's Ferry, Chickamauga, Cold Harbor, First Manassas, and Fredericksburg," I said.

"You can't compare the total destruction of entire cities and thousands of people to—" said Owen.

"That's enough, children," said Samuel. "There's been atrocities on both sides. But that's what war is about, ain't it? Killing as many people as possible?"

"While you sit in your little house out in the forest?" I said.

Samuel squinted at me. "I'll have you know, young man, that I wasn't always a hermit. I was a telegraph operator and a fine one, too, till your army cut my wires."

"I knew it!" said Owen, smiling. "You *are* one of us. Now go on, put the Yankee out of his misery," said Owen.

"Shut up," said Samuel. "I'll do the killing when I please and to whom I please."

This quieted down the Reb, who swallowed and slumped in his chair.

"There's been too much bloodshed," Samuel said, softly. "How many thousands of wives are there without husbands? How many children without fathers? It's gone on long enough. Year after bloody year. This here is a great nation. If the war continues we'll all perish, like that fella in Greece, Pyrrhus. His victory cost him everything. When enough people die, there ain't no winners anymore. Everyone loses."

"That's a right nice speech," said Owen. "How about I take you to meet General Lee and you can recite it to him personally?"

At this, I watched Samuel slowly stand up. *Uh oh,* I thought, *now the Reb's gone and done it. He's opened his mouth once too often and he's going to get us killed for sure.*

Samuel moved away from his chair and took a few steps back while still keeping the gun trained on us. Then he said, "Stand up, both of you."

I stood up as did Owen. *Here it comes,* I thought. I closed my eyes and said a silent prayer. The old man would probably shoot us then toss our bodies outside. Wild animals would undoubtedly devour our remains.

"Strip off your uniforms," said Samuel.

I glanced at Owen and he at me. Was I in some strange morphine dream?

"You heard me," said Samuel. "Take off your uniforms. You can keep on your undergarments."

Neither Owen nor I moved. Samuel held his gun and

took a step closer. I began undoing the nine brass eagle buttons on my frock coat.

"Your brogans, too," said Samuel, pointing at my feet.

I removed my boots. In a few seconds I had my uniform and kepi in my hands.

"Throw them all in a heap on the floor," said Samuel.

My dark blue coat, cap, trousers, and boots landed first, and then Owen's gray ones fell on top of mine. Samuel went over to the uniforms, picked them up, and, with one motion tossed the pile of clothing into the fireplace. The flames immediately began their work and shortly all that remained were ashes.

"All right, boys," said Samuel, reaching for some rope on a nearby table, "sit down on your chairs."

"I don't reckon I understand any of this," said Owen. "What's the idea of burning our clothes?"

"Just be glad it's your clothes I'm burning and not you," said Samuel. "Now, sit down."

We did, as Samuel placed the gun in his left hand, pulled out an Arms D Guard Bowie knife and cut a piece of rope. He threw the rope piece to Owen and said, "Tie Andrew to his chair."

Owen picked up the rope and lashed my wrists to the back of my chair with great vigor. After fashioning what felt like elaborate knots, he tested them a couple of times, then, apparently satisfied with their strength, turned to Samuel.

"Now what would you like me to do?" said Owen. "I could interrogate him regarding troop movements—"

"Sit down on your chair and place your hands behind your back," said Samuel, as he came over with the rope. He cut off a piece and tied Owen's hands to the back of the chair. When he was done he stood up.

"I am puzzled," I said. "First you preach peace, then you have us disrobe and bind us to chairs. You seem as warring as the armies you claim to have contempt for."

"A good observation; however, the difference is, thus far I have only threatened violence while *your* armies are doing far more than that."

"I don't understand," said Owen. "Here you are, living practically within spitting distance of the capital of the Confederacy, and yet you profess to hate both sides. Why?"

I saw Samuel stare at us and then, for the first time since we'd entered the cabin, he looked away, toward one of the boarded-up windows. For a minute or two he said nothing. Then he turned and faced us again.

"I suppose it don't hurt none to tell you. My wife was killed by a Union soldier. We'd just celebrated our thirty-fifth wedding anniversary."

"A Union soldier," said Owen, nodding his head and looking at me with a kind of sardonic smile.

"I had been out of town trying to get some new relays for my switchboard, my telegraph, and when I got back half the village lay in ruins. And my beloved Violet . . ." I saw him blink a few times and wipe his eyes with his sleeve.

"Untie me," said Owen. "You hate the Yankees as much as I do."

"I ain't done yet," he said. "I neglected to mention my son, Clayton. He was about your age when he joined up. They sent him to some godforsaken battlefield. All I know is, he come back in a box. Turned out he was shot by someone in his own regiment. I been told it ain't that uncommon an occurrence. Apparently, the smoke from the gunpowder and cannon fire can turn the landscape into a cloudy white sheet. A man can't see his own hand in front of his face."

"It was an accident?" asked Owen.

"Of course it was an accident, but that don't make him any less dead. That's right, boys, you see, I've had enough of this damn war, of all wars forever. Now, I'm going to go to my bedroom over there and get some sleep. I suggest you try to have yourself a little rest as well."

Samuel went to the front door, locked it, pocketed the key, then walked into the bedroom and closed the door.

I looked back at Owen. He gave me a mean stare.

"We should try to get out of here," I said. "Tomorrow he'll more than likely shoot us. Probably wants to execute us at dawn."

"What do you mean, 'we,' Billy Yank?"

"Listen," I said, "this man is insane, you heard him. His gun doesn't care which of us is blue or which is gray. We've got to work together here."

"Together?" he said, as if he'd just drunk lemon juice.

"That's right, because if we don't help each other we'll both be dead. And it'll be for nothing. It won't be for the glory of the North *or* the South. What are you going to do when you get to heaven and they ask you how you died? Tell them it was on the field of battle as a hero, fighting for what you believed in, or on the filthy floor of some crazy old man's cabin for no good reason at all. Think about it, Owen."

It was the first time I had said his name out loud. It felt unnatural, the way it does when you learn a word of a foreign language and then try to pronounce it. I saw Owen look at the ceiling.

After some time he turned back in my direction. "What'd you have in mind?" he said.

"The first thing we need to do is get out of these ropes. Let's move our chairs back to back and each try to undo the other's bonds."

He nodded and we shifted our chairs around. I felt his fingers on my ropes and then I moved mine upon his. For a few moments we worked in silence. I listened to the sound of our breathing and thought about how hungry I was.

"I sure would fancy some pepperpot about now," I said.

"What's that?" said Owen.

"It's a stew made of tripe and doughballs."

"My mouth waters at the thought."

"I can't say as I'd turn down some sweet potato pie myself."

"My girl, Bessie, makes the best pepperpot in the world."

"Well, my gal, Louisa, can bake a cracklin' bread that just about melts in your mouth. Why the very smell of it alone is enough to send you . . ." Owen's voice trailed off.

I felt his fingers start to loosen the knots of my rope. Even so, the added pressure made the rope burn into my wrists.

"What did you do before you were conscripted?" I said, pulling on his rope.

"I volunteered, but before that I was a farmer. My family owns a small farm. We grow the best corn in two counties, ask anyone. How about yourself?"

"I'm a printer, actually still an apprentice."

I managed to loosen Owen's rope a little. "Now, just so you don't get all kinds of thoughts," I said, "if you get out of your ropes first and decide to leave me and try to break down that front door, the old man will hear you and shoot you for sure. But if we are together I can help disarm him and we can get the key to the door."

"Now you're my helper, Billy Yank?"

"Just for the duration of our imprisonment in this cabin, Johnny Reb."

"Have it your way," said Owen, as I felt him loosening my rope.

As it happened, I was out of mine first. I got up and continued working on his. Eventually, his rope slipped to the floor.

Owen went over to the table and picked up the oil lamp, while I got a small log from next to the fireplace to use as a weapon.

"C'mon," I said, as we quietly made our way toward the bedroom door. When we got there, I put my ear to it and heard snoring. "It sounds like he's asleep," I said, silently testing the doorknob. It was unlocked.

We opened the door swiftly and went inside the room. The old man woke up and reached for the gun which was on his night table, but I got to it first. I dropped the piece of firewood and held the revolver steady.

"So," said Samuel, "this is the way it's going to be, is it?" From under his pillow he grabbed his knife and lunged toward us.

I fired the gun and he clutched his chest and dropped to the floor.

"I guess my plan worked," he said, smiling.

"How's that, old man?" said Owen.

"I wanted you boys to murder me," he said, his right hand over a bloody stain. "I didn't want to live no more. It ain't no life being alone, ain't no life living with this war."

"Why all the political debating?" I asked.

"And why'd you make us take off our uniforms?" said Owen.

"To show you that you're both the same, just boys. Men now. I figured I'd tie you up and then you'd have to put your differences aside against a common enemy. Me. If a couple of young bucks like you can do it, maybe the world's got a chance yet."

"There might be a doctor we could take you to," I said.

"Forget it," he replied. "Besides, I want to die. You two were the answer to months of prayers."

Samuel lay real still and his eyes stared straight ahead, unblinking. I closed his lids. Owen reached into Samuel's pocket and removed his key.

We went into the other room. I took a couple of deep breaths and set the gun down on the table.

"He was a peculiar old man," said Owen.

"Yes," I said, as I noticed the coat rack in one corner of the room. I went over, took a brown coat off a hook and tossed it to Owen. "Here," I said, "no point in running around in our undergarments."

I put on another coat, this one black, and headed toward him. To my surprise, Owen now had the gun in his hand and was pointing it at my heart. "Are you going to shoot me?" I asked.

He stared into my eyes for a long time, then replied, "I don't shoot civilians."

After that, he unlocked the door, stepped outside and disappeared into the night.

I lingered by the open door looking at the shadowy trees. A moment later I walked out of the cabin toward the quiet darkness beyond.

Blossoms and Blood

Janet Berliner

The sun rose over Bloody Pond, promising another hot and humid Tennessee day and heightening the odor of decay and death. Little moved in the stillness of that dreadful morning; little except the shoulders of the slim Union soldier who knelt at the edge of the pond, looking out across the bodies. Thinking how well the night breezes had masked the stench with the heavy smell of peach blossoms from the orchard that lay at the eastern end of what, two days before, had been dubbed the Hornet's Nest.

Next to the soldier lay an open haversack, which held a stack of papers inked with the smudged words of a lengthy war report. Working with deft hands, the soldier transformed the pages into miniature boats, the kind that children construct when they go to the park to feed the swans. They formed a flotilla, which one by one the soldier floated out into the water, watching it until it wedged between bodies, on a sea of mud and caked blood.

When the last boat had been launched, the soldier dug into the knapsack, retrieved what was obviously a journal, and began to read . . .

PETER WAS EIGHTEEN WHEN he first heard the guns of battle. They scared the living daylights out of him. Having for the last few years considered himself a lover not a fighter, the last thing he wanted was to become embroiled in the actual conflict.

By disposition of his birth in Cairo, Illinois, Peter Louis was a Yankee. By disposition of his heart, he was a Confederate. He'd become such in 1860, after spending Easter with his second cousins who lived on a farm in southern Tennessee, in the rich farmlands southwest of Pittsburg Landing known as Shiloh. The entire trip seemed magical. He rode the rivers, up the Ohio to the Tennessee and then south, which fueled a love of riverboats that started when he met a young adventurer named Clemens. On the trip, he saw a countryside so green and beautiful he almost cried, and just before his arrival, the trees burst forth with a profusion of flowers. It was as if the Lord had planned for him to be there during peach blossom season and fall in love with Lucy.

Lucy, the pretty little light-skinned, fifteen-year-old daughter of his family's slaves.

What a time they'd had, rolling around in the fragrant reds of fallen blossoms in the ten-acre peach orchard, in full bloom at the west end of the pond at the edge of his cousin's farm. How they'd laughed, scratching their initials into the trunk of the tree beneath which they had consummated their passion.

How angry he had been when, with the slim and boyish frame he remembered now distorted and heavy with child, she'd escaped and found him and shamed him before his fashionable Cairo family.

"It's your child, too," she'd said, talking like she was white folk. "You got to care for it, Peter."

Care for it? What business did she have even thinking that? He took her to the local hotel, where he made love to her once or twice, then beat her roundly until the baby loosened.

"You murdered your own child," she sobbed.

He put his ear to her bare belly. He could hear and feel nothing.

"Murderer," she said, turning her back on him.

Feeling only relief, he dispatched her back to the South where she belonged and thought about leaving home to board the Mississippi steamboat captained by his old acquaintance, twenty-five-year-old Samuel Clemens.

He thought about it much too long, off and on for more than a year. By the time he'd made up his mind, Clemens had left the river. He had been elected second lieutenant in an irregular unit of fifteen men, whose self-proclaimed duty it was to keep an eye on Grant's men.

Clemens being something of a hero to him, Peter deliberated joining the same unit. Again, he thought too long. Quickly bored by saddle sores, Clemens said the hell with it. Riding an old mule because he'd injured his foot jumping out of a hayloft, he hightailed it back to silver country to take up a career as a journalist.

To Peter, that sounded like the perfect life. He decided he'd much rather be a reporter than a soldier, and he tried to get a job with the local paper. When that didn't immediately pan out, he took a civilian job in the local telegraph office, where he figured he could read and learn from the important papers that passed regularly through his hands.

While Clemens remained his hero, Peter quickly came to detest General Sherman, a red-headed, gaunt man with a grizzled short-cropped ginger beard, wild eyes, and a hungry look. He read that Sherman had recently returned from medical leave for a nervous breakdown. The general was left with fidgeting fingers, his shoulders twitched incessantly, and he was always picking at something, twirling a button, or fiddling with his whiskers. Not wishing to be tarred with a similar brush, Peter made sure that he presented to the world a calm demeanor.

He also adopted General Grant's affect of perpetually chewing on an unlit cigar.

Though Grant was, to his regret, a Yankee, he was worthy, Peter thought, of admiration. This led to a deep interest in the Yankee reports that passed through his hands, many of which came from the pens of Generals Sherman and Grant.

When the papers particularly fascinated him, he took them home to study at his leisure, so that when the war was done—he figured that to be only a matter of a few months—he could make a name for himself by writing about them. He became familiar with the reports, returns, and information that Grant sent to Washington, telling of the strength and position of his command, as demanded by Secretary of War Stanton. Although he was a civilian, the Secretary was said to be as stern and demanding as any man in the military, which helped to earn him the nickname "Old Man Mars."

Since Peter kept the reports, they never reached their destination. Furious, Secretary Stanton complained to General Halleck, who at once suspended Grant from command and ordered him to Fort Henry.

Learning of this, Peter felt pleased with his contribution to the war effort. After all, he had caused it to happen by secreting away the documents. He thought about ceremoniously burning the valuable papers he had kept, but he could not let go of so significant a trophy. Unless they actually saw the orders, Washington Headquarters would never know whether the General had dispatched the messages or failed to do so while in some alcoholic haze. It would forever remain a mystery to which only he, Peter Louis, held the answer.

Peter's pleasure at having changed the course of the war was short-lived. Grant's replacement had received a leg injury; Grant was returned to duty to await first Buell's army, then the arrival of Halleck, who would take command.

By the end of February of the year 1862, Peter was ready to make a new contribution to the war effort. While he did not want to join the regular army and risk being wounded or killed, he had become enchanted by the romance of war and wanted to learn more firsthand. He declared himself a Confederate, packed the papers in a haversack, and took off up the Cumberland River for Nashville, which had become a fast-growing railroad and industrial center. He wanted to see for himself the arsenal of munitions and supplies in the factories there, to learn firsthand about percussion caps and muskets, about sabers and saddles. He wanted to see the looms where the gray cloth was produced for uniforms.

Later, he determined to see New Orleans. He took the railroad south to Memphis, then down the Mississippi where he tied himself to the illicit cotton trade for a while before proceeding to New Orleans. There, because he fancied himself handsome decked out in the dress blues of the Orleans Guards Battalion, he convinced them to take him on as their recorder.

By the beginning of April, Peter found that history had taken him full circle. He was headed for just what he hadn't wanted to experience firsthand, what veterans fondly called the Elephant: Combat. Worse yet, they were marching dead in the direction of the one place he would just as well have avoided, the peach orchards of Shiloh.

On a march, a battery could travel up to five miles an hour on a good road, Peter wrote in his daily journal. He also talked of the fires they built in holes in the ground, of the Confederate belief that food traveled less heavily in the belly than the haversack, so they ate their three-day rations at once and went hungry for the rest of the way. He wrote in the rain and on mud-stained pages of hearing Yankee bugles, of rumors of coughing cured by the application of red-hot pokers, of diarrhea and of nightmares of dead men yelling, "Retreat, retreat!" The only pleasant occurrence, he wrote, was the day they came across Northerners eating a breakfast of hot meat, white bread, and sweet coffee.

Stealing into their camp, he filled his belly with food and his haversack with letters and photos. General Johnston sanctioned the scavenging by acquiring for himself a Yankee tin cup. He would use it to direct battle, he said, index finger hooked through the handle.

Peter endured intermittent showers and steamy sunshine with a certain degree of stoicism. He strangely felt no real fear until he was shot at by fellow Confederates who saw the dress-blue uniforms of the Orleans Guard and, thinking them the enemy, fired upon them. At that, he and the others turned their dress-blues—"graveyard clothes" the Federals called them, when they found out what had happened—inside out and wore them with the white silk linings visible. This to prevent being killed by their own, who naturally assumed that anyone wearing blue had to be a Union soldier.

On April 5, 1862, encamped within a short distance of the enemy army that was going about its normal business, Peter wrote in his journal, unconsciously echoing what Sherman had written to Grant that very day: "I don't believe that anything much will happen today. Some picket firing maybe. Nothing more."

The rain stopped. The moon rose, lighting peach orchards in full blossom reminiscent of the spring of his youth. He took a walk toward the picket line. He would be safe there. It was an unspoken rule. No attacks were made at night on the line. It was a time for the swapping of tobacco and coffee and tall tales, a time for the gathering of firewood and courage.

"Are you not afraid, Soldier?" a muffled voice asked him.

"Yes," Peter said, surprising himself. "Grant is a clever man. He must be prepared for all eventualities."

"One can never be prepared for all eventualities," the voice went on. The face was half turned away, masked by the brim of a cap pulled low.

"I would like to forget about the war for this night," Peter said.

"I have thought of nothing else since we buried fifteen of our dead at Fallen Timbers. Would you walk with me in the orchard, Soldier?" the voice said. "Surely if we decorate ourselves with blossoms we will be protected from harm."

The Union soldier slouched, head averted, while walking awkwardly in a uniform that seemed to be much too big. They walked for a while in silence. Then, stopping several feet before a tree that stood directly in the moonlight, the young soldier pointed at the trunk.

"Look. It's still there."

"Lucy?"

"Took you long enough," she said. "I thought perhaps you had forgotten me." She removed her hat and turned to face him. In the full moonlight her face was etched more with sorrow than with hatred. "I buried him here. Our son. Here among the blossoms. He has been waiting a long time to see you, Peter."

"How could I place you in this context? How could you be a soldier?"

"Why not? After what you did to me, it was easy." She laughed, a hollow, humorless sound. "Besides, do you think I told them that I was a woman? A nigger woman?"

At 8:00 a.m. on April 6, Sherman heard picket firing in his front. Johnston, who heard it, too, hoped to drive the disorganized Federals into the swamps of Snake and Owl Creeks and destroy them.

To the Country Boys of Shiloh, the shots were an overture. They were young and inexperienced volunteers, but what they lacked in experience they made up for in valor. Advancing upon the enemy, they broke silence and sang as they marched to the band playing "Dixie."

The shelling began, every fifteen minutes, red streaks arcing against the sky. By the end of the day, the Federals had been driven back to Pittsburg Landing, but that night, while the Rebels looted from captured Yankee camps and did little to reorganize their scattered units, Grant reinforced his lines with the fresh troops of General Buell and Lew Wallace and at dawn on the seventh launched a counterattack, which, by early afternoon, had the Confederates in full retreat.

After the battle, the dead horses were burned.

Despite the shine of mercury, the odor of ammonia and turpentine, and the promise of chloroform and ether, after the battle, the Hornet's Nest was a tangle of the dead and the dying. Neither arrowroot nor belladonna, mustard or acacia or camphor, could cure their mortal wounds. The volunteers filled the shallows of Bloody Pond, knowing that no amount of quinine, of iodine and opium, could bring them back from the edge of death.

The sun rose over Bloody Pond, promising another hot and humid Tennessee day and heightening the odor of death and decay. Little moved in the stillness of that dreadful morning, little except Lucy's slim shoulders as she knelt at the edge of the Pond, looking out across the bodies.

She did not have to look down into the pond for Peter. There was no need. The bayonet was planted too deep. He could not have moved from the tree where she had left him, thinking as she did how well the night breezes would mask the stench of his decay with the heavy smell of peach blossoms.

Next to Lucy lay Peter's haversack, which held a stack of papers inked with the smudged words of a lengthy war report. Working with deft hands, she transformed the pages into miniature boats, the kind that children construct when they go to the park to feed the swans. They formed a flotilla, which one by one she floated out into the water, watching it until it wedged between bodies, on a sea of mud and caked blood.

When the last boat had been launched, she dug into the knapsack, and retrieved what was obviously a journal.

Holding it in her hand, she stared at a world that was red with bombs and blossoms and blood. Then she began to read . . .

Whistling Dixie

Billie Sue Mosiman

I tried to get Cotton to stay behind when we left for the battle at Crowley's Ridge down by Helena. I expected to find Sergeant Norman Kilpatrick on my own and kill him dead. Norman had first taken our farm away, as he was the loan officer at the Helena, Arkansas, bank before the war, and then the scoundrel bought the place himself for pennies on the dollar. He'd wanted it for years, as the land lay adjacent to his own. Then when the trouble between the states started, Norman joined up with the other side. A traitor to his people! There wasn't a man in my opinion needed dying more. The farm had been all we had after our pa died, a place that was in our family for fifty years. Once Norman foreclosed and moved us out, we drifted to Little Rock, following behind Rebel troops, hearing all the tales about General Holmes, who commanded them, and Sterling Price, his second-in-command.

While living in a tent on the outskirts of Little Rock, I waited for the army to come for me. I didn't want to leave my ma, my four sisters, and Cotton with no one to help them, but I knew it was my time to fight. The battles had been raging for a long time, and I'd neglected to join, knowing my family had

111

need of me more. But I'd heard Norman was with the Fort Curtis regiment in Helena, back in the same town he was a traitor to, back as a Union soldier and willing to turn his cannon on his fellow Confederates. I meant to make him a casualty.

It was June 1863 when the infantry recruiter came to our tent flap. He'd come down the line in our civilian tent city, looking for able men, looking to fill the ranks for a rumored plan to take back Helena. I watched him approach on horseback and the way he took off his cap at each tent as he called out the old men and the boys. Once he got to me, I was waiting, the hot sun in my eyes. Right behind me in the shadows, Cotton listened, and before I knew it he'd stepped up to my right, smart-saluted the officer, and said, "Me too, I'm going, too."

Cotton was twelve then, tall for his age, but just twelve and my only brother. I pushed him behind me and grinned nervously at the captain. "He's not right in the head, sir. He's just a boy. He won't be going."

"He's big for a boy," said the weary officer, slapping his Rebel cap on his dusty horse's flank. "We got boys with us littler than him. We got boys his age who just volunteered."

"Yessir!" Cotton said, whipping his arm from my grip so he could sidestep me and get up front again. "I'm big and I can shoot the eye from a red turkey at a hundred feet."

The captain's lips twitched into a bitter smile. "We need some sharpshooters like you, son. And you there," he said, pointing his cap at me. "How old are you now?"

"I turned seventeen this month, sir," I said, standing straight as a willow reed.

"Well, we can use both of you. Come on over to the garrison and we'll get you outfitted with caps. There ain't no uniforms to be found in the state of Arkansas. Bring what weapons you got at hand; we're short on rifles, too."

I stood staring after the captain as he rode away, his hat back on his head, a dust cloud raised in his wake that obscured him finally, and then I turned on Cotton.

"I'm taking you out to the woods and I'm bringing Daddy's razor strap." Ma had made me head of the family and look what I'd just let happen. I wanted at that moment to whip Cotton raw.

Cotton cringed at the idea. He hung his head and said, "J. T., Daddy would've let me go."

"No, he wouldn't! Who's going to stay with Ma and the girls? Who's going to keep them safe now if we both go to war? You should have stayed here."

Cotton reached into his pocket and brought out his wing-bone whistle. He put it to his lips and blew some sad melody. He'd carved the whistle from the bone of a robin and always said it was a lucky piece, but here he was blowing it on the day he offered to go get himself killed and that meant to me it wasn't lucky at all.

"God dangit, Cotton, put that away and go get your musket. Maybe they've got powder and lead, 'cause if they don't, me and you are gonna be shooting air at the Feds."

They drilled us for a month, supplied us with plenty of powder and chunks of lead that we made into balls. All the while I watched Cotton closely to make sure he was learning what he had to know. It was true he could shoot so well he could bring home supper every single night, but what would happen when the prey was shooting back? I didn't know how I was going to protect him from grapeshot and artillery bombs. I didn't know how things had gotten so bad these last years. Why all of Arkansas was in a perpetual startled state that the Union army had occupied Helena, seventy miles south of Memphis, one of our strongest agricultural and commercial centers, while the rest of the state was controlled by Confederates. How had we let them sneak in and take it over that way?

I'd heard the soldiers garrisoned down in Helena were from places like Iowa and even from way north in Pennsylvania. I heard they hated Helena's cold winters and stifling, disease-ridden summers, that they called it "Hell-in-Arkansas." I would turn my head away when I heard those tales, remembering hanging from Muscatine grapevines over deep cool ravines, remembering the rising and falling of the Mississippi behind the levee and how we swam and fished in the waters. It was my town. My home. And I'd been cheated out of it and seen it taken over by strangers.

From fifteen hundred souls, Helena once swelled by another twenty thousand when General Prentiss brought in his troops. Now I heard the twenty thousand was down to four thousand, due to the rest being sent to Vicksburg to fight.

It was rumored all around the camp that we'd take back Helena. Whispers ran from cook to drummer, from captain to private: Helena would not stand, not with most of their troops away on the march.

Cotton said one night late in June, "I'm not scared, J. T."

I scraped the last of the beans from my tin plate with a corner of cold cornbread before replying. Cutlery had been in short supply and most meals we couldn't find a spoon to save our lives. "You ought to be. If you ain't scared when we get down to Helena, you'll take the first shot."

"I just mean I won't let you down."

I looked over at him in his gray cap pulled jauntily over one eye, his dirt-encrusted clothes, and saw the little boy hiding behind the man's words. He was really scared, despite the protest. Maybe I could knock him out during the attack, just roundhouse him in the chin and then I wouldn't have to worry about him taking a gut shot or a head wound. We'd both heard how bloody these battles could be. We'd seen relatives come home missing arms and legs, hands and fingers. And now they were saying there might be a paddlewheel steamer down on the Mississippi at Helena, just waiting with its big old guns to blow us all to kingdom come. It floated on the muddy water, gun turrets poised and at the ready.

"It's not me you need to worry about letting down," I said. "It's Ma and the girls. If you don't come back from this campaign, they'll be mighty damn let down."

"What about you?" he asked. "What if . . . ?"

I waved away his worry. "Nothing's going to take me down, Cotton. I know it, somewhere down in here." I pointed to my gut. "I'm coming out of this like Old Glory after cannon fire. I'll be waving in the wind, a hero. I wouldn't be surprised if they make me a captain."

I didn't believe that, didn't really have any gut-feeling, but I had to make Cotton believe it. If he feared he'd be fighting on alone without me at his side, he'd surely collapse before we ever entered the fray. I looked around the camp and saw too many other boys who were surely as young as Cotton. Men grouped around them like hens over chicks, giving them courage, telling them tall tales of heroic deeds done in other battles and those about to commence down in Helena. If they could not impart real protection for the youths, they at least could bolster their faith, the way I was doing for my brother.

We were all on pins, sleeping restless, dreaming and waking with nightmares. The orders were forming and the battle plans were being consolidated. Holmes commanded us and Price was his man, then came Fagan, all three figuring what troops to lead against Helena and how to position them in attack. On July 2 the thousands of us were called out to parade in full summer sun and Holmes spoke from a platform raised in the center of his men. Those of us who could not hear were told in whispers by the men in front, the word passing back through the ranks like a whispering wind.

Cotton and I caught the whispers and sent them on behind us. "We're nearly sixty-two-hundred strong," Holmes shouted and the cheers went up. "The Union in Helena is smaller in number, and that's our advantage. But they have the terrain in their favor, men, and I want you all to know, those of you not from that area, that it won't be easy to overrun it. There are hills and deep ravines. There's Fort Curtis to take, and I am sure they have made fire pits, earthworks, to hide in like dogs to shoot us as we approach. If I know Prentiss, he's still smarting from defeat at Shiloh, so he'll be bound and determined to put the fire to us. But that city is our city, men! They've held it long enough. If we hit them while the battle of Vicksburg is going on, we can scatter the bastards and run them straight into the mighty Mississippi!"

The message was halting, coming as it did in bits and pieces from those in front of us, but it sounded good to me. I wanted everything back the way it had been. And I wanted to find and face the scalawag, Norman Kilpatrick. I'd stick my long blade knife through his black heart. Some way, after the war ended, I'd convince the bank to let me try to catch up on the taxes. I'd point out the ruthlessness of Norman and how he just wanted my land for his own.

It galls me now to think how I stood before him, all dejected and sad, tears coming to cloud my eyes. I'd mentioned the problem of the slaves running off and how I was doing all the work of ten men trying to save the crops. I demeaned myself before him with my begging and pleading. I promised once we got the cotton and corn to market, I'd give every single penny to the bank, but that man just sank back in his big leather chair and laughed like there was no tomorrow. "We're not waiting," he said finally in a dark voice. "We're taking that farm, and we want you off it in a fortnight."

He certainly did. And in a fortnight he had made up the papers in his name, too.

Ma cried the entire month, selling off some of her best dishes and quilts because we couldn't carry them with us. My sisters, Janie, Sugar, Marly, and Ruthanne, all looked on me with betrayed eyes as if it was my fault the slaves had absconded and the fields had gone to ruin. It wasn't my fault even if I did tell them to go if that was what they had to do. I was no abolitionist, exactly, but I'd never seen the slaves happy a day in their lives and that pulled me down, too. It was better to try to till and hoe and harvest with only Cotton and the girls to help me than to see those dark faces giving me sidelong looks of woe.

I had not come to fight against the men who would steal and set free our slaves. They'd already done that with their posters and with the war. The Emancipation Proclamation had been issued a year already, and it was said a company of free Negroes were standing fire in Helena and another company had been trained there and sent south. No, I was going to march on Helena for an altogether personal reason, and no one but Cotton had to know it.

"We leave for Helena tomorrow, men," Holmes was shouting and his words were carried back and back until they reached us. "We strike them on the Fourth of July! At the coming of the day!"

The cheers and stomping feet of the assemblage sounded like a great swell of thunder going up to greet the sky. I stomped, too, and Cotton cheered, and neither of us thought about dying, not even for a second. In our minds we had already won the battle and were mighty victors, proud to wear the Grey.

OUR ARMY REACHED THE Allen Polk house, five miles from Helena, on July 3. By that time the troops had lost some confidence in Holmes's competency to command. Here he was taking us against what was apparently a formidable defense that would take Armageddon's forces to breach. Holmes commanded Price and Marmaduke with the Calvary, to take their units, and together it would be a three-pronged attack. Holmes told Marmaduke to take his 1,750 dismounted Calvary to Rightor Hill northwest of town. On his left a Calvary brigade under L. M. Walker, a West Pointer from Tennessee, was supposed to prevent any Federal reinforcements from reaching the hill. Fagan's 1,339 men would move on Hindman Hill, southwest of town. But the main thrust would be made by Price, with 3,095 men against Graveyard Hill near the center of the defensive perimeter. "We all attack at daylight," Holmes said.

Cotton and I were under Fagan's command, and we were going to have to take a well-fortified hill. I knew the treacherous Hindman Hill, had climbed it a thousand times as a child. It was pocked with sudden drops into ravines; the hillsides were steep, densely wooded, and gloomy as a place this side of Hell could be. I had hoped we'd be with Price, for I trusted him more, but this was our orders, and I'd get up that hill if it was the last thing I ever did.

The last five miles to our rendezvous against Prentiss's batteries in Helena was a morbidly silent march. Men walked softly and glared around at the night, fearing the Union knew we were coming and might be lurking along the way. A half-mile from our position, Fagan halted us, and his officers waved their arms for us to hunker down right where we stood. We were waiting for first light. I pulled Cotton over close to my side and cupped my hand around his ear. "I want you to drop to the rear when we move on them."

Cotton jerked away his head and then caught my own ear in his cupped palm and replied, "I'll be damned if I will. I'm no yellow belly!"

I whispered to him again, this time gripping the top of his shoulder so hard I knew it would leave marks. "You do what I say or when we get through here today I'll take the hide right off your ass."

Again Cotton tore away from me and then scooted a few feet distant. Damn him, he was going to disobey me. He seemed to court jeopardy and I had to find a way to keep him alive. I shivered in the dew damp night, glancing fearfully at the dog star. We all watched the eastern sky, staring at it as if Christ in heaven was going to rise with the sun. Fog coasted along the ridges and down in the low places, hanging from tree limbs like ghosts, wrapping itself around the troops as if to swallow us.

Our muskets were primed and ready, our lead and powder hung in rawhide bags securely at our sides. I didn't have a bayonet, but I had my hunting knife strapped against my leg inside my boot. I could smell the fear rising from those thousand and more men, their sweat coming despite the early morning chill.

The light broke, struggling through milky fog like the brow of a god almighty ship sailing out of the night. It wasn't sunrise yet, and I wondered if Holmes had meant to wait till sunrise, but evidently Fagan thought he'd meant true first light. I hoped he was right, Lord, I prayed for him to be right. Before I could muster my thoughts, we were all on our feet and those in front of me were running forward. We were like a thunderous pack of wolves descending on the city's stronghold, and when we closed on the hill, the shouts and yells went up that sounded like a battalion of banshees let loose from the bowels of hell. I screamed, too, running alongside Cotton, keeping him always in my sight. I screamed in misery and disappointment that life had been so cruel, I screamed in frustration that it was still too foggy dark to know exactly where I was going, and I screamed in fury, hoping to kill the men who would keep Helena from me.

The first thing we encountered were fallen logs spread across the approach to the hill. Our men stumbled and fell, crawled and stood again only to strike up against another impediment and tumble headlong. The Feds knew we were coming now and must have been alert because artillery began to boom and the battlefield lit up with fiery blossoms of death. As I ran, my nostrils stinging with the scent of gunpowder, I wondered why Price wasn't also attacking Graveyard Hill and why we were the only troops under fire. Hadn't Price seen first light? Were we going to do this all alone, take all the fire, be wiped off the face of the earth without any help whatsoever?

"It ain't daylight!" someone screamed, and the cry was taken up even as we hurried forward under rifle fire that seemed to come from ground level, and from artillery bombs raining down overhead. "We're too early!" men shouted, and then we all understood Fagan's mistake. There were precious minutes between first light and sunrise. On this fateful day it was a discrepancy of half an hour. But there was nothing to do now but race forward and beat the terror that chased through our veins.

The rifle fire was coming from earthworks, rifle pits dug in the ground just at the ascent of Hindman Hill. I could still see Cotton, though now there were towers of acrid smoke and the fog was thick as gray velvet all around us. The sky was raining with lead and my shoulders were hunched against it. Fire burst over and over from the pits, and it was like entering the gates of Hades to go there. But the pits kept us from the hill and we would have to take them. At the zenith of Hindman Hill, cannons spewed iron balls of death at us, tearing up great gouts of dirt that sent men flying and broken bodies into the sky to mix with the falling lead.

I was breathing like a cow giving birth. My feet stumbled over Rebels lying in my way, and my face and shoulders were splattered with the blood of men caught in cannon fire. "Oh, God," I cried, never having imagined it would be this horrible. My mind fell back and my body kept going, rushing toward the rifle pits. I could see a pit in front of me now looming out of the fog and smoke. There were men in it, three firing and four or five of them reloading their weapons. "There!" I screamed to Cotton, "Shoot there and take the pit!"

Cotton slowed, brought his rifle to his shoulder and taking aim, shot one of the Feds square in the face. I had run closer, for I was not as good a shot as Cotton, and I raised my own musket and took down a second Fed. Troops behind us converged and together we fell into the pit, fighting with rifle butts and fists, kicking and screaming, our nostrils flared, our lust to kill paramount.

I had lost sight of Cotton in order to survive the next minute and then into the next, but it was over fast, the Feds falling under our attack. I pulled my knife out of the man's ribs where I'd buried it and twirled around, looking for another to attack. I saw Cotton on the far side of the bloody pit, going hand to hand with a man double his size. Before I could reach him another Rebel soldier stuck a bayonet through the big man's back and Cotton pushed him down into the pit, stomping on his head as if it were a venomous snake.

We had taken the pit, and looking to our right and left we saw our soldiers had taken the other pits, too. A victorious swell of cries went up, whoops and hollers, as I stepped on top of dead men to take Cotton into my arms. We had crossed a continent and dropped into a bower of death, but we were still whole.

All around me soldiers who had taken the pit scrambled out again and pressed forward. "Stay here!" I yelled at Cotton above the rifle shots and cannon fire. "Don't move!"

Cotton wrestled away from me, scowling, and began to fill powder into his musket. If I hit him I reasoned he'd be out long enough to escape the worst of it. I stepped to one side of him and swung the butt end of my musket against the side of his temple. The hard wood stock connected loudly with his head. He went down like a heavy sack of feed, dropping on top of the big dead man who had tried to kill him.

I checked the pulse in his wrist and then leapt from the pit. I had to move forward and get into Helena and find Norman Kilpatrick. I could taste the sweet revenge on the back of my tongue and it sung a siren song in my head. I would get back our farm. I would save my family's future.

Between the earthworks and the hill there was more impediment, more fallen logs strewn about like kindling. The fire now from the cannons on the hill came like clockwork, booming so loud my ears rang and went near deaf. I saw our men crawling into hollows and behind logs to reload.

Sunrise exploded like no day before it. My feet began to slip in the blood. The ground was littered with our men, groaning and dying, calling out for their mothers and for God's mercy. I took little sips of air through my mouth, unable to stand the stink of death everywhere around me. I fired and fell to the ground, grabbing for my powder and lead to reload my musket. I stood and ran a few feet closer and fired again, toward the blooms of fire I'd seen coming from the hillside. They were coming out to meet us! They were coming down the hill in droves and I saw our troops falter, turn back, and begin to scatter. I saw men climbing under logs and searching for deeper ravines throughout the dense woodland, this time to hide instead to reload. I heard Fagan's command to fall back, and then in just one minute more I heard his command to raise the white flag of surrender.

Now I could see it clearly. Hundreds of us were splayed out on the killing grounds, bleeding and taking last breaths. Four Feds came out of the last scraps of wispy fog, rifles pointed, and told me in excited voices to throw down my gun. A dozen men behind me did as they were told, tossing their weapons, and when I saw that, I let go of my musket to let it clatter at my feet. I worried they'd find Cotton and think him dead or bayonet him to make sure. "My little brother's back in the pit behind me," I said as they rounded a group of us up. "He's got a bruise on his temple but he's still alive."

A captain with the Feds heard me and told me he'd check for him, "Now git your Reb ass moving before I shoot it off for you, you sonovabitch."

My heart, so long beating fast and under pressure, thundered to a slow sad beat that seemed to thump right up against my ribs. We were defeated, and it was unbelievable. We'd lost so many, hundreds of us instantly shattered by artillery. By now Price might be waging a furious attack on Graveyard Hill, but that didn't help us now. Hundreds of the living and wounded were laying down guns and being rounded into groups to be marched into Helena. What they'd do with us there I could not imagine, not knowing if they had a stockade built or not.

"Have you a Sergeant Norman Kilpatrick?" I asked one of the Feds prodding me in the back with the bore of his rifle.

"He's the Orderly Sergeant up there on that hill, manning the cannon," the man said proudly. "He broke all you Reb bastards down!"

Up on the hill. Straight up Hindman Hill stood Kilpatrick with his torch for the cannon, the murdering fiend.

Sunrise had broken in the east hours before, but the light here in the near woods was still grim and smoke-filled. More Rebel soldiers lay in sorry disarray all around and it made my eyes tear up again until I took my fists and rubbed my eyes clear.

"Move on!" the Fed behind me said, burying his rifle bore deeper into my back ribs.

I couldn't even look back for Cotton.

I DIDN'T SEE MY brother until I'd been boarded on the USS *Tyler*. It was a massive paddlewheel, a hundred eighty feet long and forty-two feet wide. There was a hastily built five-inch oak bulwark over all the top of the deck to protect it from attack. It carried a thirty-pound Parrott gun and six eight-inch smoothbore cannon. This monster alone could have defended Helena for many hours.

We had heard Price and Holmes and Walker had been repulsed. They were already straggling back to Little Rock under defeat. I counted it Holmes's fault, telling his officers something so vague as to "attack at daylight." Some did attack at first light, like Fagan, but the more experienced Price, it was said, waited until sunrise. With all our troops so divided on time of attack, how could we expect our courage to win the day?

Price was the only commander to take the opposition. Twice repulsed, he tried a third time and took the battery, but when he turned the guns on the retreating Feds he found the guns disabled. When Holmes joined him, as the commanding officer he gave such confusing orders to the men that some of them tried to go to Fagan's aid and others moved to attack Fort Curtis. Finally, they were all attracting fire so fierce that the bodies piled on top of bodies and Holmes called for the retreat.

Cotton was in the hundreds of captives put aboard the *Tyler* for a trip up to Memphis. They'd kept us all garrisoned only one day and then we were marched to the river and caught first sight of the warship on the dawn of July 5. Throughout the night the Feds had celebrated their awesome victory, taunting us with the fact they had held off an army much greater in number.

"You Reb bastards couldn't fight your way out of a string-tied bale of hay," they said to us.

That was not the truth, of course, for we'd fought like the insane, moving toward nearly certain death from cannon and rifle, bombarded by artillery so hard it made the earth move. We died brave and fought hard, but we'd never be given proper credit when it was known we had to surrender and when the rest of Holmes's troops, battered by *Tyler*'s cannons and fire from the four batteries Prentiss had set up around Helena, turned back in retreat.

Cotton, thank God, was sitting against a wall of the ship, his head in his hands when I found him. When he looked up at the calling of his name, his eyes teared and he stumbled like a lame calf to his feet. "J. T.," he said, holding on to me hard, "I thought you were dead."

And then he cried, giving out hard gasps, as I held on to him tightly. "Why did you hit me?" he cried. "I was fighting good as anyone, so why did you do it?"

"I couldn't face losing you on the hill," I said. "That you got as far as the rifle pits was due to God's grace."

He saw other men watching him before turning away in shame and embarrassment, so he wiped down his grimy face and took in a big breath. "They say we're going to Memphis, to a prison there until the war's over."

"That's what they say."

"I heard Lee was routed in Gettysburg on July 3 and yesterday while we fought, Grant took Vicksburg."

I had not heard the news so that it was a slap in the face, causing me to jerk suddenly, like a man going into convulsions. The war . . . the war was finally nearing an end. And we had lost it. "Lee was beat?"

Cotton nodded and began to cry again. I put my arm around his shoulder and said to him in a low voice, "The war's 'bout over then, Cotton. You won't be long in Memphis. You'll be out and back to Little Rock before you know it."

My words sank in and Cotton raised his face, streaked with soot and the tracks of his tears. "What about you?"

"I'm getting off this tub. You won't know when or how, but I won't be aboard when she pulls into Memphis."

"But J. T., where you going? What are you going to do? Take me with you!"

"You know I can't do that. If two of us go, it will be twice the danger. And you can't swim as good as me."

Cotton knew I was right. One man might slip away, given sufficient stealth and intelligence, but two would surely be spotted. And the last time the two of us had swum across the Mississippi at Helena, when the summer had dried the riverbeds behind the levee and caused the river to shrink to no more than a large creek, he'd almost drowned before he reached the other side. He had to wait an hour, breathing heavy, his arms trembling, before he could attempt the crossing back again.

"But why are you doing this, J. T.?"

"I'm going after Norman Kilpatrick. He's back in Helena. He commanded the cannon atop Hindman Hill, and he killed all those men you saw lying over our green earth."

"He's the man took the farm?"

"Yes, and he almost took our lives, too, and he needs a killing more than any Fed ever drawed breath."

The rest of the morning Cotton tried to talk me out of my plan, but I was not to be moved. When he wasn't whining at me, I was watching the Federal guards and noting gaps in their security. They didn't have enough ropes or chains to bind us, so they stood over us with rifles and frowned in the heat, swatting away flies and scratching at flea bites.

We were the sorriest bunch of soldiers I think I'd ever seen. Our skin and clothes were so black with powder and dirt and soot that we looked like poor Negroes beaten unmercifully.

Before we'd gone far, I knew it was time to depart. "I'm going now," I whispered to Cotton. "You stay put and don't cause a row. I'll be back when the war ends, so you tell Ma, and you hug her real tight, you hear? And you tell our sisters that I love them and that they must stay away from the Federal men, especially if the rascals win the war."

Cotton clawed at my shirt sleeve when I rose, but he stayed put like I told him. I bumbled over sitting and reclining men, coughing and hacking like I had a burr in my throat. One guard looked me over and then back to his charges as I passed him by and headed for a four-foot square opening in the bulwark at the ship's side. Men, Reb and Yank alike, had been using it for pissing into the river. Beyond the opening rushed white waves stirred by the paddlewheel, and beyond that was the far shore. I would have to leap out, dive under to avoid rifle fire, and wait for the ship to slide past so that I could make for the near shore of Arkansas. It was a desperate plan, but no more than the taking of Hindman Hill, I thought, and for a much clearer ideal.

I could not stop to think, for if I mused on the liberal expanse of the opaque water I might turn back and accept my fate as captive. I glanced once behind me, saw the guard was paying no attention to me, thinking I was there to relieve myself. And then I grabbed the oaken rail with both hands and leapt up, landing with both boots there to teeter only a moment before I had flung myself over the side and down into the rolling whitecaps.

I heard men yelling immediately on reaching the surface again and I felt the tug of the ship as its wake tried to bring me back under. I had to swim toward the wrong shore first in order to free myself from the horror of being sucked beneath the boat and chewed up by the paddlewheel. Shots rang out, though I didn't hear them at first, only noting birds taking flight suddenly from trees on the opposite shore. I dived down, kicking with all my might for the bottom and for the far shore. When I could hold my breath no longer and the hard tug of the ship's wake had lessened, I broke the surface for air.

That's when I saw Cotton. He was floating like a sawmill log toward the ship's stern and the great turning wheel.

"No!" I screamed, flailing at the current, trying to swim back the way I'd come so that I might grab hold of Cotton before he went under for good.

The ship had not slowed and now it was turning another bend of the Mississippi, its hungry wake trailing out behind it like a rippling skirt. The force tugging Cotton's body toward the wheel let it go and now it turned in eddies, swirling round and round, face down in the muddy waters.

The *Tyler* was not going to slow to pick us up or to make sure we were dead. It was what I'd banked on. It was nearly gone finally, smoke from its stacks filling the sky above it. A shot rang out now and again, but they were too far distant to hit me.

My heart was a stone in my chest as I paddled closer to Cotton. I had stopped hurrying, wasting what strength I had left, for I knew what had happened and there was to be no aid or help in my hard swimming. Cotton must have followed me, coming just behind as I leaped, and they were on him, shooting at him no doubt before he ever broke the river, our skim of safety. In the end he had never listened to me, not when I asked him not to volunteer for Holmes's army, not when I told him to stay behind in the ranks, and not when I wanted him to remain in the rifle pit on the battlefield. Now he had disobeyed me for the last time, thinking that if I was going back to Helena, he would, too. He would be a hero, like his older brother. He would show the Feds what a boy could do to their plans.

I reached him and took hold of one arm, pulling on it so that his head bobbed up. I got hold of his shoulder and then his face and while kicking furiously to keep my own head above water, I pulled him closer. I flinched seeing that a shot had entered the back of his brain and exited his left eye.

I let him go immediately, throwing my arms back in the water and crying out in a shout that heaven could have heard if it had been listening. I turned my head away so that I did not have to see my brother so disfigured, and then knowing I could not let him go to the river's depths as his grave, I turned back again and hooked my arm around his bloody neck.

Finally on the Arkansas shore, I hauled Cotton over the muddy bank. I lay on my back, arms spread, gasping for breath, my eyes closed. Here we were then, Cotton and I, one of us dead and the other brokenhearted. Ma would say, in the end, that at least she had not lost us both. But this loss, the one I'd tried so hard to prevent, was too great for me.

It was all the fault of Norman Kilpatrick. If he'd been less a demon and if I'd been less bent on revenge, Cotton would have been alive.

I would bury my brother along the bank this side of the levee where we had played so many summer days. I searched and found his wing-bone whistle and stuck it into my pocket. "You can get this back later," I said.

It was dark before I had scratched red dirt deep enough to keep Cotton safe from predators. I had used my knife in one hand, a sharp river stone in the other. I gently lifted Cotton and lay him in the depression, crossing his hands on his chest. *I'll miss you forever*, I thought, and then I told God to hold on to him tight.

In the deep night I washed my face and arms in the Mississippi before I climbed the banks of the levee and slid down the other side stealthily into the city. I had buried my Rebel cap with Cotton and now looked no different from any other Helena citizen. I walked right into the streets as if I belonged there, which I did, and searched every male face as I passed it by. The Yanks were drinking and having their way with some women, victors savoring triumph.

I made my way past Graveyard Hill, where a company of men were digging graves for the Confederate dead. I pushed up Hindman Hill, carrying a pail I'd found along the way, filled with water. If asked, I would say I was sent for drinking water and if they didn't believe me, I'd pretend to be an idiot, unable to make sense. No one cared what you did if you were light in the head.

Without any incident at all I found Kilpatrick in his private tent, lying in a cot with an arm over his eyes. There was no guard posted, as the threat, he believed, had been dispatched.

Kilpatrick raised his head at my entry. "Get out of here, boy, I gave orders not to be bothered."

When I didn't move to leave, he swung his legs to the ground and fumbled for the lantern. I wanted him to see me. To know. To taste the same fear I had as I'd made my arduous way to him during battle.

Once the light was hissing, he turned to me and frowned. I watched his face carefully for signs of recognition.

"What do you want? Who are you?"

He didn't know me! It had been just over two years and he had forgotten me forever. My family and I had been nothing but victims to him, gnats to swat aside for his pleasure.

"I am J. T. Halsworthy, Sergeant. You took our land, you killed my brother, and you are a turncoat against the Southern Confederacy."

Some slight bit of understanding dawned in Kilpatrick's face just as he rose from the cot to reach for his pistol.

"I'll have none of that," I said, kicking the holster across the ground so that it landed in a corner of the tent.

"I don't know what you want, young man, but you're going to be strung up at dawn for assaulting an officer."

"No, sir." I came toward him, showing the blade of my knife as I twisted it back and forth in the lamplight. "I'll not suffer for this murder, sir. It's a venture of war. I am a Confederate soldier, and this is my land you've stolen and my people you've massacred."

He lunged for me, but his arms missed catching hold and the blade of my knife sank deeply into his chest where I brought it up and up against bone and sinew until it would rise no more.

He clutched me to stand, but as his blood spilled over my trousers and boots the look in his eyes dimmed and his hands loosened as he fell to his knees.

When I had him off the ground and back in his cot, I took out Cotton's little whistle made from the wing of a robin and I placed it carefully in his lips. When they found him dead they would wonder what he was meant to whistle, but I would know the tune, and so did Kilpatrick. For eternity, or until Cotton found him to retrieve his favorite toy, Norman Kilpatrick would whistle "Dixie."

I gently blew out the lantern and slipped from the tent flap.

It was time to walk back to Little Rock. We'd all be coming home to Helena one day soon . . . my mother, my sisters, and me.

Behind Enemy Lines

John Helfers and Carol Rondou

Mary walked into the oak-paneled dining room and surveyed the mess before her.

The cream of the Rebel army had just met here to plan the defense of Richmond, the capital of the Confederacy. The officers had left the normally stately room a cluttered mass of scrawled notes, maps, dirty dishes, and cigar butts. Smoke hung in a pallid haze above the long table, and Mary knew she'd have to beat and air the drapes again. She saw the mud tracked into the room by the generals' boots and, sighing to herself, made a mental note to have the carpet cleaned as well.

Setting down her waste bucket, Mary crossed the room, pulled open the heavy gold curtains, and opened a window. While she began collecting ashtrays, she scanned the table, sorting through the piles of maps and notes. As she worked, her eyes lighted on a neatly folded sheet of paper. Carefully unfolding it, she began to read, keeping an ear cocked for any noise outside. The paper contained a list of dates, locations, troop movements, army strengths, just the kind of information she was looking for.

The sound of bootheels clicking in the nearby hallway broke her attention. Mary quickly refolded the paper, thrusting it under the stinking pile of ashtrays, then continued her work, wiping down the table with a rag.

"Mary, what are you doing?" It was Lieutenant Martin Williams, President Jefferson Davis's new aide, immaculate in his spotless uniform. She could feel his suspicious grey eyes on her as he surveyed the room.

Rearranging her face into the mask of bovine placidity she wore whenever soldiers were around, Mary looked up and exclaimed, "Sir, the Confederates done won the war! I just cleanin' the room after they left." She gazed stupidly at the young lieutenant and waited.

Williams relaxed and smiled as if he were addressing a child. "Perhaps not yet, Mary, but soon enough. Continue with your work." He left the doorway and Mary didn't breathe until she heard him on the stairs heading to the president's office.

For Mary Elizabeth Bowser, black servant in the Confederate White House and Union spy, it was one close call too many since the lieutenant had arrived. He was always watching her, ready with his insinuating questions and surprise inspections. *That man's harder to shake off than a pack of coon dogs after a fox*, she thought.

Mary's tenure at the White House had been relatively quiet until recently. With the army drafting any able-bodied man, even blacks, for labor, the capitol had been short-staffed for months. With fewer eyes watching her, Mary's spying had been much easier. At least until the lieutenant had arrived. *I can't scarcely round a corner without him popping up somewhere*, she thought.

So far, Mary had managed not to attract any attention to herself. If Williams had suspected anything, she would either be dead or sold into hard labor by now, free woman or not. Slipping the paper into her apron pocket, she forced herself to continue working. The dining room would be needed for the family's evening meal.

As she worked, Mary shivered and pulled her shawl tighter over her shoulders, glancing at the cold, empty fireplace. January of 1864 was a time of shortage, and even the White House had limited supplies of coal and wood. With the Union Army driving General Lee farther and farther back, the South was suffering hemorrhages of men, supplies, and support.

Richmond couldn't hold on much longer, and hopefully the information she sent through the lines would hasten the city's fall. Day after day the wagons rumbled through the streets bearing their grisly cargo of dead and dying. Every building that could be commandeered became a hospital or a morgue, and often the former turned into the latter. If the war didn't end soon, there would be no one to come home.

The sound of a throat clearing made Mary look up again. Standing in the doorway was Burton Harrison, President Davis's personal secretary. Harrison was an energetic, self-contained man who prided himself on anticipating President Davis's needs. The long war years had taken their toll, etching deep lines of worry and overwork into his face. He was not an unkind man, but he was a staunch supporter of the Southern cause and had profited from the South's "peculiar institution." As such, Mary was always on her guard around him.

"Can I help you, Mr. Harrison?" she asked. *Just take whatever you need and go,* she thought.

"Mary, have you seen a stack of letters on the table?" He asked as he scanned the room, taking note of her wastebasket and brush. "President Davis needs them. He brought them in here for the meeting."

"No, sir, I haven't seen anything like that," she said.

"Why Mary, they're right here," Harrison said, shaking his head as he snatched the letters off the table and headed out. He paused at the door and glanced back at her. "Don't be concerned, Mary, everyone is overworked."

"Yessir, we certainly are," Mary replied with her wide smile. As she went to the kitchen she thought about Lieutenant

Williams, and how much he may have seen since coming to the White House. Mary had never heard of him until his arrival a month ago. He was a young graduate of West Point, and she assumed he had family connections high in the Confederate government to be the president's aide. While other young officers clamored to go into battle to protect the sacred soil of the South, he seemed content to stay in the capital and wait. Perhaps he was here to uncover the spy ring that had operated in Richmond since the beginning of the war. Perhaps they had captured one of the runaways the ring had helped, and discovered that the Confederate White House was being used as a way station for escaped slaves traveling to the North. Maybe he suspected her of passing information and was planning to catch her and her allies, perhaps leaving the papers she had found to lure her into revealing herself.

Mary watched the flames dance as she burned the trash and thought about her next move. The information had to be sent to Elizabeth Van Lew, the Union spy master and her girlhood mentor. She couldn't risk not sending this information on, it was much too important. Heading back into the kitchen, she took a deep breath to steady her nerves.

Mary reached for the egg basket and the hollow egg that would contain the message. Carefully folding the paper into a small cylinder, she slid it into the egg, sealed the hole with a paste made from flour and water, and placed the egg in the basket among the others. She would pass the false egg to one of Miss Van Lew's servants as she took the basket, by the order of the president's wife, to the military hospitals for the wounded. She cleaned her hands and was whipping them dry on her apron when Lieutenant Williams strode into the kitchen.

"What do you have there, Mary?" he asked and glanced into the basket, picking up an egg.

Mary's blood froze in her veins as he reached into the basket, but the years of living her double life helped her to stand still as stone, her face betraying none of the fear raging inside her. She showed no emotion of any kind when he selected a true egg.

"Eggs for the wounded, sir. Mrs. Davis told me to take them to the hospital for the boys," she said.

"Of course. President Davis would like some coffee. Send Liza up with a pot. Continue on your mission of mercy, Mary." He carefully replaced the egg and left the kitchen.

Liza was one of the few remaining servants in the mansion. Mary hid a smile, of course he would ask for her. *Like he wasn't haunting her steps*, she thought.

Liza was a pretty young woman about twenty years old. She had fine features, large, melting brown eyes, and mocha-colored skin. The well-spoken daughter of a planter and a mistress, her father had educated her as a house servant and had only sold her to appease a new wife. Many gentlemen who had visited the Confederate White House were taken with her beauty, but the Davis's refused to consider selling her. She had been the children's nurse since the war began, and they were devoted to her. A deft hand with pencil or ink, the children often clamored for her to sketch them or other people. Of course, she now had other duties since the war had affected the staff, but she always tried to find time for drawing. She was not free, but was part of the cell, and tomorrow night would be the next one sent through the lines to freedom.

Just then Liza entered the kitchen from the cellar, staggering under a heavy load of firewood. "Hello, Mary. I think I brought enough to last through the afternoon at least. How do people live in cold like this?" she said, placing the wood in the storage bin, then crossing over to the washbasin and scrubbing her hands.

"Don't worry, you'll get used to it," Mary said. "Lieutenant Williams has ordered a pot of coffee for the president's office, and requested you to bring it. Watch out for him, there's more to that man than he seems."

"I intend to stay as far away from him as I can. Mary . . . ," she began, only to be cut off by the chiming of a bell. "I have to answer that. Mary, I found some important papers. I'll give them to you when you get back from Miss Elizabeth's." The bell continued to chime as Liza took the coffee pot from the stove, transferred the contents into a carafe, placed it on a tray with cups and spoons, and small pots of cream and sugar, and went up the back stairs.

Mary watched her leave, tempted to wait for her but knowing if she didn't leave for the Van Lew home now, her absence would be noticed and she wouldn't make it back to the mansion by curfew. Placing her heavy wool cloak about her shoulders, Mary made sure she had her pass, then started the long walk through the city streets to the Van Lew mansion.

Winding her way through the mostly deserted city streets, Mary came to the bottom of Church Hill, which was crowned by the Van Lew mansion. The stately home commanded one of the best views of Richmond. On a clear day, one could see all the way to the Tredegar Iron Works and down to the James River.

Going to the Van Lew mansion was a return home for Mary. She had been owned by the family, but as soon as old Mr. Van Lew had died, Mary and the others had been given their freedom, and Miss Van Lew sent her to live among the Quakers in Philadelphia to be educated. She wouldn't have returned South, except Miss Elizabeth had asked for her assistance in what seemed to be a mad scheme at the time. However, the chance to help others escape to a life of freedom as she had was something she couldn't ignore. Only Elizabeth Van Lew could have convinced her to return to the danger of the South and to become a spy on top of it. *Once this war is over*, Mary thought, *I'll never come this far south again.*

AT THE MANSION, MARY knocked on the kitchen door and was greeted warmly and hustled into the cozy interior. The Van Lew household had been looked upon as eccentric since the early days of the war. Miss Van Lew was referred to as "Crazy Bet" because of her habit of whispering to herself and skipping down the street. "Crazy Bet" made it easier for her to gain access to the Union prisoners in Libby Prison and assist in their escapes.

Regardless of how she did it, Elizabeth Van Lew was playing a desperate game and some people were becoming suspicious. Last year an editorial in the *Richmond Dispatch* criticized her for visiting Federal prisoners at Libby Prison, even claiming she was giving aid and comfort to the enemy while Southern boys languished in hellish Yankee prison camps. When President Davis declared a national day of fasting, the Van Lew house dined in sumptuous fashion. During General McClellan's 1862 campaign against Richmond, Miss Van Lew and her mother had set aside the best bedroom in the house for him when he conquered the city. They called it "the McClellan room."

"Sit yoself down chile', and warm up," Nancy, the Van Lew cook, insisted, taking her cloak from her shoulders and hanging it on a peg by the fire. She was a mulatto woman in her mid-fifties, dressed in a calico dress with a starched white headscarf. She poured Mary a hot cup of tea and set a huge slab of pound cake before her. "Ain't dos Davis's feeding you none? You ain't nothin' but skin and bones. And you always was such a lil' bit of a thing."

Mary gratefully sat at the table and clasped the teacup in her hands to warm them. "Thank you, Nancy. It was a long walk today. I never remembered Richmond's being so cold."

Nancy nodded in agreement. "It won't git no better either. If de weather holds der'll be another food riot. Member de Bread Riot dis pas' April?"

Mary nodded. The harsh winter coupled with the crippled economy had seen the cost of a barrel of flour climb to $100. The desperate population had reached their breaking point in early April. A mob of over one hundred women had marched to the business district and begun smashing shop windows, grabbing whatever they could carry. The mayor had called out the city militia and ordered the crowd to disperse or they would be fired upon. The soldiers had been reluctant to fire upon a crowd of mostly poor women who were the wives, daughters, or sweethearts of their comrades at the front. Finally President Davis arrived and, in desperation, took money out of his pockets and began to throw it to the crowd. He then took out his pocket watch and gave the crowd five minutes to leave or he would give the order to fire. Fortunately, the crowd dispersed and the crisis ended as suddenly as it had begun.

"If the North carries on as it has been, the war should be over by spring," Mary said between bites of pound cake. "Tennessee has been under Federal control since November, and Vicksburg surrendered in July, which gave the Union control over the Mississippi River. Last week General Cleburne proposed freeing some slaves and training them to fight. If that doesn't mean the end, I don't know what does."

Nancy chuckled, "Dat jist puts 'em a year behind da Yankees. I wonder when we gonna see dem colored Yankee troops. What dey say about dat?"

"They refused to listen," Mary said. "Called the idea revolting and said it would demoralize the army. If the idea of their families starving isn't demoralizing, I don't know what is."

Nancy took the false egg from the basket, cracked it open, and removed the paper. "Miz Elizabeth be happy to git dis. You best git movin' or dose Patrol boys will git you."

Mary rose from the table and put on her cloak. "The last thing I need is a run-in with them. I still need to visit the hospital before I go back. There's just so much to do, even now."

"That reminds me; Liza said she found something important. I have to get back to see what it is," Mary said as she took her basket and let herself out of the kitchen.

The walk to the General Hospital Number 9 was uneventful, but seeing the wards, filled to capacity with the wounded and dying, always distressed her. She quickly made her delivery and hurried back to the White House.

Mary arrived home as the hall clock struck four. Hanging her cloak next to the fireplace, she looked around the quiet kitchen. *Odd,* she thought, *Liza should be here preparing the children's afternoon tea.* Mary called for her, but no one replied. A draft from the open cellar door caught her attention. Usually the door was always kept shut, especially during cold weather. *Another oddity,* she thought.

Mary pushed the door shut as Rebecca, the Davis's cook, came into the kitchen bearing a tray. She was an elderly black woman with a sour temper and a reputation among the other servants for carrying tales to the mistress. Mary had always treated the older woman with care, but she knew that Rebecca would have sold her out to Lieutenant Williams in a second.

"What you gawkin' at?" she demanded, glaring at Mary. "Mus' be fine to gallivant all over town while Ise doin' yo' work." She set the tray down with a clatter.

"Do you know where Liza is?" Mary asked.

"Iffen I knew, do you think Ise be haulin' dat tray fo' her?" she grumbled, walking across the kitchen to the stove to check the contents of a stewpot. "Why don't you do sumpin' useful and get some mo' firewood?"

Mary was happy to escape the kitchen and Rebecca, so she opened the cellar door and was surprised to see a light at the bottom of the stairs. Normally anyone going to the cellar brought a lantern and took it out when they were done. She continued down the stairs, concerned about the odd light.

When she reached the bottom of the stairs, she saw Lieutenant Williams kneeling by the woodpile, his back to her. He had taken his uniform jacket off, and hadn't seemed to hear her on the stairs. He appeared to be stacking wood on the pile. She stopped her descent and the stair creaked as her weight shifted. The lieutenant whirled around, and

Mary saw that his shirt was torn and there was a scratch on his cheek. Rising to his feet, Williams pulled on his jacket and stalked to the stairs.

"What the hell do you mean sneaking up on me like that?" he demanded of her.

"Cook needed wood . . ." she began, and he cut her off with a wave of his hand.

"Fine, but get it from the other end of the stack. That end is piled wrong; it could collapse if you're not careful," he said, looked at her for a long moment, his arms crossed. "Well, what are you waiting for?"

Realizing he wasn't going to leave, Mary walked over to the woodpile and gathered an armload of logs. While she worked, she stole a quick glance at the wood Williams had been crouched over. She thought she saw a piece of cloth sticking out from between the logs.

"Damn it, Mary, hurry up!" Williams said. "All of Richmond society will be here tomorrow, and I will not have it said that the food wasn't ready because a servant couldn't get the firewood fast enough!"

"Yessir. Sorry, sir," Mary said, standing up with a large armload of wood. The lieutenant stepped aside to let her pass, then followed her up the stairs.

The two emerged into the kitchen, Mary dropping the wood into the woodbin and going to a basin to wash her hands. After that she went to a table and began peeling potatoes. Williams stood in front of the cellar door and watched Mary work. Rebecca kept her head down and continued chopping vegetables, shooting venomous glares at Mary when she was sure the lieutenant wasn't looking.

After a few minutes, Williams stalked out of the kitchen. The second he left, Rebecca whirled on Mary.

"What you do to get him all riled up like dat? I'se got enuff problems without him standin' over us," she said.

"I just didn't get the firewood fast enough to suit him, that's all," Mary said.

"That kind o' trouble I don' need. Hard enough to cook tomorrow's dinner as it is. You best keep that bin full, I cain't have the stove dyin' down," Rebecca said.

"You're absolutely right," Mary said, going to the cellar door. "I'll be right back."

Once back downstairs, Mary walked over and examined the woodpile. It appeared normal in the dim light. Taking the lantern down from its peg, she brought it over to the far side of the pile. The light revealed a dark red stain on the brick wall about a foot off the ground. Bringing the light closer, Mary realized it was fresh blood. She looked for the piece of cloth she had seen earlier, and spotted a scrap of muslin sticking out from underneath a chunk of wood. Removing it revealed the sleeve of a dress with a hand sticking out. A small woman's hand. Mary jumped backward and screamed involuntarily.

"Mary? What's y'all doin' down dere?" Rebecca called from the kitchen.

"Oh—oh nothing. A mouse jumped out from the woodpile, that's all," Mary said after a moment.

"Well, kill it and get up here wit' dat wood," Rebecca said.

When she had gotten control of herself, Mary removed a few more logs. It was Liza, dead, her hair sticky and clotted with blood. Her dead brown eyes gazed into Mary's in mute appeal. Mary rocked back on her knees and gazed down at Liza's dead pale face. Choking back her revulsion, she searched Liza's apron pocket and clothing looking for the papers, shuddering whenever her fingers came in contact with Liza's cooling flesh, but found nothing. She noticed that Liza's hands were stained with ink.

Either Williams already found whatever Liza had, or else she hid it somewhere in the house, Mary thought. *If he had found it, he probably wouldn't have been so angered by me finding him in the basement.* Perhaps he hid her body so he could search her later. Speculation was pointless now. Liza was dead, and she had to find the documents and send them through the lines. There was nothing she could do for Liza but try to provide her with a decent burial. The poor girl had been so close. Tomorrow night, during the reception, she would have started on her journey to the Northern lines and freedom.

Liza's dead and I can't even accuse her murderer, Mary thought. She knew that, even with her position in the household, no one would take her word over Lieutenant Williams's about what had happened. He could make up any story he wanted, and would get away with it. *Not if I can help it,* she thought.

Murmuring a quick prayer for the dead girl's soul, Mary carefully replaced the firewood covering Liza. She then loaded one arm with logs, picked up the lantern and, with leaden legs, climbed the stairs.

MARY CONTINUED THE REST of her duties in a mechanical fashion. She was dimly aware of a search of the house being conducted by Lieutenant Williams for the missing Liza. When asked about Liza's whereabouts, she answered dully, saying she hadn't seen Liza since that afternoon, before she left for the hospital. Mr. Harrison was almost finished questioning her in the dining room when Lieutenant Williams entered and coolly announced that Liza had run off. Mary noticed him staring intently at her, and she kept her face unmovable as she returned his gaze, noting with satisfaction that his eyes dropped first. It was late when Harrison finally dismissed her to the servant quarters and the room she shared with Liza.

The bedroom was simply furnished, with two beds, a bed stand, wardrobe, two small trunks, and bare wood floors. Liza's half of the room was in disarray, as if someone had prepared for a sudden trip and left whatever they hadn't taken strewn about the room. What meager possessions she had were gone except for a few stockings, an apron, and a torn skirt.

Mary looked over her half of the room and found that her possessions had been gone through and an attempt made to replace them. Blowing out the lamp, Mary lay on her bed to prepare for an uneasy sleep. She had no way of contacting the ring to inform them of Liza's death and no idea where the documents were hidden. Assuming she could find them, the only way to deliver them would be to pass them to the contact, who was expecting to meet with Liza during the reception for top government officials being held at the mansion tomorrow.

How am I going to find the documents and get them to the courier in a house full of high ranking Confederate officials? Not to mention Lieutenant Williams, who will be watching me like a hawk on a titmouse, she thought. *Well, let's start with what I do know; the documents aren't in this room, they weren't on the body, and they weren't in the woodpile.* Beyond that, the situation seemed hopeless. Mary lay awake pondering her problem well into the early hours of the cold, gray dawn.

THAT MORNING MARY WAS assigned Liza's duties as well as her own, so the search for the missing information became much more difficult. She was able to conduct a hurried search for clues in the cellar on several trips to gather wood, but found nothing. She also searched Lieutenant Williams's office during a pretext of cleaning, on the hunch that maybe Liza had hidden the information under Williams's nose, but came up empty there as well. Mary knew Liza never would have hidden anything in the kitchen, that was the sharp-eyed Rebecca's domain, and the abrasive woman knew every hiding place like the back of her hand. She had searched everywhere in the mansion she could think of, all to no avail.

Coming out of the kitchen with a platter of smoked meats for the dining room, Mary almost stumbled over a small boy in the hallway. Looking down, she saw Joseph Davis, the youngest of the Davis children, standing before her.

"Where's Liza?" the child asked.

"Oh . . . she's away visiting kin for a few days, she'll be back soon enough," Mary said with a forced smile, hating to lie to the boy, but knowing she had to.

"She promised to fix my horse yesterday, and she hasn't yet," Joseph said, stomping his foot.

The horse was a stuffed patchwork animal loved by Joseph, and as such was often in need of repair. Every few days Liza would have to sew a limb back on or mend a seam torn from vigorous play. Of course, the toy was the boy's favorite, and he was never without it. Mary looked down and saw a trail of sawdust behind the boy leading up the stairs.

"I'm sure that's the first thing Liza will do when she gets back, child. Why don't you run upstairs and play?" Mary said.

Joseph stomped up the wide staircase towards his room, leaving another trail of sawdust in his wake. Mary watched him go, shaking her head, and went to get a broom. She finished sweeping the hallway and stairs just as the clock struck six, and Mary bustled into the dining room to put the finishing touches on the food for the reception.

When the guests began to arrive, Mary was kept busy circling among them, refilling wineglasses and bearing trays of meats and cheeses. She heard snatches of valuable conversations, but she was no closer to the lost information.

During a pass through the library, she saw Lieutenant Williams in an intense conversation with Joseph Mayo, the mayor of Richmond.

". . . and she said to me, 'Massa, the 'federates done won de war.' I wish I could have such simple faith." Lieutenant Williams and the Mayor laughed heartily and each took a glass of wine from her tray, ignoring Mary as if she wasn't there. She passed from group to group, offering drinks from the tray and soaking in the information being passed around her, all the while trying to think of where Liza might have hidden those papers.

AT A QUARTER OF eight, Mary slipped out the back door to meet Liza's contacts. Jeremiah and Joshua Clifton were a father and son from a farm outside the city, both of whom had worked with the Van Lew family since the beginning of the War.

"Where's Liza?" the older one asked.

"She was murdered last night by Lieutenant Williams, President Davis's new aide," Mary said. "Liza said she had some important information for me to send out, but she hadn't given it to me yet. I think Williams found out about her mission and killed her when she wouldn't tell him what she knew."

"Murdered? Pa, we best go away now 'afore we gets arrested," Joshua said.

"Hush, boy! Let me think," Jeremiah said as he thoughtfully stroked his beard.

"Please, I need your help. Liza died for those papers and I've got to find them," Mary pleaded. "She also needs a decent burial, if you can manage it. It's the least we can do."

"Where is the bod—where is she?" the old farmer asked.

"Pa . . ." Joshua began.

"In the cellar, this way," Mary said before the elder Clifton could change his mind.

"Hold a minute, Mary," Jeremiah said. "We can't wait forever. We can bury Liza on the farm, but we have to meet our contact in two hours. Can't you bring the papers to Missus Van Lew during your weekly drop?"

"Williams murdered Liza because he discovered she was spying. I think he suspects me now. I could be next."

"I'll give you one hour, Mary. Joshua, let's see to the poor girl. We will meet you in the barn out back in one hour. Agreed?"

"Agreed. We have to hurry." Mary led the two men down to the cellar and watched as they carefully uncovered Liza and gently wrapped her body in a blanket. She was light enough for the younger man to carry alone up the stairs.

"We meet in the barn in one hour," Jeremiah said, reaching for his pocket watch. "I have eight o'clock. If you ain't there at nine, we'll have to leave."

"If we could create a distraction to clear out the mansion, I could search without being discovered, and you and the boy could wait in the barn for me," Mary said, looking at the pile of firewood and at the lantern the old farmer was holding. He caught her meaning and a slow smile crossed his craggy face.

"You head upstairs and I'll start a fine blaze," he said. "Once I'm outside and I see smoke, I'll raise the alarm. How much time do you need?"

"Give me a few minutes before you start calling out and wait fifteen minutes after," Mary said.

"Done, but get out if the smoke gets too thick," Jeremiah replied.

Mary nodded as she dashed up the stairs.

Once she was gone, the farmer searched the cellar until he found the stores of oil. Stacking several pieces of wood in the middle of the basement, he soaked the pile and tossed the lit lantern onto it. The wood burst into flames as he escaped up the stairs.

Mary continued moving among the crowd, offering refreshment. Her eyes would often travel to the mantelclock, watching the minutes tick by. Suddenly a sharp cry split the air. It was Rebecca screaming from the kitchen.

"Fire! The cellar's on fire!"

Mary ran behind President Davis and Lieutenant Williams to the kitchen. When the door was open a cloud of thick black smoke rolled out.

"Mary, get my children out of the house," the president commanded. "Williams, organize a bucket brigade. I'll see to the guests."

Mary saw Lieutenant Williams eye her with suspicion as she rushed up the rear stairs to the top floor where the

Davis children slept. She could hear Williams commanding the remaining servants and the house guards to fight the flames.

The children were asleep in their large airy room on the mansion's top floor. The room was a sanctuary for them, filled with toys and games, far away from the hustle and bustle of life in a capital city at war. Mary shook the oldest boy awake first.

"The house is on fire. You have to help get the rest of the children out," she said. The youth sprang from his bed and helped her wake his remaining siblings and get them into their coats. By now the smoke had wafted up the stairs and was filling the room. Mary swept the youngest child out of his bed and carried him, screaming and crying, down the stairs. She led the children down the stairs through the front door to their grateful mother waiting for them in the street.

"Mummy, Mummy. Where's my horse!" Joseph Davis cried as he clung to his mother's neck.

The horse! Liza must have hidden the documents in the horse, Mary thought. *That had to be it!* "I got it!" she shouted as she ran back into the house. She could hear Mrs. Davis ordering her to come back, but she ran on.

The smoke filled the first-floor hallway, almost forcing her back, but she struggled up the stairs to the third floor. The smoke was now thicker in the nursery but she still could breathe fairly well. The stuffed horse was lying on the floor in a small pile of sawdust on the far side of the room. Running to it, Mary picked it up and saw new stitching along the toy's back. Picking the stitches apart revealed folded hand-drawn maps of the defenses of Richmond and Petersburg.

"I'll take those, Mary." Lieutenant Williams's voice came from behind her, on the top of the landing.

Mary whirled around, dropping the horse but keeping the maps in her hand as she did so. "Take what, sir?" she asked, trying to think of a plan.

"Don't insult me, Mary," the lieutenant said. "Although I will admit, you fooled me for a while. If I hadn't seen Liza with ink on her hands after she had left my office and the maps of the city out of order, you might have gotten away with it. Now you will be hung as a traitor and a spy."

Mary raised her head proudly, placed the papers in her apron, and stood there as the smoke continued to fill the room. "She and I will be replaced by a hundred others," she said.

Lieutenant Williams smiled. "Don't be foolish, Mary, there is nowhere for you to go. These stairs are the only way out. I promise you will die quickly." He stood ready for her at the top of the staircase.

"Like Liza?" Mary said.

"She refused to give me the documents," Williams said. "I knew hiding her death would bring her accomplices into the open. If you continue to resist me, I will shoot you where you stand. Without your help it will take longer to break up your ring of spies, but I will do it. Regardless, without you I am willing to bet there will be no more information coming from the White House."

Mary silently said a prayer for forgiveness for what she was about to do. Raising her hands as if surrendering, she walked towards Lieutenant Williams. She stopped in front of him.

"The maps are in my pocket," she said.

Lieutenant Williams's eyes flicked downward to her apron, then reached for her pocket. He brought the papers out and began to unfold them.

At that moment, Mary shoved him with all her strength. The lieutenant flailed, trying to regain his balance, grabbing for her arm to try to hold himself up. Mary twisted away from his grasp and watched him fall down the stairs, his body tumbling and twisting as it slid to a stop on the second-floor landing.

Mary picked up the papers from where the lieutenant had dropped them. She tucked them away again, then came down the stairs, coughing at the thick pall of smoke rising up the stairway. Lieutenant Williams lay sprawled on the landing, his head twisted at an odd angle. Carefully stepping over him, Mary poked his body with her foot. There was no response. Kneeling down by him, she leaned over and listened for the sound of his breath. The man was dead.

Mary felt sickened by what had happened. The smoke was growing thicker, and she gagged on both the smoke and the knowledge of what she had done. Rising to her feet, she continued down the stairs, heading for the kitchen. She staggered for the back door, the smoke stinging her eyes and blinding her, her chest bursting with lack of oxygen. Throwing the door open, Mary rushed to the barn, her lungs greedily drinking in the cold night air.

"Mary, did you find what you needed?" Joshua asked.

"The fire spread faster then I thought," Jeremiah explained. "I didn't think you would get out in time."

"Here are the papers. Go quickly," Mary gasped, pressing the maps into the older man's hand.

After the Cliftons were safely away, Mary left the barn to mingle with the crowd of servants and Southern aristocrats outside the mansion. By the time she got there, the fire had been put out and the Confederate White House had been saved. She saw the president, his face smeared with sweat and smoke, and Mrs. Davis comforting their children. Young Joseph saw her and started to struggle out of his mother's arms.

"Horsey! Horsey!"

Mary took a deep breath and walked over to the Davis family. "I'm sorry, ma'am. I couldn't get Master Joseph's horse."

Mrs. Davis smiled kindly at her, "Thank you for trying, Mary. It was a very brave thing to do, although I don't see for the life of me why you went back. We can always get Joseph another horse."

"It doesn't matter now, 'cause it looks like they got the fire under control," Mary said.

Burton Harrison rushed up to President Davis, slightly out of breath. "Sir, everyone has been accounted for except Lieutenant Williams. After the fire was put out in the cellar, he ran back into the mansion yelling something about the nursery."

The president frowned, and the two men exchanged suspicious looks. Before anyone else could speak, Mary addressed Harrison.

"Mr. Harrison, sir. The lieutenant came to the nursery to help me out of the house, and while coming down the stairs, I'm afraid he slipped and hurt himself quite severely. I ran down the stairs to get help, but in all the smoke got turned around and found myself in the kitchen. I came out the back door, and ran to find you."

"Thank you, Mary," the president said, breathing heavily. "Burton, get some men and see to the lieutenant. I think this has been quite enough excitement for one evening, don't you agree, dear?" he asked his wife.

Amen, Mary thought as she looked at the smoke-filled house and thought of the maps Liza had bought with her life, the maps that would hopefully bring a swift end to this terrible war. *Amen.*

The Unknown Soldier

Kristine Kathryn Rusch

He finds himself in his own nightmare. Cold deeper than any he has ever felt, wind whistling through the makeshift barracks, hunger eating away at his stomach. His feet are wrapped in ripped cloth—his shoes long worn down by marching, marching, marching. He doesn't remember throwing them away, even though the soles were gone. Perhaps someone stole them on the long train ride to this prison camp on the outskirts of a Wisconsin town.

Other men huddle around him, some clinging to thread-bare blankets, others clustered together for warmth. The fire in the stove is not as bright as before, now only a little more than glowing coals—the guards will not build another until morning. He sits as close to the stove as he can, a prime position won because he can still fight. The warmth coats his left side, making the right even colder. He stares through one of the chinks in the wood, seeing the large white flakes drift down to earth. He has heard of snow, has seen it now, day after day, week after week, but he still does not understand it. How can anything so cold be so fragile?

He asked one of the guards once, but the guard just laughed at him. *I'm assigned here same as you,* the guard said. *Only I didn't turn traitor from my country.*

Traitor. He doesn't consider himself a traitor. He is a soldier, a man called to serve, not by Jeff Davis, not by the Confederate States of America, but by his family, people who lived in New Orleans through one regime after another, who fought to protect bayous and cypress trees and warm sunlight falling on the backs of their necks. People who believed not in a cause, but in a place. A place he might never see again.

He slides closer to the stove, so close that a slight movement would cause him to burn his left arm. He doesn't know what he believes in. Used to be he believed in himself, in his future, in his own powers as a human being. But his powers disappeared along with his shoes, and his future disappeared when he took his father's horse and rode off to enlist. He has no dreams left. Only nightmares. One particular nightmare that may or may not come true.

HE FIRST HAD THE nightmare as a young boy. It was a hot July night. The shutters were closed, letting in only a slight breeze to disturb the oppressive air. His overstuffed mattress felt damp, and sweat ran off his small body. He wished himself cold, wished for cold, and dozed . . .

. . . *seeing the rags on his feet, the torn gray pants made so lovingly by his mother. The heat from a fire touched his left side, but the rest of him was cold—so cold he never thought he would be warm again. He wrapped his body into a ball, shivering. Then the wooden door opened to a world of white—and slashed across it, blood . . .*

He woke up, a scream buried in his throat. Then sat, realizing that no one was coming to him. He was in his room, safe and alone. Only when he touched his skin for reassurance, the left side was too hot, and the rest too cold.

NO ONE SPEAKS IN this godforsaken place. They all stare straight ahead, as if they are looking backward at their lives. He can see forward for some of them—a sometimes gift his mother denied. His grandmother never did. She called it "the sight," and she used it. Only after he enlisted, she would never again use it on him.

He glances around the room, sees things that are going to be: the too-thin man in the corner, dead, placed in the ice-house with the other bodies to be buried come thaw; the man asleep on the only bunk, walking home to a magnificent planta-tion in Georgia, finding nothing but ash-covered Doric columns; the man beside him, face hidden behind a white hood, whipping his horse near-death chasing a black man across a field.

Sometimes he spends hours with these future visions, but they all end the same. Used to be when he turned the sight on himself, he saw a myriad of things: sitting, as an old man, in front of a tumble-down shack, children playing around him; a book about the "old South," held in a woman's gnarled hand, his name in gold leaf on the spine; standing beside his mother in the house of his birth as blue-clad soldiers clatter in, leaving muddy tracks on the polished wood floor.

The last time he saw any of those dreams, he still lived in the New Orleans house. His father's near-lame horse remained in the barn. He called on the sight the day his grandmother introduced him to a red-haired girl, and saw even more futures: a burned Great House; their bodies, naked and entwined; a red, squalling infant; another woman, long black hair trailing to her waist. He tried to call up those images after he enlisted, but could not. When he took his father's horse and rode toward war, all those dreams disappeared. Now, when he turns the sight to himself, he sees nothing. Nothing at all.

Except his past:

"Your grandmother wants you to marry." His mother took her lemonade into the garden and sat on the wrought-iron chair, her skirts falling across her legs like a fan. A carriage rumbled past the gate, then there was silence. He always thought of the garden as a green sanctuary in the middle of the city. "I do not."

"But, Mama." He protested more out of duty than desire. He was not in love, but he wanted to do what his grandmother bade him. He gazed at the shuttered windows of the house, willing her to come outside and defend him. Since his father's death in Mexico, his mother had wielded too much power. His grandmother appeared on the porch as if she had heard his summons. She nodded once and started down the stairs.

"You don't care for this girl, and you're much too young. You have plenty of time—"

"He doesn't have time." His grandmother stopped just short of the bench. She stood on the path, the sculptured hedges behind her. "A man is remembered by doing great deeds, creating beautiful things, or having a family that lives beyond him. He has no time to do great deeds nor to create beauty. He only has time for a family."

His grandmother's words chilled him—and with the cold came the memory of the nightmare, the rags on his feet. He had had that dream every night since his father's death.

"The war will end soon," his mother said.

"Wars never end," his grandmother replied.

HE CAN'T EVEN REMEMBER the girl's name, nor her face, only the softness of her bosom against his chest as they danced. He hasn't married, hasn't had a family. Before the occupation, his mother left New Orleans to live with friends in Atlanta, and his grandmother—his grandmother died the night he left. He has heard rumors of the burning of Atlanta, and his dreams lead him to believe his mother is dead. He is the last, the keeper of his family's lives, guardian of the future. And he has created nothing of beauty, done no great deeds.

This morning, he woke up believing today is the last day of his strength. The last day of conscious choice, before he becomes as vacant as the men around him, surviving only by sheer luck or fortitude.

Perhaps the vision he has left is not a nightmare. Perhaps it is his great deed, the thing that will make him remembered.

He has been thinking of this for some time. If he can get the others to rebel, they might be able to escape, to find their own ways home. The barrack guards are strong, but the rest are mere German bumpkins, pulled in from the fields. The train station is a short ride away, and the trains are still running regularly. He can hear the whistle at the usual intervals, speaking to him of safety, of freedom, of warmth. Of home.

Great deeds. All a man needs is one. One will last him his lifetime, give him the home and family, and make him remembered. One act . . .

THE DOOR DOES NOT open until the barracks are nearly dark, the stove almost cooled. As soon as the cold air drifts in, he launches himself toward it, hitting the guard full across the chest, butting his head against the guard's chin. Blood gushes out the guard's nose and spatters the snow. A small feeling of victory rises in him, followed almost as rapidly by a sense of dis-quiet. There is more to the nightmare than he can remember.

The other men watch with disinterest from the door. He yells to them, "Come *on!*" and begins to run before he notices whether they respond. He imagines them rising on stiff legs to follow him toward freedom.

His own legs are stiff, but they move well enough. The air is cold, colder than any he has ever breathed, so cold it freezes his lungs. The snow has finished, but he can feel its remnants, wet and soggy against the rags on his feet. He will worry about that later, when he is free, when he is on the train.

He runs down a well-worn trail, past other barracks, some with light in the windows and thin curls of smoke rising from the chimneys. Not cells, surely, not anything more than guard quarters for the Northerners who keep the Southerners imprisoned.

As he passes them, another shiver of victory captures his chest. All he has is the poorly guarded gate to cross, and then he's in the open. He can hear no footsteps behind him—no guards or other prisoners tracking him. Only his own harsh breathing. The breath plumes before him like the steam from a locomotive. Free. Free. He is free.

Too late he sees one of the bumpkins beside a building. The lump isn't even wearing a uniform, just the wide home-made pants and heavy jacket of a farmer. The bumpkin raises his rifle—and he leaps to avoid the shot. In that split second, the sight comes to him, and he sees his mother recoiling as a soldier slams a rifle butt into her face. The sol-dier sets the house on fire, and as it burns, his mother lies unconscious on the floor.

"No!" he cries, and then a burning pain scrapes into his chest. He is still airborne. On the snow beneath him, the familiar bloodstain pattern blooms, the one that has haunted his dreams, and he remembers the part of the nightmare he has always forgotten upon wakening:

The pattern ends against a man's body twisted and half-buried in snow. The eyes are open, lifeless, and the skin almost blue with cold. This man is cold, as cold as a man ever gets. The body gets moved to the icehouse, to wait for the thaw, when it will be buried in a mass grave with a hundred others, all unknown.

"No!" he cries again, and lands so hard that the breath escapes his body. His arms cross, his legs bend at odd angles, and pain like he has never felt shoots through him before numbing into nearly nothing.

Soldiers, his grandmother said once about his father's death fighting Santa Anna in Mexico, *fools who die for another man's folly.*

He now knows why she wouldn't touch him, why she only used the sight on him once. He was given vision so that he could make choices. He didn't look; he didn't see. The choice he made was the one he was supposed to avoid.

Cold. He is so cold.

And alone. He wants the bumpkin to come over, anything to give him one last chance at making an impression. But no one comes. He tries to close his eyes, but his strength is gone. The last thing he sees is something he has seen before, but never understood—the zigzag pattern of his own blood on freshly fallen snow.

Cold.

He will never be warm again.

A Woman's Touch

Max Allan Collins
and Matthew V. Clemens

The unmistakable click of a cocking pistol told Sergeant James Harley he'd just made a terrible mistake. On his haunches, bent over the narrow creek, Harley knew he'd never reach his holstered Remington in time. With the sun retreating, and the dense forest all around, he may not have made a perfect target, but apparently good enough a one for that Reb—somewhere on his right, on the opposite bank—to draw a bead on him.

His voice low and tight with tension, Harley said, "Not very neighborly, shootin' a man while he's wettin' his whistle."

The Reb said nothing.

Smart, Harley thought, fingers edging ever closer toward his holster. Though the flap was unsnapped, it still covered the pistol butt and he knew the odds were long that his revolver would even clear his holster, let alone get off a shot. Sweat beaded his brow, though the promise of a cool evening hung in the September air.

Chickamauga Creek—as Harley had heard Lieutenant Patterson of Company E call it two days before—had turned into a bloodbath for the Federals, especially Harley's outfit, the 100th Illinois Infantry. Though General William Rosecrans's Army of the Cumberland had succeeded in driving the Rebs out of Chattanooga—and forced them east of Chickamauga, Georgia—the Confederates had, in the last two days, mounted a slashing counterattack that had left Rosecrans's command in tatters, sending Harley and the boys of the 100th running in any direction where they didn't see Johnny Rebs.

That was how Harley had gotten separated from his unit in the first place. When the line broke, two of Harley's best chums—Matthew Bush and Albert Deal—had been cut down right before his eyes, dropping like so much kindling. The next thing Harley knew, the entire Federal army sprinted past in full retreat, and Rebs were everywhere, separating him and his fleeing comrades-in-arms.

He'd found a good place to hide in a small swale in a stand of pines. Pulling the body of a dead Reb over him as camouflage, Harley waited for the fighting to move far away.

The Reb smelled of gunpowder, blood, and death. The body's weight pressed like a grain sack on his back, but Harley gritted his teeth, steeled himself and stayed under the corpse as long as he could, his face mashed to the earth. Still, he felt those lifeless eyes boring a hole in his head, and he wondered if ever he would be able to wash the stench of death off of him.

Now that he'd finally tossed off the foul-smelling corpse and gingerly moved to the creek bank from his hiding place— thirsty, yes, but mostly wanting to clean that smell off of him!— it seemed he'd have to pay for his impatience with his life.

"You don't have to kill me, friend," Harley said, fighting to keep his fear under control. "I'm separated from my boys. Hell, for all I know, I'm the last one. You fellers whupped us good today." As he spoke, his fingers inched ever closer to his only chance.

"Yeah, we did," came a drawl from slightly farther upstream than Harley had anticipated. "An' now I'm gonna whup you, Yank."

"No need, Reb. You got yourself a prisoner!"

"Provisions are short enough for our side, 'friend.'"

"Not even goin' to give me a chance, Johnny?" asked Harley, easing his fingers nearer the grip of the pistol.

"You're havin' your chance right now," the Reb said, a grin in his voice.

Shit! Harley thought. The Reb had been playing with him the whole time, reeling him in like a big flapping trout.

No time for further conversation; no more verbal parries and thrusts, no waiting for the Reb to say anything else, because that Reb had said everything he had to say, already . . . .

Harley drove off his haunches, and dived into the creek. Just before he splashed into the water, something drilled through his right shoulder and spun him in mid-air. As he broke the surface, his mouth opened to scream, but instead of sound coming out, the frigid creek water rushed in.

Sputtering for breath, Harley exploded out of the water, his Remington in his left hand. The Reb who had stepped out from behind a tree had only enough time for a look of shock to register before Harley—praying God or luck was with him, and that the water had not silenced his weapon—squeezed the trigger and, yes, the roar shattered the stillness of the forest as a bullet tore into the Reb's chest, a pinkish cloud puffing from the hole as he sank to the ground, sat there looking confused for perhaps a second, perhaps two—and died.

"Damn Johnny Reb," Harley muttered as he spun around looking for friends of the slain Confederate.

But as he slowly scanned the trees and foliage, he saw no one—not even a bird, the shot having scattered them—and he realized that the Reb must have been separated from his outfit as well.

"Just my damned luck," he said (already forgetting how fortunate he'd been that his Remington had fired), as he gently probed the hole in his shoulder. It didn't really hurt, at least not like he thought it would. While the skin burned, especially right around the wound, his arm felt surprisingly cold, and heavy, and useless. His stomach began to churn, his eyes burning as sweat dripped from his lank blond bangs, and his balance wanted to betray him, his head spinning.

Can't go down, he thought. If he passed out here, well, that'd pretty much be the end of the trail for him. Unsteadily, he holstered his pistol, untied the kerchief from around his neck and used it as a compress on his wound. He knew he needed a tourniquet, but didn't have anything to use and didn't know if he could tie it with one hand anyway. Maybe the dead Reb had something he could use.

Crossing the creek as quickly as he could, Harley plopped down next to the man who'd plugged him—a fellow in his late twenties with flaxen hair and sky-blue eyes, staring eyes, which Harley thumbed closed. He considered saying a brief prayer for his late opponent, then thought, *To hell with it.*

The Reb had been an officer—his uniform said so—a lieutenant . . . a lieutenant who had somehow lost his belt and replaced it with a length of rope, which Harley stripped off the corpse. He tied a slipknot at one end, then gingerly slid the loop up his arm; picking up a stick nearby, he slipped it through the knot and cinched it down tight. Biting his lip against the pain, he grabbed the Reb's pistol and jammed it into his waistband.

Darkness closed around him on every side, but he didn't feel safe. The sound of the shots could have been heard by anybody for half a mile. Harley figured it wouldn't be long before greycoats were swarming all over this spot.

Ignoring the sweat running down his face, the ringing in his ears, and the cold hard throbbing in his shoulder, he pushed himself to his feet, wobbled, nearly went down, caught himself, then stumbled off into the night. Moving slowly in the pitch blackness, blundering into low-slung branches, tripping over exposed roots, Harley tried to stay within earshot of the creek without getting too close to it.

Not long after he started out, he heard thrashing from the creek and Harley pressed himself against the trunk of a tree.

"Jesus, Lucien, what the hell are you doin'?" a voice drawled.

The answer was more nasal. "Sorry, Sarge, a piece of the bank slipped away."

A third, deeper voice said, "You keep makin' noise like that, Lucien, you gonna get us all killed. Take better care."

Sliding silently to the ground, his pistol drawn, Harley tried not to even breathe until he could no longer hear the voices from the creek. He had to get away from here. He needed to head north, get back to Chattanooga, where he'd be safe. The cloudy night sky gave him no stars to navigate by and if he stayed here, sooner or later, the Rebs would find him.

Harley was fairly sure the creek ran sort of east and west, so if he just walked away from it he'd be . . . He froze. *Which side of the creek had he ended up on, north or south?* He didn't remember. During the retreat he thought they'd crossed the creek two or three times, or was it different creeks? Harley had no damned idea.

Shit, he thought. Forcing himself back to his feet, he turned his back to the stream and moved away from it. Right or wrong, north or south, he had to move . . . .

What seemed like a lifetime later, the first hint of light appeared on the eastern horizon—on his left.

Dropping to his knees in the tall grass, he didn't know whether to laugh or cry or pray or just scream until the Rebs came and got him: he had spent the whole night walking south. The only thing that made him feel anything other than utter dejection was knowing that the going had been so difficult, he knew he couldn't have got very far.

The only other good thing was that the dense woods had given way to smoother footing and these fields of long grass. As the sun crept slowly into the sky, Harley found himself on the edge of what appeared to be someone's farm property. In front of him the grass had been mowed down and he could see several small buildings, chicken coops he guessed, and beyond those he could make out the outline of a wide, two-story house. To his right, fields stretched as far as he could see. To his left, the same. Hunkering down just within the confines of the tall grass, he looked for signs of life.

The morning breeze carried sounds from the coops that told him there were indeed at least a few chickens over there. The clucks from the chickens were nearly drowned out by the rumbling that issued from Harley's stomach. He couldn't remember the last time he'd eaten and knew he'd lost a lot of blood.

If he didn't do something soon, he'd be a goner.

Looking around, he knew that even though the place seemed deserted, someone had to be caring for those chickens. He decided to sit tight a while, and see who came to tend the birds.

A quarter-hour passed, then another, and a third before Harley heard the chickens rustling in their coops. Easing the pistol out of his belt, he crawled forward, careful to keep the coop between himself and whoever fed the creatures. He expected that he'd find a slave dishing out grain. Maybe, just maybe, he could enlist the black man's help in getting some food, a fresh bandage, and a place to hide till nightfall. Then, he could begin making his way back to his own lines.

Excitement welled in Harley's gut as he crawled painfully to the side of the coop. He still couldn't see anyone else moving around either outside the house or through the first-floor windows. Pushing himself to his feet, his back plastered against the coop wall, Harley side-stepped to the corner and carefully peeked around the edge. He saw a flash of white muslin, then it was gone.

A female, he thought. He'd caught a glimpse of a dress before she moved to the second coop. Going back the way he'd come, Harley moved around the back of the first coop, checked between the buildings, then slipped up the side of the second coop. At the corner, he again peeked around searching for the slave girl. As she worked, she hummed a melody he didn't recognize. She had her back to him, tossing grain on the ground as the chickens gathered around. It seemed like a nice enough backside to Harley. He just wished she didn't have a bonnet covering her head so he could see her hair.

Stepping from the shadow of the coop, he approached her silently and stuck the barrel of his pistol into the small of her back.

"Don't move," he whispered.

She let out a little gasp, but stood still.

"Turn around real slow. I don't wanna have to shoot you."

She turned—real slow—and Harley felt his mouth go slack as he looked into the bluest eyes he'd ever seen.

"I thought you were a slave," he said numbly.

"Have you ever seen a white slave?" the woman huffed.

"No, ma'am. My apologies—how was I to know, from behind, that you were a servant girl."

The blue eyes flared. "I'm nothing of the kind. My name is Rachel Farris—Mrs. Benjamin K. Farris—and this farm belongs to my husband and myself."

Harley's eyes darted first toward the house, then toward a barn farther to his right—a building he hadn't seen earlier, because the coops blocked his view.

"You can look all you want, brigand, but you won't see him."

"Ma'am?"

"My husband." She stood up a little straighter. "Captain Benjamin Farris of the 60th Georgia Infantry."

"An officer!"

"That's what a captain is, yes." Her eyes blazed at him and a wisp of cornsilk blonde hair escaped from the edge of her bonnet.

"And where is the good captain now?"

Looking away, she said, "I haven't seen Benjamin for two long years."

"If you're lying . . . if he's in that house . . . or off getting supplies . . ." Harley raised the pistol even with her heart-shaped face and cocked the hammer.

"I am not lying," she said. "The last letter I received from my husband said he was in Virginia. That was months ago."

"Who else is here?" he asked, the pistol still leveled between her eyes. "Kinfolk? Children?"

"I have no living kin, nor any children," she said, then added, with a note of pride in her voice, "I work the place by myself."

"No slaves?"

"Benjamin and I do not believe in keeping slaves."

Harley gave her a long appraising look. "Then why does your husband fight for the Southern cause?"

Face growing pink with anger, she said, "Just because we don't keep slaves doesn't mean that we accept the North's idea of how we should live."

"We should get into the house," Harley said almost absently, as he tried to digest what she'd said. "No telling who might wander by."

"Must you have to point that awful thing at me?" Mrs. Farris asked.

Harley looked at the Remington curiously, as if he'd forgotten the weapon was in his hand. Slowly, he lowered it, gesturing with it at the same time. "Start movin'."

"Would you be so kind as to allow me to finish feeding my chickens first?"

He shook his head. "No. You be so kind as to get your pretty self inside that house . . . ma'am."

The house had looked better from a distance. As he drew closer, Harley could see chipped paint, loose boards, and a roof that looked tired from years of wear. The chicken coops and barn lay in similar disrepair, and Harley realized these facts should have told him there was no man around.

Gonna have to be more alert, he told himself, if he was going to get back to his lines alive. As they neared the house, Harley heard the sound of hoofbeats.

"Damnit," he said, scouring the area for cover.

Mrs. Farris looked from his wounded arm to his face. "You can hide in the barn. I'll shoo whoever it is away."

"I can't do that, lady! You'd give me up . . . !"

"Do you think I want my farm shot up, for the likes of you?" she said, the blue eyes wide and flashing. "No time to argue. Go—now!"

Feeling like he was surrendering without a fight, Harley did as she told him. He crept into the shadows of the barn just as several Confederate soldiers came around the corner of the house. Two of them—officers—rode horses, while a dozen or so infantry men followed.

"Morning, Mrs. Farris," the leader said, tossing her a casual tip of his hat.

Watching from the barn, his pistol still in his good hand, Harley wondered how long it would take the woman to betray him.

"Why, good morning, Lieutenant Pettigrew," she said melodically, butter-wouldn't-melt. "What brings you fine gentlemen out this way, so early on this lovely morning?"

Looking around the area as he dismounted, the lieutenant handed the reins of his mount to one of his soldiers. "Have you noticed anything—or anyone—out of the ordinary this morning or last night, perhaps?"

Mrs. Farris tilted her head to one side, apparently perplexed. "Out of the ordinary? How so, Lieutenant Pettigrew?"

"One of our officers was killed near the creek last night."

"Oh, my. Hostilities all around us—is there nowhere safe in the entire South?"

"Well, it wasn't safe at that creek last night." Lieutenant Pettigrew sighed gravely. "About four miles from here, it was. We figure if it was a Yank he'd have taken off north, but we're checkin' out all the local homesteads, just the same. You see, he may have been wounded and taken refuge."

Leveling his pistol at the officer, Harley watched, waiting for the woman to turn him in.

"And how have you ascertained that the Yank may have been wounded?"

"A trail of blood."

She touched fingertips to her mouth. "Oh my! Did it lead here?"

"No—it barely led anywhere . . . he must have bandaged himself shortly after the altercation. Have you seen anything, Mrs. Farris?"

Harley silently thumbed back the hammer.

She seemed to think about the question for a long moment before saying, "No, Lieutenant, nothing out of the ordinary."

Though the officer nodded, he didn't seem satisfied. "As I say, he may have taken refuge. We'll just have a look around anyway. You have no objection, certainly . . ."

Keeping the pistol pointed in the general direction of the yard, Harley desperately searched the shadowy barn for a hiding place. Two stables in one corner stood empty, mounds of hay littering their floors. Next to the nearest stall a sharp-looking pitchfork leaned against the wall. Harley played out the scene in his mind and rejected the stalls. On the back wall he saw a ladder that led to the hayloft above. It might not be any safer up there, but at least he'd have the high ground.

"Of course not!" the woman was saying. "I appreciate these efforts to assure my safety . . . but I haven't seen anyone—Yankee or one of our boys—in over a week."

Harley quit listening to their conversation and as stealthily as he could he made his way to the ladder. The thing creaked as though it might give way under his weight, and he worried that the noise might be enough for the soldiers to hear. He tucked the pistol back in his belt, feeling naked as he slowly hauled himself up the ladder with his one good hand.

Harley had just slid down behind two stacked hay bales when he heard the voices.

"Leonard, you and Heyward check out the barn."

"Barn, yes, sir," Leonard drawled.

Pulling the Reb pistol from his belt and resting it on the floor in front of him, Harley unholstered his Remington and prepared to make his final stand. Beneath him, he heard the two Rebs moving around.

"Mrs. Farris sure is a fine-lookin' woman," Heyward said.

"You better get that thought right outta your head— she's married to an officer!"

"He ain't been around in nigh on two years. If I had me a woman that pretty, I wouldn't be off fightin'—I'd be right at home takin' care of what was mine."

"Be quiet, you fool, and check the damned loft."

Harley's breathing stopped as he heard the creak of the ladder as Heyward stepped on the first rung. Upon the third creak, Harley cocked the Remington.

A voice Harley didn't recognize said, "You boys findin' anything?"

"Nope," Leonard replied. "Nothin' here but hay and manure."

"C'mon then—we got lots of other places to check out."

"All right."

The men talking had drowned out the sound of Heyward on the ladder, but Harley fully expected to find the man there when he raised up. He took a deep breath and prepared to start the fight.

"C'mon, Heyward!" Leonard called from below. "We're headin' out!"

Harley froze.

"I'm on my way," Heyward answered, his voice sounding very nearby.

Then the ladder groaned several times as the Reb climbed down.

Not daring to believe his good fortune, Harley crawled on his belly to the wall that faced the yard and peered between the boards. The lieutenant was back on his horse and leading his men away from the house.

"You know you're always welcome, Lieutenant Pettigrew," Rachel Farris said as she waved to the departing column.

Pettigrew tipped his hat in her direction then led his troops back to the road.

Harley rolled over on his back, let out a long breath, and shook his head. He couldn't believe his luck!

"Are you in here?" she asked, her voice barely above a whisper.

He said nothing.

"Yankee, I asked, are you in here?" she repeated, almost yelling.

"Up here!" he answered, finally.

He heard her climbing the ladder, crossing the whining boards of the loft, then he looked up to see her peering down at him.

She asked, "Are you all right?"

"Fit as a fiddle."

"You look tired. You look as if you might pass out any second."

He swallowed. "I am tired."

"How is your arm?"

Biting his lip, he said, "It burns like hellfire."

She frowned in sympathy. "Can you manage getting down the ladder?"

"I . . . I think so."

She helped him to his feet, led him to the ladder, then went down first. He followed slowly, his arm throbbing and still hanging uselessly at his side. By the time his boots touched the floor, sweat drenched his shirt, he felt wobbly, and he wondered if he had the strength to reach the house.

Allowing himself to slip to a seated position on the floor, Harley groaned. "Need to rest."

She looked toward the yard, then at him. "All right—for a minute or two . . . then we'll move you inside the house."

"You didn't turn me over to them," he said, his eyes searching hers.

"No."

"You easily could have."

"You might have shot me."

"No. You could have screamed and scurried out of range. Why didn't you?"

"Scream and scurry?"

"Turn me over."

"I . . . I'm not entirely sure. Maybe because you're hurt. Maybe because you didn't hurt me when you could have. Maybe because I would hope some other soft-hearted, soft-headed woman might do the same for my own wounded husband . . . Maybe it's the brown of your eyes . . . or maybe I don't really know, exactly."

"Maybe you figure there's been enough killing."

"May well be."

"Well . . . thank you," he said. Awkwardly, getting a lift from her, he rose.

Her eyes locked on his.

"Did you . . . did you kill that man by the creek?"

"Yes I did."

"And he's the one who shot you?"

Harley nodded. "That's what soldiers do, in war—shoot at each other."

She shivered at the thought. "Well, let's get you inside the house and I'll bandage that arm properly. You seem to have lost a great deal of blood. Can you walk?"

"I believe so."

She ducked under his good shoulder, tucked one arm around his back and held his left hand in hers at her shoulder. "I'll help you."

Harley inhaled her fragrance. She smelled of spring flowers and soap. Such a simple combination of scents, and yet he couldn't remember anything ever smelling so sweet.

He told her so.

Blushing, she said, "Thank you."

They got into the house and she helped him ease into a chair at the kitchen table. Sweat ran down his face and he felt as though he had a fever.

"I'll fetch a pail of water, then I can dress that properly."

"Thank you, ma'am." He didn't know what else to say.

She went outside and he looked around the kitchen. The yellow room reflected the sunlight streaming through the windows and reminded him of the parson's house back home. Dishes lay stacked neatly on shelves on one wall. A stove stood against the opposite wall, a small pile of wood in a box next to it. On a counter opposite him a loaf of freshly baked bread cooled next to a jar of preserves. The aroma made him homesick.

Though he had no wife back in Illinois, his mother would come over and bake bread in his stove. He loved the smell of freshly baked bread. The room reminded him of his mother's kitchen—it too had a distinct woman's touch to it.

When she returned with the pail of water, Harley rose to take the bucket, but she motioned him back to his chair. "You just sit down. I can handle this. I've been hauling water for two years now, I'm plenty used to it."

He watched as she filled a basin, moving with the easy confidence of a man, and the grace of the beautiful woman she was.

Then she turned and said, "Let me help you upstairs."

"I can walk, ma'am."

"Not without my help."

The basin cradled in one arm, she slipped the other around his waist, and they made their way down a short hallway into the parlor. A maroon velvet chaise sat against one wall, three wing chairs in various colors and materials were scattered around the chaise and the low table that squatted in front of it. This room carried the scent of Rachel with just the faintest hint of old cigars to tell Harley that she hadn't been the only one living here.

Struggling up the front stairs, the pair paused halfway so Harley could catch his breath.

Sweat poured down his cheeks now, his head swam again, and the wound in his shoulder burned down to the bone.

"Are you all right?" she asked, huffing some herself from the exertion of holding him up.

Gritting his teeth, Harley nodded.

She led him up the rest of the stairs, and turned into the first room on the left, the master bedroom. A tall oak armoire stood against the wall next to the door, a small writing desk and chair perched under the room's large window. Sunlight filtered in through gauzy curtains, haloing the large four-poster bed.

"Sit down," she said, helping him to the edge of the bed.

Harley did as he was told. "You've been running this place alone for two years?"

She nodded. "Are you surprised by that?"

He shrugged. "A mite, I guess."

"Because I'm a woman?" she asked, trace of a smile at the corners of her mouth.

"Well . . . there's no denying you're a woman."

Looking him square in the eye, she moved in front of him, lifted the Reb pistol from his belt and laid it on the writing desk behind her. Then she unlatched his belt and holster and placed them on the desk as well. Stepping close, she began unbuttoning his blue wool shirt. "Women can do a lot if they're given half a chance."

He glanced around the room, suddenly unable to meet her eyes. Harley felt warmer than he had even a minute ago, and now he was pretty sure it wasn't just fever. She leaned in close to help him pull his injured arm out of the uniform shirt. Her bouquet filled his head with thoughts he knew he shouldn't be entertaining this far behind enemy lines, the swell of her bosom just inches away, inviting sweet surrender.

"I'll be back shortly," she said.

Woozy from both the wound and her scent, Harley managed only a nod.

Soon she returned with a white bedsheet. She removed his makeshift bandage, tore the sheet into strips and scrubbed his wound clean. His fingers throbbed as the pain worked its way down his arm. Tearing more of the sheet, she fashioned him a new bandage and wrapped his wound.

She asked, "How does that feel?"

Harley mumbled something, felt his eyelids growing heavy, his body turning to stone. His feet were lifted and he felt himself fall back for what felt like an eternity before he landed gently on fluffy pillows. He wondered if he'd landed on clouds, then suddenly remembered he was on a bed.

"It's going to be fine, just fine," she said, her voice soothing but faraway now. "You merely need a little rest."

He tried to reply, but the words wedged behind the thick brick that his tongue had become.

Easing a cool towel onto his forehead, Rachel said, "Don't try to talk—just calm yourself."

Again, Harley felt his lips move but heard no words come out, and his eyelids lowered, like a curtain on a play's first act.

When he awoke, sunshine still poured through the window and he figured he'd slept perhaps an hour. He had just managed to sit up, when she whirled through the door in a calico dress.

"How do you feel today?"

He tried to smile. "Mite better . . . that little nap sure helped . . . Today? What do you mean?"

"That 'little nap' lasted you just over twenty-four hours."

Gaping at her, he said, "You're joshing!"

She shook her head.

Harley looked around the room as if there were some way to see the passage of time on the articles scattered around. Everything looked the same, though. His guns still lay on the desk across the room, the curtains still hung the same way, nothing had changed. "Twenty-four hours?"

"Hmmm hmmm." Rachel bent over him to check his dressing. "Looks better . . . nice and clean . . . not red a'tall."

"Doesn't hurt much," he lied.

"Such strong arms," she said idly, trailing a finger over the biceps of his left arm. "I like strength in a man."

Harley's pulse pounded in his ears and finally his eyes settled on hers and locked. He saw the desire there, the same passion he felt. Pulling her to him, he pressed his lips to hers.

The urgency of her response told him he'd made the right decision. Her tongue jabbed into his mouth, hot and probing, making him forget any pain in his arm.

Then she gazed at him, breathing heavily, the cornsilk hair tousled, and said, "There are things a woman . . . a woman alone can't do for herself . . ."

They undressed each other, beside the bed, and it was by turns graceful and awkward, measured and rushed, and Harley was stunned by the beauty of the body hidden beneath the white dress and petticoats. He cupped her round, full breasts in his hands as his mouth eagerly sought the pink tips. As if doing their own bidding, his fingers traced the lines of her ribs, her hips, her thighs.

As he eased her onto the bed, her moans sounded like a choir to him as she threw her arms around his neck. Pulling his head up to her face, she kissed him and whispered, "Please, please . . . please . . ."

Needing no further encouragement, Harley slipped inside her and any thoughts of the war, the Rebs, or any world outside the two of them vanished in a whirl of desire.

Their tryst completed, each reverted to modesty and dressed quickly. Harley, discreetly turning his back as Rachel finished repairing her appearance, glanced out the window to look down upon a Confederate on horseback coming up from behind the chicken coops, just where he had approached now so long ago.

"Shit," Harley hissed. "Another damn soldier!"

"Lieutenant Pettigrew must have sent a rider back for something," Rachel said, and then looked over his shoulder, out the window, then turned toward the desk where Harley's pistols lay.

"Am I safe up here?" he asked, one eye still on the approaching rider. "You can go down and deal with that soldier, surely?"

She didn't answer.

For the second time in less than twenty-four hours, he heard the ominous sound of a pistol being cocked. He turned to find Rachel aiming the dead Reb's pistol at his chest.

"This time," she said, not unkindly, "you're not safe, and you can't hide."

"What are you saying? That you've had your tumble and now you're turning me over to them?"

Her reply was a squeeze of the trigger, and the world exploded, something hammered him in the chest and he found himself on his back, on the floor, at the foot of the bed, looking up at the ceiling. Surprisingly, he felt no pain. His brain registered what had happened and his ears rang from the sound of the shot, but no pain, no pain . . .

Her words sounded distant and didn't really make sense; she seemed to be speaking to herself, not him: "Your kind pillages and rapes . . . every soldier understands that . . ."

Trying to speak, Harley gagged on his own blood. Were those bootheels on the stairs, or some distant drum? Her final words were whispered, or seemed to be whispered; at any rate, he barely heard them before slipping into blackness.

"You see, my love, that Reb is my husband—and that makes you just another damn Yankee."

Ghost

Bradley H. Sinor

After three years of war I thought I had seen everything.

The last thing that you expect to see on a hot afternoon in Richmond is a ghost. And certainly not one standing in the front door of the Capitol Building of the Confederacy.

Well, I saw one.

I tied up my horse at a hitching post on the southeast corner of the building, in an area away from the main door. I had arrived a quarter-hour early for my appointment with General Morgan Girard, my commanding officer. A soldier, obviously on guard duty, approached me, his rifle carried low in his left hand.

"Excuse me, sir. This area is restricted to army officers only."

"As well it should be," I said. "Which is exactly why I'm leaving my horse here."

"Sir," he said. "It's for *army* officers only. The civilian areas are around the corner." He put a special bit of emphasis on the word *army*.

Because of the nature of my work, I've been more often out of uniform than in one. There are places where a uniform would stick out as much as Abraham Lincoln walking the streets of Richmond.

I held my identification where he could see it.

"Sir, I'm afraid I can't . . . read," he said.

"That's all right, son. I'm Captain Adam Thorne, military intelligence."

He eyed me for a moment. Then he snapped to attention, his rifle sliding down to rest at his side in the proper manner.

"Sir, sorry for bothering you. I've been ordered to stop any civilians from leaving their animals here."

"Not a problem. You just keep on doing your duty. I wish more of our people were as adamant as you."

"Do you have a match, Private?" I said as I pulled a cheroot from my inside coat pocket. He passed a Lucifer match to me. I had just dragged it along the bottom of my boot when I saw the ghost.

She was standing at the top of the stairway, looking off in the distance. Jenny, a vision in blue, her long red hair hung loosely on her shoulders, the parasol in one hand, to protect her from the sun.

"Jenny?" I muttered, unsure of even the sound of my own voice. Not that I expected her to hear me.

"Captain? Are you all right, sir?"

The guard was looking at me with the uncertainty that a lot of enlisted men seem to have when dealing with officers. Before I could do or say anything, pain shot through the tips of my fingers. I realized that the match had burned down and was attempting to steal a few seconds more of life by using my flesh as its home. I dropped the burning ember and stamped on it with my foot.

"Captain?"

"I'm all right. My mind was elsewhere." When I looked back, she was gone. If she had ever been there in the first place.

The memory of the headstone bearing her name was as fresh as the first time I had seen it three years before. No, it had to have been my imagination, it couldn't have been Jenny.

Yet . . .

"RIGHT ON TIME. NOT that I would expect anything less than that from you, Thorne."

Brigadier General Morgan Girard stood up from behind his desk. He was not physically a big man, standing barely five feet, eight inches tall, yet he always seemed to fill whatever room he occupied.

Girard had recruited me within a week of when the war for independence had begun. As a graduate of West Point, I had expected to serve our new country in the regular army. Instead, I found my talents being put to use in other ways. Our office was attached to the Secret Service, but they preferred not to talk too loudly about the connection.

"It's always good to see you, sir," I said. "I was sorry to hear about Mrs. Girard. I know her death must have taken a great toll on you."

"Thank you, Adam. These last few months have been very hard. But thankfully, I've had the boys, George and Derrick. They've been a source of great strength for me," he said.

"I've been told it was her heart?"

"Yes, I came into the bedroom one morning and found her. She had slipped away in the night. She just lay there, peacefully. I sat with her for an hour, before I kissed her cold blue lips and found the strength to summon the rest of the house," he said.

There were few things, outside of his job, that I had seen Girard care passionately about. His wife, Allison, had been one, his two sons the others.

"Well, I'm not the only one to have lost loved ones in this war, so enough about me. Let's talk about what you're going to be doing next. I think you'll find it not nearly as big of a problem as that matter in New Orleans," he said.

That would be a relief. I preferred not to dwell on the New Orleans matter any more than necessary. There were, at times, things a soldier had to do in service for his country. You didn't have to like them, but they had to be done. New Orleans had been one of them.

"I'm putting you in charge of security for Lord Anthony Case-Jones."

"I take it this fellow isn't your average traveler on a grand tour over here instead of in Europe."

"Far from it. He's a special representative from Prince Albert sent here to prepare recommendations on the question of diplomatic recognition."

Girard didn't have to explain the significance of that move. Diplomatic recognition would be a godsend for this country. It could bring us aid and allies, which we desperately needed. I had come to the conclusion a few months earlier that shy of a major miracle there was no way that we could win this war.

This might be that miracle.

"You'll meet his lordship tonight. He's staying with an old family friend of mine, James Collins," said Girard.

"So how does his lordship feel about having a shadow?"

"It doesn't really matter what he wants or doesn't want. He will be protected," said Girard. "I'll send a carriage for you tonight at eight. We dine at nine."

I knew when I had been dismissed.

"Captain Thorne! Captain Thorne!"

I was just fastening the last button on my waistcoat when someone started pounding on my hotel room door. My watch indicated half past six.

"Captain Thorne! Captain Thorne!"

"A moment," I answered. After slipping on my jacket I picked up a small pistol from the table. Just because someone knew my name and where to find me didn't mean that they had my best interests at heart. There are certain things that you have to do to stay alive. Better to do them and not need them than to lay bleeding and regretful minutes later.

"Yes?" I said, standing to one side of the door.

"Captain Thorne. General Girard sent me. My name is Cole Masterson," he said.

Cole Masterson turned out to be a lanky man in his thirties. He had an odd accent, one that I couldn't place.

"I wasn't expecting anyone until eight."

"I understand, sir. However, something has happened and the general wants you to come to the Collins house as soon as possible. He sent me with a carriage and orders to bring you there straight away."

"Can you tell me what happened?"

"No, sir. The general said he would brief you upon your arrival," said Masterson.

That sounded like him. I dropped the pistol into my coat pocket, picked up my hat, and motioned Masterson to follow me.

THE COLLINS FAMILY HOME was an elegant three-story affair, built at the turn of the century on the south edge of Richmond. Several rooms on the first floor were so brightly lit that they fairly glowed in the fading July sunlight.

We were met by a man in his fifties, balding with a fringe of iron gray hair, whom I presumed to be the family butler. He was accompanied by a young nigger boy who took charge of the carriage, without a word.

"If you gentlemen would come with me, you're expected," said the butler.

I didn't know too much about the Collins family. The great-grandfather had emigrated to the United States just after the first war for independence. They had extensive mine, manufacturing and farm holdings.

Girard was waiting for us in the entrance hall. He wore his usual grim expression, an unlit cigar in his mouth.

"Good evening, sir," I said.

"Ah, you made good time, Thorne. Masterson, I need you to take this to the naval office." He handed an envelope to Masterson, who promptly saluted and left without a word.

"Well, Thorne, I had hoped that this evening would be a pleasant interlude for the both of us. So much for those hopes," said Girard. He motioned for me to follow him through a pair of double doors into what proved to be the library. It was a big room with floor-to-ceiling bookcases and a fireplace at one end. Two oil lamps were the only sources of light.

The general gestured toward a wing chair in one corner. Someone sat there; a man in his late forties with heavy sideburns and a dark tropical tan. His eyes were milky gray stones sunk deep into his face. Only, now that I looked at him, it wasn't his face that caught my attention. What looked like a long red sash ran across the front of his jacket, up over his shirt, and onto a deep gash in his neck.

"Do I take it that this might happen to be the gentleman who you wanted me to keep alive, Lord Anthony Case-Jones?"

"Indeed."

Well, so much for that assignment. I glanced around the room and in a dim mirror on the far side of the room I saw the ghost again. Just for a moment, peering out from a booklined alcove on the other side of the room. Only this time it was wearing the black dress and white-collared uniform of a maid. It was Jenny! She was gone just as quickly as the first time I had seen her.

"Well, I don't know what recommendations his lordship had in mind, but I would say that someone did not approve of it," I said.

"Then you agree with me that this is very likely the work of Yankee agents," said Girard.

"Possibly," I said. "Who all is in the house?"

"Just Collins, his lordship's traveling secretary named Rodney, and us. The rest of the Collins family has been living on one of his plantations near Florida for the past six or seven months. There are several hired servants, the butler who you met, a cook along with a couple of general handyman types," said Girard.

"What about slaves?"

"Amazingly, none. The handymen are niggers, but they've both been manumitted. I honestly hope that we find out it is a personal thing, rather than a political one. That will make it far easier to explain," muttered Girard. "But whatever the reason, I want answers as soon as possible."

"If you would get everyone in the living room, I think we can begin there," I said. "I want to have a closer look at a few things about his lordship, here. Shall we say in fifteen minutes or so?"

"Agreed," said Girard.

After he left I gingerly slid my hands into the dead man's pockets. There was little there of interest; a handful of coins, a pencil, and several peanut shells. My manipulations caused him to slump to one side. That was when I noticed an inch or so of chain sticking clear of his shirt collar. It was a medallion of some sort. I thought at first it was one of those religious ones, but when I drew it free I could see a single letter engraved on each side.

"Don't you think it's about time that you came out," I said.

There was no response, certainly not from his lordship. But he wasn't who I had been speaking to.

"I saw you in the mirror. I'm going to presume you've been listening and watching since then," I said.

To my left I heard the slightest sound of metal creaking and hinges at work. Out of the corner of my eye, I caught sight of one of the bookcases swinging back into place.

"Can I get you a drink?" said the ghost. She looked every inch the proper ladies' maid. Her red hair had been wound beneath a white mob cap. At first glance it would have been hard to recognize her, but this close there was no mistaking my sister, Jenny.

"Yes. Scotch," I said.

She poured me two fingers of amber liquid from a bottle on a table near the fireplace. Then poured herself a twin of my offering.

"I hope you don't mind drinking with the hired help," she said.

"As if you were really the hired help," I said. "I imagine the only reason that you are employed on these premises is because you wanted to be."

"A girl has to earn a living," she said defensively.

"Are you saying that Davis Walker doesn't pay his spies well enough?"

I've always enjoyed being able to pull a rabbit out of my hat and surprise my sister. The astonished look on Jenny's face was enough to prove that I had not lost my skill.

"Not bad, little brother, not bad at all," she said.

Major General Davis Walker was Girard's opposite number on the Northern side. I had encountered one of his men in Cuba six months before. We had gone to West Point together and considered ourselves friends still, in spite of political differences. Besides, our particular assignments at that time did not conflict, so we spent the evening drinking and reminiscing. It was somewhere past the second bottle of rum that he mentioned to me that Jenny had gone to work for Walker.

"Looks like there are two Thornes in the spy business now," he had said.

"So, do you like working for the enemy?" I said.

"Adam, I don't consider what I do as working for the enemy. I'm working for the country that we were both born in. But let's not get started on any political discussions. I had enough of them with Father. How is he, by the way?"

"Still as hardheaded and stubborn as ever. You know that he considers you to be dead. He even went so far as to erect a headstone for you in the family plot."

I'd been there the day that he had it set in place. I suspect he would have held a formal funeral service for her, but my mother, and the local parson, had said no to that idea.

He and Jenny had disagreed on things for most of my life: slavery, politics, the proper way to respect one's parents. Their shouting matches were legend in our family. It had been her falling in love with Nathan Jackson, a Northerner, and wanting to marry him that had driven our father and her to the breaking point. It had stormed the night the two of them drove off together, four years ago. That had been the night my father had announced that as far as he, and the family, were concerned, his daughter Jennifer was dead.

So I suppose, from my father's point of view, I was talking with a ghost.

"You heard about Nathan?" she said.

"Yes, a botched bank robbery, and he was in the wrong place at the wrong time. Was that what drove you to work for Walker?"

"Among other things," she said quietly.

"You responsible for this?" I gestured at his lordship.

"Hardly. We learned he was coming, and I was sent to keep an eye on him. A dead envoy will not help the United States' relationship with Great Britain. It might even be enough to drive them into recognizing you.

"Besides, it is my understanding that he was going to file a report saying that the English should stay neutral in the whole matter. Something to the effect of letting us settle our own internal matters," she said.

"THIS IS HARDLY THE way you normally investigate a murder," said Girard. "However, you all must realize this is not a normal murder. Otherwise, we would have summoned the local police at once."

Girard was pacing back and forth in front of the leather couch that took up most of the main living room of the Collinses' house. Our host, James Collins, was a man in his mid-fifties, but seemed older. He stood near the large bay window that dominated the room. Seated near the door was Alexander Rodney, the late Lord Case-Jones's traveling secretary.

"Sir, why are you wasting your time here?" said Rodney. "It's obvious that a Yankee agent murdered his lordship. You should be pursuing him. The fiend is no doubt halfway to Washington by now."

I didn't like Rodney's tone and his presumption.

"We are pursuing all avenues of investigation, Mr. Rodney. Not just in this house, but elsewhere, as well," I said. "Do you have a particular reason to believe that the North even knows that you are in this country?"

The secretary's face burned red with anger. "Of course they know we're in this country! I have no doubt that detailed reports of our every move are making their way to Abraham Lincoln's desk in each morning's mail.

"Are you aware, sir, of the delicacy of our trip here? There are members of the government who do not want to grant the Confederacy diplomatic recognition. They want us to formally ally with the United States against you."

"The general has seen fit to brief me on your mission. I only wish I had been brought into the matter sooner. Perhaps we could have prevented this murder," I said.

"I doubt that," said Rodney.

"Mr. Collins, where were you and Mr. Rodney earlier this evening?" I asked.

"Business kept me away from the house for most of today. I had barely returned home when Morgan discovered his lordship's body. I last saw him this morning at breakfast. In fact, that's also the last place I saw Mr. Rodney," said Collins.

"Don't go trying to accuse me, sir. It was Northern assassins!" said Rodney. "In the last fifteen years I've traveled to many countries with his lordship. But this is the most vile one I think I have ever encountered!"

"General, the stories you told us of this country were enough to frighten any sane man. But all they did was make his lordship want to come here all the more," said Rodney.

"You had met Case-Jones before, General?" I asked. It was a fact that he had not mentioned.

"Yes, Allison and I spent a year in Europe and England before the war. I believe we met him at the Burton estate in Sussex," said Girard.

"Enough of this!" said Rodney. "You must stop gibbering like old women and find the killers. They are getting farther away with each passing minute!"

"Oh, I think not?"

"Really? Would you care to explain, Thorne?" said Girard.

"Actually, gentlemen, I know who killed his lordship. I have only one more matter to confirm before settling this entire matter," I said.

THE SITTING ROOM AND bedroom that had been assigned to Case-Jones was midway down the hall on the house's third floor. It wasn't locked; there was no need. So I let myself in. If the whole thing were the work of Yankee assassins, then no doubt they were, as Rodney seemed so convinced, long gone.

Everything in the room was as neat and orderly as if the maids had just finished cleaning up the room. I opened the closet and found each of Case-Jones's suits perfectly arranged. Three pairs of boots, which I suspected were shined to within an inch of their lives, sat on the floor.

I was about to inspect one when something struck me hard across the back of the head. The blow didn't knock me out, but I had to grab onto the door frame to keep on my feet. Whoever my attacker was followed with a swift kick that connected to my hip and almost sent me down.

Somewhere in that process I realized that I still had one of Case-Jones's boots in my hand. I threw it at my opponent, missing, of course, but that bought me time enough to get back on my feet and face him.

Without really thinking I threw myself against him, sending both of us tumbling down. What I presumed to be a knife went clattering to the wooden floor. My own pistol was in an inside coat pocket and caught between the two of us, essentially unreachable.

"I'd suggest that you boys call this whole thing off right now!"

Jenny! She was standing with a gun of her own in one hand. The expression on her face as cold and unfeeling as any I had ever seen.

"Are you all right, Captain Thorne?" she asked. Better not to acknowledge each other.

"Aye, and very grateful to you."

I looked down at the familiar face of my opponent. Morgan Girard.

"YOU'RE INSANE, THORNE," SAID Girard.

I'd had the butler summon the two nigger handymen who were now standing on either side of Girard. He hadn't really wanted to come back to the living room, but the barrel of the gun I had taken from Jenny and held in the small of his back provided a powerful argument in favor of doing what he was told.

Jenny had excused herself, claiming to feel close to fainting now that it was all over. Officially, she had been passing by the room, heard the scuffling, and went in to investigate. Actually, I had left her hidden in the hallway, waiting to see who might come along.

"See here, Captain Thorne, I hope that you know what you're doing," said Collins. "I've known Morgan Girard since we were both small children. I cannot conceive of the idea that he is a killer."

"Then perhaps you had best learn," I said.

"So, what is it you're claiming? Is he a Yankee spy and killer?" asked Rodney.

"Killer, yes. But I doubt he is a Yankee spy. I have no doubt of his loyalty to the Confederacy," I said. "He just wanted us to think that a Yankee spy was behind the murder. It would keep people from realizing that it was actually a matter of jealousy, revenge, and, more than likely, double murder."

"Double murder?" said Rodney and Collins at the same time. "Who?"

"Yes, I'm fairly certain that in addition to murdering Lord Case-Jones, Girard also killed his wife, Allison," I said.

"Thorne, you have become a monster. You know Allison died of a weak heart," said Girard.

"Indeed, I attended her funeral," said Collins.

"But do we know that? We have only his word and the word of a doctor who no doubt made no close examination. This morning Girard told me about discovering Allison's body. He mentioned that her lips were cold and blue. It strikes me now that that may well have indicated death by either poison or suffocation," I said.

"But why? And why kill Case-Jones?" asked Collins.

I took out the medallion that I had removed from his lordship's neck and held it out where the others could see the disk. On one side was a stylized *A* and on the other an *M*. But the *M* had been obliterated.

"This is significant?" asked Rodney.

"It is, indeed," answered Collins.

"You know?" I said.

"I was there when Morgan had those made. They were his wedding present to Allison, one for her, one for him." Collins's face had grown still, showing no emotion.

I didn't have to look to see that Girard still wore his, under his shirt. I had seen it on several occasions before.

"I would suspect that during their sojourn in England, Allison Girard and Case-Jones began an affair. That was no doubt when she gave him the medallion. At some point Girard found out about it, but opted to do nothing. Perhaps he felt having an ocean between the two lovers was enough. That was until he heard that his lordship was being sent here as a special envoy. That was when he made up his mind to have his revenge, on them both," I said.

I had wondered why he had gotten me involved in the whole matter. The only reason I could conceive of was that he thought my loyalty to him would let him conceal any-thing that was too incriminating.

"This is a fine tale you've spun, Thorne," Girard said. "But it is nothing but pure fantasy. It's obvious to me that you've gone over the edge, pressure of the war. I've seen it in others who've worked for me. Trust me, son, I'll see that you get the best medical treatment."

"Morgan, shut up," said Collins. "He's right. You told me yourself that you knew Allison had had an affair. You know the hidden passages and panels in this house almost as well as I do. We spent many hours prowling them when we were children. So I would say that the best thing to do right now is to keep quiet."

I expected Girard to do something. But not what he did. Instead of making a grab for a weapon and trying to escape, he reached into his coat pocket and brought out a small enamel snuff box. With a slow dignified manner he administered several pinches to himself.

I don't know exactly what was in it, but the reaction came a few seconds after he set the box down. He went stiff for a moment and then his head slumped forward on his chest. I didn't bother to check; if he wasn't dead, then it was only a matter of a few minutes. Perhaps this was better than the gallows or a firing squad.

Still, the whole matter left a foul taste in my mouth. I didn't say a word to Collins or Rodney as I excused myself, went out into the hallway and lit a cheroot.

A few minutes later Jenny came up beside me. "Not the most pleasant circumstances for reunions, big brother," she said.

"No, no it wasn't," I said.

Jenny reached over and plucked the cheroot out of my hand. She lifted it to her lips and took a long puff from it, then blew the smoke out in a slow series of rings.

"I know you looked up to Girard. He was a good man who went wrong, somehow," she said.

"I think we all have that potential, little one," I said.

"You know, you're a pain, but I definitely like having you around. Be careful, and don't you go wrong," she said as she passed the cheroot back to me.

"I'll try." That I was speaking to empty air didn't surprise me. My little sister is good at what she does.

"Is there a problem, sir?" The butler came from the direction of the kitchen, looking at me rather oddly.

"No, no, nothing that won't eventually right itself," I said. "I was just standing here thinking."

"Very good, sir, although I did think I heard you speaking to someone a moment ago," he said.

"Actually I was. One of the maids, the one with red hair," I said.

"Red hair? You must be mistaken, sir, we have no maids with red hair. Besides, both of them have been working in the kitchen for some time," he said. I could see the slightest sparkle in his eye.

"Perhaps I was mistaken. Who knows, maybe I was chatting with a ghost," I said.

"Quite possible, sir," he said.

The Last Day of the War

James Reasoner

The rider rode hard through the South Texas chaparral. It was a hot, humid day in May, and both man and horse were sweating. The rider shifted the strap of the leather pouch he carried. The wax-sealed documents inside it were bound to be something important, he supposed, but carrying the pouch over his shoulder was uncomfortable.

He was thinking about that when the bullet struck him in the back, knocking him out of the saddle to sprawl lifeless on the sandy ground. The horse, spooked, galloped on down the narrow trail in the low, thick brush.

The rifleman stood up from the place where he had crouched in hiding until the rider passed him. He levered another cartridge into the chamber of the new Henry rifle he carried and walked forward to check the body, nodding in satisfaction when he had made sure that the man was dead.

Like the man he had just killed, the rifleman wore the uniform of the Confederate Army.

"Wake up, Sheriff."

Dan Keller stirred and lifted his head from the desk in front of him. "Wasn't sleeping," he said as he rubbed a hand over his face. "Just resting my eyes. What do you want, Dobie?"

Keller's long-nosed, big-eared, overeager little deputy jerked a thumb over his shoulder and said, "There's a fella outside with a dead body."

Keller frowned. "What's he bringing a body here for?"

"Well, you're the law, ain't you, Sheriff?"

Keller snorted. Being the sheriff of Cameron County, Texas, in the month of May and the year of Our Lord 1865 didn't amount to a whole hell of a lot. Not with Confederate troops under the command of old Rip Ford occupying Brownsville, Union troops squatting on the sandhills of the spit of land known as Brazos de Santiago to the east, and the gamblers and saloon owners and smugglers who populated Brownsville, Matamoros, across the Rio Grande, and the port city of Bagdad on the Mexican coast to the southeast really running things. Keller knew good and well the only reason all those folks allowed him to stay in office was because they figured he wouldn't rock the boat. They knew him pretty well, he supposed. He liked to drink a bit, and it was easier just to go along and get along.

"I really think you ought to take a look at this dead man, Sheriff," Dobie went on.

Keller sighed. "And why's that, Dobie?"

"Well, for one thing, he was shot in the back. And for another, he's nekkid."

That made Keller frown. Not the back-shooting part; with all the rivalries amongst the denizens of the red-light districts on both sides of the river, bushwhackings were common. But the corpses usually had clothes on when people found them.

Keller heaved himself to his feet. He was a big man, over six feet, with broad shoulders, a massive torso, and a belly that showed the results of too many bottles of *cerveza*. His curly, reddish-brown hair was beginning to show some gray. He followed Dobie to the door and snagged a broad-brimmed Mexican sombrero from a peg in the wall beside the opening. He preferred it to an American hat because it shaded him better.

The dead man lying face-down over the back of a mule was definitely naked. Keller winced, partially from the brightness of the sun and partially from the view. A Mexican farmer was holding the mule's halter. Keller went around to the other side of the animal, being careful to stay out of range of the hooves in case the jughead decided to kick, and looked at the corpse from that angle. The man had a bullet hole in his back, all right. The wound hadn't bled a lot, which meant the bushwhacker's shot probably had found the victim's heart.

The dead man had blond hair that dangled below his head. Keller grasped it and lifted so he could see the man's face. Probably early twenties, Keller judged, and definitely a stranger.

"That ain't nothing to be putting on display in the street," Keller said to Dobie as he dropped the dead man's head. "Take him on down to the undertaker's."

"What you going to do about this, Sheriff?"

"Spread the word, I guess. If anybody's missing this gent, they can go to the undertaker's and have a look at him, see if they can identify him." Keller grimaced. "If they do it early enough in the day, that is. I reckon by this evening, he'll be better off in the ground."

"You're not going to try to find out who killed him?"

Keller turned to the farmer who had brought in the body and asked in Spanish, "Where did you find this man?" The farmer answered, and Keller turned back to Dobie. "He stumbled over him out on the Laguna Espantosa trail. You know how thick the chaparral is up there. Anybody could've ambushed him, and you couldn't ever track 'em through there."

"No, I reckon not." Dobie sounded disappointed.

Keller patted him on the shoulder with a meaty hand. "Go on along, Dobie. We ain't responsible for every dead man in the world."

As he turned back toward the office door, Keller frowned again. He supposed the oath he'd sworn as sheriff sort of made him responsible for the dead men found in Cameron County, anyway. But it was hot, and he'd never been one to beat his head against a wall for no reason, so he went back inside.

"GREAT MEN HAVE TO do great things, Colonel. It's their destiny."

Colonel Theodore H. Barrett, commander of the Union garrison on Brazos de Santiago, leaned back in his chair and looked almost hopefully at his aide-de-camp, Lieutenant Dermot Pierce. "Do you really think so, Lieutenant?" Barrett asked.

"Absolutely, Colonel," Pierce replied without hesitation. "And this may be your last chance."

Barrett frowned, torn by indecision. He knew quite well that the War Against the Southern Rebellion was coming to a close. So far, Barrett had seen no action whatsoever, and his recent posting to this obscure command in a Texas backwater did not auger well for his chances of leading men into combat, especially in light of the news he had received a few days earlier.

The voters loved a military man, especially one who had been victorious against the enemy. Barrett closed his eyes for a moment, seeing visions of himself standing on a platform draped with red, white, and blue bunting, basking in the cheers of thousands of admirers whose fondest wish it was to propel him into higher and higher offices until . . . dare he think it? . . .

Barrett sat up straight and thumped a fist on the desk. "Order the men to prepare to march, Lieutenant," he said. "By God, we're going to take Palmito Hill, whether General Brown wants us to or not!"

"SEVENTY-FIVE THOUSAND DOLLARS IN gold, I tell you," said Enrique Castillo.

Colonel Flornoy shook his head. He was a medium-sized man with close-cropped, iron-gray hair. "Where would Juarista rebels get that kind of money?"

"From the British and French cotton merchants. The Union blockade has hurt them, Colonel, you know that. They must have cotton for their mills, and if the only way to get it is to smuggle it across the Rio Grande, they will do so."

Flornoy was well aware of that. The traffic in contraband cotton had been going on for several years now. But it angered him that *French* cotton merchants would buy bales from the rebel smugglers who were trying to overthrow Maximilian's glorious empire. Did they not see that they were hurting the cause of their own nation? Did they care only about money?

Flornoy knew the answer to that, of course. And he could understand it, he supposed. Was he not on the verge of making an arrangement with one of the treacherous Mexicans himself? Castillo had no more loyalty to his supposed leaders in the revolution than . . . well, than Flornoy did to his own leaders in the Emperor's army. It was a hard thing for a man to admit, even to himself, that he would exchange his beliefs for nothing more than gold.

But still, seventy-five thousand of the American dollars! With his share of that, Flornoy thought, he could vanish into the mountains of Mexico and live well no matter who won, Juarez or Maximilian. He could have a little empire all his own.

"You say they are taking the gold across to Brownsville?"

"*Si*, tomorrow."

Flornoy nodded. "We will be ready."

LIEUTENANT PIERCE WAITED UNTIL the troops had left Brazos de Santiago before saying to Colonel Barrett, "I think I ought to scout ahead, sir."

"What if you run into Confederate skirmishers?"

Pierce smiled. "I'm not afraid of a motley bunch of Rebels, Colonel."

"A commendable attitude, Lieutenant. Would you like to take a couple of troopers with you?"

"No, sir," Pierce shook his head. "I won't be gone long."

Barrett gestured for the younger officer to ride ahead. "Good luck, son. Come back quick if you spy any Rebs."

"Oh, I will, sir, you can count on that."

Pierce spurred his horse and left the column of marching infantry behind him. He could already see the low rise of Palmito Hill up ahead, although the land around here was so flat that distances were deceptive. Pierce figured it would take most of the day for the column to reach the hill.

That would work out perfectly. At least, Pierce hoped so.

He rode for a half-hour, getting well ahead of the Union troops. He didn't stop until another rider reined his horse out of a thicket of brush and raised a hand.

"Right on time, Pierce," the second man called. Like Pierce, he wore a lieutenant's uniform—only instead of blue, it was Confederate gray. "I reckon everything's going all right?"

"Just as planned," Pierce replied. "Did you take care of your end, Blaine?"

"Damn right," said the Rebel lieutenant called Blaine. "We don't have a thing to worry about."

"What about Enrique?"

"He was supposed to talk to Colonel Flornoy today."

"You think he'll go along with it?"

Blaine snorted. "For a share of that gold? That Frenchy'll cooperate, all right."

Pierce took a deep breath and asked the question that was worrying him the most. "What about the messenger from Galveston?"

Blaine took a stub of a cigar from his tunic pocket, put it in his mouth, and said around it with a smile, "You don't have to worry about him. I burned the pouch and all the documents in it. Good thing you let me know he was on his way down here. It could have ruined everything if ol' Colonel Rip had got his hands on those papers."

"Well, then." Pierce stuck his hand out. "Here's to being rich men."

Blaine shook with him. "Rich men," the Confederate repeated, relishing the sound of it.

IN THE LATE AFTERNOON, Sheriff Keller heard hoofbeats in the street outside and hoped they would go on past the office. He'd been about to go over to one of the cantinas for some supper.

The horses stopped outside, though, and after a moment bootheels rang on the boards of the porch. A tall, rangy figure in a black hat and Confederate jacket came into the office. Colonel Rip Ford had a short white beard and a craggy face that had been leaned down by illness in the past year or so. The old Ranger hadn't let being sick stop him, though. There had been a time, a couple of years earlier, when the Yankees had controlled the whole blasted Rio Grande Valley all the way up to Eagle Pass. Then Rip Ford, who wasn't even officially a member of the Confederate Army, had formed what was variously called the Cavalry of the West and the Rio Grande Expeditionary Force. It was an irregular cavalry battalion that thought of itself as fighting for the Confederacy, and the members even outfitted themselves in whatever pieces of Confederate uniform they could get their hands on. But they took orders from the Confederate Army only when it suited them, and they got damned little support in return from the Confederates.

But that hadn't stopped them from rolling right down the valley and driving the Yankees out of town after town, including Brownsville, until the only Union presence in far South Texas was the little garrison on Brazos de Santiago. Rip Ford had done that, riding at the head of his makeshift cavalry.

Keller stood up. A fellow like Ford made other men want to get to their feet. He nodded pleasantly and said, "Hello, Colonel. Something I can do for you?"

"I heard that a dead man was brought in to you this morning, Sheriff," Ford said. "I was wondering if I could take a look at him."

Keller scratched his head. "Well, uh, I'm afraid he's already been planted, Colonel. What with it being so hot today and all."

"Are you going to try to find out who killed him?" Ford had been a Texas Ranger before the war started, and Keller supposed that once a lawman, always a lawman.

"I've been asking around . . ."

"What did he look like?"

Keller could answer that question. "He was a young fella, maybe twenty-two or twenty-three, with blond hair. I never saw him before."

"You mean he was a stranger around here?"

Keller nodded. "Yes, sir, absolutely."

"And I heard as well that he was . . . unclothed."

"Naked as a jaybird," Keller said.

"That makes me wonder—" Ford began, but then he stopped as a man came into the room. Ford looked around and asked, "What the hell is it, Sergeant?"

"Beggin' your pardon, Colonel, but a rider just come in from out at Palmito Hill. Cap'n Giddings and his men are tradin' shots with a bunch of Yankees."

Ford's eyes widened in surprise and anger. "I parleyed with General Wallace myself! We agreed there would be no more fighting until we got word from back east about the disposition of the war."

"Well, I reckon the Yankees must've changed their minds, Colonel. What're we goin' to do?"

"Send out riders to call in all the cavalry units. We're going to fight, damn it!" Ford started toward the door, then stopped abruptly and looked back at Keller. "I was about to ask you, Sheriff, why a bushwhacker would steal all of a man's clothes."

"Uh . . ." That was all Keller could manage.

"Think about it," Ford snapped, and then he was gone.

Keller didn't want to think about it. He wanted to think about a big plate of beans and peppers and tortillas, washed down by a few mugs of beer. That was all he wanted on his mind.

But despite himself, as the evening went on, he found himself trying to figure out the answer to Colonel Ford's question.

GENERAL SLAUGHTER, THE OFFICIAL commander of the Confederate forces in Brownsville, wasn't as eager as Rip Ford to fight. In fact, he had already ordered that wagons be loaded with supplies for an evacuation, and he was in the middle of packing his personal belongings when Ford found him at Confederate headquarters. The old Ranger realized what was going on, and his face twisted in a grimace of disgust. "Running out, eh?"

"I plan to order a general retreat," Slaughter replied stiffly. "At this point in the war, I have no intention of provoking a major battle."

"The damn Yankees are the ones doing the provoking," Ford snapped. "You can retreat and go to hell if you want! These are my men, and I'm going to fight."

"Colonel, you can't—" Slaughter began, but Ford had already turned on his heel and was stalking out of the general's quarters. It was too late.

Too late for a lot of things, Slaughter supposed.

SEVERAL TIMES DURING THE night, Keller thought he heard gunfire in the distance. *Could be the Yankees and the Rebs still skirmishing with each other out yonder at Palmito Hill,* he thought. Sound could sometimes travel that far, especially on a calm, quiet night. If there was a real battle, though, it wouldn't come until the next day. Rip Ford was still in town, waiting for all his scattered cavalrymen to join him.

Keller rolled over in the bedroom of his little house and sleepily patted the rump of the Mexican woman who was his mistress. She stirred and turned toward him, but he wasn't interested in that right now. Instead, to his intense disgust, he found himself sitting up in bed and thinking about what Ford had asked him.

Why *would* a bushwhacker strip his victim down to the buff, especially when the dead man was a stranger?

Because maybe, Keller thought, *if the man had been wearing his clothes, he wouldn't exactly be a stranger anymore.*

BY THE MIDDLE OF the next morning, enough of Ford's men had shown up for the colonel to move out from Brownsville. He was riding at the head of the troops as they galloped out of town and headed for Palmito Hill to fight the Yankees.

Keller stood on the porch in front of the office and watched them ride out. When the cavalry was gone, Keller stepped down into the street and walked toward Fort Brown, down at the end of the street. It wasn't much of a fort, but it served as the official Confederate headquarters in Brownsville—just as it had been Union headquarters when the Yankees were in charge. Keller had seen it change hands and never really cared either way.

Now he was interested in talking to General Slaughter. To do that, he had to go through the general's aide, a lieutenant named Blaine. The lieutenant asked him curtly, "Why do you want to see the general?"

Keller had taken off his sombrero when he came into the office. He held it in one hand and used the other to scratch his head. "I was just wondering if the general was expecting anybody to show up yesterday."

Blaine frowned. "What are you talking about?"

"A messenger, an army courier of some sort. Or anybody else who's in the army."

"Not that I know of," Blaine said without hesitation. "And I would know if a courier was expected, so I don't see any reason to bother the general with this, Sheriff."

"You're sure?" Keller asked.

"I'm positive," Blaine answered, an edge of impatience creeping into his voice now. "What's this all about, Sheriff?"

"Well, there was this dead fella brought into town yesterday, and he didn't have any clothes on. So I got to wondering if maybe he was in the army, and the hombre who bushwhacked him took his clothes all the way down through his longjohns so nobody'd know they were army issue."

Blaine looked confused. "That seems rather far-fetched, doesn't it, Sheriff?"

"Well, yeah, I reckon it does. And I couldn't figure out any reason why a killer would want to keep it a secret that the gent he shot was a soldier. But if you weren't expecting anybody to show up . . ."

"We weren't," Blaine said firmly.

"I guess I'll have to keep pondering on it, then."

"You do that, Sheriff."

Keller left the fort and walked back to his office. Blaine waited until the sheriff was gone and then left as well.

THE TWO AMERICANS, A couple of rawboned men who'd brought several wagons full of cotton bales down from central Texas, went into a saloon called *El Cabeza de Javelina*—the Head of the Boar. The owner of the saloon was an Englishman called Whitson who had named the place after the Boar's Head Tavern back in the little English village where he'd grown up. It was a little reminder of home, the only such reminder in this hellishly hot and dry place.

In the middle of the afternoon like this, the saloon wasn't very crowded. In fact, there were no customers at all, only Whitson and a single bartender. People were inside somewhere sleeping if they had any sense. The Texans nodded to Whitson, who gestured them toward the back room. Whitson was being paid to provide some privacy for this meeting, and that was all he cared about since he was not an overly ambitious man. Otherwise, he supposed he would still be in England. The Mexicans who had arrived earlier, two of them carrying a wooden chest that was evidently heavy, were already waiting in the back room to conclude the deal.

Whitson sauntered toward the doors, intending to close and lock them behind the batwings to give his visitors even more assurance of privacy. Behind the bar, the bartender lazily polished the hardwood. Whitson reached for the knob of the right-hand door. Something blocked the light coming in from outside. He looked up and saw six men shouldering through the batwings. They were all dressed in dark suits.

"Sorry, gents," Whitson said. "Closing up temporarily. Come back in an hour or so."

The man in the lead of the odd group reached under his coat. Whitson thought he was probably reaching for a wallet. The man brought out a knife instead and thrust it into Whitson's chest as hard as he could. Whitson had time to gasp in surprise before he died.

Behind the bar, the bartender saw Whitson sag and fall. He said, "Hey—"

Pistols came out from under coats. The bartender turned pale, lifted his hands, and backed against the shelves behind the bar. One of the men covered him while the other five marched toward the back room, guns drawn.

DOBIE CAME INTO THE sheriff's office and looked around. Keller wasn't there. Dobie grinned slyly. This was his chance to go behind the desk and sit in the sheriff's chair and pretend that *he* was the sheriff. He liked to do that whenever Keller wasn't around.

But Dobie stopped short as he rounded the corner of the desk and saw the bulky form sprawled on the floor behind it. Keller was lying face down, and there was a dark stain on the back of his vest.

Dobie started to back away. His mouth opened and closed but no sound came out. He heard a sound, though, and wondered where it was coming from since he knew he wasn't making it.

After a second, he realized that Keller had let out a groan. Dobie gathered up his courage and rushed forward. Keller was moving around, trying to push himself up on hands and knees. Dobie grabbed his arm to help him, and Keller heaved upright and swung his left arm in a back-handed blow that knocked Dobie all the way across the office onto the rundown couch with its broken springs. Dust puffed up from the padding as Dobie landed on it.

Keller lumbered to his feet and said, "Stab me in the back, will you!"

"I didn't stab you, Sheriff!" Dobie cried as he held his hands out, palms toward Keller, as if that would hold off the enraged lawman. For all of his slow-moving ways, Keller was sort of like a bear when he was aroused. "I didn't stab nobody!"

Keller stopped, swayed on his feet a little, blinked a few times. "Dobie?" he finally asked.

"Yeah, it's me, Sheriff. What happened to you?"

Keller frowned and shook his head. "Somebody came in the back door. I heard it scrape on the floor. I was, uh, resting my eyes again. Started to turn around, but whoever it was stuck me with a knife."

"How come you ain't dead?"

"Good question." Keller started to reach behind him, then stopped and grimaced. "Hurts like hell, I know that much. Blade must've missed anything too important."

"I reckon it helps to carry a lot of meat on your bones."

Keller glowered some, but he said, "Yeah, I reckon." Then he said, "That son of a bitch!"

Dobie swallowed. "Who?" He hoped the sheriff wasn't talking about him. Keller looked mad enough to tear somebody's head off.

"The only one who had any reason to stab me." Keller started toward the door.

"What reason?"

"Don't know," Keller said as he grabbed his sombrero and clapped it on his head. "But I reckon he knows, and I aim to find out." He went out of the sheriff's office, the bloodstain on the back of his vest slowly spreading.

BLAINE WAS WAITING IN the alley alongside the Head of the Boar. He slid up the pane and went in the window of the back room as Colonel Flornoy and four French soldiers came in the door. Of course, the colonel and his men weren't in uniform, since they were no longer representing the Emperor Maximilian. They were out for themselves now, just like Blaine.

The Mexican rebels, who were also cotton smugglers, and the two Texan wagonmasters were caught flat-footed. One of the Mexicans was holding open the lid of a wooden chest filled with gold coins. None of the men moved as Blaine and the French renegades leveled pistols at them. Blaine grinned in satisfaction. Everything was working perfectly. He would have to split the gold with Flornoy, but they'd be long gone by the time that damn fool Pierce could get here. Pierce had actually believed that Blaine would keep his end of the bargain. That was a Yankee for you.

"Y'all just sit still, and nobody will get hurt," Blaine said to the Mexicans and the Texans. "We'll be taking that chest."

One of the Texans said quietly, "Damn you. How can you betray the Confederacy like this?"

Blaine laughed. "I got news for you, mister. There isn't any—"

He was still standing close to the open window. An arm came through it, a hand grabbed the back of his uniform coat, and he was jerked backward violently, crashing out through the window in a shower of broken glass from the upper pane.

"Stab me in the back, will you!" Sheriff Keller roared.

Inside the saloon's back room, the Texans took advantage of the distraction to grab for the revolvers holstered on their hips. Colonel Flornoy opened fire, as did his men, but even though one of the Texans fell over backward in his chair, the other put a couple of slugs in Flornoy's chest. The Mexicans had gotten guns out and were shooting, too, and the whole back room was nothing but smoke and flying lead.

In the alley, Keller reached down, grabbed the stunned Blaine, picked him up, and slammed him against the wall of the building on the other side of the alley. "It had to—uh!"

Keller drove Blaine against the wall again. "Had to be you! Uh!" Another crashing impact. "You're the only one I talked to—after I figured out why that fella was naked—You must've lied to me—He was a Confederate courier, wasn't he?"

Blaine was in no shape to answer. His jaw was broken, for one thing, from one of the half-dozen times Keller had slammed him against the wall. He was only half-conscious, too, but somehow he had managed to hold on to his gun. When Keller finally let him go, Blaine sagged against the wall and started to slide down it before he caught himself. He knew now he would never get his hands on that gold, and his fury over that fueled his need for vengeance. He turned around and started to bring up the gun. If nothing else, he would kill that fat bastard of a sheriff.

One of the bullets being blasted inside the back room of the saloon hit the thin boards of the wall, punched through them, whipped past Keller's left ear, and hit Blaine in the center of the forehead. Blaine's gun was still pointing toward the floor of the alley as he fired it involuntarily in the moment of dying. He fell back against the wall in a heap.

Keller became aware of more slugs buzzing around him and went diving for the ground. He'd been mad enough at Blaine for trying to stab him that he'd gone looking for the lieutenant. But on the way to Fort Brown, he'd glanced down this alley and seen a gray-clad leg disappearing into a window. Figuring that Blaine was a likely choice to be skulking around an alley, he'd taken a look through the window, and sure enough, there was the man who'd tried to kill him.

But whatever was behind that massacre going on in the saloon's back room . . . *that* was none of his business.

He was only the sheriff, after all.

RIP FORD'S CAVALRY OF the West reached Palmito Hill and found the Union troops under Colonel Barrett still engaging the Texan pickets under Captain Giddings. Ford promptly flanked the Yankees, tore into them from the side, and sent them scurrying back toward Brazos de Santiago in a full-fledged rout. Several times along the way, Colonel Barrett tried to rally his men, but to no avail. The Yankees were beaten.

As the battle turned, Lieutenant Dermot Pierce was furious. Blaine, that damned Confederate, had assured him that regular Union troops could defeat Ford's makeshift army. Ford had been the only threat to their plan, according to Blaine, so it had been necessary to provoke this battle and get him out of town, but from a military standpoint, Ford was no threat, Blaine had assured him. It was just that the man was a former Texas Ranger, and if he'd been around when Blaine and the Frenchmen stole the gold, he probably would have said to hell with the war and come after them— especially since that gold was supposed to find its way into Confederate coffers and help the Texans prolong the war.

A war that these stupid frontiersmen didn't even know was over, had been over for more than a month. Blaine had taken care of that by killing the courier who was bringing the news from Galveston to Brownsville.

If everything had gone according to plan, the Federals would have defeated Ford's cavalry, marched on into Brownsville, and Pierce could have bided his time before deserting and rendezvousing with Blaine. Pierce had made it look good during the fighting, emptying his pistol a few times and then hanging back for the most part. As Colonel Barrett's aide, he wasn't expected to be in the front lines.

The only trouble was, once the rout started there were no front lines, and Pierce found himself fleeing for his life from a bunch of Texas devils who screeched like imps out of Hades as they attacked. All Pierce could do then was turn his horse around and ride for his life.

He made it almost a hundred yards before a Texas sharpshooter knocked him out of the saddle with a single well-placed bullet. Pierce died with his face pressed into the sand that thirstily soaked up his blood.

ONE OF THE TEXANS lived through the fight in the back room of the Head of the Boar. So did one of the Mexicans and two of the Frenchmen. Keller locked up the Frenchmen, since it seemed they had less right to be there than either the Texan or the Mexican. He got enough of the story from those two to figure out that the whole thing had been about stealing the gold in that chest. He still didn't know why Blaine had bushwhacked that courier, though he felt sure in his gut that was what had happened.

It took Rip Ford to figure that out, once the colonel got back to town from whipping the Yankees. The canny old Ranger listened to the story Keller told him, then nodded and said, "According to some of the officers we captured out there at Palmito Hill, the war is over. General Lee surrendered to Grant a little more than a month ago at a place called Appomattox. I'm sure the courier was bringing that news to us."

The local sawbones had had to rip up a sheet to make bandages big enough to go around Keller's torso over the knife wound. They were so tight they were uncomfortable, and Keller wasn't in a very good mood. "Blaine found out about it somehow, and he figured you wouldn't go out to fight the Yankees if you knew the war was over."

Ford nodded. "He must have been working with someone in the Union camp, and they plotted the whole thing with those Frenchmen. They wanted me and my men out of town when the robbery took place."

"Why would they want that?" Keller asked.

"Because then the only law they would have to deal with, Sheriff—would be you."

Keller nodded. "I reckon that makes sense, all right."

He was on his third mug of beer and his second plate of beans and tortillas that evening before he looked up abruptly from his food, frowned, and said in offended understanding, "Hey."

Valuables

Kristine Scheid

On June 8, 1861, Mrs. Rose Grenlauer, with the help of her slaves, packed all of her plantation's valuables into two railroad cars and disappeared. Willard knew the exact date because that was the day Tennessee seceded from the Union. It was also the day he got conscripted into the Confederate Army.

Ten months later, he was back in Memphis, such as it was, missing one arm, one wife, and half of his house. The Union Army had burned it just after the Battle of Shiloh, when they occupied the city. General Ulysses S. Grant now used Mrs. Rose Grenlauer's plantation as headquarters for one of his divisions and, it was said, he sat in her husband's library, drinking port and smoking his awful cigars as he made his plans to destroy the South. Colonel Rufus Grenlauer knew nothing of that, of course. He hadn't been home since he joined up right after Jefferson Davis, a friend of the Grenlauers', became president of the Confederacy.

Willard knew all that because he now begged for coins not a block from the Grenlauer estate. The damn Yankee soldiers would give him nothing for his trouble and for all his losses, but the widows and wives, most of whom were still struggling to keep their fancy homes together, usually gave him a scrap or two. Then they'd plead with him to get off the street, worried that the Yankees would somehow hurt him if they found out he was a patriot, as if they could do worse than they'd already done.

Besides, the Yankees already knew he was a patriot. A strapping local man, left sleeve pinned to his shoulder, obviously thinner than a man should be, could be nothing else. That they didn't bother him, that they didn't arrest him, showed that they no longer thought him a threat.

They were wrong.

Someday, he would prove it to them.

And Mrs. Rose Grenlauer would help.

HE DIDN'T KNOW WHEN he starting thinking about Mrs. Rose Grenlauer. Sometimes, he believed it began after he got home and saw her plantation still standing, the bricks, made by hand by the hundreds of slaves her parents had on the estate, untouched by fire or explosions or even gunshots.

His house, the bricks bought at great cost in 1855, when he was gainfully employed as a tugboat captain and which he laid by hand on hot, long summer days, had been knocked askew in a firefight he hadn't been there to see. The wooden porch his wife Selma Leigh had asked him to build just for her and for the children they would now never have, had burned, the fire licking across the plankings and eventually eating the wooden floors she had polished so lovingly after their marriage in December 1856.

The neighbors said she'd tried to defend the place all by herself, using his granddaddy's Revolutionary War musket and a hunting knife Willard had left behind. But in the end, it'd done no good.

The Yanks had captured her, done what they wanted with her, then left her for dead in the middle of the roses she'd planted that very first spring. She'd died three days later, out of her head—"a mercy," said Mrs. Cannon, who'd tended her—apparently injured too severely to live. The sheets she'd lain on had to be burned, they were covered with so much blood.

Willard found this out when he came home, too thin himself, the only thing carrying him was the memory of his pretty wife's face and the cool soothing way her hands would feel on his ruined body. He'd been afraid she wouldn't accept him, not without his arm—not even the army wanted him now, although they were hurting for men—but he knew he'd have to give it one more try.

And he'd been too late. Too late by a month, maybe more. Too late to stop any of it.

Old Mrs. Cannon, she'd said it was a blessing he hadn't been there. He'd have died, too, maybe in the gardenias or at the front of the lawn, trying to protect his wife and his home. His wife would have screamed and he would have been distracted, and the Yanks would have taken advantage, all of them—five, ten, Mrs. Cannon couldn't remember— and then his wife'd had to go through one more horrible thing, watching him die before her very eyes.

Only Mrs. Cannon couldn't have known how it would've worked, not with him home. He'd have had his rifle, and he knew how to use his granddaddy's muzzle loader. He'd have held off five men or ten. He'd have gotten his wife away.

But he hadn't been there. On the day she died, he'd been in a doctor's tent that smelled of old blood and piss, a pile of limbs outside it, and he'd been begging the man in the blood-stained uniform to let him keep his arm, let him keep it despite the bullet that had ripped through it, tearing the flesh and leaving it hanging useless at his side.

They'd gotten him drunk—the last of the army's whiskey, someone had told him later—then made him bite on a stick of wood already chewed raw by other men's teeth. That'd stopped him from biting through his own tongue, but it hadn't stopped him from screaming like he was going to die, probably as his wife'd been screaming, probably while those Yanks were enjoying her and laughing at the victory that they'd so easily won.

Then he'd asked Mrs. Cannon why his house was ruined when none of his neighbors' were, and he'd asked why his wife was dead when almost no women or children died when the Yanks took over the city, and what he'd learned upset him most of all.

His wife, Selma Leigh, had caught the eye of a Yank captain who'd decided that he wanted her and her pretty home all to himself.

I'm a married woman sir, she'd said to him, and the Yankee bastard had just laughed.

Chances are you're a widowed woman, he'd said back, *and even if you ain't, how's your husband to know what we done if you don't tell him?*

Still, she stuck to her refusal and he'd come with his men one spring afternoon, and taken what he'd wanted. Taken it, and destroyed it, so that when Willard came home, he'd have nothing. No wife, no home, and no memories worth savoring.

Because all he kept thinking was that if he hadn't brought her here, if he'd left Selma Leigh in Atlanta where he'd found her, she'd still be alive now. Alive, and using her dainty hands to grow roses and keep a home, smiling that pretty smile for someone else.

But at least that smile would still be alive. At least someone would see it.

He didn't care if he didn't get to see it, so long as someone did.

Instead, as the perennials bloomed—flowers she'd planted—he laid them on the grave his neighbors had made for her in the backyard, and he promised her, soon as he got rid of them Yankee bastards, he'd find her a proper resting place, just like he'd once promised her a proper home.

HE DIDN'T KNOW WHAT all that had to do with Mrs. Rose Grenlauer or why he started to think of her and her two railroad cars. Sometimes he wondered if he'd been thinking about Rose Grenlauer his entire life. He'd seen her when he was a boy, and she was a young woman, living in the guest cottage while her family's slaves built the most spectacular plantation in Memphis.

Back before the war, the plantation had even had artificial lights, powered by oil squeezed from linseeds, an hour's worth of light taking two days' worth of work to create. The plantation had been filled with marvels and anyone who was anyone in the city'd come to see it. Rose Grenlauer's parents, the Allens, had opened the doors to show off their new home.

He'd sat outside, of course, on the other side of the street. All he'd been able to see was the lovely landscaping, the marvelous lamps placed at the end of the long meandering sidewalk, the brick stairs and the wide white door, opened to admit people who wouldn't even meet Willard's gaze. He'd stood there most of the day, along with other folks who weren't anybody, and finally he'd gotten a chance to see Rose Grenlauer, who'd been Rose Allen then, standing by the door.

She'd worn a white dress trimmed with red to match the bows hanging all over the trees, and her lovely hair had been curled into ringlets. She'd been laughing at something a young man said to her, and then she had looked across the street.

Willard always thought she'd looked at him, but if she had, it would have been the first and only time. He'd seen her after that, had stood outside the house on one other occasion, that of her summer wedding to Rufus Grenlauer. That had been a spectacular event, too; the tents on the lawn, the musicians filling the entire outdoors with sounds Willard had never heard before, the food stacked on tables, and the servants who kept all the bugs away.

The guests had arrived looking more refined than Willard had thought possible—the women in their taffetas, the men in their best suits. Even from across the street he could smell the pomade the men used in their hair, the French perfume the women had sprayed all over themselves, and the flowers—oh, all the flowers—that the Allens had somehow convinced to bloom all over the yard.

He'd vowed then—it was June 1850—that when he married he would provide the same things for his bride: a beautiful home, more flowers than a body could behold, and wealth beyond all her imagining. That was when he'd gotten his job, and in every spare hour worked on the home, first paying for the land, then designing the house itself, and then building it, sometimes with his own hands. When he'd finally found Selma Leigh, he'd had everything he'd dreamed of, except great wealth. But he'd been better off than his parents, better off than his friends, and when the war came, he was able to give more than his service to the cause—he was able to send thousands of dollars—greenbacks—to support Jefferson Davis's new administration.

Like so many others, he'd converted the rest of his wealth into two forms: Confederate bonds and gold, kept in a safe in the house. The safe was gone, of course, gone in the fire that had destroyed half his home. He'd found some bonds, but Memphis was run by the Yankees now, and they didn't recognize what they called Jeff Davis's phony money. So Willard had nothing. No wife, no arm, no pension, and no cash with which to live. He was dependent on the charity of his friends and on the begging he did, as no one would hire him—not looking the way he did, not with his missing arm.

It was a wonder that he survived from day to day.

BUT WILLARD WASN'T A man used to being useless, and for each penny he scrounged, each jibe from a Yankee soldier, each pitiful look from one of the Southern women who used to envy his pretty wife, he grew even more despairing.

He tried finding honest work, but those who didn't stare at him with pity politely refused, saying that he had done enough in service of his country. Others asked him to take a loyalty oath to the United States, something he couldn't bear and something, he knew, that would come back to haunt him when the South won the war.

Poverty, infirmity, loss, none of those were enough to abandon your country, your state, and your dream. He knew that. Others in Memphis knew that as well. He heard them, feeling comfortable around him, talking about ways of fighting back, ways of forcing the Yankees out of Tennessee.

He even went to some meetings, when he could find them, and listened to men too old to serve or women who had no idea what the fighting was like talk about taking on the Yankees who owned his city. But he knew that the Yankees were too powerful. The help couldn't come from the inside. It had to come from outside, and right now, there was too much happening in the South for the armies to concentrate on one city, even if it was on the Mississippi River and other transportation routes.

It was up to the citizens of Memphis to remind the Confederacy of their importance. And, Willard believed, every citizen had a duty to help.

Sometimes, he thought, that was what had focused him on Rose Grenlauer and her two railroad cars full of valuables. He had learned of it from one of the widows who attended the meeting, a bitter woman whose family had sold some of the land to the Allens before they built the plantation.

Never paid us what it was worth, she would say. *Even then they were tighter with money than most—that Rose, she's just the*

worst of them—people dying for a cause, and she runs away with
the family silver.

From that moment, he dreamed of Mrs. Rose Grenlauer, thought of her, wondered if she was still as pretty as
the bride he'd seen so briefly on her wedding day, walking
underneath a bower of white roses, her veil trailing more
than a yard behind her. Was she still a delicate creature of
privilege? Or had that year of riding in railroad cars taken
some of the blush from her skin?

He wanted to find out. He needed to find out, not just
for himself, but for the sake of the Confederacy. Those two
railroad cars of hers could be used in the war effort to transport troops and supplies and weapons. And those valuables
could buy food and clothing for soldiers or help support the
widows and orphans left behind.

Yes, Mrs. Rose Grenlauer had lost her home, but only
because she had abandoned it, left it as an obvious place for
the enemy to make his headquarters.

Sometimes Willard thought she had been a collaborator
with the Union. It seemed so curious to him. She'd left the
day that Tennessee seceded. She left her home undefended
so that anyone, even that slob of a general Grant, could
move inside. She'd taken valuables in railroad cars.

Maybe, he'd found himself thinking, *maybe she'd even*
taken them up North.

He'd hated that thought the moment he had it: pretty
Rose Grenlauer using Southern heritage to fund the Union
cause. But he hadn't been able to get it out of his mind. He
would stand in his old spot across from the Grenlauer mansion and he'd stare at it, wondering if Grant was there with
Mrs. Rose Grenlauer's permission.

The very idea stuck in Willard's craw.

And he knew it was that idea, that one idea, which
forced him to take action.

IT'D BEEN HARD. FIRST he'd talked to the servants, the ones who were still in Memphis, the ones who had helped her pack the cars. They spoke of riches beyond his comprehension, silver services that had been in the family for generations, paintings by some of the old masters, jewelry that had more diamonds and emeralds than he'd ever imagined possible.

There was no way to trace the railroad cars, or so he was told, but he knew there had to be. Those cars had to be moved from place to place, whether they were pushed or pulled. It had only been a year. Someone had to remember them. Someone had to know where they were.

He'd stopped begging outside the Grenlauer plantation. Instead, he spent most of his time at the train yards. He did what work he could, voluntarily shoveling coal with his one good arm, dragging parcels from place to place, posting the weekly casualty lists.

Finally they started paying him, without the Yankees' permission of course. When the Yankees came, the train yard workers claimed he was just a bum whom they fed sometimes, and he was happy to keep up the lie. He didn't want his money, what little of it he got, coming out of the Yankees' pockets.

In return for all the work, he got to listen to the gossip. Sometimes he brought up his few stories of train travel during his brief service. Sometimes he brought up legends that he'd heard over the years—ghost trains during the night, things like that—and finally someone told him the story of Rose Grenlauer.

She'd bought the railroad cars with cash, used her own servants to load them, then hired an engineer to take her to an unfinished line where she could live and hide until the war was over.

He'd heard part of that, of course, but not all of it. He figured he could wait until he actually found the engineer, a man who might not come through Memphis again, or he could visit the unfinished lines of track himself.

A year earlier Jefferson Davis had pledged himself to finishing the rail lines, but that hadn't been possible, not with the way the war was going and the South's great need for men. Hiding was easy at the end of one of those unfinished lines—provided, of course, that no battles were being fought around it.

He'd used a map inside the stationhouse, one of the maps that showed every bit of rail ever built, and studied it for days. Some of the unfinished lines were near Shiloh, where he'd lost his arm. Only a few were in areas untouched by the war, and only one was near a small community, where a woman alone, who happened to have gold or other things to trade, could buy something to eat.

It had taken him nearly a month, but he felt he had found her. And now that he had her, it was time to make her do her duty to country.

Everyone else was paying. It was time for Mrs. Rose Grenlauer to pay, too.

OF COURSE, HE HAD no horse and no money to buy one. Stealing one was a capital crime, but, he believed, one he could justify if he had to. Why, he'd simply say that the horse was one he'd found wandering free, probably lost after one of the battles. There were so many lost horses, after all. And if he didn't get caught, he would leave the horse outside the city when he was done.

In the month he'd been searching for Mrs. Rose Grenlauer, he'd managed to buy food. The work had made his remaining arm stronger, and he actually felt like a man for the first time since he'd come home.

It was, he thought, the perfect time.

The horse theft was easy. He took one of the mares from the Grenlauer estate. He recognized the horse. It had been one of Rufus Grenlauer's, left behind by his wife when she took her railroad cars and fled. The Grenlauer horses weren't assigned to any officers, not so as he knew, and he doubted that anyone would know she was missing for at least a day or so.

That got him outside the city into the thin woods and bluffs that lined the Mississippi. He had packed his old saddlebags with food he'd saved and meal for the horse, which he'd also stolen from the Yanks. He was carrying his rifle and several hunting knives, figuring that would be enough.

When he got a few miles outside of Memphis, he doubled back through the woods to the unfinished rail line. He followed it north and cattycorner. Riding jostled him, made his stump ache, but he did it, and was proud of it. Three days over track that was weed-infested and lines that were broken, not by destructive armies, but by time and lack of use.

At times he nearly lost the track for the weeds, his horse reluctant to go through such tangles. Sometimes he doubted the wisdom of his mission—not the idea of making Mrs. Rose Grenlauer do her duty, but the idea of following this line when he had no actual evidence she was along it.

Supposition hadn't served him that well since the war started. As he rode, he was beginning to think it would fail him again.

On the fourth day, he saw rusted shovels and pickaxes abandoned on the side of the track. The wooden rails were gone—probably used as kindling—but some lengths of iron remained. His heart was in his throat as he emerged through a copse of trees and saw the line was blocked.

It looked like it was blocked by more trees. Branches covered the track in front of him, and vines tangled up it. But the branches were haphazard, the vines weaving in and out in a way they'd never do with a living tree.

He needed to know if this was Mrs. Rose Grenlauer's railroad cars and he wasn't sure how to do it, not at first. He hadn't been thinking of a plan on the ride—imagining various scenarios, yes, but not actually planning. Deep down, he never thought he would find her.

He sat on his horse for a long time, staring at the tangle ahead. Nothing moved. He heard no one, saw nothing. Maybe he was mistaken. Maybe he was just seeing an abandoned shed or an old unused car. He would have to find out.

His plan, as it evolved, was simple enough. He was a Confederate soldier, going home, his injury apparent enough. He'd stay with her until he convinced her to accompany him, taking the valuables to Richmond maybe, or Atlanta, somewhere that they could be sold for funds.

He'd always known when he met Mrs. Rose Grenlauer she'd be sweet on him. He'd use that to convince her to give her belongings to the cause.

He rode up, and as he approached the tangle he realized he was seeing box cars. Two of them attached in the middle. Someone had carefully hidden them, but had gotten careless. A lot of the branches had dried and fallen off. Others were so choked by vines that the entire works looked like a jungle from some storybook instead of a forest in Tennessee.

One of the railroad car's doors was open, revealing a small room inside, filled with furniture laid out in a comfortable pattern. He was so intrigued he pulled up right in front and stared in. Upholstered chairs with mahogany legs sat side by side, with a matching table between them, a lamp on it and a book with them. On one side were boxes. On the other, a small bed with a canopy and mosquito netting.

He was just about to dismount when a voice stopped him.

"Who goes?"

He frowned, saw a small woman in a floppy hat and a faded dress holding a rifle on him.

"Willard," he said. "Willard Harrison."

"You put up them arms, Mr. Harrison," she said. He couldn't see her face. It was shaded by the hat.

He put up his arm, keeping the reins draped over his thumb.

"Both of them, Mr. Harrison."

"Beg pardon, ma'am," he said. "I got but one."

She took a step closer. He hadn't remembered her being so small, but then he'd never seen her up close.

"I guess you do." She pushed her hat back and he saw her face. Mrs. Rose Grenlauer all right, thinner than he'd remembered, her hair tumbled around her face like a school girl's. Not the beautiful belle he'd been admiring for years, but a woman who was beginning to look her age. "What're you doing here?"

"Heading home," he said. "To Memphis."

"Then you're headed the wrong way." She didn't sound too friendly.

"I—um—I am?"

"Don't lie to me, Mr. Harrison. You came searching for me, just like them others, hearing snifflings of gold."

"No, ma'am," he lied. "I'm just a soldier on his way home."

"On my husband's mare?" She made a clicking sound with her tongue, and the mare reared. Willard slid off, unable to grab on with his remaining arm.

He landed on his back, and the wind rushed out of him. He couldn't catch his breath, and the sky revolved for a moment. Mrs. Rose Grenlauer came over to him and put a foot on his chest. A foot wearing a man's boot. She levered her rifle at him.

"I remember you," she said. "My father had the servants drive you off more than once."

Willard couldn't defend himself. He didn't have the breath.

"I'm gonna ask again. What'd you come here for?"

He finally got a gulp of air. He managed to squeeze out, "We need your railroad cars, ma'am, and your valuables. Memphis is Yankee-owned now, and the devil Lincoln made

Andrew Jackson military governor of Tennessee. We're losing. We need all the help—"

She jammed him in the chest with her rifle. "You don't need what I got," she said. "I'd tell you to take your horse and get, but it's my horse you got. Guess I'm just gonna have to shoot you."

He scrambled backward and upright faster than he'd known he could move. He grabbed the rifle and twisted it, pulling it away from her. He turned it and leveled it on her, bracing it under his arm, and holding it with his forefinger on the trigger, thumb on the hammer.

"I ain't lying to you, Mrs. Grenlauer," he said. "We need you to do what you can for the cause. The rest of us, we lost everything, but you, you're sitting here till the war's out, sitting on your hoard like what we do don't matter."

She didn't look scared of him. "I'm a woman, Mr. Harrison," she said. "I'm not expected to serve."

"There're others at home, helping with the effort. You could, too."

"I understand there's a Union general sleeping in my house and Yankee soldiers tearing up my yard. There's nothing for me to return to, Mr. Harrison."

"Nothing?" The word screeched out of him. He shoved her with the rifle, pushing her backward with the muzzle. "Nothing? You don't know what nothing is. You and your railroad cars and your fancy husband and your big house that ain't even got a bootmark on the wooden floors. You're here alive and untouched with all your treasures while my wife—"

He stopped, not liking the hysteria in his own voice. What'd his commander said? A man out of control was a man who was going to lose something. A limb, maybe a life.

How well he knew that.

He focused on Mrs. Rose Grenlauer. She no longer looked calm. Her eyes were round and her lower lip trembled. "Yes," she said in a voice that was so soothing and placating it sounded like she was talking to a child. "Yes, you're right, of course, Mr. Harrison. You're absolutely right. I should be helping with the war effort. I should donate all my goods to the cause. I was such a fool not to see it."

Her gaze darted past him, and he whirled. A black man was there, a big dark man in tattered clothes, clothes that Willard recognized as the uniform of the Grenlauer house. The man held a stick.

"Put it down," Willard said. "Put it down."

The black man looked at Mrs. Rose Grenlauer for confirmation. Willard did too, and the black man rushed him. Willard fired before he could even think. The man flew backward and Mrs. Rose Grenlauer screamed. The man landed on his side, blood gushing from a wound in his stomach.

"You idiot!" she said. "You fool!"

And she jumped on him, digging her feet into his side, kicking him, pulling at the gun. He swung his torso, trying to throw her off, trying to knock her away. She was taking his breath away, hurting him, piling into the old wounds, her hands hitting his stump, sending pain where the arm had once been. Reminding him of all the nothing he had, all he'd lost, for a cause she didn't feel she had to fight for.

With a roar, he flung her back. She slid off him and he kicked her away.

"You ignorant piece of trash," she said. "You don't understand what you're asking me to give up. You don't know—"

He shot her. Mostly to shut her up. And it did. She stared at him for a long moment, then fell forward on her face, her eyes open and fixing on the sky.

He was shaking just like he had in his first battle. He glanced over his shoulder, but there was no one to see what he had done. No one except the horse, which was watching him from the side of the railroad car.

"Didn't go like we planned, huh, girl?" he said.

The horse watched him warily.

"She didn't know. She was a traitor to the cause, sitting here on her wealth, hiding out as if what she had was the most important thing in the world."

The horse shifted skittishly from one side to the other.

He sat down, so exhausted he didn't know what to do. He glanced at her, unmoving, and the black man who was just as dead. Of course she would've brought a slave with her. Of course. To protect her and the valuables. Not that it did much good.

A shaky laugh escaped him, and it sounded just a little crazy. Of course it sounded crazy. She was dead and it was because she had pushed him to it, not understanding how things really were, how badly her railroad cars and valuables was needed. She pushed him by mentioning his wife and how he didn't understand sacrifice and—

He shook his head trying to make the thoughts stop. He had to do something. That she was dead didn't really matter, after all. He had the cars and the valuables, and he wasn't going to sit on them, not like she did. He wasn't no traitor. He'd given an arm and a wife to the cause. He wasn't going to stop now.

It would take some planning. But he had time. He could take it nice and slow.

Took him a day to bury them, using one of the rusty old shovels he'd found. He dragged them to the woods and buried them there, away from the railroad cars. That first night, he slept in her bed and knew that wasn't how he'd imagined it. From the first he'd known he'd be in Rose Grenlauer's bed, but he hadn't realized he'd be there alone.

The next day he'd closed the railroad car's doors and covered it again with brambles, hoping it'd stay hidden just long enough for him to do his duty.

That took longer than he thought, too. He couldn't go back to Memphis. That was a Union town now, and the trains, even though they had Southern boys steering, were

Union owned. He had to go farther south till he found his own men, and then he'd have to bring them back.

It took him and the mare three more days to find help, and another day after that to convince the corporal in charge to let three of his men accompany Willard back to the railroad cars. If they liked what they saw, they'd risk sending an engine in to pull everything out.

Four days back to the hiding place—counting the one day he got lost—and he was afraid someone else would have found his treasure, someone else would have stolen it, made all this work for nothing.

This was what was going to redeem him. Wouldn't make the loss of the arm or Selma Leigh worthwhile, but at least he'd help with the cause in a way that Mrs. Rose Grenlauer never did. He would have given everything—the woman he loved, a part of himself, his home, and now bounty that a lesser man would have kept as payment for all that loss. He was giving it back, giving it up, and maybe some day people would remember. They'd say, that Willard Harrison, he wasn't so crazy after all. He was the one that got the money that turned the tide in the war.

The railroad cars were as he left them. The men who'd ridden with him seemed relieved. He knew they didn't really believe him, that they thought they were getting a leave for humoring a former soldier. But when they got there, they got off their horses, tied them to some brambles, and set about opening the railroad cars' doors.

The first car was like he left it, the furniture set up, boxes on the side. The second car he'd never even looked into. It was filled with boxes and crates. One of the men whistled through his teeth as he looked in.

He pulled down the first box, opened it, and swore. Then he pulled down another. The men grabbed boxes in the first car and pulled them down. Willard saw what they did when it was opened. Letters, linens, toys, and books.

"There's supposed to be silver," he said, "and more jewels than anyone else ever had in Memphis."

And there was silver. One serving set and one set of silverware. A pearl necklace and diamond earrings. Gold leaf plates and some baby spoons, also made of gold.

But that was all. Rattles and clothing and portraits of the family, most of them recent and done with that photographic process that was so expensive, but worth nothing for resale.

The men threw things out of the box cars and kicked the boxes and ruined the little furniture grouping and cursed Willard who watched in shocked dismay.

"They'd said," he said. "They'd said there was valuables here."

"There are valuables, you dumb ass," one of the men said to him, face up close, breath smelling of rot. "Some family's mementos. Ain't got no meaning to no one else."

Willard flushed. How to save this? He thought it would be enough to finance food and clothes for an army. He'd thought it might be enough to save the South.

"The railroad cars, at least," he said. "We could use them. Troop transport or—"

"The wheels're gone," the soldier said. "We'd have to repair them first."

Willard looked. Sure enough. She'd disabled the cars so someone who came looking would think they were abandoned a long time. Only she'd never expected someone like Willard. Someone craftier than she was. Smarter. Better.

Someone who'd had a hoard of valuables and lost it to the Yankees.

Something of it must have shown on his face for the soldier who'd been yelling at him stopped, put a hand on his shoulder. "It was a good try. Next time, you make sure you know what the valuables are before you offer them to the army."

Then he whistled to the men, and they rode off, leaving Willard standing alone in a pile of boxes. A pile of memories that didn't matter to no one except Rose and Rufus Grenlauer.

The horse was watching him again, judging him, it seemed. Maybe he was no better than them Yankee bastards, killing and taking what he wanted, then realizing it wasn't worth his effort. Maybe he was no better at all.

He bent down, picked up a packet of letters wrapped in faded ribbon, and placed them back inside the box. He was better. Of course he was. He'd done this for the cause. The soldiers had had no patience, that was all. He'd find what they needed. Then he'd turn it in somewhere else.

Until then, he and the horse, they'd stay here. Where it was safe. He couldn't go back to Memphis. He didn't have a home there or a wife. Or even a dream anymore.

Just a packet of memories of a world gone by. A world he'd known mostly from the outside. Like the visions of a boy who'd stood across the street and tried to stare into a house where he'd never be invited.

A house owned by a pretty woman, with memories of her own.

The Face

Ed Gorman

The war was going badly. In the past month more than
sixty men had disgraced the Confederacy by deserting, and now the order was to shoot deserters on
sight. This was in other camps and other regiments. Fortunately, none of our men had deserted at all.

As a young doctor, I knew even better than our leaders
just how hopeless our war had become. The public knew General Lee had been forced to cross the Potomac with ten thousand men who lacked shoes and hats, and who at night had to
sleep on the ground without blankets. But I knew—in the first
six months in this post—that our men suffered from influenza,
diphtheria, smallpox, yellow fever, and even cholera; ravages
from which they would never recover; ravages more costly than
bullets and the advancing armies of the Yankees. Worse,
because toilet and bathing facilities were practically nil, virtually every man suffered from ticks and mites and many suffered from scurvy, their bodies on fire. Occasionally, you would
see a man go mad, do crazed dances in the moonlight trying
to get the bugs off him. Soon enough he would be dead.

This was the war in the spring and while I have here
referred to our troops as "men," in fact they were mostly

boys, some as young as thirteen. In the night, freezing and
sometimes wounded, they cried out for their mothers, and it
was not uncommon to hear one or two of them sob while
they prayed aloud.

I tell you this so you will have some idea of how horrible
things had become for our beloved Confederacy. But even
given the suffering and madness and despair I'd seen for the
past two years as a military doctor, nothing had prepared me
for the appearance of the Virginia man in our midst.

On the day he was brought in on a buckboard, I was
working with some troops, teaching them how to garden. If
we did not get vegetables and fruit into our diets soon, all of
us would have scurvy. I also appreciated the respite that
working in the warm sun gave me from surgery. In the past
week alone, I'd amputated three legs, two arms, and numerous hands and fingers. None had gone well, conditions were
so filthy.

Every amputation had ended in death except one and
this man—boy; he was fourteen—pleaded with me to kill
him every time I checked on him. He'd suffered a head
wound, and I'd had to relieve the pressure by trepanning
into his skull. Beneath the blood and pus in the hole I'd
dug, I could see his brain squirming. There was no anes-
thetic, of course, except whiskey and that provided little
comfort against the violence of my bone saw. It was one of
those periods when I could not get the tart odor of blood
from my nostrils, nor its feel from my skin. Sometimes,
standing at the surgery table, my boots would become
soaked with it and I would squish around in them all day.

The buckboard was parked in front of the General's
tent. The driver jumped down, ground-tied the horses, and
went quickly inside.

He returned a few moments later with General Sullivan,
the commander. Three men in familiar gray uniforms followed the General.

The entourage walked around to the rear of the wagon.
The driver, an enlisted man, pointed to something in the

buckboard. The General, a fleshy, bald man of fifty-some years, leaned over the wagon and peered downward.

Quickly, the General's head snapped back and then his whole body followed. It was as if he'd been stung by something coiled and waiting for him in the buckboard.

The General shook his head and said, "I want this man's entire face covered. Especially his face."

"But, General," the driver said. "He's not dead. We shouldn't cover his face."

"You heard what I said!" General Sullivan snapped. And with that, he strutted back into his tent, his men following.

I was curious, of course, about the man in the back of the wagon. I wondered what could have made the General start the way he had. He'd looked almost frightened.

I wasn't to know till later that night.

MY ROUNDS MADE ME late for dinner in the vast tent used for the officers' mess. I always felt badly about the inequity of officers having beef stew while the men had, at best, hardtack and salt pork. Not so bad that I refused to eat it, of course, which made me feel hypocritical on top of being sorry for the enlisted men.

Not once in my time here had I ever dined with General Sullivan. I was told on my first day here that the General, an extremely superstitious man, considered doctors bad luck. Many people feel this way. Befriend a doctor and you'll soon enough find need of his services.

So I was surprised when General Sullivan, carrying a cup of steaming coffee in a huge, battered tin cup, sat down across the table where I ate alone, my usual companions long ago gone back to their duties.

"Good evening, Doctor."

"Good evening, General."

"A little warmer tonight."

"Yes."

He smiled dourly. "Something's got to go our way, I suppose."

I returned his smile. "I suppose." I felt like a child trying to act properly for the sake of an adult. The General frightened me.

The General took out a stogie, clipped off the end, sniffed it, licked it, then put it between his lips and fired it. He did all this with a ritualistic satisfaction that made me think of better times in my home city of Charleston, of my father and uncles handling their smoking in just the same way.

"A man was brought into camp this afternoon," he said.

"Yes," I said. "In a buckboard."

He eyed me suspiciously. "You've seen him up close?"

"No. I just saw him delivered to your tent." I had to he careful of how I put my next statement. I did not want the General to think I was challenging his reasoning. "I'm told he was not taken to any of the hospital tents."

"No, he wasn't." The General wasn't going to help me.

"I'm told he was still under quarantine in a tent of his own."

"Yes."

"May I ask why?"

He blew two plump white perfect rings of smoke toward the ceiling. "Go have a look at him, then join me in my tent."

"You're afraid he may have some contagious disease?"

The General considered the length of his cigar. "Just go have a look at him, Doctor. Then we'll talk."

With that, the General stood up, his familiar brusque self once again, and was gone.

THE GUARD SET DOWN his rifle when he saw me. "Good evenin', Doctor."

"Good evening."

He nodded to the tent behind him. "You seen him yet?"

"No, not yet."

He was young. He shook his head. "Never seen anything like it. Neither has the priest. He's in there with him now." In the chill, crimson dusk I tried to get a look at the guard's face. I couldn't. My only clue to his mood was the tone of his voice—one of great sorrow.

I lifted the tent flap and went in.

A lamp guttered in the far corner of the small tent, casting huge and playful shadows across the walls. A hospital cot took up most of the space. A man's body lay beneath the covers. A sheer cloth had been draped across his face. You could see it billowing with the man's faint breath. Next to the cot stood Father Lynott. He was silver-haired and chunky. His black cassock showed months of dust and grime. Like most of us, he was rarely able to get hot water for necessities.

At first, he didn't seem to hear me. He stood over the cot torturing black rosary beads through his fingers. He stared directly down at the cloth draped on the man's face.

Only when I stood next to him did Father Lynott look up. "Good evening, Father."

"Good evening, Doctor."

"The General wanted me to look at this man."

He stared at me. "You haven't seen him, then?"

"No."

"Nothing can prepare you."

"I'm afraid I don't understand."

He looked at me out of his tired cleric's face. "You'll see soon enough. Why don't you come over to the officers' tent afterward? I'll be there drinking my nightly coffee."

He nodded, glanced down once more at the man on the cot, and then left, dropping the tent flap behind him.

I don't know how long I stood there before I could bring myself to remove the cloth from the man's face. By now, enough people had warned me of what I would see that I was both curious and apprehensive. There is a myth about doctors not being shocked by certain terrible wounds and injuries. Of course we are but we must get past that shock—or, more honestly, put it aside for a time—so that we can help the patient.

Close by, I could hear the feet of the guard in the damp grass, pacing back and forth in front of the tent. A barn owl and then a distant dog joined the sounds the guard made. Even more distant, there was cannon fire, the war never ceasing. The sky would flare silver like summer lightning. Men would suffer and die.

I reached down and took the cloth from the man's face.

"WHAT DO YOU SUPPOSE could have done that to his face, Father?" I asked the priest twenty minutes later.

We were having coffee. I smoked a cigar. The guttering candles smelled sweet and waxy.

"I'm not sure," the priest said.

"Have you ever seen anything like it?"

"Never."

I knew what I was about to say would surprise the priest. "He has no wounds."

"What?"

"I examined him thoroughly. There are no wounds anywhere on his body."

"But his face—"

I drew on my cigar, watched the expelled smoke move like a storm cloud across the flickering candle flame. "That's why I asked you if you'd ever seen anything like it."

"My God," the priest said, as if speaking to himself. "No wounds."

IN THE DREAM I was back on the battlefield on that frosty March morning two years ago, when all my medical training had deserted me. Hundreds of corpses covered the ground where the battle had gone on for two days and two nights. You could see cannons mired in mud, the horses unable to pull them out. You could see the grass littered with dishes and pans and kettles, and a blizzard of playing cards—all exploded across the battlefield when the Union army had made its final advance. But mostly there were the bodies—so young and so many—and many of them with mutilated faces. During this time of the war, both sides had begun to commit atrocities. The Yankees favored disfiguring Confederate dead, and so they moved across the battlefield with Bowie knives that had been fashioned by sharpening them with large files. They put deep gashes in the faces of the young men, tearing out eyes sometimes, even sawing off noses. In the woods that day we'd found a group of our soldiers who'd been mortally wounded but who'd lived for a time after the Yankees had left. Each corpse held in its hand some memento of the loved ones they'd left behind—a photograph, a letter, a lock of blonde hair. Their last sight had been of some homely yet profound endearment from the people they'd loved most.

This was the dream—nightmare, really—and I'd suffered it ever since I'd searched for survivors on that battlefield two years previous.

I was still in this dream-state when I heard the bugle announce the morning. I stumbled from my cot and went down to the creek to wash and shave. The day had begun.

CASUALTIES WERE MANY THAT morning. I stood in the hospital tent watching as one stretcher after another bore man after man to the operating table. Most suffered from wounds inflicted by minie balls, fired from guns that could kill a man nearly a mile away.

By noon, my boots were again soaked with blood dripping from the table.

During the long day, I heard whispers of the man General Sullivan had quarantined from others. Apparently, the man had assumed the celebrity and fascination of a carnival sideshow. From the whispers, I gathered the guards were letting men in for quick looks at him, and then lookers came away shaken and frightened. These stories had the same impact as tales of spectres told around midnight campfires. Except this was daylight and the men—even the youngest of them—hardened soldiers. They should not have been so afraid, but they were.

I couldn't get the sight of the man out of my mind, either. It haunted me no less than the battlefield I'd seen two years earlier.

During the afternoon, I went down to the creek and washed. I then went to the officers' tent and had stew and coffee. My arms were weary from surgery but I knew I would be working long into the night.

The General surprised me once again by joining me. "You've seen the soldier from Virginia?"

"Yes, sir."

"What do you make of him?"

I shrugged. "Shock, I suppose."

"But his face—"

"This is a war, General, and a damned bloody one. Not all men are like you. Not all men have iron constitutions."

He took my words as flattery, of course, as a military man would. I hadn't necessarily meant them that way. Military men could also be grossly vain and egotistical and insensitive beyond belief.

"Meaning what, exactly, Doctor?"

"Meaning that the soldier from Virginia may have become so horrified by what he saw that his face—" I shook my head. "You can see too much, too much death, General, and it can make you go insane."

"Are you saying he's insane?"

I shook my head. "I'm trying to find some explanation for his expression, General."

"You say there's no injury?"

"None that I can find."

"Yet he's not conscious."

"That's why I think of shock."

I was about to explain how shock works on the body— and how it could feasibly effect an expression like the one on the Virginia soldier's face—when a lieutenant rushed up to the General and breathlessly said, "You'd best come, sir. The tent where the soldier's quarantined—there's trouble!"

When we reached there, we found half the camp's soldiers surrounding the tent. Three and four deep, they were, and milling around idly. Not the sort of thing you wanted to see your men doing when there was a war going on. There were duties to perform and none of them were getting done.

A young soldier—thirteen or fourteen at most— stepped from the line and hurled his rifle at the General. The young soldier had tears running down his cheeks. "I don't want to fight anymore, General."

The General slammed the butt of the rifle into the soldier's stomach. "Get hold of yourself, young man. You seem to forget we're fighting to save the Confederacy."

We went on down the line of glowering faces, to where two armed guards struggled to keep soldiers from looking into the tent. I was reminded again of a sideshow—some irresistible spectacle everybody wanted to see.

The soldiers knew enough to open an avenue for the General. He strode inside the tent. The priest sat on a stool next to the cot. He had removed the cloth from the Virginia soldier's face and was staring fixedly at it.

The General pushed the priest aside, took up the cloth used as a covering, and started to drop it across the soldier's face—then stopped abruptly. Even General Sullivan, in his rage, was moved by what he saw. He jerked back momentarily, his eyes unable to lift from the soldier's face. He handed the cloth to the priest. "You cover his face now, Father. And you keep it covered. I hereby forbid any man in this camp to look at this soldier's face ever again. Do you understand?"

Then he stormed from the tent.

The priest reluctantly obliged.

Then he angled his head up to me. "It won't be the same anymore, Doctor."

"What won't?"

"The camp. Every man in here has now seen his face." He nodded back to the soldier on the cot. "They'll never be the same again. I promise you."

IN THE EVENING, I ate stew and biscuits, and sipped at a small glass of wine. I was, as usual, in the officers' tent when the priest came and found me.

For a time, he said nothing beyond his greeting. Simply watched me at my meal, and then stared out the open flap at the camp preparing for evening, the fires in the center of the encampment, the weary men bedding down. Many of them, healed now, would be back in the battle within two days or less.

"I spent an hour with him this afternoon," the priest said.

"The quarantined man?"

"Yes." The priest nodded. "Do you know some of the men have visited him five or six times?"

The way the priest spoke, I sensed he was gloating over the fact that the men were disobeying the General's orders. "Why don't the guards stop them?"

"The guards are in visiting him, too."

"The man says nothing. How can it be a visit?"

"He says nothing with his tongue. He says a great deal with his face." He paused, eyed me levelly. "I need to tell you something. You're the only man in this camp who will believe me." He sounded frantic. I almost felt sorry for him.

"Tell me what?"

"The man—he's not what we think."

"No?"

"No; his face—" He shook his head. "It's God's face."

"I see."

The priest smiled. "I know how I must sound."

"You've seen a great deal of suffering, Father. It wears on a person."

"It's God's face. I had a dream last night. The man's face shows us God's displeasure with the war. That's why the men are so moved when they see the man." He sighed, seeing he was not convincing me. "You say yourself he hasn't been wounded."

"That's true."

"And that all his vital signs seem normal."

"True enough, rather."

"Yet he's in some kind of shock."

"That seems to be his problem, yes."

The priest shook his head. "No, his real problem is that he's become overwhelmed by the suffering he's seen in this war—what both sides have done to the other. All the pain. That's why there's so much sorrow on his face—and that's what the men are responding to. The grief on his face is the same grief they feel in their hearts. God's face."

"Once we get him to a real field hospital—"

And it was then we heard the rifle shots.

The periphery of the encampment was heavily protected, we'd never heard firing this close.

The priest and I ran outside.

General Sullivan stood next to a group of young men
with weapons. Several yards ahead, near the edge of the
camp, lay three bodies, shadowy in the light of the campfire.
One of the fallen men moaned. All three men wore our own
gray uniforms.

Sullivan glowered at me. "Deserters."

"But you shot them in the back," I said.

"Perhaps you didn't hear me, Doctor. The men were
deserting. They'd packed their belongings and were heading out."

One of the young men who'd done the shooting said,
"It was the man's face, sir."

Sullivan wheeled on him. "It was what?"

"The quarantined man, sir. His face. These men said it
made them sad, and they had to see families back in Missouri, and that they were just going to leave no matter what."

"Poppycock," Sullivan said. "They left because they were
cowards."

I left to take care of the fallen man who was crying out
for help.

IN THE MIDDLE OF the night, I heard more guns being fired. I
lay on my cot, knowing it wasn't Yankees being fired at. It
was our own deserters.

I dressed and went over to the tent where the quarantined man lay. Two young farm boys in ill-fitting gray uniforms
stood over him. They might have been mourners standing
over a coffin. They said nothing. Just stared at the man.

In the dim lamplight, I knelt down next to him. His
vitals still seemed good, his heartbeat especially. I stood up,
next to the two boys, and looked down on him myself. There

was nothing remarkable about his face. He could have been any of thousands of men serving on either side.

Except for the grief.

This time I felt the tug of it myself, heard in my mind the cries of the dying I'd been unable to save, saw the families and farms and homes destroyed as the war moved across the countryside, heard children crying out for dead parents, and parents sobbing over the bodies of their dead children. It was all there in his face, perfectly reflected, and I thought then of what the priest had said, that this was God's face, God's sorrow and displeasure with us.

The explosion came, then.

While the two soldiers next to me didn't seem to hear it at all, I rushed from the tent to the center of camp.

Several young soldiers stood near the ammunition cache. Someone had set fire to it. Ammunition was exploding everywhere, flares of red and yellow and gas-jet blue against the night. Men everywhere ducked for cover behind wagons and trees and boulders.

Into this scene, seemingly unafraid and looking like the lead actor in a stage production of *King Lear* I'd once seen, strode General Sullivan, still tugging on his heavy uniform jacket.

He went over to two soldiers who stood, seemingly unfazed, before the ammunition cache. Between explosions I could hear him shouting, "Did you set this fire?"

And they nodded.

Sullivan, as much in bafflement as anger, shook his head. He signaled for the guards to come and arrest these men.

As the soldiers were passing by me I heard one of them say to a guard, "After I saw his face, I knew I had to do this. I had to stop the war."

Within an hour, the flames died and the explosions ceased. The night was almost ominously quiet. There were a few hours before dawn, so I tried to sleep some more.

I dreamed of Virginia, green Virginia in the spring, and the creek where I'd fished as a boy, and how the sun

had felt on my back and arms and head. There was no surgical table in my dream, nor were my shoes soaked with
blood.

Around dawn somebody began shaking me. It was Sullivan's personal lieutenant. "The priest has been shot. Come
quickly, Doctor."

I didn't even dress fully, just pulled on my trousers over
the legs of my long underwear.

A dozen soldiers stood outside the tent looking confused and defeated and sad. I went inside.

The priest lay in his tent. His cassock had been torn
away. A bloody hole made a target-like circle on his stomach.

Above his cot stood General Sullivan, a pistol in his hand.

I knelt next to the cot and examined the priest. His vital
signs were faint and growing fainter. He had at most a few
minutes to live.

I looked up at the General. "What happened?"

The General nodded for the lieutenant to leave. The
man saluted and then went out into the gray dawn.

"I had to shoot him," General Sullivan said.

I stood up. "You had to shoot a priest?"

"He was trying to stop me."

"From what?"

Then I noticed for the first time the knife scabbard on
the General's belt. Blood streaked its sides. The hilt of the
knife was sticky with blood. So were the General's hands. I
thought of how Yankee troops had begun disfiguring the
faces of our dead on the battlefield.

He said, "I have a war to fight, Doctor. The men—the
way they were reacting to the man's face—" He paused and
touched the bloody hilt of the knife. "I took care of him.
And the priest came in while I was doing it and went insane.
He started hitting me, trying to stop me and—" He looked
down at the priest. "I didn't have any choice, Doctor. I hope
you believe me."

A few minutes later, the priest died.

I started to leave the tent. General Sullivan put a hand on my shoulder. "I know you don't care very much for me, Doctor, but I hope you understand me at least a little. I can't win a war when men desert and blow up ammunition dumps and start questioning the worthiness of the war itself. I had to do what I did. I hope someday you'll understand."

I went out into the dawn. The air smelled of campfires and coffee. Now the men were busy scurrying around, preparing for war. The way they had been before the man had been brought here in the buckboard.

I went over to the tent where he was kept and asked the guard to let me inside. "The General said nobody's allowed inside, Doctor."

I shoved the boy aside and strode into the tent.

The cloth was still over his face, only now it was soaked with blood. I raised the cloth and looked at him. Even for a doctor, the sight was horrible. The General had ripped out his eyes and sawed off his nose. His checks carried deep gullies where the knife had been dug in deep.

He was dead. The shock of the defacement had killed him.

Sickened, I looked away.

The flap was thrown back then, and there stood General Sullivan. "We're going to bury him now, Doctor."

In minutes, the dead soldier was inside a pine box borne up a hill of long grass waving in a chill wind. The rains came, hard rains, before they'd turned even two shovelfuls of earth.

Then, from a distance over the hill, came the thunder of cannon and the cry of the dying.

The face that reminded us of what we were doing to each other was no more. It had been made ugly, robbed of its sorrowful beauty.

He was buried quickly and without benefit of clergy—the priest himself having been buried an hour earlier—and when the ceremony was finished, we returned to camp and war.

Matthew in the Morning

Gary A. Braunbeck

"We are scattered—stunned—the remnant of heart left alive with us, filled with brotherly hate."
—*Mary Chesnut's Civil War Journals*, May 16, 1865

He was found at three-forty in the morning, hanging from a tree less than a half-mile outside of the camp. He had used a set of horse reins to do the deed. So tight had the reins been pulled by his body's drop from the thick limb, so deep had they sunk into the flesh of his neck, that only the bones beneath the fragile skin had prevented his head from being separated from his body.

His name was Luther Wade, Private, Rifleman, 6th Mississippi.

He was found by the camp doctor, who had been unable to sleep, just as he'd been unable to sleep for the last three days. The doctor walked quietly back to camp and

enlisted the assistance of a private on watch. They took a
wagon and one of the more rested horses and went back to
fetch Private Wade. His body was cut down as gingerly as was
possible under the circumstances, then laid out in the buckboard and taken back to the field hospital, where the doctor
wiped his bleary eyes, shook his head at the pitiful sight, and
said, "Damn war can't last much longer now. This boy might
have been home in a few months." He didn't want to look
on a sight like this. In the last five days he'd amputated
seven legs, three arms, and numerous hands and fingers.
None of them had gone particularly well because the conditions here were unspeakably filthy. His head was still filled
with echoing screams of young men lying on the operating
table, begging him to kill them. His boots were caked with
gore. His hands, though washed, still felt like they were covered in the blood of brave young men taken too soon from
their homes and forced to fight in a war where both sides
were doomed no matter who won.

At least there was still some whiskey left for the coffee.

"What do you suppose made him do it, sir?" asked Tyler,
the young private whose terrible duty it had been to assist
the doctor in retrieving Private Wade's remains and transporting them back to camp. "Ain't we lost enough good men
on the battlefield? What kind of a coward goes out in the
night like he done and—"

The doctor waved his hand, silencing Tyler. "Be
damned careful how you use a word like *coward*, son. Every
man has his breaking point. You got no idea what made him
do this."

Tyler shrugged. "I didn't mean no offense, sir. It just
seems to me that if a man can come away from what we
seen at Cold Harbor, then he's just about seen the worst
there is."

"Has he now?"

"That's just my opinion, sir."

The doctor gestured at the body. "Did you happen to
know him?"

"Luther? Yessir, I did. I mean, we weren't best friends or nothing, but I knew him well enough to play some cards or have a pleasant enough conversation during watch. Ain't nothing he said nor did that would lead me to think he'd ever do a damn fool thing like this, no sir, not a thing at all."

"This late in the war, our beloved Confederacy is full of surprises, right down to its smallest elements," said the doctor, pulling his pipe from his pocket and tamping down what little remained of the sad, bitter tobacco he'd taken from the body of a prisoner who'd died on his table late last night. The Union soldier had known he was going to die from the severity of his wounds, and so had asked the doctor to write a note for his parents. The doctor had obliged the soldier, patiently sitting next to the table while the young man—who could not have been any older than fifteen—dictated a short letter with broken words and incomplete sentences. To show his gratitude for the doctor's help, he offered the pouch of tobacco that was in his pocket. "My father swears this is the damned finest tobacco there is, yessir," he'd said, then died without telling the doctor his last name.

The doctor still had the letter in his pocket. He would carry it with him, he suspected, until the good General Robert E. Lee came to his senses and mustered the courage to admit defeat and sent a messenger to Grant requesting terms of surrender.

The doctor looked at Luther Wade's body. "What's that?"

"Sir?" asked Tyler.

"There's something inside his coat, behind his back—see it there, son?"

"Yessir."

They lifted Wade's body, only half turning him over before the object was revealed.

Wade had pinned an envelope to the back of his uniform. It was addressed, simply, this way:

To Whoever Finds Me.

The doctor removed the envelope from Wade's uniform, then wiped off as much of the blood as was still wet enough to be wiped away. Inside, Luther Wade had wrapped the letter in a small piece of torn blanket, perhaps suspecting that rain—or his own blood—might stain the envelope and seep through to the pages within.

The first page had only a few lines on it, giving the names of his parents and asking that the reader please be kind enough to see that the following pages be posted to his parents' address, which was written in a strong, steady, legible hand.

The doctor leaned back against the buckboard, tucked the letter under his arm, and managed to get his pipe going at last. The tobacco tasted like dried manure, but he was going to smoke all of it.

The Union soldier had offered it like it was the most precious thing he possessed; it didn't seem right to simply toss it away because its flavor wasn't to his liking. Might as well have pissed on the poor kid's body, if that were the case.

The doctor puffed away on his pipe, thinking.

"You gonna read the letter, sir?" asked Tyler.

"Yes, Private, I am. And since you were the one who found him, I guess that means you've got something of a right to read it as well, considering the way he addressed the envelope."

"I don't see as how that'd be proper, sir."

The doctor stared at Tyler. "I am not one who believes that killing yourself is necessarily a coward's way out. It is my belief that a body'd have to be in a lot of pain in order to think a death the likes of *this* was preferable to breathing in the air of one more morning. So I am going to read this letter, and then you will read it, and we will at least be able to speak truthfully about Private Wade's reasons for taking his own life when others start in with their half-assed guessing. He might have killed himself, but Luther Wade was a soldier who fought for our beloved Confederacy, and that alone dictates a certain amount of respectfulness at his death. It requires we do what we can to maintain some of his dignity, for there is no man more dignified on this Earth than one of our Confederate boys in his uniform, be he alive or dead, be that death in battle or by his own hand." He offered the letter to Tyler. "Would you care to be the first to read it, Private?"

Tyler looked down at his feet and coughed. "Afraid I don't read too good, sir."

The doctor nodded. "Then cover him up and come on over to my tent. I'll make some coffee for us, and then I will read this letter aloud. Somehow I think it important that his last thoughts be shared with someone."

"Yessir."

"And Private?"

"Sir?"

"Since no one saw us cut down his body nor bring it into camp, I'll ask you to not speak of this for the time being."

"Yessir. Still seems a damned fool thing to do, hanging yourself."

"We're all hanging ourselves, son, from the moment we're born; just takes the rope fifty or sixty years to snap tight, that's all."

To My Dearest Mother and Father:

By now you have undoubtedly heard about the circumstances of my death, and for that I offer my deepest apologies. It was never my intention to disgrace my uniform or the good name of our family, but circumstances have made it necessary that I do not die a hero's death in battle or return home alive and whole.

I must also assume that the papers back home have by now told the sad tale of the battle at Cold Harbor. Though we are not privy to the papers out here, I can tell you this much: No one who wasn't there could begin to capture in words the horror of the slaughter that we took part in. I harbor no great love for the Union Army nor its soldiers, but I must confess to you here that, toward the end of their last charge, it began to turn my stomach, how easy it was to kill them. That dreadful storm of lead and iron seemed more like a volcanic blast than a battle. It did not matter that the Union Army were armed with their new repeating rifles. Our boys had dug in well, creating massive entrenchments in which we were well protected in the earthworks and suffered little from the federal fire. But still, General Grant insisted on a second charge from his soldiers.

It took almost a full day for them to prepare for their second charge, which came a little after four-thirty in the morning. Thousands of Union soldiers crawled out of their entrenchments and marched toward us. It was like shooting cans off a fence. I cannot speak for what happened farther down the line, but where I was, no Union soldier was able to get closer than twenty feet of our earthworks before being cut down—and often cut in half—by our fire. It was deafening, a boiling cauldron from the incessant pattering of shots which raised the dirt in geysers and spitting sands. The men fell and fell and fell. Blood ran thick as mud all around us. It was over in half an hour. The stunned attackers recoiled and sought the protective cover of their trenches, having left thousands upon thousands of their comrades lying on the field. Their dying screams are in my ears still, even as I write this from the relative safety of the field hospital camp.

Oh, my dear parents, I have seen the carnage in front of Marye's Hill at Fredricksburg, and on the old railroad cut which Jackson's men held at the Second Manassas, but I have seen nothing to exceed this. It was not war; it was murder.

Something took place during the battle which I need to confess, but first I must ask you to think back, if you can, to when my beloved brother Matthew and I were children. I promised you, Mother, that I would watch over Matthew during this damn war, and watch over him I did. He was never far from my side. I want you to know this, to know that I tried to be a good and loyal son and brother, one who did everything in his power to keep his word.

I remember, when we were children, the joy I would experience when I awakened to see Matthew in the morning. It never mattered to me that he was so slow-witted and deliberate of speech; a purer and more gentle soul I have never encountered—nor, I suspect, has anyone. Not this side of the angels.

Do you remember how he would always rise before any of us? How he would quietly dress himself and start the coals in the stove so it would be all warmed up when you rose, Mother? Then he would take that big old tin can of his—his "treasure chest," he called it, remember? And he would go outside and look for treasures to place within.

Lord, how I can remember those days when, trapped inside by the rain and unable to go out and play with the other children, Matthew would entertain us with a show of his treasures. "Here is a button from a king's satin shirt. Here is a feather from an angel's wing. Here is a cup once drunk from by our Lord Jesus." How I loved those moments.

Over the last several months, Matthew had taken to singing a song during the long marches to and from our battles. He sang it so much that many of the men learned the words and have been singing it ever since. It goes: Come raise me in your arms, dear brother, And let me see that glorious sun, For I am weary, faint, and dying, How could that battle lost or won; Do you ever think of mother, In that home far in the land? Watching, praying for her children, If I could see that home again!

The men would often sing that line over and over: "If I could see that home again!"

A fragile dream, with blood soaking through your boots, but at least a dream that was still kept alive.

I am sorry for the rambling nature of this. The trip from the battlefield to this new camp is still fresh in my mind. Allow me to tell you something of this journey, which for me will soon reach its end.

I held onto the tailgate of a wagon filled with the wounded, letting it pull me along because my boots had begun to fill with bloody mud. Rain fell in slanted, steely

pencilings. There was a constant murmur, the groans of
the wounded as the long slow agonized column wound
between weeping trees and wet brown fields. I could hear
their teeth grinding and even the faint scrabbling of their
fingernails against the planks of the springless wagon bed.
It was the same road we had followed into battle, only now
we were going in the opposite direction and there was no
reappearing sun nor crackle of Union gunfire to cause the
troops to hasten their steps.

Our faces were grey, the color of ashes. Some had
powder burns red on their cheeks and foreheads and running back in singed patches in their hair. Mouths were
rimmed with grime from biting cartridges, mostly a long
smear down one corner, and hands were blackened with
burnt powder off the ramrods. We'd aged three lifetimes
when Grant ordered that second, suicidal charge. The captain was calling for us to rally, rally here, rally there, but
there wasn't much rally left in any of us, not after that
damned battle. There wasn't much left in me, anyhow. I
was so empty and cold and tired it was all I could do to
hang onto the back of that wagon and let it pull me to
where the flag marked the field hospital and the encampment beyond it. I was worried, too, about not having my
rifle, but if having it meant that I had to look down at the
bearded man in whose chest I'd buried it deep and pull it
out of him, then it could damn well stay where I'd left it.
Then I happened to look down and Lord if there wasn't
one just like it lying in the mud near my feet. I picked it
up, stooping and nursing my bad arm, and nearly lost my
hold on the wagon. My arm was still seeping from the
bullet I'd taken during the last charge.

Exhausted horses and mules refused to pull; demor-
alized and badly shaken drivers, with straining eyes and
perspiring bodies, plied their whips vigorously to no effect;
difficult places in the road were choked with blazing
wagons set aflame to save their contents from falling into
the hands of the enemy.

Hundreds of men dropped from exhaustion. Even
more threw away their arms. The demoralization at last
began to spread even to the officers, who did nothing to

stop the straggling. Many of them seemed to shut their eyes to the hourly reduction of their command, and rode in advance of their brigades in dogged indifference. It was among the saddest sights I have ever seen. But still there was, if one looked closely enough in certain eyes, something left of the old spirit which had made the army of our beloved Confederacy famous throughout the world, and inscribed its banners with the most dignified and glorious names of the war.

Still I could hear the echo of tired, broken men singing: "If I could see that home again!"

Regiment by regiment the columns lurched forward as the rain grew heavier, rifles sloppily dressed at right shoulder shift and the men—as well as the too many boys—stumbling like drunkards or shuffling along like a simpleton weighed down with the shame of it all. Soon the wheels of the wagons and artillery had churned the road into shin-deep mud. There were halts and countless delays, times when the men had to trot to keep up, and other times, more frequently, when they simply stood in the rain, waiting for the man ahead of them to stumble into motion while the mud and filth grew wetter and thicker and pulled at their cold feet. The muskets grew heavy. Haversack straps began cutting into our shoulders, drawing blood. The road was littered with discarded equipment, empty boots, sabers and Bowie knives, overcoats, Bibles, playing cards. All that day as we moved along the column we came upon regiment after regiment halted by the road, the men leaning on their rifles or sitting on pieces of debris from the battle that had found their way to this spot.

As I looked at all the bitter remnants left behind, I could easily imagine Matthew in the morning, armed with his treasure chest, gathering these items and saying, "Here is a playing card from a magician's deck, here is a page from a Bible once read by a preacher with a voice of gold, here is a strap from the reins of Traveler, the finest horse in this war."

I can feel him in the morning, still. His gentleness, his wonder, his affection, and playfulness. Never has a man had a more loving brother than I had in Matthew. And when I think of the way the other children used to tease and mock him, I no longer feel anger; I feel pity—and not for Matthew, for them. In their haste to make him an object of ridicule, they denied themselves the honor of knowing the purest soul they would ever have met. The laughter he could have given to them, the mysteries of this world he could have unveiled to them. They are all the poorer. As we all are now.

And not only in the morning, but now I find that I can see Matthew in the stars at night.

I find, most especially on a night like this, that the thought gives me comfort and courage. I see and feel the Matthew we all knew, he of the slow wits and deliberate speech and tin can of treasures.

Remember him that way; I think he would have wanted you to.

I once asked him why he made up such stories to accompany every new "treasure" he found. I remember he said to me, "We don't know no different, now, do we? How do we know that this feather did not come from a angel's wing? Or this button from the shirt of a king? It's all down here, Luther, buried low in the ground. Mysteries for us to find and wonder about. Someday, maybe someone will find a button from my shirt buried low in the ground, and maybe they will hold it and clean it until it shines and say, This is a button worn by a brave soldier, and as long as I carry it with me, his spirit will protect me from harm."

I know, Father, how you always despaired that Matthew never learned to properly read or write, even when the two of us signed up he was unable to write his entire name and I had to do most of it for him. But I tell you this, dear Father, I tell you this as the son who was always a good student and quick to learn and of whom you were always so proud: I might have been well-educated as far as book-learning went, but I would gladly give all that knowledge back to have been able to see the world for just one day the way my dear brother Matthew saw it. His was a wisdom born not of books and learning, but of wonder and a joy for the details of life that few of us ever know—or if we do know it, it is only as children, and too soon crushed under the weight of adulthood.

And adulthood come fast to a boy on the battlefields of war.

War changes a boy into a man very quickly; and even more quickly does it change even the man.

I ask now, Mother and Father, that you lay aside this letter for a moment and ready yourselves for what I have next to tell you.

Matthew is dead. He died by my own hand. The bearded man I spoke of earlier, the one in whom I left my rifle buried in his chest—that was Matthew. I killed him during the final moments of the second charge at Cold Harbor. I did this with full intention in my heart of ending his life. And though I beg your forgiveness, I cannot say that I am sorry for having killed him.

The Matthew that we knew and loved, the Matthew of the morning treasures, was dead long before I attacked him in the smoke and blood and under the scream of cannon fire.

I began to notice the change in him a few months ago, after a brief but terrible encounter with a Union regiment that left many of our fellow Confederate boys dead. It was the first time Matthew had killed a man. He began to shake as he looked down upon the body of a boy no older than fifteen, then he began to weep; quietly at first, then with greater violence. I held him close and comforted him, not caring a damn about the looks some of our fellow soldiers gave us. I told him that it was all right, he had to do it, but my words did little to soothe the pain of his soul.

"It was so fast," he cried. "He was standing before me just a moment ago, and now he's dead and I killed him, and he'll never see his family again and his mother, she'll be sad for the rest of her life."

The Matthew you knew and loved began to die that moment.

Over the next days, weeks, and months, I saw Matthew's acceptance of death and violence grow from the frightened acceptance of a child to the cold-hearted disregard of a bitter, battle-weary soldier. The light in his eyes dimmed, then died altogether.

He became one of our regiment's fiercest fighters during battle.

He became something of a monster, and I was powerless to stop it. If I could have, I would have stood in the middle of the blood-soaked ground and beseeched God Almighty to stop this war for just a few hours so that I might be able to bring back the Matthew we knew. But God has recently stopped listening to the prayers of the Confederacy. Maybe He never listened at all.

There was one instance, seven nights ago, when a ghost of the old Matthew showed itself to me, and for a moment I thought perhaps he could be saved.

I found him with an injured rabbit cradled in his arms. He was stroking its head gently and singing a soft song in its ear. I remembered then, how he had found that robin when we were children, the one with the broken wing, and how he had nursed it back to health.

I reminded him of that and he smiled at me. For a moment, he was the brother I had always known and loved.

Then he grabbed the rabbit's ears and twisted its head and snapped its neck. "Everything ends up getting buried down low in the dirt," he said. "Death is terrible, and it is the end of all we try to do, so why not help it along?"

I cannot hope to describe to you the coldness in his voice and the emptiness in his eyes.

I knew then that I had failed him.

I knew then that the Matthew I loved was dead.

I knew then that I had to kill this heartless creature who stood before me.

Mother and Father, you would not have wanted him back, not the way he was, not this thing he had become. I know that you must have great disappointment—even hatred—in your hearts for me at the moment, but you know that I have never lied to you.

Our Matthew was already dead.

It was only a matter of choosing the right moment.

The second charge of Grant's men had begun their broke retreat. Smoke lay heavy on the field. Several of our men then climbed from the earthworks and continued firing on the retreating soldiers.

Matthew was among the first to leave the earthworks.

I found him a few dozen feet away, using the butt of his rifle to break open the skulls of Union boys who, though wounded and lying in their own blood, were still not dead.

Matthew was screaming, words I dare not repeat here. Worst of all was the laughter that lay underneath his cries. He continued to beat and kick and stab and kill any wounded man he could find.

All the while his screams mixed with his laughter and landed hard on my ears.

It was the sound of something nailed down and in torment. It was the sound of war's madness at its height of power.

I readied my weapon and charged at him, burying the blade of my rifle deep into his center, driving it with such force that I saw the blade finally come out his back.

He slid down the barrel of my rifle toward me, the gaping wound in his chest making a horrible wet sound, like a starving man slurping a bowl of soup.

I hefted my rifle and lifted his feet from the ground. For a moment the light of a nearby fire illuminated his face, and I saw his eyes.

In them was gratitude.

He had known all along, somehow, that what he had become was unfit to return to the world of families and shops and hard candy and music in the square and littler boys who gather their treasures in the morning.

"Forgive me," I whispered to him.

He smiled, and sang to me: "I remember you, my brother, Sent to me that fatal dart; Brothers fighting against brothers, Well, 'tis well that thus they part."

I let go of my rifle and embraced him as well as I could as he sank to the ground, pulled down by the bloody mud. I stroked his cheek and kissed his brow and told him that we would always love him.

If he understood me, he said nothing. I can only hope that heaven is merciful and allowed him to know; I can only hope that God is understanding and welcomed Matthew into Heaven with open arms, understanding that war had forever ruined the wonder that was my brother.

That is all.

It is a little before two in the morning as I write this. I cannot live with the sins my soul has acquired during this war. I cannot live knowing that I failed my brother, that I was busy killing other men while a monster crept in and took his place. My only comfort is knowing that Matthew was able to reclaim his old self at the very end.

Take me out to the battlefield, let me hear the shells flying by. Let me hear the sound of the cannons, and the cries of the brave men dying. Let me go to this place where I can feel the pain and the coldness and the loneliness that there must be for men such as myself, those who tried, those who failed, those who stood by and did nothing.

Let me take with me all my shame. Let it be buried low with me. Let my body never be found until its flesh is dust. Let the years scatter the pieces of my memory so that someday, perhaps, another child such as Matthew will come upon a trinket that once was mine, and he will wipe away the dirt until that trinket shines, and he will hold it up into the sunlight of a peaceful day and blink against its brightness, and say to himself, "This is part of a medal from an honorable man's chest. I will put it here, with the feather from an angel's wing and the button from the silken shirt of a king."

Maybe they will feel me in the morning, or see me in the stars at night.

I know Matthew will be there.

Good-bye, Mother and Father. I have always loved and respected you both deeply. I shall miss you. I hope someday you will find it in your hearts to forgive your weaker son for what he has done.

May God bless and protect you through all the lonely places that you walk.

With Love, Your Son,
Luther

THE DOCTOR STARED AT the last page in silence for several moments, then placed it atop the others on his table. He shuffled through the pages until he found the very first one, which bore the name and address of Private Luther Wade's parents. This page he set apart from the rest.

"Dear Lord," whispered Private Tyler.

"Indeed," replied the doctor.

He then poured them another cup of coffee, adding to it a generous portion of the remaining whiskey.

Outside, the sun was breaking through the night's gloom. A bird sang sweetly in the distance.

Soldiers coughed and grumbled as they awakened and began preparations to move out.

"That song Private Wade spoke of," said the doctor. "Do you know it, Tyler?"

"Only that part about wishing to see home again."

The doctor nodded, fired up the last bit of tobacco in his pipe—somehow, it didn't taste as bitter now—and puffed away for a moment.

"I know that song well," he said finally to Tyler. The last verse, in particular, I have always found haunting. It goes, 'Brother, take from me a warning, Keep that secret you have won, For it would kill our aged old mother, If she knew what you have done.'"

He then sat very still, staring at Tyler.

After a few moments of silence, Tyler took a deep breath and met the doctor's gaze. "Oh, Lordy, sir, you don't mean—"

"It's *exactly* what I mean," said the doctor firmly, and he picked up the envelope and the remaining pages of Private Wade's letter and tore them all in half, then half again. He rose from his seat and walked outside his tent and tossed the pieces into the nearest fire, then stood and watched until they were burned to black.

When he re-entered his tent, he found Tyler standing over his table, reading the only remaining page from the letter.

"Why did you do that, sir?"

"Because this goddamned stinking war has already caused enough good, decent parents too much grief, that's why. How do you think his mother and father would be able to go on if they knew the truth? Isn't it bad enough that they'll have to live through seeing their beloved Confederacy fall—and we both know it *will*, Tyler—all the while knowing they've lost both their sons? Are you so weak that your conscience cannot abide keeping this a secret so as to spare two grieving parents a burden of pain that no human being could possibly endure? *I* am not that weak, Tyler. For weeks now all I've seen is the pain and agony and pointlessness of death and violence and I've had my *fill*, do you understand me, Private? I could not take away any of these fine soldiers' pain and suffering, I couldn't take it away from their families, I was impotent in the face of war, useless and ineffectual." He snatched away the page with the Wades' address on it. "Well I can spare these two people a *little* of the pain, and that is *precisely* what I am going to do. But you have to help me, Tyler. Are you willing to do that?"

"It don't seem right, sir, I mean—"

"None of this is right, Tyler. It's up to us, as those who will survive this slaughter, to take the necessary steps to *make* it right. I cannot order you to help me, Tyler, I can only ask, and I do so now: as one battle-weary man to another, will you keep the contents of Luther Wade's letter a secret? Will you help me spare his parents that final measure of grief that might very will kill both of them?"

Tyler swallowed once. Very hard. Then nodded his head. "Yessir. And I am a man of my word."

The doctor placed a hand on Tyler's shoulder. "Thank God for that, Tyler. Thank God."

The doctor sat down at his table and found a fresh envelope and piece of stationery, then copied the Wades' address onto the new envelope.

"Sir?" asked Tyler.

"Yes?"

"Private Wade's body."

"Yes?"

"The way it is, I mean . . . how can you explain something like that?"

The doctor paused for a moment, thinking.

"It happened like this, Tyler: This morning Luther Wade asked me to look at a horse that was harnessed to one of the wagons—one of the damaged wagons. As I was examining the horse, Luther Wade was attempting to fix the undercarriage of the wagon. The horse spooked and bucked, pulling the wagon down from the rocks upon which it rested. Luther Wade's neck was caught under the weight of a wheel, nearly severing his head. That is how I will write it in my report and that is how you will tell it."

"Yessir." Then: "Doctor?"

"Yes, Tyler?"

"I'd like to say it's been an honor to spend this evening in the company of a man as fine as yourself."

The doctor smiled. "I'm just a glorified butcher these days, but I thank you for the sentiment, Private. Tell your commanding officer I wish to speak with him before you leave. I want to make sure he knows that you have been of great service to me."

"Thank you, sir."

"Thank *you*, Tyler. Now go. Look down low in the ground for buried treasure."

Tyler smiled, saluted, then left the tent.

The doctor stared at the blank page before him, then, after closing his eyes and humming a bit of a certain song to himself, set pen to page and wrote:

Dear Mr. and Mrs. Wade:

It is my sad duty to inform you of the deaths of your two sons, Luther and Matthew, at the recent battle of Cold Harbor. Both of your sons were good and decent men and fine soldiers, and both died bravely in defense of our beloved Confederacy . . .

He paused, then, and listened.

And, perhaps, somewhere deep in his soul where a weary man holds tight to the remaining dreams of childhood, he felt near him the presence of a young boy slow of wit, deliberate of speech, and pure of spirit.

"Here is a letter about heroes," he whispered. "Here is a pen once used by Shakespeare. Here is a page from a book stolen from a secret kingdom where magic never dies."

Authors' Biographies

Doug Allyn is an accomplished author whose short fiction regularly graces year's best collections. His work has appeared in *Once Upon a Crime, Cat Crimes Through Time,* and *The Year's 25 Finest Crime and Mystery Stories,* volumes 3 and 4. His stories of Talifer, the wandering minstrel, have appeared in *Ellery Queen's Mystery Magazine* and *Murder Most Scottish.* His story "The Dancing Bear," a Tallifer tale, won the Edgar Award for short fiction for 1994. His other series character is veterinarian Dr. David Westbrook, whose exploits have recently been collected in the anthology *All Creatures Dark and Dangerous.* He lives with his wife in Montrose, Michigan.

Edward D. Hoch makes his living as a writer in a way that very few other people can attest to—he works almost entirely in short fiction. With hundreds of stories, primarily in the mystery and suspense genres, he has created such notable characters as Simon Ark, the two-thousand-year-old detective; Nick Velvet, the professional thief who only steals worthless objects; and the calculating Inspector Leopold, whose appearance in the short story "The Oblong Room" won his creator the Edgar Award for best short story. He lives and writes in Rochester, New York.

Primarily known for making the New England countryside come alive in his novels and short stories, **Brendan DuBois** has written several dozen critically acclaimed short stories, and has had his work appear in several year's best anthologies. One of his latest stories, "The Dark Snow," was nominated for the Edgar Award for best short story of 1996. Recent novels include *Shattered Shell*, the third mystery featuring contemporary magazine writer/sleuth Lewis Cole, and *Resurrection Day*, a techno-thriller extrapolating what might have happened if the Cuban Missile Crisis had turned into a full-fledged war. He lives in Exeter, New Hampshire.

John Lutz is one of the most skilled mystery writers working today. His most recent novels are *The Ex* and *Final Seconds*, coauthored with David August. His settings and descriptions always have the ring of authenticity, whether he's writing about the blues scene in New Orleans or the relationships between men and women. His series characters are also in a class by themselves, whether it be the hapless Alo Nudger or the more traditional detective Fred Carver. A favorite contributor to both *Ellery Queen's Mystery Magazine* and *Alfred Hitchcock's Mystery Magazine*, his work has also appeared in numerous anthologies, most recently *Irreconcilable Differences*.

Avram Davidson (1923–1993), like many of the authors included here, wrote in several genres during his lifetime. Getting his start in speculative fiction in the 1950s, he wrote several classic stories such as "All the Seas with Oysters," and "Dagon." At the urging of the editor for *Ellery Queen's Mystery Magazine*, he turned to writing mysteries, and he won the Ellery Queen Award as well as the Edgar Allan Poe Award. When he began writing novels, he went back to the form in which he had started—science fiction and fantasy. Notable works include *The Phoenix and the Mirror* and *The Island Under the Earth*.

Marc Bilgrey's fiction has previously appeared in *First Contact, Phantoms of the Night*, and *Cat Crimes Through Time*. A native of Bellvue, Washington, he is a full-time writer.

In her twenty-five years as a writer, editor, and publishing consultant, **Janet Berliner** has worked with such authors as Peter S. Beagle, David Copperfield, Michael Crichton, and Joyce Carol Oates. Among her most recent books are the anthology *David Copperfield's Beyond Imagination*, which she created and edited, and *Children of the Dusk*, the final book of *The Madagasacar Manifesto*, a three-book series coauthored with George Guthridge. Janet divides her time between Las Vegas, where she lives and works, and Grenada, West Indies, where her heart is.

Billie Sue Mosiman has published eight suspense novels during her career, garnering an Edgar Award nomination for *Night Cruise* and a Stoker Award nomination for *Widow*. Always active as a short story writer, her work has appeared in various magazines and anthologies, including *Fathers & Daughters, Monsters in Our Midst*, and *Robert Bloch's Psychos*. She has also co-edited several anthologies, including *Death in Dixie* and a Regional Mystery series. She lives in Midway, Texas, with her husband, Lyle, and near her daughters, granddaughters, and parents.

John Helfers is a writer and editor living in Green Bay, Wisconsin. A graduate of the University of Wisconsin–Green Bay, his fiction appears in more than a dozen anthologies, including *Future Net, Once Upon a Crime, First to Fight*, and *Warrior Princesses*, among others. His first anthology project, *Black Cats and Broken Mirrors*, was published in 1998. Recent projects include the mystery anthology *Murder Most Medieval*, as well as a novel in progress.

Carol Rondou is an author and graduate of the University of Wisconsin–River Falls. A member of the Society for Creative Anachronism, she also enjoys fencing and researching Colonial American history. Other fiction by her appears in *Black Cats and Broken Mirrors*. She lives in Menasha, Wisconsin.

In 1999 **Kristine Kathryn Rusch** won three Reader's Choice Awards for three different stories in three different magazines in two different genres: mystery and science fiction. That same year, her short fiction was nominated for the Hugo, Nebula, and Locus Awards. Since she had just returned to writing short fiction after quitting her short-fiction editing job at *The Magazine of Fantasy and Science Fiction*, she was quite encouraged by this welcome back to writing. She never quit writing novels, and has sold more than forty-five of them, some under pseudonyms, in mystery, science fiction, fantasy, horror, and romance. Her most recent mystery novel is *Hitler's Angel*. Her most recent fantasy novel is *The Black Queen*.

Max Allan Collins is the author of the Shamus Award–winning "Nathan Heller" historical detective series, and the author of such bestselling tie-in novels as *Saving Private Ryan*, *Air Force One*, and *In the Line of Fire*. He has also written comic books, trading cards, and film criticism, and he is the writer/director of three independent feature films and one documentary. He lives in Muscatine, Iowa.

Matthew V. Clemens is the coauthor of the bestselling true crime book *Dead Water*, and he contributed a story to the anthology *Private Eyes*. He is the author of numerous magazine and newspaper articles and has collaborated with Max Allan Collins on several previous short stories. He is the publisher of Robin Vincent Books and lives in Davenport, Iowa.

Bradley H. Sinor is the author of the novel *Highlander: The Eye of Dawn*. He has seen his work appear in the *Merovingen Nights* anthologies; *Time of the Vampires*; *Merlin, Lord of the Fantastic*; and other places. He lives in Oklahoma with his wife, Sue, and three strange cats who are plotting to take over the world.

In a full-time writing career that has spanned a couple of decades, **James M. Reasoner** has written in virtually every category of commercial fiction. His novel *Texas Wind* is a true cult classic and his gritty crime stories about contemporary Texas are in the first rank of today's suspense fiction. He has written many books in ongoing western series, including the *Faraday, Stagecoach,* and *Abilene* novel series. Recent books include *The Civil War Battles* series, published by Cumberland House, and *The Last Good War* series, published by Forge.

Kristine Scheid is a native-born New Yorker who moved west when she was two and has yet to return to the Empire State. She has a history degree from the University of Wisconsin, where she was greatly influenced by Michael Shaara's masterpiece *The Killer Angels*. "Valuables" is her first published story.

Ed Gorman is a Midwesterner who was born in Iowa in 1941, grew up in Minneapolis, Minnesota, and Marion, Iowa, and finally settled down in Cedar Rapids, Iowa. While primarily a suspense novelist, he has written half a dozen Western novels and published a collection of Western stories. His novel *Wolf Moon* was a Spur nominee for Best Paperback Original. About his Western novels, *Publisher's Weekly* said, "Gorman writes Westerns for grown-ups," which the author says he took as a high compliment, and was indeed his goal in writing his books. "The Face" won the 1996 Spur Award for best western short fiction.

Gary A. Braunbeck is the acclaimed author of the collection *Things Left Behind* (CD Publications), released in 1998 to unanimously excellent reviews and nominated for both the Bram Stoker Award and the International Horror Guild Award for Best Collection. He has written in the fields of horror, science fiction, mystery, suspense, fantasy, and western fiction, with over 120 sales to his credit. His work has recently appeared in *Cat Crimes Through Time, The Best of Cemetery Dance, Once Upon a Crime,* and *Dark Whispers.* He is coauthor (along with Steve Perry) of *Time Was: Isaac Asimov's I-Bots,* a science fiction adventure novel being praised for its depth of characterization. His fiction, to quote *Publisher's Weekly,* ". . . stirs the mind as it chills the marrow."

Copyrights and Permissions

Murder Most Celtic

Celtic

Tall Tales of Irish Mayhem

CONTENTS

INTRODUCTION

WRITING INTRODUCTIONS IS USUALLY just a matter of research. Whether the theme is the medieval period, the Civil War, or, one of my personal favorites, food, a simple peek in an encyclopedia or a quick surf online is all that is needed to gather the necessary information.

Fate and fortune occasionally come together to produce a remarkable circumstance that is to everyone's advantage. Like this book, for example. As soon as I had returned from a week's stay on the glorious Emerald Isle, I was given the assignment to begin work on this project. At last, after writing dozens of introductions for books on subjects less familiar to me, I finally would be able to use firsthand experience to illustrate the theme of this collection. I would also have the pleasure of revisiting all that it is about Ireland that makes it so attractive to so many visitors.

Start with the landscape. Ireland is a land of amazing contrasts. From the rugged, wind-hewn majesty of the Cliffs of Mohr and the savage storms that blow on the coast to the gentle fog-shrouded hillocks and villages of the Midlands, Ireland is a study in both beauty and hostility. Peaks and mountains of slate thrust out of a starkly beautiful land to create beautiful, sun-dappled valleys. Nestled there are centuries-old towns and hamlets, where the local residents go about their lives in much the same way as did their ancestors before them. From the River Corrib winding its merry way through the city of Galway to the majestic ruins of the ancient cathedral at Cashel Rock rising over the countryside, Ireland is a land rich in tradition and a place where the people embrace their past as well as their present.

The people of Ireland are friendly, generous, and always willing to share themselves and their culture. Being among the Irish for just a few days makes it easy to understand where they get their reputation for cheerfulness and goodwill. Whether hoisting a pint in the local pub of an eighteenth-century manor house or taking up arms against enemy aggressors trying to assert their rule, the Irish are a unique people who live their lives to the fullest, no matter the circumstances.

Which brings us to the other aspect of this collection—murder. At first glance, it is hard to see how any Irishman or Irishwoman would ever bother with something so heinous. But it should also be remembered that the Irish are deeply passionate about their kinsmen, their country, their culture, and their way of life. Slow to anger and, at times, equally slow to forgive, the Irish have always been drawn to more than their fair share of, shall we say, "high-spirited activity," some of it illegal. From the revolutionaries of the Easter Rebellion to Irish mobs of the 1930s to the equally driven Irish-American policemen of the same era, the Emerald Isle's children have had plenty of experience tasting life on both sides of the law.

In this book we've assembled sixteen top mystery writers and asked them to write or contribute crime and mystery stories featuring men and women for whom being Irish is more than just a state of mind; it's a way of life. Whether it's ancient history or the modern day, the Irish prove that any time can be right for crime. Peter Tremayne's Sister Fidelma makes another welcome appearance as she gets to the bottom of a baffling case of theft and murder. Jeremiah Healy's sleuth John Cuddy investigates the disappearance of a book on Irish heritage and, along the way, discovers the close ties that bind Irish families. Brendan DuBois tells of a man whose passion for his heritage is so strong, he'll kill to protect it. From mystery master Clark Howard comes a tale of passion, revenge, and wrong choices set against the backdrop of hardscrabble Dublin. And we have Simon Clark's haunting story of a man who is forced to solve a murder to save his own life and discovers that nowhere do the waters run as deep as they do around Ireland.

The sixteen stories of Irish mystery collected here run the gamut from good men and women to bad—heroes and villains both. So raise a glass of Guinness (or any good Irish whiskey), stoke the fire, and indulge yourself in these stories of *Murder Most Celtic.*

—*John Helfers*

MURDER MOST
CELTIC

SCATTERED THORNS

(A Sister Fidelma Mystery)

Peter Tremayne

T HE BOY IS INNOCENT."
 The chief magistrate of Droim Sorn, Brehon Tuama, seemed adamant.

Sister Fidelma sat back in her chair and gazed thoughtfully at the tall man who was seated on the other side of the hearth. She had received an urgent request from Brehon Tuama to come to the small township of Droim Sorn in her capacity as *dálaigh*, advocate of the law courts. A sixteen-year-old lad named Braon had been accused of murder and theft. Brehon Tuama had suggested that Fidelma should undertake the boy's defence

In accordance with protocol, Fidelma had first made her presence in the township known to the chieftain, Odar, in whose house the boy was being held. Odar seemed to display a mixed reaction to her arrival but had offered her a few formal words of welcome before suggesting that she seek out Brehon Tuama to discuss the details of the case. She had decided, on this brief acquaintance, that Odar was not a man particularly concerned with details. She had noticed that the chieftain had an impressive array of hunting weapons on his walls and two sleek wolfhounds basking in front of his hearth. She deduced that Odar's concerns were more of the hunt than pursuit of justice.

Brehon Tuama had invited her inside his house and offered her refreshment before making his opening remark about the accused's guilt.

"Are you saying that the boy is not to be tried?" asked Fidelma. "If you have already dismissed the case against him, why was I summoned . . .?"

Brehon Tuama quickly shook his head.

"I cannot dismiss the matter yet. Odar is adamant that the boy has to go through due process. In fact . . ." The Brehon hesitated. "The victim's husband is his cousin."

Fidelma sighed softly. She disliked nepotism.

"Perhaps you should explain to me the basic facts as you know them."

Brehon Tuama stretched uneasily in his chair.

"Findach the Smith is reputed to be one of the most able craftsmen in this township. His work is apparently widely admired and has graced abbeys, chieftains' raths, and kings' fortresses. He has been able to refuse such mundane tasks as shoeing horses, making harnesses, ploughs, and weapons, to pursue more artistic work."

"It sounds as though you do not share others' appreciation of his work?" interposed Fidelma, catching the inflection in his tone.

"I don't," agreed the Brehon. "But that is by the way. Findach was commissioned to make a silver cross for the high altar of the Abbey of Cluain. He had completed the commission only a few days ago.

"The cross was extremely valuable. Findach had polished it and taken it to his house ready for collection by one of the religious from the abbey. Yesterday morning, Findach had gone to his workshop, which is a hundred yards beyond his house, to commence work. The silver cross was left in his house. His wife, Muirenn, was there.

"It was that morning that Brother Caisín had been sent by the Abbot of Cluain to collect the cross. I have questioned Brother Caisín who says that he arrived at Findach's house early in the morning. He noticed that the door was open and he went in. Muirenn lay on the floor with blood on her head. He tried to render assistance but found that she was dead, apparently killed by a sharp blow to the head.

"Brother Caisín then said that he heard a noise from a side room and found the boy, Braon, hiding there. There was blood on his clothes.

"It was then that Findach arrived back at his house and found Brother Caisín and Braon standing by the body of his wife. His cry of anguish was heard by a passerby who, ascertaining the situation, came in search of me as Brehon of Droim Sorn."

Fidelma was thoughtful.

"At what point was it discovered the silver cross was missing?" she asked.

Brehon Tuama looked surprised.

"How did you know that it was the silver cross that had been stolen? The object of the theft was not specified when I sent for you."

Fidelma made an impatient gesture with her hand.

"I did not think that you would spend so much time and detail telling me about Findach's commission from Cluain if it had no relevance to this matter."

Brehon Tuama looked crestfallen.

"What did the boy have to say?" Fidelma continued. "I presume the boy's father was sent for before you questioned him?"

Brehon Tuama looked pained.

"Of course. I know the law. As he was under the 'age of choice,' his father is deemed responsible for him in law."

"So the father was summoned and the boy was questioned?" pressed Fidelma impatiently.

"The boy said that he had been asked to go to Findach's house by Muirenn, who often used to employ him to look after a small herd of cattle they kept in the upper pastures behind the house. Braon said he found the door open. He saw the body and went inside in order to help, but Muirenn was already dead."

"And bending by the body accounted for blood on his clothes?"

"Precisely. He said that he was about to go for help when he heard someone approaching. Fearing the return of the killer, he hid in the room where Brother Caisín discovered him."

"And those are all the facts, so far as you know them?"

"Exactly. It is all circumstantial evidence. I would be inclined to dismiss the charge for lack of evidence. However, Odar insists that the boy should be prosecuted. A chieftain's orders are sometimes difficult to disregard," he added apologetically.

"What about the cross?"

Brehon Tuama was baffled for a moment.

"I mean," went on Fidelma, "where was it found? You have not mentioned that fact."

The Brehon shifted his weight.

"It has not been found," he confessed.

Fidelma made her surprise apparent.

"We made a thorough search for the cross and found no sign of it," confirmed Brehon Tuama.

"Surely, that further weakens the case against the boy? When could he have the time to hide the cross before being discovered by Brother Caisín?"

"Odar argues that he must have had an accomplice. He favours the boy's father. He suggests the boy passed the cross to his accomplice just as Brother Caisín arrived."

"A rather weak argument." Fidelma was dismissive. "What I find more interesting is the motivation for your chieftain's apparent determination to pursue the boy and his father. You tell me that it is because the dead woman's husband is his cousin? That does not seem sufficient justification. I would agree with your first conclusion, Tuama. The whole affair is based on circumstantial evidence. By the way, how big was this silver cross?"

"I do not know. We would have to ask Findach. Findach said it was valuable enough. The silver alone being worth . . ."

"I am more interested in its size, not value. Presumably, a high altar cross would be of large size and therefore of great weight?"

"Presumably," agreed the Brehon.

"Also too heavy, surely, for the boy, Braon, to have hidden it by himself?"

Brehon Tuama did not reply.

"You say that Findach's forge was a hundred yards from his house. Isn't it unusual for a smith to have a workshop at such a distance from his house?"

Brehon Tuama shook his head.

"Not in this case. Findach was a careful man. Do you know how often smiths' forges burn down because a spark from the furnace ignites them?"

"I have known of some cases," admitted Fidelma. "So Findach and his wife Muirenn lived in the house. Did they have children?"

"No. There was just the two of them . . ."

There was a sudden noise outside and the door burst open.

A wild-looking, broad-shouldered man stood on the threshold. He was dressed in the manner of a man who worked long hours in the fields. His eyes were stormy.

Brehon Tuama sprang up from his seat in annoyance.

"What is the meaning of this, Brocc?" he demanded.

The man stood breathing heavily a moment.

"You know well enough, Brehon. I heard that the *dálaigh* had arrived. She's been to see Odar and now you. Yet you told me that she was coming to defend my boy. Defend? How can she defend him when she consorts only with his persecutors?"

Fidelma examined the man coolly.

"Come forward! So you are the father of Braon?"

The burly man took a hesitant step toward her.

"My son is innocent! You must clear his name. They are trying to lay the blame on my son and on me because they hate us."

"I am here to listen to the evidence and form my opinion. Why would people hate you and your son?"

"Because I am a *bothach*!"

In the social system of the five kingdoms of Éireann, the *bothach* was one of the lowest classes in society, being a crofter or cowherder. Bethachs had no political or clan rights, but they were capable of acquiring their own plots of land by contract. While there were no restrictions placed on whom they could work for, they were not allowed to leave the clan territory except by special permission. If they worked well, they could eventually expect to acquire full citizen's rights.

"Aye," Brocc was bitter. "It is always the lower orders who are blamed when a crime is committed. Always the bottom end of the social scale who get the blame. That is why Odar is trying to make out that my boy and I were in league to rob Findach."

Fidelma was beginning to understand what Brehon Tuama had been trying to tell her about Odar's insistence that Braon stand trial.

"You and your son have nothing to fear so long as you tell the truth," she said, trying not to let it sound like a platitude. "If I believe your son is innocent then I will defend him." Fidelma paused for a moment. "You realise that under the law it will be your responsibility to pay the compensation and fines if your son is found guilty? Are you more concerned about that or whether your son is innocent?"

Brocc scowled, his features reddening.

"That is unjust. I will pay you seven séds if you simply defend him. That is a token of my faith in my son."

The sum was the value of seven milch cows.

Fidelma's face showed that she was not impressed.

"Brehon Tuama should have informed you that my fees, which are payable directly to my community and not to me, do not vary but stand at two *séds* and only change when they are remitted because of exceptional circumstances such as the poverty of those who seek my assistance."

Brocc stood uncertainly with lips compressed. Fidelma went on:

"Since you are here, Brocc, you may tell me a little about your son, Braon. Did he frequently work for Findach?"

"Not for Findach, that mean . . . !" Brocc caught himself. "No, my boy worked for his wife Muirenn. Muirenn was a kindly soul, a good soul. My boy would never have harmed her."

"How often did he work for Muirenn and in what capacity?"

"My boy and I are cowherds. We hire our labour to those who need an expert hand."

"So you knew Braon was going to work for Muirenn that morning?"

"I did. She had asked him to tend her cows in the pasture above the house."

"And that was a usual task for him?"

"Usual? It was."

"Did anyone else know he was going to Muirenn's house this morning?"

"The boy's mother knew and doubtless Muirenn told that mean husband of hers."

Fidelma was interested.

"Why do you call Findach mean?"

"The man was tightfisted. It was well known. He behaved as if he was as poor as a church mouse."

Fidelma glanced to Brehon Tuama for confirmation. The tall magistrate shrugged.

"It is true that Findach was not renowned for his generosity, Sister. He always claimed he had little money. The truth was he spent a lot on gambling. In fact, only the other day Odar told me that Findach owed him a large sum. Ten *séds*, as I recall. Yet Findach would not even employ an assistant or an apprentice at his forge."

"Yet he did pay for help with his cow herd."

Brocc laughed harshly.

"The herd was his wife's property and she paid my son."

A wife, under law, remained the owner of all the property and wealth that she brought into a marriage. Fidelma appreciated the point.

"So, as far as you knew, your son went off to work as usual. You noticed nothing unusual at all?"

"I did not."

"And during that day, you never went near Findach's house nor his forge?"

"Nowhere near."

"You cán prove it?"

Brocc glowered for a moment.

"I can prove it. I was in Lonán's pastures helping him thresh hay. I was there until someone came with the news of Braon's arrest."

"Very well." Fidelma rose abruptly. "I think I would like to see Findach's house and speak with this renowned smith."

The house of Findach the Smith stood on the edge of the township. It was isolated among a small copse of hazel and oak.

Findach was a stocky, muscular man of indiscernible age. He had a short neck and a build that one associated with a smith. He gazed distastefully at Fidelma.

"If you seek to defend my wife's killer, *dálaigh*, you are not welcome in this house." His voice was a low growl of anger.

Fidelma was not perturbed.

"Inform Findach of the law and my rights as a *dálaigh*, Tuama," she instructed, her eyes not leaving those of the smith's.

"You are obliged by law to answer all the *dálaigh's* questions and allow free access to all . . ."

Findach cut the Brehon short with a scowl and turned abruptly inside the house, leaving them to follow.

Fidelma addressed herself to Brehon Tuama.

"Show me where the body was lying."

Tuama pointed to the floor inside the first room, which was the kitchen.

"And where was the boy found?"

Findach answered this time, turning and pushing open a door sharply.

"The killer was hiding in here," he grunted.

"I understand that you knew that Brother Caisín would be arriving to collect the silver cross you had made for his abbey?"

Findach glanced at Brehon Tuama who stood stony faced. Then he shrugged. His voice was ungracious.

"I expected someone from the abbey to come to collect the piece. It was the agreed day."

"You brought the cross from your forge to the house. Wasn't that unusual?"

"I brought it here for safekeeping. There is no one at my forge at night and so I do not leave valuable items there."

"How valuable was this cross?"

"My commission price was twenty-one *séds*."

"Describe the cross, its weight and size."

"It was of silver mined at Magh Meine. Just over a metre in height and half of that across the arms. It was heavy. The only way I could carry it was by means of a rope slung across my back."

"Brother Caisín was to carry it in the same fashion?"

"I believe he arrived on an ass, realising the weight to be transported."

"And where did you leave the cross?"

"It was standing in that corner of the room."

Fidelma went and looked at the corner that he indicated.

"You believe that the boy, Braon, came into your house, saw this cross, killed your wife, and took it, as heavy as it was, and then—presumably having hidden it—returned to this house? Having done that, hearing the arrival of Brother Caisín, he then hid himself in that room, where he was discovered."

Findach scowled at her smile of skepticism.

"How else do you explain it?"

"I don't have to, as yet. What time did you leave that morning to go to your forge?"

Findach shrugged.

"Just after dawn."

"Did you know that boy was coming to help with your wife's herd?"

"I knew. I never trusted him. His father was a *bothach*, always cadging money from the better off."

"I understand that you were not one of them." Fidelma's riposte caused Findach's face to go red.

"I don't know what you mean," he said defensively.

"I heard that you were regarded as poor."

"Silver and gold costs money. When I get a commission, I have to find the metals and don't get paid until the commission is complete."

"Braon had worked for your wife often before, hadn't he?" Fidelma changed the subject.

"He had."

"And you had no cause to complain about him before? Surely you have left valuable items in your house on other occasions?"

"My wife is murdered. The silver cross is gone. The boy was a *bothach*."

"So you imply that you were always suspicious of him? As you say, he was a *bothach*. Yet you left the silver cross in your house and went to the forge. Isn't that strange?"

Findach flushed in annoyance.

"I did not suspect that he would be tempted . . ."

"Quite so," snapped Fidelma. She turned to Brehon Tuama. "I suppose that you have asked Brother Caisín to remain in Droim Sorn until the case is concluded?"

"Indeed, I have. Much to his annoyance. But I have sent a message to his abbot to explain the circumstances."

"Excellent." Fidelma swung round to Findach. "Now, I would like to see your forge."

Findach was astonished.

"I do not understand what relevance . . . ?"

Fidelma smiled mischievously.

"You do not have to understand, only to respond to my questions. I understand the forge is a hundred yards from here?"

Findach bit his lip and turned silently to lead the way.

The forge lay one hundred yards through the trees in a small clearing.

"The furnace is out," observed Fidelma as they entered.

"Of course. I have not worked here since yesterday morning."

"Obviously," Fidelma agreed easily. Then, surprising both Findach and Brehon Tuama, she thrust her right hand into the grey charcoal of the brazier. After a moment, she withdrew her hand and without any comment went to the *umar* or water trough to wash the dirt off. As she did so, she surveyed the *cartha*, the term used for a forge. It was unusual for a forge to be so isolated from the rest of the township. Smiths and their forges were usually one of the important centres of a district, often well frequented. Findach seemed to read her mind.

"I am a craftsman only in silver and gold these days. I do not make harnesses, shoe horses, nor fix farm implements. I make works of art."

His voice possessed arrogance, a boastfulness.

She did not answer.

The great anvil stood in the centre of the forge, near the blackened wood-charcoal-filled brazier and next to the water trough. A box containing the supply of wood charcoal stood nearby ready for fueling the fire. There was a bellows next to the brazier.

"Do you have examples of your work here?" she asked, peering round.

Findach shook his head.

"I have closed down my forge out of respect to my wife. Once this matter is cleared up . . ."

"But you must have moulds, casts . . . pieces you have made?"

Findach shook his head.

"I was just curious to see the work of a smith who is so renowned for his fine work. However, to the task at hand. I think, Brehon Tuama, I shall see the boy now."

They retraced their steps to Odar's house. The chieftain was out hunting, but his tanist, his heir apparent, led them to the room where the accused boy was held.

Braon was tall for his sixteen years. A thin, pale boy, fair of skin and freckled. There was no sign that he had yet begun to shave. He stood up nervously before Fidelma.

Fidelma entered the room while Brehon Tuama, by agreement, stayed outside as, under law, if she were to defend the boy, it was her privilege to see him alone. She waved him to be seated again on the small wooden bed while she herself sat on a stool before him.

"You know who I am?" she asked.

The boy nodded.

"I want you to tell me your story in your own words."

"I have already told the Brehon."

"The Brehon is to sit in judgment on you. I am a *dálaigh* who will defend you. So tell me."

The young boy seemed nervous.

"What will happen to me?"

"That depends if you are guilty or innocent."

"No one cares if a *bothach* is innocent when there is a crime to be answered for."

"That is not what the law says, Braon. The law is there to protect the innocent whoever they are and to punish the guilty whoever they may be. Do you understand?"

"That is not how Odar sees it," replied the boy.

"Tell me the events of that morning when you went to work for Muirenn," Fidelma said, thinking it best not to pursue the matter of Odar's prejudice.

"I did not kill her. She was always kind to me. She was not like her husband, Findach. He was mean, and I heard her reprimanding him often about that. He claimed that he did not have money but everyone knows that smiths have money."

"Tell me what happened that morning."

"I arrived at the house and went inside . . ."

"One moment. Was there anything out of the usual? Was there anyone about, so far as you saw?"

The boy shook his head thoughtfully.

"Nothing out of the usual. I saw no one, except for Odar's hunting dogs . . . he has two big wolfhounds. I saw them bounding into the woods by Findach's forge. But there was no one about. So I went to the house and found the door ajar. I called out and, receiving no answer, I pushed it open."

"What did you see?"

"From the open door I could see a body on the floor of the kitchen beyond. It was Muirenn. I thought she had fallen, perhaps struck her head. I bent down and felt her pulse, but the moment my hand touched her flesh I could feel a chill on it. I knew that she was dead."

"The flesh felt chilled?"

"It did."

"What then?" she prompted.

"I stood up and . . ."

"A moment. Did you see any sign of the silver cross in the room?"

"It was not there. Something as unusual as that I would have noticed even in such circumstances. In fact, I was looking round when I heard a noise. Someone was approaching. I panicked and hid myself in an adjoining room." He hesitated. "The rest you must know. Brother Caisín came in and discovered me. There was blood on my clothes where I had touched Muirenn. No one listened, and hence I am accused of theft and murder. Sister, I swear to you that I never saw such a cross nor would I have killed Muirenn. She was one of the few people here who did not treat me as if I were beneath contempt!"

Fidelma found it difficult to question the sincerity in the boy's voice.

She joined Brehon Tuama outside.

"Well?" asked the Brehon morosely. "Do you see the difficulty of this case?"

"I have seen the difficulty ever since you explained it to me," she replied shortly. "However, let us now find this Brother Caisín and see what he has to say."

"He has accommodation in the hostel."

They went to the town's *bruighean*, which was situated in the centre of Droim Sorn and provided accommodation and hospitality to whoever sought it there.

Brother Caisín was well built and, in spite of his robes, Fidelma noticed that he was muscular and more of a build associated with a warrior than that of a religieux. It was when she examined his features that she found herself distrusting the man. His eyes were close set in the narrow face, shifty and not focusing on his questioner. The lips were too thin, the nose narrow and hooked. He spoke with a soft, lisping voice that seemed at odds with his build. The line from *Juvenal* came to her mind: *fronti nulla fides*—no reliance can be placed on appearance.

"Brother Caisín?"

Caisín glanced quickly at her and then at Brehon Tuama before dropping his gaze to focus on a point midway between them.

"I suppose you are the *dálaigh* from Cashel?"

"You suppose correctly. I am Fidelma of Cashel."

The man seemed to sigh and shiver slightly.

"I have heard of your reputation, Sister. You have a way of ferreting out information."

Fidelma smiled broadly.

"I am not sure whether you mean that as a compliment, Brother. I will accept it as such."

"I must tell you something before you discover it for yourself and place a wrong interpretation on it." The monk seemed anxious. "Have you heard of Caisín of Inis Geimhleach?"

Fidelma frowned and shook her head.

"I know Inis Geimhleach, the imprisoned island, a small settlement in Loch Allua, a wild and beautiful spot."

At her side, Brehon Tuama suddenly snapped his fingers with a triumphant exclamation.

"Caisín . . . I have heard the story. Caisín was a warrior turned thief! It was ten years ago that he was found guilty of stealing from the church there. He claimed that he had repented and went into the service of the church and disappeared . . ."

Brehon Tuama's voice trailed off. His eyes narrowed on the religieux before him.

"Caisín of Inis Geimhleach? Are you saying that you are that man?" Fidelma articulated the conclusion of his thoughts.

The monk bowed his head and nodded.

Brehon Tuama turned to Fidelma with a glance of satisfaction: "Then, Sister, we . . ."

Fidelma stilled him with a warning glance.

"So, Caisín, why do you confess this now?"

"I have paid penance for my crime and have continued to serve in the abbey of Cluain. You might discover this and leap to the wrong conclusion."

"So why did you not reveal this before when the Brehon questioned you?" she demanded.

Caisín flushed.

"One does not always do the correct thing at the correct time. This last day, I have had a chance to think more carefully. I realised it was foolish not to be completely honest even though it has nothing to do with the current matter."

Fidelma sighed.

"Well, your honesty does you credit in the circumstances. Tell me, in your own words, what happened when you discovered the body of Muirenn, the wife of the smith."

Caisín spread his arms in a sort of helpless gesture.

"There is nothing complicated about it. My abbot told me that some time ago he had commissioned a new silver cross for our high altar from Findach the Smith. I was instructed to come to Droim Sorn to collect it."

"How was payment to be made to Findach?" asked Fidelma.

Caisín looked bewildered.

"The abbot made no reference to payment. He simply asked me to come and collect the cross. As it was for the high altar, I understood it to be heavy, and so I asked permission to take one of the mules from the abbey. I had been to Droim Sorn before and so I knew where to find Findach's forge."

Fidelma glanced quickly at him.

"You went to the forge directly?"

"Oh yes. Where else would I go to collect the cross?"

"Where, indeed? What then?"

"Findach was at the forge, and when I arrived he told me that the cross was at his house and I should precede him there. He would join me once he had doused his furnace."

"Was anyone else at the forge when you arrived?"

"No . . . well, I did see a man riding away."

"I don't suppose you knew who it was?"

Brother Caisín surprised her by an affirmative nod.

"I recognised him later as Odar, the chieftain. He had his hunting dogs with him. I left Findach and went to the house. I arrived at the door. It was slightly ajar. I caught sight of clothing on the floor. I pushed the door open and then I realised the clothing was a body. It was a woman. I was standing there when I heard a noise beyond an interior door. I opened it and found the youth, Braon, hiding there. He had blood on his clothes and instinct made me grasp hold of him.

A moment later, Findach, who followed me from the forge, entered and cried out when he recognised the body of his wife. His cry brought someone else who ran to fetch Brehon Tuama. That is all I know."

Outside Brehon Tuama looked worried.

"Do you think he is being honest? Once a thief . . . ? Isn't it said that opportunity makes the thief, and this man had opportunity."

"Publilius Syrus once wrote that the stolen ox sometimes puts his head out of the stall," smiled Fidelma, mysteriously.

Brehon Tuama looked bewildered. Fidelma went on without enlightening him: "I am going to ride to Cluain to see the abbot. When I return I hope to have resolved this mystery."

Brehon Tuama's eyes lightened.

"Then you think that Caisín is responsible?"

"I did not say that."

Cluain, the meadow, was the site of an abbey and community founded by Colmán Mac Lénine some sixty years before. It was evening when she reached the abbey and demanded to be announced to the abbot immediately. The abbot received her without demur for he knew that Fidelma was also the sister of the young king of Cashel.

"You have come from Droim Sorn, lady?" asked the elderly abbot when they were seated. "I suppose that you wish to speak with me of Brother Caisín?"

"Why do you suppose that?"

"His background and the circumstances make him suspect in the murder and theft there. I have had word of the event from Brehon Tuama. Caisín is a good man in spite of his history. He came to this abbey ten years ago as a penitent thief. Like the penitent thief of the Bible, he was received with rejoicing and forgiveness and never once has he given us cause to question his redemption."

"You trusted him to go to Droim Sorn to bring back a valuable cross of silver."

"It was the new cross for our high altar."

"But you did not trust him with the money to pay for it, I understand."

The old man blinked rapidly.

"There was no payment to be made."

"You mean that Findach undertook to make this cross out of charity for the abbey?" Fidelma was puzzled.

The old abbot laughed, a slightly high-pitched laugh.

"Findach never gave anything out of charity. I should know for I was uncle to his wife Muirenn. He is an impecunious man. He made the cross for us in repayment for his indebtedness to the abbey."

Fidelma raised an eyebrow in query.

"Findach spent money like water. His wife owned the house in which he dwells and kept her own money as the law allows. In fact, all Findach owns is his forge and tools."

Fidelma leant forward quickly.

"You mean that Findach will benefit from his wife's wealth now that she is dead?"

The abbot smiled sadly and shook his head.

"He does not benefit at all. Half of her money is returned to her own family in accordance with the law. She was an *aire-echta* in her own right."

Fidelma was surprised, for it was not often that a smith's wife held an equal honour price to that of her husband.

The abbot continued: "She has bequeathed the residue of her property to this abbey in my name, for she knew how I had helped her husband over the years."

Fidelma hid her disappointment at being first presented and then deprived of another motive for the murder of Muirenn.

"Findach had been asked to make some artifact for Imleach; and rather than admit to the abbot of Imleach that he had no money to purchase the silver needed to make it, he asked me for a loan. When he later confessed he could not repay it, I offered to provide him with enough silver so that he could construct a cross for our high altar. His craftsmanship was to be the repayment."

"I am beginning to understand. I am told that Caisín had been to Droim Sorn before?"

"I sent him myself," agreed the abbot. "Last month I sent him to see Findach to remind him that the time to deliver the cross was approaching. He returned and told me that Findach had assured him that the cross would be ready at the appropriate time."

Fidelma, fretting at the delay, had to spend the night at Cluain, and rode back to Droim Sorn the following morning.

She was met by Brehon Tuama whose face mirrored some degree of excitement.

"It seems that we were both wrong, Sister. The boy, Braon, announced his guilt by attempting to escape."

Fidelma exhaled sharply in her annoyance.

"The stupid boy! What happened?"

"He climbed out of a window and fled into the forest. He was recaptured early this morning. Odar let loose his hunting dogs after him and it was a wonder that the boy was not ripped apart. We caught him just in time. Odar has now demanded the imprisonment of his father as an accomplice."

Fidelma stared at the Brehon.

"And you have agreed to this?"

Brehon Tuama spread his hands in resignation.

"What is there to be done? Whatever doubts I had before are now dispelled by the boy's own admission of guilt . . . his attempt to escape."

"Does it not occur to you that the boy attempted to escape out of fear rather than out of guilt?"

"Fear? What had he to fear if he was innocent?"

"He and his father seemed to fear that, as they are of the class of *bothach*, looked down on and despised by many of the free clansmen of this place, they would not be treated fairly," she snapped. "The law is there so that no one should fear any unjust action. I regret that Odar does not appreciate that fact."

Brehon Tuama sighed.

"Sadly, the law is merely that which is written on paper. It is human beings who interpret and govern the law, and often human beings are frail creatures full of the seven deadly sins that govern their little lives."

"Are you telling me the boy is again imprisoned at Odar's rath and is unhurt?"

"Bruised a little, but unhurt."

"*Deo gratias!* And the father?"

"He has been imprisoned in the barn behind the chief's house."

"Then let us go to the chief's house and have all those involved in this matter summoned. If, after hearing what I have to say, you feel that there is a necessity for a formal trial, so be it. But the boy is not guilty."

Half an hour later they were gathered in Odar's hall. Along with Odar and his tanist were Brehon Tuama, the boy, Braon, and his father, Brocc, with Findach and Brother Caisín.

Fidelma turned to Brocc first. Her voice was brusque.

"Although you are a *bothach*, you have worked hard and gathered enough valuables to soon be able to purchase your place as a full and free clansman here. Is that correct?"

Brocc was bewildered by her question, but gave an affirmative jerk of his head.

"You would be able to pay the honour price for the death of Muirenn, the compensation due for her unlawful killing?"

"If my son were judged guilty, yes."

"Indeed. For everyone knows that your son is under age. The payment of compensation and fines incurred by his action, if found guilty, falls to you."

"I understand that."

"Indeed you do. The law is well known." Fidelma turned to Findach. "Am I right in believing that your wife Muirenn was of the social rank of *aire echta*, and her honour price was ten *séds*—that is the worth of ten milch cows?"

"That is no secret," snapped Findach belligerently.

Fidelma swung round to Odar.

"And isn't that the very sum of money that Findach owed you?"

Odar coloured a little.

"What of it? I can lend money to my own kinsman if I wish to."

"You know that Findach is penniless. If Braon was found guilty, Findach would receive the very sum of money in compensation that he owed to you, perhaps more if the claim of theft to the value of twenty-one *séds* is proved as well. Would that have any influence on your insisting on the boy's prosecution?"

Odar rose to his feet, opening his mouth to protest, but Fidelma silenced him before he could speak.

"Sit down!" Fidelma's voice was sharp. "I speak here as *dálaigh* and will not be interrupted."

There was a tense silence before she continued.

"This is a sad case. There never was a cross of silver that was stolen, was there, Findach?"

The smith turned abruptly white.

"You are known to be a gambler, often in debt to people such as Odar . . . and to your wife's uncle, the abbot of Cluain. You are also lazy. Instead of pursuing the work you have a talent for, you prefer to borrow or steal so that you may gamble. You were in debt to your wife's uncle, and when he gave you silver to fashion a cross as a means of repaying him you doubtless sold that silver.

"Having sold the silver, you had no cross to give to the abbey of Cluain. You have not used your forge in days, perhaps weeks. Your furnace was as cold as the grave. And speaking of coldness . . . when Braon touched the body of Muirenn to see if he could help, he remarked the body was cold. Muirenn could not have been killed that morning after you left. She had been dead many hours."

Findach collapsed suddenly on his chair. He slumped forward, head held in his hands.

"Muirenn . . ." The word was a piteous groan.

"Why did you kill Muirenn?" pressed Fidelma. "Did she try to stop you from faking the theft of the cross?"

Findach raised his eyes. His expression was pathetic.

"I did not mean to kill her, just silence her nagging. Faking the theft was the only way I could avoid the debts . . . I hit her. I sat in the kitchen all night by her body wondering what I should do."

"And the idea came that you could claim that the silver cross, which you had never made, was stolen by the same person who murdered your wife? You knew that Braon was coming that morning and he was a suitable scapegoat." She turned to Brehon Tuama. "*Res ipsa loquitur*," she muttered, using the Latin to indicate that the facts spoke for themselves.

When Findach had been taken away and Braon and his father released, Brehon Tuama accompanied Fidelma as she led her horse to the start of the Cashel road.

"A bad business," muttered the Brehon. "We are all at fault here."

"I think that Odar's chiefship is worthy of challenge," agreed Fidelma. "He is not fit to hold that office."

"Was it luck that made you suspicious of Findach?" queried Tuama, nodding absently.

Sister Fidelma swung up into the saddle of her horse and glanced down at the Brehon with a smile.

"A good judge must never rely on luck in deduction. Findach tried to scatter thorns across the path of our investigation, hoping that the boy or Caisín would pierce their feet on them and be adjudged guilty. He should have remembered the old proverb: He that scatters thorns must not go barefooted."

THE WEARING
OF THE GREEN

Brendan DuBois

I T WAS A COLD, wet morning in late September at Tyler Beach, New Hampshire, and Sean P. Dumont stood by the picture window of his tiny home, looking out over the seawall and to the great gray waters of the Atlantic. He stood still, strong hands behind his back, like he was standing post again, like he had done for decades as a security officer up at the Porter Naval Shipyard. He looked at the waves, at the mist pooling and dripping down the picture window, and sighed, wondering if this is what it looked like, on Galway Bay, over there, thousands of miles away.

He had on worn khaki pants and a thick natural wool sweater, sent over two years ago as a Christmas gift to himself from the great O'Greery Sweater Company of Donnegal. He loved the sweater, imagined each time he wore it that he could smell the scents of the old sod, the peat moss, the smell of the pub, the soft Irish sunshine on the green hills. Tyler Beach was a summer resort, but he loved the fall and winter the most, for that's when he imagined he could be back where his soul called to him, to Ireland.

He shifted from one foot to another, winced as his right knee twinged at him. The place was warm, and he was fortunate that even as small as the place was, it had a tiny gas fireplace in the living room. He usually didn't start a fire this early into fall, but the Atlantic was playing her usual tricks on the seacoast, and the fire felt so warm and nice. He tapped his fingers against each other, listening to the music that was playing on the CD player, just to the right of the fireplace. Tommy Makem and the Clancy Brothers were singing those old rollicking tunes, tunes that would usually make him tap his feet and whistle along as he bustled through another day of retirement.

But not today. Not today.

Traffic was fairly light on this afternoon, but he kept a close eye, a close eye indeed, and sure enough, there it was. A dark blue Ford Crown Victoria with a whip antenna on the trunk slowed down and parked across the street and was followed by a green and white Tyler police cruiser. Sean sighed. *So it begins,* he thought. The driver's door to the Crown Victoria swung open and a woman in a green parka came out and talked to a uniformed male police officer, who had emerged from the cruiser. He was wearing a bright orange raincoat that said TYLER POLICE in black letters on the rear. They conferred for a minute or two, looked right over at his home, and then crossed the road, one delivery truck going by close and spraying them with water as they made it to the sidewalk.

He rubbed his hands together, looked over at the door, and listened for the chime, which came just a few seconds after the two cops had made it to this side of the road. Sean shook his head and went to the door, opened it up.

"Mister Dumont?" the woman asked. She seemed to be in her mid-thirties, had short brown hair and a white scar on her chin. Over her shoulder she had a small black leather bag. "Mister Sean Dumont?"

"That's right," he said. "What can I do for you?"

She held out her hand, displayed a little black leather wallet with a gold shield in the center. "I'm Detective Diane Woods, with the Tyler Police Department. This is Officer Wrenn. We're working on a matter, and I was wondering if we could talk to you for a bit."

She seemed polite enough and the weather was miserable, so Sean backed away and said, "Certainly, come right in. Let me take your coats."

Within another minute, the green parka and the orange raincoat were on a wooden coatrack near the entranceway, and he seated them both on a couch that had a good view through the picture window of the beach, and where the fireplace could warm their feet. He took a simple wooden chair off to the side, after putting on a pot of water for a morning cup of tea.

"One of the few vices I have remaining," he said, crossing his legs, hearing the slight pop as a knee joint made its regular protest. "My morning and afternoon cups of tea. Are you sure I can't get you both anything?"

He noticed that the detective answered for them both, when she said, "No, we're just fine." While the detective had on blue jeans and a black turtleneck sweater, her companion was more formally dressed, with green uniform slacks and blouse, and heavy black boots. Officer Wrenn's blond hair was cut short and he had pale blue eyes, and Sean said, "Officer Wrenn, if I may?"

The officer looked over to the detective and received a slight nod in return. "Yes, what is it?"

"Your last name, it's quite Irish. Do you know where your ancestors came from?"

"Excuse me?" the cop said, and Sean immediately felt sorry for the lad. He smiled at the young man and said, "Your ancestors. Your great-grandparents. Which county in Ireland did they come from? Do you know?"

The cop smiled. "Not a clue."

"A pity," Sean said.

The detective spoke up. "If you don't mind, Mister Dumont. We're looking into something that happened in Tyler last night, and we're looking for your help. If that's all right."

Sean shrugged. "Go right ahead."

She crossed her legs, leaned forward a bit. At her feet was her small black leather bag. "The Black Rose. You're familiar with it, aren't you?"

"Of course," Sean said. "It's an Irish pub, down on M Street. I practically have my own stool down there."

Detective Woods smiled. "That's what we've been told. You go down there a lot, don't you?"

"Sure," he said. "They have imported Irish beers, good Celtic music on the jukebox, and most weekends, live music. There's no rock and roll, no youngsters looking for dates or for some action or whatever else they call it. It's just a good Irish pub, a few thousand miles away from home."

"A nice, friendly tavern, right?"

Sean nodded. "Sure, but it's more than just that. It's also a gathering place."

"A gathering place?"

"Absolutely," Sean said. "Those of us of Irish extraction, and some Irish expatriates working in the area, they like to go to the Black Rose. It either reminds them of home, or reminds them of where their ancestors came from. It's a wonderful place."

She kept her smile. "Truth be told, I have been there a couple of times. For lunch. You're right, it is a nice place."

The teakettle started whistling and Sean said, "If you'll excuse me."

"Go right ahead," the detective said, and Sean got up and went past the couch, into the small kitchen. From the cupboard he took out a white mug that said "Kiss Me I'm Irish" on the side and prepared his tea makings. There was no tea in tea bags in this household, and he let the boiling water pass through the little metal globe that held real Irish tea, bought at a specialty shop up in Porter. He called out from the kitchen, "Are you sure I can't get you anything?"

Again, the woman detective answered for them both. "No, we're fine."

When he was done, he started back into the living room and noticed that the young man was watching him with every step. He felt like sighing out loud. *Oh, what will be done?* he thought. *What will be done?* But he sat back in his chair and listened to Tommy Makem and the Clancy Brothers keep on singing, and he took a sip and enjoyed it, and felt calm.

"Well," Sean said. "I'm sorry for interrupting you. We were talking about the Black Rose."

"Yes, we were," she said. "Excuse me, do you mind if I take some notes here? My memory is awful."

Sean laughed. "If you think it's awful now, Miss, wait until you get to be my age."

She managed a smile in reply, as she pulled a notebook out of her bag. "I'm sure you're right, Mister Dumont. Now, I just want to make sure I've got all the facts clear. Your name is Sean P. Dumont, right?"

"That's right," he said.

"And what does the *P* stand for?"

"Patrick, what else."

"Unh-hunh," she said. "And you're retired?"

"Yes, I am," he said. "Spent some time in the merchant marine, and then got a job working security at the Porter Naval Shipyard."

"And what did you do at the shipyard?"

"Security."

Her smile now seemed forced. "Besides that, Mister Dumont."

He took another sip from his tea. "I'm sorry, Detective Woods. The nice people up at the shipyard, they work for the Department of Defense and work on nuclear-powered and nuclear-armed submarines. When I left their employ, I had to sign a nondisclosure form. The only way I'll say anything more than that is if you get a lawyer in here from the shipyard."

"Really?" the detective said, and Sean noticed that the white scar on her chin was getting more pronounced.

"Really, and I'm sorry I can't be more gentlemanly about that, detective, but that's the way it is."

"All right," she said. "I guess we can move on. So you worked all these years up in Porter. Why did you come to Tyler?"

"This was my parents' place," he said. "Why should I buy anything else? And besides, there was the pub."

The detective looked up from her notebook. "The pub? You would decide where to live because of a pub?"

Sean looked at her youthful and attractive face and felt a flash of envy for the number of years ahead for her. He put his teacup down in his saucer and said, "Miss, look at me, will you? I'm nearing my seventh decade. I've never married. Except for the merchant marine and the shipyard, I've done nothing else with my life. I have no siblings, my parents and uncles and aunts have long passed on. I'll be damned if I'll sit here and watch the soaps and the daytime nonsense on television, and slip away until I'm wearing adult diapers and eating oatmeal three times a day. I like to go out, I like to go to a place that's homey and that welcomes me, and that reminds me of my heritage. So be it. I've had a good life and I have nothing to apologize for. Nothing."

Officer Wrenn's look was blank, and Detective Woods went back to her notebook. "You said something about your heritage. I find that interesting."

"And why's that?"

Another scribble in her notebook. "Because of your last name, Mister Dumont. That's not very Irish, is it?"

Sean said flatly, "No, it's not. It's French-Canadian."

Detective Woods looked about the living room, and Sean knew what she was looking at. The framed prints of Irish castles. The books on Ireland in the bookshelf. The little statuettes and knickknacks of leprechauns and Saint Patrick in the little glass case in the corner of the room. She had a half-smile on her face. "So, why the Irish first name and the French last name?"

Now, he sighed. The old story, once again. "My paternal grandfather's real last name was Lindsay. He was adopted as a boy by a French-Canadian family named Dumont. But he was Irish, through and through. As were my other grandparents, and my parents. Names like Callaghan, Hanratty, Mullen, and O'Neil. We're quite Irish."

"But with a French last name . . ."

He shrugged. "My family history. I can't do much about it."

"And where did your family come from?"

"County Armagh, in the northern part of Ireland. Almost all of my ancestors came from that one place."

"And what's it like?"

"Excuse me?"

She turned over a page in her notebook. "Ireland. What's it like? I'm sure you've been there, haven't you?"

He said nothing. She looked up. "You mean . . . you've never been to Ireland?"

"No," he said, feeling a flush of shame.

"Really?"

"Look," he said, his voice rising. "When I was working, I was working hard, trying to support elderly parents. So that's where a lot of my paycheck went. And then I had to help pay for them in a nursing home. And when they were gone, I was broke, Miss, quite broke. And it didn't take long after that I was retired myself, and every time I saved enough or thought enough about doing it, then something would happen. A new roof for the house. A new furnace. My prescription pill prices going up. No, I've never been to Ireland. Not yet. But I will. You can count on that."

Officer Wrenn was beginning to look like a breathing statue, for he had hardly moved since sitting down on the couch. Sean had a very good idea of what the man was doing here with the detective. He was the muscle, the backup. *How sweet*, he thought, though it sure looked like the woman detective could take care of herself.

"I see," Detective Woods said. "So you've never been to Ireland, but you've been to the Black Rose Pub, am I right?"

"Yes," he said.

"How often?"

"Three or four times a week," he said.

"Really? Wouldn't you get bored after a while?"

"No, not at all. There's always good music, good talk, good things going on. And there's always new faces there. May I ask you something, Detective Woods?"

She shifted in her seat. "Sure. Go ahead."

"You said you're here because of something that happened last night at the beach. Am I right in thinking that whatever happened is connected to the Black Rose Pub?"

Now the male officer seemed even more attentive. Detective Woods slowly nodded. "Yes. You're right. Something happened at the Black Rose Pub last night. You were there, right?"

Sean held his teacup carefully in his hands. "I was."

"And who else was there?"

"The usuals," he said. "I'm sure if you talk to Pat Boyle, the owner, he'll give you a list of the regulars who go there all the time. Just like me. Plus the few tourists and the expats."

"The expats?"

Sean said, "The expatriates. The Irish who are here working in the States. You know, don't you, that's one of the many things Ireland has given to the world—its people."

"Really," Detective Woods said.

"Really," Sean said firmly. "The young have always left the country, to seek their fortunes elsewhere. They've also gone to help the less fortunate, the ones who need help. You read any story or see any television program about a famine or a civil war, the Irish are there. Either they are there as doctors and nurses, or as UN peacekeepers. The Irish are first to volunteer, to help out."

"I see, but—"

Sean interrupted, his voice rising some. "Ever since the 1840s, when the potato famine struck and millions died and millions left to live somewhere else, the Irish have been a wandering, helpful people. That's where the term comes from, you know. The Wild Geese. The young Irish men who traveled the world, seeking their fortune. And they're still doing it, spreading their culture about and contributing to dozens of other countries. There you go, Detective Woods. Even today, there are expats here in the United States. The newest generation of the Wild Geese. Both men and women."

Detective Woods looked quickly to her side, and then said, "All right. Expatriates still go to the Black Rose Pub, am I correct?"

"Yes," he said.

"And what kind of Irish people go to a pub like the one here in Tyler Beach?" she asked.

He sipped from the last of his tea. "Sometimes it's college students. They get visas where they can work here for the summer, at the hotels or restaurants. They make good American money, lots of tips, and if the weather is warm all summer long, they get better weather than they would at home. Other times it's specialists, whether computer or finance. There was a time, Detective Woods, when the only kind of labor that the Irish could export was physical labor. Those times are changing. You have very bright men and women, coming out from Dublin and Belfast and Cork and other places."

"And some of them come to New Hampshire, and some come to Tyler, and even a few make it to the Black Rose Pub."

"Yes," he said, "but I'm sure you already knew that."

Detective Woods again made another glance to the officer at her side. "That's right. We do."

"And something happened last night."

"Yes, something did. At the Black Rose Pub. Were you there last night, Mister Dumont?"

"If I said no, you'd know I was lying, so I won't do that. So yes, Detective Woods, I was there. I arrived at 6:00 P.M., had a meat pie and two glasses of Guinness stout. Mister Boyle, he had a tape delay running of a European football final, Ireland versus France. Soccer, as we call it over here. The place was fairly crowded, and I left by 10:00 P.M."

"Did anybody see you leave?"

"Sure," he said. "Pat Boyle did, right when I left."

"And where did you go when you left the pub?"

"I came right home."

"Did you drive?"

"No, I walked."

Detective Woods looked skeptical. "All the way from the main beach to here? That's quite a walk."

"It surely is, but I enjoy it. Especially after a couple of Guinnesses. It clears my head and gets me ready for sleep."

"I'm sure it does," she said. "Tell me, when you were at the pub, who did you talk to?"

"Talk to? I'm sure I talked to a lot of fellows there."

"Yes, but did you talk to anybody in particular?"

Sean hesitated, then said, "I think you already have an idea of who I talked with, Miss. Am I right?"

"Perhaps," she said. "Let me try it this way. Did you talk to any, as you say, expats from Ireland when you were at the pub last night?"

In his lap the teacup began to shake just a little bit, as if a heavy truck had driven by the house and had caused the foundation to vibrate. But no traffic was going by. Sean looked at the detective and her officer companion, knew what was going on behind those polite looks.

"Yes," Sean said, "yes, I did."

"Do you know who they were? What their names were?"

"There were two of them, two young men. Brian and Neil, I think, that's what their names were. Both were in their mid-twenties."

"Both from Ireland?"

"Yes, Dublin," he said. "They told me that they were over here at a trade show up in Porter, a computer trade show. They work for a software company in Dublin and were in the States for a week."

"Unh-hunh," the detective said. "And what did you three talk about?"

"The usual," he said.

She looked at him, pen held firmly in her hand. "Humor me, Mister Dumont. What's considered the usual?"

"What most Irish men talk about in a pub," he said. "Sports, beer, women, politics. All that and more. But, as an aside, Miss Woods, the Irish are more than just good talkers, you know. Did you know that the Irish saved civilization?"

Officer Wrenn brought a hand up to his face, perhaps to hide a tiny smile. Detective Woods's face looked just a bit irritated, Sean thought. She said, "Really? And how did they do that?"

Sean said, "During the Dark Ages, the monasteries in Ireland kept the old books and records. Irish monks kept reading and writing alive, and Irish monks also traveled to Europe and other places, spreading the gospel. They kept civilization alive while the rest of Europe descended into barbarism. And that's how the Irish saved civilization, Miss Woods."

"Thanks for the lesson," she said quietly. "These two men, Brian and Neil, did you get their last names?"

"Perhaps, but I don't remember," he said.

"And your conversation with them, it was polite, wasn't it?"

Sean felt the teacup begin to rattle again. "Define polite, Miss Woods."

She crossed her legs, kept her notebook in plain view. "I think it's like pornography. I can't define it, but I know it if I see it."

"All right," Sean said.

"And if I had been at the Black Rose Pub last night, I think I would have been able to see conversation that wasn't polite."

"Really."

"Truly," Detective Woods said. "A conversation among an older American and two young Irishmen. A conversation that started out polite enough, and then got louder and louder. With angry words. With curses. And with the American storming out of the pub, his face red with anger. That would be an example to me, at least, of a conversation that wasn't polite. Wouldn't you agree, Mister Dumont?"

"Perhaps," he said, finding it odd that he was now almost enjoying this little give and take with the woman detective. "But we Irish tend to argue hard, especially if we've had a few. It's part of our nature.

We argue hard and respond to any slight, however real or imaginary. I mean, look at some of the bombers over there, still working in Northern Ireland. They're working on slights and grudges and defeats that happened hundreds of years ago. And it's still as new to them as if it had happened yesterday."

"Or perhaps last night," Detective Woods responded, and Sean admired how deftly she had steered the conversation back to her turf. "Perhaps something happened last night with you and those two men that resulted in a grudge on your behalf. A sense of wrong, of something that needed to be righted. Would that be possible?"

"As my mother would say, anything's possible under the sun," Sean said, "and let me tell you, my mother was one for not forgetting a slight. A number of years back, I don't rightly remember when, some banker had given her a hard time over a late deposit. Oh, the language she used, and I don't mean vulgarities. My mother would never let such a word slip through her lips. No, she told the banker— a Mister Wilson—that if he didn't straighten the matter out, that she would tell all of her friends and acquaintances and women at the parish and at the social clubs what he did. She went on and on, almost cursing him and his family for generations to come. It was quite the performance."

"And last night, at the pub," Detective Woods said, "was that a performance? Is that what you're saying? Because the people I've spoken to, who were in that pub last night, said they had never seen you so angry. Correct?"

Now it came back to him and Sean nodded, keeping his lips firm. "Yes, I was angry with them. Quite angry."

"Over your conversation, true?"

"True."

"And what did you talk about, the three of you?"

He waited, the cold cup in his hands. On the CD player, Tommy Makem and the Clancy Brothers were singing again of heartbreak and loneliness. He looked down at the cup for a moment and then looked up at the two members of the Tyler Police Department.

"Are . . . are you sure I can't get you a cup of tea?" he asked, realizing how soft his voice now sounded.

"No," she said. "We're fine."

"But perhaps your friend there—"

"No," she repeated, a bit more strongly. "We're fine, Mister Dumont. Please, could you tell me what the three of you talked about?"

He shook his head, wiped at his cheek, and then said, "It started out just grand, that's all. I struck up a conversation with them about Ireland, about their families, about their jobs. Just friendly stuff, and then we watched the football on the big-screen TV. That's all."

She said, "You mentioned it started out grand. What happened then?"

He sighed. "That's the problem with the Irish. We drink our liquor and then voices get raised, and then the harshness starts. Miss Woods, I—"

"Mister Dumont, please," she said firmly. "I appreciate your knowledge and love of all things Irish, but can we concentrate on what happened last night? You said everything started out grand. Then what happened?"

He rubbed at his cheek again. "One of the two boy-os, I'm not sure if it was Brian or Neil, he started making fun of the pub. That's what he did. He started saying something under his breath to his friend, about the silly Americans. I mean, why did he have to start insulting everything like that? We were just trying to show them a good time, that's all."

Detective Woods scribbled something in her notebook, said nothing. Sean cleared his throat and continued. "At first, I thought they were just joking with me. I mean, I had bought them a round of beers and we had cheered on the Irish football team and that, but they started making fun of the pub and its decorations. The pictures of Ireland and Saint Patrick. The green bunting. The old walking sticks. The statues of Brian Boru and the other old Irish kings. The little model of Blarney Castle."

Sean felt his throat tighten up and bowed his head for a moment, then went on. "They said . . . they said everything was so fake and unreal, not Irish at all. They laughed and said it was typical of us silly Americans. The fake Irish, the Saint Patrick's Day Irish they called us."

"What does that mean, the Saint Patrick's Day Irish?" Detective Woods asked.

Now his throat was quite tight, and he was finding it hard to continue, but the story was now tumbling out of him. "Saint Patrick's Day Irish, that's what they called us. We're just regular Americans, 364 days out of the year. But every March 17, we put on green sweaters or green neckties, drink green beer, and have drunken parades down the middle of our cities. While in Ireland, the real Ireland as they pointed out, Saint Patrick's Day is just a religious holiday, that's all. And to think of dressing up in green and drinking green beer and stumbling drunk down a parade route wouldn't even be considered. Then they laughed some more."

"And what did you say?"

He found that the teacup and saucer in his lap was getting heavier, like it was slowly transmuting into lead, but he didn't dare move it from his lap. He was afraid that it would fall to the floor and shatter.

"I . . . I played along with them at first, thinking it was just a big joke, that they were having fun with me, but no, they were cutting loose. They went on about how fake everything in the pub was, how unreal it was, and that they were tired of being from a place that so many thought was a theme park, like Euro Disney. So I said back to them, if the place was so fake and so silly, why were they there, and they said because it was the only place they knew in the area that would be showing the football match. And that's why they were there. And besides, the place had a rotten selection of beers. Oh, they were going on for a while, they were."

Detective Woods said, "Is that when your voice started to get loud?"

Sean didn't answer the question, decided just to keep going. "Ireland's different now, they said. It was prosperous and working toward a real peace up north, and its economy was so strong that it was nicknamed the 'Celtic Tiger.' And that instead of people leaving the country each year, like the Wild Geese of old, that refugees and immigrants from Bosnia and Croatia and Bulgaria were trying to get in. They laughed and called me a silly old man, that I didn't even know one thing about modern Ireland, and . . . um . . ."

Detective Woods was now gazing straight at him, as was Officer Wrenn. "Go on, Mister Dumont, what else did the two men say to you?"

"They looked at the way I was dressed and the way I talked, and the way I rooted for the Irish football team to win, and they laughed and said I should be rooting for the French team, since I had a froggie last name," Sean said.

"I take it you explained to them what you told me, about your grandfather, didn't you?"

Sean felt himself sit up straighter in the chair. "They didn't believe me! Not for a moment. They thought I was faking it, that I was a typical American mongrel, a mix of everything European, and that I was trying to hook up with the Irish because they had the better beer and better music and prettier girls and . . . I . . . I even showed them my driver's license, showed them that my first and middle names were Irish, and by then, they had turned their backs on me. They called me a silly old froggie, and that was that."

The teacup and saucer were trembling again. "I even asked Pat Boyle, the owner, to help me out, but they wouldn't listen to him either. They just laughed and went back to watching the football match. Then I left."

Detective Woods glanced again at the officer next to her. "I see. That's when you walked home, correct?"

Sean nodded. Detective Woods made another mark in her notebook and said, "Tell me, Mister Dumont, and this is very important."

"All right."

"How long did you stay home when you got here?"

Sean said nothing.

"When you got home, was there anybody who saw you come in? Did anybody see you go to bed for the night? A neighbor? Somebody walking by? Anybody?"

Sean said nothing.

"You see, Mister Dumont, we have a problem here. We truly do. And I think you might know what I'm talking about."

Sean cleared his throat again. "Perhaps you could make it clearer."

"All right, I will," she said, flipping through the pages of her notebook. "This is the problem we have. After you left, about an hour later, the two gentlemen—Brian O'Halloran and Neil Glynn, both from Brass Cannon Software Limited of Dublin—they left the pub. But they didn't return to their hotel room in Porter. In fact, their rental car was found parked near the pub, where it had spent the night. Are you with me so far, Mister Dumont?"

"Yes, Miss, I am."

"Good. Because a number of hours ago, both Mister O'Halloran and Mister Glynn were located, right on the sands of Tyler Beach, across from M Street. They were found by a state park cleaning crew, cleaning up the beach sands. They're both dead, Mister Dumont, both shot in the head."

"I see," Sean said.

"Well, I don't think you see the trouble here, Mister Dumont," she said gently. "Two young men from Ireland, shot dead at Tyler Beach, just a while after you've been seen, arguing with them at the Black Rose Pub. Can you see the problem, Mister Dumont?"

"I surely can," Sean said.

"Right now, you're the person we're talking to, the only person we're talking to. Their rental car was still there, as were their wallets and watches and rings. So robbery wasn't a motive, not at all."

"Yes, I see what you're driving at."

"I'm glad you do. You're the only person who had an argument with these two, the only person who might be considered a suspect. Do you understand that, Mister Dumont?"

"I do," Sean said.

"I mean, prison can be hard for a man of your age, and perhaps if we knew about what was going on, what was happening in your mind—"

"Don't threaten me with prison," he said sharply. "Some of the best and brightest from Ireland have spent time in prison, for their beliefs and their actions. So don't threaten me with prison. It won't work."

"All right, I won't then," she said. "You've told us plenty about your beliefs, Mister Dumont. Don't you think it's time to talk about your actions?"

By now the CD player had stopped, the soothing voices of Tommy Makem and the Clancy Brothers had been stilled. Sean looked around his snug little house and the memories and memorabilia for a homeland he had never been to, and then gingerly moved the teacup and saucer off his lap and placed it on a nearby coffee table.

Sean said, "I came home, just like I said, but I was pacing. I was wound up. I could not sleep. I felt like I could not leave those boys back in the bar thinking that they had bested me. So I walked back, walked back as fast as I could. And as luck would have it, they were both walking out from the bar, heading down to the beach. Maybe they were going to look at the stars. Maybe they were going to drain their bladders. Who knows. All I know is that I followed them, and I started talking to them."

"And what did you say?"

"I said they should be more considerate. That their descendants here and other places around the world still loved the old Ireland, loved the old stories. That they should be gracious to the descendants of their ancestors, descendants who had supported them and sent them money and arms during their wars, descendants who had kept the stories and memories alive of Ireland. Saint Patrick, Saint Brigit, Saint Kevin, Brian Boru, Yeats, all the great names, all the great tales . . . I asked them to be more considerate, that's what I asked them. I said the Irish who lived here looked out for each other and so should the Irish from back home."

Detective Woods said, "And what did they say in return?"

"They told me to piss off, froggie."

"I see. And then what?"

Sean shrugged. "I shot them both."

"Okay," she said. "What kind of weapon did you use, and where did you get it from?"

"My old .38 revolver, from when I was a security officer. I brought it back with me when I went back to the pub. I thought they'd pay me better attention if they saw I had a gun with me, that they would take me seriously."

"I guess they didn't," Detective Woods said.

"No, they didn't," he said.

"Where's the revolver now, Mister Dumont?"

"Upstairs, bedroom closet, in a shoe box in the rear."

Officer Wrenn spoke up for the first time in a long time. "Detective?"

"Yes, please."

Officer Wrenn got up and took the staircase by the kitchen, and when Sean looked back at Detective Woods, she was sitting such that a part of her sweater had ridden up, revealing a holstered pistol. She noted his look and said, "Just so there's no misunderstanding, Mister Dumont, I want you to stay nice and still in your chair. All right?"

"Of course," he said. "You've treated me politely, Miss, and I'm glad to return the favor."

There came a clumping sound as the officer descended the stairs and handed a tan shoe box over to the detective. She lifted the lid, nodded, and looked over. Sean sat there, hands clasped.

"A word of advice, Mister Dumont?"

"Certainly," he said.

"Get yourself a good attorney. There might be a diminished capacity defense for you, though I'm not sure."

"Thank you," he said.

"Now, Mister Dumont, will you please stand up? Officer Wrenn is going to put handcuffs on you. I'm afraid you're under arrest."

Sean felt his throat tighten up, and then stood up and held his arms behind him, hoping to help the officer along, for he had seen such matters before on the television. He thought of the patriots of the Easter 1916 rebellion and the troubles they went through, and he was heartened, just for a moment, at the thought of ending up in prison. So many great Irish had ended up in a prison. Why not him?

And when the handcuffs snapped about his wrists, Sean thought of something else. "Do you suppose," he said, "that I might be getting a judge that's Irish?"

Detective Woods shrugged. "I couldn't say. All the judges I know are American."

THE WORLD IS MINE; OR, DEEDS THAT MAKE HEAVEN WEEP

P. M. Carlson

W E'D ALL SCRUBBED OFF our greasepaint and changed from our rags and finery into street clothes when Jimmy O'Neill asked me, "Bridget, you speak beautifully for a child of ould Ireland. How did you train your voice?"

Jimmy was, as Shakespeare has it, a young man of excellent growth and presence. I replied, "I had the kind offer of a letter of introduction from a relative of the illustrious actress Mrs. Fanny Kemble, who deigned to give me lessons." Well yes, I must admit the letter had been more coerced than kindly offered—but that's another story. Besides, my Aunt Mollie always said a girl was foolish to tell every detail of her life to handsome new acquaintances. I went on,

"One could make the same observation about your voice, Jimmy. Who tutored you?"

Jimmy laughed and shifted to brogue. "I tutored meself, colleen! But didn't a pair o' great Edwins give me hope? Edwin Forrest said—"

"But Jimmy, you're too young to have met Mr. Forrest!"

"'Twas his last tour, and I was little more than a boy. He said—" Here Jimmy's voice suddenly became gruff and bombastic and terribly British—"Harrumph! If that young man manages to forget his brogue, he is going to make a capital actor."

I laughed and quoted, "'May the brogue of ould Ireland niver forsake your tongue—may her music niver lave your voice!'"

He beamed at me—and didn't he have lovely white teeth and manly, chiseled features! "A mustached Adonis," the papers called him. He said, "Bridget, have you too played in *The Colleen Bawn*? It was my first venture onstage!"

"And mine also!"

I soon learned that Jimmy O'Neill and I had much in common. Like Papa, Jimmy's father had immigrated with high hopes for the future but then had drunk up his money in barrooms. So Jimmy and I had both been raised hungry as little birds, subsisting on the few coins earned by the women and children in our families. Both of us had scrambled from one desperate job of work to another. Both of us dreamed that the theatre might allow us to escape poverty, despite being Irish, if we persevered.

And both of us had worked our way up to Mr. Palmer's lovely production of *The Two Orphans* in the fashionable Union Square Theatre. My role was small but Jimmy, a few years older and recently triumphant in San Francisco and Chicago theatres, was one of the two leading gentlemen—not the Chevalier, but the crippled Pierre, even though Jimmy's strong voice and magnetic stage presence made him perhaps overly powerful in the role.

Ever eager to learn, I said, "But Jimmy, please tell me about the other Edwin, for Mr. Booth is the finest Shakespearean actor alive today."

"Indeed he is. And at McVicker's theatre in Chicago, I had the good fortune to be cast as Othello to his Iago, with an ancient scimitar to punctuate my speeches." He swept an imaginary sword through the air. "'Do deeds that make heaven weep!' And Mr. Booth was kind enough to say—"

He trailed off, and I realized that something behind me had distracted his luminous gaze. I turned to see a lovely young lady of nineteen or twenty years, taller than I and expensively gowned. I was not surprised—Jimmy's manly vigor and good looks attracted young ladies and schoolgirls in droves, to say nothing of actresses like Adelaide Nielson, said to be the loveliest Juliet on two continents, and Nettie Walsh, who claimed to be his wife though he denied it, and Louise Hawthorne, who had thrown herself from a Chicago hotel window for Jimmy's sake, though he denied that, too. The thought of adding myself to his list had great appeal, yes indeed; but I prefer prosperous gentlemen.

Tonight's pretty visitor had a sweet face and a rich cascade of curls that glinted bronze and copper in the gaslight. Her eyes, big and brown and as lustrous as Jimmy's, locked on his for an instant, then looked away in fluttery confusion. Jimmy said, "Miss Quinlan? Can it be?"

She took courage and said, "Uncle, may I present Mr. James O'Neill? Mr. O'Neill, my uncle Mr. Brennan, who kindly brought me to see your wonderful play."

"I'm happy to meet you, sir," said Jimmy. He introduced us all and added, "I'm very glad Miss Quinlan enjoyed tonight's performance."

Mr. Brennan smiled. "Ella gave me no peace until I agreed to bring her! She remembered you as a friend of her late father's."

"My mother and I appreciated your note of sympathy, Mr. O'Neill. Though I can hardly believe that he's gone—" A shadow flitted across Ella's childlike face. "Well! I mustn't think of that! And now my mother and I can live here in New York."

"Why, I thought you were going to stay in South Bend and become a nun!" Jimmy teased.

Her hand patted her curls nervously. "For now I want a home in New York, just like my father's. And you are here, too! My friends in South Bend will be so envious!"

Her innocent smile combined with her roguish glances was having a devastating effect on the worldly Jimmy. He said, "Dear Miss Quinlan, the hour is late now, but perhaps you would allow me to call on you and your esteemed mother tomorrow."

"Oh, that would be lovely!" she exclaimed, pulling a card from her sleeve and pressing it into Jimmy's hand. He smiled at her, which threw her into confusion again, and she slipped her hand into her uncle's elbow as they bade us good-bye.

I murmured, "A pretty child. Who is she?"

He was gazing after her, memories in his eyes. "Miss Ella Quinlan is the daughter of my friend Thomas Quinlan, who crossed from Ireland the same time we did. Thomas always welcomed actors to his liquor store in Cleveland, especially fellow Irishmen. He worked hard, invested wisely in property, and became quite prosperous. He sent Ella to Saint Mary's Academy in South Bend for a first-rate education."

I was thinking that Shakespeare had it right when he said, "foolish over-careful fathers Have broke their sleep with thoughts, their brains with care, Their bones with industry." Foolish over-careful Thomas Quinlan's hard work had left behind a lovely daughter with much education and so little knowledge of the world that she treated Jimmy as though he were truly as rich and eligible as the characters he played, instead of that doubly disreputable creature, an Irish immigrant and an actor. But I didn't want to cast aspersions on Jimmy's old friends, so I said, "How pleasant for her!"

Jimmy said seriously, "I admire Thomas for creating such a lovely world for her. I dream of doing the same someday," and I realized that Jimmy had a deep gnawing hunger to be rich and respectable. Well, I knew that hunger, too. And I knew that if Ella Quinlan represented that ideal to him, she'd best beware. In a moment Jimmy came back to himself and smiled at me. "But what's an Irish lad without his dream? Pay me no heed, Bridget! Let's go to supper at O'Riley's, for we Irish must stick together and help each other prosper, right?"

I was happy to go to supper, though thoughtful, because Jimmy's remark about the Irish sticking together had put me in mind of Mora Corrigan.

I'd met Mora a few weeks before, when I was still looking for work. Mora was approaching her middle years, still slender but with a few silvery streaks in the raven-black hair around her honest blue-eyed Irish face. A red burn scar on her right forearm attested to her profession of cook and housekeeper. She had come to the corner of Union Square where actors hoping for work gathered each day. My training with Mrs. Kemble was exactly what she was looking for, she told me, if I was willing to take on a job paying good money. Well, of course I was, as I'd had little to eat for a month.

Still, it was disappointing to learn that I had to hire on as an English chambermaid in the rich Pritchard house where Mora worked. "But Mora, that's just what I'm trying to avoid!" I complained. "Everyone knows that servant girls are soon ruined by the man of the house!"

"And aren't you a silly goose to be worrying about that!" Mora scolded, sounding exactly like my dear departed Aunt Mollie. "Old Mrs. Pritchard is a widow and can't abide her son's wife, so he doesn't visit often, even though the old lady's on her deathbed. And you should see the lovely jewels she has! And generous—she gave Sadie a silver necklace when she married."

Well, that made the position seem more attractive, yes indeed. But I was disheartened to learn that the last chambermaid had been let go when she'd been caught attempting to steal a brooch. "And didn't old Mrs. P raise a ruckus! That girl was Irish, so her son told me this time I must find an English chambermaid." Mora snorted. "As though I'd ever trust those sneaking English vermin! No, we Irish must stick together."

So I agreed. Oh, I know, it's not proper to mislead a rich dying lady, but what's a poor girl to do when hunger gnaws and an honest fellow Irishwoman offers her plenty of good food, wages steadier than a theatrical living, and the possibility of some lovely jewels?

Almost everything at Mrs. Pritchard's was as Mora had described it—a richly furnished house, a mistress who was pleased to have an English chambermaid, a handsome jewel case filled with lovely emerald brooches and ruby necklaces in a drawer close by Mrs. Pritchard's bed. I had changed my red hair to blonde so as to appear more English, and wore a plain black frock and white apron, and ran up and down the steep back stairs dozens of times every day to dust Mrs. P's camphor-scented rooms, or bring her tea, or help her with unmentionable tasks involving the chamberpot, or listen to her stories.

One thing did not fit Mora's description, for Mrs. P was hardly on her deathbed. She was bedridden, but still sharp as could be, with a prominent beaky nose, quick hazel eyes, skimpy white hair, and a hearty appetite. One day, as she took another big bite of Mora's chestnut-stuffed chicken, she mumbled, "You seem a good lass, who has had a little schooling."

"Only a little, mum," I replied, bobbing a curtsey.

"Well, you're much better than those Irish wenches. I hope you will remain with me many years, and then marry an industrious young fellow of English extraction. I'll see to it that you receive a nice emerald brooch for your wedding. Dear Mr. Pritchard would have approved," and she was off again with yet another story about the dear departed.

Kind as Mrs. P meant to be in the future, I saw little likelihood that she would soon fulfill Mora's dream of bestowing gifts on us. I had now eaten well for nearly two weeks and secretly hidden away enough apples and potatoes from Mora's stores to see me through a lean winter if necessary. But I would wait a few days before giving notice, for I wished to repay the kindness Mora had shown me, and besides, I couldn't collect the week's wages until Friday.

On Wednesday, Mora handed me a supper tray as usual, straightened my apron and cap, and sent me up with Mrs. P's meal of roast beef, potatoes, and boiled greens with bacon. Mrs. P thanked me warmly and attacked the food and, simultaneously, a tale about a roast-beef meal she'd had with the dear departed Mr. P. After a few minutes she began to look rather queasy and said, "I have quite lost my appetite, lass. Please take it away!"

I obliged, though she'd left half the beef and potatoes. As I reached the door she called weakly, "And do return soon!"

"Yes, mum." I carried the tray down the two flights to the scullery, then climbed wearily back up again. When I pushed open her chamber door I was greeted by the pungent odor of someone who has been very ill and saw Mrs. P curled up in pain and mumbling incoherently.

"Mrs. Pritchard, mum! What is it?" I cried, running to the bedside. But she only coughed and slipped into a faint.

I looked about the room. I found some smelling salts, but they failed to revive her. I ran to the door and called the housemaid, who tried to help but was no more successful than I. A boot boy, wide-eyed, peered into the room, and I asked him to run for a doctor. To the housemaid I said, "Wait with her a moment, and I'll go fetch some rum. It helped my uncle."

Halfway down the back stairs I put my hand in my apron pocket and realized something was there. I pulled out an empty packet of Paris green, so useful for killing ants and other pests.

Lordie, it gave me a turn! I stared at the dreadful little packet and in a flash saw how I'd been betrayed.

I continued down the stairs to the kitchen, where Mora was laying the table for the servants' supper, and cried, "Oh, Mora, the most dreadful thing has happened!"

"Why, what is it?" There was concern in her honest blue eyes.

I threw myself into her arms. "It's dear Mrs. P! We tried to revive her but I fear—oh, Mora, you can help her, you know more than I! I'll go fetch help." I snatched my cloak from the peg. "Please go up to her. Maybe some rum will help?" I ran out the door and up the steps to the street.

At the corner of the avenue I found a policeman. "Oh, please, sir, poor dear Mrs. Pritchard has been poisoned by her cook!"

"Mrs. Pritchard?" he said, looking down the block.

"Just there, where the doctor is entering," I said. He bustled off after the doctor, and I after him. We all ascended the front stairs to Mrs. P's room. The doctor looked carefully at her poor little body and said, "She has been poisoned."

Mora cried, "Poisoned? That's impossible, sir, begging your pardon! Haven't I prepared wholesome meals for these three months now?" The other servants were nodding agreement and she added, "Unless—the only other to touch the tray was the new chambermaid!"

"The chambermaid? There she is!" cried the housemaid, pointing at me.

The policeman approached, scowling. "Now, me girl, did you poison the old lady's victuals?"

"Of course not!" I exclaimed.

"Perhaps you should look in her pockets!" Mora suggested.

Hang it, isn't that about as low-down as you've ever heard? I reckon when Saint Patrick drove the serpents out of Ireland, he left one behind and it was Mora's great-grandfather!

The officer searched my pockets, but, of course, there was nothing there. I said to him, "Sir, perhaps you should be looking in the cook's pockets instead!"

He did, and to Mora's astonishment he discovered the empty packet of Paris green, together with some necklaces and brooches that the housemaid—and later Mrs. P's son—identified as coming from the jewel case by the bedside. Oh, 'twas sad indeed, having to part with the jewels I'd scooped up before I'd called for the housemaid! But of course I couldn't allow a policeman to find jewels in my apron, so I had nobly sacrificed them to make certain that a poisoner and cruel betrayer of her fellow Irishwoman was discovered with the evidence in her pockets. Sometimes the law needs a little help.

Mora was taken away to the Tombs. Well fed now, but not much richer, I returned to Union Square and soon had the good fortune to be chosen by Mr. Palmer for the role in *The Two Orphans*, where I met Jimmy O'Neill.

Alas, life in the theatrical profession is not predictable, and at the end of the year Jimmy's path diverged from mine. Mr. Palmer decided to send *The Two Orphans* to the Brooklyn Theatre across the river and off we went, all except for Jimmy, who stayed behind to play the lead in Mr. Palmer's next Union Square show. You may have heard of the dreadful fire at the Brooklyn Theatre—but that's another story. I remind you of it here only because one of the actors who died in that horrid conflagration was dear Mr. Murdoch, who had replaced Jimmy as the crippled Pierre.

Everyone was amazed by Jimmy's good luck. And he was lucky again, we all believed, in persuading the rich Miss Ella Quinlan to become his wife the next year, and lucky again in finding a splendid play to make him rich and famous.

And now, as in that play, we must jump a dozen years to our second act, and—You don't know the play? You don't know *The Count of Monte Cristo*? Poor thing, you were born too late! 'Twas a grand play, the most popular in the nation for the thirty years before the Great War, and it was all because of Jimmy O'Neill. Playing the hero, Edmond Dantes, demonstrated his great versatility. In the first act Edmond is a frisky, handsome young seaman with a new bride, about to be promoted to captain. But jealous, corrupt rivals conspire to have him arrested on trumped-up charges at the end of Act I. Next comes that jump of a dozen years. The second act finds a dirty, bearded Edmond Dantes still in prison. A fellow prisoner, on his deathbed, reveals to him where the treasures of Monte Cristo are hidden. Edmond puts his friend's dead body in his own bed, then crawls into the corpse's bag. Guards fling the bag out of the prison into the sea, and soon, in a great storm—oh, it makes my spine tingle just thinking about the moment, Jimmy did it so well!—a ragged, sodden figure pulls himself from the sea, raises his arm to heaven amid the crashing waves and salt spray, and cries in that great melodious voice, "The world is mine!"

Matrons wept, schoolgirls swooned, and all were delighted after intermission when Jimmy—now shaven, combed, and ravishingly handsome as the rich Count of Monte Cristo—revenged himself on one after another of the scalawags who had plotted against him.

So, that chilly January of 1889, a dozen years after meeting Jimmy, I was looking for work in Chicago and feeling low because I would have preferred to stay longer with my dear little six-year-old niece in Saint Louis. But I brightened when I saw a young advance man, red-nosed in the bitter wind, supervising the posting of bills for *Monte Cristo* with James O'Neill, coming soon to the Columbia Theatre. "Oh, good, Jimmy O'Neill is coming!" I exclaimed. "We have been friends ever since we shared the stage in Union Square."

The young man smiled at my red hair and freckles. "If you are as Irish as you look, I'm sure Mr. O'Neill will be happy to see you again when he arrives. He says to me, 'George, if you ever need a favor, find someone whose name begins with O'. We stick together, we O's.'"

I laughed. "It's true, he's proud to be Irish. Are you?"

"I fear I am a mere Tyler. George Tyler, his advance man."

"A pleasure. I am Bridget Mooney. No O', but just as Irish, and an actress. I've acted with Edwin Booth and Tommaso Salvini, as well as Jimmy O'Neill."

"Oh, that's capital! Miss Mooney, I am so eager to learn about theatrical matters. I'm nearly finished here—would you be kind enough to join me at supper, and tell me about Mr. Booth and Mr. Salvini?"

Well, he was a polite and pleasant young fellow, and I happily agreed to sup with him at his hotel. "I would take you to Rector's Restaurant if I could," George explained, "but part of my duties as advance man are to settle Mrs. O'Neill and the baby into a comfortable hotel while Mr. O'Neill plays those dreaded one-night stands.

This week he's in Columbus and Dayton, Lima and Fort Wayne—not suitable for an infant. So I must stay nearby in the hotel to run errands until he arrives."

"Oh, is there another baby? I was abroad for a while and hadn't heard. A friend told me that Mrs. O'Neill was so heartbroken when the second baby died of the measles that she could hardly move."

"Yes, poor lady. She is so frail. The older boy was a solace to her, but they've just left him at his school in South Bend. Mr. O'Neill says we mustn't let her dwell on her child's death. His hope is that the new baby will draw her mind away from morbid thoughts. But now, tell me of Mr. Booth!" So young George Tyler and I had a pleasant supper and quite a lengthy discussion, so engrossing that I was still with him at 4:00 A.M. Oh, I know, but what do you expect a poor girl to do when the wind is bitter and she hasn't yet found work? Sleep in the snow?

Suddenly, there was an urgent knock on the door of his room. He cracked it open, and I had a glimpse of a plump arm and a heap of silvery hair. George said, "Mrs. O'Hara! What is it?"

"Oh, Mr. Tyler, sir, it's the baby! He's colicky, and Mrs. O'Neill is beside herself! Please, come help!"

"Yes, of course, just a moment." George closed the door and reached for some clothes. "Bridget, come with me, please do! You say you have a little niece, so I'm sure you know more about babies than I do! Oh, this is dreadful, if the little fellow is ill—poor Mrs. O'Neill!"

I refastened my bustle, pulled my hair into a hasty swirl atop my head, and followed George down the rose-carpeted hall. The heartfelt yowls of the infant were evident from some distance, despite the thick walls. Mrs. O'Hara opened the door to us, glanced at me in surprise, then ducked her head deferentially.

Ella Quinlan O'Neill was still beautiful, and wore a rich blue breakfast jacket, but her eyes were huge and shadowed with grief. She clutched the screaming child to her breast and cried, "Oh, George, George, my baby is dying! And I didn't leave him this time, I didn't, I'm right here!"

"Of course you are, Mrs. O'Neill," said George uncomfortably. "Here is Miss Mooney to help. She is good with infants."

"Oh, Miss Mooney, I haven't arranged my hair, I must look dreadful—" Ella O'Neill's hand fluttered to her beautiful coppery-bronze tresses. "But please, can you help my baby? He's inconsolable! George, please, you must go for the doctor!"

"Yes, of course!" George ran hotfoot out of the room, relieved to have a task that did not require remaining with the squalling infant. The little fellow was perhaps three months old and had certainly worked himself into a pet, gasping and hiccupping between bellows, his little face purple with fury. I said as reassuringly as I could, "He's probably just got colic."

Ella O'Neill said doubtfully, "That's what Mrs. O'Hara thinks too, isn't it?"

"Yes, mum." Mrs. O'Hara was in the corner, arranging blankets in the little crib.

Ella continued, "But my first boy, Jamie, was never like this, and neither was—but no, I mustn't think about—oh, my baby is dying, I just know it!"

I said, "Mrs. O'Neill, please, calm yourself. If you are upset the baby will be, too."

"Oh, I know I mustn't—but my nerves—When I married James, you know, he said we would have a home in New York. A lovely home like my father's. How can I be a good mother without a home?"

What a silly creature she'd been, to believe an actor's promise to stay in one place! I said, "With *Monte Cristo*, your husband has achieved every actor's dream of large profits and a vast adoring public. But success requires travel."

"Yes, Miss Mooney, that is what James says, too. And we both find it painful to be apart for long. But hotels are not homes!"

She was certainly right about that. I said, "I leave my dear little niece with a reliable woman in Saint Louis while I travel."

Ella's eyes brimmed. "Once I left my babies behind in the care of my mother. And they caught measles and the little one—but no, I mustn't think of that!"

Hang it, my heart quite went out to her. If anything happened to my precious niece while I was away earning money for her, I might never recover. Ella continued miserably, "Miss Mooney, do you think God is punishing me? You see, I was going to be a nun—but then I fell in love with James O'Neill—oh, it's my fault! My nerves—Mrs. O'Hara, are you quite certain there is no more nerve tonic?"

Mrs. O'Hara's blue eyes glanced up from where she was working in the corner. "Sorry, mum, there's none."

Ella cried, "If only I had a home, I could—but he's dying!"

Well, I was made a bit uneasy by the baby's purple color and by plump Mrs. O'Hara lurking in the corner, but I thought it best to calm the mother. I said, "Mrs. O'Neill, the boy is obviously healthy. He's strong, and his lungs are certainly powerful. He's nursing still, isn't he? He gets no other food?"

"None at all! Sometimes Mrs. O'Hara gives him a sweet to quiet him, that's all."

A dreadful suspicion was forming in my mind. "Perhaps I can help Mrs. O'Hara find a more suitable sweet. Yes! Here come Mr. Tyler and the doctor now."

The doctor, unshaven and as hastily garbed as young George, entered. Ella wailed, "Oh, doctor, my baby is dying!"

He took one look at the angry, gasping infant and said, "Colic, madam. He's not dying. You must calm yourself, for your distress is disturbing him."

"Oh, I know, it's my fault! Please, doctor, may I have something for my nerves?"

The doctor obligingly pulled something from his bag and Ella held out her arm to him. I took advantage of the diversion to seize the nanny's plump elbow and march her from the room, saying, "Mrs. O'Hara and I will return in a few moments." She came along willingly enough, though when I reached the gaslight and pushed up her right sleeve she jerked her arm back. But I had already seen the red burn scar on her arm. Mora Corrigan, silver-haired now and grown plump as butter on Jimmy O'Neill's generosity. "I thought you'd been hung, Mora!" I exclaimed. "How did you escape the Tombs?"

"In a laundry bag."

Well, Jimmy O'Neill's wonderful play gave ideas to all the wrong people. I said, "And just what are you doing here?'"

"Working hard! I've reformed, Bridget, and Mr. O'Neill likes to hire the Irish."

"You deny that you've been feeding Paris green or worse to that poor little baby?"

"I've done no such thing! I swear it, Bridget! I would never hurt Mr. O'Neill's child, and him as Irish as I am!"

Well, I thought Mora was low before, poisoning an old lady, but only the rottenest skunk would do in a little baby, don't you agree? I said, "I shall tell them immediately about the nanny they have hired!"

I saw the long glint of the kitchen knife in her hand before she could raise it, so I skedaddled down the hall to the stairs. Mora ran after. My skin shivered at the thought of that knife, and I galloped down the stairs and out the door into the bitter wind. There was nary a policeman to be seen, and she was only a few steps behind. I raced down the street and turned a corner. At a construction site I paused to pick up a brick, but before I could throw it, Mora and the knife were almost upon me. I felt the fabric of my skirt rip as the blade sliced through it, so I ran again.

The icy wind blew, and no one was about to help, and I could hear her panting close behind me.

In moments we had reached the inky Chicago River. In the faint light from a streetlamp a block away, I could see a few boats rocking on the frigid ripples.

I hoisted my skirts, leaped sideways, and kicked out my foot to trip Mora as she came plunging past me. As she fell, she dropped the knife and it skittered across the cobblestones. She began to get up, so I lifted the brick high and cracked it down twice on her silvery head.

I know, I know, the Irish should stick together, and perhaps Mora should have had her day in court. But we'd tried that already, when all she'd poisoned was an old lady, and the law had failed us. And did you really believe her when she said she had reformed? I thought Jimmy's poor wee miserable son would have a happier, longer life in a world without Mora.

I rolled her into the river and returned shivering to the warmth of the hotel.

A few days later Jimmy O'Neill came to town and had his usual grand success playing *Monte Cristo* and making heaps of money. He was annoyed that the Irish nanny he'd been so pleased to find had suddenly left without a trace. "But Bridget, what a joy to see you! I'd hire you for my company, but I've signed these pesky contracts," he said ruefully. I took work instead in a spectacle called *A Dark Secret*, which featured scenes on the River Thames, with real water in the river, real dories and racing shells in the water, and a real dog circus on the shore. But the river stirred up unpleasant memories for me, so I gave notice, deciding to try my hand in New York again. My last night in Chicago I accepted Jimmy's invitation to sit backstage with Ella while he enacted the Count.

The O'Neill baby was still colicky and nervous, though his color was better. In the greenroom Ella, as lovely and expensively dressed as when I first saw her, held him out to me and said, "Please hold little Eugene for a moment. It's my nerves. I know I must be calm, and not think of sad things. I love James dearly—but it's so difficult to be calm in theatres and trains and hotels. And I can't keep good servants; they know it's not a real home. Like Mrs. O'Hara—" Her back to me, she was rustling through a valise. From the stage we heard the roar of the fake storm, the rumbling of the metal thunder sheets. Ella turned back to me with a happy smile.

I looked at that smile, and then at the fussy baby I was handing back to his mother, and remembered how eagerly she'd held out her arm to the doctor. I stepped around her to peek into the valise. Inside were several little ampoules and a hypodermic.

The baby whimpered, and from the stage, the storm raged on.

Hang it, I owed an apology to Mora Corrigan, who poisoned old ladies but perhaps not babies as well. If I'd known I would have cracked her head only once. I said gently, "Mrs. O'Neill, I have heard that it is best not to take morphine when you are nursing a baby, for it sometimes makes them colicky and irritable."

She smiled at me sunnily. "Oh, he's not colicky! He's a fine healthy baby, and we couldn't be happier!"

From the stage Jimmy's voice cried, "The world is mine!"

Yes, indeed.

A roar of applause filled the house. They were still cheering a moment later when an unkempt bearded prisoner's head smelling of spirit gum poked into the room. "And how's our little one, dear?" asked Jimmy's lovely voice.

Ella gave him a melting smile. "Doing well. Miss Mooney is so helpful!"

Jimmy said to me, "Thank you! And isn't Ella a beautiful mother? Fairer than the dawn!" Even through the scruffy beard his smile dazzled and his eyes were luminous and happy, and I decided I didn't want to be the one who told him. He added, "I'm sorry we can't spend much time with you after the show, because we must pack to go on to Michigan."

"I too am traveling, to New York on the first train."

Jimmy O'Neill kissed my hand, and Ella O'Neill smiled vaguely, and baby Eugene O'Neill clasped my finger in his angry little fist, and we said our good-byes, for ahead of us all lay a long day's journey.

BLACK IRISH

Doug Allyn

BITTER MORNING. NOVEMBER. WIND off the Detroit River chasing scraps of newsprint and Big Mac boxes down the alleys. Chasing Irish Mick Shannon down the Cass Corridor on his morning run.

Mick was used to the cold, liked it, in fact. Icy wind in his teeth, overcast skies painting Motown a monotone, grimy gray. On sunny days, training was a downer. Who the hell wanted to run five miles, work weights, then spar or pound the bags when you could be catching some rays on Belle Isle or a Detroit Tigers home game?

But on grim, gray days? Might as well be boxing or working out. Or running. And thinking.

Couldn't get the woman out of his mind. Theresa Garcia. Schoolteacher. Spotted her the day she moved into the Alamo Apartments with her nine-year-old daughter. Took Mick weeks to meet her accidentally on purpose so he could introduce himself. Irish Mickey Shannon. The fighter.

She wasn't impressed. Only curious.

"Isn't calling yourself Irish Mickey Shannon . . . redundant?" she asked. "I mean, isn't someone named Mick Shannon automatically Irish?" That was Theresa. Direct as a right cross.

"In Dublin, any Mick Shannon would probably be Irish," he conceded. "In Detroit, *Irish* is a code word for *white*."

"I don't understand."

"Most Motown boxers are black or Hispanic. They put Irish in front of my name on fight cards to show I'm white. Saves the promoters the price of printing my picture, that's all."

"But not all Irishmen are white," she countered. "Aren't some of them called Black Irish?"

And like a moron, he started to explain the whole deal of shipwrecked sailors from the Spanish Armada swimming ashore in Ireland. To a history teacher, for chrissake. She listened politely, never cracked a smile. He hadn't realized she was joking until much later.

They'd had a half-dozen dates over the past month, but he still couldn't be sure she was joking unless she smiled. He didn't mind. Her smile was worth it—damn! A wind gust rocketed out of an alley, nearly blew him into the street.

Definitely a Michigan November. Up north, in Tawas, Alpena, Onaway, hunting season would open in a few days. In Motown it never closed. Open season on chumps, year 'round.

He'd spotted the car a few blocks earlier. Big car, black four-door sedan. Noticed when it whipped around, making a quick U-turn. Coming for him? Didn't wait to find out. Ducking into the alley, Mick broke into a flat-out sprint, pounding down the narrow drive. If he could make it to the loading area in the middle of the block he could lose anything on wheels.

Halfway down the alley he glanced over his shoulder. Nothing. No car, nobody following. False alarm. Probably getting paranoid— suddenly the car screeched across the alley ahead of him, blocking it off. Mick whirled—too late! A black guy was strolling casually toward him from the alley mouth, an automatic in his hand. Not aimed at anything, just showing it. No point in running now. Nowhere to go.

Ahead of him, the driver stepped out of the car, tall guy, Latin, maybe. Also with a gun. And showing a badge in his free hand. Cops? Sweet Jesus. Now what?

Raising his hands to show he was unarmed, Mick continued down the alley toward the car. The driver was well dressed, dark suit, tailored from the look of it. Loden London Fog raincoat.

"Mick Shannon?"

"Yeah."

"Face the wall and assume the position. Now."

Mick did as he was told, leaning against the wall, ankles spread, while the black cop patted him down. He was bigger, solid as a linebacker, wearing a navy peacoat and black watch cap.

"He's clean," he said, stepping back.

"Turn around, Shannon. I'm Lieutenant Menendez. This is Detective Bennett. Do you know why we stopped you?"

"Speeding?" Mick asked.

"We could have. Why did you take off?"

"Thought you might be somebody else."

"Like who? Is somebody looking for you, Shannon?"

"Anybody who bet on my last fight. Besides, this is a rough part of town."

"The whole town's rough. What are you doing out here?"

"Running. I run to the gym every other day. Why?"

"Where were you last night?" the black cop put in. "From dark until now."

"Ummm . . . had dinner with a friend from about seven to eight-thirty, Papa Doc's in Greektown."

"You eat at Doc's?" Bennett asked, surprised. "You're a little light for the color scheme in there, ain'tcha?"

"The owner was a pretty good light-heavy once. Lets fighters run a tab."

"He's an ex-con, too. Did you know that?"

"Nope. He's just Papa Doc to me. After dinner I went for a walk with my date, just talking, you know. Got home about . . . nine-thirty, I guess. Hit the rack, watched the news on Channel 50, zonked about halfway through. Up at seven, did isometrics, two hundred marine push-ups, three hundred crunches, stretched out some, suited up, headed out, and here we are. And now it's your turn. What's this about?"

"Can anybody besides your girlfriend confirm your story?" Menendez asked.

"It's not a story, it's what happened. And the *lady* can only vouch for the dinner-and-walk part. I spent the night alone."

"Tough luck for you on both counts. You know a guy named Brooks? Tony Brooks? Runs a karate dojo on Dequinder?"

Damn. "I've met him," Mick said warily.

"Met him?" Bennett snorted. "We hear you two mixed it up."

"It wasn't like that."

"No? Then what was it like?"

"A . . . misunderstanding, that's all. A guy I know asked me to talk to Brooks, straighten him out. Said Brooks was bothering his sister."

The two detectives exchanged a glance. "You'll have to do better than that," Menendez said. "Brooks was gay."

"I know but—what do you mean *was?*"

"He's dead," Bennett said. "Somebody whacked him last night."

"I'm sorry to hear that, he seemed like a nice guy. But I sure didn't do it, and I don't know anything about it."

"Maybe you do," Menendez said. "Tell us more about how you straightened him out."

"I didn't. I went to his studio, dojo, whatever you call it, but before I laid a hand on him he pulled some karate move, kicked my feet out from under me. So there I sat feelin' dumber than a coal bucket while Brooks explained the situation. The girl was one of his personal training clients. She hit on him, he turned her down, she went crying to her brother. End of story."

"She didn't know Brooks was gay?"

"Nah. I've known this girl a long time. She's . . . nice, but she ain't the brightest crayon in the box, you know? She's kinda plain, takes care of her mom and her grandfather, doesn't get out much. I doubt she had a clue about Brooks."

"So what happened after your conversation with Brooks? What did you tell the girl's brother?"

"The truth. That I talked to Brooks and he'd never bother Ma— the girl—again. And that was the end of it."

"Really? And if we talk to this brother he'll confirm all this?"

Mick hesitated. "Maybe. Maybe not."

"Why not?"

Mick took a deep breath. "This guy . . . doesn't talk to cops much. It's a religious thing, I think. He's Sicilian. His family made a lot of money in Prohibition. Get the picture?"

"He's mobbed up?"

"I wouldn't know. It's not the kind of thing you ask a guy like him, you know?"

"Who is he?"

"What's the difference? He won't talk to you."

"And that's supposed to explain why we can't check out your story?" Menendez said, shaking his head. "Jesus, Irish, who do you think you're playin' with? I gotta tell you, you're real high on our hit list for this. You tangled with Brooks, he told people about it, you were seen in the neighborhood. And any brain-dead doper could come up with a better alibi than yours. I thought Irishmen were supposed to be mighty storytellers."

"We are. And there's your proof."

"What proof?"

"The Irish are a race of poets, Lieutenant. If I was lyin' to ya, I'd make a better job of it. Maybe work in a leprechaun and a pot o' gold. The truth isn't as interesting, but it's all I've got. So. You gonna bust me for this?"

Menendez eyed him for a moment, thinking. Then he shook his head slowly. "No. Not today. Maybe later. You sure you won't give me the brother's name?"

"Not today. Maybe later."

"Later may be too late for you, Irish," Bennett put in. "I saw you fight Killer Kroffut a few weeks back. Tough luck."

"Better than no luck at all," Mick said. "Are we done, fellas? I still got roadwork to do."

"Yeah, go ahead on, Shannon. We'll be in touch."

"Right," Mick sighed, trotting back toward the mouth of the alley. "I expect so."

THE SIGN OVER PAPA DOC'S said Best Barbequed Baby Backs in East Detroit. It was half right. The city changed its name to Eastpointe back in the eighties but Doc's sign remained as it was. The rest of the diner dated from the fifties. Or before. Formica counter with chrome stools, dark booths upholstered in naugahyde, ribs revolving over an open barbecue pit in the front window, filling the air with an aroma that could convert Gandhi to a carnivore.

Ordinarily, Papa slid a Diet Coke across the counter whenever Mick walked in. Not today. Instead he casually carried it down to the end of the counter, away from the other customers.

"You in trouble?" Papa asked as Mick eased down on the stool. Papa was crowding sixty but was as hard and scarred as an ebony fist.

"Could be. Why?"

"Two guys in earlier, lookin' for ya."

"Cops? They found me."

"Not cops, Easties, that Irish bunch. Dolan and Doyle. Know 'em?"

"I've seen 'em around," Mick said. "Mutt and Jeff, right?"

"Both mutts, you ask me. Legbreakers. Mostly do collections for Eastside bookies. What'd the cops want?"

"Me. Or thought they did. A guy I know got whacked last night."

"Tony Brooks?"

"Yeah," Mick said, surprised. "You know him?"

"Know about him," Papa nodded. "The one they call Black Irish?"

"What do you mean, Irish? Brooks was a black guy."

"Half black, and definitely half Irish. His mama was Dinah Brooks, the soul singer? Had some hit records for Motown in the sixties. Send me your looooove . . ." Papa crooned in a gravelly baritone, drawing a few stares from his customers. "His daddy is Big Danny Guinn, the Wayne County Drain Commissioner."

"The guy they call the Irish pope?" Mick whistled.

"The Man himself. Controls all them city jobs and contracts. Guinn's got more juice than the mayor of Detroit."

"And Tony Brooks was his son?"

"Guinn never admitted to it, had a wife and kids in Grosse Pointe. But everybody on our side of town knew about him and Dinah. Not so many knew on yours, I expect."

"What do you mean *my* side of town? I live in the same neighborhood you do."

"Same 'hood, maybe," Papa nodded. "But you ain't never lived on the black side of Detroit. Irish."

Papa stalked off to wait on other customers, leaving Mick puzzled. He'd known Papa Doc for years, now all of a sudden they were back to basic black and white? What the hell was up with him?

He was still mulling over Papa's mood when two guys in dark overcoats and silk scarves walked in, spotted him, and sauntered over, standing behind him, one on each side.

"I know you," the smaller one said. "Irish Mickey Shannon, right? The fighter?"

"Guilty," Mick said, swiveling to face them. Smaller was a relative term. Dolan was probably six foot, two hundred pounds, with reddish hair and a permanent Irish grin. Doyle topped him by six inches and a hundred pounds, darker hair, darker outlook. Mick doubted he ever smiled at all. "Something I can do for you boys?"

"Actually, there is," Dolan said. "We'd like you to come along with us to meet a fella. Big fan of yours. *Big* fan."

"Nice to know I have one, but I'm afraid I can't, guys. I'm meeting my manager in a few minutes. Business. Some other time, maybe."

"You know who we are," Dolan said quietly. It wasn't a question. "You probably even know who we work for. So you know I'm not kiddin' when I say you're comin' along. Easy or hard, Shannon. But you're comin'."

Mick didn't answer for a moment, eyeing the smaller man. Dolan's smile was still in place. But his eyes had gone stone cold. Fifteen years in the ring, Mick was good at reading eyes.

"I know what you're thinkin'," Dolan murmured, leaning down, his voice barely a whisper. "You're thinkin' you're a pro fighter, maybe you can take us both. Well, maybe you could. In a fair fight." He opened his coat just enough to show the gun. "But it wouldn't be a fair fight, boyo. And we wouldn't leave any witnesses. So we're just gonna walk outa here, three friends goin' for a drive. Okay?"

"Since you put it that way," Mick sighed, rising.

"Mick?" Papa said, strolling over, a meat cleaver in his scarred fist. "Everything all right?"

"No problem, Papa," Mick said. "They're fans. From my side of town."

Maybe they were. Their maroon Lincoln Town Car had all the comforts of home: telephone, color TV, even a wet bar. Dolan offered him a drink but Mick passed. In training, he said. Dolan didn't drink either. Instead he kept up a cheery banter about the weather and the eternally lousy Lions while Doyle drove them through the noon-hour crush down along Jefferson Avenue. Doyle still hadn't said a word. Mick was beginning to wonder if the big guy could talk.

Tuning out Dolan's blather, Mick tried to guess where they were taking him. Waterfront district. Only a few years ago the area was an eyesore, abandoned warehouses with eyeless windows, empty factories. Now it was booming. Spurred by the success of the Renaissance Center and the Ojibwa casinos, the waterfront was a fever of construction.

Parking the Town Car in one of the casino lots, the three men walked a few blocks away from the river to a spanking new high rise, still under construction, its skeletal frame soaring twenty-five stories above its neighbors.

"It'll be called the Golden Shamrock," Dolan explained, as he led them beneath a catwalk to a freight elevator. Tools and wheelbarrows were scattered about, but no workmen were in sight.

Mick glanced the question at Dolan.

"Temporary labor problems," Dolan shrugged. "That's why the Man's here. To fix things. It's what he does. This way."

Mick followed Dolan onto the elevator as Doyle pulled the lift-gate shut then cranked the toggle over. Shuddering, the lift clattered its way upward. Five stories, ten. At the twelfth floor they left the masonry walls behind, nothing around them now but naked steel girders, pulleys, chains, and overhead cranes. And still they climbed, finally rattling to a halt on the twentieth floor.

Half a floor, actually. It was really just a platform, plywood sheets scattered over half-inch steel mesh. No real barriers. Nylon safety lines that were strictly decorative. A clear view for ten miles in any direction. And a twenty-story drop to the concrete below. The only furnishings were a couple of work tables covered with architectural drawings.

And the Man. Sitting on a tall drawing stool, Daniel Guinn looked larger than life. Round-faced and rosy-cheeked with a comfortable paunch he didn't bother to camouflage, the Man looked sleek as a TV preacher, a pussycat in a five-thousand-dollar cashmere overcoat and felt Homberg. He eyed Mick in silence a moment, wind whistling through the iron H-beams framing the floor, nothing around them but scaffolding and a dull November sky.

"Irish Mickey Shannon," Guinn said at last, keeping his hands in his overcoat pockets. "I've seen you fight a time or two over the years. Weren't always victorious but you gave your best. Can't ask for more than that. Still fightin', are ya?"

"Now and again."

"But in the twilight of it all, I'd guess. Must be hard for a man like yourself, when the cheers start to fade."

"It's not as much fun as it was," Mick acknowledged. "Is that why I'm here? To talk about my crummy career?"

"A direct man," Guinn smiled. "A rare thing amongst the Gaels. Most Micks greet the world with a smile. Makes it easier to catch the bastards off-guard. Personally, I prefer the direct approach. Saves time. The police believe you're involved in the death of Tony Brooks."

"I'm not. I only met him once. Liked him, in fact."

"He liked you as well. He told me what happened, that somebody rented you to scare Tony away from some girl. Is that how it was?"

"Something like that," Mick nodded warily.

"He also said he dumped you on your arse."

"Sad but true. He used a karate move. It was embarrassing, but if you've followed my career at all, you know it wasn't the first time I've been dumped on the deck. Or even the tenth."

"So you bore the lad no hard feelings? Is that what you're tellin' me?"

"It's the truth."

"Maybe. Tony thought you took it well, but he could have been mistaken. He was a sweet boy. I doubt he thought he had an enemy in the world. And now he's dead. Somebody blew his head off last night. Maybe someone who bore him a grudge. Someone who already knew he couldn't take him on the square. Someone like you, Shannon?"

"No way. I had no beef with him and I've never owned a gun in my life."

"You were in the marines, boyo. I expect you know one end of a weapon from the other. And Tony was killed with a shotgun anyway. Any moron can pull a trigger. Do you know what a plea bargain is, Shannon?"

"More or less."

"Well, that's what I'm givin' you. A chance to save your life. Tony Brooks was my son, Shannon. I want Tony's killer, but I want the man who hired it done even more. Give me his name and you can walk away from this. Hell, I'll even double what he paid you."

Mick said nothing.

"Unless you think you can fly, I'd answer the man," Dolan put in.

"Don't know if I can fly or not," Mick said with a shrug. "Never tried. But it still won't get you anything, Mr. Guinn. I talked to Tony as a favor to a friend. It was a misunderstanding that came to nothing. I didn't kill him, and my friend had no reason to either."

"Then give me his name."

"No. You offered me a plea bargain a minute ago, suppose I offer you one? I'll ask my friend about this. If I think there's even an out-side chance he knows anything about it, I'll give him to you. No charge."

"And I'm supposed to take your word for that? Sorry, Shannon, the stakes are too high. I've lost too much already. Come here a minute, let me show you something." Rising, Guinn sauntered over to the edge of the platform, standing at the rim of the abyss with the city spread out below and the November wind whipping his slacks around his ankles.

Mick joined him warily, keeping an eye on Dolan and Doyle. But if they meant him harm, they gave no sign.

"Do you know where we are?" Guinn shouted over the wind.

"I'm not sure what you mean—"

"Corktown," Guinn said, cutting him off. "In my granddad's day and even when my father was a boy, this whole district was Irish. From Lafayette to Myrtle, east to First Street, west to Brooklyn, all Irish. We controlled the police, the courts, the Detroit mayor's office, half the legislature. Even won the governorship, most years."

"And your point is . . . ?"

"In those days, no man would have dared to harm any friend of mine, to say nothing of my son. Then the Greeks came, and the Dagos and the blacks. And they got good jobs at Ford and G.M. and they think Detroit is their town now. That they can do as they please. Even kill one of us. I intend to prove they're wrong. To send them a mes-sage. Like the old days. You want to talk to your friend? Go ahead. I'll give you one day to find where the guilt lies. But if you can't give me a name by tomorrow, then you'll be the message I send. Right or wrong. Do we understand each other, Mr. Shannon? Or are you one of those dumb Micks they tell all the jokes about?"

"No sir, I'm not. But understanding's a two-way street, Mr. Guinn. If you figure on teaching me to fly, you'd better buy a set of wings for anybody you send after me. I won't be flying solo."

IT WAS LATE AFTERNOON when Mick finally tracked down Tommy Ducatti at his dealership. New Millenium Motors occupied a whole city block in Hamtramck. Premium, Pre-owned Vehicles, Fleet Leases, and Repossessions. A used-car lot, but a classy one.

Tommy Duke's office was equally classy. Thick green carpet, a massively carved desk, and a brag wall covered with awards and photographs. Tommy Ducatti with Muhammad Ali and with Evander Holyfield. At Kronk's gym with Emmanuel Lewis, at banquets with Mayors Archer and Coleman Young. And even one with Irish Mickey Shannon, back when he was winning. When Mick was somebody.

Time hadn't been kind to either of them. Mick had scar tissue around his eyes now, and his nose was wider.

Tommy looked like the picture Dorian Gray had hidden in the attic. Tall, fleshy, and forty, his eyes were red-rimmed, hands trembling, skin patchy. Mick guessed he was in rehab mode from another hard night on the town.

Fidel Ramos, Tommy's bodyguard, was leaning against one of the narrow windows, looking out over the lot. Cool, slender as a stiletto, impeccably turned out in a gray sharkskin suit, Fidel scarcely gave Mick a glance when Tommy's secretary showed him in.

"Hey, Irish," Tommy said absently, scanning some paperwork, "how's it going?"

"Not good, Tommy. We've got a problem."

"I don't do problems," Tommy sighed without looking up. "Problems are Fidel's department."

"Not this time. Remember that guy you asked me to talk to a few weeks back? Tony Brooks?"

"Brooks?" Tommy echoed blankly.

"That black guy who was giving Maria a bad time," Ramos prompted.

"Oh, yeah, right," Tommy nodded, wincing at the movement. "I forgot. What about him?"

"He's dead, Tommy. Somebody blew him away last night. The cops heard I had a beef with Brooks, tracked me down this morning to ask me about it."

"Cops?" Mick had their attention now. Tommy's father and grandfather were hard-core mobsters, gunsels for the Purple gang, both of them. His father died in a gangland shoot-out when Tommy was away at college. Tommy supposedly went legit afterward, but he hustled used cars, owned fighters, and promoted bouts. Which meant on any given day he was probably guilty of something.

"I kept you out of it, Tommy. So far. Wanted to talk to you first. Do you know anything about this?"

"About what? Brooks? Hell no! You straightened him out, that was the end of it far as I was concerned. Maria was off my back and . . . that was all I cared about."

Mick caught the hesitation, but let it pass. "And that was it? I talked to Brooks; you forgot about it?"

"I just said so," Tommy said sullenly. Avoiding Mick's eyes.

"How about you, Fidel? You ever meet Brooks?"

"Wouldn't know him if he walked in the door. Guess that ain't likely, though. How'd he buy it?"

"Shotgun, the cops said."

"Amateur night," Ramos snorted. "Noisy, splatters blood all over everything, hard to carry concealed. Besides, they mess up the cut of my suit. Never use one."

"Look, we don't know squat about this, Irish," Tommy said. "You've got my word. But I don't want to talk to the cops about it or have 'em bugging Maria, getting her all upset. Can you keep me out of it? It's worth a c-note to me."

"Yeah, I guess I can do that. Can't promise they won't turn something up on their own, though."

"I don't see how," Tommy said, opening his desk drawer, peeling two fifties off a roll he kept there. Next to a gun. "We're the only ones who know about this, right?"

"Brooks could have told somebody."

"If he had, I'd be talkin' to the cops already. This finishes it, Irish. We're done. Paid in full." He slid the bills across to Mick.

"Right," Mick said, eyeing him warily as he picked up the fifties. "Paid in full."

NOT QUITE. MICK HAD planned to head for the gym after talking to Tommy. He didn't. Walked along Woodward Avenue instead, thinking. Fighting for a living, you get good at reading faces, especially a man's eyes.

Maybe Tommy wasn't involved in Brooks's killing, but he knew something about it. For one thing, he'd given Mick his word. In the fight game, deals up to a hundred grand are often done over the phone, no contracts, no lawyers. Word alone. Welshing on a deal isn't an option. You don't get sued, you get busted up or killed. Tommy was a serious player so his word had to be rock solid. That was a given. And yet he swore to Mick he wasn't involved. And that was overkill. Obviously, he wanted Mick to believe him.

Why? To keep the cops away? Maybe. But Mick had a hunch something else was going on. It was in his eyes when . . . he said Maria was off his back and that was all he cared about. And again when he said he didn't want the cops bothering her. Why not? Could Maria be involved somehow?

Not a chance. He'd known Maria Ducatti since she was a gawky teenager mooning around the gym, plain as a crowbar and not much brighter. She thought boxers were romantic, like knights or something. Yeah, right.

Hadn't seen as much of Maria in recent years. She'd grown out of her crush on boxing, disliked the violence. But not much else had changed for her.

The ugly duckling grew into an awkward horse of a woman, as tall as Tommy and with a similar build. But with a good heart. She'd never worked or had much of a life of her own. She'd stayed home to tend her ailing mother and grandfather instead.

He could see Maria falling for Brooks. Could even see her whining to Tommy after Brooks politely gave her the brush. But blowing his head off? Hardly.

Still, there'd been something in Tommy's eyes . . . Unfortunately, Mick had no idea what it could be. Something to do with Maria, perhaps? It seemed unlikely but . . . maybe. And he wondered if Maria

had heard the bad news about Tony Brooks yet. The kid they called
Black Irish.

THE DUCATTI PLACE WAS in a real neighborhood, an all-Italian
enclave cut off by the freeway back in the sixties. Tall, ornate older
homes of brick or stucco standing shoulder-to-shoulder, largely
unchanged since the days of Prohibition, when illegal booze had paid
for a good many of them.

Maria had definitely heard about Tony. Mick knew it the moment
she opened the door. Her pudgy face was tear-streaked and she was
still in her bathrobe and pajamas.

"Mick? What are you doing here?"

"Hi, Maria, sorry to bother you. I was in the neighborhood and I
wondered, well, if you'd heard about Tony."

"I . . . heard earlier," she said swallowing. "What an awful thing."

Maria looked equally awful. Haggard and hurting. But what
struck Mick most strongly was an emotion he recognized instantly
from the ring. Fear. Maria Ducatti was as terrified as she was grief-
stricken. Why?

"Can I come in for a minute?"

"I, um, of course," she said reluctantly. "Come to the kitchen, I
was just making a little snack for my mom."

He followed her through the beautifully furnished home, richly
carpeted, with comfortable, overstuffed furniture, a decorator's mix of
maroon and gray.

But dark. The day was overcast, a standard sunless November
afternoon, yet the living room blinds were drawn. Permanent twilight.

Brighter in the kitchen, a sprawling affair with brick ovens, dozens
of copper pots suspended from a rotating rack that probably dated
from the days the Ducattis had servants. Hell, maybe they still did.

"Sit down," Maria sniffled, waving him to the small enameled
kitchen table against the wall. "Coffee?"

"Please," Mick said, easing down in the ladder-back chair, watching her. "Black is fine."

"How did you . . . hear about Tony?" she asked, filling a mug from a percolator.

"The police told me. They thought I might know something about it."

"You?" she said, puzzled. "I don't understand."

"Maria, I'm the one Tommy sent to talk to Brooks when he was . . . bothering you."

She winced as though he'd slapped her. But when she handed him the mug of steaming Italian coffee, her face was a blank. A Sicilian mask. "I knew Tommy . . . straightened things out, but . . ." Her voice faded away, as though she'd forgotten she was speaking. She shook her head, swallowing hard.

Mick didn't get it. She was clearly overwrought, only a word away from breaking down completely. Could she have cared about Brooks that much? Or was something else—

"Maria!" The old man's voice cracked like a whip as he strode angrily into the kitchen. "Are you deaf? Angelina calls you—who is this man? Why is he here?"

"A friend of Tommy's, Grandfather. *Un pugile Irlandese*, the Irish boxer. Please tell Mama I'll just be a moment, Nonno."

"I know you," the old man said, eyeing Mick suspiciously, ignoring Maria. Taller than Tommy and gaunt as Death, he was carefully dressed, white shirt, old-fashioned string tie, black vest, silver watch fob.

"Irish Mickey Shannon, Mr. Ducatti." Mick rose, offering his hand. Salvatore Ducatti was eighty if he was a day, but his grip was like iron.

"No," he said, frowning. "Not Shannon . . . I remember now. You're the one is going to fight Barrow, no?"

"Barrow?"

"Louis Barrow, the black champion. Joe Louis he calls himself now. An *infamia*, a curse, this black champion of America. He was nothing when we brought him up from Saint Louis. Now he thinks he's a big shot, a *pezzonovante*. But any white man can beat him. They have no heart for a real fight, the blacks."

"I, um, I won't be fighting Louis, sir," Mick stammered, his mind reeling. "Joe's a heavy, I'm a middleweight. I think . . . Marciano's scheduled to fight him."

"Yeah, that's right, Marciano. I forgot. Maria! Angelina calls you. She's hungry." He started to turn away, but stopped when he noticed Mick. "Who are you?" he asked.

Mick met Maria's pleading eyes, and in that moment he understood. All of it.

"I'm a friend of Tommy's, Mr. Ducatti," Mick said carefully. "And I was just leaving."

HE HURRIED AWAY FROM the house, not slowing his pace for a good six blocks, trying to assemble the pieces of what he'd seen. When had Joe Louis died? The eighties? Earlier? But he was an old man then. He fought Marciano for the championship back in . . . Mick couldn't remember the year. But he knew the fight had taken place long before he was born.

"HAVE AN OYSTER," DANIEL GUINN said, waving Mick to a seat. Guinn was in the middle of supper at the Top of the Ponch, the exclusive restaurant atop the Ponchartrain Hotel, downtown Motown. His reserved table was piled high with the wreckage of a lobster, prime rib, french fries smothered in gravy, cherries swimming in brandy, and two slices of pecan pie, one topped with cheddar, one with ice cream. The meal could have fed a stable of fighters for a week. Guinn was dining alone.

"No thank you, Mr. Guinn. I only have a few minutes."

"You may have less than that," Guinn observed, glancing pointedly at Dolan and Doyle, who were seated two tables away, sipping coffee. And watching Mick like bird dogs on point. "What do you have for me, Shannon?"

"A theory," Mick said, and quickly outlined what he thought had happened. That when Maria had confided her unhappiness to her brother, her grandfather overheard. Or perhaps she poured out her heart to the old man as well, never dreaming that in his confusion he'd actually act on it.

"You're saying that old man killed Tony?" Guinn interrupted. "Not a chance. Tony was a karate teacher, forgodsake."

"Which is probably why he let Mr. Ducatti in without a qualm. But physically, the old man's fine. He's got a grip like a vise, and how strong do you have to be to pull a trigger? Years back he was a hit man. And in what's left of his mind, it's still 1950. He thought he was defending his granddaughter's honor. With a shotgun. The way they did in those 'good old days' you're so fond of. When a guy like Ducatti could kill a black man in this town and expect to get away with it."

"But he's not going to get away with it! I don't give a damn how old he is or whose kin he is—"

"What are you going to do, Mr. Guinn? Have your goons throw him off a building? What would that prove? He won't understand what's happening or why. And killing him won't be the end of it. You'll have Tommy and his crew to deal with afterward. And maybe more people will die. For what? Vengeance against a crazy old man?"

"Then what would you suggest I do? Go to the police?"

"No," Mick sighed. "I have no real proof and Tommy's got top-notch lawyers on his payroll. Needs 'em in his line of work. The law can't touch the old man. And you don't want the cops sniffing around your business any more than Tommy does."

"What then?" Guinn continued his meal as he talked, wolfing his food as though he hadn't eaten in a month.

"A plea bargain. You offered me one this morning. Do the same for Tommy. He's guessed what happened, I saw it in his eyes when I told him about Tony. Suppose Tommy puts his grandfather away in a place where he can't hurt anyone else? That's all the courts would do anyway."

"It's not enough. Not for a life."

"Maybe not, but we're not talking about what's right, we're talking about what's possible. Do you really think Tony would want more killing over this? Do you?"

Guinn stopped chewing, a forkful of lobster poised in mid-air. Then he lowered it to the plate. "No," he said quietly. "I suppose he wouldn't. But it's not that simple. I can't just . . . let this go. As though Tony's life didn't matter."

"No, of course not. But nothing can bring your son back, Mr. Guinn. All you can do is see that he's not forgotten."

"How do you mean?"

"A memorial. Right downtown. A big one. In honor of the Corktown Irish who helped build this great city. Something made of stone that'll last a thousand years. In your son's name."

Guinn didn't answer for a moment, thinking. "Perhaps you're right," he said at last. "Perhaps that would be best, but . . . Tony was only half Irish."

"The first Black Irishmen were Spaniards. But their children were Irish. How could a son of Daniel Guinn be anything but Irish at heart?"

"You've the devil's own tongue, Shannon," Guinn nodded, showing the faintest trace of a smile. "Black Irish. I like it. I like it a lot."

Murder in Kilcurry

Mary Ryan

T HE MARCH WIND WHISTLED down Sliabh Rua and swept across the townland of Kilcurry. Mary O'Farrell felt it as soon as she left the fire. Her cough was still bothering her. Her chestiness was exacerbated by the turf smoke that scented the room, but she blamed it on the east wind that sneaked under the door. Poor Hannah's efforts to draught-proof the door with canvas bought in Bandon had not been successful.

Hannah was Mary's daughter. The latter observed her now through the window as she fed the hens, throwing out handfuls of mash. The birds squawked and bobbed for the food; the boldest of them flapped awkwardly to land on the edge of the basin.

"Get down out of that, you *oinseach!*" Hannah cried crossly, "before I wring your impudent neck!" Hannah did not know about the visitors who had called earlier; Mary did not want to worry her.

MARY'S EYES SEARCHED THE yard. It was a square farmyard, puddled
from last night's squall, with a fuschia hedge along the side that bordered the road. To the left was the old iron pump, painted a long-
faded green, from which the family obtained their drinking water;
behind it were the outhouses where the cows were milked and the
pony had its quarters. Above the stable was the hayloft in which
Mary's elder son, Paddy, had his bedroom. They had not seen sign
nor light of him for nearly two weeks. He had gone to the fair in
Bandon and had not returned.

It could be over yet another woman, Mary acknowledged. You
wouldn't know with Paddy. But he obviously didn't give two straws for
the worry he caused his family. When did he ever think of anyone but
himself?

For years his mother and siblings had endured his overbearing
ways. They had no other option; since his father Patrick's death, the
farm belonged to him. It was he who held the purse strings.

"Sure maybe he'll grow into a decent man yet!" Mary consoled herself. And then she remembered that Paddy was already in his forties
and the chances of a sea change in temperament were not enormous.

SHE SCANNED THE GATEWAY and the road beyond, looking for any sign
of Con, or of Billy, his dog, whose panting arrival would mean that her
second son was not far behind. She often wondered why Con was so
different than his brother; there wasn't a mean bone in *his* body. She
remembered his rueful grin of that morning when she had advised him
to wrap up against the wind:

*"Sure I don't take one bit of heed of the cold, Mam! Don't be worrying
your head."*

She had heard the bravado. It was a shame, she thought, that Con had
not even a warm coat to show for all his work on the farm.

What would he say when she told him her news? Or maybe he already
knew? Maybe he had met the two *gardaí*; they might have seen him crossing the fields.

THE TWO POLICEMEN MARY was thinking of had called a little earlier. Hannah had been in the village at the time, shopping for tea and flour. Con had been out on the farm. He had returned from the Travers place where he worked most mornings, eaten a quick bite before rushing off again, muttering that a farmer's work was never done. A couple of hours later the *gardaí* had arrived on bicycles. She heard the voices and the rattle of their machines.

"Lift the latch, let ye," Mary called from her seat by the fire when she heard their knock. She thought it was some of the neighbours and was astonished when the door opened and two uniformed policemen stood on the threshold. She gasped and put her hand to her heart.

"Would Con be about, Mrs. O'Farrell?" the sergeant asked politely.

"Musha he's around somewhere all right . . ."

"We'll look for him so, ma'am . . ." he replied, and both had moved back to take their bicycles from where they had propped them against the stable wall.

Mary got up with difficulty and went to the door.

"What is it ye want him for?" she called after them. "He's not in some kind of trouble?"

The younger of the pair, who had blue eyes and an important little moustache, opened his mouth to say something. But the sergeant silenced him with a look.

"No, ma'am," he said gently, coming back a few paces to answer her question. "We just thought he might be able to help with a few inquiries . . ."

As they went out the gate she saw the sergeant look meaningfully at his younger colleague. The latter said something, but the wind carried away his words and she could not catch them.

Mary narrowed her eyes and muttered aloud, "Now what would they be after . . . ?"

Maybe it was that Con had been out on his bicycle after dark without a light?

She shut the door, wondering at the weight on her heart. It had been there these two last weeks, a nameless dread. She knew it was because Paddy had not come home. But it did not occur to her that the visit from the police had anything to do with him. She knew in her bones that he would turn up sooner or later.

Her eyes wandered to the grey clouds. The rain would be back later, maybe turn to sleet. She glanced up uneasily at the thatch that could be seen through the rafters. They would have to renew it in summer; it would not see them through another storm. The last thatching had been done in that glorious June four years ago, just before Patrick had died. His yellowing photograph was on the mantleshelf under the framed picture of the Sacred Heart. He was holding himself stiffly for the camera.

Mary's heart quickened with memory as she looked up at the portrait of her late husband.

Oh, Patrick, a chroí, do you watch out for us at all?

PATRICK HAD FOLLOWED RURAL tradition in leaving the farm to his firstborn son. He had also bequeathed a right of residence for the rest of the family—Mary as his widow, and Con and Hannah for as long as they might need a place to reside.

What would he have made of Paddy's absence? Mary wondered. Would he agree that it was as likely as not to do with another wild filly with red hair? Like Nora O'Keefe, the publican's daughter, the girl he had had such a great notion of some months ago, even though she had been more or less engaged to Dan Riley the blacksmith? Mary was glad that had ended before there was trouble. The girl had gone off to England and there had been no word of her since.

But the *gardaí*'s visit had sharpened her anxiety. She searched in her pocket for her rosary beads and eased herself back into the settle by the fire. Gráinne, the tabby cat, looked up from the hearth and jumped into her lap.

"Sure you're nothing but an ashy pet!" Mary told her, looking with dismay at the marks on her black dress. "And the four feet of you covered! And you thinking only of cat affairs and knowing no more than myself about what's happening in the parish . . ."

What Mary did not know was that a ten-year-old local boy, on his way home from school, had discovered a potato sack in the hedge bordering the O'Farrell land and, on inspecting the contents, had flung it back into the brambles and raced for home. His father had listened to his story and alerted the police.

IN A FIELD BY the road bordering the O'Farrell farm, the two *gardaí* who had earlier spoken to Mary O'Farrell—Sergeant Touhy and Garda McHugh—were examining the hedgerow.

Con O'Farrell was standing beside the officers of the law in an old gaberdine coat with missing buttons. The coat was open at his chest and disclosed a grimy V-neck jumper. Under it a striped collarless shirt was held at the neck by a single stud. Con's cheeks were wind-flayed and had red thread veins, but his face was strong and kind.

The light was almost gone now, but the *gardaí* had bicycle lamps. They shone them around the edge of the field and into the hedgerow where Billy was nosing with increasing excitement.

"There's something there!" the sergeant announced suddenly, pointing his lamp at a spot in the hedge where a bundle was partially concealed by the brambles.

Young Garda McHugh leant down and pulled at the bundle. It emerged into the torchlight, a jute sack of the kind commonly used for carrying potatoes.

"There's something in it right enough!" he said doubtfully, holding it up and shaking it a little. He turned to Con and asked.

"What's in it?"

"Wisha, how would I know?"

"It's your land!"

"Faith 'tis not!" Con said with a short laugh. "It belongs to my brother. And divil a one of us patrols the road!"

An unpleasant sweetish smell rose from the sack. The *garda* gently tipped its contents onto the wet grass. They rolled a foot or so, and came to rest against the sergeant's boot, stared up at him. In the torchlight they saw half-open eyes, a mouth agape. They were looking at a crude-ly decapitated human head.

The *garda* exclaimed in horror. The sergeant started back. The beam of his lamp wavered, then found the dead countenance once more. He turned grimly to Con.

"Is this your brother Paddy?"

Con stared at the head for several seconds without moving.

"If you could move it so that I might see the temples better . . ."

The sergeant nodded, and the garda gingerly held up the grisly find by the hair while the sergeant played the beam of his torch over it. The nose was smashed, a deep indentation marked the side of the skull; the dead flesh was mottled, blue and ghastly white, already beginning to slough from the skull.

Con showed no emotion.

"Yes," he said eventually. "That is Paddy sure enough."

"Where is the rest of him?"

"How would I know?"

It was March 7, 1925.

AT FIRST LIGHT THE search began again and, as the day wore on, the farm began to disgorge its secrets. In a field adjoining the one where the head had been discovered was another potato sack, concealed like the first. It contained a human arm, still wearing its shirtsleeve. It had been severed at the shoulder.

In the afternoon fresh discoveries were made; a human leg was found, then a torso, then the second leg. They were all concealed in the same manner. Toward evening Billy came trotting from the wood. In his mouth was a human arm. The body parts were assembled. Only the genitalia were still missing.

THE GARDAÍ ASKED CON to accompany them. They brought the remains to the nearby village and placed them, still wrapped in sacking, on a table in a room at the back of O'Keefe's public house, which had been shut temporarily at their request. The superintendant now took charge of the case. He sent for the local doctor and for Hannah, watched as she came cycling up the village street, a well-built woman pushing forty, with a handsome face that was closed and tense. When she entered the pub she looked around for Con, saw him seated in the corner, and made to speak to him, but Con shook his head. He had said nothing about what had been found on the farm in the last twenty-four hours, dreading the effect it would have on his womenfolk. Now he evaded his sister's interrogative glance.

"Do you know where your brother Paddy is?" the superintendant asked the woman.

"I do not. He went to Bandon fair to buy a colt two weeks ago."

"Why didn't you make inquiries about him when he failed to return?"

"Paddy was his own master. He wouldn't have taken kindly to inquiries. We were expecting him back any day!"

"Would you be surprised if I told you he was dead?"

Hannah's eyes widened, but the superintendant detected no sign of grief.

"I wouldn't believe you. He was a fine stout man."

"Would you be frightened if I told you someone had killed him?"

Hannah paled. "Sure who would do a thing like that?"

The superintendant looked at the doctor.

"Would you come in here, please," he said to Hannah, opening the door to the back room. Con made to follow, but the sergeant barred his path.

Hannah entered the little room, followed by the doctor. Her nose twitched at the unpleasant smell; her gorge rose. *'Tis like rotting meat,* she thought with disgust.

The superintendant took the head out of the sack and placed it on the table.

Hannah glanced at it without flinching, and then directed her gaze around the room as though desperately seeking any other object on which to rest her eyes.

"Will you look at the head again, ma'am," the superintendant said, "and try to identify it for us."

Hannah glanced at it sideways. She shook her head.

"I don't know him."

The superintendant, who had already recognised Paddy O'Farrell from his own acquaintance with him, stared at the dead man's sister with disbelief.

"Are you sure?"

"Paddy was not so thin in the poll," Hannah added after a moment, glancing at the head again.

"Your brother Con has already identified it for us!" Hannah redirected her eyes to the evidence. After a moment she said in a calm, toneless voice:

"I am beginning to think it is Paddy! Yes, it is him, right enough!"

IN THE THATCHED FARMHOUSE at Kilcurry, Mary O'Farrell sat propped up with pillows in the fireside settle. Hannah had fussed over her today, for her cough was worse and she croaked occasionally, trying to shift the mucus from her lungs. Above the mantleshelf the Sacred Heart looked down on the flagged kitchen, the old woman in the settle, the young cat that lay curled by the embers. The deal table had been scrubbed by Hannah that morning; the dresser with willow pattern cups and plates had been dusted. The old clock with weights and chains, bought years before by Patrick, struck a sudden, melodious 4:00 P.M.

Mary's arthritic hands moved over her rosary beads. She was praying for Paddy. Her anxiety over him had escalated during the night when she had woken from a nightmare unable to breathe, and now she was besieging heaven for him. Why hadn't he come home? Had he followed the O'Keefe hussy to England? Was Hannah keeping something from her?

She called "Hannah," but there was no reply.

She finished the Rosary, put the beads back in her pocket.

It was strange to have the house so empty. Hannah was generally around all day, cleaning and cooking, washing and ironing, preparing mash for the hens. She was a great housekeeper and would have made someone a grand wife, some children a devoted mother. But it had not worked out like that and the waste of a passionate life weighed on her mother. Mary longed for grandchildren; she could also remember the yearnings of her own heart when it was young.

She sighed. It was hard for a woman not to have her own man. Only a year ago things had looked good for Hannah. Denis Donnelly from the next parish—a man who had inherited ninety good acres—had taken to visiting regularly, and it was clear that he was set on Hannah. It was a great chance for her daughter, and she had never seen her so happy.

"Do you mean to have him?" she had whispered conspiratorially to Hannah one evening after the men had retired—Paddy to his room in the hayloft, Con to his bed in the small bedroom. "Are you for marrying Denis?"

"Oh, Mam, the truth is that I'd marry him in the morning. He's decent and kind and we'd rub along grand together. But I'd need some class of a dowry, for Denis has to think of his sister . . ."

"I've no money, *a stór* . . ."

"I know, but Paddy has."

Hannah drew her chair closer to her mother and continued eagerly. "Do you think he'd let me have something, a hundred pounds, even fifty . . . I'll give up my right of residence here, so it's not as though I'd be asking something for nothing."

"Sure all you can do is put the question to him."

Mary did not divulge her misgivings. She knew that not only was her firstborn miserly, but he was arrogant and brutal as well. He had attacked Con for taking a job in the Travers place—a neighbouring farm of some two hundred acres—telling him he was a disgrace to abandon his home place to work for strangers. The row had taken place in the yard one moonlit night. Mary had woken, gone to the window, heard Con's voice and his attempt at reason.

"I can't live without a shilling in my pocket. There are things a man needs besides work . . ."

Then Mary saw Paddy lift the stout blackthorn stick he carried around with him and deliver a blow to his brother's chest that made the latter gasp and double over.

"God damn you to hell!" Con cried when he got his wind back, lifting his fists and approaching his brother, "for there's five devils in you—one for every season of the year and one for yourself . . ."

Mary had opened the kitchen door and screeched:

"Stop that . . . stop it now!"

"Stay out of this, old Mother O'Farrell," Paddy shouted back. "Mind your own business, woman . . ."

But it had been Con who had hurried to help her back to the settle bed, soothing her. "It's all right, Mam . . . Just a tiff . . ."

"It's not lucky!" Mary whispered. "For brothers to behave so . . ."

This happened around the time that Con had taken to staying out late of an evening, but was always noncommittal about where he went.

Is it the drink? his mother had wondered. Is my poor Con down there in O'Keefe's propping up that bar with the rest of the *amadáns*, spending the few bob he gets from Dick Travers?

But apparently not. Con always returned at midnight with no sign of liquor on him, but with a glow that told his mother more than he realised.

Who was it? she wondered with a sinking heart. If he wanted to marry, he could not bring a wife into his brother's house.

Next day Paddy went to the Travers' and made a scene, his chest shoved out, his blackthorn stick thumping the ground.

"Mr. Travers . . . It's one thing to have Con over here, working like a slave for youself, but his home place needs him . . . It's neither right nor decent to have him spending himself here . . ."

WHEN MARY EVENTUALLY FOUND out from Hannah that Con was walking out with little Minnie Dwyer who kept house for her half brother, Séamus, near the main road, a lot of things fell into place for her. She had heard that Séamus was about to be married and knew that Minnie must be desperate to escape. "Minnie says that if she can't have Con, it's the boat to America . . ." Hannah confided. "And he's dead set on her, Mam . . ."

Mary's heart ached for Con. He was a trapped, landless man. Even if he went to Dublin there would be nothing for him. Many a one had tried it, but had ended up in the slums—dreadful places where a body would sicken for the breezes from the hills and the clean, wild sky.

And he was too old to emigrate. When he had mooted it years before, his brother had persuaded him to stay, with vague promises, never honoured, of putting the farm into joint names.

And now his job at Travers was about to disappear. Dick Travers, fed up with Paddy's loud-mouthed interference, had given Con notice. And Minnie, too, had been as good as her word. A cousin in New York had sent her a steamship ticket and she was due to sail from Cobh within the month.

MARY'S THOUGHTS RETURNED TO Hannah. She had been offered a real chance. Denis would have made a good husband and she would have wanted for nothing. But when she asked Paddy if he would let her have a small dowry, he had refused.

"No, no, no. Sure where would I get that kind of money? Anyway, we need you here. What would the house do? . . . Who would look after your mother? If Denis Donnelly wants you he'll have to take you in your shift . . ."

This had been communicated to Denis whose visits had ceased. Hannah had waited every evening for almost three weeks, her apron off, her hair coiffed, but he had not come. She had gone around white-faced, too proud to show how deep was the wound until, one night, Mary had taxed her on it:

"I know how you feel, Hannah *a croí* . . ." she had whispered when they were alone together in the kitchen. "If it's any comfort to you . . ."

Hannah burst into tears.

"Is it to be a skivvy here for all the days of my life, Mam? Is it never to have my own home, my own children? Oh, Mam, I wish I had never been born . . ."

This from the daughter whose laughter had once filled the house!

MARY SURFACED, WONDERING IF she was dreaming that Billy was whining outside the door. But it was him all right. He normally accompanied Con around the farm and his presence alarmed her. She got up and let him in.

"Where has Con got to?" she asked him. "Where's Hannah?"

The dog wagged his tail and lay down by the door. The cat, from her warm spot by the hearth, opened one eye in a cautious slit.

"Has Hannah gone to the village again . . . ?" Mary continued. But Billy was uninformative.

Mary returned to the settle and said the Hail Mary in Irish under her breath. It always comforted her:

A naomh Mhuire.

A mhátair Dé . . ."

the cadence of the old language reaching into her soul. Holy Mary, Mother of God, Pray for us sinners now and at the hour of our death.

Her mind turned to the past, the sweet, safe place in which she always found refuge.

SHE REMEMBERED HER WEDDING day, Patrick beaming at her when he turned at the altar, the blue poplin dress that she had made herself crisp and cool against her young flesh, like the starched sheets when Patrick had reached for her that night, shy and urgent and so full of love. There had been a shadow on that day, because Patrick's illegitimate half brother, Liam Ward, had arrived drunk. He was the family's shameful secret, Patrick's elder by five years, a man bitter at his illegitimate status and resentful that he could never hope to inherit his father's acres. His mother had been a sultry tinker woman who had been ostracised by her tribe.

"Bad cess to ye," he had shouted at Patrick when the latter told him to leave. "Ye'll have no luck out of this land . . . nor yeer children after ye . . ."

"Don't be talking like that!" Mary cried. "On our wedding day and all . . ."

"Oh, you think you're doing well for yourself, pretty Mary McCarthy . . . marrying into this farm. But the day will come, mark my words, when you will wish you had never set eyes on your fine bridegroom here . . ."

A tinker's curse on my wedding day? Mary thought in disbelief and prayed silently that God would avert it.

FOR A LONG TIME there were no children. One miscarriage followed another. Novenas—prayers said over nine consecutive days—succeeded each other until Mary was desperate.

Why could she not have babies? She longed for them with a passion, could feel their gentle skin, their little bodies against her heart.

"God—if you send me children I will ask for nothing else; I will work all my days for them . . ."

Seven years to the day from her wedding, Mary went into a labour that seemed without end. Two days of torture passed and still she fought and strained, gripping the iron bedstead, while the midwife, old Molly Kerrigan, muttered between her teeth at the baby that didn't want to be born. Eventually, Patrick had sent for a doctor all the way to Bandon. He arrived in a motor car, examined the labouring woman and went into the kitchen.

"I can save only one of them, Mr. O'Farrell. . . . Which do you want, mother or child?"

Although the Church said the child must be preferred above the mother in such circumstances, Patrick replied through the tears that started in his eyes:

"Save my Mary!"

Molly, listening at the bedroom door, turned and whispered to her moaning patient:

"There's a man out there that loves ye sore! So never mind the fancy oul' doctor! Let's have that baby, girleen . . . *Let it come* . . ."

And then she had begun a stroking of Mary's abdomen, while she set up a soft crooning in Irish. Mary felt herself in a dream, slipping somewhere between this world and the next, alternately racked as though her bones and sinews were being sundered, alternately strangely comforted by the noble language her race had spoken for thousands of years. She collected the last of her strength. Even as the Bandon doctor made dismissive comments on the midwife's chant, even as he took from his black bag the instruments that would have drawn the infant from her in pieces, Mary with a last terrible effort cried aloud in triumph as she felt the child's head break from her in a gush of blood and water.

Death had been cheated. Patrick had come in to embrace her a little later, full of joy. They had named the baby after his father and almost immediately called him Paddy.

A year later Con had arrived, easily, followed in just another year by Hannah. Now, across the reach of forty years, their mother's heart remembered their little heads pressed against her breast, their small toes clenching as they nursed. All three had grown into fine, handsome children.

And she had honoured her promise to God. She had never complained, although the years had been hard. She had milked the cows, and kept the hens, and run the house, and made clothes, and cooked and cleaned until she became arthritic. She had been so proud of her beautiful family, knew that if there had only been the money for their education they could have held their own anywhere in the world.

Patrick had been a kind father. But, no matter how hard he had worked, luck seemed to have left him. Harvests had been disappointing; cows dropped their calves. Someone had suggested it was because his father had ploughed a fairy fort, a well-known cause of such ills. Someone else suggested, with a knowing inclination of his head, that if it had *only* been a *fort* that had been ploughed by his father . . .

In those long-ago days Mary had thought that their love would overcome everything. But even it had been squeezed hollow by the grinding effort to live.

MARY ROUSED HERSELF FROM her reverie. Her mouth was parched and she longed for a cup of tea. She called Hannah's name again.

She must be still at the village. Poor girl! How desperate she had been when her romance with Denis had ended, how she still had wept at night thinking no one could hear.

Sometimes, Mary mused, *I am glad God gave me no more children, for their sorrows are breaking my heart.*

There was a step in the yard. The door opened and Hannah's form filled the doorway. She was wearing her hat and coat.

"I didn't know you had gone to the village," Mary said reproachfully.

"Oh, Mam," Hannah said in a voice full of anguish, "I have something terrible to tell you . . ."

THE INQUEST WAS HELD the next day. Con gave evidence about his brother's disappearance and how he had expected to see him return any day. Hannah refused to give evidence. The coroner returned a verdict of homicide by person or persons unknown.

"Hannah has ruined us!" Con confided to Garda McHugh afterward.

"How is that, Con?"

"She should have given evidence," Con replied. "She should have told them how we thought Paddy would walk through the door any minute."

Garda McHugh turned to him.

"Will you be having the funeral tomorrow!"

"Aye."

They passed the forge. Dan Riley's bulky form could be glimpsed within as he swung the hammer onto the anvil with a mighty clang and a shower of sparks. He had become taciturn since Nora O'Keefe had gone to England. The forge was no longer the centre for badinage and *craic* as it once had been.

But everyone understood. The man, for all his size and strength, had a broken heart.

THE FOLLOWING DAY MARY O'FARRELL felt her mind was wandering. They had a coffin in the parlour. Poor Paddy was in it, they told her, for he had been killed.

But how could he be killed? There was peace in the country these days. The troubles were over.

They would not let her see the remains. They made her stay by the kitchen fire, where she closed her eyes and fingered her beads while tears crept down her face and her mind struggled to find answers to the riddle of her life.

THE NEIGHBOURS CAME TO the wake, shook hands with the family; the women knelt to say the Rosary around the coffin; the men joined them, bareheaded. When the prayers were over, they stood around uneasily, accepted whisky or stout and spoke in whispers. Con and Hannah served the drinks, accepted the condolences, lifted the coffin lid when Willie Cassidy asked to see the corpse.

"I must say," the latter blurted, "that it is a terrible state of affairs, Con, to see your brother cut up in pieces and you not a bit worried over it!"

"There is nothing I can do about it," Con replied. "And *my* hands are clean."

DAN RILEY CAME LATE to the wake. He spoke to Hannah briefly, shook Con's hand, and then he left.

Mrs. Travers and Mrs. Coonihan, the priest's housekeeper, followed him as quickly as they could. The atmosphere in the O'Farrell house was oppressive.

"Poor Dan Riley was looking very strange in himself . . ." Mrs. Travers confided, after the two women had exchanged horrified comment on the murder.

"It's the O'Keefe girl! He would have done anything for her, but she ran off to England!"

"Her mother told me she has a good job there and won't be coming home!"

"A good job?" Mrs. Coonihan remarked, pursing her lips and glancing sideways at her companion. "Between ourselves, Mrs. Travers, that girl had more in her purse when she left Killcurry than a decent girl should have . . . if you take my meaning . . ."

Mrs. Travers widened her eyes. She knew Mrs. Coonihan knew more than anyone else in the parish, except the parish priest.

ON THE DAY FOLLOWING the funeral the police investigation continued. They knew Paddy O'Farrell had died by repeated blows to the head. It was clear that he had not gone to the Bandon fair as both his siblings had claimed; the murder had been committed while he was still in bed asleep. His room in the hayloft bore the marks of the assault. The headboard of his bed showed evidence of having been wiped, but wormholes in the wood still contained dried blood. The bed frame and the floor beneath were bloodstained; the inside of the loft roof was stained rust red from arterial spouting. But the bed clothes were free of stains, and looked fresh. The mattress was missing, but pieces of bloodstained mattress were found in a field near the house.

WHEN THEY HAD COMPLETED their inspection of the loft, Garda McHugh and Sergeant Troy came to the house. Hannah was giving Con his dinner. The two policemen came in and stood uneasily.

"Will ye have a bite to eat?" Hannah asked them.

"No . . . We have something to say to you and Con . . ." the sergeant replied, glancing meaningfully at the old lady by the fire.

"Say it then, man," Con replied. "We've nothing to hide!"

The sergeant took a deep breath.

"Cornelius O'Farrell and Hannah O'Farrell, I am arresting you both for the murder of your brother Paddy. You are not obliged to say anything, but anything you do say may be taken down and used in evidence against you . . ."

There was a cry from the old lady in the settle.

"Oh, Mam . . ." Hannah cried. "Oh, Mam . . ."

But Mary gave a deranged, keening wail. The hairs on the back of the sergeant's neck stood up.

God blast this job, he thought.

AT THE TRIAL THE state pathologist gave evidence that the dismemberment had been effected by a blunt, nonsurgical instrument. The right side of victim's face had been reduced to pulp, possibly by a hammer or the blunt end of a hatchet; the base of the skull, left cheekbone, and nose were extensively fractured.

But Con's clothes, which had been taken away for examination, showed no bloodstains of any kind. Hannah's had not been investigated.

Con and Hannah exercised their right not to give evidence, and, in his address to the jury, Mr. Justice Hanna commented unfavourably on their failure to do so. The jury returned within half an hour with a verdict of guilty for both accused.

Turning to the dock where the two O'Farrells stood like creatures turned to stone, the judge asked:

"Cornelius O'Farrell, have you anything to say as to why sentence of death should not be passed on you?" Con said in a ringing voice:

"I had not hand, act, or part in Paddy's murder."

The judge put on the black cap.

"It is the sentence of this court," he said, "that on the 28th July you be taken to a lawful place of execution and there be hanged by the neck until you are dead, and may God have mercy on your soul."

Con replied: "I am going to die an innocent man!"

Hannah cried out as the judge turned to her: "I did not kill my brother."

At the back of the court Dan Riley slipped from his seat and left, closing the heavy door carefully so that it made no sound.

CON O'FARRELL WAS HANGED on 28 July 1925. Hannah's death sentence was commuted to life imprisonment. The locals were left to ponder the fate of their neighbours; they gave the O'Farrell farm a wide berth. No one would buy it or graze it. The *mí-ádh*, the bad luck, was on it, they said, and crossed themselves when it was mentioned. And when a man by the name of Michael Casey came down from Dublin and quietly assumed possession, no one hindered him. They knew he was Liam Ward's son, blood kin from the wrong side of the blanket. But better him to have the farm, even though he was a tinker woman's son, than have it overgrown, with silent windows and mouldering thatch.

DAN RILEY RETREATED INTO himself. He worked night and day, had to be reminded to charge his customers, and eventually took so heavily to whisky that the forge became cold and Dan's eyes as red as the furnace over which he had once hammered the hot iron. Some said he grieved still for the red-haired vixen Nora O'Keefe.

* * *

THE COUNTY MENTAL HOSPITAL had high walls of limestone. Behind them were two acres of shrubbery and well-kept grounds and the old hospital itself with its barred windows. The deranged were housed according to the severity of illness—those likely to be dangerous to themselves or others in locked and padded cells, those dwelling in a cloudland of their own making, in dormitories. Despite the efforts of the well-meaning staff, there clung to the whole establishment the miasma of bewilderment and despair.

But in the midst of the tormented, one woman stood out. Everyone who looked at her felt cheered; for, although she was old, her face was luminous with serenity and peace. Mary O'Farrell had good reason for her serenity: her three beloved children—Paddy, Con, and Hannah—played happily all day at her feet.

(This story is loosely based on a murder committed in County Cork, Ireland, in 1925.)

Great Day for the Irish

Edward D. Hoch

B RENDA CONWAY HAD BEEN working her Saint Patrick's Day scam for seven years, and it seemed to grow more successful each time. Perhaps it was just that the economy was good and she was becoming a better actress. She always started the day over on Fifth Avenue, before the parade began, standing for a moment in the middle of the street looking north along that long green line that the city so generously painted down its center each year. Then she retreated to the sidelines as the rumble of the first drums reached her ears and watched the spectacle from afar.

There was a certain ritual after seven years, and Brenda was careful to abide by it. She waved to her friend Tom O'Toole when he marched by in his kilt with the Saint Bridget Bagpipers and cheered wildly as the contingent from Holy Apostles in White Plains came into view with their banner flapping in the March breeze. A decade earlier she'd been a senior at Holy Apostles herself, carrying one end of that very same banner.

After the parade passed the reviewing stand along Central Park, it was traditional for the marchers and many of the spectators to congregate at various private parties and Irish bars around midtown Manhattan. Brenda always waited till evening when the revelers were at their loudest, and she never picked the same bar twice. Last year it had been that place on Fifty-seventh Street near Lexington, and this time she made her way down Eighth Avenue to a block near Forty-second that boasted Irish pubs almost side by side. Both had live music and it made no difference that the one she wanted, the Harp & Shamrock, was actually owned by a restaurant chain that bought it from the original owners. Tonight it was as Irish as any place in New York.

Brenda, who now became Molly Malone for purposes of her scam, entered and managed to squeeze her way up to the bar at the near end. Her father always said she had the map of Ireland on her face, and it served her well at this time each year. "Here! Let this fine colleen through!" a young dark-haired man insisted, making room for her. He was dressed for the office and held a laptop computer carrier in his nondrinking hand.

"Thank you, sir," she said, trying not to lay the Irish accent on too thick.

"What'll it be? A pint of Guinness?"

"A lager. Harp will do me nicely."

"Harp it is, Rocky!" The bartender in a green hat nodded and poured a foamy pint, smoothing off its head before presenting it to her.

"How much?" she asked, fumbling for her kelly green purse with the sequin shamrock on it.

"On me," the dark-haired man said. "I'm Michael Behan." He held out his hand, and as Brenda stepped closer to grasp it she could smell the beer on his breath.

"Molly Malone, like the girl in the song."

"Wouldn't you know it? They were playing that a while ago."

She glanced at a couple of young men who were strumming guitars and singing on a low platform at the far end of the noisy barroom. "I hear it a great deal back in Ireland. It's a favorite in the pubs."

"You're a true Irish lass! I should have known from your brogue. What are you doing here in New York?"

"I live here now, but I'm flying home for a visit tomorrow."

"Great! Let's drink to a lovely trip."

They touched glasses and she glanced around, taking in the scene. The place was so crowded it was impossible to tell where the tables started, or even if there were any tables. There was green everywhere, from the ceiling banners and crepe paper to the customers' apparel. Caps and shamrocks and Kiss-Me-I'm-Irish buttons. The bartenders, wearing paper hats, were working as hard as they could to keep up with the demand.

Brenda spotted the rest room sign she'd been seeking and turned her attention back to Behan and the other men who'd clustered around. "Do you boys come here regular?"

Most of them confessed to frequenting other bars, but this one was close to the bus terminal and a good place to stop on the way to their homes in Jersey. Behan simply shrugged and said, "I'm meeting someone here later."

"Ah! A girlfriend!"

"It's business." He shifted the conversation back to her. "Where's your family live in Ireland?"

"Killarney. I'll be almost there by this time tomorrow. I'll take the bus from Shannon Airport. Just another Molly Malone coming back to the old sod."

One of the others, a jovial red-haired stockbroker named Ken, caught the name this time. "Hey," he shouted at the musicians. "We've got the real Molly Malone here!"

She hardly resisted as the crowd propelled her forward and the lead guitarist helped her onto the low bandstand. "Is it true your name is Molly Malone?" he asked into the microphone. His name was Slim and his partner was Roy. Slim & Roy, the Irish Troubadours, the banner behind them read.

"That's me," Brenda agreed, and of course they launched into the song.

"*In Dublin's fair city where girls are so pretty I first set my eyes on sweet Molly Malone . . .*"

Brenda started singing along, and the crowd at the Harp & Shamrock joined in, rocking the place with their voices until the emotion was so great it brought her close to tears. Finally, she had to run off the stage to the ladies' room.

She emerged a few minutes later, looking puzzled and just a bit distraught. "Where's my purse?" she asked around the bandstand. "Has anybody seen my purse?"

"What does it look like?" Slim asked, putting down his guitar.

"It's kelly green with a sequin shamrock on it. All the money for my trip is inside!"

Some of the men she'd been drinking with remembered the purse. "I saw it," Ken the stockbroker said. "I thought you had it with you on the bandstand."

"I thought so, too, but it's gone."

They looked all over the bar and the floor, even making an announcement that the purse was missing. She returned to the ladies' room with one of the other girls, but it was not to be found.

"Was your plane ticket in there, too, Molly?" Slim asked.

"No, just the money. I took it out of the bank this afternoon before I came here. I know I should have gotten travelers' checks, but I was in a hurry. I had almost a thousand dollars. I was planning to give some to my mother." The tears came now, rolling down her cheeks and ruining her makeup. Brenda had always been good at crying on cue.

After another five minutes' searching, Slim held up his hands. "Folks, folks, listen to me! We've got the real Molly Malone here, and she's going back to Ireland in the morning to visit her mom. The purse with her money in it is gone. I'm not saying anyone here took it, but it's gone and so is the money. Let's pass the hat for Molly Malone!"

He picked up a big cowboy hat he sometimes wore and dropped a twenty-dollar bill into it, starting it around the far side of the room. Brenda saw Ken adding a twenty. She tried to find Behan in the crowded pub but he was nowhere to be seen. While the hat was passed there were more cheers as Slim and Roy launched into another rendering of "Molly Malone."

When the hat had been passed through all corners of the room Slim made a show of dumping the collected bills into a paper bag and presenting it to Brenda. Roy had slipped off to the men's room. "There now, lass. Don't lose it this time."

"I won't!" she assured them. "Thanks to everyone! I'll never forget you!"

She would have been out the door in another minute, safely on her way, had not a strong hand gripped her shoulder as she made her way through the noisy crowd. "Hello, Brenda."

She was so startled to hear her real name that she swerved around to see who it was. "Tom! What are you—"

Tom O'Toole smiled at her. "—doing here?" he completed "Well, it's Saint Patrick's Day and this is an Irish pub. What more reason do I need? I just came in and saw them passing the hat for you." He was still in his kilt and carrying a big leather pouch with his bagpipe inside.

"I waved to you in the parade," she said, trying to cover her embarrassment.

"I saw you. What's this?" he asked, tapping the paper bag. "Don't tell me you lost your purse again this year!"

"Tom, can't we go outside? It's too noisy in here." She didn't want anyone overhearing them.

But before they could reach the door there was a commotion at the far end of the bar. "Call the cops!" a man was shouting. "There's a dead guy in the men's room!"

AFTER THAT, NO ONE left. Brenda stood there with her bag full of money, frozen in position next to Tom O'Toole. He was several inches taller, a good six feet, and he'd told her once that the kilt only came out for the annual parade. She'd met him two years earlier at a pub on Saint Patrick's night when she was working her scam, and they'd gone out drinking a few times after that. He'd remained a friend, but she'd never told him that the lost purse and passing the hat were all a scam she repeated annually.

The police arrived and it quickly became obvious that no one would be leaving the Harp & Shamrock for a while. Ken, the stockbroker who'd been standing at the bar with Brenda and Michael Behan, had worked his way through the crowd to her. "It's Behan," he said. "Someone killed him in the men's room."

"Oh no!"

"I'll want to talk to you," he told her, and suddenly his demeanor had changed. He was no longer a carefree Irishman celebrating the holiday. He showed her a badge and ID for Kenneth Wagner, Federal Bureau of Investigation. "We can use the office back here."

He led the way to a little room behind the bar, and she had time only for a quick appealing glance at Tom O'Toole. "What's this all about?" she asked the FBI agent. "What were you doing here?"

"We've been watching Behan for some time now. We suspect he was a conduit supplying American money to a violent Irish splinter group. Do you know anything about that?"

Brenda shook her head. "I only met the man a couple of hours ago. You were standing there. You saw me come in."

"He'd told me he was meeting someone here tonight on business. It could have been you. You're flying to Ireland tomorrow."

"I'm not—" she began and then decided she couldn't admit too much. "I have a mother back in Ireland. There are no ties to any splinter groups." When Wagner remained silent she added, "Look, there are over two hundred people out there. Any one of them might have killed him."

"Almost certainly it was a man. He was found in one of the men's room stalls, seated on the closed toilet and fully clothed. He'd been stabbed twice in the chest and died almost immediately. I think he went in there to meet the person who killed him. His carrying case was empty on the floor. If it held a laptop computer, the killer stole it."

"Maybe that's all he wanted. They're not cheap."

"There could be another motive. That laptop might have an address list of contributors to Irish causes."

Brenda was doubtful. "Would someone kill for that?"

"Quite possibly. There could be a great deal of money at stake. The police are out there searching for the laptop right now."

"And you suspect me because I'm going to Ireland tomorrow?"

"You said your mother lived in Killarney, didn't you?"

"That's right." Somehow she felt everything was closing in on her.

"Behan lived just long enough to start writing a word in his own blood, on the wall of the toilet stall. He wrote *kill*. Maybe he was trying to write *killarney*."

"How could I have gotten into the men's room unnoticed?"

"The place was crowded, noisy. Somebody got in there to stab him, why not you?"

Before she could respond, there was a knock on the office door. It was the bartender, Rocky. "Lieutenant wants to see you."

The FBI agent stepped outside but left his fingers on the door's edge, not quite closing it. She heard the police lieutenant say something about laptops, and Wagner replied, "Get everyone's name and address. Make sure they have IDs."

"Are you letting them go?" she asked when he came back inside.

He nodded. "There were only two laptops in the place, and each had an owner who could prove it was his."

"Why wouldn't the killer have taken the carrying case, too?"

"It has Behan's initials on it."

"If you're releasing the others, does that mean I can go, too?"

"As soon as you show me some ID with your New York address."

"I—it was in my purse that got stolen."

Kenneth Wagner allowed himself a slight smile that seemed more menacing than friendly. His hand dipped into the side pocket of his jacket and pulled out her little green purse. "This one?"

"Where did you find it?"

"The police just located it in the disposal bin for paper towels, in the ladies' room."

"Thank you." She reached out for it but he didn't immediately let go.

"There's nothing in it, Molly. That is your name, isn't it? Molly Malone?"

She nodded. "The thief must have cleaned it out."

He sighed and motioned for her to leave. "I'll talk to you again later."

She put her purse in the bag with the money and went back into the bar. Patrons were lined up, showing their identification to a police officer who carefully noted names and addresses before allowing them to leave. Slim and Roy were putting their guitars away and taking down their banner. She walked over to them and Slim said, "You'd better get out of here."

"I'm trying," she assured him.

But she had no identification in the name of Molly Malone, and one of the bar's patrons was sure to overhear if she gave the officer the name of Brenda Conway.

Tom O'Toole was standing in line, his bagpipe in its case over his shoulder. "Let's get out of here and go somewhere else," he suggested.

"These cops are unbelievable! I had to unzip my pouch and show them the bagpipe. It's a wonder they didn't make me play a tune."

"The dead man had a laptop that was stolen. That's what they're searching for."

"You knew this guy?"

"I just met him here tonight."

He rested his hand on her shoulder. "I don't know what you're into, Brenda, but be careful. There's lots of stuff going on here that you don't know about."

"I know enough. I know that Behan was supposed to receive money from someone that could be sent to an Irish splinter group. Only that someone killed him instead, and stole his laptop with a list of other donors."

"Stick to singing 'Molly Malone,' " he suggested. "You sounded great doing that."

"Oh, Tom!" She felt a sudden sadness, as if she'd lost a close friend. She walked away from him blindly, clutching her paper bag. Somehow the money didn't seem important any longer.

"We have to talk," Slim said as she walked past him.

"Later."

She found Kenneth Wagner with the police, standing at the entrance to the men's room. Inside, they were preparing to remove the body. "I can tell you who killed him," she said. "I can tell you where that missing laptop is."

He studied her face for a moment. "Go on."

She pointed across the room at the line of people waiting to leave. "The third man in line. The laptop is in that leather pouch under his bagpipe. His name is Tom O'Toole and he's your killer."

TOM SAW THEM COMING and tried to bolt through the door, but they had him. The laptop was in there, and also the knife that was the murder weapon. When it was over, Wagner simply looked at her and shook his head. "How did you know?"

"He thought I was great singing 'Molly Malone,' but he'd told me earlier he'd just come in while they were passing the hat. That was a good fifteen minutes after I sang. He was here all the time, but I didn't notice him in the crowd. He went to the men's room, carrying his pouch, at the agreed time, and killed Behan for that computer and its lists. Behan didn't know his name, and in his dying moment he tried to identify him with a single word."

"Killarney?"

"No, I was Molly to him. He would have written that if he'd meant me. He didn't write *kill*, he wrote *kilt*, meaning that his murderer was wearing one. He didn't live long enough to cross the *t*, and with his dying scrawl it probably looks like an *l.*"

"It does," Wagner confirmed grimly. "But how did you know where the stolen laptop was hidden?"

"If Tom was the killer, where else could it be? He unzipped the pouch for the police, but probably only enough to show the bagpipes. They didn't go feeling around underneath." She thought of something else. "Actually, he'd have made his escape if he hadn't stopped to talk with me on the way out. Someone found the body and then we were all stuck here."

Kenneth Wagner nodded. "You'd better get going yourself. And take care of that money."

A while later, at a coffee shop in the Port Authority bus terminal, she met Slim and Roy. "How much did you get?" Slim asked, resting his guitar case next to the booth.

"Twenty-one hundred and thirty dollars. Better than last year. Here's the five hundred I promised you."

"They were tanked up and generous. It's always a great day for the Irish."

"Unless they get killed, like Behan."

"We'll let you know where we'll be playing next year."

Brenda shook her head. "Don't bother. I'm retiring from these scams. Tonight was too much for me."

Slim shrugged. "What are you going to do with the money?"

Brenda thought about it. "Hey, maybe I'll take a trip to Ireland."

Stealing the Dark

Jane Adams

A MONGST THOSE ITEMS RECOVERED was an album of faded photographs. Sepia-toned faces gazed out at him from foxed pages decorated with roses and twining tendrils of honeysuckle. The cream boards that formed the cover had pulled loose from their binding and flapped limply as he removed the book from the evidence bag and lay it down on the wooden table of the interview room. *It was,* he thought, *a sad little volume, filled with the faces of the long dead, stiffly posed and their eyes gazing from the book at a world so changed it made him wince to think of it.*

The young man accused of theft sat opposite him, blank-eyed and sullen. His chair had been pushed back from the table and his long legs stretched beneath it, the air of studied nonchalance designed to make him look hard, though all it did, to Colm's practised eye, was emphasize how scared this kid was.

Colm checked the tape and announced himself and the others in the room for the benefit of posterity, then, gently, careful not to dislodge any of the fragile images, he began to turn the pages of the book.

"Where'd you get this, Michael?"

The boy glanced at the book, a mere flick of his eyes sideways and down.

"Where'd I get what?"

"It's an album, Michael. Family pictures. Someone's grieving for this loss." He paused, again noted the swift sideways look, but aimed at him this time and not at the book upon the table.

"Some old book?" the boy said boldly. "You going to charge me with stealing some old book." He jerked upright and then sat forward, pushing the album back toward Colm.

"Well, no," Colm said. "I thought we'd charge you for the video recorders and the bits of jewellery that we found first, but I'd like you to tell me about the book. Call it curiosity."

The boy shifted awkwardly. He was baffled by this, Colm knew, by Colm's interest in some tatty old photo album full of people who'd most likely been dead even before the lad was born.

"It's me auntie's, ain't it?" he said at last.

"And which auntie would that be, Michael? Your auntie May that lives in Galway or your auntie Joan that married the teacher and won't have anything to do with your lot now?" Colm shook his head and allowed the creases on his ugly face to compose themselves into a look of deep sorrow at the boy's situation.

"Your mam told me you were going straight, Michael. She told me you'd even got a job. What was it Michael, couldn't earn enough honestly, you had to make a bit extra thieving from those who worked hard for the things they've got?"

"What, like that scrappy old thing? Look at it. It's filthy dirty and falling to bits." He lunged forward and gave the book a shove that sent it to the floor, the poor old covers flapping and flailing in flight and the back one breaking away as it hit the floor.

Colm crossed the room and bent to pick up the book, an anger burning in his chest that was quite out of proportion to the boy's action.

"It's people's lives you're wrecking," he almost shouted at the boy. "People like the ones here in this book. Ordinary working folk that can't afford what your thieving costs them, never mind about thinking what it's costing you, lad."

"Like you care."

"Like I care!" Colm sighed and returned to his seat, placing the book once more upon the wooden table. "To be honest with you, lad, I don't know that I do care any more," he said more softly. "Three more days I have until I'm gone from here. Retired. Three more days and I'll be away from the likes of you and all the other little thieves and tow rags and scrotes and clowns, and shall I miss it? Shall I damn, so you see, lad, you're quite right when you say I don't care. I'm leaving the caring to someone else and I'll be on my way." He paused, not looking at the boy, and was silent for such a long time that the young constable standing by the door felt compelled to record the fact on tape. Colm's fingers traced the outline of the book, the worn covers with the frayed binding and the thick cardboard showing through where the cloth had worn away. There were words embossed and inked in black. "Family Album" they said, and inside the cover, neatly scribed in a rounded old-fashioned hand, the words, "For Sarah, who steals the dark."

COLM KNEW WHAT THEY were saying, even while they slapped his back and brought him drinks and fed him the sweet iced cake someone's wife had made for him. Even while they got him drunk—or near as dammit—Colm knew what they were saying about him.

"The old man's lost it."

"Retirement coming just about the right time. Just as well, he can go with a bit of dignity."

"He's been a good officer. Straight as they come, our Colm."

"Best he go now then, he's a dying breed!"

"Away with yer. Don't you be spreading them rumours again."

"You should have seen him with that kid, Mick Brady. Thought he were going to thump him. His face! God, you should have seen it, and all over some old book or other."

He knew what they were saying as he emptied his desk for the final time and carried the taped-up box away to the pub, and he felt . . . a part of him felt . . . that they were right, that the old man *was* losing it, while the rest of his heart shouted aloud that this was a new beginning and he no longer had a thing to prove.

"No," he said out loud, knowing that everyone else was too drunk and too loud to hear. "Never anything to prove."

COLM LIVED ALONE IN a big old place his mother had left to him. Once it had been a farm but the family had long since sold the land, and the stone house, sprawling and cold in winter, was all that now remained. He got up early on his first day of freedom and went downstairs in his dressing gown to make his tea instead of dressing straight the way, feeling that he ought to make some statement, however small, that his life was changed.

Waiting for the kettle to boil, he opened up the cardboard box, spilling the assortment of pens and pads and cards from well-wishers out onto the kitchen table, then reaching down for the thing hidden in the bottom.

Colm had only stolen twice in all his life. The first time had been chocolate and a comic when he was nine years old and his mother had lambasted his backside with a wooden spoon so well that he couldn't sit for days. The second had been yesterday and now he retrieved his prize, sliding from the evidence bag the dirty, board-covered book that almost fell apart between his hands but which felt like treasure.

COLM HAD NEVER KNOWN a day pass so slowly. Used to imposed routine, finding he had none of his own was a major shock and Colm knew, even from that first day, that he could not live long like this. He tended to his garden, a job usually reserved for weekends off, and scrubbed the kitchen table, a task his mother had carried out twice daily but which he could not remember doing for himself. And then feeling idle and unwanted rather than glorying in his freedom, he made more tea and sat beside the garden window to look once again through Sarah's book.

There were thirty pages and pictures on all of them. Most were posed studio shots, many of couples or families, and he guessed that three or four must have been for weddings. A man in a uniform he did not recognise, wearing cavalry boots and epaulettes, stared proudly from a picture, a cloth backdrop of forest behind him. The date on the picture was 1915. As he touched it, the photograph fell from the page, the four little dots of glue holding it there finally giving in to age. Curiously, Colm turned it over.

"Uncle George," he read. "1892 to 1915."

He turned it about once more, looking closely into the youthful, eager face of the man who stood so proudly in his uniform, and it struck Colm how often men felt the need to dress for death as though the garments of every day were not fine enough.

Carefully, he began to detach other pictures from the frames. Most were stuck only lightly and came away almost eagerly, falling into his hands. Many were blank behind as though the images were so well known to the owner that she needed no reminder of the who or when, but some were dated and given names, and from these Colm gained vague knowledge of George and Edward, Gracie and her sister Jo. Elizabeth on her wedding day—her husband, oddly, unnamed—and Sarah herself in a high-necked blouse, the throat decorated with a simple beaded pin and her hair piled high away from a broad forehead and decided eyebrows arching over intense dark eyes. Unlike so many of the other pictures, this was no studio shot. It was taken in the open air with a line of hills behind her, faded and distant. She was seated and her skirts were spread upon the grass and one tightly buttoned boot peeped from beneath them. Sarah's name was written on the back, Sarah Connelly, 1917, and also a brief line of description beneath.

"Beautiful day," the note said, in the same rounded hand that had written Sarah's name at the front of the book. "Beautiful day. March 1917, Glendalough. Wicklow."

Gently, Colm slipped the other pictures back into the album, careful to place them in the proper order, but the picture of Sarah he kept aside and that night when he slept he placed it on his bedside table propped against the light.

"I'm sorry to bother you, sir."

"Not sir anymore, Robbie, and it's just Colm now. You'd better come in."

The young man was out of uniform, just come off shift, and Colm knew why he was there.

He opened the drawer in the kitchen table and handed Robbie the evidence bag, the album safely back inside.

"I expect it was still on your desk," the young man said. "I mean, when you were packing stuff away ready to be gone. It was a bit mad that day." He smiled, a real affectionate smile, Colm was glad to see. "We thought that's what you'd done, just picked it up along with all your other things."

Colm nodded, relieved not to have had to make up a lie. The fact that the book had been bagged and tagged and left with the other evidence in care of the property master was not mentioned. He handed the album over and enquired as to the health of Robbie's new wife, delighted in the fact that they were expecting a child, and pretended sorrow that the young man did not have time to stay for tea or something a little stronger. The truth was, Colm was relieved when he had gone. He stood beside the door, watching the car maneuvre through the farm gate and back onto the lane. One day only but already the gulf was widening between himself and those he had called colleagues if not friends.

He closed the door and went upstairs as though needing to be certain of something. To be certain that he had not done wrong, that she would not reproach him for giving her family away so freely and keeping her there, but Sarah gazed at him from her place beside his bed and there was neither sadness nor reproach in the dark blue eyes—and he knew that they were blue—he saw only understanding and compassion in her smile.

LEAVING WAS EASY AND took little preparation. He had no one to say good-bye to and little to pack aside from a few clothes. He saw no reason to wait until the morning.

He drove north, to Wicklow, the hills when he reached them hidden by a curtain of fine grey rain that parted with the wind to give him only a fragile glimpse. Glendalough was on the farthest side and not easy to find on badly signed lanes and in a veil of rain. Finally, he pulled the car over into a farm gate and, covering himself with the car blanket he had ready in the back seat, he fell asleep and waited for the daylight.

"DID HE SAY ANYTHING, Colm, I mean, when you collected the album?"

Robbie shook his head. "Asked about Dierdre and the baby. I said to him like you told me to, that we thought he must have picked up the book by accident, like, when he packed to go."

"Good, good," Superintendent Philips nodded approvingly. "And he seemed fine aside from that?"

"Yes, sir. He seemed well enough."

"That's all right then. Best left at that." Philips frowned, "Funny, though, but when we interviewed the Brady boy again he asked about the book. Said he didn't know why he'd taken it, rambling on about some woman . . ." He shrugged, losing interest, his mind already onto other things.

COLM WOKE, STIFF AND cold, to a dawn that was more mist than daylight. His limbs were stiff and aching and he almost fell getting out of the car, stumbling about amongst the tussocks of grass and the ruts left from his tyres until his feet came back to life and the feeling in his legs was not just the pain of returning blood.

Leaving his car he walked farther up the lane, the road climbing steeply and bending about the hill until it reached the summit after a quarter mile.

The mist was thick about him, deadening his footsteps and filling his ears with the sound of water, the air so thick with it that it seemed to drip into the silence and run constantly beneath his feet. His own breath returned to him, sodden and chilled against his face, and in time he gave up, returned to his car, and drove back along the lane in search of breakfast and a place to get warm.

ROBBIE WAS NOT QUITE sure what had piqued his curiosity, but the nagging at the back of his mind had grown throughout the day and drew him to the photograph album. It was back in the evidence store, wedged between two seized video players and a box filled with car radios. He turned the pages slowly, examining the faces of those whom the camera had caught in time, exposed for the examination of future generations. A woman, the boy Michael had said. Something about a woman. There were women aplenty in the album, but Robbie had the impression he had meant a woman alone and there were none like that in the little book. All had accompaniments, a sister, a husband, a clutch of children clinging to their skirts. An old couple pictured with a single girl was the clearest he could get to a lone woman and Robbie knew instinctively that this was not the image he sought.

And there was another thing, something he was certain had changed since the album had been in Colm's possession. Every image had been eased free of its page then placed back carefully between the leaves. Robbie would have been willing to swear that when he had first seen the album on the table in the interview room the pictures had been glued down, not floating free and ready to fall from the book if you tilted it too far.

Slowly and carefully he placed each one back in its space, pausing only to read the brief inscriptions on the back identifying Uncle George or Great Aunt Rose, and when he had finished, he was sure. One image was missing, not a large picture if you went by the glue marks on the page, but one, Robbie was sure, which had been the picture of the woman.

Puzzled, he put the album carefully away and replaced it in the evidence store.

COLM HAD WAITED FOR the sun to rise fully enough to burn away the mist. He had found a place for breakfast, sitting outside until the cafe opened and ignoring the curious looks from its proprietors, Colm being neither local nor tourist and therefore something of a novelty. As he paid his bill he took Sarah's photograph from his pocket and showed it to the woman behind the counter.

"I'm looking for family," he explained. "This woman and her family . . ."

He stopped, the quizzical expression on the woman's face bringing him to his senses.

"Ay, well, like I said," he blustered, "old family . . ."

He left, feeling like a fool. The woman's gaze burning at his back. Showing a photograph as old as this to someone and expecting her to say, *Oh, yes, she lives in Dunscomb Street just down the way,* was patently ridiculous. He'd be the talk of the village by mid-morning, no doubt. Colm made a note to himself not to pass back that way.

HE RETURNED TO WHERE he had parked the night before and again walked up the hill, the narrow road becoming less than a farm track as it rounded the bend to overlook the valley. This time there was no mist and the valley of Glendalough opened out below him. Weak autumn sunshine sparkled on the surface of the two lakes from which it took its name and, at the farthest end of the steep-sided valley, stood the round tower and small squat church that he recalled they named Saint Kevin's kitchen after the saint who had made his home there.

The road to Wicklow and Kildare curved at the valley's closer end, the road back to Colm's world. Colm turned his gaze away and began to scramble down.

ROBBIE LOOKED CURIOUSLY AT the balding, round-faced man who had come into the front office enquiring for his property.

"Your belongings have been laid out in the interview room, sir, but I don't know if I can release them to you yet; you'll have to have words with the sergeant."

He led Mr. Williams through to the interview room and stood by while the man inspected his video recorder and his little portable television and the bits and pieces of cheap jewellery that the boy Michael Brady had said came from the same house.

The VCR had been postcoded and the television had a sticky label fixed to its underside with its owner's address, something Michael Brady had not thought to look for. He would never make even a good thief, thought Robbie, and he seemed to have little talent for anything else.

"Anything wrong, Mr. Williams?" Robbie asked.

"No, no." The man paused awkwardly, something clearly on his mind. "There was a little book along with the things I had taken," he said at last. "A book of pictures, photos, you know. A family thing. I wondered . . ."

"Ah, yes, the family album."

"Oh? So you have it here?"

"We have an album, yes, that might be yours. Perhaps you could describe it to me, just to be sure?"

Williams hesitated, "It's, well, it's old, very old, and with creamy covers. Rather worn and dirty like. And there's a picture inside I'm fond of. A woman in a high-necked blouse. Her name was Sarah, I believe. The book was hers."

"She was a relative of yours was she, this Sarah?"

Mr. Williams shuffled his feet uncomfortably.

"I suppose she must have been," he said. "She was a pretty woman
. . ." He caught sight of Robbie's frown. "Is something wrong, officer?"

Robbie recovered himself. That woman again. "I'll get it for you to
look at, sir," he said, "if you could just hang on here for a minute or two?"

Mr. Williams nodded eagerly. Too eagerly perhaps, and on impulse
Robbie turned back, his hand on the handle of the door. "Mr. Williams,
this isn't a family album, is it? Not from your family? Is there maybe
something you'd be telling me?"

"Oh God, how did you know?" The man crumpled and sat down
in the nearest chair, his plump face flushed to the roots of his balding
head and then ran pale with such speed that Robbie thought that he
was going to faint.

"Are you all right, sir? That's right, you sit down there." He left
the door and came back across the room, perching himself on the
table edge. The truth was, Robbie had known nothing until that
moment. Some blend of instinct and pure mischief had led him to the
question, no more than that, but now he was intrigued. "Tell me,
Mr. Williams," he invited. "Maybe I can get you a cup of tea? And the
two of us can have a little chat."

ROBBIE PUSHED OPEN THE door of the dusty little shop and went inside,
avoiding the stacks of books piled on the windowsill and balanced
precariously on the floor beside it.

Shelves stood floor to ceiling around the musty little room, a converted parlour before the big windows had been fitted and the shop
sign hung outside.

Other shelves were crammed so close there was scarcely space for
Robbie to slide between as he made his way to the rear of the shop and
rang the counter bell. "Yes, can I help you?"

The man was younger than Robbie had expected.

"Are you the owner, sir?"

"That's my father, he's not here today." He examined Robbie
thoughtfully, taking in the uniform, his eye falling upon the package
tucked under Robbie's arm.

"The album!" he said. He sounded startled. "Where on earth did you find that old thing? My dad's been going mad about it these past months."

"It came from here, then?"

"Well, yes, we got it from a house clearance, somewhere out near Wicklow."

"So it's not a family thing?"

"No, but from the fuss Dad made when it was gone, you'd think it had been. He hardly spoke to me for weeks afterward, but I mean, how was I to know he wanted to keep that old thing. I just put it out in the bargain box with all the other cheap books." Robbie nodded. That fitted well with what Mr. Williams had told him.

"Did you look at the pictures inside?" he asked.

The shopkeeper shook his head. "We'd that lot arrive and three other house clearance batches all within the one weekend. My dad had to go away for a day or two and I did what I always do, look through for the odd first edition, shelve anything that seems worth the trouble of pricing, and shove the others in the box. To be truthful, I don't know why he bothers with that stuff; most times it costs us as much in diesel to collect as we'll ever make, but he won't be told."

Robbie lay the evidence bag on the counter and withdrew the album. At first glance it did indeed look like a tatty piece of rubbish, but, had he been in this man's place, Robbie knew that he would have at least looked inside and have been fascinated by the old-fashioned pictures. He found it hard to understand such lack of curiosity; though, to be fair, he supposed working in a shop as packed to the gills as this, with what to even Robbie's untrained eye was clearly unremarkable, it might become a little difficult to maintain enthusiasm.

"You have records, I suppose, of where this stuff comes from."

"Of course we do, though all they'll say is the address and how many boxes we took."

"That should do," Robbie told him. "That should do very well." He paused, then asked, "Did your father say why he liked this old book so much?"

The other man laughed. "Quite right he did, something about a woman's picture and how he wanted to frame it. He gets these odd notions from time to time." He leaned across the counter toward Robbie. "Privately, you know, I don't think he'd sell any of this stuff

unless he'd been forced. He'd keep the lot and just keep adding to it."
He frowned. "I thought it was funny though, you know. As I say, the
book was in the bargain box. Ten pence a shot we charge for that stuff.
Ten pence and some bugger still had to go and steal it."

COLM HAD REACHED THE valley floor. Breathless and hot despite the
chill of the day, he stood on the banks of the lower lake and gazed
across its ruffled surface feeling more than a little foolish and wondering what he should do.

He had hoped for revelation, for a wonderful thing about to happen that would help him to make sense of his newfound freedom.
That would help him to make sense of these feelings that he had for a
woman he had never known.

He tried to rationalise his actions, this wild-goose chase in search
of the location in a photograph. He told himself that it was the
inscription in the front of the book that had so drawn him, that it
reminded him of things long past and it was nostalgia that had drawn
him here, not the overfull, overblown feelings for some woman he had
never even seen.

"For Sarah," he said out loud. "Sarah who steals the dark." It came
close to something his mother was fond of saying in those days when
there'd been just the two of them trying to run the old farm alone.

"To let the daylight in," his mother had told him, "sometimes you
just have to steal the dark." It was like a proverb to her, words of wisdom to be said when life was at its worst and the debts were piling at
their door. Finally, they had been forced to sell the land and they were
left only with the garden to tend, all that was left of the rich black
earth that his mother had grieved for all the remainder of her days.

"For Sarah," he said again. "Who steals the dark." He stared hard
into the depths of the peaty waters, his eyes filling with tears.

COLM'S HOUSE LOOKED EMPTY and deserted even as Robbie turned into the lane. Colm's old red car was absent from the drive and when he tried the door it was locked up tight. Robbie could not explain the feelings of dread that gripped him when he realised that the man was gone.

He walked down the road to the nearest farm a quarter mile away and enquired after their neighbour, but they had nothing to tell. They saw Colm little enough at any time, and for them not to see him now was nothing to be wondered at. But they had heard a car go by in the early hours, last morning or the one before, it was hard to say, and noticed only because the world was so quiet in the hours before the dawn.

Robbie fetched his car and went back to work, telling himself that he was not Colm's keeper and the chances were he had gone out only to shop or visit friends, until he remembered that Colm never mentioned friends. That Colm never mentioned anyone or anything outside of work and duty and that hours went by, unbooked and unnoticed when Colm would work a case deep into the night rather than go home.

Robbie let his anxiety ride through the afternoon until he could stand no more of it.

"I may be foolish, sir," he told his superintendent, "but I can't get out of my mind that something's happened to him."

"And you think he'd be grateful to you if you go looking for him and the man most likely just taking a holiday."

"I'll risk that. I'd rather he told me to get lost and mind my own than go on being bothered by this feeling."

Superintendent Philips frowned at him disapprovingly. "I always deplored too much imagination in the young," he said. "And in this profession, lad, it can lead to nothing but grief. But go your way, see if any of our lot spot him on his travels. Tell them that you found a window insecure or some such when you went out to Colm's farm."

Robbie thanked him. "I will, sir," he said gratefully, wondering just why he should feel so relieved when it was clear that his superior officer thought he was making an idiot of himself and that, surely, could do his career not one bit of good.

"THE LAKE IS CALLED LOCH PEIST, you know. It means the lake of the water monster. I used to think he must lie very still in the peat and mud waiting for the little boats to float by."

"You still think that?" He dared hardly breathe, watching her reflection in the tea-coloured water. Afraid to turn, just knowing if he did that she would disappear.

"I'd like to think it, but my auntie reckons he moved out long ago when the tourists came and he got tired of being pointed at and of having grown men fishing for him all the summer."

"And where did he go to? Did she tell you that?"

"Oh, along the hill a little way. To the Loch na h'Onchon I've no doubt. It would be more peaceful there."

"And *Onchon* does mean monster," Colm agreed with her. "It would be a good place for a water dragon to be at home."

He took a deep, quavering breath and held it in, still afraid to turn, like Orpheus in the story fearing to lose Euridice. But he could not bear to be so close, so close that he could hear the rustle of her dress when she moved, catch the lavender hint of her perfume, and not be able to look her in the face.

"Sarah," he whispered softly, and he slowly twisted his head around and she stood still behind him, holding out her hand.

THEY HAD FOUND COLM'S car. A full day and night had passed since Robbie had spoken of his anxiety and another day would have gone by if the farmer had not complained of a car blocking the gate to his top field. They had moved the car, Robbie was told, pushing it farther up onto the grass verge, and the farmer said that he thought he had seen a man walk from it up the hill and then disappear over the crest as if he had gone down on the other side.

Robbie followed, walking more swiftly than Colm had done, breasting the hill and then almost running down the vast and variable slope to the wide valley below.

It had been too much to hope that he would see Colm there. The valley was peopled only by sheep and three skittish horses that bolted at the suddenness of his descent and a few walkers, distant, colourful figures set against the green. But of Colm there was no sign but for boot marks in the mud beside the lake, half obscured by the impressions of sheep pads and the hooves of horses. Desperately, Robbie stared about him, willing the man to appear; but there was no one close, no Colm, no hunched-shouldered man in tweeds looking as though life bore down on him, only, as Robbie looked, a woman standing on the far-side shore, her long skirt blowing in the brisk wind and a white blouse fastened high against her throat.

COLM HAD DRIFTED IN deep waters, the coldness closing above his head and the darkness surrounding him; but aside from the cold he felt no discomfort and experienced no regrets. Sarah's hand was clasped tightly in his own and he had never felt so much at peace or more beloved.

THE DOCTOR CAME THROUGH the double glass doors to the waiting room and approached Robbie.

"Your friend was lucky," he said quietly. "He was half dead when the fishermen pulled him from the lake. Just as well, one of them knew some first aid, and they had the good sense to wrap him warm and bundle him into their car. Then they brought him here. He's still shocked, but he's taken no great harm." The doctor hesitated before he asked. "He says he's just retired?"

Robbie nodded. "Just a few days ago."

"And he's maybe been depressed? It's hard to cope sometimes when the job's been your life."

"He'll be all right," Robbie said defensively. "Anyone can fall into a bloody lake."

"He didn't fall . . ." the doctor began, then paused, shaking his head beneath Robbie's glare. "Yes, well, we can talk about this later on. Now, I'm sure you just want to see your friend."

Robbie nodded. "And I'd like a word with the men that pulled him out. Thank them."

"They're tourists," the doctor said, "but I've got their details ready for you. It's a funny thing, though, they said there was another helping them. A woman in a long black skirt and white blouse that waded in and grabbed your man even before they realized what was going on. She held onto him until they reached her and then they pulled the two of them into their boat and rowed ashore. She must have been local, though, because the men said when they looked up from seeing to your friend she'd taken off somewhere and neither saw the way she went."

ROBBIE SAT QUIETLY AT Colm's bedside waiting for him to open his eyes. Colm looked more peaceful and rested than Robbie could ever remember seeing him. He sat watching the older man's face, seeing the fleeting expressions pass across it like a man who dreams and the dreams are pleasant ones, until at last Colm opened his eyes.

"You found her then?" Robbie asked him softly.

"I found her," Colm answered him. "She reached out her hand for me and I have never felt so warm nor so safe before in all my life. It's a good feeling, Robbie, for a man to know that he is loved."

Robbie nodded but Colm didn't see him, he had closed his eyes again and gone back to dreaming. Dreaming of Sarah who had stolen the dark and let the daylight stream, warm and golden, back into his heart.

A Book of Kells

(A John Francis Cuddy Story)

Jeremiah Healy

T HE IRISH-AMERICAN HERITAGE CENTER was located in a red-brick building three blocks off East Broadway in South Boston. Growing up in the neighborhood, I remembered the structure as a public elementary school, but when the city fell on hard times in the seventies, the mayor and council sold a number of municipal properties to keep real-estate taxes from rocketing skyward. As I parked my old Honda at the curb, I got the impression that the Center was doing a lot better by the building than the school department ever had.

The main entrance consisted of three separate doors, the one to the left having a sign in gold calligraphy, reading TRY THIS ONE FIRST, which I thought was a nice touch. Inside the lobby area, the same ornate lettering adorned the walls, including a mural with the homily: MAY YOUR TROUBLES BE LESS/YOUR BLESSINGS BE MORE/AND NOTHING BUT HAPPINESS/COME THROUGH YOUR DOOR.

On my right was an office complex, probably where the principal used to hold court. A woman sitting behind a reception counter rose when she saw me.

"John Cuddy," I said, "here to see Hugh McGlachlin."

"Oh, yes." Her expression shifted from concerned to relieved. "Please come in."

A buzzer sounded. She opened the door nearest her counter and showed me through a second inner door. "Hugh, Mr. Cuddy," she said.

A voice with just a lick of the brogue said, "Thank you, Grace. And hold any calls, if you would, please."

Grace nodded and closed the inner door behind me.

The man rising from the other side of the carved teak desk was about five-nine and slight of build, wearing a long-sleeved dress shirt and a tie. His hair was gray and short, combed a little forward like a Roman emperor's. Despite the gray hair, his face was unlined around the blue eyes, and his smile shone brightly enough for a toothpaste commercial.

A woman occupied one of the chairs in front of McGlachlin's desk, but instead of standing as well, she turned toward me while twisting a lace handkerchief in her lap. I pegged her as middle forties, with florid skin and a rat's nest of red hair. She wore the drab, baggy clothes of someone catching up on her housework, a canvas tote bag that had seen better days at her feet.

The man came around his desk and extended his right hand. "Hugh McGlachlin, executive director of the Center here. Thanks so much for coming so quickly."

I shook hands with him, and McGlachlin turned to the seated woman. "This is Mrs. Nora Clooney."

She swallowed and shook hands with me as well, hers trembling in mine.

"Well," said McGlachlin, tapping the back of the other chair in front of his desk, "I'm not sure of the protocol, but I think I'd be most comfortable using first names."

"Fine with me."

He and I sat down at the same time, and McGlachlin studied me briefly. "I didn't tell Michael O'Dell why we needed a private investigator," he said.

O'Dell was a lawyer in Back Bay who'd fed me a lot of cases over the years. "Probably why he didn't tell me."

The toothpaste smile again. "Michael is a member of our advisory board. And he assured me you were the soul of discretion and someone to be trusted."

"I'll be sure to thank him."

McGlachlin leaned back in his chair. "I think you may be just the man for the job, John."

"Which is?"

He pursed his lips. "How much do you know about the Heritage Center?"

"Only what I've seen so far this morning."

Hugh McGlachlin rose again, picking up a manila envelope from the corner of his desk. "In that event, I think a brief tour might prove instructive. Nora?"

Clooney preceded us out the inner door.

"We incorporated as a nonprofit institution in '75," said McGlachlin, "and moved into this building four years later. I don't mind telling you, John, the city left it quite the mess." He made a sweeping gesture with the envelope. "But thanks to some Irish-American tradesmen generously donating their time and talents, we've been able to renovate the interior a bit at a time and rejuvenate the community we serve."

I sensed that the operative word for me was *donating*.

The three of us were moving down a hallway festooned with the various crests of the thirty-two counties of Ireland, that signature gold calligraphy naming each. On the left, double doors opened onto a large and beautifully rendered country-house room, sporting an exposed-beam ceiling, slate floor, and massive fieldstone fireplace on the shorter wall. In the hearth was a cauldron suspended by metal bars over an unlit fire, an iron milk jug bigger than a beer keg to the side.

I said, "Hugh, what exactly is the Center's problem?"

McGlachlin just stopped, but Clooney seemed to freeze in her tracks. He looked up at the crests over our heads. "Would you know where your forebears hailed from, John?"

"County Kerry on my father's side, Cork on my mother's."

"Ah." McGlachlin pointed first to a shield with a white castle and gold harp. "Kerry . . ." and then to a crest with a galleon sailing between two red towers, "and Cork."

He took a step into the room. "In both places, John, they would have broken their backs hoisting jugs like that one onto a pony cart to carry their cows' milk to town." He fixed me with those blue eyes.

"'Tis a marvelous thing that we who emigrated are more fortunate, don't you think?"

"Hugh," I said, "until I know why you called Michael O'Dell—and probably why Clooney seems nervous as a wet cat—I won't be able to tell you whether I can help the Center for free."

McGlachlin grinned this time, but without showing any teeth, and I had the feeling that despite my being six inches taller and fifty pounds heavier, I'd hate to meet him in an alley. He said, "Yes, I do believe you're the man for our job. This way, please."

We took an elevator to the second floor. As I followed McGlachlin down the hallway, I tried to stay abreast of Clooney. No matter how I adjusted my stride, though, she always stayed a step behind me.

McGlachlin stopped again, this time outside a large classroom where the chairs and tables were shoved against the walls. Perhaps a dozen girls and young women were moving in a circle, their hands joined but held high. "We have step-dancing classes in here," he said, "though we also host Lithuanian folk dancing for our neighbors of that extraction. The Nimble Thimbles teach needlework over there, and every Wednesday we have instruction in Gaelic."

I nodded.

Another toothy smile. "All right, then. The next floor is the one that concerns us most at the moment."

"THIS IS OUR MUSEUM, John."

McGlachlin used a key to open a heavy security door in a corridor filled with construction odds and ends, plaster dust on every surface. The area at the end of the hallway was still just undefined space, only a few wall studs in place.

The security door opened into a large viewing room, glass-faced cases along two walls displaying china in all shapes and sizes, lots of pastel green "icing" on the edges of plates and pitchers.

"Recognize it?" asked McGlachlin.

My mother had a piece she prized. "Belleek."

"Very good. The finest of Irish porcelain." He waved a hand at the third wall. "And there's the loveliest collection of lace you may ever see."

I took in the white fabric spread on trays of green velvet. "You said downstairs that—"

"—this is the floor that concerns us most right now. Yes, indeed I did." McGlachlin's voice dropped to the subdued tone of a devout man entering his church. "Over here, John."

We went through a doorway into a smaller room with soft, recessed lighting. In the center was a freestanding case about two feet square. Its top, or cover, evidently had been glass, though it was hard to judge further because it was shattered into crumbly crystals lying fairly evenly on the otherwise empty green velvet.

I said, "You've had a theft."

McGlachlin looked my way as Clooney began twisting her hankie again. After glancing at her, he turned back to me. "John, you recognized the Belleek. Would you also know about *The Book of Kells?*"

"Something the Irish monks did back in the Middle Ages?"

"Close enough. During the eighth and ninth centuries, Celtic scribes painstakingly copied each passage of the four Gospels onto 'paper' made from the stomach lining of lambs. Every page is an artist's palette of flowing script and glorious colors, with the original book carefully guarded at Trinity College in Dublin. However, in 1974 some reproductions were permitted—they called them 'facsimiles.' Only five hundred copies. But they are works of art themselves, down to the wormholes in the pages."

I looked at the smashed case. "And you had one of those."

"The Center purchased its facsimile in 1990 for twenty thousand dollars."

I thought back to my time as a claims investigator. "You've notified your insurance carrier."

McGlachlin shook his head. "On the collector's market now, the price is ten times what we paid; but the money is largely irrelevant: Nobody who has a facsimile is willing to part with it."

"Still, the policy would pay—"

"It's not a check I want, John. It's the book itself. There'll never be any more facsimiles produced, at least not in our lifetime. The Center needs its copy back as a matter of"—another sweeping gesture with the manila envelope—"heritage."

I looked at him. "Let me save you some time. The Boston police have an excellent—"

"Not yet, John." McGlachlin seemed pained. "I'm rather hoping this can be resolved without resorting to our insurance company or the police." He opened the manila envelope and slid a single piece of paper from it. "This was on top of the shards there."

I stepped sideways so I could read it without touching it. In simple block lettering on white photocopy stock, the words were TAKEN, BUT NOT STOLEN, AND WILL BE RETURNED.

"Who found this?"

"I did, sir," said Clooney, the first words I'd heard her speak.

McGlachlin cleared his throat. "Nora volunteers her time to clean for us. Given all the plaster dust from the ongoing renovation, it's no small task."

I looked at her. "Where was this piece of paper when you first saw it?"

Clooney glanced at her boss. "It was just like Mr. McGlachlin told you. The note was lying atop all the broken glass." The brogue was woven through her voice much more than her boss's.

"And the glass hasn't been disturbed since?"

McGlachlin said, "I've kept the room locked since Nora came to me this morning with the news."

I let my eyes roam around before returning to Clooney. "Do you clean this room the same time every day?"

"First thing in the morning, sir. Eight o'clock. It wouldn't do for visitors not to be able to see the book for the plaster dust covering its blessed case."

"And nothing was wrong yesterday at eight?"

"No, sir." The lace hankie was getting wrung some more.

I glanced around again. "Other than the locked door, what kind of security do you have for this room?"

"None," said McGlachlin. "We've been spending every available penny on the renovations."

I stared at him. "But what about visitors wandering in?"

"Access to these museum rooms is restricted solely to those of us with a key to that door. As anyone can plainly see, there's been no attempt to jimmy it or the windows, even assuming the bastard—

sorry, Nora—thought to bring a ladder with him to lean against the outside wall."

I thought about it. "I can see why you haven't gone to the police."

McGlachlin sighed. "Exactly so. This had to be—is it still called 'an inside job'?"

I turned back to Clooney. "So the incident must have occurred sometime between 8:00 A.M. or so yesterday—"

"More like nine, sir, the time I finished in here—"

"To eight this morning?"

"Yes, sir."

I looked at McGlachlin. "All right, how many people have keys to that door?"

"I do, as executive director. And Nora, for her cleaning and turn-ing."

"Turning?"

She said, "Every day, sir, I go up to the book and turn a page."

McGlachlin pointed to the windows. "So the sun fades the ink only a tiny bit, and more or less evenly."

I looked at the shattered glass. "How did you open it?"

They both stared at me.

"The glass cover, or top. How did you open it to turn the pages?"

"Oh," said Clooney, and moved to a wall panel. She threw a switch, and the remaining structure of the glass top clicked upward.

McGlachlin went to demonstrate. "You can then lift this—"

"Don't touch it," I said. "Fingerprints."

"Ah, yes. Of course."

I gestured toward the paper he still held in his hand. "And please don't let anybody else touch that. As it is, the police will need elimi-nation prints from you, and—"

"Harking back to what I said earlier, John, we hope we won't be needing the police, thanks to you."

I waited before asking, "Who else has keys to the security door?"

McGlachlin raised a finger. "The chairman of our advisory board, Conor Donnelly. He's a professor of Irish studies." He named the col-lege. Another finger went up. "Conor's brother, Denis, was a generous contributor to the Center, so he received a key as well."

"Denis Donnelly, the venture capitalist?"

"The very one."

"The man kicks in enough, he gets his own key?"

McGlachlin cleared his throat again. "Given the amount of Denis's contribution, John, that would be an awkward request to deny."

"Anybody else?"

"Only Sean Kilpatrick. The carpenter donating his time to do our work down the hall."

I looked around one last time. "These museum rooms look pretty well completed. Why would Kilpatrick need access to them?"

"In the event anything went wrong," he said. "But, John, Sean's somebody who's completely trustworthy."

"Hugh, at least one somebody with a key obviously isn't."

WE WERE BACK IN the executive director's office, the door closed. "Mr. McGlachlin, will you or Mr. Cuddy be needing me anymore today?"

McGlachlin glanced at me, and I shook my head. "Go home, then, Nora," he said. "And tell Bill I'll be by to visit after work."

After Clooney picked up her tote bag and left us, I said, "Bill's her husband?"

"Just so. And a fine, generous man to boot, but suffering from the cancer. You know how that can be."

Though I figured McGlachlin meant his comment rhetorically, I still pictured my wife, Beth, asleep in her hillside less than a mile away. "I do."

He shook his head sadly. "They met each other here at one of the Center's first socials. But then, we've sparked a lot of unions from our activities."

"Who else besides Nora—and you—actually knew how the cover over your *Book of Kells* opened?"

McGlachlin grew wary. "And what difference would that make, John? The case was smashed."

"That 'ransom' note—it was lying on top of the broken glass. Being a single sheet of paper, it's pretty light."

More wary now. "Agreed, but—"

"—so the note wouldn't have disturbed the broken glass under it very much, if at all."

McGlachlin seemed to work it through.

To save time, I said, "And since the glass shards were spread almost evenly . . ."

The executive director closed his eyes. ". . . the book was probably taken out of the case before the cover was smashed."

"Somebody wanted you to think that the glass had to be broken in order to take the book. So my question still stands: Who else knew about the cover mechanism?"

McGlachlin fixed me with his blue eyes. "John, I just don't know. But I do know this. Nora wouldn't know what to do with our book. And she's honest as the day is long."

I filed that with his endorsement of the carpenter, Sean Kilpatrick. "You didn't mention if Grace, your receptionist, also had a key."

"She does not. But given where Grace sits, she's in a position to see who comes and goes."

"Assuming everyone comes through the main doors."

"The other outside doors are alarmed, John. And besides, Grace tells me she saw all three of our key holders walk by her yesterday."

"Both in and out?"

"No, but each of them had either a knapsack or briefcase or tool-box big enough to hold the book."

"You have any suggestions on where I should start?"

"More a question on *how* you should start." McGlachlin paused. "So far, only Nora, Grace, and you know about what's happened."

"And given the tenor of that ransom note, you're hoping the book will be back by the time anyone else has to know?"

"On the button, John. There's an advisory board meeting here next week—five days hence, to be exact. The members have a tradition of reading a passage from the book—as a benediction, you might say."

"Meaning the book is taken from the case?"

"No. No, we all troop up to the room, and thanks to Nora's turning the page each morning, there're always different passages to choose from."

"Anything else about this situation you haven't told me?"

"One of the reasons I'm trying to resolve things quickly." McGlachlin pursed his lips. "You see, Conor—our board chairman—was asked by his brother, Denis, a few months ago to loan out the book for a party. Denis was giving a la-di-da affair at his home, and he wanted to have our facsimile on display for his guests."

"And what did Conor say?"

"That he'd have to put it to the Center's advisory board, which he did. And they voted not to allow the book to leave its case."

"How did Denis take that?"

"Not well. He stomped in here the next day, gave me holy hell. He thought I could perhaps permit him to borrow the book anyway."

"For a small . . . stipend?"

He nodded. "I told him I couldn't do that." McGlachlin winced. "You could have heard him yelling all over the building."

"Denis believed he should have been accommodated because of that large contribution you mentioned?"

"More specific than that, I'm afraid. You see, John, 'twas Denis's money that let our Center buy the book in the first place."

After getting McGlachlin's home number—"Call, John, any time of the day or night"—I drove from the Center to another repository of memories. Irish-American also, but different. And more personal.

Leaving the Honda on the wide path, I walked through the garden of stones until I found hers. The words ELIZABETH MARY DEVLIN CUDDY never changed, but they became a little fainter, the freeze/thaw of Boston winters taking their toll even on polished granite.

"I've been asked to find a book, Beth."

A book?

I explained the problem to her.

After a pause, she said, *I remember seeing an illuminated page from it, in an art-history text, I think.*

"That would make sense."

An incredible collector's item.

As I nodded at her comment, my eye caught the plodding movement of a lobster boat down in the harbor, chugging along in the light chop of a northeast wind that smelled of rain to come. Its skipper seemed intent on collecting his pots before the storm began to . . .

John?

I came back to her stone. "Sorry?"

How are you going to approach these three men without tipping them to who you are and what you're doing?

"It took a while, but coming here has shown me the way."

I fooled myself into thinking I could hear the confusion in Beth's next, unspoken question.

PICTURE THE KIND OF campus that would bring tears of joy to a high-school guidance counselor. The classroom and dormitory buildings were a Gothic design like the lower, auxiliary structures tacked onto cathedrals—imposing mullioned windows, ivy winding from the ground nearly to the rooflines.

After stopping three students with enough earrings piercing them to fill a jewelry box, I was directed by the last to a sallow, four-story affair. Inside, red arrows with small signs beneath them directed me to the second floor, and a receptionist swamped by students picking up exams waved me toward the office on her immediate right. The stenciling on the door reminded me of my own office's pebbled glass, but instead of JOHN FRANCIS CUDDY, CONFIDENTIAL INVESTIGATIONS in black, this one read CONOR DONNELLY, IRISH STUDIES in green.

I knocked and received a "Come," repeated three times like an oft-intoned litany.

The door opened into a large office with a high ceiling and two banks of fluorescent lights suspended over the bookshelved wall. The opposite wall had five of the multipaned windows throwing as much sunshine as the day was offering onto the head and shoulders of a standing man.

Conor Donnelly scribbled in a loose-leaf notebook lying on one of those bread-box lecterns you can lift onto a table to make a podium. His shoulders were rounded under a V-neck sweater over a flannel shirt. The brown hair was thinned enough that he had resorted to one of those low-part comb-overs, the scalp showing through between the strands that were left. His bushy eyebrows made up a little for the hairline, though. As he stepped toward me, Donnelly had to shuffle around stacks of papers on the floor.

His gray eyes blinked. "You're not a student." Brooklyn instead of brogue in his voice.

"No, but I'm hoping you're Conor Donnelly."

"A fair assumption, given where you've found me." Donnelly returned to his notebook. "But these are office hours for the students, so I can't spare you much time, Mr. . . ."

"Francis, John Francis," I said, which amounted to only one-third of a lie. "I'd like to speak with you about *The Book of Kells*."

That seemed to catch Donnelly's interest, because he motioned me toward a captain's chair across from his desk, though he stayed at the lectern. "We can speak about it, but you're a good three thousand miles from the original."

"All right, *A Book of Kells*, then. I represent a collector who'd very much like to own one of those limited-edition facsimiles, and I understand you have access to such."

Donnelly cocked his head. "In a functional sense, yes. However, I'm afraid ours at the Heritage Center is not for sale."

"No matter the money involved?"

Now Donnelly frowned. "Well, as chair of the advisory board, I'd be honor-bound to entertain any serious offer—subject, of course, to board approval."

"Professor, I'm aware that the going rate for a reproduction is tenfold what the Center paid, and my client is prepared to substantially sweeten even that inflated price. Provided, of course, that you can open that glass cover over the book so she can inspect the item."

No reaction to my "cover-opening" comment, which told me Donnelly already knew of the mechanism. "Well, Mr. Francis, you're welcome to submit your offer in writing, but I must inform you, I doubt the board will approve it. We take great pride in our copy of the book, and frankly, I don't know that any owner not desperate for money would part with one of the facsimiles."

I decided to explore what might be a gambit from Donnelly. "Would it have to be the technical owner who was desperate for money?"

He looked confused. "I don't follow you."

Leaning forward in the captain's chair and lowering my voice, I said, "Or would a person even have to be desperate for money just to be interested in having himself a little—no, a lot—more of it?"

"Ah," said Donnelly, "the light dawns. A bribe, eh?"

I shrugged.

Conor Donnelly smiled and returned again to his notebook. "Mr. Francis, get the hell out of my office before I call campus security and have you thrown out."

HIS BROTHER'S RECEPTIONIST, IN a lovely office suite overlooking Faneuil Hall, told me politely, if firmly, that Denis Donnelly would not be in that day. Both of Boston's daily newspapers had run profiles on him, though, and in each story the venture capitalist's obsession with his home in Weston Hills shone through. It didn't take long to find the place—read *estate*—and once I gave the hard-eyed man at the driveway's security gate two-thirds of my name and mentioned *The Book of Kells*, I was escorted by a younger hard-eyed guard up the drive and into a mansion on a par with the gold-domed statehouse on Beacon Hill.

The second guard watched me admire—without touching—a dozen paintings, sculptures, and vases in the parlorlike anteroom before a pair of gilded doors opened and a man I recognized from his newspaper photos came out from a spectacular atrium to greet me.

The financier was a glossy version of his brother the professor. A hair weave of some kind made this Donnelly look as if a lush bush had been planted in the middle of his head and was spreading symmetrically outward. He'd colored his eyebrows to match the new do, and his gray eyes had that jump in them I associate with race-car drivers and serial killers. He wore a silk shirt over his rounded shoulders. A pair of painfully casual, stonewashed jeans ended an inch above some loafers, no benefit of socks.

After we shook hands, Donnelly glanced at his security man. "I'll be fine with Mr. Francis, Rick," he said, his brother's Brooklyn accent on his words, too. "But advise Curt no more visitors until I'm done here."

Rick nodded, gave me a look that said, *Don't make me come back for you*, and left us.

Donnelly suggested the Queen Anne love seat might hold me, while he sank into a leather, brass-studded smoking chair. "So, Mr. Francis, you mentioned to Curt *A Book of Kells*."

"Actually, *The Book of Kells*, but I'm sure we mean the same thing."

A look of frank appraisal. "You want to buy a facsimile, or sell one?"

"Buy, as intermediary for a client of mine."

No change of expression. "I'm in and out of the art market quite a bit. I don't recall anyone with judgment I respect ever mentioning your name."

"It's an easy one to forget."

A grin that you couldn't exactly call a smile. "You, my friend, are trying to scam me. Why?"

"No scam. My client wants one of the reproductions, and I understand you have a brother with—shall we say—sway over one of them."

"Hah!" said Donnelly, though it came out more as a bray. "I haven't so much as spit in Conor's face for a good two months now."

I tried to look disappointed. "Why?"

Donnelly lazed back in his chair. "I'm guessing you already know. I'm guessing also that you're playing me for some reason I can't figure. But I also can't see how this bit of information can hurt me. Come along."

I followed him into the atrium room, even on a dark day spectacularly lit by a rotunda skylight. I couldn't describe the furnishings if I had an hour to write about them. Except for one piece. It rested on a pedestal in a corner, shielded from potential sunlight by a glass cover that was smoke-colored on top but crystal clear on the sides. Donnelly moved directly toward it, beckoning me.

As I looked down at the large and open book, Donnelly said, "You've never seen one before, have you?"

"No," I said, my voice a little clogged as I took in, up close and personal, the filigreed detail on the capital letter at the top of the left-hand page, the depictions of people and animals—some real, some fantastical—occupying the margins and trailing after the end of paragraphs, even just the calligraphy in the text—some version of Latin, I thought.

"My brother thinks I wanted to borrow his Center's copy just to show it off for a party here. And I did." Donnelly's voice wavered. "But once I got a look at it, even in that pop-top candy case in their museum room, something—a kind of tribal memory, maybe—kicked in. What Conor seemed to forget is that I could have had the Center's own copy by just buying it for myself ten years ago. And once he and his snotty board turned me down on the party idea, I went out last month and quietly—bought another one."

I tore my eyes away from the pages in front of me. "For how many times the twenty thousand you shelled out for the first?"

Donnelly moved over to twin columns extruding from his wall. He pushed a button, and I looked back at the book pedestal, expecting its glass case to open the way the one at the Center had. It was maybe five seconds before the button's purpose hit me.

I heard a noise behind my back and wheeled around. The two hard-eyed security guys were standing inside the double doors of the atrium, arms folded in front of their chests. Looking a little more critically now at each, I didn't see any evident weapons.

I said to Donnelly, "That business of 'no other visitors' was code for 'hang close,' right?"

A nod with the bad grin. "And now, since you've obviously wasted my time on some sort of false pretenses, I think I'll enjoy watching Curt and Rick bounce you around a bit."

I tilted my head toward the door, my eyes still on Donnelly. "Just the two of them?"

The venture capitalist's eyes went neon. "Oh, I might jump in at the appropriate time."

I turned to Rick and Curt. "Denis, you're one man short."

Rick, the younger one, stepped up to the plate first. He extended both his hands to push on my chest, just like a demonstration of unarmed defense back in the sawdust pit when I was an MP lieutenant. I danced to Rick's lead for two steps, then reversed my feet and sent him over with a hip throw. When he landed on the floor, the sound of his lungs purging air was a lot easier on the ears than the gagging and dry-heaving that followed.

Curt was on me before I could turn back, clamping a choke hold across my throat with one of his forearms. I smashed my left heel down hard on his left instep and he cried out, lifting the foot. I hammered

back with my left elbow and found his rib cage, feeling some of his car-
tilage separating as I drove into it.

Curt slid off me and cradled his left side with both hands, eyes
squinched shut like a little kid who really doesn't want to cry but
doesn't see how to avoid it. When I looked at Rick, he was still trying to give himself mouth-to-mouth resuscitation.

Denis Donnelly said, "So much as touch me, and I'll sue you and
your client for every cent you've got."

I walked up to him, Donnelly apparently forgetting that those
twin columns behind him significantly limited his mobility. He tried
to kick me in the groin, but I caught his ankle in my right hand, then
bent upward until he began to moan.

"Denis, I lift six more inches and you lose at least a hamstring,
maybe an achilles tendon as well. We communicating?"

A strangled "Yes."

"Okay. I was never here."

"Right, right."

"And I'm never going to have to worry about Rick or Curt or any
of their successors trying to find me, am I?"

"No. No, of course not."

I left him then, but not before taking a last look at Denis Donnelly's
Book of Kells. I'd found one facsimile, but Donnelly's arrogance seemed
more consistent with his trumping story of buying a facsimile for himself than with stealing the copy he had in essence donated to the
Center. Which left me just one last key holder to the museum rooms.

It was nearly dark by the time Sean Kilpatrick's carpentry truck
pulled into the driveway across the street from where I was sitting behind
the wheel of the Honda. When the pickup approached the garage of the
modest ranch, security floods came on, bathing the front yard in a
yellow glow. Thanks to the lights, I could see that his truck had a
primered front fender and the tailgate was held in place by bungee cords.

As Kilpatrick got out of his vehicle, I got out of mine and began
crossing over to him. At the sound of my footsteps, he straightened up
and turned to me.

Kilpatrick stood about six feet, with broad shoulders and curly
black hair. He was wearing a sweatshirt with the sleeves cut off at the
armpits over jeans and work boots. By the time I reached the foot of
his driveway, his right hand had a claw hammer in it.

I stopped short of his rear bumper. "Mr. Kilpatrick?"

"And you'd be?" A brogue heavy enough that if you didn't listen for the rhythm of his cadence, you might not catch the words themselves.

"John Francis. I understand you're doing some work over at the Heritage Center."

I'd expected him to tense even more at the mention of the place, but instead he visibly relaxed, tossing the hammer toward the passenger's seat of his pickup before wiping his right palm on his thigh and approaching me to shake hands. Up close, he had a pleasant face around a genuine smile with crooked front teeth.

"Mr. Francis, pleased to make your acquaintance. What can I do for you?"

Letting go of his hand, I said, "A client of mine is a collector."

Confusion on the pleasant face. "Collector? You mean of bills, now?"

"No. Art, sculpture, rare . . . books."

"And what would that be to me?" Kilpatrick gestured toward the truck. "I'm just a carpenter."

"But a carpenter with access to the Heritage Center's museum."

"Yes." He actually started to pull out a key ring from his back pocket, the ring itself anchored to his belt by a clasp and coiled cord. "I've got—" Kilpatrick reined up short. "Wait a minute, now. What are you saying?"

"I'm saying there's a particularly valuable book under a glass case in one of those museum rooms, and a considerable commission to be earned by the person who obtains it for us."

Kilpatrick lost the crooked smile, the face now anything but pleasant. "You're wanting me to steal *The Book of Kells?*"

"Let's not say 'steal.' Let's just say you flip open the thing's glass cover before knocking off one night, and you slip the book itself into a—"

"Boyo, if you're not out of my sight in ten seconds, I'll kick every fooking tooth in your head down your fooking throat."

No need to listen for the rhythm there to know what he meant. "Sorry to have troubled you," I said.

I turned, half listening for those heavy work boots to come clumping after me. But as I got back into the Honda, Sean Kilpatrick was still standing at the rear of his battered pickup, fists on hips and staring me down.

EVEN AFTER DARK, YOU can see the dome of the Massachusetts state-house from my office window on Tremont Street. It's a pretty impressive effect, the gold leaf painstakingly reapplied by artisans a few years ago for what it probably cost the Navy to buy a carrier jet. But the dome also helps me to think somehow, especially when I'm stuck.

And I was stuck fast that night.

A very valuable reproduction of *The Book of Kells* disappears from the locked room in which it's kept, the glass top of its case smashed. Most people with access to the museum know that this top opens to allow Nora Clooney to turn a page each day, but the thief smashes it anyway, maybe to deflect suspicion onto others less informed. Hugh McGlachlin as executive director of the Center has a key, though he's the one calling me into the matter, through a member of the advisory board, Michael O'Dell. On the other hand, reacting immediately and internally like that might be a good cover story for McGlachlin himself. Of the three people he "reluctantly" suspects, none acts suspiciously—or even smugly—about my suggesting the book could be pinched: Professor Conor Donnelly orders me to leave his office, brother Denis wants me beaten up for "scamming" him, and carpenter Sean Kilpatrick stops just short of mayhem himself when I imply he could steal the Center's copy for me.

Which, according to the note left on the broken glass, wasn't actually what had happened, anyway. "Taken, but not stolen, and will be returned." No apparent sarcasm in the words or even a double meaning.

If the one person who'd asked to borrow the book had now apparently acquired a copy for himself, who would need the facsimile only temporarily?

Then, staring at the statehouse dome reminded me of something else I'd seen at the Center. It was a long shot, but worth at least a call to a certain home phone.

After dialing, I got a tentative, "Hello?"

"Hugh, it's John Cuddy."

"Ah, John. You've found something, then?"

"Maybe, but I need to ask you a question first. Who did all that calligraphy work at the Center?"

THE FRONT DOOR TO the three-decker in Southie opened only about four inches on its chain inside. The one eye I could see through the crack seemed troubled. "Oh, my. Mr. Cuddy, how could I be helping you at this hour?"

"I'd like to meet with your husband," I said.

Nora Clooney tried to tough it out. "He's asleep. Perhaps in the morning?"

I shook my head.

She squeezed her lips to thin lines. "Then let me just pop up there, sir, make sure my Bill hasn't—"

"Nora, we both know what I'll see. Can we just get it over with?"

Her head dipping in defeat, she undid the chain on the door. "That'd probably be best, I suppose."

Terminal cancer has a certain aura to it. Not always a smell, though. More an edge in the air, a sense that something's very wrong but also irreparable. Bill Clooney's bedroom projected that aura.

His wife led me into the ten-by-twelve space. There were matching mahogany bureaus with brass handles and framed photos of a younger couple wearing the clothes and hairstyles of the late seventies. The bed was of mahogany too, a four-poster that I could see newlyweds buying shortly after their ceremony. A set to last a lifetime.

Bill Clooney lay under sheets and a quilt, his head nestled in a cloud of pillows. There were a few wisps of gray hair on top of his head, a patchy fringe around his ears. His eyes were closed, but the mouth was open, a snoring so faint you might lose it in the hum of the electric space heater near one corner of the room. His hands lay atop the quilt, bony and heavily veined.

Centered between Clooney's throat and waist, a bed tray straddled his torso. A very large book was open on the tray, a couch cushion propping the text at an angle toward his face.

"My Bill was a graphic artist," said Nora Clooney, her voice barely louder than her husband's snoring. "He came over from Ireland five
years before me, and he was ten years older to start with. The charmer
told me he fell in love the moment he laid eyes on me, but I wasn't
sure of him till I saw his wondrous calligraphy, after a social at the
Center that very same night. Modest about it though, my Bill was,
telling me that I'd not use the word 'wondrous' for his lettering once
I saw *The Book of Kells*."

I kept my voice low as well. "You wanted to bring the book home
so your husband could see it again."

"See it, yes sir, and touch it and even breathe it as well. But after
the terrible row between Mr. McGlachlin and that Mr. Donnelly at
the Center, I knew the board would never grant my Bill what it
refused a rich man."

"You took the book out of its case before you broke the glass."

"Yes, sir." She made a sign of the cross. "I'd never have forgiven
myself if I'd damaged so much as a page of it."

"And you carried the book out in your tote bag."

"Brazen, I was. Walked right by Grace behind the reception
counter, her not suspecting a thing."

"Then why did you leave the note?"

She blew out a breath. "I thought it might keep Mr. McGlachlin
from calling in the police right away, sir. Buy me the time to let my Bill
pore over the book during his last days before I took it back to the
Center unharmed." She turned toward her husband, and I had the sense
that Nora Clooney always looked at him this way, with the same expression. A loving one that went beyond duty and maybe even devotion as
well.

"Every morning he was able, my Bill would come to the Center
with me. Oh, his eyes would shine, sir, watching me turn that day's
page, him feeling honored as though he was the first modern man to
look upon the work of those long-ago scribes."

I waited a moment before saying, "Nora, I need to make a phone call."

She closed her eyes and dipped her head again. "The one in the
kitchen, please. So we don't disturb my Bill."

As I followed her down the stairs, I said, "You wouldn't know
whether Hugh McGlachlin has Caller ID on his home phone,
would you?"

From the look on her upturned face, I could tell that Nora Clooney thought I was crazy.

I dialed and got that tentative hello.

"Hugh, John Cuddy again."

"John, are you calling from the Clooneys, then?"

"No," I lied, "a pay phone. I'm afraid Nora and Bill couldn't help me. But listen, Hugh, I've traced your *Book of Kells*."

"Traced it?" His voice was thick with hope.

"Yes," I said. "The book'll be back in the Center before your board meets next week."

A long pause on the other end. "John, is there something you're not telling me?"

"There is."

An even longer pause. "Michael O'Dell said I could trust you."

"And you can."

No pause at all now, but a considerable sigh. "Then I will. Good night, John Cuddy, and thank you."

As I hung up the phone in Nora Clooney's kitchen she blinked three times before kissing the pads of the index and middle fingers on her right hand and then touching them to my forehead.

SKIV

Wendi Lee

THE PHONE RANG FIVE times before Maggie O'Malley picked it up. There had been a robbery last night in Kill, a tiny village ten miles from Rathcoole, and she had been called to assist the *garda* until nearly two in the morning. To be awakened at seven in the morning seemed unfair, but she propped herself up on her elbow and reached for the receiver.

"Yeah," she croaked into it, "O'Malley here."

"Maggie?" It was her boss, Detective Chief Superintendent Aidan O'Rourke. "We've got a murder down in Saint Jude's. Thought you'd like to take it." Saint Jude's, a boarding school for boys of wealthy Protestants, was located five miles outside of Rathcoole.

"Don't tell me—one of the students finally murdered one of the masters," she replied.

"No, actually, it's a missing student."

So, she thought, one of the masters finally killed one of his students and hid the body. But she didn't say it out loud. Maggie knew that the reason she was being handed this assignment—her first case—was because she had once worked at Saint Jude's as kitchen help.

She dropped onto her back and peered out at the weather. Gray and misty. Not unusual for Rathcoole. "Yeah. I'll be ready in fifteen minutes." Time enough to splash her face with water, brush her hair, and put on her uniform with the new shoulder tabs.

"Sergeant Leary will be ready with an auto," O'Rourke replied before hanging up.

Donal Leary had recently advanced from *garda* to sergeant. As the first woman to advance to detective within the Rathcoole police force, Maggie was often paired with the newest *garda* recruits, so she was grateful to have someone with experience by her side. Ireland had a long way to go when it came to equality for women, so she tried not to show her impatience when she was watched more closely than her male peers, or when a man with less years on the force advanced before she did.

WITHIN HALF AN HOUR, Maggie and Sergeant Leary pulled up to the main building on Saint Jude's grounds. Students and staff headed to their next class slowed down and watched Maggie and Leary, both in uniform, head for the school warden's office.

The school warden—still Mr. Jack Garvey—was waiting for them in his dark, wood-paneled office. Garvey was a tall man, in his fifties, still handsome.

Maggie stepped up and introduced herself. Garvey peered at her as if he was trying to place her. She wasn't wearing her usual kitchen scrubs, and it had been five years since she set foot on Saint Jude property as a *skiv*, the derogatory word used to describe the menial workers.

Maggie recalled the social order she'd had to endure when she left the farm eight years ago. She was just out of secondary school and in need of a job. She came to work at the school as a *skiv*. Skivs got up at five in the morning to bring in the fifty-pound cans of milk and lug the food trays up to the dining hall before serving it to the students and faculty. They cleaned up the dining hall after meals and scrubbed up the dishes, flatware, pots, pans, and serving trays. The work was hard, dirty, and the pay was embarrassing. The only advantage to the job was that room and board were provided, making it easy to save up her money—as long as she didn't spend her money at the pubs.

As a skiv, she had been at the bottom of the social order and had been treated accordingly. She had worked there for three years and had barely been able to stay on. One of the cooks, Nora, had been a nasty piece of work who spent much time standing in the doorway of the washing-up room and screaming at them like a taskmaster to "stop lagging and work until you drop." All Nora needed was a whip to complete her image.

Maggie shook her head and turned to the school warden. "Tell me the situation, Mr. Garvey. What is the name of the missing student?"

"Trent Taylor."

"How old?"

"Seventeen."

"What kind of student is he?"

"A fair student, from his grades."

"Has he ever been in trouble?"

Garvey made a show of studying the file in front of him. "No."

"Is it possible that Mr. Taylor slipped away from the school last night to go drinking?" Maggie knew that a certain percentage of the students at Saint Jude's would obtain fake ID's and slip out of school to go to the pubs.

The warden looked shocked, but it was a practiced expression. "I don't know what kind of school you think I'm running, but—"

She smiled and patted the air. "I'm not suggesting anything, Mr. Garvey. I know you don't approve, but it's common knowledge that some of the boys here can get themselves into trouble with fake ID's."

Garvey paused and studied her. "Forgive me for saying this, but you seem familiar to me. Not that I spend a lot of time at the Rathcoole police station—"

Maggie gave him her professional smile. "I attend a lot of charity dinners," she said evasively. She didn't want him to remember her as a skiv. Not that she was ashamed of the job she had once done, but it would color his view of what he would tell her. "Is there anything else you can tell me about Trent Taylor?"

"He has a younger brother here named Brad."

"Do the brothers share a room?"

"I don't believe so, but to be certain, you'll have to ask the house-keeper, Mrs. Crawford."

She turned to Sergeant Leary. "You take Mrs. Crawford and ask her where Trent Taylor's room is located. Search it for anything that might shed light on why he disappeared." She turned back to the school warden. "Thank you, Mr. Garvey," she said, snapping her note-book shut. "I'll get back to you."

There was no point asking him any more questions. He was so high up on the food chain at the school that it was doubtful that he knew much about the Taylor boy other than how much his parents forked over in tuition, room, and board.

As they left the office, Maggie saw Christopher Ferrot, one of the masters, passing by. He glanced at her and smiled in recognition.

Maggie had always liked Ferrot, the literature master, when she was a skiv. He was a vegetarian, always introducing himself as "Ferrot, which rhymes with carrot."

"Ah, a former coworker. How are you—Maggie O'Malley, isn't it?" His head always appeared too large for his body. The thinning hair and small glasses didn't help alleviate that illusion. Ferrot was bony to the point of emaciation. Maggie remembered often overhearing stu-dents making fun of the quirky master.

"Yes. How are you, Master Ferrot?" she asked.

"Christopher, please," he insisted.

Maggie smiled. She found Christopher Ferrot charming. But she was here on duty. "Sorry. It will have to be Master Ferrot for now."

"This is about Trent Taylor, isn't it?"

"'Tis," she replied. "Do you know him well?"

Ferrot nodded. "I had him in class last term."

"Good student?"

Ferrot shrugged. "It depends on what you call good. He received good grades, but there's no spark there. He's just marking time until he graduates."

"Has he ever been in trouble?"

"He fancies himself a ladies' man. I don't know for certain, but I suspect that he and his friends have slipped out of the school and gone to the pub down the road."

That would be Kavanagh's Pub, Maggie recalled. It was approximately a mile down the road. An easy enough walk.

"Can you give me the names of his friends?" she asked.

Ferrot gave her two names: Reg Fortune and Feroze Pappas.

"Do you happen to know if they were in class today?"

Ferrot thought. "I was on breakfast duty this morning, and I saw both of them. But I didn't see Trent."

"How did they seem to you?"

Ferrot shook his head. "The same as always. As if nothing happened."

Maggie found that odd, considering that their friend was missing. Wouldn't they be concerned?

"So they didn't come to anyone with their concern for their missing friend? Do you know who reported his disappearance?"

"That would be his brother, Brad. In fact, he came to me with his worry."

Leary was at her side and she excused herself, thanking Ferrot for his cooperation.

"You seem to be familiar with himself," Leary observed, slipping into the vernacular.

She smiled grimly. "I'm familiar with most of the masters here. I need a room to interview the brother and friends."

They went to the dormitory where Trent stayed and found an empty office near the common room. Leary went away to gather up the boys Maggie needed to interview. A few minutes later, he returned with Brad Taylor, a slight blond boy, large teary blue eyes, American accent, southern. Expensive designer frames perched on his narrow nose. His navy blue uniform blazer seemed to float, it was so big on him.

Maggie introduced herself and began immediately. "Tell me the last time you saw Trent."

Brad frowned. "I'm two years behind him, so we don't travel in the same circles, see?"

Maggie nodded encouragement. "What is your brother like? Is he quiet?"

Brad laughed, but there was no humor behind it. "Trent quiet? Definitely not a good description. You knew Trent was coming for miles. He was loud, and when he entered a room, you knew it five minutes before he was there. He was very athletic, playing on the soccer team, and cricket and golf for fun." A tear slipped down his pale cheek.

"I noticed that you're using the past tense with your brother," Maggie observed. "Do you think something happened to him?"

Brad looked guilty. "No," he said quickly. "No, I'm sure he's fine. I guess . . . I'm just concerned and afraid something's happened."

"Can you think of any reason why he might have disappeared? Had he appeared troubled lately?"

Brad shook his head. "No, Trent was—is—always the same—always one for the girls."

"So you think he went out last night and just might not have made it back here? Maybe he's with some girl?"

"Not that I'm aware of," Brad said wearily.

"Did he have any habits?" Maggie searched for a way to phrase the question. "Sometimes boys do things like drink or smoke or do drugs . . ."

Brad sighed heavily. "He went out drinking a couple of times."

"Do you know where?"

Brad shrugged. "The pub down the road, I imagine. Sometimes Trent and a few of his buddies would go there."

Maggie raised her eyebrows. Kavanagh's Pub again. "Trent and his friends had fake ID's?"

The boy nodded.

"Trent liked the girls?"

Brad smiled shyly. "The girls like Trent, too."

Of course. With his American accent, his designer clothes, the money he probably flashed around, what girl wouldn't be attracted to him?

"Are your parents notified?" she asked gently.

"Headmaster Garvey doesn't seem to think it's necessary for at least a day. I hope you find him, Inspector. He's going to be in trouble at the school, but I worry what kind of trouble he might be in right now."

She verified the names of the students whom Maser Ferrot had mentioned as being friends of Trent Taylor.

"Yes, both of those boys are his friends," Brad replied.

"Can you think of any other names of friends?"

Brad shook his head. "Those are his buddies."

Maggie thanked him and told him to get to class. A moment later, Sergeant Leary slipped into the office.

"Do you have the other boys ready for an interview with me?" she asked.

"I do, but we just received a call from Aidan Kavanagh."

"The pub owner down the road."

Leary nodded. "He's found a body. The body of a student from here."

FIFTEEN MINUTES LATER, THEY were in the field back of the pub. Gardai from the neighboring town had joined them—a photographer, a medical examiner, a forensic specialist, and several *gardai* to keep the curious away.

The boy was about sixteen years old and looked like an older version of Brad Taylor. There was no doubt in Maggie's mind that this was Trent Taylor. He wore jeans and a nice shirt. His jeans were unbuttoned and a red windbreaker was wadded up next to him. He had been hit in the head, and the murder weapon was one of any number of rocks scattered in the field. Three *garda* were combing the area, literally turning up rocks.

Maggie inspected the body. "Can you tell me anything I might need to know about this murder?" she asked Dr. Reagan, the medical examiner.

Dr. Reagan straightened up. "He was killed by several blows to the back of the head. He didn't die immediately, which is why he's turned up. He was also sexually active before he was murdered."

Maggie wrote it all down.

Master Ferrot was brought to the scene to make a preliminary identification. Maggie hadn't wanted the younger brother to do it and Christopher Ferrot knew Trent well enough to confirm whether it was the missing student or not. A sheet covered the body now that the photographer had taken pictures of the crime scene, and Maggie escorted Ferrot carefully up to the body and had a *garda* pull down enough of the sheet to expose the face.

The master nodded reluctantly, swallowing hard. "Yes, that's him. That's Trent Taylor."

"Thank you, Master Ferrot. I'll have one of the *garda* bring you back to the school."

"Thanks, but I think I'll walk." He looked a little green. "I need some air before I go back to teaching class."

"Master Ferrot," she called after him. He turned around, a sad look in his eyes. "I don't have to tell you to please keep the news quiet. The school warden may know, but neither of you should say anything to the students yet."

He nodded that he understood and turned his back for the long mile back to school.

"SERGEANT," SHE CALLED TO Leary, "I'll be interviewing Aidan Kavanagh now."

Leary led her into the pub to the back where Kavanagh kept his rooms. He was a beefy man, red-faced from too much of his own product, and had an unkempt beard.

"How did you find the body?" she asked.

The pub owner ran a hand over his face, clearly still upset by his discovery. "I was heading out to milk the cow. I saw something red in the field and—I found him."

"Do you recognize him?"

Kavanagh hesitated.

"Mr. Kavanagh," she said, "I know that he's a Saint Jude's boy. I used to work at the school about five years ago, and I'm aware that the boys try to get into the pub with fake ID's."

Kavanagh let out a breath. "Well, I try to keep 'em out, but I'm not always successful. Sometimes the ID's are just so good, and the pub is so busy, I don't always succeed."

"Do you happen to remember his face from last night?"

The pub owner was clearly reluctant to say, but he finally nodded. "I remember him, only because the boys with him were clearly too young, and I threw 'em all out."

"Do you remember anything else unusual about last night?"

Kavanagh paused, then said, "There were a couple of young girls who tried to get in as well, and I threw one of them out about the same time."

"They had fake ID's as well?"

He nodded. "I don't know how they thought they'd get away with it. I'm friends with their da. The older one can drink, so she stayed for a half-pint, but I turned the other girl away."

"Who are these girls?"

"It's the Herlihy girls. Both of 'em work as kitchen help at Saint Jude's."

MAGGIE AND LEARY DROVE back to the school. "Round up the boys for interviews. I'm going to the kitchen to talk to some of the help."

"Do you need directions?" Leary asked.

"I know where it is, sergeant. Carry on."

Both cooks, Nora and Bernie, were working for the noon meal. Three younger girls were helping. The kitchen was a large room with industrial gas ranges and ovens, whitewashed concrete walls, and a brick floor. The wonderful smells coming from the oven made Maggie's stomach growl in response.

Nora was the first to notice Maggie's appearance. "Well, if it isn't herself come to see how the little folk are doing." She was a short, big-busted woman with a homely face and dark stringy hair. She'd made Maggie's year at Saint Jude's miserable.

Maggie crossed her arms. "Is Nora seeing leprechauns again, Bernie?"

Nora glared at her and made a harrumphing sound.

Bernie, a tall rangy woman with frizzy red hair and pale freckles scattered across her friendly face, suppressed a smile. "How are ye, Maggie? I heard ye became a *garda*. The uniform looks good on ye."

"I made detective recently," she said, not being able to help boasting a bit.

Bernie looked interested. "And what would you be doin' here?"

"A disappearance."

Bernie turned to Nora. "I told you there was somethin' funny goin' on when that boy didn't show."

Nora snorted.

"What do you mean, Bernie?" Maggie asked. She noted that Bernie was making scones. She'd loved Bernie's scones when she worked here.

"We're short two today and Nora and I had to cover breakfast. One of the boys didn't show. Someone told a master that the boy was sick and in his room, but when the master went to check on the boy, he wasn't in his room."

"Do you know who it was who reported Trent Taylor as sick?"

Bernie thought. One of the kitchen workers spoke up. "I think it was his brother, the young one."

Maggie made a note to check on that bit of information. "You said you're two short today."

"Aye," Bernie said. "The sisters went back home for a visit."

"The sisters?" she asked, already knowing the answer.

"Siobhan and Nuala Herlihy. They called this morning to say their da took sick and needed tending. Siobhan said they'd be back tomorrow." She gestured to the other girls. "Now these three have to work an extra shift."

"Thanks for the help. Good to see you, Bernie," Maggie said.

"'Tis good to see yourself, Maggie. Come back on a good day and we'll have scones and tea." Before Maggie could leave, Bernie said, "I hope you find out what happened to that poor boy."

Ignoring Nora, who did likewise, Maggie left for the dorm to talk to the friends of Trent Taylor. She took up residence in the small office she'd used earlier. Maggie consulted the names Master Ferrot had given her, Reg Fortune and Feroze Pappas, and instructed the sergeant to bring in the Fortune boy.

Reg Fortune was about sixteen or seventeen, fair-haired, athletic build, light brown eyes, and a killer smile. And he knew it. When he came into the office, he looked Maggie up and down in appreciation, then sat down across from her.

She ignored his leer. "I'm Inspector O'Malley. I need to ask you a few questions about Trent Taylor's movements last night and this morning. When was the last time you saw him?"

"Last night. We went to the library to study."

Maggie doubted he was telling the truth. She raised her eyebrows. "When I worked here in the kitchens, we often went out to Kavanagh's Pub, and we often met boys from Saint Jude's there. I imagine things haven't changed that much over the past five years."

"You worked here?" he asked, a spark of interest in his eyes.

"In the kitchen."

His face closed up and a sneer replaced the interest. "A *skiv*."

"A kitchen worker," she said evenly. "Where were you last night?"

"We went to the library," he insisted.

"You didn't meet the Herlihy sisters?"

"I don't know what you're talking about," he replied.

Maggie asked him a few more questions, but felt he was lying.

"Can I go now?" He stood up.

"For now. I may want to ask you additional questions, so don't leave the grounds."

Feroze Pappas was next, a striking combination of Arabic and Greek parentage. His dark good looks and tousled black hair made him appear older than Reg. It was clear that he came from money and had the European worldliness to pull off looking older. Maggie doubted Feroze needed to show his fake ID to get into a pub. If he had gone to the pub alone, he might have passed as eighteen or older.

He sat down and looked coolly at her.

"To begin, it has been established that Trent, Reg, and yourself went to Kavanagh's last night. There was some trouble." She was taking a chance, to make a guess like this about something that happened.

Feroze's expression froze. "I don't know what you're talking about."

She gave him a severe look. "I talked to Mr. Kavanagh and he remembers all of you well."

"He's mistaken. We weren't there. We were at the library."

Neither boy was willing to admit that he was at Kavanagh's Pub. Maggie was tempted to take both boys by the scruff of the neck and haul them in front of Kavanagh, but decided to wait on that.

"You can go," she told Feroze in a severe tone, "but you are not to leave the premises until I say so."

He gave her a haughty look. "My father will hear about the way you're treating me, and it will cost you your job."

Leary popped his head in the door. "What now, Detective?"

Maggie sighed. "Take this boy out of my sight," she said in a disgusted tone. She had a good notion of what had gone on, but she needed to fit a few pieces into place before presenting her theory.

SHE GOT DIRECTIONS TO the Herlihy farm, a ten-mile drive. Men along the side of the road were cutting peat and tending sheep.

The cottage was whitewashed stone with a gaily painted red door. Laundry hung out to dry, even though it had rained a bit that morning.

Maggie knocked on the red door. She could hear movement inside and a moment later, a young girl answered the door. She looked at Maggie, then beyond to the police car. She shut the door on Maggie, who imagined there was some discussion about whether to let the *gardai* into their home.

Maggie knocked forcefully to distract the girls from concocting a story. They finally allowed Maggie and Leary inside.

Siobhan was the older of the two girls. She told Maggie she was just eighteen and had been working at the school for a little over a year. She was petite, small-boned, and had a mass of dark curls that floated around a face with sharp, not unpleasant features.

Her fifteen-year-old sister, Nuala, had just left school six months ago and taken her first job at Saint Jude's. She sat in a dark corner, and Sergeant Leary made a move toward her, reaching out to steer the younger girl toward a chair. Nuala looked at Leary with frightened eyes and shrank away from him.

Maggie eyed the younger girl—taller than her older sister, gawky, but with a certain charm. "Sergeant, will you do me the favor of going out to the auto and waiting?"

He hesitated, then nodded.

"Now girls, I think there's something you want to tell me."

"What are you talking about, Inspector?" Siobhan asked.

"Girls, there's a student who's been murdered down at Kavanagh's Pub."

Siobhan sat at the table, cool as a soft day in Ireland, her hands clasped in front of her on the kitchen table. "I don't know what you're talking about, ma'am."

Maggie turned to Nuala. "Do you know what I'm talking about, Nuala? You were down at the pub last night, you tried to get in with a fake ID, you were turned away. So were three boys from Saint Jude's—"

"She doesn't know what you're after, Inspector," Siobhan broke in. "She waited for me to come out after I had me half-pint of Guinness, and we walked home from there."

Maggie turned to the younger sister. "Is that true, Nuala?" she asked softly.

Nuala looked about to break, but Siobhan kept stonewalling, keeping Maggie from doing her job.

After half an hour of trying, Maggie stood up. "It's clear to me that you're withholding information about Trent Taylor's death. It's also clear that Nuala here has been seriously hurt, perhaps sexually attacked. Why are ye not talkin' to me?" She asked this last question plaintively.

Siobhan glanced at Nuala, who looked up at Maggie with dark, haunted eyes. "We have nothin' to tell you, Detective. We walked back to the school last night by ourselves, then received word that our da was sick."

Maggie looked around. "And where is he now?"

Siobhan thrust her chin up. "In hospital."

"I can check on that."

Nuala stood up and came toward Maggie. "Why are ye question-in' us? We're not the criminals here," she said, her voice about to break.

Maggie stood her ground, but it was difficult. Siobhan came between them. She stood nose to nose with Maggie. "We have noth-in' to say. And if you continue to persecute us, we will report you to your superior."

Maggie shook her head and turned to leave. As she opened the door, she said, "I suspect Nuala has been molested. Why are you pro-tecting them? Why are you denying it? It's clear that it was self-defense."

Siobhan looked back stonily. "I don't know what you're talking about."

Maggie said more softly, "Your sister is going to need more help than you can give her. Call me if you want some resources in Dublin."

Siobhan shut the door on Maggie, but a moment before the door closed, she saw the expression of the older sister, the desperation and vulnerability that told her that she'd hit on something important.

BACK AT THE SCHOOL, she pounded away at Reg Fortune and pushed Feroze as far as she dared. Neither boy gave an inch. She brought Kavanagh to the school and had him identify the two boys.

"What about the other boy?" he said. "Don't you want me to identify the fourth boy?"

"Oh?" she asked, feeling slightly stupid for not asking how many boys he'd turned away. She had just assumed it was the trio. "And what was he like?"

"I told you that one of the boys looked too young." Maggie had assumed it was Reg, who was the youngest-looking of the group. Kavanagh went on to describe Brad Taylor to a *T*.

MAGGIE STOOD WHEN BRAD TAYLOR was brought into her office. "Sit," she said. "You were with the other boys, with your brother last night. I know about the girl."

"I don't know what you're talking about," the boy muttered, keeping his head down, avoiding Maggie's eyes.

Maggie had always heard that silence spoke louder than words, so she remained silent. Less than a minute later, she detected Brad's shoulders shaking.

"You're carrying a heavy burden, young sir," she said gently, "and you're not the only one to bear it. Those two girls are denying everything now, as are Trent's friends. But eventually one of you will break down. Maybe not the two tough cases I've had in here previously, but—"

"I killed him, all right?" Brad looked up, his face streaked with tears. "I killed my own brother." He got up and paced. Everything came tumbling out as if he'd been holding back by the skin of his teeth.

Trent had gotten Brad a fake ID and took him along last night to go, as he put it, "trolling for girls." "He wanted easy girls. He told me it was time I had sex." Brad paused, shaking, unshed tears brimming, threatening to spill. "He told me he'd had sex for the first time at my age, and he said it was my time. I didn't want to go, Inspector, but I was bullied into it by Reg and Feroze. I knew I wouldn't pass as eighteen even with an ID, so I went along to the pub. I thought I'd be thrown out and that would be the end of it."

He sobbed. "But the pub owner threw all of us out. We saw the two girls go into the pub, and the younger one came out a few minutes later. Trent recognized them as kitchen help from Saint Jude's. He whispered to me that they were skivs and skivs were known to be easy. I told him I just wanted to go back to the school. I could tell the younger girl was scared, and I offered to walk her home." He stopped, as if he wasn't sure he could go on.

Maggie gently prompted him. "Trent wouldn't let you, would he?"

A heavy sigh. "He said we'd all walk them home and he knew a shortcut through the back of the pub. When we were away from the lighted area, Trent took hold of the girl and started ripping her clothes off. Reg and Feroze just stood and watched—"

Maggie waited, knowing this was difficult for him.

"—she fought and got away, but Reg and Feroze went after her. I just stood there, not believing that this was happening, that my brother could be this cruel. Feroze came back and dragged me to where Trent was—" it was clearly difficult for Brad to talk about this."—raping the girl. She didn't have any fight left in her, but she was crying and kept saying that he was hurting her and she kept saying no. I finally found my voice and told him to stop." Brad looked up at Maggie. "He wouldn't. I felt so sorry for her. She's probably my age."

"How did you feel about what was happening?"

"I hated my brother. I was scared and angry at the same time."

"What happened next?"

He sobbed again, a heart-ripping sound. "I tried to pull him off but I'm not very athletic and he threw me off easily. So I finally picked up a rock, only meaning to knock him out." His face was in his hands and an animal cry came from him. "I killed my brother. I killed him. It was an accident. I'm sorry, I'm sorry—"

Maggie pulled him up gently and put an arm around him. "There, there. We'll get you some help. Don't you feel better for telling?"

But she knew she was giving him empty words. He would never feel better, never be able to reconcile killing his brother, choosing a girl's dignity over his brother's life. Nothing would ever make it better for him.

So Where've You Buried the Missus Then, Paddy?

Mat Coward

WHEN I FIRST MET Polish Pat he was a single man, albeit single in a peculiarly Irish way—his wife, the lovely but enormous Charmaine, was "off visiting the family in Dublin." I was so young in those days, my barman's towel so new you could still read the print on it, that I took this time-tried euphemism entirely at face value. Luckily, I never did say to Polish Pat, "That's a long visit your wife's having, Paddy," as otherwise I suspect that Pat, sweet little feller though he was, might have punched my nose clean off my face.

(Would this be a good place to explain about the names? Polish Pat—known as Paddy to everyone who knew him, and not known at all to those who didn't—was not Polish, but Irish. However, when he first began drinking in the Old Boar, there was already a Paddy Pat amongst the regulars, and so Paddy—*our* Paddy, the Paddy of this story—became Polish Pat, on the unspoken understanding that he would succeed to the title of Paddy Pat upon the demise or departure of the incumbent. Paddy was never in the least Polish, but nobody was too bothered by that, since Paddy Pat himself was not Irish, but Californian. It must seem confusing to anyone unfamiliar with the pubs of north London. All I can say in our defence is that it makes sense to us; or at least, it doesn't make *sense*, exactly, but it keeps us busy, which is the next best thing.)

Anyway, Paddy seemed to be enjoying his long separation from his lovely but enormous wife, judging by the number of impromptu after-hours parties he hosted in his unpleasant but spacious basement flat, about five minutes' walk from the pub.

I attended several of these do's, not because I was a particular pal of Paddy's, but simply because I was a human being who looked as though he could do with a drop of friendly company. "Come on over when you've finished here, son," he'd say to me, at closing time.

One day I'm going to write a book of advice for young lads finding themselves alone in a big city for the first time. Advice like, "Don't smile at strangers in public lavatories," and "If you're offered a job by a man in a pub at three times your present salary, consider the possibility that there might be a catch." But the biggest piece of advice, printed large on the first page to make sure no one misses it, will be this: "Get yourself in with an Irish crowd." For the Irish man or woman who can bear to see a poor boy without a glass in his hand and a plate of beans-on-toast on his lap has yet to be born. I say this as an Englishman, of my own free will.

It was whilst enjoying Paddy's good hospitality one late Friday night in August that I asked a fellow guest whether Charmaine perhaps had illness in the family.

"Illness?" replied Rasta Jack. "Not that I know of. Why?"

"I was just wondering. She seems to have been away in Ireland an awful long time; ever since I've been working at the Boar, in fact."

Rasta Jack laughed. "The thing is, son, they've not been getting on so well lately, Paddy and his missus. But not to worry, I'm sure she'll turn up again sooner or later. She always does."

I looked across at Paddy, playing cards on the other side of the large, under-furnished room with a bunch of lads from the pub. He was a short, wiry man, with bow legs, thin ginger hair, and jug ears. He worked, in an informal sort of way, in the building trade, but was out of work more often than he was in, due, so he often told us, to a wickedly infirm back.

"It's hard to imagine such an easygoing bloke falling out with his wife," I said. "Or with anyone else."

Rasta Jack shrugged. "She's five times his size," he said, "and has ten times his brains. Maybe she just gets fed up with looking after him every now and then and needs to get away for a while. Now pass me that bottle, will you—what sort of barman are you, that allows a man to die of thirst sitting right next to you?"

An off-duty one, I thought. But I passed the bottle, anyway.

IT WASN'T UNTIL CHARMAINE had gone unseen for nearly three months that people began to think it odd. Previous occasions on which she had been "off visiting the family" had never lasted more than a month, and it was generally agreed amongst the regulars at the Old Boar that three months was significantly longer than four weeks, whichever way you looked at it.

"He's done her in," suggested Mike the Bike one evening. "That must be it."

"Can't be," countered another concerned drinker. "There's no garden to that flat of theirs, where would he bury her? And she's a big woman, you'd never get her under the floorboards."

"Besides," added a third, "it'd be more believable the other way around. She's a lovely woman, is Charmaine, but she's got a temper on her. And her the size she is, you'd need a gang of fit men to get her down."

"Poison," said Mike. "That takes no strength at all."

"Poison's a woman's weapon," declared Big Rick definitively. "And whatever Paddy is or isn't, he's certainly a man's man by anybody's standards. If he was to kill a wife, it'd be with straightforward strangulation, or a decent blow to the head—not something as dirty as poison."

"You're right, of course," said Mike, "and I apologise to all concerned for raising the matter."

Conversation then turned to someone else who hadn't been seen
for a while, Jonathan Lansdowne—"Hungry Jon" as he was known,
not because he was poor (he was a millionaire by anybody's standards),
but because he was always hungry. He would often come in to the
Boar and order a beer, half a dozen sandwiches, three bags of crisps,
and a packet of peanuts. And then go off to a restaurant for lunch.
The regulars used to tease him—"Does she not feed you at home,
Jon?"—but nobody said that any more, since he'd recently become a
widower.

Of the two mildly missing persons, I have to admit that I found
Hungry Jon the more immediately interesting. No offence to
Charmaine; it was just that Jon had been a pop star in the sixties, and
although he now worked as a record company executive, wore a plain
suit and a sensibly outdated haircut, he still carried with him a certain
cachet of celebrity.

As time went on, however, with still no sign of Charmaine, my
fickle attention returned to her case. If a recording executive is away
for a few weeks, after all, however uncharacteristically, it is no big surprise. But an Irish housewife, whose husband continues to host post-
pub parties throughout her absence . . .

"Tell me about Charmaine," I invited Rasta Jack, one night when
a Siberian wind had kept most of the pub's potential customers at
home with their televisions. "I always hear her described as 'lovely
but enormous.'"

"So she is," said Rasta. (Picture a white man, completely bald, who
worked in insurance, wore faded corduroys, and spent all his money on
operatic LPs.)

"How enormous?" I asked.

"She's tall," he said. "She's taller than me, and I'm five-ten. And
big, with it. She must be thirteen, fourteen stone. And if you think a
two-pound bag of sugar weighs two pounds, which it does, and there's
fourteen pounds to a stone, then you're talking about someone who
weighs roughly the same as ninety-eight bags of sugar."

"That *is* fairly enormous, isn't it," I agreed, "by anybody's standards. Especially given that her husband is, what, five-foot-six?"

"And if he's a chocolate biscuit over nine stone, I'd be significantly surprised."

I tried to picture this woman I'd never met; this couple I'd only ever seen half of—or less than half, by the sound of it. I tried to picture a six-foot-tall pile of sugar bags walking down the aisle with a mostly eaten packet of chocolate biscuits. And as for the honeymoon—it was like that old joke about the Rottweiler and the Chihuahua.

"I'd know her if I saw her, then?"

"You would that," Rasta agreed.

"And what about 'lovely'?"

"Oh, she's lovely, all right. Charmaine is a lovely girl." He took a sip from his pint. "Just, you know, not to look at."

She sounded more fascinating than ever. I looked forward to meeting her.

THE FIRST TIME I ever heard it *seriously* suggested that I might never get a chance to meet the lovely but enormous Charmaine was when a quite large, middle-aged woman, with a southern Irish accent, arrived in the pub one Saturday lunchtime inquiring after the whereabouts of her estranged sister.

"Sure, you'd know Charmaine if you saw her," said Tessie, after introductions had been made and drinks served.

"Oh, yes," said Griff, the landlord, a Yorkshireman with a prematurely grey beard and posthumously raven sideburns. "I know who you mean, all right. It's just that—"

"Or failing that," interrupted Tessie, "I'll settle for her husband, wee Paddy. I certainly expected to find *him* in here. Don't tell me he's gone crazy and actually taken a day's work somewhere! I knocked at their flat, but there was no answer."

"Well, it's just that . . ." Griff's voice trailed off and his face showed anguish. A pub landlord's job description is notoriously infinite in its scope and most definitely includes the role of diplomat. Nonetheless, I got the impression that this particular tricky situation was a new one on him. He looked for aid to his patrons, but seemed to find it hard to catch an eye. "The thing is, Tessie," he said, "we understood, we *all* understood, that the lovely but—er, that is, the lovely Charmaine was currently staying with your family."

"With *my* family?" said the quite large but soft-spoken Tessie, plainly bewildered.

"Well, with your parents. In Dublin."

"But *I* live with my parents," said Tessie. Many eyes flicked to her left hand. "And you'd not find Charmaine there, not as long as my mother is alive." She lowered her voice and added, somewhat superfluously I thought: "They don't get on, you see." This was her first-ever visit to Britain, she explained, and she wouldn't be able to stay long; she'd come on a peace mission. Her mother was poorly, with heart trouble, and anxious to be reconciled with her other daughter.

Once Tessie had left, in a taxi operated by one of the Boar's customers, to book into a small hotel managed by another, and with the promise of an immediate news flash from Griff should either Paddy or Charmaine be sighted in the vicinity, those of us left behind gave full vent to our speculation.

The consensus view, I have to report, was that "obviously he's done her in, else why would he have lied about her trip to Ireland?"

Over that weekend, Paddy himself joined the absent-without-leave list, which did nothing to reduce the suspicions of his friends.

Until then, the parties at his flat had continued on a regular basis, though old hands had begun to complain that the gatherings lacked a certain something. They couldn't quite put their fingers on precisely what the lovely but enormous Charmaine had contributed to the scene—but whatever it was, many agreed, had been the essential element that transforms a mundane booze-up into a social occasion of note.

I MUST INTRODUCE YOU at this point to another man who was a regular of the Boar in those days. He too was an Irishman—as so many in north London are, of course; and even those who aren't tend to know at least three verses and the chorus of "Wild Rover."

O'Nuff was an interesting chap. A Protestant from the South, a man of broadly Republican-Marxist outlook, an independent specula-tor upon the Stock Exchange by profession, and a graduate with high honours of Dublin University, in a subject so intensely esoteric that he claimed to be unable even to pronounce it, let alone to remember what it actually meant. He was also the only person any of us had ever met who held a private eye's license, valid in the state of New York. How he came to own such a thing was one of the very few subjects on which he was known to be reticent.

On top of all that, O'Nuff was a handsome fellow, in his late thir-ties, strong and healthy, popular with men and women alike, erudite without ever being condescending, and kindly to a fault. Needless to say, there were those in the pub who couldn't stand the sight nor sound of him.

I am not ashamed to admit that I admired him as a kind of hero. He made me feel that, as long as there were such men in the world, it meant the rest of us could happily fritter away whatever talents and energies we might have been born with, secure in the knowledge that better people than us would always be around to take care of the dif-ficult stuff.

Late one autumn evening, after a particularly sweaty session behind the bar, I was standing in the Old Boar's small courtyard, smoking a cigarette and enjoying the fresh air and thinking whatever thoughts I had left in my head by that time of night, when a voice spoke a few inches from my ear.

"Did I scare you?" were the first words it said to me, and the first intimation of any sort I'd had that I was not alone. I took this to be an example of the globally fabled Irish humour, rather than a sincere attempt at homicide by startlement.

"You did," I admitted. "You scared all of it right out of me. I'll be needing a dustpan and brush here."

"Oh, sure 'nuff. Sorry about that, kiddo. I just wanted a private word."

"A private word? With me?" I hoped it was nothing to do with the Theory of Relativity.

"Oh, sure 'nuff," said O'Nuff, again; thus relieving me, I trust, of the burden of explaining his nickname. "Now, the thing is, a young man in your position—polishing all those glasses, pouring all those pints—you'd be ideally placed to overhear all sorts of interesting items from the careless lips of your clientele. That's so, no?"

Was he suggesting that I was some sort of eavesdropper? It wasn't an accusation I'd take kindly. Especially since it was one I could hardly deny. "What is it you think I might have overheard, O'Nuff?"

"Well, now," he said, taking out a packet of Major and offering me one—possibly to replace the Benson I'd dropped when he'd first appeared. "You're aware, naturally, that there is some concern in the air about the current whereabouts of our friend Hungry Jon?"

"Naturally," I agreed, wondering—not for the first time—how it was that the Irish could be so good at beer and so very bad at cigarettes. "And the same goes ditto for our friend Charmaine."

"Oh, sure 'nuff. Indeed. But whereas I am quite confident that she will turn up when turning-up time comes, I am less sanguine about him. About Hungry Jon, I mean."

That was unpleasantly exciting news. "Why so?"

"Well, now. You know, of course, that I lived for a while in America."

"New York, wasn't it? I've often wondered, if you don't mind me asking, what brought you back? I should have thought that being a private eye in the Big, Bad Apple—"

"Green beer," he said, with a bitter grimace. "Green beer and shamrock hats."

The words meant nothing to me, but they clearly meant something to him, so I left it at that. "And your time amongst the diaspora is in some way connected to your worries about Hungry Jon?"

"It is, so. And what I would like to ask of you, my friend, is this: if you were to hear anything which you feel might go toward explaining why the aforementioned gent has not been seen in this pub for some time, and why there is no answer at his door or upon his telephone, I would be most grateful if you would bring that same information to me. Only to me, you see? And without unreasonable delay." He extinguished his cigarette underfoot. "I mean, finish serving the round, obviously, but don't leave it until the next Bank Holiday."

"Well . . ." I said, which meant—as it so often does—*I'm not too happy about this.*

"You needn't worry, at all. No ill will is meant toward Hungry Jon. I am merely acting for some folk back in America, who are eager for news of the evanesced popster. It's nothing heavy—you have my word as a licensed private detective."

He smiled, to show that his words were intended both humorously and seriously. It was an honest and broad smile, but even so I couldn't help remembering that his license to privately detect was valid only in a place far away from the Old Boar.

IN THE END, IT was I who found Paddy.

Pub-goers in this part of the world are naturally territorial, and in any case no loyal habitue of the Old Boar would be seen dead or alive in the King's Head, ever since an unfortunate incident during a darts match seven years earlier. I wouldn't have been there myself, but for the presence of a particular barmaid (another story; not relevant here).

Which made it, of course, a perfect place for Paddy—who had heard of the arrival on the scene of his sister-in-law—to lie low.

Acting upon my report of his location, a deputation hurried to escort Paddy back to the Boar and confront him with the accusation that he had malice aforethought'd his good wife.

Any thought of fight or flight had quite gone out of the little man, as he slumped in his usual chair at the bar, all stubble and weary eyes.

"You might as well know," he told us, "Charmaine is—"

"Is she under the floorboards, Paddy?" called out Big Rick, who I believe had been wagering on the subject with Mike the Bike. "Or should we be digging up the Heath?"

"She's left me," said Paddy, in a horribly quiet voice. "That's the truth, and I'll hide it no longer. My wife has abandoned me for another man."

This admission produced deep sighs from Paddy's audience; sighs of sympathy, of course, but also of disappointment at a mystery too easily solved.

"It's true," the self-proclaimed cuckold continued, running his bony fingers through his thin hair. "She has run off with Hungry

Jon—and who can blame her? He can offer her so much more than I ever could."

Perhaps so, the rest of us thought. But what could *she* offer *him*? (Lovely though she was.)

The meeting adjourned to Hungry Jon's doorstep, just across the street from the Boar. Paddy, "too ashamed to face that man," stayed in the pub, bravely forcing down a nourishing pint of stout.

Prolonged ringing on Hungry Jon's doorbell eventually produced the ex-pop star, looking a lot more ex than star that day, and he reluctantly admitted us to the immense, white-carpeted sitting room of his four-storey house. A fully equipped bar, fitted out in white leather, stood at one end of the room, a white piano at the other.

"I don't know what you're talking about," Jon insisted, when Paddy's allegations had been put to him by Griff, our duly elected spokesman. "I'd heard she was away in Dublin, visiting her family? As for me—well, I've been busy, that's all, no time for socialising. Big album deal on the cooker."

He seemed convincing enough. In the cold light of that white room, the idea of him eloping with poor Paddy's missus did seem a little unlikely.

"So, Jon," said Griff, uncomfortably, "let me just get this a hundred percent clear. You are not now, nor have you ever been, insanely enamoured of the lovely but enormous Charmaine?"

Jon treated us to a distinctly ungallant laugh. "Come on, guys! Can you really imagine—"

And that was when the singing started. Loud, lusty, but undeniably tuneful. An old Irish rebel song.

Coming from the cellar.

"Ah!" said one of the older members of our little mob, clicking his fingers in revelation. "*That's* what was missing from Paddy's parties. Of course—his dear wife's enormous but lovely voice!"

THE ANSWER, AT LAST, seemed clear. Recently widowed, and entering a difficult period of middle-age, poor Hungry Jon had, indeed, been driven mad by his love for Charmaine—so mad, that he had kept her locked in his cellar for months, an unwilling love slave.

Not a murder, then, but something which was, for those regulars privileged to witness its climactic moments, almost as enjoyable, and just as retellable.

Upon her release from her luxuriously appointed prison, however, Charmaine herself shot that one down.

"Love slave?" she gasped, restored at last to her own kitchen. "Sweet Jesus, isn't that just like a load of men, to think of sex, sex, sex, and nothing but!" It was a small kitchen, and there was barely room enough for the dozen or so men present to look suitably abashed. We did our best.

"But if not love," asked Griff, neatly summarising the question of the moment, "then what?"

"An insurance swindle," said Big Rick, authoritatively. "I always knew Paddy was in on it." He wouldn't have said that if Paddy had been around to defend himself, but Paddy wasn't. He was busy in the bedroom, sleeping off the regrettable side effects of being left alone for thirty minutes in an unattended pub.

"Nothing of the sort!" snorted Charmaine. "If you must know, Jon wanted to turn me into a recording star."

This announcement was met with a loud silence.

"He'd heard me singing here at the flat, during one of our wee soirees," she continued. "He said he could make me into the Irish Cher."

"But," said Griff eventually, "you weren't keen?"

"I was not. Though Jon wouldn't take no for an answer. I was flattered, of course. But, you see—Paddy has very strong views on married women pursuing careers outside the home." As the silence got longer and louder, she added, by way of clarification: "He's against it, I mean."

The illusions of marriage, eh? Where would we all be without them?

No charges were pressed. "The poor man wasn't himself," Charmaine ruled, displaying the innate kindness for which she was so well known. And besides, as Griff's own wife pointed out later, those weeks of well-fed captivity were probably the only ones in Charmaine's life during which she had not been required to cook, clean, or run errands. An unorthodox kind of holiday, to be sure, but sometimes a rest can be as good as a change.

A week later, she and Paddy returned to Ireland, permanently, which was bad news for the Old Boar and its patrons, but good news, no doubt, for Ireland, a country that has suffered more than most over the years from excessive emigration.

We never saw Hungry Jon in the pub again, even after he had returned from treatment in a private clinic for nervous exhaustion. Too embarrassed, I suppose; about the white piano, one can but hope, if not the kidnapping.

Paddy and the lovely but enormous Charmaine send the pub a collectively affectionate card every Christmas, but in the years since their departure they have never appeared here in person. Charmaine, so it's said, reconciled with her family, has sworn never to leave her native land again; while Paddy, I suspect, would not care to make a solo visit.

People in pubs have long memories (long *long*-term memories, at any rate), and Paddy would naturally dread the prospect of walking into the Old Boar on his own and being greeted after all these years with cheery cries of "So—*where did you bury the missus this time then, Paddy?*"

All of which, I am well aware, leaves one loose end; and it's not even a small one. You'll forgive me, I hope, but you see I have learned my storytelling manner, such as it is, from my Irish neighbours—and as you'll know if you've ever sat in a pub in north London (or, I daresay, in Boston, or Sydney, or Hong Kong), there is a right way and there is a wrong way to end an Irish story. Even one told by an Englishman.

The right way is to finish it just a little after your listeners think it is already finished. The wrong way is to finish it before closing time.

Following our crepuscular conversation in the Boar's courtyard, I didn't see O'Nuff again for some weeks. Which, given the givens, struck me as a little odd.

About a month after Paddy and Charmaine had left us, we held a Christmas football match one Sunday afternoon, up on the Heath. It was not a formal affair. All were invited, and all were guaranteed a game, if they wished to play; those who didn't were welcome to watch,and encouraged to barrack.

The day was fine and the turnout good. There must have been thirty or more of us gathered there, and many bottles of beer and hip flasks of whiskey were in evidence. Some people even brought sand-wiches—though the purists amongst the crowd muttered that such preparedness was evidence of an orderliness of mind that bordered on the clinically obsessive.

Men and women took part—even one or two kids—and substitu-tion was frequent and liberal. You would simply play until you got tired, or bored, at which point you would jog off the pitch and your place would be taken by whoever felt like doing so.

I was not much of a footballer and had no deep knowledge of the rules, so I confined my own active participation to one or two spells as referee. This brought me many offers of free drinks in exchange for particular interpretations of the laws of the game, all of which I hap-pily accepted, and none of which, as I remember, were subsequently honoured.

We were about twenty minutes into the match, with the score standing at six-all (or not, depending on who you asked), when I saw the skinny Greek girl who had been keeping goal at the south end trot off the field, to be replaced by O'Nuff. I surrendered my whistle to the nearest unoccupied person and took a long route round the pitch to arrive right behind the goal.

I was about to reach out and tap him on the shoulder and say, "Did I give you a scare?" when, without turning around, O'Nuff spoke.

"Now then, kiddo—I've been hoping for a chat with you."

"I'm glad to see you. It's been a while."

"Oh, sure 'nuff. I wouldn't miss this; it's a great laugh for a Sunday afternoon. Have you ever been to a pub up West, called the Irish House?"

"I have, yes."

"Good. I'll meet you there tomorrow lunchtime, if that would be convenient to yourself?"

"It would, so," I said, which made him laugh. I watched him for a short while and saw him let in two goals. (Or not, depending on who you asked). He was wearing smart clothes, and he got them dirty diving after the ball, but he didn't seem to mind.

THE IRISH HOUSE WAS famous for serving the best stout in London, and the slowest. The customer would place his order at the bar in the centre of the big room, and then go to his table. When the pint had been poured, and allowed to settle, and topped off with a palette knife, and topped up from the tap, and allowed to settle again, it would eventually be delivered to its dry-throated purchaser by a waiter.

When you wanted a refill, you did not take your empty glass with you to the bar—that would be a faux pas. It was all very different from the Old Boar.

"When people think of the Irish in Britain," said O'Nuff, as I sank my face into the black-and-white elixir, "and *pace* our cousins in the North, they think only of County Kilburn. But every city in the country has an Irish centre, or an Irish club, or at least a couple of Irish pubs. Now, do you think of London as an English city?"

I thought before answering. It was that sort of conversation. "English," I said. "And Scottish and Welsh and Irish and Bangladeshi and Jewish and Nigerian and—"

"Exactly!" said O'Nuff. He drank a slow throat-full of his beer and sighed. "That's good. My father was over here in the fifties, you know. Working on the roads, laying the tarmac. In those days, you would still see signs in boardinghouse windows: 'No Coloured, No Irish, No Dogs.'"

"Awful."

"Oh, sure 'nuff, inexcusable. But my father was a man of strong opinions, particularly where men of the cloth were concerned, and relating to the rights of the working man, and he found it easier to hold those opinions, at that time, in this country than in his own."

"Did he find lodgings?"

"He did." O'Nuff nodded. "With a Jamaican woman who bred poodles."

I had to laugh at that. So I did.

"Did you know that Irish citizens can vote in British elections?"

"I didn't."

"Oh, sure 'nuff. But, naturally, British citizens cannot vote in Irish elections. Now, does that strike you as unfair?"

I shrugged and finished my pint. O'Nuff went to order two more. "It's not unfair, obviously," he said on his return. "And I'll tell you why: because what British person would ever want to vote in an Irish election? *That's* the point."

If that was the point, then I was none the wiser. "I do know it wasn't Hungry Jon you were interested in," I said, "when you spoke to me that time outside the Boar."

"Ah, well," said O'Nuff. We sat quietly and smoked, until our beers arrived.

"You told me that Jon wasn't answering his doorbell or his phone. But when we all went over to his place from the pub, he did answer the bell eventually."

"Bet you rang it awful hard, mind." O'Nuff sipped, nodded his head, and sipped some more. "Fair enough. What was the final score in the football yesterday, do you know?"

"It depends who you ask."

"Ah well, then, I reckon we won. Let's drink to that."

We drank to that. "It wasn't really me you were hoping for a word with that night. You just said all that about Hungry Jon to stop me wondering what you were actually doing, loitering outside the pub in the dark," I said. "Were you really a private detective in America?"

"I was, so. Did night classes and everything." He offered me one of his Majors, which I declined. Politely, I hope.

"Unless there was yet another missing person, who I know nothing about, then I'd guess that it was Paddy you were watching for."

"The Boar was his local, right enough, but there were one or two other pubs where he would put in the odd guest appearance. I did the circuit that evening and ended up back at the Boar, just on the off-chance."

"And through him you were hoping to learn the whereabouts of his wife."

"The lovely but etcetera," he confirmed. "Quite so."

I set my drink to one side and thought it through. All the while, O'Nuff watched me closely. After a time, I realised that I had one more question. "So, who was it thought that Paddy had killed his wife?"

He cocked an eyebrow at me. "Apart from everyone in the pub, you mean?"

I shook my head. "That was just messing around. No one who knew Paddy could really think such a thing of him."

"I feel at home in this city," said O'Nuff, after a pause. "Britain, Ireland, America—home for me is wherever I happen to find myself when I wake up in the morning. But not everybody's like that. My client was away from home for the first time, amongst strangers— kindly strangers, but strangers nonetheless. She was confused, afraid, not sure how best to discharge her responsibilities. It's natural enough to fear the worst in such circumstances."

She? The sister: Charmaine's sister. "How did she get on to you?"

He laughed. "Ah, you'd have to be Irish. Or Romany, maybe. The short version is, she phoned a cousin in New York, who phoned a fellow member of the Grand Order of This and That in Boston, who remembered that he used to know a PI, a reliable man, Irish, too, and sure, didn't he happen to be living in London just now? The diaspora, you know."

"So the reason I didn't see you in the pub after that . . ."

"Oh, sure 'nuff. I was busy looking for Charmaine, or Paddy, or— I hoped—both. Looking in all the wrong places, as it transpired. If I really *had* been looking for Hungry Jon, I'd likely have found Charmaine a lot sooner, wouldn't I?"

"And does Paddy know that—"

"Nobody knows. You, me, and my client. No one else." He didn't ask me for my silence—obviously didn't consider it necessary to ask— which, young as I was, I found flattering.

I sat and stared at my beer. O'Nuff read my face and read it correctly. "Look, son. As we now know, no one was killed. There was no murderer. There was some foolishness, true enough, but that's supplied as standard where human beings are concerned. On the other hand, we have a family reunited and a marriage born afresh."

I said nothing. When he held his cigarettes out to me across the table, I took one absentmindedly.

"What we have here, in summation, is a happy story. Am I right? Not a sad one. So, that being the case, my friend—why the long face? As the psychiatrist said to the horse."

It seemed to me a story with a not-unhappy ending, true, but with a lump of irredeemable sadness at its core; of suspicion and fear and misjudgment. Perhaps it was because I wasn't Irish—except by adoption, so to speak. Which, it struck me then, was precisely what O'Nuff had been trying to tell me earlier.

He leant over and put a hand on my shoulder. "I'll tell you what. I see you don't accept what I've said, and that's fair enough. But as a personal favour to me, as a mark of our friendship . . ."

I looked up at him. "Yes?"

"Will you just take my bloody *word* for it?" He drained his glass. "Now, up to the bar with you, and two more of the same, please."

My glass was still three-quarters full. "I haven't finished this one, yet."

O'Nuff laughed, and shook his head. "You make me feel very Irish, kiddo, you really do. Look: you'll have finished drinking *that* one by the time they've finished pouring the *next* one!"

He was right, of course. He was, so.

Green Legs and Glam

(A "Henry Po" Story)

Robert J. Randisi

1

I WAS NOT IN NEW ORLEANS specifically to ogle naked women, but I figured what the hell? Where was the harm?

I was actually in the Big Easy as a favor to my boss, J. Howard Biel, the Chairman of the New York State Racing Club. He had asked me if I would help out a friend of his who had a problem. Requests like these were not outside of my job description. Recently, one of them had taken me to Ireland for a few days. I figured why turn down an all-expenses-paid trip to New Orleans, the French Quarter, and the Fairgrounds Race Track.

The Fairgrounds was where Biel's friend hung his hat. Not the big magilla Biel was in New York, his friend, Andrew Cone, was still the number-two man at the Louisiana track.

Cone had handled all the travel arrangements and had booked me into a hotel right in the Quarter, on Bourbon Street, called the Bourbon Orleans. When I arrived at 2:00 P.M. there was a message waiting for me at the desk, in writing. I waited until I got to my room before reading it.

"Enjoy what the Quarter has to offer," it said, "and meet me at the Blue Orleans Gentlemen's Club at 1:00 A.M."

It was signed, "With thanks, A. C."

I assumed by "Gentlemen's Club" we were referring to a strip joint. I wondered about the lateness of the meeting, but Cone was footing the bills, so I decided to keep the appointment.

Oh, did I mention it was Saint Patrick's Eve? March 17 was never a big holiday for me. I wasn't one of those people who suddenly became one-quarter Irish when Saint Paddy's Day rolled around, so it didn't bother me to be away from New York and miss the parade.

Since the meeting was for one in the morning, it would actually take place on Saint Patrick's Day. I spent the rest of Saint Paddy's Eve walking around the Quarter and—as Cone had suggested—taking advantage of what it had to offer. That meant great food and music and an interesting few hours spent in Jackson Square, getting sketched, read—tarot and palm—and fed.

I went back to my hotel after a late dinner to take a two-hour nap before meeting Cone at the Blue Orleans. I left a wake-up call, because I was pretty groggy after the flight and spending the day walking around.

Now, I had spent a short time walking down Bourbon Street because it was so famous and I had never been there before, but that had been during the day. I left my hotel at 12:30 A.M. to give myself plenty of time to find the club, but I needn't have bothered. After midnight Bourbon Street was like no street I had ever seen before, even in New York.

For one thing the street was closed to all vehicles, so people were just walking in the center of the street, as well as up and down the sidewalks. There were gentlemen's clubs everywhere, each with a unique way of advertising itself. One had a girl on a swing moving in and out of a window, apparently naked, but to be sure one had to go inside—and pay the cover charge. All you could see from outside was a pair of excellent bare legs and maybe—if she swung out too far—just the hint of a bare bottom.

Some of the clubs just had one or two girls loitering at the doors, just inside, so that as you passed you got a glimpse of a nice set of boobs or an excellent derriere.

Other clubs had girls dancing in the windows, but the windows were opaque, so that all you saw was a very shapely silhouette dancing and touching herself.

Music emanated from all these clubs, as well as the regular bars and jazz clubs along the street. There were vendors open that late still selling the traditional New Orleans hotdog called "a Lucky Dog." On almost every corner there was a daiquiri shop selling the icy drink in all flavors, and people strolled and sucked them up through straws while they stepped in and out of the gift shops. Amazingly—at least, amazing to me—each of the daiquiri shops and a lot of the gift shops had their own ATM machines. I had never seen so many bank machines on one street before; but then they were necessary, because everyone you saw on that street was either buying or selling something.

I found the Blue Orleans Gentleman's Club with no problem. It was one of the ones that had a naked girl or two right at the front door. As I entered I immediately had a nude girl on each arm, pressing a bare boob against me. I had a B-cup on one side and a D-cup on the other. Being a D-cup fan, I gave her most of my attention.

"You here to see me, honey?" she asked. "I'm Alicia."

"I'm here to see you," I said, "and to meet a friend."

"I can be very friendly," she said, rubbing her boob up and down my arm, now. It was very firm and warm and the sensation was anything but unpleasant. Both girls were wearing that patented "stripper scent" that most strippers seem to wear. They must all buy it from the same central location. It's very sweet and heady and stays with you a long time after you've left the place.

Okay, yeah, this wasn't my first time in a strip—excuse me—a gentlemen's club.

"Would you like me to come to your table later and show you?" she asked.

"I won't leave here until you do."

"You want to sit down in front or in the back?"

"What's the advantage of down front?"

Now she wiggled both boobs at me, the magic of silicone keeping them from jiggling uncontrollably, and said, "Well, a bird's-eye view, for one."

"And for another?"

"You never know when a naked girl will plop herself down in your lap."

"Well," I said, "my friend and I are going to be discussing some business, so I guess you better put me in the back."

She pouted at me and said, "I'll have to come find you, then."

"You do that."

She brightened and said, "I'll show you to your table and then I'll know where you are."

"Sounds like a plan."

Somewhere along the line the B-cup had disentangled herself. Guess I hadn't noticed.

What can I say? I'm a boob man.

2

BY 2:30 I WAS starting to wonder if Cone was going to show, and I was considering moving down front. I was still working on my first five-dollar beer, which had been dyed green for Saint Patrick's Day.

"There you are!" Alicia said, running up to me.

"I saw you up there," I said. She had been up on one of the stages doing her thing a little while ago. Her thing was to be noticed, and she did it very well.

She sat down next to me and said, "Your friend stood you up?"

"Maybe," I said. "It's been an hour, but I guess I'll give him a little more time."

"How about a lap dance while you wait?" she asked. She leaned over so that her stripper smell was very strong in my nostrils and put her hand on my arm. "For twenty bucks I slide into your lap and wiggle all around!"

Having her think she had to explain a lap dance to me made me realize how young she probably was. I started to feel like a dirty old man.

"Wow," I said, "I'm tempted, but I better put it off until a little later."

I had given her a five-dollar bill just for showing me to the table, and now I slipped her another so she wouldn't forget about me.

"Gents," the announcer said into the microphone, "put your hands together and give a nice Saint Patrick's Day welcome to . . . Glam!"

The lights went down, a spotlight hit the center stage, and a girl stepped into it. She had green hair, and green legs, and her name was Glam. All of a sudden I was reminded of Dr. Seuss—but that didn't last long. Once she started moving she was nothing like the Cat in the Hat, at all!

She was different from the other girls. For one thing, as the spot hit her she was already naked, except for the green stockings, or leggings, whatever they were. The other girls all strutted on stage with little outfits on and proceeded to move around in some parody of a dance, stripping the outfit off little by little. This girl had the body and the moves of a trained dancer so she was actually more of an entertainer than a stripper, since she had nothing to strip off.

Her body was lean and muscular, her breasts small but solid. When she moved you could see the muscles in her calves and thighs rippling, when she turned the muscles in her buttocks were evident. While she danced to Joe Cocker singing "You Can Leave Your Hat On," everything else in the place stopped.

Then the music stopped and the spot went off, and when it came back on she was gone.

There was a collective sigh from the spectators, me included. We all knew we'd just seen something special.

At this point I realized Alicia had not left, but had remained seated there during "Glam's" number.

"Is she the headliner?" I asked.

"Hmph," Alicia said, "she thinks she is."

"How long has she been dancing here?"

"Only a week, and already she's got her own dressing room."

Well, I thought, somebody else thinks she's the headliner, too—like maybe the boss?

"And what about the green wig and stockings? Does she always wear that?"

"No," Alicia said, "that's for Saint Patrick's Day. Who is she kidding? She's not even Irish."

At this point I saw a man come in the front door, accosted by a B-cup and another girl, probably a C. He shook them off and spoke to a man who came walking over. Unmistakably, there was a handoff between them, but some people passed into my line of sight at the crucial moment and I couldn't tell which way it went.

"I'll be back later to see if you want that dance," Alicia said, and went stalking off, obviously upset that I had enjoyed Glam's number. She didn't know that, if she was a bit older, she'd still be more my preferred body type.

I looked for the customer involved in the handoff and was surprised to see him coming toward me.

"Henry Po?" he asked, as he reached the table.

"That's right," I said, standing up.

"Andy Cone." He extended his hand and I shook it. He was younger than I had expected, maybe because Biel—who was in his sixties—had described him as being a friend. This man was closer to my own age, somewhere in the mid to late thirties. "Sorry I'm late. I got caught up in something."

"That's okay," I said. "I've been entertained."

"I thought you might, that's why I had you meet me here," Cone said. "I come here a lot. Who showed you to your table?"

"A girl named Alicia."

"Ah," he said, his eyes lighting up, "nice."

"A little young," I said, for some reason.

"Maybe," he said. "Look, I hate to do this, but how about having another beer on me. I have to go in the back and talk to one of the girls, but then I'll come out and join you."

I shrugged and said, "It's your party, and your dime."

"Great," Cone said. "Thanks for being understanding."

Actually, I didn't understand at all, but the girls were naked and the beer was green and . . . well, none of that mattered. I was feeling pretty relaxed and mellow, at the moment. The pulse of Bourbon Street was dancing in my head and in my veins, it seemed. I'd never been anyplace like it, and I liked it; so I was quite willing to sit there and wait. Having nothing to do was a luxury for me.

Cone disappeared, somehow managing to get backstage. A waitress came over, topless and pert, and I ordered another beer.

3

THE BEER HADN'T ARRIVED when Cone reappeared, moving a lot faster than when he had disappeared. He looked at me and stopped, fidgeting, appearing to be in a quandary over whether to come over to me or head for the door. Suddenly, there was a scream from somewhere in the back and Cone froze, unable to even fidget.

Nobody seemed to know what to do. Patrons looked around, torn between the girls on the stage and the scream. Even the girl on stage seemed unsure. I sighed; Nothing was going to get done unless I did it. So much for relaxing.

I got up and rushed over to Cone, grabbed his arm.

"What happened?"

"I didn't . . ." he stammered, " . . . I didn't know . . ."

"Take me there."

"What?"

"Take me into the back!" I probably wouldn't get back there without him.

"Come on." I pushed him in the direction he had come. He led me to a curtained doorway I couldn't see from my table. A man was blocking it, obviously a bouncer.

"Hold it!" he said.

"Police," I said, not knowing the penalty in New Orleans for impersonating a cop, and not wanting to know.

"Oh," he said, "okay. What's goin' on?"

"That's what I'm gonna find out," I said, and pushed Cone ahead of me again.

We went through the curtain into a hall, and from there I didn't need Cone anymore. There was a small crowd in front of a door at the end of the hall. I didn't need him, but I pulled him along anyway, pulled this time, instead of pushing.

When we reached the door the crowd parted, probably something in my eyes or the way I was moving.

"Stay here," I said to Cone.

"But—"

"Don't make me have to find you."

He nodded, and started fidgeting. I turned and went into a small dressing room.

She was on the floor, arms and green legs askew, her green wig half on and half off, revealing red hair underneath. She wasn't naked anymore, wearing what looked like a silk dressing gown that was half on and half off. Her red pubic thatch was peeking up at me. There was blood under her head, soaked into the wig and spreading. The bullet had entered dead center in her forehead. The bloody puddle beneath her stood out in stark contrast to her pale skin.

There was a man in the room, wearing a cheap suit, a cheap hairpiece, and a frightened look.

"I don't know what to do," he said to me. I guess I looked as if I did. He was sweating so bad I could smell him.

"Who are you?" I asked.

"The manager."

"How many bouncers you got working?"

"Five"

"How many ways in and out?"

"Three."

"Block them," I said, "nobody in and nobody out."

"Okay," he said, glad to finally have something to do.

"And call nine-one-one."

"The police?" he asked, looking frightened again.

"They usually get called to the scene of a homicide."

He reached for a phone on a dressing table.

"Not from here," I shouted. "Go to your office and call them."

"But . . . I pay, I'm protected."

"Not against murder, friend."

4

UNIFORMS ARRIVED FIRST, THEN detectives. It was the same in every state, I guess.

They got the back hallway cleared out, probably putting everyone in the club. The music had been stopped a long time, and the girls had probably all covered up. There were two detectives, and they were in the dressing room with me and the dead girl.

"From what I've been told, you're the only one who knew what to do," one of them said.

"Somebody had to do something."

"Why you?" he asked. "I mean, how did you know what to do?"

I took out my wallet and handed him my ID.

"Private?"

"That's right."

"From New York."

That wasn't a question. It was on my ID. He handed it back.

"The manager says you made him call us."

"That's right. He told me he was protected. I assumed that a little protection money didn't include murder."

He impressed me by not denying anything, but simply saying, "You assumed right."

He looked at his partner, who nodded. They were the same age, forties, and had all the signs of having worked together a long time. The nod was one of the signs. They had communicated without saying a word, and had come to a decision.

"Mr. Po," the first man said, "my name's Detective LaSalle, this is my partner, Detective Batiste."

Batiste and I exchanged a nod. I had the feeling I had just gone up several notches in their estimation. With most cops, when they see your PI ticket, you go down; but I had known what to do in this situation, and that worked for me.

"Quick thinking to keep everyone inside," LaSalle said. "Now just tell me one other thing."

"What's that?"

"Who killed her?"

"I wish I knew," I said. "She was . . . special."

"How do you know that?" he snapped.

"I saw her dance," I said. "She was different from all the others."

"You don't know how different," LaSalle said, looking down at her. No one from the Medical Examiner's office had arrived, so they hadn't moved her. "She was one of ours."

"A snitch?"

He shook his head and looked at me with tremendous sadness in his eyes.

"A cop," I said.

He nodded. "She was working undercover."

"One of the girls said she came in a week ago."

"That's right," LaSalle said.

"And she already had her own dressing room."

"She has—had—dance background. That was why they sent her in here."

"Too bad."

"About what?"

"If she hadn't had the dance background, hadn't distinguished herself from the others, she might have shared a dressing room and not been alone."

He nodded. "I see what you mean."

"What was she working on?" I asked.

"Somebody is selling drugs from inside the club," LaSalle said. "It was thought that all that was needed was somebody on the inside who would keep their eyes on something other than the girls. That's why they sent in a woman."

I frowned, thinking back to what I had seen in the club.

"You didn't hear a shot?" LaSalle asked.

"No," I said, "just the scream of the girl who found her."

"Must have been suppressed, then," LaSalle said.

"The murder was planned," Batiste said.

"Somebody sniffed her out," LaSalle said. "She was a good cop, but somebody spotted her."

"One of the other girls, maybe," I said. "Even if she had her own dressing room they still saw more of her than anyone else."

"This is not the way a woman kills," LaSalle said.

I shrugged. "A woman may have fingered her."

LaSalle looked down at Glam again. Each time he did the pain in his eyes was evident. Batiste's glances at her were more dispassionate.

"I want this guy," LaSalle said.

I looked at Batiste, who simply stared back at me without expression, and yet I felt as if he'd passed me something.

"Look, Detective," I said, "I'm not from here, and I don't mean to try and do your job, but . . . if I could have a minute to leave the room?"

"If you can do anything to give me the killer," LaSalle said, "you can leave the state and come back."

"No," I said, "just the room."

"Go."

As I left he was still sitting, his shoulders slumped, and I thought I saw his partner put his hand on his shoulder.

5

I WENT OUT INTO the club and looked around. There was still a bouncer standing at the front door and one that I could see at a side door. In each case a uniformed policeman had joined him. Since there were three ways out, I assumed that there was also a bouncer and a cop on that door, as well.

I found Andrew Cone seated at the table I had been sitting at, with three other people, none of whom seemed to know each other. The police had simply made everyone sit down, so that most of the seats were taken.

"Cone," I said, "come with me for a minute."

"What for?" He looked frightened.

"Just come on."

He stood up, and I walked him over into a corner where we could talk alone.

"Tell me what happened in the back." I said.

"Did you tell them—"

"I didn't tell them anything," I said, "and if you answer all my questions I might not. Why did you go into the back?"

"I—I'm having a thing with one of the girls. I went in the back to see her."

"And what happened?"

"I—I saw the new girl's dressing room door open and I . . . I saw green legs on the floor. I . . I walked over and took a look. She was on the floor . . . there was blood . . . I wanted to get out . . ."

"Why?"

"I . . ." He stopped, as if answering that question was harder than the others.

"Is it because you have drugs on you that you're afraid would be found in a search?"

His eyes widened and he looked around to see if anyone had heard me.

"No one can hear us," I said, keeping my voice low. "When you walked in I happened to be looking at the door." That was when I found out how young and dumb Alicia was, and I lost interest in her, D cups or not. If not for that I might not have seen what I did. "I saw a hand-off when you walked in, but I didn't see what was exchanged. Were you selling, or buying?"

He didn't answer right away.

"Come on, Andrew," I said, "you can answer me or the cops."

"Buying," he said, quickly in a barely audible voice. "I was buying."

"So the bouncer is the one selling drugs out of the club?"

"That's right."

"Which one?" I asked him. The sale had taken place at the door, but that didn't mean that the bouncer on that door was the one. As it turned out, it was.

"That one," Cone said, and pointed at the man.

The bouncer must have been watching us. Maybe Cone was the last person he had sold drugs to, maybe the only one in the club he had made a sale to. In any case, when Andrew Cone pointed him out the man bolted for the door.

"Stop him!" I shouted to the cop who had been standing with him. "Stop that man!"

Too late. The cop was too slow and the bouncer was out the door. I took off after him, ran out the door myself before the cop could intercept me.

Out into the combination of people and sounds and lights and music that was Bourbon Street after midnight.

6

THE BOUNCERS IN THE club all wore the same thing, black pants and a black T-shirt with the club's logo on it which—luckily—was yellow. As I ran out the door onto the street I looked both ways and spotted the yellow logo hightailing it up Bourbon Street. I took off after him, and then we were both dodging two-way traffic of people who were having a good time, moving slowly, men and women trying to stop us to throw beads on us or flash us. The bouncer literally ran over three or four people, knocking them to the ground, scattering green daiquiris onto the street, forcing me to try to avoid them and in the process knocking one or two people down. The only difference is that although neither of us stopped, I tried to toss apologies over my shoulder.

The bouncer stayed on Bourbon Street, probably figuring to lose himself in the people, rather than turning off on a side street. However, he was knocking so many people over that he was leaving a trail behind him. Neither one of us was making much progress, me in catching him or he in getting away. He risked a look over his shoulder once or twice and saw me chasing. I didn't know if there were cops running behind me or not, and I didn't take a look, not wanting to risk taking my eyes off him.

Finally, he decided he wasn't getting anywhere and turned down a side street. When I reached it I saw that it was Orleans Street. Now we were away from people and running down a darker street. I could still see him ahead of me and hear his feet pounding on the ground. With fewer people to avoid—literally only one or two of them—he was able to pick up speed, but so was I. He ran one block and turned right at the corner, trying to lose me. As I turned the corner I saw him make a quick left and duck into Pirate's Alley, a street I had been on earlier in the day. I had been to the Faulkner House bookstore and I knew that the alley would give out onto Jackson Square. In the afternoon the square was teeming with as much life as Bourbon Street was at night. At this time of the night it would be empty. I had to keep him in sight to see which way he would go when he reached the square.

As luck would have it we were now running on a cobblestoned street, something the bouncer was probably not used to. Truth be told, neither was I, but I didn't stumble and fall and he did. It happened in every movie, and it happens in real life. Sometimes you're just running too fast for your feet to keep up with, or you simply trip. He did one of those things and went down flat on his belly. I could hear him slide as he hit the cobblestones, then the sound his hands and feet made as he scrambled to get up. He had just gotten his balance when I hit him, tackling him low around the knees. He was a lot bigger than me, and I still didn't know if I had help behind me. I took him at the knees because it's easier to fight a man who is bigger than you if you take him off his feet.

We went down together. His hands and knees must have been smarting from his first fall, and I heard the wind go out of him as he hit this second time.

I scrambled this time, trying to get on top of him so I could keep him down. I got into his back and as I did he heaved himself up and me with him. He was big and strong, and if I was alone in this alley with him I was going to be in trouble.

Luckily, that was not the case.

As he tossed me off him and tried to get to his feet two uniformed NOPD cops hit him and took him down for a third and final time.

7

"SO YOU SAW AN exchange take place at the door, but you didn't see what was exchanged," LaSalle asked me, about half an hour later, "or who the exchange was made with."

"Right."

"And you figured drug buy?"

"What can I say?" I asked. "I have an extremely suspicious mind."

He stared at me, not sure whether I was telling the whole truth or not. I was trying to keep Andrew Cone out of it, because I believed what he had told me. He'd simply chosen the wrong night to make a drug buy and to have a meeting with me to discuss whatever problem it was he needed help with. I didn't know what that problem was, or if it had anything to do with drugs, but I knew I wasn't going to hang around to find out. If LaSalle would let me I was going to be on the first plane home the next day.

"So you went out into the club to see if he was still there?"

"Right."

"One of my boys said you talked to someone else."

"Right," I said. "I came here to meet someone, and I wanted to check in with him when I had the chance. Then I started toward the bouncer, and he took off."

"Why would you figure he was the killer?"

"Well, if it was a drug buy, it fit in with what you told me about, uh, the girl, Glam, and what she was doing here."

"And how did you come to see this buy?"

"I told you," I said. "I just happened to be looking at the door."

"With all these naked girls here you were looking at the door?" he asked, doubtfully.

"Like I said," I replied, "I was waiting for someone."

"Yeah," the detective said, "you did say that. I'm going to need his name by the way."

I gave it to him. I figured they'd question Cone, but not search him. What happened while they were questioning him would depend on how guilty he felt. That was his problem, not mine.

At that moment the M.E.'s men came out of the back carrying the body of the dead cop. We both waited until they had passed and gone out the front door. Batiste was gone, having taken the bouncer to wherever they'd take him to question him and book him.

LaSalle looked back at me.

"How do you figure the bouncer got back there to kill her?"

"He works here, he's got access. According to the manager there are five bouncers working and three ways out. Put one on each door, and one on the door to the dressing rooms, and you got one guy who can float. He was probably the floater when he went back and killed her. Check with the bouncer who was on that door and see if he went back there."

"We did," LaSalle said. "He says the guy went back there only for a minute and came right out again."

"Then it fits."

"There were girls going in and out, too."

"Like you said," I reminded him, "not a woman's crime."

"I wonder how he made her."

I thought about Alicia, and how jealous she seemed of "Glam."

Some of the other girls probably felt the same way. I wondered if one of them had made her for the killer, maybe even innocently.

His cell phone rang then, and he plucked it from his belt and answered it by saying his name. He listened, nodded, grunted, said, "Thanks," and hung up.

At that moment a uniformed cop came over with a gun in a plastic bag. Also in the bag was a suppressor.

"Where'd you find it?"

"In a garbage bag in the back. Had to go through a bunch. The bags had all been tied off, but whoever had the gun was able to shove the gun and suppressor through a hole without untying it."

"Good. Get it down to the lab. We should be able to get some prints off it."

"And they'll match those of the bouncer," I said, helpfully.

As the uniformed cop walked away LaSalle said, "Yeah, they will. That was my partner on the phone. The guy confessed. He did it. He killed her."

"All right," I said. "You got him."

"You got him, Mr. Po," LaSalle said, and I was surprised to see that he was close to tears. "And I'm very grateful."

"Detective . . ." I said, then decided not to ask.

"You got a right to know," he said. "She and I . . . we were . . . well, close."

"I'm sorry."

"Yeah," he said. "Listen, if you'll come down and make a statement tomorrow, I don't think we'll have to detain you in town any longer."

"Thanks. I'll be down first thing."

He handed me his card with the address of the police station I was to go to, then turned to walk away.

"Can I ask . . ." I said, and he turned around ". . . what her real name was?"

"Shannon," he said, "her name was Detective Shannon O'Brien."

"So she was Irish, after all?"

"Oh yeah," he said, "she was definitely Irish. She loved Saint Paddy's Day."

Neither one of us appreciated the irony.

ONE OF OUR LEPRECHAUNS IS MISSING

Bill Crider

1

BEING ON RETAINER TO Gober Studios can be pretty strange sometimes. Once, for example, the Easter Bunny slept off a drunk in the back seat of my car.

Usually, though, I'm on the run, trying to keep Mr. Gober's stars from disgracing themselves, and incidentally the studio, by getting their names in some scandal rag because of their odd, to put it politely, behavior. You just never know what some of those fun-loving Hollywood characters will get up to. The big war with Germany and Japan had been over for a couple or three years, but maybe the stars were still celebrating the victory.

Take Monty Raines, star of a series of black-and-white oaters about a character called Dan the Drifter. For some reason no one was quite able to explain, Raines had developed a sudden affection for livestock during the making of a ranchers-versus-sheepherders movie and set off to deflower all the virgin sheep in California.

It's not easy to find sheep in California, much less virgins, so Raines crossed the state line and headed for greener pastures, so to speak. I caught up with him in West Texas and dragged him back to Tinsel Town after dealing with irate sheep owners in three states.

Raines wasn't any happier than the sheep owners, but Mr. Gober was pleased. And if he was pleased, so was I. He was the one writing the checks, which is exactly what he was doing at the moment as he sat behind his big desk with a top about the right size for landing a P-38.

"Good work, Ferrell," he said in a voice like a rock crusher at work. He tore my bonus check from the checkbook and waved it in the air to let the ink dry. "You're sure no one from *Inside Secrets* heard about Raines?"

"I can't guarantee it," I said. I was sitting across from him, and my fingers were itching to get hold of the check. "One of the sheep might have squealed."

Actually, I'm pretty sure some of them squealed when Monty got to them, though I was hoping no one had heard them except other sheep.

"Goddamnit, Ferrell, I don't want to hear any cheap jokes, I want to know if the studio is protected."

"I think so. I paid off enough sheep owners."

"All right, then."

He handed over the check, and I tried not to look too pleased as I folded it and put it in my wallet.

"Now that we have that settled," Mr. Gober said, "there's another little problem."

I didn't want to hear about it. I was tired, I smelled like sheep, and I wanted to take a bath and sleep for a week. Besides, as far as my experience went, there was no such thing as a *little* problem where the studio was concerned. But Mr. Gober was the man with the checkbook.

"Tell me about it," I said.

"One of our leprechauns is missing," he said.

I didn't laugh. A man who's hauled the Easter Bunny around in his car is ready for anything.

"I suppose there's a pot of gold involved, too," I said.

Gober sat up straight and glared at me over the top of his enormous desk.

"Goddamnit, Ferrell, who told you?"

"Let's just call it a lucky guess. How can you lose a leprechaun, anyway?"

"Lost? I didn't say lost. I said missing."

I didn't see the difference, but I said, "Okay. So what do you want me to do?"

"What the hell do you think I want you to do? I want you to find him. Now. There's another bonus in it for you when you do."

"Okay," I said.

GOBER STUDIOS WASN'T ONE of the biggest. It wasn't one of the best, either, but it made money, and now and then it even came up with a genuine hit. That's what happened with a musical called *Smilin' Irish Eyes*. It was set in Ireland (naturally) and starred Jackson Kendall (from Fort Worth, Texas) as a young lad named Sean O'Grady, who fell in love with a visiting British lass (Karen Swan, from Kansas) whose family hated all things Irish. The sly local priest, played by Basil Cooperworth (real name: Harry Melon, from Saint Louis), played cupid, and of course all was well in the end.

Kendall and Swan sang a couple of solos apiece and a humdinger of a duet on the sort-of title song, "When Irish Eyes Are Smiling," but the real success story of the movie was a group of three girls whom Gober had dubbed "The Singing Shamrocks," sort of an Irish Andrews Sisters. Their recording of "You Can Kiss the Blarney Stone, but You Can't Kiss Me" played on every jukebox and radio in the country for months. The movie was big box office for nearly as long.

With all that success, the studio naturally had to make another movie as much like the first one as possible. So *Leaping Leprechauns* was born. It would be bigger and better, of course. It would even be in color, which was unusual for a Gober project. It was getting the full treatment.

It must have seemed like a good idea at the time. But someone should have thought about the fact that less than ten years earlier, *The Wizard of Oz* hadn't done especially well with its cast of singers and dancers and little people. There was plenty of room for things to go wrong, and they did.

"We hired the wrong guy," Gober admitted to me. "He was a problem on the Oz set, but he swore to me that all that was behind him. The goddamned little liar."

The little liar was Jerry Fitzgerald, a midget with a practically authentic Irish heritage, or at least name, and the perfect man to play the leprechaun that led Jackson Kendall astray in a search for the pot of gold that leprechauns were supposed to guard.

"Or maybe he wasn't so perfect," Gober said. "Leprechauns are boozers, aren't they?" He didn't wait for me to answer. He said, "So is Fitzgerald."

"Leprechauns are supposed to disappear, too," I said. "Take your eyes off them, and they're gone."

"That's the way it happened with Fitzgerald. I had a man assigned to watch him, and he must've blinked."

"And now I have to find him. I hope they're shooting on location. I've always wanted to go to Ireland."

"Try the back lot," Gober said.

2

IT WAS A GOOD deal like Ireland, I guess, if you could ignore the thick black cables snaking around, the cameras, the Klieg lights, the crew, the scaffolding, the dollies, and all the rest of it. The grass was green (painted, of course), the sky was blue, and the air was full of the sound of bleating and the smell of sheep.

I was all too familiar with the smell. I thought immediately of Monty Raines, and I wondered if any of the sheep were friends of his. I hoped he didn't hear about this movie. He'd move heaven and earth to get a part in it. There was no way that could happen, however. I'd stashed him in a little bungalow way out near Coldwater Canyon with a hypnotist that Gober had imported from Australia. "An expert in human/sheep relations," was the way Gober had put it, though I thought the real expert on that topic was probably Raines. Not that I mentioned my thought to Gober.

The crew was swarming around setting up a scene, and I didn't see any of the stars. They were probably in their trailers getting a massage or whatever it was that they got. I did spot Lenny Jorkens, however. Lenny was a guy I knew slightly, and he was the leprechaun wrangler. He was standing in the midst of a swarm of little people. They were jumping around excitedly, and they wore green hats with giant shamrocks stuck in the bands, green shirts and pants with a leather apron over them, and gold-buckled shoes. Each one had a fringe of beard along the jawline.

I walked over to see what was going on and also to have a private word with Lenny if I could get him off to himself. I wanted to find out just how he'd managed to let Jerry Fitzgerald disappear.

As it turned out, I didn't ask. Jerry had already been found. That's what all the excitement was about.

"I tell you, he's lying behind the Blarney Stone," one of the leprechauns said. "Dead as a doornail, too."

"Dead drunk is more like it," Lenny Jorkens said.

He was a real string bean of a guy, with a prominent Adam's apple, a shock of black hair, and thick glasses. Surrounded by leprechauns, he looked even taller and skinnier than he normally did.

"Why don't we go have a look," I said, walking up to the group.

"Hey, Bill," Lenny said. "I didn't know you were on the set. Gober send you?"

"Right the first time. I'm here to check on Jerry Fitzgerald."

"He's dead," one of the leprechauns told me. "And the pot of gold's missing."

"It's not real gold," Lenny said.

"Jerry said it was real," the leprechaun said.

"We'll see what we can find out," I said. "Why don't you and Lenny come with me. The rest of you take a break."

The other leprechauns scattered, and I asked the one who remained his name.

"Michael O'Shea. You can call me Mike."

"You're pulling my leg."

"Nope, that's my name. I'm as Irish as they come."

He sounded more like Oklahoma to me, but I didn't care. I said, "Where's Blarney Castle?"

"Castle?"

"Yeah. That's where the Blarney Stone is. Blarney Castle."

Lenny laughed. "Maybe it is in Ireland, but not in this movie. This is Gober Studios, remember. Our Blarney Stone is in the woods."

It figured. Gober wasn't going to spring for a castle, not if he figured nobody in the audience would miss it.

"Fine," I said "Let's go to the woods."

To get there, we had to go down the village street and through the flock of sheep that was grazing just beyond. The village was mostly false fronts, and it was usually a western town. Take away the fake trees and the painted grass, change the fronts a little, and it would be a western town again.

The sheep herd was fairly small, all in keeping with Gober's economics. One of the sheep bleated as I came along. Probably thought he smelled a friend.

We got to the woods pretty quickly. It wasn't much of a woods, but at least there were some trees. I don't know much about trees, but I thought I could identify a few oaks, some cottonwoods, and maybe even a eucalyptus. It didn't matter whether these trees were native to Ireland or not. This same wooded area had served as England in Robin Hood's day, Texas in the time of the Texas Rangers, and even a Florida swamp. Gober figured that the audience's knowledge of trees was about equal to mine.

Just inside the trees was a big rock. The amazing thing about it was that it was real. It just happened to be there, and it was too big to move. It had been seen in many a western.

"There's the Blarney Stone," Mike said, as if I couldn't have figured it out for myself.

Lenny ran ahead of us and looked behind the rock. He sang out, "He's here," and bent down.

When Mike and I got there, Lenny was straddling Fitzgerald, slapping his face and yelling at him. Fitzgerald wasn't much bigger than a good-sized doll.

"Wake up! Come on, you lazy bum! You're gonna cost me my job."

Fitzgerald just lay there beside the rock. His little green hat was lying beside him, and a leaf of the giant shamrock was clutched in his hand, as if someone had placed it there. The rest of the shamrock was lying on Fitzgerald's stomach. A bottle of Old Skullbanger lay nearby. It figured.

Mike ran over to Lenny on his short little legs and grabbed Lenny's arm.

"Stop it!" Mike said. "Don't you have any respect?"

Lenny looked surprised. "For a drunk? Hell, no."

By that time I'd had a pretty good look at Fitzgerald's face, and also the side of his head. I could tell he wasn't drunk.

"Get up, Lenny," I said.

"You're not the boss around here," Lenny said.

"You want to call Mr. Gober and check on that?"

Lenny thought about that, but not for long. He stood up and moved away from Fitzgerald, and I knelt down to feel for a pulse. There wasn't one, of course. There was blood under Fitzgerald's head, and he was already turning cold. I stood up and took off my hat.

"He's dead," I said.

"Yeah," O'Shea said, giving Lenny a look. "Like I tried to tell you."

3

THE ONE THING YOU don't do if you work for Gober Studios is call the cops. Not until you have to, that is. First you figure out how you're going to keep the studio from getting any bad publicity. Which in this case was most likely impossible. All I could do was delay things for a while.

"It's easy to see what happened here," I said, putting my hat back on. "Jerry was rehearsing a scene, a dance on the Blarney Stone, maybe, and he fell off. He hit his head on the stone, and that's what killed him."

O'Shea said, "Baloney."

"Call Doc Sloane in about an hour," I told Jorkens. "I'm sure he knows someone on the cops who can stall things for an hour or two."

O'Shea said, "Baloney." This time he said it in a much louder voice, however.

"Don't worry," I told him. "The fall is just the story we'll give out for the press until I find out what really happened."

"Baloney," O'Shea said. He was like a broken record. "The press will never hear what really happened, and neither will anyone else."

"Calm down," Jorkens told him. "Ferrell's okay. He handles jobs for Gober all the time. He'll do the right thing. You and I will keep mum."

O'Shea opened his mouth as if to say *baloney* again, but he didn't. He just shut his mouth and looked at me.

"Trust me," I said, giving him my sincere look.

"Baloney," he said.

AFTER I GOT RID of them, I looked things over more closely. There was no blood on the rock, but there was blood on the whiskey bottle, which was about half full. The blood pretty much ruled out a fall, unless Fitzgerald had fallen on the bottle, which was highly unlikely, no matter how drunk he might have been. Even if he had fallen on the bottle, it wouldn't have killed him. He'd been hit pretty hard.

The grass around the body was disturbed as if there'd been a scuffle. So all I had to do was find out who'd been doing the scuffling. Then I'd know who'd swung the bottle, which I didn't touch. I figured there were bound to be fingerprints on it. That would be the clincher, but fingerprints were for the cops to find.

And then they'd have to find a match. If matching prints were on file, that would make it easy for them, but they'd have to find a suspect to match them with. That was my job.

If the prints weren't on file, things would be a lot tougher. Fingerprinting a movie star who has a high-powered lawyer isn't an easy task. Of course, it was always possible that no stars were involved. Maybe Jerry Fitzgerald had been killed by a member of the crew.

I doubted it, however. The cops and I were never that lucky.

I looked at the hat again. It was lying right beside the body. The brim was crushed where the bottle had hit it.

I looked around for a few minutes longer, hoping I might see the pot of gold. It wasn't there, but something glittered at the edge of the stone. I bent down and had a look. It was a gold foil package with the words "Sold for the prevention of disease only" stamped on it. Well, well. I picked it up by the edges and put it in my pocket. Then I walked back to the fake village to see if I could find Mike.

I LOCATED THE LEPRECHAUN along with a few of his pals in the building that served as the saloon in the studio's westerns. Take off the top, get rid of the bat-wing doors, put up a few shrubs, add a new thatched roof, and *voilá!* you had an Irish pub.

I called O'Shea outside and asked if he'd kept quiet about Fitzgerald.

"Sure. But half that bunch already knew. They were with me when I found the body. God knows who they've told."

It figured. "Kendall? Swan? Cooperworth? They all know?"

"Probably not. They don't talk to us much. We're not pretty enough for them."

"How about the Singing Shamrocks?"

O'Shea looked at the dirt street. My detecting instincts detected that I was on to something.

"Sure, and the Irish love to tell a lie," I said. "But now 'tis not the time for one."

"That was awful," O'Shea said, looking up. "Probably the worst Irish accent I've ever heard."

"But it came from the heart."

"Yeah."

"About the Singing Shamrocks," I said.

"Jerry liked the women," O'Shea said. "Even the big ones. Maybe especially the big ones."

"So he liked the Shamrocks?"

O'Shea got a feisty look on his face. "Nothing wrong with that, is there? Or do you have something against midgets?"

"Nothing wrong with a little romance as far as I'm concerned, as long as it's confined to members of the same species. Was it a problem for anyone else?"

O'Shea clammed up again. I looked at him and waited. Finally, he said, "Kendall."

"Kendall?"

"Kendall liked Brenda, too. He told Jerry that if he bothered her again, he'd kill him."

Ah-ha. The old detecting instincts had been right on the money.

"Brenda's one of the Shamrocks, I take it," I said.

"Their names are Brenda, Betty, and Beryl. Or so they tell me. I don't believe it for a minute."

"I believe your name is Michael O'Shea."

"Baloney."

"Yeah. Anything else you want to tell me?"

"Cooperworth."

"Cooperworth?"

"He was after Betty."

"I thought you said that Jerry liked Brenda."

O'Shea gave a leprechaun shrug.

"I told you he liked women. Brenda and Betty are women, and they didn't give us the brush-off like the big stars of the picture did."

"Right. So that's it?"

"Jorkens."

"Jorkens?"

"Have you noticed the echo around here?"

"Never mind the cracks," I said. "What about Jorkens?"

"He was after Beryl."

"And so was Jerry?"

"Like I told you."

I thought it over for a second. "What about Karen Swan? She's a real looker. Wasn't anyone after her?"

"You don't know about her?"

"No."

"She doesn't like guys. She prefers other women."

"Oh," I said. "Was she after any of the Shamrocks?"

"Sure," O'Shea said.

"Which one?"

"All of them."

"Damn," I said, not that I cared who or what Karen Swan liked. I'd just rounded up a guy who preferred sheep, after all. I just hoped nobody from *Inside Secrets* found out about Swan. That would be another job I'd have to handle.

"What about that pot of gold you mentioned?" I asked.

"It's gone. Jerry was the one who carried it around. He told me it was real."

"This is a movie set," I said. "Nothing's real. Except that rock out there, and the trees." I looked down at the green stain on my shoes. "The grass isn't even really green."

O'Shea shook his head stubbornly.

"All I know is what Jerry told me. 'Pure gold.' That's what he said."

Hollywood people, I thought. In some ways they were shrewd, but in others they were like children. They spend their whole lives with illusions. Not that I'm much different. I've dealt with a cockatoo that posed as a parrot and a dog that posed as a wolf that turned out to be . . . well, you get the idea. It's no wonder that as the days go by it gets harder and harder for Hollywood people to tell the difference between the illusions and what is real. Maybe that's why we're sometimes so easy to fool. Maybe that's why I work so hard at not being fooled.

4

I HAD TO CALL Gober and get him to come to the set. He wasn't happy about it, but he came. It took all his powers of persuasion and a number of threats about paychecks and people "never working in this town again" to get everyone I wanted to see rounded up together in the pub. No one was happy to be there, but at least some of them were honest.

"Sure, I said I'd kill him," Jackson Kendall told me. "But I didn't. I don't mind that somebody beat me to it, though, if you want to know the truth."

Kendall was one of those guys who looked even better in person than on the screen, where he looked pretty darn good. And his voice was deep and rich and powerful, just the way it sounded when he sang. He was shorter than he looked on screen, though. Probably not over five feet and six inches tall. Even at that, he towered over O'Shea.

"I told him to stay away from Brenda," Kendall went on. "I didn't like the way the little bastard would run up to her and bump into her all the time."

Brenda and the other two Singing Shamrocks were seated at a nearby table. They were all buxom women wearing Irish country dresses, and they all had glossy red hair, creamy complexions, and green eyes. What their real hair color might have been was anybody's guess.

Brenda was the one who was blushing. I figured the blush might have been genuine, but I didn't know the reason for it. Kendall was ready to explain, however.

"You know how short Fitzgerald was," he said, as if he were a giant among men himself. "Where do you think he'd strike Brenda when he bumped into her?"

I got it then, and Brenda blushed a bit more brightly.

"Sure and he did the same thing to Betty," Basil Cooperworth said in his phony Irish accent, which I had to admit was a lot better than mine. Cooperworth looked the part of a priest wearing his clerical collar and a pair of little half-glasses. He didn't sound like a priest when he talked about Fitzgerald, however.

"I told him to stay away from Betty or I'd break his scrawny little neck," he said, losing the accent.

It was Betty's turn to blush, but she didn't bother. She said, "He played the same game with Beryl. Isn't that right?"

Beryl didn't blush either. She just nodded, while Lenny Jorkens looked at her fondly.

"Which one of you did he lure out to the Blarney Stone today?" I asked.

"Goddamnit, Ferrell, what are you trying to do here?"

That was Mr. Gober, of course. I'd tried to get him to leave, but after walking all the way to the back lot, he wasn't going anywhere until things were settled satisfactorily. Having someone practically accuse one of his prized singers of killing Fitzgerald didn't fit his definition of "satisfactorily."

Lenny Jorkens didn't like it any better than Gober did.

"You'd better watch what you say, Ferrell," he said, an ugly twist to his mouth.

I thought about the way he'd slapped a dead man's face. There was a lot of hate in a person who'd do something like that. But I didn't think he'd killed Jerry Fitzgerald.

"Yes," Beryl said. She was the prettiest of the Shamrocks, and her alto voice was nice and low. "You should be careful of what you say, Mr. Ferrell. There are laws about libel and slander, you know."

"Tell that to the people at *Inside Secrets*," I said. "If they get wind of this mess, they'll make my little accusations sound like a bedtime story."

Gober turned red when I mentioned the magazine. He looked around the room as if some sleazy reporter might be lurking in a dark corner.

"That's all your accusations are," Kendall said. "A bedtime story. You can't prove a thing."

"Probably not. But the police might be able to. You know what I'd like?"

Nobody said a word. I guess they weren't interested. I'd thought Mr. Gober might help me out, but he just sat there, still red-faced, staring at me as if he thought I'd lost my mind.

Maybe I had. I said, "Since nobody wants to guess, I'll tell you what I'd like: I'd like to hear the Shamrocks sing a song."

"Faith and begorra," Cooperworth said. "The man's turned daft."

The accent was just as good as before, but it irritated me more this time.

"I'm not asking much," I said. "Maybe just part of a song."

"Why should we?" Betty wanted to know.

"Because Mr. Gober would appreciate it," I said, hoping he'd back me up this time.

And he did. Maybe he remembered all those other times I'd saved the studio. Or maybe he just wanted to get things over with. The reason didn't matter, as long as he did it.

"Sing him a song," he said. "What could it hurt?"

The Shamrock Sisters looked at each other. Beryl nodded, and they stood up.

"Over there would be fine," I said, pointing to a cleared area in front of the bar.

They walked over and stood side by side. Brenda was a bit taller than the other two, while Betty was on the stocky side. But they were all very attractive. I could see why Fitzgerald had liked them.

"Any requests?" Betty asked.

"Do your hit," I said.

Betty hummed a note, and they launched into a lively *a capella* version of "You Can Kiss the Blarney Stone, but You Can't Kiss Me."

They swayed in time to the music, and their skirts billowed out with their movements. I looked down at their shoes. They were black, but I could see the stains from the painted grass on them. Or at least I could see the stains on Beryl's and Brenda's shoes. There were no stains on Betty's.

That was interesting, because nearly everyone had walked on the grass that day, and they'd be walking on it again. Why bother to clean the shoes?

When the song was over, everyone applauded, and I took an empty glass over to Betty and handed it to her.

"That was great," I said. "I'd like to buy you a drink."

"There's no real liquor in here, Ferrell," Lenny said. "It's all just weak tea."

There was a general laugh at my stupidity. I joined in, and Betty put the glass down on the bar.

"I guess that's it, then," I said. "Thanks for the song."

Everyone seemed to think I was completely nuts, but they didn't ask questions. They just left. Except for Mr. Gober.

"Goddamnit, Ferrell," he said, "what the hell was all that about?"

"It's about this," I said, and I pulled the prophylactic out of my pocket.

"Jesus Christ!" Gober said, looking all around. "Put that away! What are you, anyway? Some kind of pervert?"

"That's always a possibility," I admitted. "But this isn't mine. I found it near Fitzgerald's body."

"In the woods? That's where you usually find things like that."

I didn't ask him how he knew. I said, "I think it was Fitzgerald's. He probably had it in his little pot of gold, the one he kept telling people was real. My idea is that he about halfway convinced Betty that he was telling the truth about the gold and got her to go out to the woods with him to have a little drink and take a look at his treasure. When they got to the Blarney Stone, she asked to see the gold, and this is what Fitzgerald pulled out of the pot. That's when she clobbered him with the bottle. She took the gold. She probably still hoped it was real. But she missed this."

"Knowing that damned lying Fitzgerald," Gober said, "I can see how that might have happened the way you say. But how do you know it was Betty who was with him?"

"I knew it had to be one of the Shamrocks," I said. "Before he died, Fitzgerald pulled the fake clover out of his hat and clutched one of the leaves in his hand."

"How do you know that, for God's sake?"

"When he was hit by the bottle, it dented the brim of his hat. He was hit so hard that the blow should have knocked the hat away from him. But it was lying right beside him. I think he pulled it over to him and grabbed the shamrock to leave a clue about his killer."

Gober nodded as if he might believe me, but he wasn't entirely convinced.

"If it happened that way," he said, "which I'm not sure it did, why single out Betty?"

"Her shoes."

"Shoes?"

I saw what O'Shea meant about the echo.

"Her shoes didn't have any green paint on them. From the grass. She'd wiped it all off. She wasn't thinking clearly, I guess, and she must have believed the paint would give away the fact that she'd been to the woods. But the paint was everywhere. Even you have a little on your shoes."

Gober looked down. "All right. I suppose that's why you wanted them to sing. So you could have a look at the shoes."

"I'd already seen the shoes when she came in. I wanted a reason to congratulate them and get her to hold a glass."

"Fingerprints," Gober said, looking over at the glass that still sat on the bar.

"Right. If the prints on that glass match the ones on the whiskey bottle, the cops will have a pretty good case against Betty. And they'll probably find that she has the pot of gold, too."

"And that's the end of the Singing Shamrocks," Gober said. "The end of the picture, too. Goddamnit, Ferrell, you're supposed to help the studio, not shut it down."

Shutting down the picture wasn't the same thing as shutting down the studio, but there was no need to point that out. Gober already knew it.

"You won't have to shut down the picture," I said.

"The hell you say. What about the Shamrocks?"

"That's easy. Find you someone else who can sing and who looks like Betty. Dye her hair red, and that's that."

"It's not as easy as you make it sound," Gober said.

"Sure it is. This town is full of pretty women who want to be movie stars and singers. You'll find someone."

"Maybe. But what about leprechauns? They aren't as easy to find as singers."

"O'Shea is pretty good. He could carry the part. He even has an Irish name."

Gober nodded. "He does, doesn't he? But the trial and the publicity will be ugly."

"You know what short memories people have. There won't be much publicity if Betty is already replaced by the time she's arrested."

He knew I was right. He said, "When do the cops get here?"

"It won't be long. They may be here already. Dr. Sloane is coming first. He's going to confuse things for a while."

"Come back to the office when you're finished. I'll have another bonus check for you. Then you need to go home. You smell like sheep."

I PUT THE GLASS in a safe place under the bar and went outside to watch Gober walk down the village street. The production obviously hadn't shut down. Jackson Kendall and Karen Swan, along with the whole crew, were at the edge of the village, getting ready to film a scene with the sheep. I could hear the herd's gentle bleating. It didn't do much for me, but then I wasn't Monty Raines. I hoped the hypnotist would be able to help him.

I skirted the shooting area and walked on back to the woods to sit with Jerry Fitzgerald until Dr. Sloane and the police arrived. There was something in my pocket that I needed to return to the scene. And besides, I didn't like the idea of a leprechaun having to wait alone.

THE DUBLIN EYE

Clark Howard

K ILKENNY HEARD THE PHONE ring as he was unlocking his office door. He hurried in to answer it.

"Kilkenny," he said.

"Is this Mr. Royal Kilkenny?" a hesitant female voice asked. The caller sounded very young. "Mr. Royal Kilkenny, the query man?"

"Yes. How can I help you?"

"Mr. Kilkenny, my name is Darlynn Devalain. I'm the daughter of Joe Devalain, of Belfast."

An image mushroomed in Kilkenny's mind. Not of Joe Devalain, but of the woman Joe had married. Of Sharmon. This girl on the phone was probably Sharmon's daughter.

"How is your dad, then?" Kilkenny asked. "And your mother?"

"My dad's not so good, Mr. Kilkenny," the girl replied, and Kilkenny, though he had never laid eyes on her, could almost see her lip quivering as her voice broke. "He's been in a bad accident. An explosion in his shop. They've got him over at Saint Bartholomew's Hospital, but it's not known if he'll live or—"

"Did your mother tell you to call me?" Kilkenny asked, frowning. It had been eighteen years since Sharmon Cavan had picked Joe Devalain over him, and he had gone off to America to try and forget her.

"No, she doesn't even know I'm after calling you," Darlynn Devalain said. "Me dad told me once that he knew you before you went to America. When he heard you'd come back and set up as a query man down in Dublin, he told me you were a man he could always count on. He said if I should ever find myself in serious trouble of any kind to get hold of you and tell you I'm the daughter of Joe Devalain. You'd help me just as if I were your own. So that's why I'm calling, sor. Not for me, but for me dad. He needs somebody to look after his interests. The police, they don't seem to care much about who blew up his shop."

"How badly was he hurt in the explosion?" Kilkenny asked.

"As badly as one can be and still be called alive," the girl said. "Oh, Mr. Kilkenny, he's in terrible shape. Can you come, sor? Please."

The girl's voice reminded Kilkenny of Sharmon. Sharmon, with her deep-rust-colored hair and dancing emerald eyes, the smile that showed crooked teeth that somehow made her even prettier, the wide, wide shoulders, and the strong peasant thighs that even at sixteen could lock a man where she wanted him, for as long as she wanted him there.

"Yes, I'll come," Kilkenny said. "I'll take the train up and meet you at the hospital this evening."

KILKENNY BOUGHT A FIRST-CLASS seat on the *Enterprise Express*, which made the Dublin-Belfast run in two hours and twenty minutes. Dundalk, an hour north of Dublin, was the last stop in the Irish Free State. After Dundalk, the train crossed into Country Armagh, which was part of Northern Ireland.

At Portadown, the first stop in Armagh, British soldiers boarded the coaches and checked all passengers. From Portadown on into Belfast an armed British soldier rode at each end of every coach. Most passengers didn't leave their seats even to go to the lavatory during that leg of the journey.

At Belfast Central the passengers stood for a pat-down baggage search and questioning at a British Army checkpoint in the middle of the station.

"Identification, please," a pink-cheeked, young lieutenant requested. Kilkenny handed over his billfold. "What's your business in Belfast, sir?"

"To see a friend who's in hospital."

"What's the duration of your stay, sir?"

"I don't know. No more than forty-eight hours, I shouldn't expect."

"Your occupation is listed as a 'personal enquiries representative.' What is that, exactly?"

"I'm a private investigator. A detective."

The young officer's expression brightened. "You mean like one of those American private eyes? Like that Magnum bloke?"

"Yes, sort of. Less hectic, though."

The lieutenant frowned. "Not armed, I hope."

"No." Kilkenny wondered why he asked. A sergeant had already patted Kilkenny down and two privates had rummaged through his overnighter.

"Pass through," the officer said, returning Kilkenny's billfold.

Outside the terminal Kilkenny got into a square black taxi. "Saint Bartholomew's Hospital," he said.

The driver glanced at him in the rearview mirror, then looked out the side window at the darkening late-afternoon sky. "That's in the Flats," he said.

"The Flats?"

"Aye. Unity Flats. The Catholic section. I'll take you in, but I can't wait for you or come back to get you. I'm not Catholic, so I can't risk being in the Flats after dark."

"Just drop me at the hospital," Kilkenny said. "That'll be fine."

ON THE WAY THROUGH the city, it started to rain—one of those sudden, blustery rains that seemed to be forever blowing in off the North

Channel and turning the already dreary gray streets a drearier black. Kilkenny hadn't thought to bring a raincoat—it had been so long since he'd been to Belfast he had forgotten how unpredictable the weather could be.

"Bit of a heavy dew out there," he said.

"Aye," the driver replied, turning on the wipers. He made no attempt at further conversation.

Kilkenny wasn't familiar with the section called Unity Flats. He, Joe Devalain, and Sharmon Cavan had grown up in a slum known as Ballymurphy. It was a savagely poor place, worse than anything Kilkenny had seen during his ten years as a New York City policeman. In New York he had worked both Spanish Harlem and the South Bronx, and neither of them was nearly as poor, ugly, or deprived as Ballymurphy. Ballymurphy wasn't the gutter, it was the sewer. Both Kilkenny and Joe Devalain had sworn to Sharmon that they would take her away from the life of poverty in which they had all grown to adolescence.

It had not been Kilkenny that Sharmon picked to do it. "I've decided in favor of Joe," she told Kilkenny one night after they had made love under the back stairs of Sharmon's tenement building.

"I thought you loved *me*," Kilkenny had said.

"I love you both," Sharmon had answered. "Do y'think I'd do this with the two of you if I didn't love you both? It's just that I can't *have* you both, so I must choose, mustn't I? And I've chosen Joe."

"But why? Why him and not me?"

"Lots of reasons," she said lightly. "I like the name Sharmon Devalain better than I like Sharmon Kilkenny. And I think Joe will do better in life than you. He's got a good job at the linen plant— someday he'll probably be a foreman. While you've done nothing at all to better yourself."

"I go to school," Kilkenny protested. "I want to be a policeman, someday—"

"I don't like policemen," she said loftily. "They're a smug lot. Anyway, Joe'll earn lots more when he works his way up to plant foreman than you'll ever earn being a policeman."

Kilkenny had been sick with disappointment. "If it's just the money, maybe I could be something else—"

"It's not just that," she said.

"What else, then?"

"Well, y'see," she replied with a little reluctance, "Joe is—well, *better* at—well, you know—" She sighed impatiently. "He's a bit more of a man, if y'know what I mean."

Kilkenny had thought he would never get over that remark. It left him impotent for six months. Only after leaving Ireland, going to Southampton, boarding a ship for America, and meeting on board a fleshy Czech girl just beginning to feel her new freedom after escaping from behind the Iron Curtain, was he able to function physically as a man again. He had never had a problem since—but he had never forgotten Sharmon's words.

"Here you are," the driver said. "Saint Bartholomew's."

Kilkenny collected his bag and got out. The driver made change for him, glanced up at the waning daylight again, and sped off.

FROM THE FRONT STEPS of the hospital Kilkenny looked around at what he could see of Unity Flats. It was a slum, as Ballymurphy had been, though not quite as stark and dirty. But definitely a ghetto. Sharmon hadn't made it very far with Joe, he thought.

In the hospital lobby, a young nun, wearing the habit of the Ulster Sisters of Charity, consulted a name file and directed Kilkenny to a ward on the third floor. He waited for the lift with several women visitors. The women in the north were not as attractive as the women down south, he noticed. Most of them wore white *T*-necks that clearly outlined their brassieres, wide-legged, baggy slacks or skirts that were too short, no stockings, and shoes with straps that made their ankles look thick. Their hair seemed to be combed and in control only down to their cheeks, then appeared to grow wild on its own, as if it was too much to take care of. They were poor women, clearly. As they grew older, Kilkenny knew, they would all become noble mother figures who would strive to keep their husbands sober, their children God-fearing and Catholic, and their homes decent. They were the silent strength of the poor Northern Irish Catholic household. Kilkenny wondered if Sharmon had become like them.

At the third-floor ward, Kilkenny stepped through double swinging doors and looked around. The instant he saw Darlynn Devalain, he knew who she was. She looked nothing at all like Joe, but though he saw only a trace of Sharmon, there was enough so there was no mistaking who she was. Burnt-blonde hair, eyes a little too close together, lips a little crooked, almost mismatched, there was something distinctly urchin about her. That touch of the gutter, Kilkenny thought. It never entirely leaves us.

She was standing just outside a portable screen that kept the last bed on the ward partitioned from the others. She was staring out at nothing as if in a trance. Kilkenny put his bag by the wall and walked down the ward toward her. When he came into her field of vision, it seemed to break her concentration and she watched him as he walked up to her. Their eyes met and held.

"You're Darlynn," he said. "I'm Royal Kilkenny."

She put out her hand. "Thanks for coming." She bobbed her chin at the bed behind the screen. "Me dad's there. What's left of him."

There were a doctor and two nurses on one side of the bed, the nurses just turning away with covered aluminum trays in their hands, walking past Kilkenny on their way out. When they left, Kilkenny had an unobstructed view of the bed. What he saw did not look like a man at all; it looked like a large pillow under a sheet with a head placed above it and several rubber tubes running down to it from jars of liquid hung on racks next to the bed. There was an oxygen mask over part of the face. Kilkenny saw no arms or legs under the sheet and felt his mouth go dry.

"Who are you, please?" the doctor asked, noticing Kilkenny.

"A friend. Up from Dublin. His daughter called me." Kilkenny tried to swallow but could not. "Is he still alive?" he asked. The form did not appear to be breathing.

"Yes. Why or how, I don't know. The explosion totally devastated him. Apparently, he was right on top of whatever detonated. The flash of the explosion blinded him; the noise destroyed his eardrums so that he's now completely deaf; and the hot gases got into his open mouth and burned up his tongue and vocal cords, making him mute. The force of the blast damaged his lungs and shattered his limbs so badly we had to amputate both arms above the elbow and both legs above the knee. So here he lies, unable to see, hear, or speak, unable to breathe without an oxygen mask, and with no arms or legs. But he's alive." He led Kilkenny out to where Darlynn stood. "I've sedated him for the night," he told the girl. "You go home and rest, young lady. That's an order."

Kilkenny took Darlynn by the arm and gently led her out of the ward, picking up his bag on the way. There was a snack shop still open on the ground floor and Kilkenny took her there, found a remote table, and ordered tea.

"How's your mother taking it?" he asked.

Darlynn shrugged. "It's not the end of the world for her. She and Dad haven't got on that great the past few years."

Kilkenny decided not to pursue that topic. "What kind of explosion was it? How'd it happen?"

"We don't know. It's supposedly being investigated by the RUC. But you know how that is."

The RUC was the Royal Ulster Constabulary, Northern Ireland's civilian police force. Like all other civil service in Ireland's British-aligned six northern counties, it was controlled by London and more than 90 percent Protestant.

"They're trying to put the blame on the IRA," Darlynn added.

"Of course." *It would be the natural thing for them to do*, Kilkenny thought. But he knew, as most Irishmen did, that for the IRA to be responsible for every crime attributed to it, the outlaw organization would have to be fifty thousand strong instead of the less than a thousand it actually was. "Was your dad still active in the IRA?" he asked.

Darlynn glanced at him and hesitated a beat before answering. Kilkenny expected as much. He was, despite her father's recommendation, still a stranger to her, and to speak of the IRA to strangers could be dangerous. But something about him apparently prompted her trust.

"No, he hadn't been active for about five years. He still supported the organization financially, as much as he could afford, but he no longer took part in raids or anything like that."

"Had he any trouble with the Orangemen?" Kilkenny asked, referring to the pseudo-Masonic order of Protestants that opposed a united Ireland. Their activities were often as violent as the IRA, though never as well publicized.

"Dad had no trouble with them that I know about," Darlynn said. "Except for his IRA donations, he stayed pretty much out of politics. All he cared about these past few years was that shop of his. He was very proud of that shop."

"What sort of shop?" Kilkenny asked. The last he'd heard, Joe Devalain was still trying to work his way up the ladder at the linen factory.

"It was a linen shop. Tablecloths, napkins, handkerchiefs, a few bedcovers, a small line of curtains. If there was one thing Dad knew, it was cloth. He worked in the linen factory for eighteen years and never got a single promotion, but he learned all there was to know about cloth. Finally, he decided to pack it in. He drew out all his pension benefits and opened the shop. Mum was furious about it, said those benefits were half hers, for her old age as well as his. But Da did it anyway."

"Was that when things started going bad between them?"

"Not really. They'd been at each other off and on for a long time." Darlynn looked down at the tabletop. "Mum's had a boyfriend or two."

"Did you tell your mother you were calling me?" Kilkenny asked.

"I told her after."

"What was her reaction?"

"She got a funny kind of look on her face, like I haven't seen in a long time. When I was a little girl, she used to get a look like that whenever Da would bring her a bouquet of posies. When I mentioned your name, it was like I had done something special for her. Were you and my mother close?"

Kilkenny nodded. "Your mum and dad and me were all three close. Your dad and me were best friends, but we were rivals for your mum, too. Your dad won her. He was too much a match for me."

"He wouldn't be much competition now, would he?" she asked. Suddenly, tears streaked her cheeks.

Kilkenny calmed her down and got her to finish her tea, then walked the two miles home with her because she didn't feel like riding a bus. It had stopped raining and the bleak, poorly lighted streets smelled wet and the air was heavy. Kilkenny's palm sweated from carrying the suitcase. There was something about the way Darlynn's hair bounced in back that reminded him of Sharmon.

Somewhere along the way, he promised the girl he would look into the matter of the explosion that had destroyed everything about her father except his life.

THE DEVALAINS LIVED AS tenants in a little timeworn house that looked like wet newspaper. As Kilkenny and Darlynn got to the door, Sharmon Devalain opened it for them.

"Hello, Roy," she said.

"Hello, Sharmon."

The sight of her reduced him to astonishment. She seemed not to have aged as he had. There were no plump cheeks, no wide hips, nothing even remotely in common with the women he had seen at the lift in the hospital. She didn't look a day over thirty, if that.

"Come in, Roy. I'll make tea."

"We've just had tea, actually. And I've got to go get a room."

"You can stay here. I can sleep with Darlynn. The place isn't much, but it's clean."

"Thanks anyway, but I'd better stay downtown. I told Darlynn I'd try and find out about the explosion."

Sharmon threw her daughter a quick, irritated glance. "She's quick to ask for anything she wants. Even with strangers."

"I don't really feel like a stranger to her. After all, she *is* yours. And Joe's."

"Yes. Well, I'm sure the RUC will appreciate any help you can give them." Her eyes flicked up and down his tall frame. "You're looking well, Roy. Prosperous."

"Hardly that. I make a comfortable living is all. But it's what I want to do."

"Well, you're one of the lucky ones, then. Most people never get what they want out of life. Are you sure about tea? Or staying the night?"

"Yes, thanks. I'll be off. Is there a bus at the corner?"

Sharmon nodded. "Number Five. It'll take you to Great Victoria Street. Will I see you again?"

"Sure," Kilkenny said. "I'll be around."

Only when he was walking down the street did Kilkenny realize that he had not said he was sorry about Joe.

HE GOT A ROOM at the Europa Hotel downtown and spent the night alternating between restless, fitful sleep and sitting on the windowsill, staring out at the night city, remembering.

When the night finally ended and daylight broke over Belfast Lough, when from his hotel window Kilkenny saw smoke rising from the great stacks of Harland and Wolff, the mammoth shipbuilding complex, and when civil servants began hurrying along Howard Street to their jobs in nearby Donegall Square, he showered and shaved and went down for breakfast.

After he ate, he walked over to Oxford Street where the Royal Courts of Justice were located and found that the Royal Ulster Constabulary headquarters were still situated nearby. After telling his business to a receptionist in the lobby, he was sent up to the first floor and shown to the desk of Sergeant Bill O'Marn of the Bomb Investigation section.

"Well, well," O'Marn said, looking at Kilkenny's identification. "A real flesh-and-blood private eye, just like on the telly." He was a handsome man of forty, with great bushy black eyebrows. One of the "Black Irish" that women seemed to find so attractive. He wore a sprig of light green heather on the lapel of his Harris tweed jacket. *Dapper,* Kilkenny thought. "You realize your detective license is no good up here, don't you?" O'Marn asked.

"Certainly," said Kilkenny. "I'm only making inquiry at the request of Mr. Devalain's daughter."

"Who, I believe, is a minor."

"Yes, I believe she is. As I started to say, though, I haven't been retained or anything like that. The girl just wants to know who detonated her father. As I'm sure you do also."

"We already know," O'Marn said. "It was the IRA."

"I see. May I ask *how* you know?"

"The explosion was caused by gelignite. Nobody but the IRA uses gelignite. Every time we raid an IRA headquarters, we confiscate a footlocker full of the stuff."

Kilkenny nodded. "What reason, I wonder, would the IRA have for blowing up Joe Devalain."

"They don't need reasons for what they do," O'Marn scoffed. "They're madmen, the lot of them."

"Are you saying they simply decided to blow up a shop—any shop—and picked Joe Devalain's place randomly?"

"Looks that way to us."

This time Kilkenny shook his head. "I'm sorry, Sergeant O'Marn, but I can't accept that premise. It's always been my understanding that the IRA was much more precise in its operations than that. I thought it only set off bombs in strategic locations where the British Army mustered or patrolled, or where the explosion would produce some subsequent economic impact. I don't see how blowing up a small linen shop is going to do them any good at all."

"Neither do I," O'Marn agreed with an artificial smile. "But then, you and I aren't IRA terrorists, are we?"

"Is the matter still under investigation?" Kilkenny asked, ignoring the sergeant's question.

"Technically, yes."

"But it isn't being worked?"

"I didn't say that, Mr. Kilkenny."

Kilkenny rose. "You didn't have to. I wonder what you'll do about your crime statistics if the IRA ever disbands. Anyway, thanks for your time, Sergeant. Good day."

FROM RUC HEADQUARTERS, KILKENNY rode a bus back out to Unity Flats. On the way he became aware of some of the graffiti that scarred the city. NO POPE HERE! read one. NO QUEEN HERE! countered another. PROVISIONALS FOR FREEDOM, GOD SAVE OUR POPE! was offset by NO SURRENDER, GOD SAVE THE QUEEN! Some city blocks warned: ARMY

KEEP OUT! SOLDIERS ARE BASTARDS! Others proclaimed: ULSTER WILL FIGHT! The most ominous said simply: INFORMERS BEWARE.

Twice along the way, the bus passed moving Saracens, big six-wheeled armored vehicles that carried three soldiers and patrolled the Catholic sections. The great tanks lumbered past children playing on the sidewalk. They didn't even glance at it, never having known streets without such patrols.

At Saint Bart's hospital, Kilkenny found Darlynn sitting by her father's bed, gently stroking the stump of one arm above the bandage. She looked scrubbed and fresh, like a schoolgirl. Kilkenny drew a chair around and sat by her.

"When your dad was active in the IRA, did you ever know any of his contacts?" he asked very quietly.

Darlynn shook her head. "The only time the organization was ever mentioned was when he and Mum would fight about it. She claimed it was because he was suspected of being IRA that he never got promoted at the linen factory. According to her, it's been the IRA that's kept us in Unity Flats all these years."

"Did you ever know of any meeting places he went to?"

"I'm not sure. There was a pub out on Falls Road—Bushmills', it was called. I used to find matchboxes from the place when I emptied the pockets of Da's trousers for the wash. I know after he left the IRA I never found them again."

While she was talking, Darlynn had unintentionally stopped stroking her father's mutilated arm. To Kilkenny's surprise, the reduced figure on the bed began emitting from under the oxygen mask a pitiful, begging noise. Darlynn resumed stroking at once, and what was left of Joe Devalain calmed down.

"I don't even know if he's aware of me," Darlynn said.

"I'm sure he is," Kilkenny told her, though he wasn't sure at all.

"I wish there was some way to communicate with him," the girl said. "Maybe he'd know who did this to him."

Yes, Kilkenny thought, he might. But how *did* one communicate with a living soul who could not see, hear, or speak, and had no hands with which to write or feel or make signals?

"Would you like to come for supper tonight?" Darlynn asked. "Mum's going out, but I'm a better cook, anyway—at least, Da's always said I was. It wouldn't be anything fancy, you understand."

"I'm sorry, I'll be busy tonight, Darlynn. I want to make contact with the IRA if I can."

She put her free hand on his knee. "Stop by later, then. Just so I'll know you're all right?"

He promised he would.

As he left the hospital, Kilkenny imagined that his leg felt warm where she had touched him.

BUSHMILLS' WAS NOT UNLIKE a hundred other neighborhood pubs in Belfast. It had a stained-glass window or two, a few secluded nooks, one private booth with frosted glass, and a bar as shiny as a little girl's cheeks on First Holy Communion Day. There was always an accordion player about, and always a stale beer odor in the air. Anyone ordering anything except a pint of stout drawn from the tap got a sidelong glance. All conversation ceased when a stranger entered.

Kilkenny stood in the silence at the end of the bar and ordered his pint. When it came, he paid for it and drank it down in a single, long, continuous swallow. Wiping off the foam with the back of his hand, he then spoke to the bartender in a tone that every man on the premises could hear.

"My name is Royal Kilkenny. I'm a detective down in the Free State, but I grew up here in Belfast, over in Ballymurphy. My father was Doyle Kilkenny. My mother was Faye Quinn Kilkenny. My grandfather on my mother's side was Darcy Quinn, who was Padraic Pearse's man in County Longford and served four years in His Majesty's prison at Wormwood Scrubs for the privilege. I'm up here because a friend of mine named Joe Devalain was blown up in his linen shop three days ago. He's still alive, what there is left of him, but that doesn't include eyes, ears, voice, hands, or feet. The RUC tells me the IRA did it. I don't believe that. But I want to hear it from the mouth of a man who knows for sure. I'm at the Europa Hotel, room 719. I'll be back there within the hour."

AS KILKENNY SUSPECTED, IT worked. Two men came for him just after dark, escorted him to a panel truck parked near the hotel, put him in the back, and blindfolded him. The truck was driven for about thirty minutes, on rough streets, making many turns. When finally it stopped, Kilkenny was taken out, led into a building and down some stairs, and finally had his blindfold removed in a small, cluttered room in which a white-haired man sat behind a scarred desk.

"My father was in prison with your grandfather," the white-haired man said. "I'm Michael McGuire."

"It's an honor to meet you, sir," Kilkenny said. Iron Mike McGuire was a legend in Northern Ireland. A third-generation Irish freedom fighter, he was the most-wanted man in the country. There wasn't a child over six in Belfast who didn't know his name, yet fewer than a dozen people had seen his face in nearly a decade.

"I know about Joe Devalain's misfortune," Iron Mike said. "I was saddened to hear of it. Joe was once a loyal soldier fighting for a united Ireland. He left the cause some years back, for reasons of his own, but I understand he continued to contribute money to us, for which we are grateful. There was no ill will when he left us. There never is. A man does what he can, for as long as he can, and that's all we ask. If Joe still had been one of us, actively, we'd right now be after finding out who bombed him. Since he was not, we choose to stay out of it. I can assure you, however, that the IRA had nothing to do with the incident."

Kilkenny nodded. "I see. Well, I thank you for telling me, sir, and for the trouble of bringing me here."

"It's not been that much trouble. I'd be particular, though, if I were you, where I made that little speech you gave in Bushmills'. There's some pubs you'd not've walked out of. Pubs that are patronized by the other side."

"I understand," Kilkenny said. "I appreciate the advice. May I ask for a bit more?"

"A man can always ask."

"How would I go about contacting the Orangemen?"

McGuire exchanged a fleeting glance with the two men who had brought Kilkenny. "For what purpose?" he asked.

"The same purpose as my coming here. To see if they were responsible. If it was political, what happened to Joe, then I'll let the matter go. But if the Orangemen also disclaim the act, then I've still got work to do."

Pursing his lips, McGuire silently drummed the thick, stubby fingers of one hand on the scarred desktop. "All right," he said after a moment. "I don't believe the Orangemen were involved, but I could be wrong. At any rate, the only Order of Orange faction that is authorized to take lives is the Black Preceptories. It's an internal terrorist group that specializes in kidnapping, torture, and house-burning. It was them that torched the two hundred Catholic homes in Bogside back in '78. The leader of the bunch is Black Jack Longmuir. He works in the shipyards. You can usually find him through the union office." McGuire smiled as cold a smile as Kilkenny had ever seen. "When y'see him, tell him I'm thinking about him. Day and night. Always thinking about him."

With those words, McGuire nodded and Kilkenny was once again blindfolded and led away.

THE UNION OFFICE WAS open around the clock, because Harland and Wolff Shipbuilding was running three shifts. The office was situated in a little corrugated metal building just outside the shipyard entrance. There was no doubt where the union's sympathy and support lay. Immediately inside the door was an Order of Orange flag and a framed rhyme:

> Catholics beware! For your time has come!
> Listen to the dread sound of our Protestant drum!
> In memory of William, we'll hoist up our flag!
> We'll raise the bright orange and burn your green rag!

William was William of Orange, who married the daughter of the last Catholic king of England, James II, then betrayed him, drove him from the throne, and turned Britain into a Protestant country. Five years later the Orange Society was formed in Ireland by the new gentry to whom William had distributed the land. Its

purpose, by its own charter, was to maintain the Protestant constitution of the country. Nearly two hundred years later, it was still trying to do that, although it had since met failure in twenty-six of
Ireland's thirty-two counties. The organization was strongest in
Belfast, where it controlled the trade unions. Nowhere was there a
better example of that strength than at Harland and Wolff, Ulster's
greatest single industrial complex. Of ten thousand employees, only
one hundred were Catholic.

"Might I be of some service, sor?" a bulldog of a man asked
Kilkenny when he entered.

"I was told I might find Jack Longmuir here," Kilkenny said. Several
men in the little office glanced at him, then looked away quickly.

"May I ask what your business is, sor?"

"I'm a detective from Dublin. An old mate of mine was seriously
injured by a bomb in his shop three days ago. I'd like to ask
Mr. Longmuir's advice about how best to go about finding out who did it."

The little bulldog cocked his head. "What makes y'think he'd give
you advice on a matter like that?"

"What makes *you* think he wouldn't?" Kilkenny countered. "Or
are you authorized to speak for him?"

The little man turned red. "I'll see if he's here."

Several minutes later, a young man in coveralls, with metal shav-
ings and dust on his sleeves, came to fetch Kilkenny. Giving him a
visitor's pass, he led Kilkenny past a security gate and into the shipyard. They walked in silence for two hundred yards, then the escort
guided him into a welding hangar where at least thirty men were
working on sections of steel hull. Pointing, he directed Kilkenny up
a metal ladder to a catwalk where a tall man stood with a clipboard
in his hand.

Kilkenny climbed the ladder and moved around the metal catwalk
until he was near enough to speak. But the tall man spoke first.

"I'm Longmuir. What d'you want?"

"Do you know of Joe Devalain?" Kilkenny asked.

Longmuir nodded. He was a cadaverous man with a jaw that was
steel blue from a lifetime of using a straight razor. His eyes looked like
two perfect bullet holes.

"I'd like to find out who did it to him," Kilkenny said. "But only
if it was nonpolitical. If it was a political act, I'll leave it be."

"Why come to me?" Longmuir asked. "I'm a law-abiding British subject. I work, take care of my family, and support the Presbyterian Church and my trade union. I know nothing of bombings and such. Who sent you to me?"

"Michael McGuire."

For just an instant Longmuir's face registered surprise, but he quickly contained it. "Iron Mike, eh?" he said, as if the words were a foul taste in his mouth. "You saw him, did you?"

"Yes. He assured me the IRA wasn't involved in what happened to Joe. He said only you could tell me whether the Black Preceptories did it."

"How does Iron Mike look?" Longmuir asked curiously. "I've not seen even a photograph of him in ten years."

Kilkenny thought for a moment, then said: "He looks old. And tired."

Longmuir grunted softly. "Aye. Like me." He squinted at Kilkenny. "Did he say anything about me?"

"Yes. That he thinks about you a lot."

Longmuir smiled a smile as hateful as McGuire's had been. "I hope he's thinking of me when he draws his last breath." The tall man stared out at nothing for a moment, deep in thought. Then he emitted a quiet sigh. "No one associated with the Order of Orange had anything to do with blowing up your friend," he told Kilkenny. "You'll have to look elsewhere for them that's guilty."

Kilkenny thanked him, and Black Jack Longmuir had him escorted out of the shipyard complex.

IT WASN'T TOO LATE, so Kilkenny rode a bus out to the Devalain house to ask how Joe had fared that day and to question Sharmon and Darlynn, now that a political motive had been eliminated, about who else might have reason to harm Joe. When he got to the house and knocked, no one answered right away. Kilkenny thought they might already have gone to bed. The past few days had to have been very trying for them. Darlynn, especially, looked on the verge of exhaustion.

Kilkenny had just turned to leave when Sharmon opened the door, wearing a housecoat.

"Hello, Roy. Darlynn's not here—she's staying at the hospital all night. Joe's mind seems to be going. He's bucking up and down on the bed, making that pathetic sound he makes, raising havoc. The only thing that seems to calm him is to have Darlynn there, patting him. The doctor says her touch is all he relates to now; he's been reduced to the primitive level, whatever that means. I'd offer you tea, but I'm just out."

She had not stepped away from the doorway or invited him inside.

"Tea's not necessary," Kilkenny said, "But I would like to ask you a few questions."

"I was just ready for bed, Roy. Can we do it tomorrow?" She must have noticed the curious expression that came over his face, because she amended her reply at once. "I suppose we can do it now. It won't take long, will it?"

"Shouldn't."

She led him to the modest parlor with its threadbare sofa, worn rug, and scratched coffee table. She conducted herself very much like a lady, keeping the housecoat well around her, even holding it closed at the throat. Her reserved demeanor brought back Darlynn's words to him: "Mum's had a boyfriend or two." Kilkenny had expected Sharmon to make advances on him first chance she got. Now it appeared she was doing just the opposite.

"I'm sorry Darlynn isn't here," she said. "She'll be sorry she missed you. She fancies you, y'know."

"Nonsense," Kilkenny scoffed. "She's only a girl."

"Look again, Roy. She's older than I was when we first went under the stairs together."

"That was different. I'm sure she only looks on me as an uncle or something." He sat down. "Now then, to business. I've made contact with the IRA and the Black Preceptories. From both quarters I've been assured that there was no involvement in blowing up Joe's shop."

"And you believe them?" Sharmon asked.

Kilkenny nodded. "No reason not to. If either group had done it, there would have been a purpose—the IRA because Joe had betrayed it in some way, the Black Preceps because he was still providing financial support to the IRA or some other unknown reason. Whatever, the bombing would have been to make an example of him. Not to take credit for it would be defeating the purpose of the act. If either group had done it, they'd have claimed it and said why."

"So who d'you think did it, then?"

"That's where I go from here. Who do *you* think might have done it?"

"I haven't a notion."

"Did he have any enemies?"

"Joe? Not likely. You have to *do* something to make enemies. Joe never did anything. Sure, he joined the IRA, but only because a lot of his mates was doing the same. And he ended up quitting that. The only thing he ever done on his own was leaving the linen factory and opening up that silly shop. That was the only independent decision he ever made in his life, and you see how that turned out."

"Was he gambling, d'you know? Could he have been in debt and you not know it?"

Sharmon grunted scornfully. "He didn't have the guts to gamble."

"Do you think there could have been another woman? A jealous husband or a boyfriend?"

She shook her head. "Never."

"Well, *somebody* didn't like him," Kilkenny said. "Can't you think of anybody?"

"Just me," Sharmon answered evenly.

"You?" Kilkenny had known it, but had never expected her to be so candid about it.

"Yes, me." With just a hint of defiance. "And why not? Look around you," she challenged, waving an arm. "This here is what my whole *life* is like. Worn, tattered, musty, colorless. This here is what I gave up my *youth* for, Roy. This here is all I *have*. It's all he's ever given me. Oh yes, I disliked him. And if he'd been poisoned or cut up with a kitchen knife, I'd be your number-one suspect. But I wouldn't know how to make a bomb even if I had the proper stuff."

"No, you wouldn't," Kilkenny said. He thought he heard a noise from the rear of the house—a creaking, as if someone had stepped on an unsteady floorboard. "Could that be Darlynn home?"

"No. She always uses the front. It's probably a loose shutter. Listen, can we finish this another time, Roy? I've a raging headache and really would like to get to bed."

"Sure."

On his way to the front door, Kilkenny noticed an ashtray on one of the tables with something purplish in it. He saw it only for a second, for just as his eyes came to rest on it Sharmon picked it up and emptied it in a wastebasket under the table. "Goodnight then, Roy," she said. "God bless."

"Goodnight, Sharmon."

He did not return her "God Bless" because it had just registered in his mind what the purplish thing in the ashtray was.

Irish heather. Green Irish heather. It turned purple when it died.

KILKENNY WENT TO THE hospital and found Darlynn asleep on a couch in the waiting room. "She was all wore out," the nun in charge of the ward told him. "When her father finally got calmed, we made her come in here and lie down. She was asleep that quick."

"Is he asleep, too?" Kilkenny asked of Joe.

"We never know, do we?" the nun replied quietly. "He doesn't have to close his eyelids to sleep."

Kilkenny went into the ward and stood by Joe's bed. Devalain's form was still, his eyes wide and fixed. "I might know who did this to you, Joe," Kilkenny whispered. "But I must be sure before I do anything."

Stepping to the window at the end of the long room, Kilkenny stared out at the blackness, seeing only his own dim reflection from the night-light next to Joe's bed. *If only I could ask him simple questions he could answer with a nod or a shake of his head,* he thought. But how in bloody hell can you communicate with somebody who can't hear or see? If he had fingers, he could use children's wooden alphabet blocks. Joe could feel the letters.

If, sure, Kilkenny thought with frustration. If he had fingers, if he had eyes. If I could work goddamned miracles, I could read his bleeding mind! He turned from the window and looked at Joe again. Sighing, he walked into the hall, wondering if he should wake Darlynn and take her home. Across the hall, above the door to one of the other rooms, a red light was blinking on and off. One of the patients had pressed the call button to summon a nurse. Kilkenny walked away from it. Then he stopped, turned, and stared at it.

Blink-blink. Blink-blink.

Dot-dash.

Hurrying back into the ward, Kilkenny drew a chair up to Joe's bed and sat down. It had been a long time, thirty years, perhaps too long. Yet if there was a chance . . .

Gently, Kilkenny placed the palm of his hand on Joe's sternum, just below the clavicle. Joe stirred. Kilkenny thought back thirty years. Thought back to the blue neckerchiefs and khaki caps, the gold patches they pinned to their shirts with the letters BSI on them. Boy Scouts International. It was the only youth organization that had ever come into the Ballymurphy slum to help the kids there. The first thing they had learned in the Morse Code class, Kilkenny remembered, was how to do their names.

With his index finger, he began to tap lightly on Joe Devalain's sternum. Dot-dash-dash-dash. That was *J*. Dash-dash-dash. That was *O*. Dot. That was *E. J O E.* Joe.

Joe Devalain frowned. Kilkenny began tapping again. He repeated the same letters. *J O E.*

Under the oxygen mask, Joe's lips parted. He began breathing a little faster. He's got it, Kilkenny thought. *He understands it!*

Kilkenny rubbed his hand in a brief circle to indicate he was erasing and starting a new message. He tapped dot-dash-dot for *R*. Dash-dash-dash for *O*. Dash-dot-dash-dash for *Y*. His name. Roy.

Joe's lips parted even more and he forced a guttural sound from his throat. All it sounded like was a long "Aaaggghhh" but it was beautiful to Kilkenny. It meant he had reached Joe Devalain's mind.

Kilkenny began tapping again, slowly, carefully. Making his message as brief and simple as possible. He tapped: Use eyelids. Dot short blink. Dash long blink. Then he waited.

For a brief, terrible instant, he was afraid Joe wasn't going to be able to do it; his lips remained parted, his sightless eyes unblinking. But then the eyelids closed, remained closed, opened, blinked once, closed again and remained closed for a second, and opened. Dash-dot-dash. That was the letter *K*. He was doing it!

Kilkenny watched the eyelids as they closed, opened, blinked. The letters they were making etched in his mind. *K-I-R-R-G.* Then the blinking stopped.

K-I-R-R-G? What the hell did that mean?

Kilkenny took out his pen and tore a sheet of paper from the medical chart hanging on the end of the bed. Turning the paper to its blank side, he wrote down the entire International Code that he and Joe had learned as Boy Scouts. Then he went to work breaking down the blinks Joe had used. The *K* and the *I* were all right, he decided. But the two *R* signals had to be wrong. Unable to quickly decide how they were wrong, he moved on to the G. That, in all likelihood, was *M-E.* One of the most common mistakes in Morse was to misread M (dash-dash) and *E* (dot) as G (dash-dash-dot). Simply a case of too short a pause between letters, causing the receiver to think it was a single signal.

Kilkenny now had *K-I-R-R-M-E.* Frowning, he scanned the code symbols he had just written. What was similar to *R* (dot-dash-dot)?

Then it hit him. Dot-dash-dot-dot. Two dots at the end instead of one. The letter was *L.* Joe had signaled *K-I-L-L-M-E.*

Kill me.

Kilkenny tapped a new message: No.

Devalain blinked back: Please. Pain. Going crazy.

Kilkenny: No.

Why?

Kilkenny tapped: Darlynn.

Joe shook his head furiously and blinked: Burden.

Kilkenny tapped: Sharmon.

The answer came: Finish me. Please.

Who bomb? Kilkenny wanted to know.

Why?

Pay back.

Again the emphatic shake of the head: Hurt Darlynn.

How?

Sharmon.

She bomb?

No.

How hurt Darlynn?

Sharmon.

Involved?

This time Joe nodded as he blinked: Maybe. No matter. Finish me. No. Who bomb?

Then finish me? Joe asked, blinking a question mark at the end of his signal.

Kilkenny thought about it for several long moments. Then he tapped: Okay.

Joe's next message read: *O-M-A-R-N*.

Kilkenny nodded to himself. O'Marn. The Bomb Investigation sergeant. Neat. He had access to explosives that had been confiscated from the IRA. He knew how to use them. And he was in a position to bury the case without resolving it.

O'Marn. Yes, Kilkenny had suspected as much when he saw the sprig of dying heather in Sharmon's ashtray. The same kind of sprig O'Marn wore on his lapel. He wondered how O'Marn and Sharmon had met. How long they had been lovers. Sharmon, who didn't like policemen, who had picked Joe over him when he told her he was going to become a policeman.

He wondered exactly how much Sharmon knew about the bombing. Not that it mattered. If she was still seeing O'Marn after what had happened to Joe, that was enough. And Kilkenny was sure she was still seeing him. That noise he had heard earlier from the back of the Devalain house. Along with Sharmon's eagerness to send him on his way. O'Marn had been there, listening.

Another guttural sound from the bed drew Kilkenny's attention back to Joe. He was blinking rapidly, repeating a message over and over. Do it. You promised. Do it. You prom—

Kilkenny put his hand back on Joe's sternum. He tapped: Later.

Darlynn was still deeply asleep on the couch in the waiting room. One of the nuns had covered her with a blanket. Kilkenny quietly opened her purse and took her door key.

IT WAS VERY LATE now, dark and quiet in Unity Flats. He walked the two miles to the Devalain house, passing no one, seeing no one. When he arrived, he let himself in and stood just inside the door. The house was silent. A night-light burned dimly in the hall. Kilkenny moved slowly toward the rear of the house, taking care to stay close to the wall where the floorboards were less likely to creak.

At the door to a bedroom, he saw in the faint glow two naked bodies asleep on the bed. On the doorknob hung a Harris tweed sport coat. Kilkenny moved into the room and over to the single window. It was shut tight and locked.

Slipping back out of the bedroom, he edged along the hall until he found the kitchen. Its window was also shut. Pulling a handkerchief from his pocket, he turned on all the gas jets on the stove.

Before he left, Kilkenny shut the door to Darlynn's small bedroom and the parlor, closing off all the house except the kitchen and the bedroom in which the two lovers slept. Then he let himself back out.

He waited down at the corner, concealed in the dark doorway of a small store, watching the house. No light came on and there was no sign of movement anywhere. Kilkenny gave it an hour. Then he returned to the hospital.

DARLYNN WAS STILL ASLEEP when he put her door key back in her purse. But Joe was wide awake and responded instantly when Kilkenny tapped his first message: Paid back.

Who? Joe blinked.

Kilkenny signaled: O'Marn. Sharmon.

A great, weary sigh escaped Joe's chest, the first sound Kilkenny had heard from him that sounded human. Then he blinked: Now me.

And Kilkenny answered: Yes.

Kilkenny reached over and pinched the tube that was feeding oxygen to Joe Devalain's lungs. As his breathing started to become labored Joe blinked: Darlynn.

With his free hand, Kilkenny responded: Yes.

Joe's throat began to constrict, his face contorting as what was left of his body struggled for oxygen. He had time for only one more message. God bless, he blinked . . .

Kilkenny sat in the waiting room watching the sleeping Darlynn Devalain until daylight came and the buses began running. Then he woke her and they left the hospital together. On the bus downtown, he told her how her parents had died, but not who killed them. Her mother and O'Marn would be considered suicides. Her father simply had not survived his trauma.

When the bus reached Great Victoria Street, they got off.

"Where are we going?" Darlynn asked.

"First to the hotel to get my things."

"And then?"

"The part of Ireland that's free. Dublin."

Darlynn accompanied him with no further questions.

The Male and Female Hogan

Jon L. Breen

F AIRWAY FLATS WAS ONE of those condominium communities that
line the water-guzzling golf courses in the California desert near
Palm Springs. The residents would have a nice view of the San
Jacinto Mountains as well as the greens and bunkers, Al Hasp reflected
as he drove his well-used Mercedes through the gate. A nice place to
retire to, unless you hated the desert or hated golf or, like Al Hasp,
hated both. Parking in an inconsiderately shade-deprived visitors' area,
Al could still hear his partner Norm Carpenter's well-meant but unwelcome instructions playing over in his head: "These people are old, Al.
You have to be patient with them. You can't rush them or bully them.
They need special handling. Listen to everything they say carefully."

As if Al Hasp, with his years of experience as cop and private
investigator, didn't know how to interview all sorts of people, regardless of age, sex, nationality, ethnicity, sexual preference, whatever. But

that was Norm, always ready to lecture his partner on everything from theology to his taste in clothes.

Seconds after Al walked up a cactus-lined path and pressed the doorbell of the seventh-hole condo, the door opened and an aged but still lovely face looked up at him cheerfully. It belonged to a small, white-haired, and slightly stooped woman of seventy or eighty. "Mr. Hasp?"

"Yes. Mrs. Hogan? Pleased to meet you. And thanks for agreeing to talk to me."

"Our pleasure. It's not every day we're visited by a private eye. Do you mind that term, by the way?"

"Well, it's not the worst thing I've been called."

She laughed. "Do come in. My husband can't wait to meet you."

Al crossed the threshold from hundred-degree heat into air-conditioned comfort and wondered fleetingly what the Hogans' electric bills must be like. Mrs. Hogan led him through a short hallway lined with old photographs and motion picture lobby cards into a similarly decorated study where a tall, very thin, and militarily straight man of similar age rose from in front of a computer screen to greet him.

"Al Hasp!" The old man gripped his hand firmly. "Grant Hogan. How were my directions?"

"Perfect."

Various social rituals followed. He would be Al; they would be Grant and Marge. Yes, he'd love some iced tea and some freshly baked brownies. The photos and lobby cards were terrific, reminded Al of his boyhood watching western movies at kids' matinees, and was that cowboy bronze in the corner really a Remington? Statistics emerged: Grant was eighty-four and received a hundred jokes a day via e-mail; Marge was eighty-three and had a file of two thousand recipes. While noting to himself that they almost looked those proudly trumpeted ages, the fifty-four-year-old Al truthfully claimed to envy their energy. About fifteen minutes into his visit, the three of them sat in the living room around a glass coffee table supported by what appeared to be moose antlers, and Al was able to broach the reason for his visit.

"You both heard about the death of Clinton Bortner?"

The faces of Grant and Marge turned solemn.

"Wasn't that awful?" said Marge.

"Did they ever find out who did it?" Grant demanded.

"Ah, no, they didn't. Did the police ever come out here to interview you about it?"

"No," said Grant.

"I'm not surprised."

"Should they have?" Marge asked, more intrigued than concerned. "Are we suspects?"

"You're certainly not suspects, and they probably didn't interview you because they figured Bortner was killed in the course of a routine burglary. They decided he surprised some kid looking for drug money, and nothing could get them off that. As an old cop myself, I can't really blame them. The crime happened on a weekend—"

"Why, I thought it happened on a Tuesday," Marge said. "Didn't it happen on a Tuesday?"

"I thought it was a Wednesday myself," Grant said.

"No, we heard about it on a Wednesday, but I thought you told me it happened the day before, on the Tuesday."

"Believe me," Al said, "it happened on a Sunday. There were a lot of visitors at the retirement home where he lived, and it would be easier for a stranger to sneak onto the property. Their drug-crazed youth seems a lot more likely to have bludgeoned Bortner with a fireplace poker than a fellow resident."

"Senior citizens are often underestimated, Al," Grant said with a smile. "Clint went back a long way with some of the people who live there. Through happy times and times that were, well, not so happy. Grievances can fester. You never know."

"I gather Bortner was an old friend of you both. Did you ever visit him in that retirement home?"

"No," said Marge.

"Driving to L.A. is a major expedition for us these days, Al," Grant explained. "We've become homebodies."

"You went to that western memorabilia show quick enough a while back," Marge pointed out.

"Well, that was special."

"I'm told three of Bortner's old cronies from his movie days live in that same retirement home," Al said.

Grant nodded. "Right. And we knew 'em all, didn't we, Mother?"

Marge said, "They were like family in a way."

"According to people at the home," Al said, "two of them seemed to be on good terms with Bortner, spent a lot of time with him, but the third one he never had anything to do with."

"And I guess we know which one that is, don't we?" Grant said, throwing a knowing look his wife's way.

"Emmett Donnelly," Marge said, nodding her head briskly. "They fell out when Clint married his sister Bridget."

"No, Mother, it was after they got married."

"Well, not long after. The next day maybe."

"Bridget's drinking was none of Clint's doing."

"Well, she never drank before she married him. And when she drove her car off that bridge—"

"Clint wasn't there, you know."

"Well, some of us think Clint should have been there. Now, I don't take Emmett's side, but I think Clint had to answer for some of it."

Al could tell this was no new discussion, and the old couple aired their disagreement good-naturedly, not heatedly at all. Al already knew that Bridget Donnelly Bortner had been an alcoholic who died in an accident and that her brother had blamed her husband for driving her to drink. It didn't appeal to him as a motive for a forty-year-delayed murder, but who knew?

"How did two such bitter enemies wind up living in the same retirement home anyway?" Al asked.

"It's just a place old movie people go," Marge said sadly. "Poor souls."

"Aren't we lucky not to be old?" her husband said with a smile.

"There are other places, though," said Al. "That one in Woodland Hills is bigger and better known."

"It was because of Gimp and Terry," Grant said, as if it were obvious. Al knew he was referring to Calvin "Gimp" O'Reilly and Terence O'Neil, two western movie contemporaries of Clinton Bortner. "Those two sons-of-guns have been close buddies all their lives, and they managed to stay friendly with both Clint and Emmett."

Al nodded. "That's what I'm told. O'Reilly and O'Neil always together. Bortner and Donnelly would hang out with them but never at the same time."

Grant chuckled. "I think Gimp and Terry worked on Clint and Emmett separately to come live there, without either knowing about the other one. If they had known, neither of them probably would have gone there. We all went in for practical jokes in the old days."

"I don't think Gimp and Terry would have meant it as a joke, though," Marge said. "They may have thought Clint and Emmett could bury the hatchet after all these years."

"Right you are, Mother. And maybe they could. In each other's skulls."

"I gather you know these three guys well," Al said. "O'Reilly, O'Neil, and Donnelly, I mean. I haven't met them yet. What can you tell me about them? I don't mean personal history so much, but what kind of people are they?"

"We haven't really seen them in years, but they were all good friends," Marge said. "Good men. Not murderers, I don't think."

"We can do better than that for Al, can't we, Mother?" Grant said. "Come on. Let's consider them one by one. We'll do it like one of those word-association tests."

"Okay," Al said. "Start with Donnelly."

"Angry," Marge said. "Always worried about something. And much too serious. But decent."

"Great horseman," Grant offered. "Fearless. Loyal. Little wiry guy. Came back from more serious injuries than any stuntman I can think of, and in later years it started to show. Not much sense of humor."

"Okay," Al said. "How about Gimp O'Reilly?"

"A lot of fun," Marge said. "He liked to put on this dumb cowpoke persona, bad grammar and all, but Gimp was nobody's fool. Kind of wearing to be around for too long at a stretch, I always thought."

Her husband nodded his agreement. "Had to be the center of attention at all times. Knew a lot of jokes. Loved to needle people. Kind of a mean streak with it sometimes."

"That leaves Terry O'Neil," Al said.

"Quiet," Marge said. "Dreamy. Kind of sweet really."

Grant snorted. "Not the horseman he thought he was. Unrealistic about everything really. Might have believed in Santa Claus, the Easter Bunny, and the Tooth Fairy. Oh, and leprechauns. Phony auld sod brogue."

"Oh, you're much too hard on him," Marge scolded.

"Now, Al," Grant said, "walking down memory lane is always fun for us old codgers—"

"Speak for yourself," Marge said lightly.

"—but why are we discussing these old-timers we haven't crossed paths with in years?"

"Bortner's daughter and son-in-law aren't happy with the way the case was handled, so they came to my partner and me. They thought the police were too quick to blame Bortner's death on some anonymous outsider. They thought the detectives should have followed up on some leads they ignored."

"I get it," said Grant. "The younger generation think one of Clint's old movie cronies took that poker to his skull. And you're investigating Clint's murder."

Al raised a hand. "Not really. We need to get that straight. Private investigators do not investigate murders."

"Why, in every book I ever read or movie I ever saw they do," said Marge.

"Right. But in real life it would only get us in trouble."

"Naturally. But then trouble is your business, isn't it?"

Al smiled. "Making money is my business, and I wouldn't make much without my license. Police departments don't take kindly to private operatives looking into murders. No, I'm just trying to find out the meaning of some things Bortner had written in his notebook the day before he died. If the meaning of those notations should turn out to have some bearing on his death, well, we'll consider that a bonus."

Like a witness on the stand, Al was anticipating the next logical question: what did it say in the notebook? But Grant Hogan took a sudden ninety-degree turn.

"Can I take your picture, Al?"

"Huh?"

"I like to take everybody's picture who visits us here. I've always been a photographer. An amateur, mind you."

"But with an artist's eye," Marge said.

"I do my best. Most of what you see on these walls I took myself. Just as a hobby. You had to do something to fill all that time on a movie set between saloon fights and horse falls." Grant got to his feet, more limberly than Al. "Come out back. I have a great idea for a shot."

Moments later, Grant was posing Al standing in the back doorway, with the seventh hole and the San Jacintos behind him.

"Yeah, stand right there. Light's perfect right now. Look like a tough hombre. Won't be hard." Grant went down on one knee and aimed his Canon slightly upward at Al. "That's better. Don't want the damn golf course in the shot. Just you, the doorway, the mountains." He took the picture and rose to his feet with nary a creak. "Great. I love doorway shots. John Ford loved doorway shots, you know. Ever count all the doorway shots in a John Ford picture?"

"Can't say I have, no."

"Ever see *The Searchers*? Full of doorway shots, out of the farmhouse, out of the tipi. I didn't get to work on that one. Wish I had."

Grant led Al back to the living room where Marge was waiting for them. Their iced-tea glasses had been refilled, and more brownies had appeared.

"So did you say Clint kept a notebook?" Marge asked.

"Yes."

"Didn't know he could write," Grant said with a cackle. "Oh, I don't mean to disrespect the dead, but Clint would laugh as much as anybody, believe me. We had a good time with old Clint."

"Mr. Bortner didn't write complete sentences in this notebook," Al said. "It would make my job easier if he had. But his daughter says he was making notes for his memoirs."

Grant snorted. "Hope he could afford a ghostwriter."

"The notebook was full of lists of things from out of his past. Some of the references are obvious, some not."

"Aids to memory," Marge suggested. "They only had to make sense to him."

"Bortner's notebook was lying open on a table in his room when he was found. There were four phrases on that last page, dated the day before. It would be helpful if you tell me what, if anything, they mean to you." Though he remembered all of Bortner's notations, Al took out his own notebook for reference. "The first phrase was 'Back to Ireland.' "

"Clint Bortner wasn't Irish," Marge said.

"But all three of your suspects, if that's what they are, have Irish surnames," Grant Hogan pointed out. "Donnelly, O'Reilly, O'Neil. Not to mention Hogan."

"But we're not suspects," his wife pointed out.

Al smiled. "Right, you're not. Were any of them born in Ireland?"

"No, but they probably had family there," Grant said. "What's your point?"

"I was thinking if O'Neil effected a brogue—"

Grant shook his head. "That didn't make him an Irishman, just an uncured ham. What else did Clint write in his notebook?"

"'The Male and Female Hogan.'"

"Yeah? I guess now we know what brought you to us."

"Well, Bortner's daughter remembers you fondly, and you two were the only male and female Hogans she could think of."

"Melissa was a beautiful child," Marge said. "Haven't seen her since she was, oh, junior high age. I'll bet she's a lovely young woman now."

Though neither young nor lovely had sprung to Al's mind when he met the Bortner daughter, he just said, "Oh, yes."

"Melissa was never really all that interested in her father's movie work," Grant said. "Embarrassed by it, if anything. If she'd paid more attention, she might have saved you a trip down here. Not that we aren't glad to have you, you understand. What else did Clint write?"

"The third phrase was 'The Three Sisters.' Somebody in our office thought that might have been a reference to Bortner's acting career. There's a famous play—"

Grant interrupted with a snort of laughter. "Oh, no! That's rich, that is."

"Why is that funny?"

"When you say Clint Bortner was an actor, that's funny enough. Oh, he made some movies and read some lines, but he got into it the same way most of those guys did, as a stuntman. Not me, mind you. I went to college and was an actor before I started doing stunts. I could do whatever they wanted on a horse, but they valued me more for the way I could read lines. But a guy like Clint, it was the way he handled a horse that kept him working. He looked like a cowboy, hell, he'd *been* a cowboy, so he made himself a career playing ranch hands and villains' henchmen. I don't know if he ever appeared on a stage, but if he did, he wasn't playing in anything by Chekhov. I bet he'd never even heard of Chekhov."

"What was the fourth phrase?" Marge asked.

"It said, 'Told Pappy.'"

"I can't imagine—" Marge began, then broke off when she saw the changed look on her husband's face. "What is it, honey?"

"Hm? Oh, not a thing." Grant turned to Al and said with forced brightness, "Want to see my photo album?"

"Your photo album?" Marge laughed. "You've got a hundred photo albums, my dear, and Al probably hasn't got all day."

"I mean one particular photo album. I can put my hand on it easy. Come on back in the study."

Grant was up from his chair and out the door. Al could only follow.

Hogan closed the door of the study behind them and said softly, "That bastard. I know just what he was up to. Marge doesn't need to know about this. It would just upset her, turn sour a lot of happy memories. You understand?"

Al didn't, but he nodded his head anyway and waited to see what else was coming.

Grant Hogan's photo albums, which filled one small bookcase in the study, looked identical to Al, but Grant was able to find the one he was looking for right away. He leafed through the pages quickly. Al saw shots of horses, rock formations, movie cameras, and vaguely familiar-looking actors fly by until Grant got to the one he wanted, a photo of a man with an eye patch sitting in a director's chair.

"That's the man himself, John Ford. Sometimes known as Pappy. I took this on the set of *Cheyenne Autumn*, not one of his best I'm afraid. Folks said it was his apology to the Indians for the lousy way he'd treated them in his pictures, but he didn't owe an apology to anybody. He always treated Indians with dignity. Well, usually. People always associate Ford with westerns, cavalry, and Indians, but he made all sorts of pictures. And he was an Irishman through and through. Real family name was Feeney. Back in the thirties, he made a great movie out of *The Informer*, the Sean O'Casey play, coaxed and bullied an Academy Award performance out of Victor McLaglen, and you remember how funny McLaglen was as an Irish sergeant in the cavalry movies, don't you?"

"Haven't seen one in a while," Al said, trying to remember if he'd ever seen one.

"Rent 'em. Hell, buy 'em. I think *Fort Apache* was the best one. Now, Marge is partial to *She Wore a Yellow Ribbon*, for the color photography, like Remington's paintings come to life. But my point is, Pappy's heart was in Ireland. That last picture in the cavalry trilogy, *Rio Grande*, he made at Republic so old man Yates would let him take his company to the Emerald Isle and make *The Quiet Man*. Did you ever see *The Quiet Man?*"

"I guess I must have."

"If you don't remember it, you didn't see it. Do yourself a favor. Rent it. Hell, buy it. I usually buy myself. If I rent, Marge gets on me, says I can remember what I had for breakfast on a location shoot in 1945 and can't remember when to take a tape back to the video store. There's something to that."

Al thought Grant's garrulousness was a way to put off discussing something unpleasant. Unless—and this was a less-attractive alternative—the old-timer's mind was starting to cut in and out like a cell phone. When he thought Grant had wound down—don't rush him, Al, whatever you do—Al ventured, "So you think the phrase 'Back to Ireland' might be a reference to John Ford?"

"Yep. No question in my mind."

"John Ford's been dead a long time," Al said, and soon regretted it. It set Grant Hogan off on another round of reminiscences.

"Oh, well, sure, most of 'em have. George O'Brien's gone. Ward Bond's gone. Duke Wayne's gone. Even old Ben Johnson's gone now. Dobe Carey's still around, though. You know, Harry Carey Jr. His dad was Ford's first cowboy star, but they had a professional falling-out and didn't work together for years. Lots of people got on Ford's bad side one time or another, sometimes didn't even know why. The old man was funny that way. Dobe Carey wrote a swell book about his days with Ford. You should read that, Al."

"Yeah, I should. What about those other references in the notebook?"

Grant took to flipping the pages of his album again, stopping at a photo of three tall rock formations in a group. They looked vaguely familiar. "There's your Three Sisters. They're in Monument Valley, on the big Four Corners Navajo reservation, where Ford used to shoot his westerns. Some of the most beautiful scenery in the world, made for a lot of dramatic shots. All of us who worked for Ford on westerns spent a lot of time there. They gave names to all the red-rock buttes and spires, like the Mittens, the Big Indian, the Totem Pole. These three are supposed to look like three nuns. I think just the one on the left really looks like a nun. What do you think?"

"Well, I don't know."

"Depends on the angle you look at 'em from, of course. Anyhow, that's the Three Sisters, and lemme see here." He flipped a few more pages and pointed out a picture of a primitive triangular structure. "There you have the male hogan." He turned a page and pointed to a similar structure, more conical in shape. "And this is the female hogan. They're the traditional Navajo dwellings. Why there's a male one and a female one and where the door goes and who gets to sit where, I won't go into. You could look it up. But that's to show you it's nothing to do with me and Marge. Happy you came to visit, though, don't get me wrong."

Al knew Hogan had something more in mind and hoped he would reveal it in his own good time. Don't rush him, Al, just keep the conversation going. "I guess you worked on a lot of pictures with John Ford, huh?"

"As many as I could. I was one of his regulars. Oh, I had my dry spells when he wouldn't give me any work, just like anybody else, never knew why. When a new Ford picture was about to shoot, I'd go by to see Ford in his office. He'd shoot the breeze for a while, very pleasant, ask me how was Marge, how were the kids, and so forth. I'd never ask him if he had a part for me. That was out. He'd talk a little about the picture he was going to do, and if there was a part for me, he'd say so. If not, well, he wouldn't. All his regulars went through that same ritual. And like I said, you couldn't always know why Ford would give you a job in a whole string of movies, then suddenly never give you any work for years maybe, then start using you again like nothing had happened. It happened to everybody—George O'Brien, Ben Johnson, everybody. Sometimes you could trace it to some particular incident, but sometimes not."

"Was Bortner a Ford regular, too?"

"Yeah, he worked on Ford pictures off and on for years."

"What about Donnelly, O'Reilly, and O'Neil? Were they regulars with Ford?"

"Yep, and of course I'd see them all on other western shoots. Only Ford flick all five of us worked on was *She Wore a Yellow Ribbon*. We were all close in those days. The misunderstandings came later. The picture was shot in Monument Valley, of course. And that's where you'll find the key to your whole mystery."

"You think so?"

"I know so."

"I should go to Monument Valley?"

"Don't take me that literally. But you should talk to those three guys up at the retirement home: Donnelly, O'Reilly, and O'Neil."

"Did one of them kill Bortner?"

Grant Hogan shrugged.

"Do you know who killed Bortner, Grant?"

"I'm not going to make it easy for you," Grant said. "Why should I? But I do have a little story to tell you. Just don't say anything about it to Marge. It'd just upset her."

"Okay."

Grant Hogan talked in a low voice for about five minutes. The story he told Al sounded unlikely, but he seemed to believe it. Then he replaced the album he'd been showing Al and pulled another one from the shelf. "Now one more thing that might interest you."

Grant Hogan turned a few pages and pointed to a photo of a solemn-faced young man in a cowboy hat. "There's the guy that killed Clint Bortner." Grant took the photo out of the album and handed it to Al.

"Are you sure?"

"Oh, you probably can't prove it or anything. Not sure I'd want you to, now that I know what that bastard Bortner pulled on the four of us."

Al turned the picture over. There was no identification of the young cowboy. "But who is this?"

"I'm not making this easy for you," I said. Take it up to L.A. and show it to those three old pals of mine, see what they have to say. When you find out the truth, think about what you want to do next. If anything. Remember he was old, they're all old, and everything will be over soon for everybody. Okay?"

Before Al Hasp left the desert, he was on his cell phone to Norm Carpenter to tell him, "I figured it out."

THE CHARLES KING MEMORIAL RETIREMENT HOME was called by some of its denizens "Owlhoots' Roost" or "Henchmen's Haven" or

"Just Deserts." Well endowed by an anonymous donor, it accepted the money of those movie old-timers, mostly from the long-lost days of the western, who could afford to pay and quietly subsidized those who couldn't. A building the size of a country hotel, surrounded by meticulously kept gardens, it was more grandly appointed than the Hogans' golf course condo—yes, those certainly were real Remingtons that decorated the spacious public rooms—but just because of what it was, it made Al Hasp feel hemmed in and claustrophobic. The three old men he was facing in a circle of easy chairs wore stern faces that made him no more comfortable. If one of these old faces went with the young one in the photograph, Al couldn't tell which one it was, but he could make a case for any of them. The eyes, the part of the face that provided the most clues over time, were shaded in the photo.

"The investigation's over," Emmett Donnelly said. He was a tiny, spider-like man with a terrible toupee, misshapen arthritic hands, and a way of moving that suggested too many falls off too many horses. "Some kid druggie murdered Clint."

"They've found the kid?" Al asked mildly.

"No, they ain't found the kid," Gimp O'Reilly roared. Though he had walked with a limp since a rodeo accident in his twenties, he was the best physical specimen of the three, big and powerful with a surprisingly unlined face under the ten-gallon hat that never left his head. The strength of his bass voice, able to reach any back row, suggested this cowboy might once have worked on the stage. "But that don't mean the case ain't over. Police don't got the manpower or the political backing to do their jobs, that's it in a nutshell. People get away with murder in this city every day."

"I've been out to the desert to talk to Grant Hogan," Al said.

Terry O'Neil asked, "And Margie? Did you see Margie?" O'Neil was the quietest of the three, round-faced and pudgy, looking more like a retired banker than a poverty-row cowpoke. Now his face had gone from a determined sternness that matched the others to a wistful softening. "She was a darlin' was my Margie. Wasn't she somethin', Gimp?"

"Oh, she was somethin' all right," O'Reilly replied, as always a few decibels louder than anyone else. "But she was never your Margie."

"I won't hear a word against her."

"That was a word in her favor, you horny old sidewinder."

"Jealousy, jealousy," murmured O'Neil in his affected Irish brogue.

"I gather Mrs. Hogan was well-liked," Al commented.

"We all were sweet on her," said O'Reilly, "but only Grant Hogan got her."

"Everybody loved her," Emmett Donnelly said, and the other two nodded.

"And what about Grant Hogan? Did everybody love him, too?"

The three old cowboys looked at each other during a significant pause. Finally, O'Neil said, "He was all right, I suppose. Can't say I loved him."

"He had more education than the rest of us," Donnelly said carefully. "Some thought he was kind of, what's the word, patronizing. He grew up with horses, just like we did, but he'd been to college and he'd read a lot of books and sometimes he seemed to feel superior to others."

"He knew Chekhov," Al said.

Donnelly looked blank. "I don't know him. Either of you guys know a Chekhov?"

"Never mind that," Al said. "I was just thinking out loud. Was Hogan jealous?"

"No reason to be," O'Reilly roared. "Marge never looked at another man. And if she hadda, it'da been somebody higher up the food chain than us dusty cowpokes."

"Nobody should ever marry a cowpoke," Donnelly muttered. "And that includes me."

"Didn't think you wanted to marry a cowpoke, Emmett," O'Reilly said.

"You know damn well what I meant."

"Grant Hogan suggested you fellows might be able to help me out on those three notations in Bortner's notebook," Al said. "His daughter Melissa wants to know what they mean."

"Well, go ahead," O'Reilly said impatiently. "What were they? Nobody mentioned any notebook to us." Clearly, they'd compared notes.

"How about the 'Three Sisters'?"

"Why, I think Clint had three sisters," O'Neil said. "Yes, I believe he did. Now, what were their names?"

"Bortner didn't have sisters," Donnelly said. "It was me had three sisters. At one time. They died one by one. One I can blame on Bortner, I don't mind telling you."

"What about 'Back to Ireland'?"

"That's a laugh," O'Reilly said. "Bortner wasn't Irish."

"Hogan told me a little story when I was down there," Al said. "About the time when you three and he and Bortner all went to Monument Valley to work on John Ford's *She Wore a Yellow Ribbon*."

For a moment, none of the three spoke. Then Donnelly said, "Do you have any idea how many western movies the three of us made, together or separately?"

"True, that is," chimed in O'Reilly, "from Gower Gulch to the soundstages of Fox and MGM. Lots more than we can remember."

"Lots more," O'Neil agreed.

They're making this too easy for me, Al thought. "So your time working with John Ford on a classic film wasn't all that memorable?"

Donnelly shrugged. "Work was work. It all runs together."

"Did you guys do a lot of drinking on movie locations?"

"We did a lot of drinking in those days, yes," O'Neil said, "but not while we were working."

"And the Navajo Reservation was dry back then," O'Reilly said. "Probably still is."

"But wasn't John Ford quite a drinker in his own right?" said Al. "Wouldn't he have had a supply of booze on hand for his own use?"

O'Neil shook his head. "You couldn't drink on a Ford location. That I do remember. Ford didn't drink when he was working, and he didn't allow anybody else to either."

"Did any of you fellows," Al asked casually, "get to go to Ireland with Ford when he made *The Quiet Man*?"

The three looked at each other in the silence that followed. O'Reilly spoke for the group, dropping completely the ignorant cowboy persona. "Not a lot of stunt work in *The Quiet Man*. It was a romance, not a western. We were all basically stuntmen, you see."

"But you all could read lines," Al said. "And Ford took lots of his regulars along. Ken Curtis, the old band singer."

Donnelly snorted. "He was Ford's son-in-law."

"And isn't it true Hogan and the three of you were all having tough times and were badly in need of a job at that time?"

"Hell, that was true at most times," O'Reilly said.

Enough sparring, Al decided. "I'm starting to think all three of you are in this together. Oh, I suppose only one of you swung that poker that cracked Clint Bortner's skull, but you're stonewalling me like a tag team, aren't you? All the times you've been to Monument Valley, how the hell could you not know what the Three Sisters are?"

"You get old, the memory goes," Donnelly said, and the looks he got from his two cronies told him how unconvincing that sounded.

"Here's what happened," Al said. "When *She Wore a Yellow Ribbon* was filming, some members of the cast or crew—I don't know who or how many—were smuggling booze onto the Navajo reservation, hiding the bottles at various strategic locations. Empty bottles were found at a male hogan and a female hogan—and don't tell me you don't know what those are—not far from Goulding's Trading Post, where the Ford unit was headquartered. Other bottles were found around the base of the Three Sisters. Ford was furious that somebody was sneaking drinks and he wasn't able to find out who it was. A few years later, when Ford was about to do *The Quiet Man* in Ireland, all of you were hoping to be a part of it. Besides being desperate for work, you were proud of your Irish heritage. You still had relatives there. You wanted to go. But you weren't chosen, and adding insult to injury, Clint Bortner, who wasn't even Irish, somehow was selected for a small part in the movie. You never knew why you were left out. Then one of you, while visiting Bortner in his apartment, saw his notebook lying on the table, figured out what those four phrases meant, and you realized that he had been the cause of your not getting that trip to Ireland, that he had somehow convinced Ford, whether it was true or not, that you were the ones smuggling liquor into Monument Valley during the shooting of *She Wore a Yellow Ribbon*. You, or one of you, got so angry, you picked up that fireplace poker and brained Bortner with it, then did what you could to make it look like a burglary."

"That's some fancy story," O'Reilly bellowed. "But you can't prove a thing."

"You wouldn'ta found me in Bortner's room," Donnelly said.

"That's what your friend Hogan said. You were the most logical suspect, a guy who hated Bortner for your sister's death, but you were automatically eliminated from consideration because you wouldn't have been visiting Bortner in his room. That left you other two, O'Neil and O'Reilly."

"You can't prove a thing," O'Reilly said again. "Are you going to try to? You can tell Bortner's daughter Melissa what the notebook means—that's what she hired you for—and let it go at that, can't you? If what you and Hogan have come up with is true, and I'm not saying it is, old Clint Bortner was a poisonous critter who sold out his friends out of pure nastiness. Didn't he deserve to die?"

"Maybe he did. But I'd still like to know the truth."

"I have a question," Emmett Donnelly said. "I'm out of this, but I want to defend my friends here. If somebody murdered Clint Bortner because of what it said in his notebook, wouldn't that person have taken the notebook or at least torn out that page in order to avoid drawing suspicion to himself?"

"Seems like that wasn't necessary, Emmett," O'Neil pointed out.

Al said, "Maybe the killer found out some other way about what Bortner had done. Or maybe he had other grievances against Bortner and this just added to them."

"And which one of us desperate characters supposedly did this?" O'Reilly demanded. "According to our imaginative friend Hogan, I mean."

Al took out the picture of the scowling young cowboy from Hogan's album and passed it across to the three old cowboys. Donnelly looked at it first, gripping it with his gnarled hands and gaping at it. Then he passed it over to O'Neil, whose eyes widened in surprise. O'Reilly got it last and responded with a whoop of laughter.

"And which one of us do you think this is?" O'Reilly demanded.

"I've been trying to figure that out," Al said. "You've all changed over the years, obviously. But you remember what you all used to look like, don't you?"

Donnelly looked at O'Reilly. "What do you think? Could it be?"

"Sure. It was the day after that memorabilia convention Clint Bortner spoke at. Maybe Clint told the story of what he did to us there. Funny to him, a good joke, but very serious to us." O'Reilly poked a finger at the picture. "He was at that convention. He could have stuck around overnight. He could have come here the next day, done the deed, never seen the notebook references. Maybe Bortner wrote 'em *after* he told the story at the convention, to remember them for his memoirs. I never saw him here, but one more old fart could kind of blend into the woodwork."

"But poor Margie," said O'Neil.

"The guy confessed!" Donnelly said.

O'Reilly waved an impatient hand. "Ah, it means nothin'. He could say it's just a joke. He could say he wasn't serious. Still, I'll bet he was."

"What are you all talking about?" Al asked.

"A good joke on you, Mr. Private Eye. He's changed a good bit in fifty-some years, but this is a picture of Grant Hogan."

CELTIC NOIR

Paul Bishop

A

S EE, BOYO, I DON'T much give a frig iffin you're offended.

So, iffin you're being one of them gobshite bastards wots always gettin your knickers in a knot over a little sex and violence then best you be stoppin here.

Surely, aren't I always ready for a fight? But when Kink and Turner smashed open the door to Brigit's flat, I would have shite me shorts iffin I'd been wearing any. I thought it was the Garda at first, but the filth doesn't bother messing with good Catholic girls like Brigit.

I bounced instantly away from Brigit's fat bum—the girl might be named after the saint herself, but isn't she at least three times her size—and groped blindly for the fireplace poker I knew she kept beside the bed.

The flat is a one-room nothing with a thin mattress on the floor where Brigit and I had been doin' the business, so Kink and Turner didn't have far to go once they were through the door. Brigit scrambled away from me and started screaming. I will give her points for taking the time to throw an empty bottle of Guinness at Turner, but it didn't even slow him down.

Kink grabbed for me. The stupid berk must have thought I wouldn't fight knowing he and Turner works for Mandrake.

Unfortunately for him, I couldn't have given a frig iffin he worked for the Pope himself.

As Kink reached for me, I smashed the poker across his wrists, and then swung it back and caught him on the side of the throat. He's a big bastard with muscles on top of muscles, but he still fell to the floor howling like a stuck pig.

Turner backed off, his hands raised in a calming gesture I didn't believe for a second. "What the frig do you want?" I said, whipping the poker back and forth.

"Mandrake wants to see you, shite bucket," Turner said, keeping just out of me range. Kink was still moaning on the floor, and Brigit had turned up the volume of her screeching. She was struggling to cover herself with the bedsheet. That almost made me laugh. The last thing anybody in the room was concerned about was Brigit's udders.

"I've never borrowed from Mandrake."

"This ain't about money. He wants to talk to you."

"He can twirl his arse on a corkscrew."

I swung the poker again and brought it down across Kink's legs just for the sheer pleasure of it.

Brigit's screeching rose another octave to keep pace with Kink's new notes. "Shut up, you stupid slag," I yelled at her. "You're getting on me friggin pip."

When I bent down to snag me jeans off the floor, Turner made his move. And, wasn't I was ready for him to come? I brought the poker up square between his legs, trying to bat his testicles for six. His hands didn't even make it to his goolies. His eyes simply rolled up in his head, and he collapsed like the bag of shite he was.

"What's happening, Decco?" Brigit took a break from her screeching. Tears and sweat had run her eye makeup and she looked worse than ever. It made me fancy her again.

"Not to worry, luv," I said, stepping into me jeans and Doc Marten's. I ran a hand over the short black stubble on me head. "They won't touch you when they see I'm gone."

Brigit's eyes widened. "You can't leave me here with them!"

"Watch me," I said. I blew her a kiss, pulled on me leather jacket, and sprinted for the front door.

B

ON THE STREET, I stuck a fag in me gob before nicking an almost new Trident a pair of stupid sods—who shall remain nameless, but you can guess—had trustingly left out.

As I drove, I wondered what Mandrake wanted. Dublin isn't Belfast, but it's still a hard town that don't forgive when you screw up. Mandrake was your man when it came to crime—a mean little willie with ambitions.

At five-foot-six and a massive one hundred forty pounds of tattooed punk, I didn't fit the usual hardman category. Compared to Mandrake, I was a pissant, and I knew it. Mandrake was a right evil bastard, so I had two choices—run like hell, or talk to him.

I cranked the Trident's radio up loud. Me nose twitched. Something was in the air, but I wasn't sure if it was money or aggro. Either way, I was ready for it.

C

AS I STOOD WATCHING Mandrake's wrecking yard, a Garda car rolled by. The twits inside didn't even give me a second look. How that lot ever catch anybody is beyond me. Some of them—like Blake—are right bastards who take no stick from nobody. They're who you gots to worry about. The rest of them couldn't find their arse in the dark with both hands and a torch.

You might think I'm stupid. I ain't. I done loads of them Open University courses on the telly. I ain't stupid. I just ain't like you, and I don't want to be.

I hate effin squares like you—sitting there on your arse reading books. You're boring. I hate boring. Get up, get out, smash somebody's face in. That's what it's all about—a little aggro makes the world go round.

I don't give a shite if you understand me, but I'll give it one shot. Some people likes to drink. Some people likes to smoke. Some idiots like to stick shite in their veins and would swallow anything to get high. Meself? Me, now don't I likes to fight? I likes to feel me fist smash some spotty twat's nose across his face and put the boot in when he goes down. I like to smash me nut into some berk's face and walk away with the blood flowing. Shite that feels good. And isn't that the way of it?

Mandrake ran his business from a beat-up office at the back of his yard. It wasn't high class, but then neither was he. You had to give the bastard the truth of his roots. Corrugated metal fencing ran around the perimeter, and the tops of a couple of cranes could be seen above the fence line along with several stacks of flattened, junked cars.

I made me way around the back of the yard until I found a gap in the corrugated sheeting. There were a couple of big mongrel dogs in the yard who sniffed me out and came running. They were silent and salivating, but I have no fear of dogs and they know it. And aren't dogs almost worse than women when it comes to falling for bad boys?

As the two sleek lumps of fur and teeth charged forward, I extended an arm toward them and lowered it as I bent down. I whistled low through me teeth, and the two dogs suddenly started wagging their tails. They trotted happily behind me through the stacks of junked cars until I could see Mandrake's office.

The noise coming from inside was Mandrake going spare at Kink and Turner. I smiled and waltzed in unannounced, all attitude and cool.

"Wotcher, lads," I said to Turner and Kink. "Mr. Mandrake," I added with a touch of respect.

"You effin toe rag," Turner said.

"Temper," I said with a smug smile, and then kicked him square in the jewels. He went down puking all over himself.

I slid a straight razor out of me jacket sleeve. A sharp flick of the wrist and it whipped open like a switchblade, only deadlier. It was me weapon of choice, and even Kink knew me reputation with it. "Don't even fink about it," I said, pulling him up short on the balls of his feet. "I'll effin gut you from here to your mum's Sunday dinner."

"Put it away, you stupid git." This was from Mandrake. His voice was harsh from too many cigars and too much booze. I flicked the razor closed and disappeared it up me sleeve.

"How did you get past the dogs?" Mandrake asked.

"Nufing to worry about. Right welcoming wasn't they?"

"I don't like smart mouths," Mandrake said.

"And I don't like your effin bully boys disturbing me while I'm getting me end away. Scared piss out of Brigit they did."

Mandrake was a big man, all barrel chest and weightlifters' arms. He wore a flash waistcoat over a black dress shirt done up to the neck. The top button was covered by a diamond stud. "I should have you stuffed in a crusher and sent back to your mother in a soup can."

"Probably," I said, not of a mind to apologize. "Look, Mr. Mandrake. Iffin your messenger boys want to play rough, they shouldn't be surprised when somebody plays rough back." Kink stepped forward, but the razor was back in me hand and he pulled up short again.

"Get him out of here," Mandrake said to Kink with a nod of his head toward Turner. The bigger man hadn't moved since his testicles were introduced to his tonsils. Kink moved slowly away, dragging Turner by the pits.

"Sit down, Decco." Mandrake said me name awkwardly, as if it left a bad taste. "And put that silly razor away."

He wouldn't fink it was silly iffin I slashed him across the face from temple to chin, but I stowed the urge and slipped the cool steel into its familiar dark hole.

"You're like watching a bad movie," Mandrake said. "But I've been told you're useful despite acting like a dog dropping."

I knew the part about money or aggro was coming.

"I've got a job I want you to do," Mandrake said suddenly, as if coming to a decision. He sat down in the big leather chair behind his desk and swiveled back and forth. "I want you to find my daughter."

D

WELL, THAT WAS A bit of a surprise. Hadn't I been in school with
Mandrake's daughter—Maureen by name? She was a brain. Knew
everything and never seemed to study. Now, though, wasn't she a little punk slut of all things? She was a club raver, one of those I was
telling you about wot would swallow anything to get high. The stupid
bint was probably passed out in some back room, or colder than concrete on a slab.

There was always something odd about Maureen. Nasty rumor
said Mandrake was impotent. Mrs. Mandrake once drunkenly said as
much in a local pub. Next day she had a nasty fall, broke her nose, and
blacked both eyes.

It kept her quiet for a while, but word was Mrs. Mandrake had
recently been a bit loose with her tongue again and had been sent to
visit her mother. Interesting, since her mother was dead.

"Where's she got to then?"

"If I knew, I wouldn't need to bother with a piece of shite like you."

I kept me mouth shut. I needed money more than aggro at the
moment.

We exchanged stares for a moment before he said, "You take care
of this little chore, and maybe I can find some other efforts to put your
way."

"Iffin you say so," I said, a bit happier. "When did little Maureen
do her Amelia Earhart?"

"She's been gone for three days."

"Is that unusual?" I asked.

"Not particularly," Mandrake said. "I rarely see the little cow these
days."

So much for fatherly love. "Where'd you see her last then?"

"Here, in the office."

Mandrake wasn't being exactly forthcoming.

"Is there somefink I'm missing? You tell me you want me to find your
kid, but it don't seem like you're burning up your Jockeys to get her back."

"Maureen took something that belongs to me."

"Right, yeah, go on. Wot? Money? Jewelry?"

"A book."

"A book? Now, that doesn't sound like somefink to get yourself
knotted about."

Mandrake launched himself across his desk, and didn't he back-hand me so hard he nearly tore me head off? I hit the back wall of the office with a thump and slid down to the floor. The razor gots as far as me hand when Mandrake stepped on me knuckles and ground them into the floor.

I tried to give him a steel toe cap in the back of the knee, but me leverage wasn't right and he took the blow on his thigh. He didn't like it much, but it didn't do no damage. To him that is. He hit me six or four times with a fist as hard as me own skull.

When he was done exercising, he crouched down. There was blood in me mouth, and one of me eyes was down to a slit.

"Friggin' hell," I said.

"Shut up, you five-fingered shite hawk. You do as I tell you, or I'll cut your arsehole open and pull you through backwards. You've got forty-eight hours to find Maureen and get my friggin' book back. After hour forty-nine, nobody will even remember your name. Got it?"

E

THE PHYSICAL DAMAGE MANDRAKE had done me was mostly minor. In the bathroom of an Esso station, I hawked out a wad of blood before splashing water over me face.

The shiny, steel mirror over the basin showed a swollen eye and a bruise the size of a cricket ball. It was nothing time wouldn't solve. The fingers on me right hand, however, still throbbed like soddin' hell. I'd be lucky if I could make a fist, let alone hold me razor. Could be a problem.

As I left the Esso, me nose started twitchin overtime.

Two black Rovers suddenly pulled into the petrol station and dis-gorged a swarm of plainclothes Garda. They were all big and mean, with nasty little truncheons already exposed.

I took to me heels, but a third Rover cut off me escape, and two of the Garda caught up with me from behind. I was taken down to the ground, me already abused face scraping hard.

One of the filthy bastards stamped squarely on me spine before pulling me arms back and shaking me razor out of its hiding place. He knew it was there, so this was no case of mistaken identity.

"You're friggin nicked, mate," he said, as he clamped down on the manacles he'd slipped over me wrists.

"Get off me, you gob stupid berk!" I yelled.

As he hauled me to me feet by me chained wrists, I gave him a back heel in the goolies. He let me go and I took off running, but it was no good. Three steps later, another bastard smacked me in the back of the head with his truncheon and I went down like a ton of coal.

F

I WOKE UP ALONE in a cell. The bracelets had been taken off, but me head throbbed like a miners' brass band playing an off-key melody.

I heard the *look-in* slide open on the cell's metal door. After a few moments, the door itself swung open and a woman walked in wearing a dapper top coat. She had black hair cut short in ragged layers. Trouble. She was the filth. The Irish police. The bloody frigging An Garda Siochana's. Inspector Siobhan Blake took no prisoners, ever.

"Well, Declan," Blake said in a sweet tone. She was the only person who could ever get away with using me real name. "How nice to see you."

I sat up, even though it took a major effort. "Allo, Blakey." I tried a grin. "I'd have come to sees you iffin you'd asked."

It was Blake's turn to smile, but I could see the shark behind it. She wasn't a big lezbo bitch, but she was as hard as they come, and as crooked.

"Of course you would, Declan. But then I wouldn't have had this to hold over your grotty little head." She held up me razor, opening it to let the light from the bare electric bulb flash off the blade. "Carrying an offensive weapon with your record." Blake shook her head sadly. "How many years do you think that's good for? At least two, I'd say."

Me throat felt swollen closed. "Be reasonable, Blakey," I said. "Isn't it only a family heirloom? I'd never think of using it on anyone."

Blake laughed. A full-bodied boomer, it was, but it cut off as quickly as it started, and I knew trouble was coming.

"Don't try to be funny with me, guttersnipe. It's Inspector Blake to you. If I tell you to shite, you ask how much and what color, got it? If you don't, I'll use this heirloom and you'll be air-wanking for the rest of your life."

"Yes, Inspector Blake," I said. I had no doubt Blake could cut me willy off and never bat an eye. She'd get away with it, too. Had half the judges in her pocket and was sleeping with the other half. You didn't piss Blake off.

"That's better, Declan. Much better." Blake undid her coat to show a nice bit of blue sheath dress underneath. It was tight across her full breasts. "Now, you've been a naughty boy, haven't you?" Blake ran her thumb down the edge of me razor. She didn't flinch, but closed her eyes and shuddered slightly. I knew how sharp that blade was. Watching Blake play with it was making me sweat. Suddenly, she flipped the blade closed and stuffed it into her coat pocket.

"Aren't you going to ask me what particular bit of naughtiness I'm interested in?"

"Wasn't I sure you'd tell me?" I was still trying to figure a way out of this alive.

Blake's lips twitched. "How is Mandrake these days?"

Not good.

"Isn't he doin fine?"

"How's his daughter?"

"Maureen?" I was trying to stall. Blake. Mandrake. Not much difference between them.

Blake leaned forward. "Mandrake doesn't have but one effin daughter," she said quietly.

I held me hands out in surrender. "Look, just ask me what you wants to know."

"Where's Maureen?"

"I don't know. She's done a runner, and doesn't Mandrake think I can find her?"

"You?" Blake looked astounded. That stung.

"Yeah, me," I said. "Why not?"

"Because you are nothing more than a pimple on a pig's arse, Declan. An effin' waste of human protoplasm."

I sat on the edge of the metal cell bed and sulked.

"Did Maureen take Mandrake's book?"

"What book?" I asked. "Mandrake is worried about his daughter. She's into the punk scene and he thinks I can find her."

"That's rich," she said. Then she hit me. I hadn't noticed her getting closer, but suddenly her fist was deep in me gut. I found meself retching on the damp stone floor.

Blake crouched on her haunches next to me. "Don't ever lie to me, sunbeam. I'm a human lie detector." She smoothed her hand over me close-cropped scalp. It was a curiously intimate gesture, like a mother touching her son. However, the brass knuckles over her fingers shattered the illusion.

Blake's mouth was close to me ear. "Listen, sunbeam. I know Maureen's got Mandrake's book. She was supposed to bring it to me. Now either she's got a bad case of stupid and had a change of heart, or somebody's changed it for her. Either way, I want that book. Understand?"

"Yes." Even in me condition, her breath on me neck and the breast pushing into me shoulder were getting a rise out of me.

"You may be nothing but a grotty little scrote, but you're my grotty little scrote. Got that? You bring me that book and there's a hundred nicker in it for you. If you don't, I'll bury you and piss on the gravestone."

With that, she stood up, straightened her coat, and walked out of the cell. She left the door open.

Fifteen minutes later, I found the strength and the nerve to follow her.

G

MANDRAKE, HIS DAUGHTER, AND a hundred pounds on offer from the bitch herself Inspector Siobhan Blake. There was something effin weird about the setup, but for a ton in readies I was more than willing to ignore it. There was also a mass of aggro I was due to pay back. The pain of me bruises felt good, but it would feel even better when somebody else was on the receiving end.

I started searching at Copperface Jacks off Saint Stephen's Green. It weren't the most likely spot to find Maureen Mandrake, but word would travel and sooner or later aggro would happen—and aggro would lead me to the stupid slag.

The downstairs bar was packed. There were a few tasty bits about, but nothin that would look at me twice. The beer was lousy and bloody expensive. I downed one pint on the arm from the bartender, and snagged two others from tables when their owners weren't looking. The manager said he'd never even heard of Maureen—liar—and the DJ said he hadn't seen her in a week since selling her some quaaludes.

It was the same story at Buskers in Temple bar (a major quim spot if you pay the lolly to get into their Boomerang club), at the Brazen Head across the river (decent beer, too many tourists, crap music), the Palace Bar (darts, old dozers, and a punk gathering that scares everyone off on weekends), the Bridge (yuppie-crap-punk-wannabees), and McTurkel's (a guaranteed punch-up).

In McTurkle's, however, I spotted Jimmy Riddle, arsehole extraordinaire and purveyor of mayhem. From the boot of his car, he sold me two straight razors. One went up me sleeve, and the other down the side of me left Doc Marten. Armed and happy, it was time to downscale.

At Angels on lower Leeson Street (lap-dancing whores), I was met with blank stares (and wasn't that a good sign word was traveling?), and further down the street at Strings (more lap, less dancing), I was told Maureen was putting it about earlier at Red Box (punks and ravers). Shite, how thick did people think I was? Wasn't this the obvious setup? I certainly hoped so. I'd had enough piss beer to last a month and I needed to hit somebody.

At Red Box, I forced the emergency exit and slipped in. The new Harcourt Street train station was behind me, and inside BiggZ were whamming away on their first set—all attitude and cocaine.

Red Box was a dross bucket of a club knocked through on a cheap refurbish of the old train station. As its name implied, it was a giant square inside, the walls painted red with red strobes strung from the ceiling on unconcealed wires. The stage supporting BiggZ was nothing more than scaffolding, the planking matching the bar on the opposite wall, which had the rough wood supported on ancient beer kegs. And wasn't I less than surprised when Nicky Ryan—all six-foot-six of him—came up behind me?

"Upstairs, you," he yelled over the music, one of his meaty hands grabbing me shoulder. What he makes up for in height, he lacks in brains. Big, but slow. I left the hand there for the moment.

Upstairs, he shoved me into O'Malley's office. Sean O'Malley runs Red Box, but kickbacks to the Bray brothers—Mandrake's biggest competitors.

O'Malley is a little runt, but along with Nicky, he had two other heavies to back his play. I could feel meself getting aroused. This was what I lived for. Me pulse rate went up a notch.

"Decco, me old son," O'Malley said. He threw a dart past me head and into a cork board on the back of the closed door behind me. I didn't flinch. The music from downstairs was only partially muted, so conversation was loud.

"Wot do you want?" I asked.

"It's not me that wants something, now is it, Decco?" He threw another dart, closer to me head this time. I still didn't move. "Aren't you the one wandering all over town looking for something?"

"Somebody."

"Something. Somebody. No difference, since you're going to stop." He threw the third dart.

I exploded with pent-up lust. I snatched the dart out of the air, stomped on Nicky's instep with me Doc Marten's, and smashed me head back into his face. Staying in motion, I threw the dart at the biggest heavy, hitting him in the eye. He went down screeching.

O'Malley and his other goon stood flatfooted in shock staring at their mate. I couldn't have cared less. I elbowed Nicky in the face and then spun around to give him a steel toe to the knee. Two down.

With me razor out of me sleeve and flashing in the overhead light, I took a step and slashed the side of the other goon's face. Three down, and I was on to O'Malley himself. I had the little bastard by the hair with the razor at his throat.

"Right, me old son," I said, throwing his bog Irish back at him. "Where the fook is she?"

"I'll kill you for this, Decco."

I let the razor sink into the flabby skin of his neck. "Last chance. Where the effin hell is she?" With me other hand I wiped me fingers through the blood trickle and held them up for him to see. "See some sense, old son."

His eyes flickered. "Down the hall. The Brays have got her work-ing a room. They think it's funny. If you take her, I might not get you, but they will."

"Won't we all be having fun in hell together then?" I said and smashed his head down onto his desk. It left a dent before it bounced off and he slummed to the floor.

The hallway was a knocking shop. The Brays ran whores on the streets and used the upper floor of Red Box for the mattress action. The Garda knew, but took their readies and stayed away.

I found Maureen in the third room on the right. She was doped up and laying under some sweaty bastard puffing himself out on top of her. I kicked him hard enough to curl him up and then rolled him clear.

Maureen wasn't registering any of this. I hauled her to her feet, grabbed a cotton dress from the floor and pulled it over her head, before half-walking her, half-dragging her out to the street.

The cold air seemed to revive her. "Who the fook are you?"

"Sir effin Lancelot," I said.

"I need a smoke," she said.

"Later." I dragged her to the side of a parked Fiesta and smashed the window with me elbow. I popped the locks and pushed her into the rear seat. I was about to get in and connect the wires under the dash, when another wire was slipped around me throat from behind. It bit into me skin as it pulled tight.

"Gotcha, you fooking weasel," Kink said.

Turner moved into me peripheral vision. The bastards must have been following me the entire time. He smiled and then hit me in the kidneys.

"Where are we going?" Maureen asked, from her unconcerned sprawl on the back seat.

Turner smiled. "Hell," he said.

H

HELL TURNED OUT TO be Mandrake's wrecking yard. I'd been bundled into the passenger seat and the wire around me neck secured to the headrest. Turner had tied me hands with a rough piece of rope and tethered them to the stick shift. He'd then driven while Kink sat in the back giggling and touching Maureen up as he tied her.

I couldn't say I was comfortable, but I was alive and in with a chance. Turner had, of course, relieved me of the razor in me sleeve, but he hadn't even thought to take a gander for the one down the side of me boot.

At the yard, Maureen and I had been left in the car while the two bully boys consulted with Mandrake. We were parked in a wide-open spot, and I figured I knew wot was comin. Apparently, so did Maureen.

"You stupid wanker. Why did you have to stick your face in?"

Now is that gratitude, I ask you?

"You like being humped by one sweaty geezer after another?"

"It beats the alternative."

I would have asked her what was the alternative, but at that moment it became clear. I could see Kink climbing into the driver's seat of a massive crane and crank over the engine. He maneuvered some gears and the huge magnet controlled by the crane began to raise up and swing our way.

"Why don't you just give Mandrake the effin book he's rabbiting on about?" I asked this knowing nobody had mentioned the book since Kink and Turner had grabbed us.

"I don't have his flaming book," Maureen said. It came out high pitched as she had started to pant with fear.

I gave this particular answer some thought. Remembering Maureen's performance in school, I connected the dots. "You gots one of them photogenic memories, don't you? That's why you always gots perfect scores on all the tests in school."

"And aren't you just the little Einstein?"

"You memorized his books, didn't you? Not his wrecking business books—his real business books."

"You're as thick as two planks. Not his business books, his bloody diary. Every filthy thing the bastard ever did."

"Well, shite."

The crane's magnet swayed back and forth above us before dropping down and smashing onto the Fiesta's roof.

"Flippin hell!" I said. "He's your father. Can't you make him stop?"

"He's not me fooking father!" Maureen was screaming. I felt like joining her, but instead I thought rapidly about what she'd just said.

"Your mother was heard blathering on about Mandrake being impotent—"

"And the bastard finally killed her for it."

Stuck to the magnet on its roof, the Fiesta shuddered as the crane lifted it off the ground. The car swung through the air.

"Is she in one of Mandrake's crushed soup cans?" If she was Blake and her Garda thugs could probably still find traces.

"Where else would she be? And isn't he going to put us in the same place?"

"Why go to the Garda with what you memorized from the books?"

"It would have fixed the bastard good." Maureen was straining against the ropes that bound her, yelling to fight her fear and be heard over the noise of the crane. "For hell's sake, he killed me mother."

"But why Blake, the head bitch herself?"

"Because Mandrake killed me father, too. Blake is me half-sister. It was her father, a copper himself wasn't he? He got me mother pregnant while trying to turn her against Mandrake. When Mandrake found out, he had him killed and terrorized me mother into silence. But the years of booze and pressure finally got to her, and she started telling anyone who would listen—including me."

"Why didn't you go straight to Blake?"

"I wanted the bastard to sweat. And then the Brays got a hold of me."

Maureen screamed again as the crane lowered and then dropped the Fiesta into the slot of the crusher. Thick metal walls clanged into both sides of the car. It was time to move.

I scrunched up and wiggled around to where me fingers could draw the second razor out of me boot. I fumbled with it for a second, the wire around me throat cutting deep as I struggled to see what I was doing.

I managed to slice through the rope tethering me hands to the gear shift without fuss, but the wire at me neck proved tougher. It wasn't pretty, and blood flowed, but I finally found some purchase on the wire where it went around the headrest and forced the blade through. The blade was sharp, the wire thin, and I was getting desperate as the sound of the crusher drove me on.

"What are you doing?" Maureen asked. Her eyes were huge as I scrambled past her and into the Fiesta's hatch area.

I lay on me back and kicked out with me Doc Marten's. It took three grunting tries, but eventually the hatch window shattered and showered me with safety glass. I jumped out of the car as the crusher made its first inward motion.

"You can't leave me here!" Maureen screamed when the car began to crease. And where had I heard that line before?

As soon as I popped out of the crusher's bay, Kink spotted me from his position in the crane cab. He shouted and pointed. Turner and Mandrake looked over from where they stood by the crusher's controls. Mandrake jabbed Turner, who stopped the crusher's movement. They wanted me inside, not out.

Mandrake's yard dogs were beside him. He immediately sent them after me and I loved him for it. As the dogs raced toward me, I extended me hand, palm down, and gave a low whistle—or tried to whistle. Me throat was clamped up.

I swallowed hard and tried again. This time sound came out and I lowered me hand as I crouched down. The dogs stopped, confused, wagging their tails slowly and looking back and forth from Mandrake to me.

"Good lads," I said, moving among them and fondling their ears. "Now, get him!" I sent them back racing toward Mandrake.

He saw them coming, disbelief in his eyes. The dogs were only too happy to have a direct command to obey. Mandrake called out to them, but they didn't so much as slow down. He turned and ran. Bad mistake. It turned him into lunch.

That left Kink and Turner. I flashed me blade at them. "Come on, boyos, let's dance." I must have looked crazed with the blood still flowing from me neck.

Neither of the bastards wanted to face me, but Turner was the one in the position to do something about it. With a malicious grin, he threw the switch to start the crusher moving again. He then picked up a discarded wrench and smashed the switch. He and Kink turned to run for the wrecking yard's front gate.

Shite! Turner and Kink or Maureen? Life is one effin decision after another.

The choice was made for me when Siobhan Blake and a clutch of uniformed Garda appeared across the yard entrance. And wasn't it a case of the followers following the followers.

With Mandrake a dog's dinner, and Kink and Turner under wraps. I turned to jump back up on the crusher. And should we praise the saints that Mandrake had been a cheap bastard. The crusher was donkey's years old and slow as me granny getting her leg over.

I ducked in through the hatch and sliced through Maureen's bonds. She scratched out at me with her nails, so I knuckled her in the face before dragging her clear. I dropped her over the side and jumped down next to her. Blake was standing, waiting.

The Fiesta popped and creased as the crusher finally forced it together with a solid crunch.

"And didn't you pull that one a bit fine?" Blake said.

"Where's me hundred nicker?" I asked.

"Where's the book?"

I pointed at Maureen. "Ask your sister."

Blake shot me a look. "You're on dangerous ground, Declan."

I sneered. "While you're at it, have your boffins look through the stacks of crushed cars."

"What for?"

"Wouldn't they be finding something of Mrs. Mandrake? At least enough to take to court."

"You'll get your money." Blake smiled. "You're still a wanker, Decco, but you're my wanker."

Fenian Ram

Simon Clark

John Philip Holland (1840–1914), educated in Limerick, Ireland, emigrated to America in 1873 where he invented the first viable submarine. The U.S. Navy purchased the Holland, ordered six more, and the age of the submersible warship was born. Legend has it that he built his first submarine as a young man after the unsuccessful Irish uprising of 1867. Little remains of his early work, however, but a few tantalizing sketches . . .
   —From *Birth of the Submarine*, by Captain E.A. Woolcombe; Curlew Press, 1967

D ecember 5th, 1872

MY DARLING KATHLEEN,

ISN'T it a lunatic thing to sit here writing this letter? Isn't it madness to be writing to you to kill time when time is killing me? Isn't it even madder to be writing this when you are only four yours old? And isn't it the ultimate insanity that this letter can never ever reach you?

But this letter unburdens me. And if, God willing, this should ever find you, you will be a grown woman with a husband and fine sons and daughters of your own, no doubt, and you will be breathing sweet air that will be all the sweeter because it rides to you over mountains and great plains that are home to men and women who are free. The land and people who I write about now will be strange to you, and perhaps none stranger than I, your own father, one Augustus Nash Lamb. Augustus? Is that really a fine Irish name I hear you ask. No. Not at all, I'd reply. My widowed mother was housekeeper to a Quaker academic in the wild and windy county of Donegal. His was a house that sits as far north in Ireland as you can get without soaking your feet. There I was born (my father's posthumous son), received my rare name, and grew up amid a family of intellectuals. I gained enough learning to be forever a handicap to me and that would make me a stranger to my fellow countrymen.

Later the cancer took my mother, leaving me to return alone to her hometown of Cullenagh on the shores of County Kerry. I had just turned fifteen, a foreigner in my own homeland.

With a chip on my shoulder so big you could have driven a coach-and-four through, I drank away my youth, blacked the eyes of my compatriots in the Cullenagh pubs, womanized, and ruined the reputation of a wealthy widow who lived in the big house of Oisin that stood at the top of Cullenagh Falls. She fled to Dublin. Within months rumors came back like homing pigeons of a newborn child that shared my scowling eyes.

You can't employ a man like me who is eternally angry at the world, so I earned my shilling by setting lines for cod on the scaurs that run out in long fingers of rock from the beach. There, the Atlantic seethes and boils all white around the end of the rocks. A restless anger with no cause that mirrors my own.

Yet even on the darkest of stormy days sometimes a shaft of brilliant golden sunlight will pierce the cloud. Just for a moment or so it's as warm and as bright as summer. So it happened to me. How, I don't know, but I fell in love with your mother. Colleen was a golden-hearted soul with blue eyes, fair hair, and a way that could make me as gentle as the lamb that was my namesake. You were born the year after we married. Another burst of sunlight in my life. But like those short-lived flashes of light on a stormy day my happiness was over before it had seemingly begun. Colleen died of consumption on your second birthday. Once more I was angry at the world and all it held. I knew I had to give you up. At least, thank heaven, you were taken into my sister's family to be brought up as their own.

So, for me, it was a time of turmoil. I returned to my terrible ways, drank the booze like it was milk, blacked eyes, and roamed mountaintops where I raged at heaven.

I did not like Cullenagh or its people. They did not like me. Yet I continued to circle the town like some dark raven. Not wanting to stay, yet somehow never able to break away. I was a son of that briny soil after all.

A year ago Lord Featherstone doubled the rents of his tenant farmers. Already dirt-poor, they pleaded that he reconsider. Within forty-eight hours the English soldiers had turned out the tenant farmers from their homes. Now families endure the winter in hovels made of sticks on common land. Menfolk are in hiding because Featherstone issued arrest warrants for unpaid rent that will put them in debtor's jail where they'll pick hemp until hell freezes over.

INTO THIS TURBULENT WORLD came one Mr. Holland, a young schoolteacher with mild eyes, and a voice that rarely rose above a whisper. He brought with him the *Fenian Ram*. Not a farm animal as you might think but a wee boat that, he told me, would right many a wrong and set Ireland free. You see, he wished to conduct secret sea trials on that remote coast far from prying eyes.

Picture an iron fish with a tail and a long point of a spear for a nose. A big black fish; big enough to house four men in its belly, where panting and running with sweat they work a massive crank. The crank turns a propeller that, in turn, drives the boat through water. On top of this craft is something like a diver's helmet of brass set with little round windows. There, head and shoulders inside this brass dome, stands the captain of the *Fenian Ram*. "Crank faster, lads," he orders. Or: "Slower. Stop. Back crank!" And he steers with a rudder bar that's as long as a broom handle. Insanity again I can hear you say. There I am with three other fellows cranking away like a mad thing until we grunt with sheer effort. Even more insane when I tell you that the iron cylinder can dive under the sea like a whale. But wasn't it a fine, fine occupation for a man like me? Sixpence a day to funnel my dark rage into that crank handle. I didn't have to think; I didn't have to consider my future; or that my beloved daughter would grow up not knowing me. All I had to do was crank, crank, crank. Crank until our breath condensed on the cold iron walls as if that tiny ship were cracking open; crank until my heart beat with all the rhythm of a drum played by a lunatic.

So this was my life. Me, a crew member on this secret ship built by the freedom-fighting schoolmaster. Me, with my back to the world, its woes, its injustices: me, scowling into my metaphorical corner. And so this life would continue, I believed. But this morning everything changed when I found the man in Lord Featherstone's wood.

HE LAY ON HIS back beneath a tree. His arms were above his head, reaching out for the base of the tree as if to claw the bark with his fingernails. Whoever had cut his throat had the skill of a butcher, the cut through the gullet exposing a valley of raw meat that reached the bone at the back of the neck.

A cold wind ran up from the sea, but when I touched the man's face his flesh was somehow colder.

"Augustus Lamb. I knew you were a brawler, but a murderer?" The constable shook his head. "No. But it seems as if I'm mistaken."

I watched the uniformed man looking at me down the length of his rifle.

"It wasn't me, O'Ryan. I've just found the poor devil."

"A murderer always returns to the scene of the crime, doesn't he, Lamb?"

"I'm not the murderer and you know it."

"I do, do I, Lamb? Why's that then, man? You have an alibi?" He held the rifle steady, aiming at my heart. "No. I didn't think so."

"I was—"

"Sleeping the whiskey off in a hayloft. Yes. I don't doubt. After you'd cut this poor wretch's throat."

"It wasn't having his throat slit that killed him."

"Cut himself shaving, did he? Nasty cut, eh? Then what? He tripped over that root while out walking?"

"No."

"Oh, so you do know something then? Come on, man, keep working that tongue of yours. Do you know him?"

"No."

"No, eh?" O'Ryan moved closer to get a better look at the body. "Well, I haven't seen the feller before. Must be a stranger to the town. But he hasn't traveled here recently. His boots look a might too clean to have been walking far in this weather." He jerked his head back at the muddy road. The constable's own boots were smeared with sandy mud that was as pale as whitewash.

"He wasn't walking out last night, either," I added.

"And why do you suppose that?"

"He's not wearing a coat, only shirtsleeves."

"Then someone stole his coat after he was dead. Do you own a blood-stained coat, Lamb?"

"He wasn't wearing a coat when he was outside. His shirtsleeves are rolled up to the elbow. Surely he would have rolled them down before putting on his coat."

"Perhaps," the constable allowed reluctantly. "Now sit yourself down on the ground, Lamb."

"What are you going to do?"

"I'm going to put a chain on you. I don't want you running, do I now? And I don't propose to stand here all day pointing this gun at you."

"Surely you don't think I did this?"

"I'd wager you'd beat a man to death in a bar before long, but I didn't think you'd kill in cold blood."

As he locked the handcuffs to my wrists behind my back I said, "You're going to arrest me?"

"I'll not be charging you yet, but I'll be obtaining a warrant of restraint from Lord Featherstone, then you'll be held in jail pending the magistrate's investigation."

"You're no friend of Featherstone," I told him, angry.

"I'm executing my duty as town constable, Lamb."

"What was in that sack you've got there, O'Ryan?"

"None of your business."

"I know you have sisters living out on the common. Featherstone turned them and their husbands out of their homes. You've been taking them food, haven't you? Featherstone wouldn't thank you for that, would he?"

"You keep that mouth shut of yours, Lamb. I'll break your head into a dozen pieces if you mention that to his Lordship."

"Why should I worry? They'll hang me anyway."

"Maybe."

"I didn't kill this man, O'Ryan."

"Stop lying to me then and tell me what you know."

"I'm not lying, but you can see the man wasn't even killed here."

"How do you know that?"

I nodded at the corpse. "See? He never walked here."

"He flew then, I suppose."

"Look at the soles of his boots. They don't have a fleck of mud on them. They're clean. The man was taken from his house and carried here. Look nearby and you'll find fresh hoofprints from a horse or mule."

"I'd heard you were a clever so-and-so."

"I've never claimed that."

The constable looked at me with knowing eyes. "You can read and write?"

"Yes."

"That sets you apart from nine-tenths of the town, then. Now what does that big brain of yours tell you about the dead man there?"

"He was dead before the killer cut his throat. If he were still alive he'd have bled all over the ground. There's scarcely a drop. If you were to open a vein I'd wager you'd find the blood's already congealed there."

"Then how did he die?"

"There's a little blood in the nose, but no wounds I can see other than the one to the throat—and that was made to disguise the real cause of death."

The constable squatted beside the body that was the color of clay there in the cold morning light. "There is blood in the nose. I daresay there was more on the face but it looks to have been wiped away."

"Are the fingernails torn?"

O'Ryan shot me a surprised look. "Yes," he said, "they are. The knuckles are grazed, too. He fought his attacker before he was overwhelmed."

I shook my head. "No, he *was* fighting to escape, but not from a man."

"You're playing games with me, Lamb. You know what happened, don't you?"

"The man was asphyxiated. That's why there are no marks on his body. A symptom of asphyxiation is bleeding from the nose."

The constable was a man of strong instincts. He knew I hadn't been as free with the truth as I ought. "Speak out, now. Who is this man?"

I sighed. "He's a Frenchie. Guy Drancourt. I worked with him. He and I were crew members on a . . ." I checked myself just in time. "On a fishing smack."

"You're a poor liar, Lamb. I know you're working on the schoolteacher's daft little boat. Was he?"

"Yes." I shook my head in surprise. "But you mean to say you know about—"

"Of course I do, man. It's my job to know what goes on round here. I know that Charlie Bibby's been poaching his Lordship's land every night for the past month. He took the herd's stag last night."

My look of bewilderment must have said it all.

The constable explained. "Bibby's been feeding those poor devils living up on the common, my relatives included. I'd be no better than Lucifer himself if I arrested him for that."

"But you must know that the submersible has been built to sink English battleships. Once this thing has been made to work then we'll be building—"

"There you go with your runaway tongue again, Lamb. I don't know any such thing about the schoolteacher's boat being a warship. As far as I'm concerned it's just a harmless bit of eccentricity on Mr. Holland's part. A man's entitled to that. Now." He jerked a thumb at the corpse. "How did that man die—exactly how."

"I don't know."

The constable shot me an angry look. Clearly, he didn't want taking for a fool any longer.

"I swear, O'Ryan. I don't know the exact details of his death. But yes, I do know the man, and when I saw him three days ago he was alive. But my guess is that there has been an accident with the submersible. He was trapped in the vessel and stifled as the air was used up. See, he ripped his hands trying to claw his way out."

"When was the last time you went out on the vessel?"

"Three days ago when I saw Drancourt."

"What have you been doing since then?"

"I've been away to Kilbarron."

"Which is the only place hereabouts that will serve you drink no doubt."

"What are you doing?"

"What does it look like? I'm going to take the chain off you."

"I thought you were putting me in jail?"

"I still might do that. But first you can show me where the school-teacher hides this miracle boat of his."

O'RYAN WAS GOOD TO his word. He took the cuffs from my wrists and we walked side-by-side through the wood to the clifftop. The wind had dropped by this time but the sea still ran a ferocious swell onto the rocks below. Every so often a wave hit the cliff bottom with a mighty thump that sent spray up a hundred feet to wet our faces. And all the time the gray December cloud streamed from those far-flung reaches of the ocean.

At last I voiced what had been on my mind. "There's a detail that's been troubling me, O'Ryan."

"And what's that?"

"Why haven't you reported the murder to the magistrate first before bringing me down here?"

"The corpse is not likely to stroll away, is he?"

"There's more to it than that, isn't there?"

"So you are a shrewd man, Augustus Lamb." He paused for a moment, catching his breath while looking out to sea. "But you're right. If I were to report a killing such as this—a possibly politically motivated murder—the magistrate might suppose then he'd call in the English soldiers to occupy the town until he was convinced otherwise."

"You'll have to report the crime sometime."

"And I will, Lamb. I've decided to file my report tomorrow." He looked at me. "You see, a number of Lord Featherstone's tenants have had more than a belly full of being treated no better than slaves." He walked briskly away, still talking. "A schooner is leaving on the evening tide for America. Officially, it's carrying bales of wool." He gave a shrug that amply conveyed the rest.

"Your sisters will be on there, too."

"Aye, and their husbands. But as there are debtors' warrants on them, they have to leave like thieves in the night. I wish it wasn't so. But there you have it. Their only desire is to live like human beings." He shot me a look. "Your own sister is leaving with her family, too. But you didn't know that?"

"No." I shrugged my shoulders, feeling ice in the pit of my stomach. "But I don't communicate that well round here as you know."

"Aye, you're a black sheep, no doubting that. And you've only yourself to blame, man. Now, is the boat in this cove?"

"The next. Below the old abbey ruin."

"Well, come on then, what's wrong with you, man?"

"My daughter will be on that schooner, too, then."

"Aye, she will. But take heart, Lamb, she'll be away to a better life in America." Those direct eyes on me again. "There's no point mewling about it. You're no good as a father to her now, are you?"

NEWTON, ONE OF MY fellow crewmen, coiled rope on the little jetty. Bobbing beside it was the *Fenian Ram*. Painted Bible black, the craft appeared as a tear-shaped shadow there in the water.

"Keep out of sight while I ask Newton some questions," I told O'Ryan. "If he sees a constable he'll scarper before we get anyway near."

Slipping the rifle from his shoulder, O'Ryan nodded his agreement and ducked behind a line of bushes. I continued down as if nothing were amiss. I walked with my hands in my pockets, kicking stones, whistling a jaunty air. Newton looked up at me as if nothing were amiss, too. For all the world it looked as if he were readying the *Fenian Ram* for another of her sea trials.

"We taking her out, Newton?" I asked.

"Only into the bay," he said, working the rope into a huge, dripping coil.

"But Mr. Holland won't be back until the end of the week, will he?"

"He sent word to test her against the old wreck with the torpedo."

I noticed a pair of strangers watching me from the hut on shore that served as the secret workshop. "Is this new crew?" I asked.

"Mr. Holland said we needed to train more men to sail her." Casually, Newton put the coiled rope over one of the jetty posts. "While you're here," he said, "you can get on board and check the steering gear. Her rudder's seized."

"It looks all right to me."

"It comes and goes. I reckon one of the tiller lines is frayed where it runs over the pulley aft. You go down below and check. I'll shout down and let you know if the rudder's moving freely enough."

"Right you are." I hopped onto the iron back of the boat, raised the hatch, and climbed down into the belly. Inside, there was barely room to stand straight and the entire cabin wasn't much more than fifteen feet from end to end.

Enough light came through the portholes in the dome atop the hull to see the lines running at either side of the cabin back to the steering gear.

"How is it?" Newton called.

"They seem all right to me. Are you sure they're—hey! Wait! What the devil are you doing!"

With a clang Newton slammed the hatch shut. The moment I scrambled back to it, I saw blood smears around the hatch on the iron walls. So this is how they'd finished Drancourt. He'd been tricked down here on some pretext like me. Newton had swung down the hatch and barred it from the other side. Of course the vessel was airtight. Within a few hours the air would have turned foul and the Frenchman would have suffocated. No wounds on the body. No fatal ones anyway. But here were the bloodstains on the hatch where he'd clawed his hands to raw flesh trying to escape. Then he'd been carried away up to Featherstone's wood where his throat had been cut to make it look like the work of some common bandit. But why was Newton doing this? For the last six months we'd stood side-by-side working the crank. And who were those strangers on the beach?

I climbed up to the portholes. There I could see Newton walking along the jetty to meet the two men. They were talking. But what they were saying heaven alone knows, because this iron cylinder was sealed against sound as well as fresh air. There was little doubt now, however, that they'd leave me to choke on my exhaled breath. That might take four or five hours, but they looked patient enough. One took out a pipe and lit it. What struck me then was that all three seemed peculiarly interested in what was happening out at sea.

My view from the porthole in the brass dome wasn't a particularly good one, and for a good few minutes, I couldn't see what they were looking at. But at last I made out smoke, a funnel, then the sea swell lifted the *Fenian Ram* up a good two feet and I saw it.

A British gunboat had steamed into the mouth of the bay. The muzzles of its great cannon gleamed silver. It had all the stealthy might of a monster waiting for its prey to happen by.

When I turned back to the three men, they appeared to be so unperturbed by the presence of the gunboat that they'd taken to sitting on the jetty. Then I identified the reason for this: O'Ryan had that rifle of his aimed at them. I watched as he chained them together. Then he talked to them for upwards of twenty minutes. When he didn't appear to get the kind of answers he was hoping for, he poked the muzzle of the rifle non-too-gently into the side of Newton's neck.

Newton's head bobbed and he had such a look of fear on his face that I wondered if he wouldn't start wailing. Presently, O'Ryan walked down the jetty and I heard the clang of his boots on the boat's hull. In a moment he'd opened the hatch to admit that sweet cold air.

"Newton killed Drancourt," I told the constable as I climbed out. "You can see the bloodstains on the inside of the hatch where the man tried to claw his way out."

"So the man told me. With encouragement." He shrugged the rifle onto his shoulder. "He and his two cronies planned to sell the school-teacher's little miracle boat here to the English."

"And Mr. Holland would be none the wiser. He won't be back until the end of the week."

"You'll also realize that the Frenchman discovered their intentions, so Newton shut him up in that floating coffin and watched him stifle himself."

"What now?"

"I'll keep these three locked up somewhere quiet for a couple of days, but the problem is that beast." O'Ryan nodded out where the gunboat sat guarding the bay. "The English have been told there's a valuable prize waiting for them somewhere hereabouts. A boat that can swim through water like a fish to sink the biggest battleship? Why, it's going to be worth more than its weight in gold. When these fellers don't deliver, the English are going to come looking for it. What's more, they're going to blockade the approaches to Cullenagh harbor. They'll search every ship in and out to make sure that little boat isn't spirited away."

"They'll stop the schooner tonight?"

O'Ryan nodded. "So they will. And they'll find that half-starved parcel of humanity bound for America. Just what I can do about that I don't know."

"I have an idea," I told him. "But I will need the use of your cuffs."

"THIS IS INSANITY!" NEWTON screamed the words at me. *"Insanity! Do you hear me!"*

"I hear you, Newton. Crank faster."

"No, we'll not do that."

"You've no choice. I'll put this axe through your head if you choose to mutiny now."

"Mutiny! You're insane, Lamb."

"Of course I am. You know that, Newton. I've been mad with anger for years. I've drank like a fish. I've brawled. But now I've the opportunity to redeem myself. You, too."

"No, Lamb. I'm not doing this. You're going to kill us."

But he did do it. And maybe Newton did redeem himself after all. Picture us, my dear Kathleen. I'd chained Newton and one of the strangers to the crank. I took the tiller, and standing there, head and shoulders in the brass dome, I guided the *Fenian Ram* away from her dock and into the bay. The swell had quieted somewhat, yet still it lifted her high onto those glassy mounds then dropped her into the dark hollows of the ocean. The sea slid over her hull leaving only the dome above the surface. With the help of O'Ryan I'd primed the torpedo. The constable is a good-hearted Irishmen, I realized at last. Even with all his blarney about breaking my head.

So there we were, the two men cranking like mad things (the sharp axe a reminder of my orders). Myself steering. At the end of the long pole that juts out from the vessel's nose was the hefty cylinder that contained a hundred fifty pounds of blasting powder. Two hundred yards ahead was the gunboat, sitting at anchor. I knew that in a few hours it would seize the schooner bound for America with its fragile cargo and you, my beautiful clear-eyed daughter.

Moments later, I sang out: "One hundred yards."

So this is the right thing to do, isn't it? If only Mr. Holland could know that his brave little craft can operate as well with a crew of just three.

"Eighty yards."

I looked out through the porthole, the tiller in my hand, the waves rolling the *Fenian Ram* from side to side, spray dashing against the glass, but still she held true to course.

"Fifty yards."

The slumbering leviathan lay at anchor. The guns were turned toward the harbor town ready to blaze at any ship daring to run. I saw the crew standing on decks, waiting for their orders. Still we hadn't been seen. But then, who'd notice this dome little bigger than a stew pot resting in the water, with the black hull of the boat lying invisible beneath the surface?

"Thirty yards and closing."

At that moment the sun pierced the gray winter cloud. An immense wash of radiance enfolded our craft. The sea turned the purest blue; the foam tipping the waves shone whiter than altar cloth. And at that moment it seemed we were sailing toward the gates of paradise.

"Twenty yards."

Mr. Holland had intended that magnets would fix the explosive charge to the side of a ship. Then the *Fenian Ram* would move to a safe distance before detonating the torpedo by a connecting line.

"Ten yards."

There were no magnets in the workshop; those were the items that Mr. Holland was himself collecting in Dublin.

"Five yards."

The torpedo at the end of the spar struck the gunboat below the water line. That was the moment I pulled the firing cord.

For a dozen or more years I carried a furnace of anger in my heart that roared and blazed and seared me from within. Anger that all the drink in Ireland couldn't douse. But at that instant my anger left me. It seemed to me it blazed like a shooting star from my fingertips, along the firing line, along the wooden spar and into the drum of blasting powder. It was my anger that exploded. It was my fury that ripped open the iron monster that would have claimed my daughter. It was my rage—red as blood—that drove the gunboat over onto its side, then down to the bottom of the Atlantic.

IT'S BRIGHTER HERE ON the seabed than I could have thought possible. Sunlight filters down through shifting veils of blue. The sand is rippled and it is the color of gold. Fish move like living diamonds. Light that appears to be the stuff of halos cascades through the portholes. And it is bright enough to see the hairs on the back of my hand. Mr. Holland would be pleased to learn that although his *Fenian Ram* lies deep in the ocean, dragged down by the passing of the gunboat, it is still watertight. The two men here have made their peace with God. I've sat for an hour or more scribbling with this pencil in the ship's log.

But enough is enough, isn't it, Kathleen? I've said my piece. The anger is gone. I am serene. Now I will seal this book inside an oilskin and lay my head down to sleep. I hope I dream of you walking on a beach on the other side of the world. You will have your mother's beautiful eyes, your mother's grace and gentleness. May I dream, dear Lord, that this book is washed upon that other shore; that you find it—and you know that even though I could not be there, I always loved you.

Your loving father,
Augustus Nash Lamb

Authors' Bios

Peter Tremayne is the pseudonym of Peter Berresford Ellis, a Celtic scholar who lives in London, England. He conceived the idea for Sister Fidelma, a seventh-century Celtic lawyer, to demonstrate that women could be legal advocates under the Irish system of law. Sister Fidelma has since appeared in eight novels, the most recent being *The Monk Who Vanished*, and many short stories that have been collected in the anthology *Hemlock at Vespers and other Sister Fidelma Mysteries*. He has also written, under his own name, more than twenty-five books on history, biography, and Irish and Celtic mythology, including *Celtic Women: Women in Celtic Society and Literature* and *Celt and Greek: Celts in the Hellenic World*.

Brendan DuBois is the award-winning author of short stories and novels. His short fiction has appeared in *Playboy*, *Ellery Queen's Mystery Magazine*, *Alfred Hitchcock's Mystery Magazine*, *Mary Higgins Clark Mystery Magazine*, and numerous anthologies. He has received the Shamus Award from the Private Eye Writers of America for one of his short stories and has been nominated three times for an Edgar Allan Poe Award by the Mystery Writers of America. He's also the author of the Lewis Cole mystery series—*Dead Sand*, *Black Tide*, and *Shattered Shell*. His most recent novel, *Resurrection Day*, is a suspense thriller that looks at what might have happened had the Cuban Missile Crisis of 1962 erupted into a nuclear war between the United States and the Soviet Union. This book also recently received the Sidewise Award for best alternative history novel of 1999. He lives in New Hampshire with his wife, Mona.

P. M. Carlson taught psychology and statistics at Cornell University before deciding that mystery writing would be more fun. Carlson's novels have been nominated for the Edgar Award, the Macavity Award, two Anthony Awards, and selection to the *Drood Review of Mystery's* top ten list. Ten earlier Bridget Mooney stories, including two nominated for the Agatha Christie Award, are collected in *Renowned Be Thy Grave*. She was also the 1992–93 president of Sisters in Crime.

Doug Allyn is an accomplished author whose short fiction regularly graces year's best collections. His work has appeared in *Once Upon a Crime*, *Cat Crimes Through Time*, and *The Year's 25 Finest Criman and Mystery Stories*, volumes 3 and 4. His stories of Tallifer, the wandering minstrel, have appeared in *Ellery Queen's Mystery Magazine* and *Murder Most Scottish*. His story "The Dancing Bear," a Tallifer tale, won the Edgar Award for short fiction for 1995. His other series character is veterinarian Dr. David Westbrook, whose exploits have been collected in the anthology *All Creatures Dark and Dangerous*. Allyn lives with his wife in Montrose, Michigan.

Mary Ryan lives in Dublin, Ireland, and has bought a house near Carcassone, France, where she seeks the peace and quiet to write her novels. Married with two sons, she is a graduate of University College, Dublin, and a qualified lawyer, but has now given up her practice to concentrate on her writing. Published in the United Kingdom, Eire, United States, France, and Germany, her titles include *Glenallen*, *Whispers in the Wind*, *The Seduction of Mrs. Caine*, *The Promise*, *Summer's End*, *Mask of the Night*, and *Song of the Tide*.

Edward D. Hoch is probably the only man in the world who supports himself exclusively by writing short stories. He has appeared in every issue of *Ellery Queen's Mystery Magazine* since the early 1970s and manages to write for several other markets as well. He has probably created more short story series characters than anybody who ever worked in the crime fiction field. And what great characters, too—Michael Vlado, a Gypsy detective; Dr. Sam Hawthorne, a small-town GP of the 1920s who solves impossible crimes while dispensing good health; and, among many others, his outre and bedazzling Simon Ark, who claims, in the proper mood, to be two thousand years old. Locked room, espionage, cozy, hard-boiled, suspense, Ed Hoch has done it all and done it well.

Jane Adams, who lives in Leicestershire, England, is married with a son and daughter. She has a degree in sociology and was once the lead singer in a folk rock band. In 1995, she was nominated for the prestigious John Creasey Award for best new crime writer for her novel *The Greenway*. Her other novels include *Cast the First Stone*, *Bird*, *Fade to Grey*, *Final Frame*, and *The Angel Getaway*. Her works have been published in the United Kingdom and translated in Denmark, Germany, Japan, and France.

Jeremiah Healy's street-smart detective John Francis Cuddy has appeared in several novels, most recently *Invasion of Privacy*. He's also made several appearances in anthologies, including *Legal Briefs*, *Cat Crimes II*, and several of *The Year's 25 Finest Crime and Mystery* volumes. A former president of the Private Eye Writers of America, he has spoken extensively about mystery writing around the world, including at the Smithsonian Institution's Literature series. Recently he was elected president of the International Association of Crime Writers.

Wendi Lee is the author of four novels featuring PI Angela Matelli, the latest being *Deadbeat* and *He Who Dies . . . .* Her westerns include the "Jefferson

Birch" series and *The Overland Trail*. She has published numerous short stories in the western, horror, and mystery genres, and is free-lance editor.

Mat Coward is a British writer of crime, SF, horror, children's, and humorous fiction, whose stories have been broadcast on BBC Radio, and published in numerous anthologies, magazines, e-zines in the UK, U.S., and Europe. According to Ian Rankin, "Mat Coward's stories resemble distilled novels." His first nondistilled novel—a whodunit called *Up and Down*—was published in the USA in 2000. Short stories have recently appeared in *Ellery Queen's Mystery Magazine*, *The World's Finest Crime and Mystery Stories*, *Felonious Felines*, and *Murder Through the Ages*.

Robert J. Randisi has had more than 350 books published since 1982. He has written in the mystery, western, men's adventure, fantasy, historical, and spy genres. He is the author of the Nick Delvecchio series and the Miles Jacoby series, and is the creator and writer of *The Gunsmith* series, a 230-book series for which he writes under the pseudonym of J. R. Roberts. He is the founder and executive director of the Private Eye Writers of America.

Bill Crider won the Anthony Award for his first novel in the Sheriff Dan Rhodes series, *Too Late to Die*. His first novel in the Truman Smith series, *Dead on the Island*, was nominated for a Shamus Award, and a third series features college English professor Carl Burns. His short stories have appeared in numerous anthologies, including past *Cat Crimes II* and *III*, *Celebrity Vampires*, *Once Upon a Crime*, and *Werewolves*. His recent work includes collaborating on a series of cozy mysteries with television personality Willard Scott. The first novel, *Death Under Blue Skies*, was published in 1997, and the second, *Murder in the Mist*, was released in 1999.

The short story is arguably the most demanding of all literary art forms, and few people ever master it. **Clark Howard** is one of the few. While his thirteen novels, including *The Hunter* and *Love's Blood*, are all exciting and rewarding books, his short stories display an even greater number of gifts and talents. His two stories, "Animals" and "Horn Man," are among the best written by anyone of his literary generation. And the amazing fact is that he continues to work at that level. Born in Tennessee, he has also written several true-crime books, including exposés on Alcatraz prison, the infamous Zebra serial killer, and the book *Brothers in Blood*, dealing with a case of murder in Georgia.

Jon L. Breen has written six mystery novels—most recently *Hot Air*—and over seventy short stories; contributes review columns to *Ellery Queen's Mystery Magazine* and *The Armchair Detective*; was shortlisted for the Dagger Awards for his novel *Touch of the Past*; and has won two Edgars, Two Anthonys, a Macavity, and an American Mystery Award for his critical writings.

Paul Bishop divides his time between writing best-selling mystery novels and heading up the Sex Crimes and Major Assault Crimes departments of the Los Angeles Police Department. During his twenty-year tenure, he has worked on a federal task force that coordinated with the L.A. Sheriff's Department, the FBI, CIA, and the Secret Service. Although his main series character is a female homicide detective named Fey Croaker, he also writes about a one-eyed ex-soccer goalie-turned-private-eye. His latest book is a collection of his short fiction entitled *Patterns of Behavior*.

Born in 1956, **Simon Clark** has contributed many stories to anthologies and magazines in the United Kingdom, United States, and to the BBC. His novels have been published in both Great Britain and America, and translations have appeared in Greece, Norway, and Russia. His novels include *Nailed by the Heart*, *Blood Crazy*, *Darker*, *King Blood*, *Vampyrrhic*, and *The Fall*. His latest work, inspired by the late John Wyndham and set to be published in Summer 2001, is entitled *Night of the Triffids*.

COPYRIGHTS AND PERMISSIONS

Murder MERRY most

CREEPY CRIMES CONTRARY TO THE CHRISTMAS SPIRIT

CONTENTS

CONTENTS

CONTENTS

INTRODUCTION

The Yuletide season has proven irresistible ground for mystery writers, and *Murder Most Merry* is a collection of the best in Christmas crimes. These 32 stories from *Ellery Queen's Mystery Magazine* and *Alfred Hitchcock's Mystery Magazine* span from hard-boiled police procedurals to cozy mysteries to fantasy adventures. With mysteries embracing sentiments ranging from world-weary cynicism to uplifting joy, this collection provides a holiday feast for mystery fans.

On his "Santa Claus Beat," Rex Stout's Art Hipple pines for a Christmas Eve murder truly befitting the season. In John D. MacDonald's story, a young woman ends up "Dead on Christmas Street," and the cops corner the desperate murderer using unconventional resources. Robert Turner offers a "Christmas Gift" anyone would be pleased to receive, and solving mysteries means more than just finding criminals when we go along with "Inspector Tierce and the Christmas Visits," by Jeffry Scott.

Professional thief Nick Velvet welcomes the holiday spirit when he attempts "The Theft of the Christmas Stocking," by Edward D. Hoch, while Thomas Larry Adcock's "Christmas Cop" stumbles across a gang of criminals who understand that it is better to give than to receive.

In a trio of tales featuring the bespectacled Mr. Albert Campion, Margery Allingham explores the darker side of the human spirit and lifts it into the light. "On Christmas Day in the Morning," an elderly woman embraces the enduring love and promise of Christmas in the face of life's tragedies. When there's "Murder Under the Mistletoe," an old acquaintance of Campion's draws on his expertise to solve an impossible crime. And, "The Case is Altered" on holiday in the country, when Campion explores a series of peculiar events.

From the first perplexing and then intriguing "Supper With Miss Shivers," by Peter Lovesey, to the "Christmas Party" with a twist by Martin Werner, to "The Adventure of the Blue Carbuncle" classic by Sir Arthur Conan Doyle, here are Christmas crimes every mystery reader will love to unwrap, one clue at a time.

Abigail Browning
April 2002

Murder MERRY

most

CREEPY CRIMES CONTRARY TO THE CHRISTMAS SPIRIT

Ann Cleeves

A WINTER'S TALE

In the hills there had been snow for five days, the first real snow of the winter. In town it had turned to rain, bitter and unrelenting, and in Otterbridge it had seemed to be dark all day. As Ramsay drove out of the coastal plain and began the climb up Cheviot the clouds broke and there was a shaft of sunshine which reflected blindingly on the snow. For days he had been depressed by the weather and the gaudy festivities of the season, but as the cloud lifted he felt suddenly more optimistic.

Hunter, sitting hunched beside him, remained gloomy. It was the Saturday before Christmas and he had better things to do. He always left his shopping until the last minute—he enjoyed being part of the crowd in Newcastle. Christmas meant getting pissed in the heaving pubs on the Big Market, sharing drinks with tipsy secretaries who seemed to spend the last week of work in a continuous office party, It meant wandering up Northumberland Street where children queued to peer in at the magic of Fenwick's window and listening to the Sally Army band playing carols at the entrance to Eldon Square. It had nothing to do with all this space and the bloody cold. Like a Roman stationed on Hadrian's Wall, Hunter thought the wilderness was barbaric.

Ramsay said nothing. The road had been cleared of snow but was slippery, and driving took concentration. Hunter was itching to get at the wheel—he had been invited to a party in a club in Blyth and it took him as long as a teenage girl to get ready for a special evening out.

Ramsay turned carefully off the road, across a cattle grid, and onto a track.

"Bloody hell!" Hunter said. "Are we going to get up there?"

"The farmer said it was passable. He's been down with a tractor."

"I'd better get the map," Hunter said miserably. "I suppose we've got a grid reference. I don't fancy getting lost out here."

"I don't think that'll be necessary," Ramsay said. "I've been to the house before."

Hunter did not ask about Ramsay's previous visit to Blackstoneburn. The inspector rarely volunteered information about his social life or friends. And apart from an occasional salacious curiosity about Ramsay's troubled marriage and divorce, Hunter did not care. Nothing about the inspector would have surprised him.

The track no longer climbed but crossed a high and empty moor. The horizon was broken by a dry stone wall and a derelict barn, but otherwise there was no sign of habitation. Hunter felt increasingly uneasy. Six geese flew from a small reservoir to circle overhead and settle back once the car had passed.

"Greylags," Ramsay said. "Wouldn't you say?"

"I don't bloody know." Hunter had not been able to identify them even as geese. And I don't bloody care, he thought.

The sun was low in the sky ahead of them. Soon it would be dark. They must have driven over an imperceptible ridge because suddenly, caught in the orange sunlight, there was a house, grey, small-windowed, a fortress of a place surrounded by byres and outbuildings.

"That's it, is it?" Hunter said, relieved. It hadn't, after all, taken so long. The party wouldn't warm up until the pubs shut. He would make it in time.

"No," Ramsay said. "That's the farm. It's another couple of miles yet."

He was surprised by the pleasure he took in Hunter's discomfort, and a little ashamed. He thought his relationship with his sergeant was improving. Yet it wouldn't do Hunter any harm, he thought, to feel anxious and out of place. On his home ground he was intolerably confident.

The track dipped to a ford. The path through the water was rocky and the burn was frozen at the edges. Ramsay accelerated carefully up the bank and as the back wheels spun he remembered his previous visit to Blackstoneburn. It had been high summer, the moor scorched with drought, the burn dried up almost to a trickle. He had thought he would never come to the house again.

As they climbed away from the ford they saw the Black Stone, surrounded by open moor. It was eight feet high, truly black with the setting sun behind it, throwing a shadow onto the snow.

Hunter stared and whistled under his breath but said nothing. He would not give his boss the satisfaction of asking for information. The information came anyway. Hunter thought Ramsay could have been one of those guides in bobble hats and walking boots who worked at weekends for the National Park.

"It's a part of a circle of prehistoric stones," the inspector said. "Even if there weren't any snow you wouldn't see the others at this distance. The bracken's grown over them." He seemed lost for a moment in memory. "The house was named after the stone, of course. There's been a dwelling on this site since the fourteenth century."

"A bloody daft place to put a house," Hunter muttered. "If you ask me. . . ."

They looked down into a valley onto an L-shaped house built around a flagged yard, surrounded by windblown trees and shrubs.

"According to the farmer," Ramsay said, "the dead woman wasn't one of the owner's family. . . ."

"So what the hell was she doing here?" Hunter demanded. The emptiness made him belligerent. "It's not the sort of place you'd stumble on by chance."

"It's a holiday cottage," Ramsay said. "Of sorts. Owned by a family from Otterbridge called Shaftoe. They don't let it out commercially but friends know that they can stay here. . . . The strange thing is that the farmer said there was no car. . . ."

The track continued up the hill and had, Hunter supposed, some obscure agricultural use. Ramsay turned off it down a potholed drive and stopped in the yard, which because of the way the wind had been blowing was almost clear of snow. A dirty green Land Rover was already parked there, and as they approached a tall, bearded man got out and stood impassively, waiting for them to emerge from the warmth of their car. The sun had disappeared and the air was icy.

"Mr. Helms." The inspector held out his hand. "I'm Ramsay. Northumbria Police."

"Aye," the man said. "Well, I'd not have expected it to be anyone else."

"Can we go in?" Hunter demanded. "It's freezing out here."

Without a word the farmer led them to the front of the house. The wall was half covered with ivy and already the leaves were beginning to be tinged with frost. The front door led directly into a living room. In a grate the remains of a fire smouldered, but there was little warmth. The three men stood awkwardly just inside the room.

"Where is she?" Hunter asked.

"In the kitchen," the farmer said. "Out the back."

Hunter stamped his feet impatiently, expecting Ramsay to lead the way. He knew the house. But Ramsay stood, looking around him.

"Had Mr. Shaftoe asked you to keep an eye on the place?" he asked. "Or did something attract your attention?"

"There was someone here last night," Helms said. "I saw a light from the back."

"Was there a car?"

"Don't know. Didn't notice."

"By man, you're a lot of help," Hunter muttered. Helms pretended not to hear.

"But you might have noticed," Ramsay persisted, "fresh tyre tracks on the drive."

"Look," Helms said. "Shaftoe lets me use one of his barns. I'm up and down the track every day. If someone had driven down using my tracks how would I know?"

"Were you surprised to see a light?" Ramsay asked.

"Not really," Helms said. "They don't have to tell me when they're coming up."

"Could they have made it up the track from the road?"

"Shaftoe could. He's got one of those posh Japanese four-wheel-drive jobs."

"Is it usual for him to come up in the winter?"

"Aye." Helms was faintly contemptuous. "They have a big do on Christmas Eve. I'd thought maybe they'd come up to air the house for that. No one's been in the place for months."

"You didn't hear a vehicle go back down the track last night?"

"No. But I wouldn't have done. The father-in-law's stopping with us and he's deaf as a post. He had the telly so loud you can't hear a thing."

"What time did you see the light?"

Helms shrugged. "Seven o'clock maybe. I didn't go out after that."

"But you didn't expect them to be staying?"

"No. Like I said, I expected them to light a fire, check the calor gas, clean up a bit, and then go back."

"So what caught your attention this morning?"

"The gas light was still on," Helms said.

"In the same room?"

Helms nodded. "The kitchen. It was early, still pretty dark outside, and I thought they must have stayed and were getting their breakfasts. It was only later, when the kids got me to bring them over, that I thought it was strange."

"I don't understand," Ramsay said. "Why did your children want to come?"

"Because they're sharp little buggers. It's just before Christmas. They thought Shaftoe would have a present for them. He usually brings them something, Christmas or not."

"So you drove them down in the Land Rover? What time was that?"

"Just before dinner. Twelvish. They'd been out sledging and Chrissie, my wife, said there was more snow on her kitchen floor than out on the fell. I thought I'd earn a few brownie points by getting them out of her hair." He paused and for the first time he smiled. "I thought I'd get a drink for my trouble. Shaftoe always kept a supply of malt whisky in the place, and he was never mean with it."

"Did you park in the yard?"

"Aye. Like I always do."

"That's when you noticed the light was still on?"

Helms nodded.

"What did you do then?"

"Walked round here to the front."

"Had it been snowing?" Ramsay asked.

"There were a couple of inches in the night but it was clear by dawn."

"What about footprints on the path? You would have noticed if the snow had been disturbed."

"Aye," Helms said. "I might have done if I'd got the chance. But I let the dog and the bairns out of the Land Rover first and they chased round to the front before me."

"But your children might have noticed," Ramsay insisted.

"Aye," Helms said without much hope. "They might."

"Did they go into the house before you?"

"No. They were still on the front lawn throwing snowballs about when I joined them. That's when I saw the door was open and I started to think something was up. I told the kids to wait outside and came in on my own. I stood in here feeling a bit daft and shouted out the back to Shaftoe. When there was no reply I went on through."

"What state was the fire in?" Ramsay asked.

"Not much different from what it's like now. If you bank it up it stays like that for hours."

There was a pause. "Come on then," Ramsay said. "We'd best go through and look at her."

The kitchen was lit by two gas lamps mounted on one wall. The room was small and functional. There was a small window covered on the outside by bacterial-shaped whirls of ice, a stainless-steel sink, and a row of units. The woman, lying with one cheek against the red tiles, took up most of the available floor space. Ramsay, looking down, recognised her immediately.

"Joyce," he said. "Rebecca Joyce." He looked at Helms. "She was a friend of the Shaftoe family. You don't recognise her?"

The farmer shook his head.

Ramsay had met Rebecca Joyce at Blackstoneburn. Diana had invited him to the house when their marriage was in its final throes and he had gone out of desperation, thinking that on her own ground, surrounded by her family and friends, she might be calmer. Diana was related to the Shaftoes by marriage. Her younger sister Isobel had married one of the Shaftoe sons and at that summer house party they were all there: old man Shaftoe, who had made his money out of scrap, Isobel, and her husband Stuart, a grey, thin-lipped man who had brought the family respectability by proposing to the daughter of one of the most established landowners in Northumberland.

Rebecca had been invited as a friend, solely, it seemed, to provide entertainment. She had been at school with Diana and Isobel and had been outrageous, apparently, even then. Looking down at the body on the cold kitchen floor, Ramsay thought that despite the battered skull he still saw a trace of the old spirit.

"I'll be off then. . . ." Helms interrupted his daydream. "If there's nothing else."

"No," Ramsay said. "I'll know where to find you."

"Aye. Well." He sloped off, relieved. They heard the Land Rover drive away up the track and then it was very quiet.

"The murder weapon was a poker," Hunter said. "Hardly original."

"Effective though." It still lay on the kitchen floor, the ornate brass knob covered with blood.

"What now?" Hunter demanded. Time was moving on. It was already six o'clock. In another hour his friends would be gathering in the pubs of Otterbridge preparing for the party.

"Nothing," Ramsay said, "until the pathologist and the scene-of-crime team arrive." He knew that Hunter wanted to be away. He could have sent him off in the car, arranged a lift for himself with the colleagues who would arrive later, earned for a while some gratitude and peace, but a perverseness kept him quiet and they sat in the freezing living room, waiting.

When Ramsay met Rebecca Joyce it had been hot, astoundingly hot for the Northumberland hills, and they had taken their drinks outside onto the lawn. Someone had slung a hammock between two Scotch pines and Diana had lain there moodily, not speaking, refusing to acknowledge his presence. They had argued in the car on the way to Blackstoneburn and he was forced to introduce himself to Tom Shaftoe, a small, squat man with silver sideburns. Priggish Isobel and anonymous Stuart he had met before. The row had been his fault. Diana had not come home the night before, and he had asked quietly, restraining his jealousy, where she had been. She had lashed out in a fury, condemning him for his Methodist morals, his dullness.

"You're just like your mother," she had said. The final insult. "All hypocrisy and thrift."

Then she had fallen stubbornly and guiltily silent and had said nothing more to him all evening.

Was it because of her taunts that he had gone with Rebecca to look at the Black Stone? Rebecca wore a red Lycra tube which left her shoulders bare and scarcely covered her buttocks. She had glossy red lipstick and black curls pinned back with combs. She had been flirting shamelessly with Stuart all evening and then suddenly to Ramsay she said:

"Have you ever seen the stone circle?"

He shook his head, surprised, confused by her sudden interest.

"Come on then," she had said. "I'll show you."

In the freezing room at Blackstoneburn, Hunter looked at his boss and thought he was a mean bastard, a kill-joy. There was no need for them both to be there. He nodded towards the kitchen door, bored by the silence, irritated because Ramsay would not share information about the dead woman.

"What did she do then?" he asked. "For a living."

Ramsay took a long time to reply and Hunter wondered if he was ill, if he was losing his grip completely.

"She would say," the inspector answered at last, "that she lived off her wits."

He had assumed that because she had been to school with Diana and Isobel her family were wealthy, but discovered later that her father had been a hopeless and irresponsible businessman. A wild scheme to develop a Roman theme park on some land close to Hadrian's Wall had led to bankruptcy, and Rebecca had left school early because the fees could not be paid. It was said that the teachers were glad of an excuse to be rid of her.

"By man," said Hunter, "what does that mean?"

"She had a few jobs," Ramsay said. "She managed a small hotel for a while, ran the office of the agricultural supply place in Otterbridge. But she couldn't stick any of them. I suppose it means she lived off men."

"She was a whore?"

"I suppose," Ramsay said, "it was something like that."

"You seem to know a lot about her. Did you know her well, like?"

The insolence was intended. Ramsay ignored it.

"No," he said. "I only met her once."

But I was interested, he thought, interested enough to find out more about her, attracted not so much by the body in the red Lycra dress, but by her kindness. It was the show, the decadent image, which put me off. If I had been braver I would have ignored it.

Her attempt to seduce him on that hot summer night had been a kindness, an offer of comfort. Away from the house she had taken his hand and they had crossed the burn by stepping stones, like children. She had shown him the round black stones hidden by bracken and then put his hand on her round, Lycra-covered breast.

He had hesitated, held back by his Methodist morals and the thought of sad Diana lying in the hammock on the lawn. Rebecca had been kind again, unoffended.

"Don't worry," she said, laughing, kissing him lightly on the cheek. "Not now. If you need me you'll be able to find out where I am."

And she had run away back to the others, leaving him to follow slowly, giving him time to compose himself..

Ramsay was so engrossed in the memory of his encounter with Rebecca Joyce that he did not hear the vehicles outside or the sound of voices. He was jolted back to the present by Hunter shouting: "There they are. About bloody time, too." And by the scene-of-crime team at the door bending to change their shoes, complaining cheerfully about the cold.

"Right then," Hunter said. "We can leave it to the reinforcements." He looked at his watch. Seven o'clock. The timing would be tight but not impossible. "I suppose someone should see the Shaftoes tonight," he said. "They're the most likely suspects. I'd volunteer for the overtime myself but I'm all tied up this evening."

"I'll talk to the Shaftoes," Ramsay said. It was the least he could do.

Outside in the dark it was colder than ever. Ramsay's car would not start immediately and Hunter swore under his breath. At last it pulled away slowly, the heater began to work, and Hunter began to relax.

"I want to call at the farm," Ramsay said. "Just to clear up a few things."

"Bloody hell!" Hunter said, convinced that Ramsay was prolonging the journey just to spite him. "What's the matter now?"

"This is a murder enquiry," Ramsay said sharply. "Not just an interruption to your social life."

"You'll not get anything from that Helms," Hunter said. "What could he know, living up there? It's enough to drive anyone crazy."

Ramsay said nothing. He thought that Helms was unhappy, not mad.

"Rebecca always goes for lonely men," Diana had said cruelly on the drive back from Blackstoneburn that summer. "It's the only way she can justify screwing around."

"What's your justification?" he could have said, but Diana was unhappy too, and there had seemed little point.

They parked in the farm yard. In a shed cattle moved and made gentle noises. A small woman with fine pale hair tied back in an untidy ponytail let them into the kitchen where Helms was sitting in a high-backed chair, his stockinged feet stretched ahead of him. He was not surprised to see them. The room was warm despite the flagstone floor. A clothes horse, held together with binder twine, was propped in front of the range and children's jeans and jerseys steamed gently. The uncurtained window was misted with condensation. Against one wall was a large square table covered by a patterned oilcloth, with a pile of drawing books and a scattering of felt-tipped pens. From another room came the sound of a television and the occasional shriek of a small child.

Chrissie Helms sat by the table. She had big hands, red and chapped, which she clasped around her knees.

"I need to know," Ramsay said gently, "exactly what happened."

Hunter looked at the fat clock ticking on the mantelpiece and thought his boss was mad. Ramsay turned to the farmer.

"You were lying," he said. "It's so far-fetched, you see. Contrived. A strange and beautiful woman found miles from anywhere in the snow. Like a film. It must be simpler than that. You would have seen tracks when you took the tractor up to the road to clear a path for us. It's lonely out here. If you'd seen a light in Blackstoneburn last night you'd have gone in. Glad of the company and old

Shaftoe's whisky."

Helms shook his head helplessly.

"Did he pay you to keep quiet?" Hunter demanded. Suddenly, with a reluctant witness to bully he was in his element. "Or did he threaten you?"

"No," Helms said, "it were nothing like that."

"But she was there with some man?" Hunter was jubilant.

"Oh," Helms's wife said quietly, shocking them with her interruption, "she was there with some man."

Ramsay turned to the farmer. "She was your mistress?" he said, and Hunter realised he had known all along.

Helms said nothing.

"You must have met her at the agricultural suppliers in Otterbridge. Perhaps when you went to pay your bill. Perhaps she recognised you. She often came to Blackstoneburn."

"I recognised her," Helms said.

"You'd hardly miss her," the woman said. "The way she flaunted herself."

"No." The farmer shook his head. "No, it wasn't like that."

He paused.

"You felt sorry for her . . . ?" Ramsay prompted.

"Aye!" Helms looked up, relieved to be understood at last.

"Why did you bring her here?" Ramsay asked.

"I didn't. Not here."

"But to Blackstoneburn. You had a key? Or Rebecca did?"

Helms nodded. "She was lonely," he said. "In town. Everyone thinking of Christmas. You know."

"So you brought her up to Blackstoneburn," Hunter said unpleasantly. "For a dirty weekend. Thinking you'd sneak over to spend some time with her. Thinking your wife wouldn't notice."

Helms said nothing.

"What went wrong?" Hunter demanded. "Did she get greedy? Want more money? Blackmail? Is that why you killed her?"

"You fool!" It was almost a scream, and as she spoke the woman stood up with her huge red hands laid flat on the table. "He wouldn't have harmed her. He didn't kill her. I did."

"You must tell me," Ramsay said again, "exactly what happened."

But she needed no prompting. She was desperate for their understanding. "You don't know what it's like here," she said. "Especially in the winter. Dark all day. Every year it drives me mad. . . ." She stopped, realising she was making little sense, and continued more rationally. "I knew he had a woman, guessed. Then I saw them in town and I recognised her too. She was wearing black stockings and high heels, a dress that cost a fortune. How could I compete with that?" She looked down at her shapeless jersey and jumble-sale trousers. "I thought he'd grow out of it, that if I ignored it, he'd stop. I never thought he'd bring her here." She paused.

"How did you find out?" Ramsay asked.

"Yesterday afternoon I went out for a walk. I left the boys with my dad. I'd been in the house all day and just needed to get away from them all. It was half-past three, starting to get dark. I saw the light in Blackstoneburn and Joe's Land Rover parked outside. Like you said, we're desperate here for company, so I went around to the front and knocked at the door. I thought Tom Shaftoe was giving him a drink."

"There was no car," Ramsay said.

"No," she said. "But Tom parks it sometimes in one of the sheds. I didn't suspect a thing."

"Did you go in?"

"Not then," she said calmly. "When there was no reply I looked through the window. They were lying together in front of the fire. Then I went in. . . ." She paused again. "When she saw me she got up and straightened her clothes. She laughed. I suppose she was embarrassed. She said it was an awkward situation and why didn't we all discuss it over a cup of tea. Then she turned her back on me and walked through to the kitchen." Chrissie Helms caught her breath in a sob. "She shouldn't have turned her back," she said. "I deserved more than that. . . ."

"So you hit her," Ramsay said.

"I lost control," Chrissie said. "I picked up the poker from the grate and I hit her."

"Did you mean to kill her?"

"I wasn't thinking clearly enough to mean something."

"But you didn't stop to help her?"

"No," she said. "I came home. I left it to Joe to sort out. He owed me that. He did his best, but I knew we'd not be able to carry it through." She looked at her husband. "I'll miss you and the boys," she said. "But I'll not miss this place. Prison'll not be much different from this."

Hunter walked to the window to wait for the police Land Rover. He rubbed a space in the condensation and saw that it was snowing again, heavily. He thought that he agreed with her.

James Powell

GRIST FOR THE MILLS
OF CHRISTMAS

The tabloid press dubbed the corner of southern Ontario bounded by Windsor, Sarnia, and St. Thomas "The Christmas Triangle" after holiday travelers began vanishing there in substantial numbers. When the disappearances reached twenty-seven, Wayne Sorley, editor-at-large of *The Traveling Gourmet* magazine, ever on the alert for offbeat articles, penciled in a story on "Bed-and-Breakfasting Through the Triangle of Death" for an upcoming Christmas number, intending to combine seasonal decorations and homey breakfast recipes (including a side article on "Muffins from Hell") with whatever details of the mysterious triangle came his way.

So when the middle of December rolled around, Sorley flew to Detroit, rented a car, and drove across the border into snow, wind, and falling temperatures.

He quickly discovered the bed-and-breakfast people weren't really crazy about the Christmas Triangle slant. Some thought it was bad for business. Few took the disappearances as lightly as Sorley did. To make matters worse, his reputation had preceded him. The current issue of *The Traveling Gourmet* contained his "Haunted Inns of the Coast of Maine" and his side article "Cod Cakes from Hell," marking him as a dangerous guest to have around. Some places on Sorley's itinerary received him grudgingly. Others claimed no record of his reservations and threatened to loose the dog on him if he didn't go away.

On the evening of the twenty-third of December, and well behind schedule, Sorley arrived at the last bed-and-breakfast on his prearranged itinerary to find a handwritten notice on the door. "Closed by the Board of Health." Shaking his fist at the dark windows, Sorley decided then and there to throw in the towel. To hell with the damn Christmas Triangle! So he found a motel for the night, resolving to get back across the border and catch the first available flight for New York City. But he awoke late to find a fresh fall of snow and a dead car battery.

It was midafternoon before Sorley, determined as ever, was on the road again. By six o'clock the snow was coming down heavily and aslant and he was still far from his destination. He drove on wearily. What he really needed now, he told himself, was a couple of weeks in Hawaii. How about an article on "The Twelve Luaus of Christmas"? This late they'd have to fake it. But what the hell, in Hawaii they have to fake the holidays anyway.

Finally Sorley couldn't take the driving anymore and turned off the highway to find a place for the night. That's when he saw the "Double Kay B & B" sign with the shingle hanging under it that said "Vacancy." On the front lawn beside the sign stood a fine old pickle-dish sleigh decorated with Christmas tree lights. Plastic reindeer lit electrically from within stood in the traces. Sorley pulled into the driveway and a moment later was up on the porch ringing the bell.

Mrs. Kay was a short, stoutish, white-haired woman with a pleasant face which, except for an old scar from a sharp-edged instrument across the left cheekbone, seemed untouched by care. She ushered Sorley inside and down a carpeted hallway and up the stairs. The house was small, tidy, bright, and comfortably arranged. Sorley couldn't quite find the word to describe it until Mrs. Kay showed him the available bedroom. The framed naval charts on the walls, the boat in a bottle, and the scrimshawed narwhal tusk on the mantel gave him the word he was looking for. The house was ship-shape.

Sorley took the room. But when he asked Mrs. Kay to recommend a place to eat nearby she insisted he share their dinner. "After all, it's Christmas Eve," she said. "You just freshen up, then, and come downstairs." Sorley smiled his thanks. The kitchen smells when she led him through the house had been delicious.

Sorley went back out to his car for his suitcase. The wind had ratcheted up its howl by several notches and was chasing streamers of snow down the road and across the drifts. But that was all right. He wasn't going anywhere. As he started back up the walk someone inside the house switched off the light on the bed-and-breakfast sign.

Sorley came out of his room pleased with his luck. Here he was settled in for the night with a roof over his head and a hot meal and a warm bed in the bargain. Suddenly Sorley felt eyes watching him, a sensation as strong as a torch on the nape of his neck. But when he looked back over his shoulder the hall was empty. Or had something tiny just disappeared behind the low-boy against the wall? Frowning, he turned his head around. As he did he caught the glimpse of a scurry, not the thing itself, but the turbulence of air left in the wake of some small creature vanishing down the stairs ahead of him. A mouse, perhaps. Or, if they were seagoing people, maybe the Kays kept rats. Sorley made a face. Then, shaking his head at his overheated imagination, he went downstairs.

Mrs. Kay fed him at a dining room table of polished wood with a single place setting. "I've already eaten," she explained. "I like my supper early. And Father, Mr. Kay, never takes anything before he goes to work. He'll just heat his up in the microwave when he gets home." The meal was baked finnan haddie. Creamed smoked haddock was a favorite Sorley had not seen for a long time. She served it with a half bottle of Alsatian Gewurtztraminer. There was Stilton cheese and a fresh pear for dessert. "Father hopes you'll join him later in the study for an after-dinner drink," said Mrs. Kay.

The study was a book-lined room decorated once again with relics and artifacts of the sea. The light came from a small lamp on the desk by the door and the fire burning in the grate. A painting of a brigantine under sail in a gray sea hung above the mantel. Mr. Kay, a tall, thin man with a long, sallow, clean-shaven face, heavy white eyebrows, and patches of white hair around his ears, rose from one of two wing-backed chairs facing the fire. As he shook his guest's hand he examined him and seemed pleased with what he saw. "Welcome, Mr. Sorley." Here was a voice that might once have boomed in the teeth of a gale. "Come sit by the fire."

Before sitting, Sorley paused to admire a grouping of three small statues on the mantel. They were realistic representations of pirates, each with a tarred pigtail and a brace of pistols, all three as ugly as sin and none more than six inches tall. A peglegged pirate. Another with a hook for a hand. The third wore a black eye patch. Seeing his interest, Mr. Kay took peg leg down and displayed it in his palm. "Nicely done, are they not? I'm something of a collector in the buccaneer line. Most people's family trees are hung about with horse thieves. Pirates swing from mine." He set the statue back on the mantel. "And I'm not ashamed of it. With all this what-do-you-call-it going round, this historical revisionism, who knows what's next? Take Christopher Columbus, eh? He started out a saint. Today he's worse than a pirate. Some call him a devil. And Geronimo has gone from devil incarnate to the noble leader of his people. But here, Mr. Sorley. Forgive my running on. Sit down and join me in a hot grog."

Sorley's host poured several fingers of a thick dark rum from a heavy green bottle by his foot, added water from the electric teakettle steaming on the hearth, urging as he passed him the glass, "Wrap yourself around that."

The drink was strong. It warmed Sorley's body like the sun on a cold spring day. "Thank you," he said. "And thanks for the excellent meal."

"Oh, we keep a good table, Mother and I. We live well. Not from the bed-and-breakfast business, I can tell you that. After all, we only open one night a year and accept only a single guest."

When Sorley expressed his surprise, Mr. Kay explained, "Call it a tradition. I mean, we certainly don't need the money. I deal in gold coins—you know, doubloons, moidore—obtained when the price was right. A steal, you might say. So, yes, we live well." He looked at his guest. "And what do you do for a living, Mr. Sorley?"

Sorley wasn't listening. For a moment he thought he'd noticed something small move behind Mr. Kay, back there in the corner where two eight-foot-long bamboo poles were leaning, and was watching to catch sight of it again. When Mr. Kay repeated his question Sorley told him what he did and briefly related his adventures connected with the aborted article.

Mr. Kay laughed like thunder, slapped his knees, and said, "Then we are indeed well met. If you like, I'll tell you the whole story about the Christmas Triangle. What an evening we have ahead of us, Mr. Sorley. Outside a storm howls and butts against the windows. And here we sit snug by the fire with hot drinks in our fists, a willing taleteller and . . ."

". . . an eager listener," said Sorley, congratulating himself once again on how well things had worked out. He might get his article yet.

Mr. Kay toasted his guest silently, thought for a moment, and then began. "Now years ago, when piracy was in flower, a gangly young Canadian boy named Scattergood Crandal who had run off to join the pirate trade in the Caribbean finally earned his master-pirate papers and set out on a life's journey in buccaneering. But no pantywaist, warm-water pirating for him, no rummy palm-tree days under blue skies. Young Crandal dreamed of home, of cool gray summers plundering the shipping lanes of the Great Lakes, of frosty winter raiding parties skating up frozen rivers with mufflers around their necks and cutlasses in their teeth, surprising sleeping townspeople under their eiderdowns.

"So with his wife's dowry Crandal bought a ship, the *Olson Nickelhouse*, and sailed north with his bride, arriving in the Thousand Islands just as winter was closing the St. Lawrence. The captain and his wife and crew spent a desperate four months caught in the ice. Crandal gave the men daily skating lessons. But they were slow learners and there were to be no raiding parties that winter. By the end of February, with supplies running low, the men ate the captain's parrot. And once having eaten talkative flesh, it was a small step to utter cannibalism. One snowy day Crandal came upon them dividing up the carcasses of three ice fishermen. He warned them, 'Don't do it, you fellows. Eating human flesh'll stunt your growth and curl your toes!' But it was too late. Those men were already slaves to that vile dish whose name no menu dares speak."

As Mr. Kay elaborated on the hardships of that first year he took his guest's glass, busied himself with the rum and hot water, and made them both fresh drinks. For his part, Sorley was distracted by bits of movement on the edges of his vision. But when he turned to look, there was never anything there. He decided it was only the jitters brought on by fatigue from his long drive in bad weather. That and the play of light from the fire.

"Now Crandal knew terror was half the pirate game," continued Mr. Kay. "So the loss of the parrot hit him hard. You see, Mr. Sorley, this Canadian lad had never mastered the strong language expected from pirate captains and counted on the parrot to hold up that end of things. The blue jay he later trained to stride his shoulder hadn't quite the same effect and was incredibly messy. Still, pirates know to go with the best they have. So he had these flyers printed up announcing that Captain Crandal, his wife (for Mrs. Crandal was no slouch with the cutlass on boarding parties), and his cannibal crew, pirates late of the Caribbean, were now operating locally, vowing Death and Destruction to all offering resistance. At the bottom he included a drawing of his flag, a skeleton with a cutlass in one bony hand and in the other a frying pan to underscore the cannibal reference.

"Well, the flyer and flag made Crandal the hit of the season when things started up again on the Lakes that spring. In fact, the frying pan and Crandal's pale, beanpole appearance and his outfit of pirate black earned him the nickname Death-Warmed-Over. And as Death-Warmed-Over the Pirate he so terrorized the shipping lanes that soon the cold booty was just rolling in, cargoes of mittens and headcheese, sensible swag of potatoes and shoes, and vast plunder in the hardware line, anvils, door hinges, and barrels of three-penny nails which Crandal sold for gold in the colorful and clamorous thieves' bazaars of Rochester and Detroit."

"How about Niagara Falls?" asked Sorley, to show he knew how to play along with a tall tale. He was amused to detect a slur in his voice from the rum.

"What indeed?" smiled Mr. Kay, happy with the question. He rose and lifted the painting down from its nail above the mantel and rested it across Sorley's knees. "See those iron rings along the water line? We fitted long poles through them, hoisted the *Olson Nickelhouse* out of the water, and made heavy portage of her around the falls."

As Mr. Kay replaced the painting Sorley noticed that the group of three pirates on the mantel had rearranged themselves. Or was the strong drink and the heat from the fire affecting his concentration?

"Well," said Mr. Kay, "as cream rises, soon Crandal was Pirate King with a pirate fleet at his back. And there was no manjack on land or sea that didn't tremble at the mention of Death-Warmed-Over. Or any city either. Except for one.

"One city on the Canadian side sat smugly behind the islands in its bay and resisted Crandal's assaults. Its long Indian name with a broadside of o's in it translated out as 'Gathering Place for Virtuous Moccasins.' But Crandal called it 'Goody Two-Shoes City' because of its reek of self-righteousness. Oh, he hated the world as a pirate must and wished to do creation all the harm he could. But Goody Two-Shoes City he hated with a special passion. Early on he even tried a Sunday attack to catch the city by surprise. But the inhabitants came boiling out of the churches and up onto the battlements to pepper him with cannonballs with such a will that, if their elected officials hadn't decided they were enjoying themselves too much on the Sabbath and ordered a cease-fire, they might have blown the *Olson Nickelhouse* out of the water."

Here Mr. Kay broke off his narrative to poke the fire and then to stare into the flames. As he did, Sorley once again had the distinct impression he was being watched. He turned and was startled to find another grouping of little pirate statues he hadn't noticed before on a shelf right at the level of his eye in the bookcase beside the fireplace. They held drawn dirks and cutlasses in their earnest little hands and had pistols stuck in their belts. And, oh, what ugly little specimens they were!

"Then, early one December," Mr. Kay continued, "Crandal captured a cargo of novelty items from the toy mines of Bavaria. Of course, in those days toys were quite unknown. Parents gave their children sensible gifts like socks or celluloid collars or pencil boxes at Christmas. Suddenly Crandal broke into a happy hornpipe on the frosty deck, for it had come to him how he could harm Goody Two-Shoes City and make it curse his name forever. But he would need a disguise to get by the guards at the city gate who had strict orders to keep a sharp eye out for Death-Warmed-Over. So he changed his black outfit for a red one with a pillow for fatness, rouge for his gray cheeks, a white beard to make him look older, and a jolly laugh to cover his pirate gloom. Then, on Christmas Eve, he put the *Olson Nickelhouse* in close to shore and sneaked into Goody Two-Shoes City with a wagonload of toys crated up like hymnals. That night he crept across the rooftops and down chimneys and by morning every boy and girl had a real toy under the Christmas tree.

"Well, of course, the parents knew right away who'd done the deed and what Crandal was up to. Next Christmas, they knew, they'd have to go and buy a toy in case Crandal didn't show up again or risk a disappointed child. But suppose he came next year, too? Well, that would mean that the following year the parents would have to buy two toys. Then three. And on and on until children no longer knew the meaning of the word 'enough.'

" 'Curse Crandal and the visit from the *Olson Nickelhouse,*' the parents muttered through clenched teeth. But their eavesdropping children misheard and thought they said 'Kris Kringle' and something about a visit from 'Old Saint Nicholas.' As if a saint would give a boy a toy drum or saxophone to drive his father mad with, as if a saint would give a girl a Little Dolly Clotheshorse doll and set her dreaming over fashion magazines when she should be helping her mother in the kitchen." Mr. Kay laughed until the tears came to his eyes. "Well, the Pirate King knew he'd hit upon a better game than making fat landlubbers walk an icy gangplank over cold gray water. And since the Crandals had salted away a fortune in gold coins they settled down here and started a reindeer farm so Crandal could Kringle full-time with the missus as Mrs. Kringle and the crew as his little helpers." Mr. Kay looked up. "Isn't that right, Mother?"

Mrs. Kay had appeared in the doorway with a red costume and a white beard over her arm and a pair of boots in her hand. "That's right, Father. But it's time to get ready. I've loaded the sleigh and harnessed the reindeer."

Mr. Kay got to his feet. "And here's the wonderfully strange and miraculous thing, Mr. Sorley. As the years passed we didn't age. Not one bit. What did you call it, Mother?"

"The Tinker Bell Effect," said Mrs. Kay, putting down the boots and holding up the heavily padded red jumpsuit trimmed with white for Mr. Kay to step into.

"If children believe in you," explained Mr. Kay, as he did up the Velcro fasteners, "why then you're eternal and evergreen. Plus you can fly through the air and so can your damn livestock!"

Mrs. Kay laughed a fine contralto laugh. "And somewhere along the line children must have started believing in Santa's little helpers, too," she said. "Because our pirate crew didn't age either. They just got shorter."

Mr. Kay nodded. "Which fitted in real well with their end of the operation."

"The toy workshop?" asked Sorley.

Mr. Kay smiled and shook his head. "No, that's only a myth. We buy our toys, you see. Not that Mother and I were going to spend our own hard-earned money for the damn stuff. No, the crew's little fingers make the counterfeit plates to print what cash we need to buy the toys. Electronic ones, mostly. Wonderful for stunting the brain, cramping the soul, and making ugly noises that just won't quit."

"Hold it." Sorley wagged a disbelieving finger. "You're telling me you started out as Death-Warmed-Over the Pirate and now you're Santa Claus?"

"Mr. Sorley, I'm as surprised as you how things worked out. Talk about revisionism, eh? Yesterday's yo-ho-ho is today's ho-ho-ho." Mr. Kay stood back and let his wife attach his white beard with its built-in red plastic cheeks.

"But where does the Christmas Triangle business fit in?" demanded Sorley. "We've got twenty-seven people who disappeared around here last year alone."

"Copycats," insisted Mr. Kay. "As I said, Mother and I only take one a year, what we call our Gift from the Night. But of course, when the media got onto it the copycats weren't far behind. Little Mary Housewife can't think of a present for Tommy Tiresome who has everything, so she gives him a slug from a thirty-eight between the eyes and buries him in the basement, telling the neighbors he went to visit his mother in Sarnia. Little Billy Bank Manager with a shortage in the books and a yen for high living in warmer climes vanishes into the Christmas Triangle with a suitcase of money from the vault and reemerges under another name in Rio. And so on and so on. Copycats."

"Father's right. We only take one," said Mrs. Kay. "That's what our agreement calls for."

Mr. Kay nodded. "Last year it was an arrogant young bastard from the SPCA investigating reports on mistreated reindeer. Tell me my business, would he?" Mr. Kay's chest swelled and his eyes flashed. "Well, Mother and I harnessed him to the sleigh right between Dancer and Prancer. And his sluggard backside got more than its share of the lash that Christmas Eve, let me tell you. He was blubbering like a baby by the time I turned him over to my scurvy crew."

"I don't understand," said Sorley. But he was beginning to. He stood up slowly, utterly clearheaded and sober. "You mean your cannibal crew ate him?" he demanded in a horrified voice.

"Consider the fool from the SPCA part of our employee benefits package," shrugged Mr. Kay. "Oh, all right," he conceded when he saw Sorley's outrage, "so my little shipmates are evil. Evil. They've got wolfish little teeth and pointed carnivore ears. And don't think those missing legs and arms were honestly come by in pirate combat. Not a bit of it. There's this game they play. Like strip poker but without the clothes. They're terrible, there's no denying it. But you know, few of us get to pick the people we work with. Besides, I don't give a damn about naughty or nice."

Sorley's voice was shrill and outraged. "But this is hideous. Hideous. I'll go to the police."

"Go, then," said Mr. Kay. "Be our guest. Mother and I won't stand in your way."

"You'd better not try!" warned Sorley defiantly, intending to storm from the room. But when he tried he found his shoelaces were tied together. He fell forward like a dead weight and struck his head, blacking out for a moment. When he regained consciousness he was lying on his stomach with his thumbs lashed together behind his back. Before Sorley's head cleared he felt something being shoved up the back of his pant legs, over his buttocks, and up under his belt. When they emerged out beyond the back of his shirt collar he saw they were the bamboo poles that had been leaning in the corner.

Before Sorley could try to struggle free, a little pirate appeared close to his face, a grizzled thing with a hook for an arm, little curly-toed shoes and a bandanna pulled down over the pointed tops of its ears. With a cruel smile it placed the point of its cutlass a menacing fraction of an inch from Sorley's left eyeball and in language no less vile because of the tiny voice that uttered it, the creature warned him not to move.

Mrs. Kay was smiling down at him. "Now don't trouble yourself over your car, Mr. Sorley. I'll drive into the city later tonight and park it where the car strippers can't miss it. Father'll pick me up in the sleigh on his way back."

Mr. Kay had been stamping his boots to get them on properly. Now he said, "Give us a kiss, Mother. I'm on my way." Then the toes of the boots hove into view on the edge of Sorley's vision. "Good-bye, Mr. Sorley," said his host. "Thanks for coming. Consider yourself grist for the mills of Christmas."

As soon as Mr. Kay left the room, Sorley heard little feet scramble around him and more little pirates rushed to man the ends of the bamboo poles in front of him. At a tiny command the crew put the cutlasses in their teeth and, holding their arms over their heads, hoisted Sorley up off the floor. He hung there helplessly, suspended front and back.

The little pirates lugged Sorley out into the hall and headed down the carpet toward the front door. He didn't know where they were taking him. But their progress was funereally slow, and, swaying there, Sorley conceived a frantic plan of escape. He knew his captors were tiring under their load. If they had to set him down to rest, he would dig in with his toes and, somehow, work his way to his knees. At least there he'd stand a chance.

Sorley heard sleigh bells. He raised his chin. Through the pane of beveled glass in the front door he saw the sleigh on the lawn rise steeply into the night, Christmas tree lights and all, and he heard Mr. Kay's booming "Yo-ho-ho-ho."

Suddenly Sorley's caravan stopped. He got ready, waiting for them to put him down. But they were only adjusting their grips. The little pirates turned him sideways and Sorley saw the open door and the top of the cellar steps and smelled the darkness as musty as a tomb. Then he felt the beginning of their big heave-ho. It was too damn late to escape now. Grist for the mills of Christmas? Hell, he was meat for the stew pots of elfdom.

Lawrence Block

AS DARK AS CHRISTMAS GETS

It was 9:45 in the morning when I got to the little bookshop on West Fifty-sixth Street. Before I went to work for Leo Haig I probably wouldn't have bothered to look at my watch, if I was even wearing one in the first place, and the best I'd have been able to say was it was around ten o'clock. But Haig wanted me to be his legs and eyes, and sometimes his ear, nose, and throat, and if he was going to play in Nero Wolfe's league, that meant I had to turn into Archie Goodwin, for Pete's sake, noticing everything and getting the details right and reporting conversations verbatim.

Well, forget that last part. My memory's getting better—Haig's right about that part—but what follows won't be word for word, because all I am is a human being. If you want a tape recorder, buy one.

There was a lot of fake snow in the window, and a Santa Claus doll in handcuffs, and some toy guns and knives, and a lot of mysteries with a Christmas theme, including the one by Fredric Brown where the murderer dresses up as a department store Santa. (Someone pulled that a year ago, put on a red suit and a white beard and shot a man at the corner of Broadway and Thirty-seventh, and I told Haig how ingenious I thought it was. He gave me a look, left the room, and came back with a book. I read it—that's what I do when Haig hands me a book—and found out Brown had had the idea fifty years earlier. Which doesn't mean that's where the killer got the idea. The book's long out of print—the one I read was a paperback, and falling apart, not like the handsome hardcover copy in the window. And how many killers get their ideas out of old books?)

Now if you're a detective yourself you'll have figured out two things by now—the bookshop specialized in mysteries, and it was the Christmas season. And if you'd noticed the sign in the window you'd have made one more deduction: i.e., that they were closed.

I went down the half flight of steps and poked the buzzer. When nothing happened I poked it again, and eventually the door was opened by a little man with white hair and a white beard—all he needed was padding and a red suit, and someone to teach him to be jolly. "I'm terribly sorry," he said, "but I'm afraid we're closed. It's Christmas morning, and it's not even ten o'clock."

"You called us," I said, "and it wasn't even nine o'clock."

He took a good look at me, and light dawned. "You're Harrison," he said. "And I know your first name, but I can't—"

"Chip," I supplied.

"Of course. But where's Haig? I know he thinks he's Nero Wolfe, but he's not gone housebound, has he? He's been here often enough in the past."

"Haig gets out and about," I agreed, "but Wolfe went all the way to Montana once, as far as that goes. What Wolfe refused to do was leave the house on business, and Haig's with him on that one. Besides, he just spawned some unspawnable cichlids from Lake Chad, and you'd think the aquarium was a television set and they were showing *Midnight Blue.*"

"Fish." He sounded more reflective than contemptuous. "Well, at least you're here. That's something." He locked the door and led me up a spiral staircase to a room full of books, full as well with the residue of a party. There were empty glasses here and there, hors d'oeuvres trays that held nothing but crumbs, and a cut-glass dish with a sole remaining cashew.

"Christmas," he said, and shuddered. "I had a houseful of people here last night. All of them eating, all of them drinking, and many of them actually singing." He made a face. "I didn't sing," he said, "but I certainly ate and drank. And eventually they all went home and I went upstairs to bed. I must have, because that's where I was when I woke up two hours ago."

"But you don't remember."

"Well, no," he said, "but then, what would there be to remember? The guests leave and you're alone with vague feelings of sadness." His gaze turned inward. "If she'd stayed," he said, "I'd have remembered."

"She?"

"Never mind. I awoke this morning, alone in my own bed. I swallowed some aspirin and came downstairs. I went into the library."

"You mean this room?"

"This is the salesroom. These books are for sale."

"Well, I figured. I mean, this is a bookshop."

"You've never seen the library?" He didn't wait for an answer but turned to open a door and lead me down a hallway to another room twice the size of the first. It was lined with floor-to-ceiling hardwood shelves, and the shelves were filled with double rows of hardcover books. It was hard to identify the books, though, because all but one section was wrapped in plastic sheeting.

"This is my collection," he announced. "These books are not for sale. I'll only part with one if I've replaced it with a finer copy. Your employer doesn't collect, does he?"

"Haig? He's got thousands of books."

"Yes, and he's bought some of them from me. But he doesn't give a damn about first editions. He doesn't care what kind of shape a book is in, or even if it's got a dust jacket. He'd as soon have a Grosset reprint or a book-club edition or even a paperback."

"He just wants to read them."

"It takes all kinds, doesn't it?" He shook his head in wonder. "Last night's party filled this room as well as the salesroom. I put up plastic to keep the books from getting handled and possibly damaged. Or—how shall I put this?"

Any way you want, I thought. You're the client.

"Some of these books are extremely valuable," he said. "And my guests were all extremely reputable people, but many of them are good customers, and that means they're collectors. Ardent, even rabid collectors."

"And you didn't want them stealing the books."

"You're very direct," he said. "I suppose that's a useful quality in your line of work. But no, I didn't want to tempt anyone, especially when alcoholic indulgence might make temptation particularly difficult to resist."

"So you hung up plastic sheets."

"And came downstairs this morning to remove the plastic, and pick up some dirty glasses and clear some of the debris. I puttered around. I took down the plastic from this one section, as you can see. I did a bit of tidying. And then I saw it."

"Saw what?"

He pointed to a set of glassed-in shelves, on top of which stood a three-foot row of leather-bound volumes. "There," he said. "What do you see?"

"Leather-bound books, but—"

"Boxes," he corrected. "Wrapped in leather and stamped in gold, and each one holding a manuscript. They're fashioned to look like finely bound books, but they're original manuscripts."

"Very nice," I said. "I suppose they must be very rare."

"They're unique."

"That too."

He made a face. "One of a kind. The author's original manuscript, with corrections in his own hand. Most are typed, but the Elmore Leonard is handwritten. The Westlake, of course, is typed on that famous Smith-Corona manual portable of his. The Paul Kavanagh is the author's first novel. He only wrote three, you know."

I didn't, but Haig would.

"They're very nice," I said politely. "And I don't suppose they're for sale."

"Of course not. They're in the library. They're part of the collection."

"Right," I said, and paused for him to continue. When he didn't I said, "Uh,

I was thinking. Maybe you could tell me . . ."

"Why I summoned you here." He sighed. "Look at the boxed manuscript between the Westlake and the Kavanagh."

"Between them?"

"Yes."

"The Kavanagh is *Such Men Are Dangerous*," I said, "and the Westlake is *Drowned Hopes*. But there's nothing at all between them but a three-inch gap."

"Exactly," he said.

"As Dark as It Gets," I said. "By Cornell Woolrich."

Haig frowned. "I don't know the book," he said. "Not under that title, not with Woolrich's name on it, nor William Irish or George Hopley. Those were his pen names."

"I know," I said. "You don't know the book because it was never published. The manuscript was found among Woolrich's effects after his death."

"There was a posthumous book, Chip."

"Into the Night," I said. "Another writer completed it, writing replacement scenes for some that had gone missing in the original. It wound up being publishable."

"It wound up being published," Haig said. "That's not necessarily the same thing. But this manuscript, *As Dark*—"

"—*As It Gets*. It wasn't publishable, according to our client. Woolrich evidently worked on it over the years, and what survived him incorporated unresolved portions of several drafts. There are characters who die early on and then reappear with no explanation. There's supposed to be some great writing and plenty of Woolrich's trademark paranoid suspense, but it doesn't add up to a book, or even something that could be edited into a book. But to a collector—"

"Collectors," Haig said heavily.

"Yes, sir. I asked what the manuscript was worth. He said, 'Well, I paid five thousand dollars for it.' That's verbatim, but don't ask me if the thing's worth more or less than that, because I don't know if he was bragging that he was a big spender or a slick trader."

"It doesn't matter," Haig said. "The money's the least of it. He added it to his collection and he wants it back."

"And the person who stole it," I said, "is either a friend or a customer or both."

"And so he called us and not the police. The manuscript was there when the party started?"

"Yes."

"And gone this morning?"

"Yes."

"And there were how many in attendance?"

"Forty or fifty," I said, "including the caterer and her staff."

"If the party was catered," he mused, "why was the room a mess when you saw it? Wouldn't the catering staff have cleaned up at the party's end?"

"I asked him that question myself. The party lasted longer than the caterer had signed on for. She hung around herself for a while after her employees packed it in, but she stopped working and became a guest. Our client was hoping she would stay."

"But you just said she did."

"After everybody else went home. He lives upstairs from the bookshop, and he was hoping for a chance to show her his living quarters."

Haig shrugged. He's not quite the misogynist his idol is, but he hasn't been at it as long. Give him time. He said, "Chip, it's hopeless. Fifty suspects?"

"Six."

"How so?"

"By two o'clock," I said, "just about everybody had called it a night. The ones remaining got a reward."

"And what was that?"

"Some fifty-year-old Armagnac, served in Waterford pony glasses. We counted the glasses, and there were seven of them. Six guests and the host."

"And the manuscript?"

"Was still there at the time, and still sheathed in plastic. See, he'd covered all the boxed manuscripts, same as the books on the shelves. But the cut-glass ship's decanter was serving as a sort of bookend to the manuscript section, and he took off the plastic to get at it. And while he was at it he took out one of the manuscripts and showed it off to his guests."

"Not the Woolrich, I don't suppose."

"No, it was a Peter Straub novel, elegantly handwritten in a leatherbound journal. Straub collects Chandler, and our client had traded a couple of Chandler firsts for the manuscript, and he was proud of himself."

"I shouldn't wonder."

"But the Woolrich was present and accounted for when he took off the plastic wrap, and it may have been there when he put the Straub back. He didn't notice."

"And this morning it was gone."

"Yes."

"Six suspects," he said. "Name them."

I took out my notebook. "Jon and Jayne Corn-Wallace," I said. "He's a retired stockbroker, she's an actress in a daytime drama. That's a soap opera."

"Piffle."

"Yes, sir. They've been friends of our client for years, and customers for about as long. They're mystery fans, and he got them started on first editions."

"Including Woolrich?"

"He's a favorite of Jayne's. I gather Jon can take him or leave him."

"I wonder which he did last night. Do the Corn-Wallaces collect manuscripts?"

"Just books. First editions, though they're starting to get interested in fancy bindings and limited editions. The one with a special interest in manuscripts is Zoltan Mihalyi."

"The violinist?"

Trust Haig to know that. I'd never heard of him myself. "A big mystery fan," I said. "I guess reading passes the time on those long concert tours."

"I don't suppose a man can spend all his free hours with other men's wives," Haig said. "And who's to say that all the stories are true? He collects manuscripts, does he?"

"He was begging for a chance to buy the Straub, but our friend wouldn't sell."

"Which would make him a likely suspect. Who else?"

"Philip Perigord."

"The writer?"

"Right, and I didn't even know he was still alive. He hasn't written anything in years."

"Almost twenty years. *More Than Murder* was published in nineteen eighty."

Trust him to know that, too. "Anyway," I said, "he didn't die. He didn't even stop writing. He just quit writing books. He went to Hollywood and became a screenwriter."

"That's the same as stopping writing," Haig reflected. "It's very nearly the same as being dead. Does he collect books?"

"No."

"Manuscripts?"

"No."

"Perhaps he wanted the manuscripts for scrap paper," Haig said. "He could turn the pages over and write on their backs. Who else was present?"

"Edward Everett Stokes."

"The small-press publisher. Bought out his partner, Geoffrey Poges, to became sole owner of Stokes-Poges Press."

"They do limited editions, according to our client. Leather bindings, small runs, special tip-in sheets."

"All well and good," he said, "but what's useful about Stokes-Poges is that they issue a reasonably priced trade edition of each title as well, and publish works otherwise unavailable, including collections of short fiction from otherwise uncollected writers."

"Do they publish Woolrich?"

"All his work has been published by mainstream publishers, and all his stories collected. Is Stokes a collector himself?"

"Our client didn't say."

"No matter. How many is that? The Corn-Wallaces, Zoltan Mihalyi, Philip Perigord, E. E. Stokes. And the sixth is—"

"Harriet Quinlan."

He looked puzzled, then nodded in recognition. "The literary agent."

"She represents Perigord," I said, "or at least she would, if he ever went back to novel-writing. She's placed books with Stokes-Poges. And she may have left the party with Zoltan Mihalyi."

"I don't suppose her client list includes the Woolrich estate. Or that she's a rabid collector of books and manuscripts."

"He didn't say."

"No matter. You said six suspects, Chip. I count seven."

I ticked them off. "Jon Corn-Wallace. Jayne Corn-Wallace. Zoltan Mihalyi. Philip Perigord. Edward Everett Stokes. Harriet Quinlan. Isn't that six? Or do you want to include our client, the little man with the palindromic first name? That seems farfetched to me, but—"

"The caterer, Chip."

"Oh. Well, he says she was just there to do a job. No interest in books, no interest in manuscripts, no real interest in the world of mysteries. Certainly no interest in Cornell Woolrich."

"And she stayed when her staff went home."

"To have a drink and be sociable. He had hopes she'd spend the night, but it didn't happen. I suppose technically she's a suspect, but—"

"At the very least she's a witness," he said. "Bring her."

"Bring her?"

He nodded. "Bring them all."

It's a shame this is a short story. If it were a novel, now would be the time for me to give you a full description of the off-street carriage house on West Twentieth Street, which Leo Haig owns and where he occupies the top two floors, having rented out the lower two stories to Madam Juana and her All-Girl Enterprise. You'd hear how Haig had lived for years in two rooms in the Bronx, breeding tropical fish and reading detective stories, until a modest inheritance allowed him to set up shop as a poor man's Nero Wolfe.

He's quirky, God knows, and I could fill a few pleasant pages recounting his quirks, including his having hired me as much for my writing ability as for my potential value as a detective. I'm expected to write up his cases the same way

AS DARK AS CHRISTMAS GETS

Archie Goodwin writes up Wolfe's, and this case was a slam-dunk, really, and he says it wouldn't stretch into a novel, but that it should work nicely as a short story.

So all I'll say is this: Haig's best quirk is his unshakable belief that Nero Wolfe exists. Under another name, of course, to protect his inviolable privacy. And the legendary brownstone, with all its different fictitious street numbers, isn't on West Thirty-fifth Street at all but in another part of town entirely.

And someday, if Leo Haig performs with sufficient brilliance as a private investigator, he hopes to get the ultimate reward—an invitation to dinner at Nero Wolfe's table.

Well, that gives you an idea. If you want more in the way of background, I can only refer you to my previous writings on the subject. There have been two novels so far, *Make Out With Murder* and *The Topless Tulip Caper*, and they're full of inside stuff about Leo Haig. (There were two earlier books from before I met Haig, *No Score* and *Chip Harrison Scores Again*, but they're not mysteries and Haig's not in them. All they do, really, is tell you more than you'd probably care to know about me.)

Well, end of commercial. Haig said I should put it in, and I generally do what he tells me. After all, the man pays my salary.

And, in his own quiet way, he's a genius. As you'll see.

"They'll never come here," I told him. "Not today. I know it will always live in your memory as The Day the Cichlids Spawned, but to everybody else it's Christmas, and they'll want to spend it in the bosoms of their families, and—"

"Not everyone has a family," he pointed out, "and not every family has a bosom."

"The Corn-Wallaces have a family. Zoltan Mihalyi doesn't, but he's probably got somebody with a bosom lined up to spend the day with. I don't know about the others, but—"

"Bring them," he said, "but not here. I want them all assembled at five o'clock this afternoon at the scene of the crime."

"The bookshop? You're willing to leave the house?"

"It's not entirely business," he said. "Our client is more than a client. He's a friend, and an important source of books. The reading copies he so disdains have enriched our own library immeasurably. And you know how important that is."

If there's anything you need to know, you can find it in the pages of a detective novel. That's Haig's personal conviction, and I'm beginning to believe he's right.

"I'll pay him a visit," he went on. "I'll arrive at four-thirty or so, and perhaps I'll come across a book or two that I'll want for our library. You'll arrange that they all arrive around five, and we'll clear up this little business." He frowned in thought. "I'll tell Wong we'll want Christmas dinner at eight tonight. That should give us more than enough time."

Again, if this were a novel, I'd spend a full chapter telling you what I went through getting them all present and accounted for. It was hard enough finding them, and then I had to sell them on coming. I pitched the event as a second stage of last night's party—their host had arranged, for their entertainment and edification, that they should be present while a real-life private detective solved an actual crime before their very eyes.

According to Haig, all we'd need to spin this yarn into a full-length book would be a dead body, although two would be better. If, say, our client had wandered into his library that morning to find a corpse seated in his favorite chair, *and* the Woolrich manuscript gone, then I could easily stretch all this to sixty thousand words. If the dead man had been wearing a deerstalker cap and holding a violin, we'd be especially well off; when the book came out, all the Sherlockian completists would be compelled to buy it.

Sorry. No murders, no Baker Street Irregulars, no dogs barking or not barking. I had to get them all there, and I did, but don't ask me how. I can't take the time to tell you.

"Now," Zoltan Mihalyi said. "We are all here. So can someone please tell me why we are all here?" There was a twinkle in his dark eyes as he spoke, and the trace of a knowing smile on his lips. He wanted an answer, but he was going to remain charming while he got it. I could believe he swept a lot of women off their feet.

"First of all," Jeanne Botleigh said, "I think we should each have a glass of eggnog. It's festive, and it will help put us all in the spirit of the day."

She was the caterer, and she was some cupcake, all right. Close-cut brown hair framed her small oval face and set off a pair of China-blue eyes. She had an English accent, roughed up some by ten years in New York, and she was short and slender and curvy, and I could see why our client had hoped she would stick around.

And now she'd whipped up a batch of eggnog, and ladled out cups for each of us. I waited until someone else tasted it—after all the mystery novels Haig's forced on me, I've developed an imagination—but once the Corn-Wallaces had tossed off theirs with no apparent effect, I took a sip. It was smooth and delicious, and it had a kick like a mule. I looked over at Haig, who's not much of a drinker, and he was smacking his lips over it.

"Why are we here?" he said, echoing the violinist's question. "Well, sir, I shall tell you. We are here as friends and customers of our host, whom we may be able to assist in the solution of a puzzle. Last night all of us, with the exception of course of myself and my young assistant, were present in this room. Also present was the original manuscript of an unpublished novel by Cornell Woolrich. This morning we were all gone, and so was the manuscript. Now we have returned. The manuscript, alas, has not."

"Wait a minute," Jon Corn-Wallace said. "You're saying one of us took it?"

"I say only that it has gone, sir. It is possible that someone within this room was involved in its disappearance, but there are diverse other possibilities as well. What impels me, what has prompted me to summon you here, is the likelihood that one or more of you knows something that will shed light on the incident."

"But the only person who would know anything would be the person who took it," Harriet Quinlan said. She was what they call a woman of a certain age, which generally means a woman of an uncertain age. Her figure was a few pounds beyond girlish, and I had a hunch she dyed her hair and might have had her face lifted somewhere along the way, but whatever she'd done had paid off. She was probably old enough to be my mother's older sister, but that didn't keep me from having the sort of ideas a nephew's not supposed to have.

Haig told her anyone could have observed something, and not just the guilty party, and Philip Perigord started to ask a question, and Haig held up a hand and cut him off in mid-sentence. Most people probably would have finished what they were saying, but I guess Perigord was used to studio executives shutting him up at pitch meetings. He bit off his word in the middle of a syllable and stayed mute.

"It is a holiday," Haig said, "and we all have other things to do, so we'd best avoid distraction. Hence, I will ask the questions and you will answer them. Mr. Corn-Wallace. You are a book collector. Have you given a thought to collecting manuscripts?"

"I've thought about it," Jon Corn-Wallace said. He was the best-dressed man in the room, looking remarkably comfortable in a dark blue suit and a striped tie. He wore bull-and-bear cufflinks and one of those watches that's worth five thousand dollars if it's real or twenty-five if you bought it from a Nigerian street vendor. "He tried to get me interested," he said, with a nod toward our client. "But I was always the kind of trader who stuck to listed stocks."

"Meaning?"

"Meaning it's impossible to pinpoint the market value of a one-of-a-kind item like a manuscript. There's too much guesswork involved. I'm not buying books with an eye to selling them, that's something my heirs will have to worry about, but I do like to know what my collection is worth and whether or not it's been a good investment. It's part of the pleasure of collecting, as far as I'm concerned. So I've stayed away from manuscripts. They're too iffy."

"And had you had a look at *As Dark as It Gets?*"

"No. I'm not interested in manuscripts, and I don't care at all for Woolrich."

"Jon likes hardboiled fiction," his wife put in, "but Woolrich is a little weird for his taste. I think he was a genius myself. Quirky and tormented, maybe, but what genius isn't?"

Haig, I thought. You couldn't call him tormented, but maybe he made up for it by exceeding the usual quota of quirkiness.

"Anyway," Jayne Corn-Wallace said, "I'm the Woolrich fan in the family. Though I agree with Jon as far as manuscripts are concerned. The value is pure speculation. And who wants to buy something and then have to get a box made for it? It's like buying an unframed canvas and having to get it framed."

"The Woolrich manuscript was already boxed," Haig pointed out.

"I mean generally, as an area for collecting. As a collector, I wasn't interested in *As Dark as It Gets*. If someone fixed it up and completed it, and if someone published it, I'd have been glad to buy it. I'd have bought two copies."

"Two copies, madam?"

She nodded. "One to read and one to own."

Haig's face darkened, and I thought he might offer his opinion of people who were afraid to damage their books by reading them. But he kept it to himself, and I was just as glad. Jayne Corn-Wallace was a tall, handsome woman, radiating self-confidence, and I sensed she'd give as good as she got in an exchange with Haig.

"You might have wanted to read the manuscript," Haig suggested.

She shook her head. "I like Woolrich," she said, "but as a stylist he was choppy enough *after* editing and polishing. I wouldn't want to try him in manuscript, let alone an unfinished manuscript like that one."

"Mr. Mihalyi," Haig said. "You collect manuscripts, don't you?"

"I do."

"And do you care for Woolrich?"

The violinist smiled. "If I had the chance to buy the original manuscript of *The Bride Wore Black*," he said, "I would leap at it. If it were close at hand, and if strong drink had undermined my moral fiber, I might even slip it under my coat and walk off with it." A wink showed us he was kidding. "Or at least I'd have been tempted. The work in question, however, tempted me not a whit."

"And why is that, sir?"

Mihalyi frowned. "There are people," he said, "who attend open rehearsals and make surreptitious recordings of the music. They treasure them and even bootleg them to other like-minded fans. I despise such people."

"Why?"

"They violate the artist's privacy," he said. "A rehearsal is a time when one refines one's approach to a piece of music. One takes chances, one uses the occasion as the equivalent of an artist's sketch pad. The person who records it is in essence spraying a rough sketch with fixative and hanging it on the wall of his personal museum. I find it unsettling enough that listeners record concert performances, making permanent what was supposed to be a transitory experience. But to record a rehearsal is an atrocity."

"And a manuscript?"

"A manuscript is the writer's completed work. It provides a record of how he arranged and revised his ideas, and how they were in turn adjusted for better or worse by an editor. But it is finished work. An unfinished manuscript . . ."

"Is a rehearsal?"

"That or something worse. I ask myself, what would Woolrich have wanted?"

"Another drink," Edward Everett Stokes said, and leaned forward to help himself to more eggnog. "I take your point, Mihalyi. And Woolrich might well have preferred to have his unfinished work destroyed upon his death, but he left no instructions to that effect, so how can we presume to guess his wishes? Perhaps, for all we know, there is a single scene in the book that meant as much to him as anything he'd written. Or less than a scene—a bit of dialogue, a paragraph of description, perhaps no more than a single sentence. Who are we to say it should not survive?"

"Perigord," Mihalyi said. "You are a writer. Would you care to have your unfinished work published after your death? Would you not recoil at that, or at having it completed by others?"

Philip Perigord cocked an eyebrow. "I'm the wrong person to ask," he said. "I've spent twenty years in Hollywood. Forget unfinished work. My *finished* work doesn't get published, or 'produced,' as they so revealingly term it. I get paid, and the work winds up on a shelf. And, when it comes to having one's work completed by others, in Hollywood you don't have to wait until you're dead. It happens during your lifetime, and you learn to live with it."

"We don't know the author's wishes," Harriet Quinlan put in, "and I wonder how relevant they are."

"But it's his work," Mihalyi pointed out.

"Is it, Zoltan? Or does it belong to the ages? Finished or not, the author has left it to us. Schubert did not finish one of his greatest symphonies. Would you have laid its two completed movements in the casket with him?"

"It has been argued that the work was complete, that he intended it to be but two movements long."

"That begs the question, Zoltan."

"It does, dear lady," he said with a wink. "I'd rather beg the question than be undone by it. Of course I'd keep the *Unfinished Symphony* in the repertoire. On the other hand, I'd hate to see some fool attempt to finish it."

"No one has, have they?"

"Not to my knowledge. But several writers have had the effrontery to finish *The Mystery of Edwin Drood*, and I do think Dickens would have been better served if the manuscript had gone in the box with his bones. And as for sequels, like those for *Pride and Prejudice* and *The Big Sleep*, or that young fellow who had the colossal gall to tread in Rex Stout's immortal footsteps . . . "

Now we were getting onto sensitive ground. As far as Leo Haig was concerned, Archie Goodwin had always written up Wolfe's cases, using the transparent pseudonym of Rex Stout. (Rex Stout = fat king, an allusion to Wolfe's own regal corpulence.) Robert Goldsborough, credited with the books written since the "death" of Stout, was, as Haig saw it, a ghostwriter employed by Goodwin, who was no longer up to the chore of hammering out the books. He'd relate them to Goldsborough, who transcribed them and polished them up. While they might not have all the narrative verve of Goodwin's own work, still they provided an important and accurate account of Wolfe's more recent cases.

See, Haig feels the great man's still alive and still raising orchids and nailing killers. Maybe somewhere on the Upper East Side. Maybe in Murray Hill, or just off Gramercy Park . . .

The discussion about Goldsborough, and about sequels in general, roused Haig from a torpor that Wolfe himself might have envied. "Enough," he said with authority. "There's no time for meandering literary conversations, nor would Chip have room for them in a short-story-length report. So let us get to it. One of you took the manuscript, box and all, from its place on the shelf. Mr. Mihalyi, you have the air of one who protests too much. You profess no interest in the manuscripts of unpublished novels, and I can accept that you did not yearn to possess *As Dark as It Gets*, but you wanted a look at it, didn't you?"

"I don't own a Woolrich manuscript," he said, "and of course I was interested in seeing what one looked like. How he typed, how he entered corrections . . . "

"So you took the manuscript from the shelf."

"Yes," the violinist agreed. "I went into the other room with it, opened the box, and flipped through the pages. You can taste the flavor of the man's work in the visual appearance of his manuscript pages. The words and phrases x'd out, the pencil notations, the crossovers, even the typographical errors. The computer age puts paid to all that, doesn't it? Imagine Chandler running Spel-Chek, or Hammett with justified margins." He sighed. "A few minutes with the script made me long to own one of Woolrich's. But not this one, for reasons I've already explained."

"You spent how long with the book?"

"Fifteen minutes at the most. Probably more like ten."

"And returned to this room?"

"Yes."

"And brought the manuscript with you?"

"Yes. I intended to return it to the shelf, but someone was standing in the way. It may have been you, Jon. It was someone tall, and you're the tallest person here." He turned to our client. "It wasn't you. But I think you may have been talking with Jon. Someone was, at any rate, and I'd have had to step between the two of you to put the box back, and that might have led to questions as to why I'd picked it up in the first place. So I put it down."

"Where?"

"On a table. That one, I think."

"It's not there now," Jon Corn-Wallace said.

"It's not," Haig agreed. "One of you took it from that table. I could, through an exhausting process of cross-questioning, establish who that person is. But it would save us all time if the person would simply recount what happened next."

There was a silence while they all looked at each other. "Well, I guess this is where I come in," Jayne Corn-Wallace said. "I was sitting in the red chair, where Phil Perigord is sitting now. And whoever I'd been talking to went to get another drink, and I looked around, and there it was on the table."

"The manuscript, madam?"

"Yes, but I didn't know that was what it was, not at first. I thought it was a finely bound limited edition. Because the manuscripts are all kept on that shelf, you know, and this one wasn't. And it hadn't been on the table a few minutes earlier, either. I knew that much. So I assumed it was a book someone had been leafing through, and I saw it was by Cornell Woolrich, and I didn't recognize the title, so I thought I'd try leafing through it myself."

"And you found it was a manuscript."

"Well, that didn't take too keen an eye, did it? I suppose I glanced at the first twenty pages, just riffled through them while the party went on around me. I stopped after a chapter or so. That was plenty."

"You didn't like what you read?"

"There were corrections," she said disdainfully. "Words and whole sentences crossed out, new words penciled in. I realize writers have to work that way, but when I read a book I like to believe it emerged from the writer's mind fully formed."

"Like Athena from the brow of What's-his-name," her husband said.

"Zeus. I don't want to know there was a writer at work, making decisions, putting words down and then changing them. I want to forget about the writer entirely and lose myself in the story."

"Everybody wants to forget about the writer," Philip Perigord said, helping himself to more eggnog. "At the Oscars each year some ninny intones, 'In the beginning was the Word,' before he hands out the screenwriting awards. And you hear the usual crap about how they owe it all to chaps like me who put words in their mouths. They say it, but nobody believes it. Jack Warner called us schmucks with Underwoods. Well, we've come a long way. Now we're schmucks with Power Macs."

"Indeed," Haig said. "You looked at the manuscript, didn't you, Mr. Perigord?"

"I never read unpublished work. Can't risk leaving myself open to a plagiarism charge."

"Oh? But didn't you have a special interest in Woolrich? Didn't you once adapt a story of his?"

"How did you know about that? I was one of several who made a living off that particular piece of crap. It was never produced."

"And you looked at this manuscript in the hope that you might adapt it?"

The writer shook his head. "I'm through wasting myself out there."

"They're through with you," Harriet Quinlan said. "Nothing personal, Phil, but it's a town that uses up writers and throws them away. You couldn't get arrested out there. So you've come back East to write books."

"And you'll be representing him, madam?"

"I may, if he brings me something I can sell. I saw him paging through a manuscript and figured he was looking for something he could steal. Oh, don't look so outraged, Phil. Why not steal from Woolrich, for God's sake? He's not going to sue. He left everything to Columbia University, and you could knock off anything of his, published or unpublished, and they'd never know the difference. Ever since I saw you reading, I've been wondering. Did you come across anything worth stealing?"

"I don't steal," Perigord said. "Still, perfectly legitimate inspiration can result from a glance at another man's work—"

"I'll say it can. And did it?"

He shook his head. "If there was a strong idea anywhere in that manuscript, I couldn't find it in the few minutes I spent looking. What about you, Harriet? I know you had a look at it, because I saw you."

"I just wanted to see what it was you'd been so caught up in. And I wondered if the manuscript might be salvageable. One of my writers might be able to pull it off, and do a better job than the hack who finished *Into the Night*."

"Ah," Haig said. "And what did you determine, madam?"

"I didn't read enough to form a judgment. Anyway, *Into the Night* was no great commercial success, so why tag along in its wake?"

"So you put the manuscript . . . "

"Back in its box, and left it on the table where I'd found it."

Our client shook his head in wonder. *"Murder on the Orient Express,"* he said. "Or in the Calais coach, depending on whether you're English or American. It's beginning to look as though everyone read that manuscript. And I never noticed a thing!"

"Well, you were hitting the sauce pretty good," Jon Corn-Wallace reminded him. "And you were, uh, concentrating all your social energy in one direction."

"How's that?"

Corn-Wallace nodded toward Jeanne Botleigh, who was refilling someone's cup. "As far as you were concerned, our lovely caterer was the only person in the room."

There was an awkward silence, with our host coloring and his caterer lowering her eyes demurely. Haig broke it. "To continue," he said abruptly. "Miss Quinlan returned the manuscript to its box and to its place upon the table. Then—"

"But she didn't," Perigord said. "Harriet, I wanted another look at Woolrich. Maybe I'd missed something. But first I saw you reading it, and when I looked a second time it was gone. You weren't reading it and it wasn't on the table, either."

"I put it back," the agent said.

"But not where you found it," said Edward Everett Stokes. "You set it down not on the table but on that revolving bookcase."

"Did I? I suppose it's possible. But how did you know that?"

"Because I saw you," said the small-press publisher. "And because I wanted a look at the manuscript myself. I knew about it, including the fact that it was not restorable in the fashion of *Into the Night*. That made it valueless to a commercial publisher, but the idea of a Woolrich novel going unpublished ate away at me. I mean, we're talking about Cornell Woolrich."

"And you thought—"

"I thought, why not publish it as is, warts and all? I could do it, in an edition of two or three hundred copies, for collectors who'd happily accept inconsistencies and omissions for the sake of having something otherwise unobtainable. I wanted a few minutes' peace and quiet with the book, so I took it into the lavatory."

"And?"

"And I read it, or at least paged through it. I must have spent half an hour in there, or close to it."

"I remember you were gone awhile," Jon Corn-Wallace said. "I thought you'd headed on home."

"I thought he was in the other room," Jayne said, "cavorting on the pile of coats with Harriet here. But I guess that must have been someone else."

"It was Zoltan," the agent said, "and we were hardly cavorting."

"Kanoodling, then, but—"

"He was teaching me a yogic breathing technique, not that it's any of your business. Stokes, you took the manuscript into the john. I trust you brought it back?"

"Well, no."

"You took it home? You're the person responsible for its disappearance?"

"Certainly not. I didn't take it home, and I hope I'm not responsible for its disappearance. I left it in the lavatory."

"You just left it there?"

"In its box, on the shelf over the vanity. I set it down there while I washed my hands, and I'm afraid I forgot it. And no, it's not there now. I went and looked as soon as I realized what all this was about, and I'm afraid some other hands than mine must have moved it. I'll tell you this—when it does turn up, I definitely want to publish it."

"If it turns up," our client said darkly. "Once E. E. left it in the bathroom, anyone could have slipped it under his coat without being seen. And I'll probably never see it again."

"But that means one of us is a thief," somebody said.

"I know, and that's out of the question. You're all my friends. But we were all drinking last night, and drink can confuse a person. Suppose one of you did take it from the bathroom and carried it home as a joke, the kind of joke that can seem funny after a few drinks. If you could contrive to return it, perhaps in such a way that no one could know your identity . . . Haig, you ought to be able to work that out."

"I could," Haig agreed. "If that were how it happened. But it didn't."

"It didn't?"

"You forget the least obvious suspect."

"Me? Dammit, Haig, are you saying I stole my own manuscript?"

"I'm saying the butler did it," Haig said, "or the closest thing we have to a butler. Miss Botleigh, your upper lip has been trembling almost since we all sat down. You've been on the point of an admission throughout and haven't said a word. Have you in fact read the manuscript of *As Dark as It Gets*?"

"Yes."

The client gasped. "You have? When?"

"Last night."

"But—"

"I had to use the lavatory," she said, "and the book was there, although I could see it wasn't an ordinary bound book but pages in a box. I didn't think I would hurt it by looking at it. So I sat there and read the first two chapters."

"What did you think?" Haig asked her.

"It was very powerful. Parts of it were hard to follow, but the scenes were strong, and I got caught up in them."

"That's Woolrich," Jayne Corn-Wallace said. "He can grab you, all right."

"And then you took it with you when you went home," our client said. "You were so involved you couldn't bear to leave it unfinished, so you, uh, borrowed it." He reached to pat her hand. "Perfectly understandable," he said, "and perfectly innocent. You were going to bring it back once you'd finished it. So all this fuss has been over nothing."

"That's not what happened."

"It's not?"

"I read two chapters," she said, "and I thought I'd ask to borrow it some other time, or maybe not. But I put the pages back in the box and left them there."

"In the bathroom?"

"Yes."

"So you never did finish the book," our client said. "Well, if it ever turns up I'll be more than happy to lend it to you, but until then—"

"But perhaps Miss Botleigh has already finished the book," Haig suggested.

"How could she? She just told you she left it in the bathroom."

Haig said, "Miss Botleigh?"

"I finished the book," she said. "When everybody else went home, I stayed."

"My word," Zoltan Mihalyi said. "Woolrich never had a more devoted fan, or one half so beautiful."

"Not to finish the manuscript," she said, and turned to our host. "You asked me to stay," she said.

"I *wanted* you to stay," he agreed. "I wanted to *ask* you to stay. But I don't remember . . . "

"I guess you'd had quite a bit to drink," she said, "although you didn't show it. But you asked me to stay, and I'd been hoping you would ask me, because I wanted to stay."

"You must have had rather a lot to drink yourself," Harriet Quinlan murmured.

"Not that much," said the caterer. "I wanted to stay because he's a very attractive man."

Our client positively glowed, then turned red with embarrassment. "I knew I had a hole in my memory," he said, "but I didn't think anything significant could have fallen through it. So you actually stayed? God. What, uh, happened?"

"We went upstairs," Jeanne Botleigh said. "And we went to the bedroom, and we went to bed."

"Indeed," said Haig.

"And it was . . . "

"Quite wonderful," she said.

"And I don't remember. I think I'm going to kill myself."

"Not on Christmas Day," E. E. Stokes said. "And not with a mystery still unsolved. Haig, what became of the bloody manuscript?"

"Miss Botleigh?"

She looked at our host, then lowered her eyes. "You went to sleep afterward," she said, "and I felt entirely energized, and knew I couldn't sleep, and I thought I'd read for a while. And I remembered the manuscript, so I came down here and fetched it."

"And read it?"

"In bed. I thought you might wake up, in fact I was hoping you would. But you didn't."

"Damn it," our client said, with feeling.

"So I finished the manuscript and still didn't feel sleepy. And I got dressed and let myself out and went home."

There was a silence, broken at length by Zoltan Mihalyi, offering our client congratulations on his triumph and sympathy for the memory loss. "When you write your memoirs," he said, "you'll have to leave that chapter blank."

"Or have someone ghost it for you," Philip Perigord offered.

"The manuscript," Stokes said. "What became of it?"

"I don't know," the caterer said. "I finished it—"

"Which is more than Woolrich could say," Jayne Corn-Wallace said.

"—and I left it there."

"There?"

"In its box. On the bedside table, where you'd be sure to find it first thing in the morning. But I guess you didn't."

"The manuscript? Haig, you're telling me you want the *manuscript?*"

"You find my fee excessive?"

"But it wasn't even lost. No one took it. It was next to my bed. I'd have found it sooner or later."

"But you didn't," Haig said. "Not until you'd cost me and my young associate the better part of our holiday. You've been reading mysteries all your life. Now you got to see one solved in front of you, and in your own magnificent library."

He brightened. "It is a nice room, isn't it?"

"It's first-rate."

"Thanks. But Haig, listen to reason. You did solve the puzzle and recover the manuscript, but now you're demanding what you recovered as compensation. That's like rescuing a kidnap victim and insisting on adopting the child yourself."

"Nonsense. It's nothing like that."

"All right, then it's like recovering stolen jewels and demanding the jewels themselves as reward. It's just plain disproportionate. I hired you because I wanted the manuscript in my collection, and now you expect to wind up with it in your collection."

It did sound a little weird to me, but I kept my mouth shut. Haig had the ball, and I wanted to see where he'd go with it.

He put his fingertips together. "In *Black Orchids,*" he said, "Wolfe's client was his friend Lewis Hewitt. As recompense for his work, Wolfe insisted on all of the black orchid plants Hewitt had bred. Not one. All of them."

"That always seemed greedy to me."

"If we were speaking of fish," Haig went on, "I might be similarly inclined. But books are of use to me only as reading material. I want to read that book, sir, and I want to have it close to hand if I need to refer to it." He shrugged. "But I don't need the original that you prize so highly. Make me a copy."

"A copy?"

"Indeed. Have the manuscript photocopied."

"You'd be content with a . . . a copy?"

"And a credit," I said quickly, before Haig could give away the store. We'd put in a full day, and he ought to get more than a few hours' reading out of it. "A two-thousand-dollar store credit," I added, "which Mr. Haig can use up as he sees fit."

"Buying paperbacks and book-club editions," our client said. "It should last you for years." He heaved a sigh. "A photocopy and a store credit. Well, if that makes you happy . . . "

And that pretty much wrapped it up. I ran straight home and sat down at the typewriter, and if the story seems a little hurried it's because I was in a rush when I wrote it. See, our client tried for a second date with Jeanne Botleigh, to refresh his memory, I suppose, but a woman tends to feel less than flattered when you forget having gone to bed with her, and she wasn't having any.

So I called her the minute I got home, and we talked about this and that, and we've got a date in an hour and a half. I'll tell you this much, if I get lucky, I'll remember. So wish me luck, huh?

And, by the way . . .

Merry Christmas!

John Mortimer

RUMPOLE AND THE SPIRIT OF CHRISTMAS

I realized that Christmas was upon us when I saw a sprig of holly over the list of prisoners hung on the wall of the cells under the Old Bailey.

I pulled out a new box of small cigars and found its opening obstructed by a tinseled band on which a scarlet-faced Santa was seen hurrying a sleigh full of carcinoma-packed goodies to the Rejoicing World. I lit one as the lethargic screw, with a complexion the color of faded Bronco, regretfully left his doorstep sandwich and mug of sweet tea to unlock the gate.

"Good morning, Mr. Rumpole. Come to visit a customer?"

"Happy Christmas, officer," I said as cheerfully as possible. "Is Mr. Timson at home?"

"Well, I don't believe he's slipped down to his little place in the country."

Such were the pleasantries that were exchanged between us legal hacks and discontented screws; jokes that no doubt have changed little since the turnkeys unlocked the door at Newgate to let in a pessimistic advocate, or the cells under the Coliseum were opened to admit the unwelcome news of the Imperial thumbs-down.

"My mum wants me home for Christmas."

Which Christmas? It would have been an unreasonable remark and I refrained from it. Instead, I said, "All things are possible."

As I sat in the interviewing room, an Old Bailey hack of some considerable experience, looking through my brief and inadvertently using my waistcoat as an ashtray, I hoped I wasn't on another loser. I had had a run of bad luck during that autumn season, and young Edward Timson was part of that huge south London family whose criminal activities provided such welcome grist to the Rumpole mill. The charge in the seventeen-year-old Eddie's case was nothing less than wilful murder.

"We're in with a chance, though, Mr. Rumpole, ain't we?"

Like all his family, young Timson was a confirmed optimist. And yet, of course, the merest outsider in the Grand National, the hundred-to-one shot, is in with a chance, and nothing is more like going round the course at Aintree than living through a murder trial. In this particular case, a fanatical prosecutor named Wrigglesworth, known to me as the Mad Monk, was to represent Beechers, and Mr. Justice Vosper, a bright but wintry-hearted judge who always felt it his duty to lead for the prosecution, was to play the part of a particularly menacing fence at the Canal Turn.

"A chance. Well, yes, of course you've got a chance, if they can't establish common purpose, and no one knows which of you bright lads had the weapon."

No doubt the time had come for a brief glance at the prosecution case, not an entirely cheering prospect. Eddie, also known as "Turpin" Timson, lived in a kind of decaying barracks, a sort of highrise Lubianka, known as Keir Hardie Court, somewhere in south London, together with his parents, his various brothers, and his thirteen-year-old sister, Noreen. This particular branch of the Timson family lived on the thirteenth floor. Below them, on the twelfth, lived the large clan of the O'Dowds. The war between the Timsons and the O'Dowds began, it seems, with the casting of the Nativity play at the local comprehensive school.

Christmas comes earlier each year and the school show was planned about September. When Bridget O'Dowd was chosen to play the lead in the face of strong competition from Noreen Timson, an incident occurred comparable in historical importance to the assassination of an obscure Austrian archduke at Sarejevo. Noreen Timson announced in the playground that Bridget O'Dowd was a spotty little tart unsuited to play any role of which the most notable characteristic was virginity.

Hearing this, Bridget O'Dowd kicked Noreen Timson behind the anthracite bunkers. Within a few days, war was declared between the Timson and O'Dowd children, and a present of lit fireworks was posted through the O'Dowd front door. On what is known as the "night in question," reinforcements of O'Dowds and Timsons arrived in old bangers from a number of south London addresses and battle was joined on the stone staircase, a bleak terrain of peeling walls scrawled with graffiti, blowing empty Coca-cola tins and torn newspapers. The weapons seemed to have been articles in general domestic use, such as bread knives, carving knives, broom handles, and a heavy screwdriver. At the end of the day it appeared that the upstairs flat had repelled the invaders, and Kevin O'Dowd lay on the stairs. Having been stabbed with a slender and pointed blade, he was in a condition to become known as "the deceased" in the case of the Queen against Edward Timson. I made an appli-

627

cation for bail for my client which was refused, but a speedy trial was ordered.

So even as Bridget O'Dowd was giving her Virgin Mary at the comprehensive, the rest of the family was waiting to give evidence against Eddie Timson in that home of British drama, Number One Court at the Old Bailey.

"I never had no cutter, Mr. Rumpole. Straight up, I never had one," the defendant told me in the cells. He was an appealing-looking lad with soft brown eyes, who had already won the heart of the highly susceptible lady who wrote his social inquiry report. ("Although the charge is a serious one, this is a young man who might respond well to a period of probation." I could imagine the steely contempt in Mr. Justice Vosper's eye when he read that.)

"Well, tell me, Edward. Who had?"

"I never seen no cutters on no one, honest I didn't. We wasn't none of us tooled up, Mr. Rumpole."

"Come on, Eddie. Someone must have been. They say even young Noreen was brandishing a potato peeler."

"Not me, honest."

"What about your sword?"

There was one part of the prosecution evidence that I found particularly distasteful. It was agreed that on the previous Sunday morning, Eddie "Turpin" Timson had appeared on the stairs of Keir Hardie Court and flourished what appeared to be an antique cavalry saber at the assembled O'Dowds, who were just popping out to Mass.

"Me sword I bought up the Portobello? I didn't have that there, honest."

"The prosecution can't introduce evidence about the sword. It was an entirely different occasion." Mr. Barnard, my instructing solicitor who fancied himself as an infallible lawyer, spoke with a confidence which I couldn't feel. He, after all, wouldn't have to stand up on his hind legs and argue the legal toss with Mr. Justice Vosper.

"It rather depends on who's prosecuting us. I mean, if it's some fairly reasonable fellow—"

"I think," Mr. Barnard reminded me, shattering my faint optimism and ensuring that we were all in for a very rough Christmas indeed, "I think it's Mr. Wrigglesworth. Will he try to introduce the sword?"

I looked at "Turpin" Timson with a kind of pity. "If it is the Mad Monk, he undoubtedly will."

When I went into Court, Basil Wrigglesworth was standing with his shoulders hunched up round his large, red ears, his gown dropped to his elbows, his bony wrists protruding from the sleeves of his frayed jacket, his wig pushed back, and his huge hands joined on his lectern in what seemed to be an attitude of devoted prayer. A lump of cotton wool clung to his chin where he had cut himself shaving. Although well into his sixties, he preserved a look of boyish clumsiness. He appeared, as he always did when about to prosecute on a charge carrying a major punishment, radiantly happy.

"Ah, Rumpole," he said, lifting his eyes from the police verbals as though they were his breviary. "Are you defending *as usual?*"

"Yes, Wrigglesworth. And you're prosecuting *as usual?*" It wasn't much of a riposte but it was all I could think of at the time.

"Of course, I don't defend. One doesn't like to call witnesses who may not be telling the truth."

"You must have a few unhappy moments then, calling certain members of the Constabulary."

"I can honestly tell you, Rumpole—" his curiously innocent blue eyes looked at me with a sort of pain, as though I had questioned the doctrine of the immaculate conception "—I have never called a dishonest policeman."

"Yours must be a singularly simple faith, Wrigglesworth."

"As for the Detective Inspector in this case," counsel for the prosecution went on, "I've known Wainwright for years. In fact, this is his last trial before he retires. He could no more invent a verbal against a defendant than fly."

Any more on that tack, I thought, and we should soon be debating how many angels could dance on the point of a pin.

"Look here, Wrigglesworth. That evidence about my client having a sword: it's quite irrelevant. I'm sure you'd agree."

"Why is it irrelevant?" Wrigglesworth frowned.

"Because the murder clearly wasn't done with an antique cavalry saber. It was done with a small, thin blade."

"If he's a man who carries weapons, why isn't that relevant?"

"A man? Why do you call him a man? He's a child. A boy of seventeen!"

"Man enough to commit a serious crime."

"*If* he did."

"If he didn't, he'd hardly be in the dock."

"That's the difference between us, Wrigglesworth," I told him. "I believe in the presumption of innocence. You believe in original sin. Look here, old darling." I tried to give the Mad Monk a smile of friendship and became conscious of the fact that it looked, no doubt, like an ingratiating sneer. "Give us a chance. You won't introduce the evidence of the sword, will you?"

"Why ever not?"

"Well," I told him, "the Timsons are an industrious family of criminals. They work hard, they never go on strike. If it weren't for people like the Timsons, you and I would be out of a job."

"They sound in great need of prosecution and punishment. Why shouldn't I tell the jury about your client's sword? Can you give me one good reason?"

"Yes," I said, as convincingly as possible.

"What is it?" He peered at me, I thought, unfairly.

"Well, after all," I said, doing my best, "it is Christmas."

It would be idle to pretend that the first day in Court went well, although Wrigglesworth restrained himself from mentioning the sword in his opening speech, and told me that he was considering whether or not to call evidence about it the next day. I cross-examined a few members of the clan O'Dowd on the presence of lethal articles in the hands of the attacking force. The evidence about this varied, and weapons came and went in the hands of the inhabitants of Number Twelve as the witnesses were blown hither and thither in the winds of Rumpole's cross-examination. An interested observer from one of the other flats spoke of having seen a machete.

"Could that terrible weapon have been in the hands of Mr. Kevin O'Dowd, the deceased in this case?"

"I don't think so."

"But can you rule out the possibility?"

"No, I can't rule it out," the witness admitted, to my temporary delight.

"You can never rule out the possibility of anything in this world, Mr. Rumpole. But he doesn't think so. You have your answer."

Mr. Justice Vosper, in a voice like a splintering iceberg, gave me this unwelcome Christmas present. The case wasn't going well, but at least, by the end of the first day, the Mad Monk had kept out all mention of the sword. The next day he was to call young Bridget O'Dowd, fresh from her triumph in the Nativity play.

"I say, Rumpole, I'd be *so* grateful for a little help."

I was in Pommeroy's Wine Bar, drowning the sorrows of the day in my usual bottle of the cheapest Chateau Fleet Street (made from grapes which, judging from the bouquet, might have been not so much trodden as kicked to death by sturdy peasants in gum boots) when I looked up to see Wrigglesworth, dressed in an old mackintosh, doing business with Jack Pommeroy at the sales counter. When I crossed to him, he was not buying the jumbo-sized bottle of ginger beer which I imagined might be his celebratory Christmas tipple, but a tempting and respectably aged bottle of Chateau Pichon Longueville.

"What can I do for you, Wrigglesworth?"

"Well, as you know, Rumpole, I live in Croydon."

"Happiness is given to few of us on this earth," I said piously.

"And the Anglican Sisters of St. Agnes, Croydon, are anxious to buy a

630

present for their Bishop," Wrigglesworth explained. "A dozen bottles for Christmas. They've asked my advice, Rumpole. I know so little about wine. You wouldn't care to try this for me? I mean, if you're not especially busy."

"I should be hurrying home to dinner." My wife, Hilda (She Who Must Be Obeyed), was laying on rissoles and frozen peas, washed down by my last bottle of Pommeroy's extremely ordinary. "However, as it's Christmas, I don't mind helping you out, Wrigglesworth."

The Mad Monk was clearly quite unused to wine. As we sampled the claret together, I saw the chance of getting him to commit himself on the vital question of the evidence of the sword, as well as absorbing an unusually decent bottle. After the Pichon Longueville I was kind enough to help him by sampling a Boyd-Cantenac and then I said, "Excellent, this. But of course the Bishop might be a burgundy man. The nuns might care to invest in a decent Macon."

"Shall we try a bottle?" Wrigglesworth suggested. "I'd be grateful for your advice."

"I'll do my best to help you, my old darling. And while we're on the subject, that ridiculous bit of evidence about young Timson and the sword—"

"I remember you saying I shouldn't bring that out because it's Christmas."

"Exactly." Jack Pommeroy had uncorked the Macon and it was mingling with the claret to produce a feeling of peace and goodwill towards men. Wrigglesworth frowned, as though trying to absorb an obscure point of theology.

"I don't quite see the relevance of Christmas to the question of your man Timson threatening his neighbors with a sword."

"Surely, Wrigglesworth—" I knew my prosecutor well "—you're of a religious disposition?" The Mad Monk was the product of some bleak northern Catholic boarding school. He lived alone, and no doubt wore a hair shirt under his black waistcoat and was vowed to celibacy. The fact that he had his nose deep into a glass of burgundy at the moment was due to the benign influence of Rumpole.

"I'm a Christian, yes."

"Then practice a little Christian tolerance."

"Tolerance towards evil?"

"Evil?" I asked. "What do you mean, evil?"

"Couldn't that be your trouble, Rumpole? That you really don't recognize evil when you see it."

"I suppose," I said, "evil might be locking up a seventeen-year-old during Her Majesty's pleasure, when Her Majesty may very probably forget all about him, banging him up with a couple of hard and violent cases and their own chamber-pots for twenty-two hours a day, so he won't come out till he's a real, genuine, middle-aged murderer."

"I did hear the Reverend Mother say—" Wrigglesworth was gazing vacantly at the empty Macon bottle "—that the Bishop likes his glass of port."

"Then in the spirit of Christmas tolerance I'll help you to sample some of Pommeroy's Light and Tawny."

A little later, Wrigglesworth held up his port glass in a reverent sort of fashion.

"You're suggesting, are you, that I should make some special concession in this case because it's Christmastime?"

"Look here, old darling." I absorbed half my glass, relishing the gentle fruitiness and the slight tang of wood. "If you spent your whole life in that highrise hell-hole called Keir Hardie Court, if you had no fat prosecutions to occupy your attention and no prospect of any job at all, if you had no sort of occupation except war with the O'Dowds—"

"My own flat isn't particularly comfortable. I don't know a great deal about *your* home life, Rumpole, but you don't seem to be in a tearing hurry to experience it."

"Touché, Wrigglesworth, my old darling." I ordered us a couple of refills of Pommeroy's port to further postpone the encounter with She Who Must Be Obeyed and her rissoles.

"But we don't have to fight to the death on the staircase," Wrigglesworth pointed out.

"We don't have to fight at all, Wrigglesworth."

"As your client did. "

"As my client *may* have done. Remember the presumption of innocence."

"This is rather funny, this is." The prosecutor pulled back his lips to reveal strong, yellowish teeth and laughed appreciatively. "You know why your man Timson is called 'Turpin'?"

"No." I drank port uneasily, fearing an unwelcome revelation.

"Because he's always fighting with that sword of his. He's called after Dick Turpin, you see, who's always dueling on television. Do you watch television, Rumpole?"

"Hardly at all."

"I watch a great deal of television, as I'm alone rather a lot." Wrigglesworth referred to the box as though it were a sort of penance, like fasting or flagellation. "Detective Inspector Wainwright told me about your client. Rather amusing, I thought it was. He's retiring this Christmas."

"My client?"

"No. D.I. Wainwright. Do you think we should settle on this port for the

632

Bishop? Or would you like to try a glass of something else?"

"Christmas," I told Wrigglesworth severely as we sampled the Cockburn, "is not just a material, pagan celebration. It's not just an occasion for absorbing superior vintages, old darling. It must be a time when you try to do good, spiritual good to our enemies."

"To your client, you mean?"

"And to me."

"To you, Rumpole?"

"For God's sake, Wrigglesworth!" I was conscious of the fact that my appeal was growing desperate. "I've had six losers in a row down the Old Bailey. Can't I be included in any Christmas spirit that's going around?"

"You mean, at Christmas especially it is more blessed to give than to receive?"

"I mean exactly that." I was glad that he seemed, at last, to be following my drift.

"And you think I might give this case to someone, like a Christmas present?"

"If you care to put it that way, yes."

"I do not care to put it in *exactly* that way." He turned his pale-blue eyes on me with what I thought was genuine sympathy. "But I shall try and do the case of R. *v.* Timson in the way most appropriate to the greatest feast of the Christian year. It is a time, I quite agree, for the giving of presents."

When they finally threw us out of Pommeroy's, and after we had considered the possibility of buying the Bishop brandy in the Cock Tavern, and even beer in the Devereux, I let my instinct, like an aged horse, carry me on to the Underground and home to Gloucester Road, and there discovered the rissoles, like some traces of a vanished civilization, fossilized in the oven. She Who Must Be Obeyed was already in bed, feigning sleep. When I climbed in beside her, she opened a hostile eye.

"You're drunk, Rumpole!" she said. "What on earth have you been doing?"

"I've been having a legal discussion," I told her, "on the subject of the admissibility of certain evidence. Vital, from my client's point of view. And, just for a change, Hilda, I think I've won."

"Well, you'd better try and get some sleep." And she added with a sort of satisfaction, "I'm sure you'll be feeling quite terrible in the morning."

As with all the grimmer predictions of She Who Must Be Obeyed, this one turned out to be true. I sat in the Court the next day with the wig feeling like a lead weight on the brain and the stiff collar sawing the neck like a blunt execution. My mouth tasted of matured birdcage and from a long way off I heard Wrigglesworth say to Bridget O'Dowd, who stood looking particularly saintly and virginal in the witness box, "About a week before this, did you see the defendant, Edward Timson, on your staircase flourishing any sort of weapon?"

It is no exaggeration to say that I felt deeply shocked and considerably betrayed. After his promise to me, Wrigglesworth had turned his back on the spirit of the great Christmas festival. He came not to bring peace but a sword.

I clambered with some difficulty to my feet. After my forensic efforts of the evening before, I was scarcely in the mood for a legal argument. Mr. Justice Vosper looked up in surprise and greeted me in his usual chilly fashion.

"Yes, Mr. Rumpole. Do you object to this evidence?"

Of course I object, I wanted to say. It's inhuman, unnecessary, unmerciful, and likely to lead to my losing another case. Also, it's clearly contrary to a solemn and binding contract entered into after a number of glasses of the Bishop's putative port. All I seemed to manage was a strangled, "Yes."

"I suppose Mr. Wrigglesworth would say—" Vosper, J., was, as ever, anxious to supply any argument that might not yet have occurred to the prosecution "—that it is evidence of 'system.' "

"System?" I heard my voice faintly and from a long way off. "It may be, I suppose. But the Court has a discretion to omit evidence which may be irrelevant and purely prejudicial."

"I feel sure Mr. Wrigglesworth has considered the matter most carefully and that he would not lead this evidence unless he considered it entirely relevant."

I looked at the Mad Monk on the seat beside me. He was smiling at me with a mixture of hearty cheerfulness and supreme pity, as though I were sinking rapidly and he had come to administer extreme unction. I made a few ill-chosen remarks to the Court, but I was in no condition, that morning, to enter into a complicated legal argument on the admissibility of evidence.

It wasn't long before Bridget O'Dowd had told a deeply disapproving jury all about Eddie "Turpin" Timson's sword. "A man," the judge said later in his summing up about young Edward, "clearly prepared to attack with cold steel whenever it suited him."

When the trial was over, I called in for refreshment at my favorite watering hole and there, to my surprise, was my opponent Wrigglesworth, sharing an expensive-looking bottle with Detective Inspector Wainwright, the officer in charge of the case. I stood at the bar, absorbing a consoling glass of Pommeroy's ordinary, when the D.I. came up to the bar for cigarettes. He gave me a friendly and maddeningly sympathetic smile.

"Sorry about that, sir. Still, win a few, lose a few. Isn't that it?"

"In my case lately, it's been win a few, lose a lot!"

"You couldn't have this one, sir. You see, Mr. Wrigglesworth had promised it to me."

"He had *what?*"

"Well, I'm retiring, as you know. And Mr. Wrigglesworth promised me faithfully that my last case would be a win. He promised me that, in a manner of speaking, as a Christmas present. Great man is our Mr. Wrigglesworth, sir, for the spirit of Christmas."

I looked across at the Mad Monk and a terrible suspicion entered my head. What was all that about a present for the Bishop? I searched my memory and I could find no trace of our having, in fact, bought wine for any sort of cleric. And was Wrigglesworth as inexperienced as he would have had me believe in the art of selecting claret?

As I watched him pour and sniff a glass from his superior bottle and hold it critically to the light, a horrible suspicion crossed my mind. Had the whole evening's events been nothing but a deception, a sinister attempt to nobble Rumpole, to present him with such a stupendous hangover that he would stumble in his legal argument? Was it all in aid of D.I. Wainwright's Christmas present?

I looked at Wrigglesworth, and it would be no exaggeration to say the mind boggled. He was, of course, perfectly right about me. I just didn't recognize evil when I saw it.

John D. MacDonald

DEAD ON
CHRISTMAS STREET

The police in the first prowl car on the
scene got out a tarpaulin. A traffic policeman threw it over the body and herded the crowd back. They moved uneasily in the gray slush. Some of them looked up from time to time.

In the newspaper picture the window would be marked with a bold X. A dotted line would descend from the X to the spot where the covered body now lay. Some of the spectators, laden with tinsel- and evergreen-decorated packages, turned away, suppressing a nameless guilt.

But the curious stayed on. Across the street, in the window of a department store, a vast mechanical Santa rocked back and forth, slapping a mechanical hand against a padded thigh, roaring forever, "Whaw haw ho ho ho. Whaw haw ho ho ho." The slapping hand had worn the red plush from the padded thigh.

The ambulance arrived, with a brisk intern to make out the DOA. Sawdust was shoveled onto the sidewalk, then pushed off into the sewer drain. Wet snow fell into the city. And there was nothing else to see. The corner Santa, a leathery man with a pinched, blue nose, began to ring his hand bell again.

Daniel Fowler, one of the young Assistant District Attorneys, was at his desk when the call came through from Lieutenant Shinn of the Detective Squad. "Dan? This is Gil. You heard about the Garrity girl yet?"

For a moment the name meant nothing, and then suddenly he remembered: Loreen Garrity was the witness in the Sheridan City Loan Company case. She had made positive identification of two of the three kids who had tried to pull that holdup, and the case was on the calendar for February. Provided the kids didn't confess before it came up, Dan was going to prosecute. He had the Garrity girl's statement, and her promise to appear.

"What about her, Gil?" he asked.

636

"She took a high dive out of her office window—about an hour ago. Seventeen stories, and right into the Christmas rush. How come she didn't land on somebody, we'll never know. Connie Wyant is handling it. He remembered she figured in the loan-company deal, and he told me. Look, Dan. She was a big girl, and she tried hard not to go out that window. She was shoved. That's how come Connie has it. Nice Christmas present for him."

"Nice Christmas present for the lads who pushed over the loan company, too," Dan said grimly. "Without her there's no case. Tell Connie that. It ought to give him the right line."

Dan Fowler set aside the brief he was working on and walked down the hall. The District Attorney's secretary was at her desk. "Boss busy, Jane?"

She was a small girl with wide, gray eyes, a mass of dark hair, a soft mouth. She raised one eyebrow and looked at him speculatively. "I could be bribed, you know."

He looked around with exaggerated caution, went around her desk on tiptoe, bent and kissed her upraised lips. He smiled down at her. "People are beginning to talk," he whispered, not getting it as light as he meant it to be.

She tilted her head to one side, frowned, and said, "What is it, Dan?"

He sat on the corner of her desk and took her hands in his, and he told her about the big, dark-haired, swaggering woman who had gone out the window. He knew Jane would want to know. He had regretted bringing Jane in on the case, but he had had the unhappy hunch that Garrity might sell out, if the offer was high enough. And so he had enlisted Jane, depending on her intuition. He had taken the two of them to lunch, and had invented an excuse to duck out and leave them alone.

Afterward, Jane had said, "I guess I don't really like her, Dan. She was suspicious of me, of course, and she's a terribly vital sort of person. But I would say that she'll be willing to testify. And I don't think she'll sell out."

Now as he told her about the girl, he saw the sudden tears of sympathy in her gray eyes. "Oh, Dan! How dreadful! You'd better tell the boss right away. That Vince Servius must have hired somebody to do it."

"Easy, lady," he said softly.

He touched her dark hair with his fingertips, smiled at her, and crossed to the door of the inner office, opened it and went in.

Jim Heglon, the District Attorney, was a narrow-faced man with glasses that had heavy frames. He had a professional look, a dry wit, and a driving energy.

"Every time I see you, Dan, I have to conceal my annoyance," Heglon said. "You're going to cart away the best secretary I ever had."

"Maybe I'll keep her working for a while. Keep her out of trouble."

"Excellent! And speaking of trouble—"

"Does it show, Jim?" Dan sat on the arm of a heavy leather chair which faced Heglon's desk. "I do have some. Remember the Sheridan City Loan case?"

"Vaguely. Give me an outline."

"October. Five o'clock one afternoon, just as the loan office was closing. Three punks tried to knock it over. Two of them, Castrella and Kelly, are eighteen. The leader, Johnny Servius, is nineteen. Johnny is Vince Servius's kid brother.

"They went into the loan company wearing masks and waving guns. The manager had more guts than sense. He was loading the safe. He saw them and slammed the door and spun the knob. They beat on him, but he convinced them it was a time lock, which it wasn't. They took fifteen dollars out of his pants, and four dollars from the girl behind the counter and took off.

"Right across the hall is the office of an accountant named Thomas Kistner. He'd already left. His secretary, Loreen Garrity, was closing up the office. She had the door open a crack. She saw the three kids come out of the loan company, taking their masks off. Fortunately, they didn't see her.

"She went to headquarters and looked at the gallery, and picked out Servius and Castrella. They were picked up. Kelly was with them, so they took him in, too. In the lineup the Garrity girl made a positive identification of Servius and Castrella again. The manager thought he could recognize Kelly's voice.

"Bail was set high, because we expected Vince Servius would get them out. Much to everybody's surprise, he's left them in there. The only thing he did was line up George Terrafierro to defend them, which makes it tough from our point of view, but not too tough—if we could put the Garrity girl on the stand. She was the type to make a good witness. Very positive sort of girl."

"Was? Past tense?"

"This afternoon she was pushed out the window of the office where she works. Seventeen stories above the sidewalk. Gil Shinn tells me that Connie Wyant has it definitely tagged as homicide."

"If Connie says it is, then it is. What would conviction have meant to the three lads?"

"Servius had one previous conviction—car theft; Castrella had one conviction for assault with a deadly weapon. Kelly is clean, Jim."

Heglon frowned. "Odd, isn't it? In this state, armed robbery has a mandatory sentence of seven to fifteen years for a first offense in that category. With the weight Vince can swing, his kid brother would do about five years. Murder seems a little extreme as a way of avoiding a five-year sentence."

"Perhaps, Jim, the answer is in the relationship between Vince and the kid. There's quite a difference in ages. Vince must be nearly forty. He was in the big time early enough to give Johnny all the breaks. The kid has been thrown out of three good schools I know of. According to Vince, Johnny can do no wrong. Maybe that's why he left those three in jail awaiting trial—to keep them in the clear on this killing."

"It could be, Dan," Heglon said. "Go ahead with your investigation. And let me know."

Dan Fowler found out at the desk that Lieutenant Connie Wyant and Sergeant Levandowski were in the Interrogation Room. Dan sat down and waited.

After a few moments Connie waddled through the doorway and came over to him. He had bulging blue eyes and a dull expression.

Dan stood up, towering over the squat lieutenant. "Well, what's the picture, Connie?"

"No case against the kids, Gil says. Me, I wish it was just somebody thought it would be nice to jump out a window. But she grabbed the casing so hard, she broke her fingernails down to the quick.

"Marks you can see, in oak as hard as iron. Banged her head on the sill and left black hair on the rough edge of the casing. Lab matched it up. And one shoe up there, under the radiator. The radiator sits right in front of the window. Come listen to Kistner."

Dan followed him back to the Interrogation Room. Thomas Kistner sat at one side of the long table. A cigar lay dead on the glass ashtray near his elbow. As they opened the door, he glanced up quickly. He was a big, bloated man with an unhealthy grayish complexion and an important manner.

He said, "I was just telling the sergeant the tribulations of an accountant."

"We all got troubles," Connie said. "This is Mr. Fowler from the D.A.'s office, Kistner."

Mr. Kistner got up laboriously. "Happy to meet you, sir," he said. "Sorry that it has to be such an unpleasant occasion, however."

Connie sat down heavily. "Kistner, I want you to go through your story again. If it makes it easier, tell it to Mr. Fowler instead of me. He hasn't heard it before."

"I'll do anything in my power to help, Lieutenant," Kistner said firmly. He turned toward Dan. "I am out of my office a great deal. I do accounting on a contract basis for thirty-three small retail establishments. I visit them frequently.

"When Loreen came in this morning, she seemed nervous. I asked her what the trouble was, and she said that she felt quite sure somebody had been following her for the past week.

"She described him to me. Slim, middle height, pearl-gray felt hat, tan

639

raglan topcoat, swarthy complexion. I told her that because she was the witness in a trial coming up, she should maybe report it to the police and ask for protection. She said she didn't like the idea of yelling for help. She was a very—ah—independent sort of girl."

"I got that impression," Dan said.

"I went out then and didn't think anything more about what she'd said. I spent most of the morning at Finch Pharmacy, on the north side. I had a sandwich there and then drove back to the office, later than usual. Nearly two.

"I came up to the seventeenth floor. Going down the corridor, I pass the Men's Room before I get to my office. I unlocked the door with my key and went in. I was in there maybe three minutes.

"I came out and a man brushes by me in the corridor. He had his collar up, and was pulling down on his hatbrim and walking fast. At the moment, you understand, it meant nothing to me.

"I went into the office. The window was wide open, and the snow was blowing in. No Loreen. I couldn't figure it. I thought she'd gone to the Ladies' Room and had left the window open for some crazy reason. I started to shut it, and then I heard all the screaming down in the street.

"I leaned out. I saw her, right under me, sprawled on the sidewalk. I recognized the cocoa-colored suit. A new suit, I think. I stood in a state of shock, I guess, and then suddenly I remembered about the man following her, and I remembered the man in the hall—he had a gray hat and a tan topcoat, and I had the impression he was swarthy-faced.

"The first thing I did was call the police, naturally. While they were on the way, I called my wife. It just about broke her up. We were both fond of Loreen."

The big man smiled sadly. "And it seems to me I've been telling the story over and over again ever since. Oh, I don't mind, you understand. But it's a dreadful thing. The way I see it, when a person witnesses a crime, they ought to be given police protection until the trial is all over."

"We don't have that many cops," Connie said glumly. "How big was the man you saw in the corridor?"

"Medium size. A little on the thin side."

"How old?"

"I don't know. Twenty-five, forty-five. I couldn't see his face, and you understand I wasn't looking closely."

Connie turned toward Dan. "Nothing from the elevator boys about this guy. He probably took the stairs. The lobby is too busy for anybody to notice him coming through by way of the fire door. Did the Garrity girl ever lock herself in the office, Kistner?"

"I never knew of her doing that, Lieutenant."

Connie said, "Okay, so the guy could breeze in and clip her one. Then, from the way the rug was pulled up, he lugged her across to the window. She came to as he was trying to work her out the window, and she put up a battle. People in the office three stories underneath say she was screaming as she went by."

"How about the offices across the way?" Dan asked.

"It's a wide street, Dan, and they couldn't see through the snow. It started snowing hard about fifteen minutes before she was pushed out the window. I think the killer waited for that snow. It gave him a curtain to hide behind."

"Any chance that she marked the killer, Connie?" Dan asked.

"Doubt it. From the marks of her fingernails, he lifted her up and slid her feet out first, so her back was to him. She grabbed the sill on each side. Her head hit the window sash. All he had to do was hold her shoulders, and bang her in the small of the back with his knee. Once her fanny slid off the sill, she couldn't hold on with her hands any longer. And from the looks of the doorknobs, he wore gloves."

Dan turned to Kistner. "What was her home situation? I tried to question her. She was pretty evasive."

Kistner shrugged. "Big family. She didn't get along with them. Seven girls, I think, and she was next to oldest. She moved out when she got her first job. She lived alone in a one-room apartment on Leeds Avenue, near the bridge."

"You know of any boyfriend?" Connie asked.

"Nobody special. She used to go out a lot, but nobody special."

Connie rapped his knuckles on the edge of the table. "You ever make a pass at her, Kistner?"

The room was silent. Kistner stared at his dead cigar. "I don't want to lie to you, but I don't want any trouble at home, either. I got a boy in the Army, and I got a girl in her last year of high. But you work in a small office alone with a girl like Loreen, and it can get you.

"About six months ago I had to go to the state Capital on a tax thing. I asked her to come along. She did. It was a damn fool thing to do. And it— didn't work out so good. We agreed to forget it ever happened.

"We were awkward around the office for a couple of weeks, and then I guess we sort of forgot. She was a good worker, and I was paying her well, so it was to both our advantages to be practical and not get emotional. I didn't have to tell you men this, but, like I said, I don't see any point in lying to the police. Hell, you might have found out some way, and that might make it look like I killed her or something."

"Thanks for leveling," Connie said expressionlessly. "We'll call you if we need you."

Kistner ceremoniously shook hands all around and left with obvious relief.

As soon as the door shut behind him, Connie said, "I'll buy it. A long time ago I learned you can't jail a guy for being a jerk. Funny how many honest people I meet I don't like at all, and how many thieves make good guys to knock over a beer with. How's your girl?"

Dan looked at his watch. "Dressing for dinner, and I should be, too," he said. "How are the steaks out at the Cat and Fiddle?"

Connie half closed his eyes. After a time he sighed. "Okay. That might be a good way to go at the guy. Phone me and give me the reaction if he does talk. If not, don't bother."

Jane was in holiday mood until Dan told her where they were headed. She said tartly, "I admit freely that I am a working girl. But do I get overtime for this?"

Dan said slowly, carefully, "Darling, you better understand, if you don't already, that there's one part of me I can't change. I can't shut the office door and forget the cases piled up in there. I have a nasty habit of carrying them around with me. So we go someplace else and I try like blazes to be gay, or we go to the Cat and Fiddle and get something off my mind."

She moved closer to him. "Dull old work horse," she said.

"Guilty."

"All right, now I'll confess," Jane said. "I was going to suggest we go out there later. I just got sore when you beat me to the draw."

He laughed, and at the next stop light he kissed her hurriedly.

The Cat and Fiddle was eight miles beyond the city line. At last Dan saw the green-and-blue neon sign, and he turned into the asphalt parking area. There were about forty other cars there.

They went from the check room into the low-ceilinged bar and lounge. The only sign of Christmas was a small silver tree on the bar; a tiny blue spot was focused on it.

They sat at the bar and ordered drinks. Several other couples were at the tables, talking in low voices. A pianist played softly in the dining room.

Dan took out a business card and wrote on it: *Only if you happen to have an opinion.*

He called the nearest bartender over. "Would you please see that Vince gets this?"

The man glanced at the name. "I'll see if Mr. Servius is in." He said something to the other bartender and left through a paneled door at the rear of the bar. He was back in less than a minute, smiling politely.

"Please go up the stair. Mr. Servius is in his office—the second door on the right."

"I'll wait here, Dan," Jane said.

"If you are Miss Raymer, Mr. Servius would like to have you join him, too," the bartender said.

Jane looked at Dan. He nodded and she slid off the stool.

As they went up the stairs, Jane said, "I seem to be known here."

"Notorious female. I suspect he wants a witness."

Vincent Servius was standing at a small corner bar mixing himself a drink when they entered. He turned and smiled. "Fowler, Miss Raymer. Nice of you to stop by. Can I mix you something?"

Dan refused politely, and they sat down.

Vince was a compact man with cropped, prematurely white hair, a sun-lamp tan, and beautifully cut clothes. He had not been directly concerned with violence in many years. In that time he had eliminated most of the traces of the hoodlum.

The overall impression he gave was that of the up-and-coming clubman. Golf lessons, voice lessons, plastic surgery, and a good tailor—these had all helped; but nothing had been able to destroy a certain aura of alertness, ruthlessness. He was a man you would never joke with. He had made his own laws, and he carried the awareness of his own ultimate authority around with him, as unmistakable as a loaded gun.

Vince went over to the fieldstone fireplace, drink in hand, and turned, resting his elbow on the mantel.

"Very clever, Fowler. 'Only if you happen to have an opinion.' I have an opinion. The kid is no good. That's my opinion. He's a cheap punk. I didn't admit that to myself until he tried to put the hook on that loan company. He was working for me at the time. I was trying to break him in here—buying foods.

"But now I'm through, Fowler. You can tell Jim Heglon that for me. Terrafierro will back it up. Ask him what I told him. I said, 'Defend the kid. Get him off if you can, and no hard feelings if you can't. If you get him off, I'm having him run out of town, out of the state. I don't want him around.' I told George that.

"Now there's this Garrity thing. It looks like I went out on a limb for the kid. Going out on limbs was yesterday, Fowler. Not today and not tomorrow. I was a sucker long enough."

He took out a crisp handkerchief and mopped his forehead. "I go right up in the air," he said. "I talk too loud."

"You can see how Heglon is thinking," Dan said quietly. "And the police, too."

"That's the hell of it. I swear I had nothing to do with it." He half smiled. "It would have helped if I'd had a tape recorder up here last month when the Garrity girl came to see what she could sell me."

Dan leaned forward. "She came here?"

"With bells on. Nothing coy about that kid. Pay off, Mr. Servius, and I'll change my identification of your brother."

"What part of last month?"

"Let me think. The tenth it was. Monday the tenth."

Jane said softly, "That's why I got the impression she wouldn't sell out, Dan. I had lunch with her later that same week. She had tried to and couldn't."

Vince took a sip of his drink. "She started with big money and worked her way down. I let her go ahead. Finally, after I'd had my laughs, I told her even one dollar was too much. I told her I wanted the kid sent up.

"She blew her top. For a couple of minutes I thought I might have to clip her to shut her up. But after a couple of drinks she quieted down. That gave me a chance to find out something that had been bothering me. It seemed too pat, kind of."

"What do you mean, Servius?" Dan asked.

"The setup was too neat, the way the door *happened* to be open a crack, and the way she *happened* to be working late, and the way she *happened* to see the kids come out.

"I couldn't get her to admit anything at first, because she was making a little play for me, but when I convinced her I wasn't having any, she let me in on what really happened. She was hanging around waiting for the manager of that loan outfit to quit work.

"They had a system. She'd wait in the accountant's office with the light out, watching his door. Then, when the manager left, she'd wait about five minutes and leave herself. That would give him time to get his car out of the parking lot. He'd pick her up at the corner. She said he was the super-cautious, married type. They just dated once in a while. I wasn't having any of that. Too rough for me, Fowler."

There was a long silence. Dan asked, "How about friends of your brother, Servius, or friends of Kelly and Castrella?"

Vince walked over and sat down, facing them. "One—Johnny didn't have a friend who'd bring a bucket of water if he was on fire. And two—I sent the word out."

"What does that mean?"

"I like things quiet in this end of the state. I didn't want anyone helping those three punks. Everybody got the word. So who would do anything? Now both of you please tell Heglon exactly what I said. Tell him to check with

Terrafierro. Tell him to have the cops check their pigeons. Ask the kid himself. I paid him a little visit. Now, if you don't mind, I've got another appointment."

They had finished their steaks before Dan was able to get any line on Connie Wyant. On the third telephone call he was given a message. Lieutenant Wyant was waiting for Mr. Fowler at 311 Leeds Street, Apartment 6A, and would Mr. Fowler please bring Miss Raymer with him.

They drove back to the city. A department car was parked in front of the building. Sergeant Levandowski was half asleep behind the wheel. "Go right in. Ground floor in the back. 6A."

Connie greeted them gravely and listened without question to Dan's report of the conversation with Vince Servius. After Dan had finished, Connie nodded casually, as though it was of little importance, and said, "Miss Raymer, I'm not so good at this, so I thought maybe you could help. There's the Garrity girl's closet. Go through it and give me an estimate on the cost."

Jane went to the open closet. She began to examine the clothes. "Hey!" she exclaimed.

"What do you think?" Connie asked.

"If this suit cost a nickel under two hundred, I'll eat it. And look at this coat. Four hundred, anyway." She bent over and picked up a shoe. "For ages I've dreamed of owning a pair of these. Thirty-seven fifty, at least."

"Care to make an estimate on the total?" Connie asked her.

"Gosh, thousands. I don't know. There are nine dresses in there that must have cost at least a hundred apiece. Do you have to have it accurate?"

"That's close enough, thanks." He took a small blue bankbook out of his pocket and flipped it to Dan. Dan caught it and looked inside. Loreen Garrity had more than $1100 on hand. There had been large deposits and large with-drawals—nothing small.

Connie said, "I've been to see her family. They're good people. They didn't want to talk mean about the dead, so it took a little time. But I found out our Loreen was one for the angles—a chiseler—no conscience and less morals. A rough, tough cookie to get tied up with.

"From there, I went to see the Kistners. Every time the old lady would try to answer a question, Kistner'd jump in with all four feet. I finally had to have Levandowski take him downtown just to get him out of the way. Then the old lady talked.

"She had a lot to say about how lousy business is. How they're scrimping and scraping along, and how the girl couldn't have a new formal for the Christmas dance tomorrow night at the high school gym.

"Then I called up an accountant friend after I left her. I asked him how Kistner had been doing. He cussed out Kistner and said he'd been doing fine;

in fact, he had stolen some nice retail accounts out from under the other boys in the same racket. So I came over here and it looked like this was where the profit was going. So I waited for you so I could make sure."

"What can you do about it?" Dan demanded, anger in his voice, anger at the big puffy man who hadn't wanted to lie to the police.

"I've been thinking. It's eleven o'clock. He's been sitting down there sweating. I've got to get my Christmas shopping done tomorrow, and the only way I'll ever get around to it is to break him fast."

Jane had been listening, wide-eyed. "They always forget some little thing, don't they?" she asked. "Or there is something they don't know about. Like a clock that is five minutes slow, or something. I mean, in the stories . . ." Her voice trailed off uncertainly.

"Give her a badge, Connie," Dan said with amusement.

Connie rubbed his chin. "I might do that, Dan. I just might do that. Miss Raymer, you got a strong stomach? If so, maybe you get to watch your idea in operation."

It was nearly midnight, and Connie had left Dan and Jane alone in a small office at headquarters for nearly a half hour. He opened the door and stuck his head in. "Come on, people. Just don't say a word."

They went to the Interrogation Room. Kistner jumped up the moment they came in. Levandowski sat at the long table, looking bored.

Kistner said heatedly, " As you know, Lieutenant, I was perfectly willing to cooperate. But you are being high-handed. I demand to know why I was brought down here. I want to know why I can't phone a lawyer. You are exceeding your authority, and I—"

"Siddown!" Connie roared with all the power of his lungs.

Kistner's mouth worked silently. He sat down, shocked by the unexpected roar. A tired young man slouched in, sat at the table, flipped open a notebook, and placed three sharp pencils within easy reach.

Connie motioned Dan and Jane over toward chairs in a shadowed corner of the room. They sat side by side, and Jane held Dan's wrist, her nails sharp against his skin.

"Kistner, tell us again about how you came back to the office," Connie said.

Kistner replied in a tone of excruciating patience, as though talking to children, "I parked my car in my parking space in the lot behind the building. I used the back way into the lobby. I went up—"

"You went to the cigar counter."

"So I did! I had forgotten that. I went to the cigar counter. I bought three cigars and chatted with Barney. Then I took an elevator up."

"And talked to the elevator boy."

"I usually do. Is there a law?"

"No law, Kistner. Go on."

"And then I opened the Men's Room door with my key, and I was in there maybe three minutes. And then when I came out, the man I described brushed by me. I went to the office and found the window open. I was shutting it when I heard—"

"All this was at two o'clock, give or take a couple of minutes?"

"That's right, Lieutenant." Talking had restored Kistner's self-assurance.

Connie nodded to Levandowski. The sergeant got up lazily, walked to the door, and opened it. A burly, diffident young man came in. He wore khaki pants and a leather jacket.

"Sit down," Connie said casually. "What's your name?"

"Paul Hilbert, officer."

The tired young man was taking notes.

"What's your occupation?"

"I'm a plumber, officer. Central Plumbing, Incorporated."

"Did you get a call today from the Associated Bank Building?"

"Well, I didn't get the call, but I was sent out on the job. I talked to the super, and he sent me up to the seventeenth floor. Sink drain clogged in the Men's Room."

"What time did you get there?"

"That's on my report, officer. Quarter after one."

"How long did it take you to finish the job?"

"About three o'clock."

"Did you leave the Men's Room at any time during that period?"

"No, I didn't."

"I suppose people tried to come in there?"

"Three or four. But I had all the water connections turned off, so I told them to go down to sixteen. The super had the door unlocked down there."

"Did you get a look at everybody who came in?"

"Sure, officer."

"You said three or four. Is one of them at this table?"

The shy young man looked around. He shook his head. "No, sir."

"Thanks, Hilbert. Wait outside. We'll want you to sign the statement when it's typed up."

Hilbert's footsteps sounded loud as he walked to the door. Everyone was watching Kistner. His face was still, and he seemed to be looking into a remote and alien future, as cold as the back of the moon.

Kistner said in a husky, barely audible voice. "A bad break. A stupid thing. Ten seconds it would have taken me to look in there. I had to establish the time. I talked to Barney. And to the elevator boy. They'd know when she fell. But I had to be some place else. Not in the office.

"You don't know how it was. She kept wanting more money. She wouldn't have anything to do with me, except when there was money. And I didn't have any more, finally.

"I guess I was crazy. I started to milk the accounts. That wasn't hard; the clients trust me. Take a little here and a little there. She found out. She wanted more and more. And that gave her a new angle. Give me more, or I'll tell.

"I thought it over. I kept thinking about her being a witness. All I had to do was make it look like she was killed to keep her from testifying. I don't care what you do to me. Now it's over, and I feel glad."

He gave Connie a long, wondering look. "Is that crazy? To feel glad it's over? Do other people feel that way?"

Connie asked Dan and Jane to wait in the small office. He came in ten minutes later; he looked tired. The plumber came in with him.

Connie said, "Me, I hate this business. I'm after him, and I bust him, and then I start bleeding for him. What the hell? Anyway, you get your badge, Miss Raymer."

"But wouldn't you have found out about the plumber anyway?" Jane asked.

Connie grinned ruefully at her. He jerked a thumb toward the plumber. "Meet Patrolman Hilbert. Doesn't know a pipe wrench from a faucet. We just took the chance that Kistner was too eager to toss the girl out the window— so eager he didn't make a quick check of the Men's Room. If he had, he could have laughed us under the table. As it is, I can get my Christmas shopping done tomorrow. Or is it today?"

Dan and Jane left headquarters. They walked down the street, arm in arm. There was holly, and a big tree in front of the courthouse, and a car went by with a lot of people in it singing about We Three Kings of Orient Are. Kistner was a stain, fading slowly.

They walked until it was entirely Christmas Eve, and they were entirely alone in the snow that began to fall again, making tiny perfect stars of lace that lingered in her dark hair.

Malcolm Gray

MISS CRINDLE AND FATHER CHRISTMAS

Christmas comes reluctantly to Much Cluning. Huddling in its valley, the village looks even drearier than usual under grey December skies. There is no tree outside the village hall, and the single string of fairy lights along the High Street hardly creates an air of festivity. The housewives complain about the extra work Christmas brings and the men about the expense. They only do it for the kids, they say. All the same, it is doubtful if they really mean it, or if they would want to see the season abolished even if they could, and a fair number go to church or chapel on Christmas morning.

A few days before Christmas last year, Harriet Richards stood in the yard at her brother's farm giving him a piece of her mind. At twenty-two, Harriet was as generous and warm-hearted as she was pretty. "Do you have to be such a Scrooge?" she demanded angrily.

"Go away," Jason told her coldly. He was nine years older than his sister and he had no use for the season of goodwill. The only good thing about it to his mind was the profit he made on his flock of chickens and turkeys. He was damned if he was going to give any of them away to layabouts who weren't prepared to get off their backsides and work. He said as much to Harriet.

"Layabouts!" she exclaimed furiously. "Do you call old Mrs. Randall a layabout?"

"It's her husband's job to provide for her, not mine."

"When he's nearly eighty and crippled with arthritis?"

"Ach!" Jason said, disgusted.

"And she's not the only one," Harriet went on. "There's Josie Gardner with her three kids. And Bert Renwick and Phoebe," she added, forestalling her brother's attempt to interrupt her. "It's not their fault they can't afford anything but the bare necessities."

"They get their pensions," Jason retorted. "And benefits. They wouldn't

649

get those if people like me didn't pay too damned much in taxes."

"Oh," Harriet said, exasperated, "I don't know how Sheila puts up with you!" And, turning, she started toward the house.

"If you think I breed those birds to feed all the lame ducks in the village, you'd better think again!" Jason called after her.

There were times when she could strangle him, Harriet thought furiously. It wasn't as if he couldn't afford three or four turkeys. By local standards, he was well off. But he seemed to feel that people expected him to give them. It put him on the defensive, and he resented it.

Her sister-in-law was in the kitchen. "Have you and Jason been arguing again?" she asked, amused.

"You could say so." Harriet, still boiling with indignation, explained.

"He works hard," Sheila reminded her. "And he's inclined to think other people don't. There's so much to do at this time of year, he gets worn out."

"He could afford to pay another man if he wasn't so mean," Harriet said bitterly. "Anyway, it's not just this time, it's always."

Soon afterward, she left. Sheila watched her go, thinking.

Later that evening Harriet had a very public quarrel with Colin Loates, her boy friend. Nobody who heard it was quite sure what it was about, but Harriet went home in tears.

Miss Crindle met her in the street the next day. Miss Crindle was a large woman with greying hair and a cheerful manner. Until her retirement three years ago, she had taught at Much Cluning Primary School for more than thirty years, and both Harriet and Colin had been among her brightest pupils. So had Jason, who hadn't been as clever as his sister but by hard work had gained a scholarship to Leobury School and gone on to university. Harriet could have gone, too, but she preferred to stay home and work with the horses her father bred for show jumping.

Colin had been the brightest of the three, a cheeky little boy with charm and a talent for mischief. Miss Crindle had never quite forgiven him for leaving school at sixteen to go into his father's grocery shop.

"And how is Colin?" Miss Crindle inquired that morning.

Harriet looked surprised. "Haven't you heard, Miss Crindle? I thought everybody had. We had a row last night and it's all over."

Miss Crindle noticed that Harriet's left eye was twitching and that she looked embarrassed. All the same, she didn't seem too distressed. She had always been a sensible girl, Miss Crindle thought, and things were different nowadays. In her time, if a girl and her boy friend split up she would be upset for days. "I'm sorry," she said.

Harriet shrugged. "I'll get over it," she said ruefully.

Miss Crindle was sure she would. A girl like Harriet, vivacious and attractive, would find no shortage of young men.

That afternoon, Colin, driving back from Leobury, slewed off the road into a ditch two miles from the village. He explained that he had swerved to avoid a pheasant and skidded, but the popular theory was that his mind hadn't been on his driving, he was thinking about Harriet and their row. Whatever the cause, his car was well and truly stuck and he had to walk to the nearest house and phone the garage to come and tow him out.

They were still doing it when Billy Powis, having run all the way home, blurted out breathlessly to his mother that he had just seen Santa Claus. Mary Powis was busy making mince pies. She laughed but didn't pay too much attention. She was used to her son's tales.

"Oh, dear?" she said.

"But I did, Mum," the seven-year-old insisted.

"Had he got his sledge and reindeer?"

Billy hesitated. He was a truthful little boy and he couldn't really remember, he had been too excited. "He'd got something," he mumbled. More certainly he added, "And he had a sack over his shoulder."

"Where was he?"

"I told you, at the edge of Brackett's Wood. He went into the trees."

"You shouldn't make up stories, Billy," Mary told him mildly. "It's telling fibs, and that's naughty."

"I did see him," Billy persisted. He was learning early that it is bad enough to be suspected when one is guilty, but much worse when one is innocent. "He was all in red, with white stuff on his coat, and he had a big red hood and boots. Like he does when he comes to our school party."

Oh, dear, Mary thought. She decided that the best course would be to ignore her son's tale. "Go and wash your hands," she said.

At the same time, Sheila Richards was trying without success to ring her sister-in-law. Harriet's mother told her Harry was out. She didn't know where, but she didn't suppose she would be long. Sheila thanked her and said she would try again later.

Billy Powis wasn't the only inhabitant of Much Cluning to see Father Christmas. Two other people saw him, and they were grownups. The first was George Townley, the owner of the general store-cum-post office. While Billy was running home to tell his mother what he had seen, George was returning from visiting his sister at Little Cluning. As he drove down the hill into the village, he saw a figure in red with a hood and carrying a sack disappear into the trees beside the road. He was unwise enough to mention it to one of his customers, and soon the story was all over the village. George Townley had started seeing things, and he believed in Santa Claus.

It had been getting colder during the day, and about five o'clock it started to snow. By the time most of Much Cluning went to bed, there was a three-inch covering over everything and it was still snowing. It stopped during the night, but the temperature dropped further.

The second adult to see Father Christmas was Miss Crindle. At one o'clock in the morning of December the twenty-third, she had to get out of bed to go to the bathroom. On her way back, she looked out of the window. It was a fine clear night with a moon. There was never much noise in the valley, but now every sound was muffled by the thick layer of snow.

Just across the road, a figure dressed in scarlet and white, its head covered by a hood, was turning the corner round the back of the Renwicks' cottage. It was bowed under the weight of the sack slung over its right shoulder. Miss Crindle blinked. There were no children's parties at that hour, and any devoted father who was inclined to go to the lengths of dressing up to deliver his offsprings' presents would hardly do so two days before Christmas.

Miss Crindle told herself that if it wasn't a fond father, it must be a burglar. She considered calling the police. But she disliked the idea of being thought an overimaginative old fool and, anyway, everybody knew the Renwicks were almost destitute. No burglar would try his luck there. She climbed back into bed, and the next day she kept what she had seen to herself.

She said nothing even when Phoebe Renwick, who was well over seventy and worn out from caring for her invalid husband, told her her news. When she came down that morning and opened the back door, there on the doorstep there had been a parcel wrapped in gift paper. In it there was a small turkey already plucked and drawn and a tiny Christmas pudding.

"I couldn't believe it," Phoebe said. She was close to tears. "We haven't been able to have a turkey for over twenty years. Not since soon after Bert was first ill and had to give up work. We can't keep it, of course, it wouldn't be right, but it was a lovely thought."

"Of course you can keep it," Miss Crindle told her with spirit.

"No. We were brought up not to accept what we hadn't paid for, or to ask for charity, and we never have, neither of us."

"You call a present charity? Anyway," Miss Crindle added reasonably, "who would you give it back to?"

"I hadn't thought of that," Phoebe admitted.

"You keep it and be glad there are people in the village who think of others," Miss Crindle told her. "You can say a prayer for them in chapel on Christmas morning."

The old lady's eyes moistened. "I will tonight, too," she said.

Busy with her thoughts, Miss Crindle went back indoors and resumed the cleaning she had been doing when she heard Mrs. Renwick calling her. Who was the kind soul who had left the parcel on the old couple's step? She had no doubt that it was the person in Santa Claus costume she had seen during the night, but who was he? Or she?

Not that it mattered: if somebody wanted to do the old couple a good turn surreptitiously, good luck to them. Only why the fancy dress? Such ostentation seemed out of keeping with leaving the parcel secretly in the middle of the night. It was like a disguise, and it made her a little uneasy.

The Renwicks weren't the only beneficiaries of Much Cluning's own Santa Claus: the Randalls, Josie Gardner, and an elderly lady named Willings with a crippled son had found similar parcels at their back doors that morning. By evening the story was all over the village.

Miss Crindle heard it, and she wondered still more.

Neither of the Richardses had heard about the parcels. Bracketts Farm was a mile out of Much Cluning and they'd been busy there all day. Thus there was no reason for Sheila to suspect anything when Jason came into the kitchen during the afternoon and asked her, "Has Mrs. Grundy been for her bird?"

Sheila had been right, he was tired. The woman who helped deal with the turkeys was ill with flu and he had been driving himself hard for days. He was also suspicious.

"No," Sheila answered without looking up from what she was doing at the sink. "She said she'd come tomorrow."

Jason swore.

"Why, what's the matter? It doesn't make any difference."

"It's gone."

Sheila looked up then. "What do you mean?"

"What I say," Jason told her angrily. "It's clear enough, isn't it? It's been pinched."

His wife stared at him. "Are you sure?" she asked. But she could see from Jason's face he was. "Have any of the others gone?"

"I don't know. I was only looking for hers."

"Can't she have another one?" Sheila tried to be practical, but she knew it wouldn't assuage Jason's anger.

"Of course she bloody well can't," he retorted. "The others are all sold, you know that. And you know how fussy she is."

Sheila did know. Mrs. Grundy lived at Much Cluning Hall and, although she was pleasant enough, she disliked being thwarted or inconvenienced. Her manner implied that she expected her life to run as smoothly as the Rolls-

Royce her husband drove. Oh, God, Sheila thought, it looked like being a miserable Christmas. Jason would be in a foul mood for days. A terrible thought occurred to her. "Hadn't you better count them?" she asked.

"I'm going to."

Jason strode across the yard to the big shed where the dead birds, plucked and drawn, were laid out in rows along the shelves. Sheila followed and watched while he counted them. There should be ninety, she knew. Christmas turkeys might be profitable, but they were only a sideline to the main business of the farm, the crops and sheep.

"There are four gone!" Jason shouted. "Four! That's the best part of fifty pounds!" He turned furiously. "I'm going to ring the police!"

"Jason, do you think—?" Sheila asked weakly.

But he was in no mood to pay attention, and she followed him uneasily into the house.

It was nearly an hour before P.C. Tom Roberts arrived. He had been at the site of a road accident four miles away and the theft of four turkeys hadn't seemed like the crime of the century, even in Much Cluning. Clearly Jason Richards didn't agree with him.

"They must have got in during the night," he said. Waiting had done nothing to soothe his anger. "You can see their tracks."

He led the way through the churned-up slush in the yard, past the farm buildings to a small meadow bounded on the far side by a low hedge. It was still freezing hard, and the snow, several inches deep, was crisp and unbroken save for a clearly designed set of footprints leading from the yard to the hedge near the point where it met the road. Jason had said "they," Roberts thought, but there was only one set. Smallish prints, too.

"Looks like he came this way," he agreed. "Was the shed locked at night?"

"No." Jason sounded as if he were daring the policeman to criticize him. "The padlock's fastened with a peg. We've never had anything stolen before."

Roberts walked back across the yard.

"Where are you going?" Jason demanded.

"Don't want to disturb the tracks then, do we, sir?" Roberts said. He walked along the road and across to the point where, it seemed, the thief had forced his way through the hedge. There was still just enough light for him to make out the tuft of material caught on a twig. He picked it out carefully and frowned. It was bright-red and thin. Hardly the sort of clothing a man would wear to go stealing turkeys on a freezing-cold night. Not what most men would wear at any time, come to that. He tucked the fragment away between two pages of his notebook and returned to where the farmer was watching.

The turkeys must have been stolen on one of the last two nights, Jason told him. He had counted them two days ago.

Tom Roberts lived in the village. He knew about George Townley's seeing a figure dressed like Santa Claus disappearing into Brackett's Wood and about the mysterious parcels which had appeared on certain doorsteps last night. There had been four of them, each one containing a turkey. And four turkeys had been taken from Jason's shed. Roberts was well aware of the dangers of putting two and two together and making sixteen, but it looked to him very much as if some joker had been playing twin roles, Robin Hood and Santa Claus.

Of all the people in the village, he could think of only one who possessed the sort of mind to think up a ploy like that and the cheek to carry it out: Colin Loates. Colin had never been suspected of dishonesty, but he was— what was the word? —unpredictable. Sometimes his sense of humor ran away with him. After all, everybody knew Jason Richards could well afford the loss of four birds, and the recipients of the parcels were genuinely deserving cases. If it had been up to him personally, Roberts would have felt inclined to say, "Good luck to him," and write the case off as unsolved. But it wasn't, and theft was theft, however good the motive. So he promised Jason he would make inquiries and went to see Colin.

He found him at his father's shop, making up orders for the next day.

When Colin heard why he was there, he laughed. "Serve Jason right," he said.

"You've no idea who might have done it?" Roberts asked him.

"Me? No. I don't know why you should come to me about it. You're the one who's supposed to know about all the crime that goes on here."

"Where were you the last two nights?" Roberts asked him.

"What time?"

"Anytime."

"Home in bed. "

They eyed each other. Colin seemed to think the whole business was a great joke, and that annoyed Roberts a little. He looked down at the other man's feet. They must be size nines, at least. The boots which made the tracks in the snow on Jason Richards' meadow had been no bigger than sevens. All the same, "Have you got any wellingtons?" he asked.

"Course I have," Colin answered.

"Where are they?"

"In the boot of my car. Why?"

"Do you mind if I have a look at them?"

"Not if you want to."

They went out to the yard at the back of the shop where Colin's old Escort was parked. He opened the boot and brought out a pair of worn grey wellingtons. Roberts studied them. They were size ten.

"All right, thanks," he said.

Colin just grinned. "Do you think I took Jason's turkeys?" he asked.

Roberts didn't answer.

Miss Crindle heard about the theft the next morning when she was doing her last-minute Christmas shopping. It seemed to justify her fears, and she decided that she must talk to Tom Roberts.

"You think the turkeys the Renwicks and the others got were the ones somebody stole from Jason Richards' shed, don't you?" she asked him.

"I can't say, Miss Crindle," the policeman replied cautiously.

"Of course you can, everybody else is." Miss Crindle swept his objection aside. "And you suspect you know who it was, don't you?"

Roberts eyed his visitor. Muffled up in what looked like two or three layers of jumpers and cardigans under her coat, she looked bigger than ever. It would have been easy to put her down as a silly busybody, but Roberts knew better. Miss Crindle was an intelligent woman. And if she took a keen interest in what went on in Much Cluning, she was no mischief-maker. "We're pursuing our inquiries," he said.

"So I should hope," she told him briskly. "Although I must confess, my sympathies are rather with the thief." She paused, then continued with obvious embarrassment, "I thought I should tell you, I saw Father Christmas last night."

Roberts gaped at her. For a moment he wondered if she had suddenly gone queer. "I'm sorry?" he stammered.

"Somebody dressed as Santa Claus left the parcels. I happened to look out of my window about one o'clock and I saw them going round behind the Renwicks' house. I didn't say anything about it, there didn't seem any point, and I've no wish to be thought mad, but if the birds were stolen—"

"You've no idea who it was?" Roberts asked, recovering a little.

"None," Miss Crindle answered firmly. "I can't even say if it was a man or a woman. I suppose you know George Townley saw them, too, two or three days ago?"

Roberts nodded. "It looks as if whoever took the turkeys was wearing red," he said grimly. "He left this caught on the hedge where he pushed through." He took out his notebook and showed Miss Crindle the fragment of cloth.

She studied it with interest. "It looks like a piece from a Santa Claus costume," she observed. She gave the policeman a shrewd look. "I suppose you think it was Colin Loates?"

This time Tom Roberts wasn't startled, he knew half the village would be supposing the same thing. "It wasn't him," he said.

"Oh?" Miss Crindle couldn't quite conceal her curiosity.

Roberts was undecided how much he should reveal. He knew the old girl had helped the police when Ralph Johns was murdered and the Chief Inspector had a high regard for her. And he could do with some help now. "The thief left footprints from the hedge across to the shed," he explained. "They were sixes or sevens, and Colin takes tens. I've seen his boots. Besides, when George Townley saw his Santa Claus, they were towing Colin's car out of a ditch along the Leobury road."

Miss Crindle hadn't known that, but she was rather glad. "Have you any idea who it may have been?" she inquired.

"No," Roberts admitted.

Miss Crindle was afraid *she* had, and after Roberts had gone she walked across the road. The Renwicks had few visitors—even the milkman called only every other day—and the footprints in the snow along the side of the cottage were still as clear as when they were made. She studied them thoughtfully, then she went to see Harriet Richards.

She didn't beat about the bush. "What do you know about Father Christmas and Jason's stolen turkeys?" she demanded.

"Me?" The girl looked surprised. "Nothing, Miss Crindle."

"Harriet," Miss Crindle told her sternly, "your eyelid's twitching. That's the second time it's done it in the last four days."

For some unaccountable reason Harriet blushed.

"Theft is a crime," Miss Crindle continued. "It can have very serious consequences. Sometimes for the wrong person. You may disapprove of Jason but, even if you aren't having anything to do with Colin now, you wouldn't want him to get into trouble, would you?"

"No," Harriet said.

Miss Crindle nodded. "Good. What size wellingtons do you take?"

"Sevens."

"And where were you at one o'clock the night before last?"

Harriet smiled, and for the first time that morning there was a hint of her old mischief. "At Leobury," she answered. "I went to see Pat Dellar. It started to freeze hard, there was a lot of slush on the road, and I stayed the night."

Miss Crindle gazed at the girl for quite a long time. Then, "Think about it, my dear," she said.

On her way home, she met Mary Powis and Billy.

"I've seen Father Christmas," the little boy announced triumphantly.

"Billy!" his mother reproved him. "You thought you saw him on Monday, and you know he doesn't come out until Christmas Eve. And only after dark then." She smiled apologetically at Miss Crindle.

But Miss Crindle was interested. "Where did you see him, Billy?" she asked.

"By Brackett's Wood," Billy replied.

"What time was it?"

"I don't know. But it got dark soon."

"You aren't the only person who saw him," Miss Crindle said. "I saw him, too, and so did Mr. Townley." It was too much, she thought.

When she got home, she phoned Pat Dellar, who was one of her old pupils. Pat confirmed that Harriet had spent last night there.

Miss Crindle asked after her parents, they talked for a minute or two longer, and when Miss Crindle put down the phone she sat for some time, thinking. It was clear that Colin hadn't stolen the turkeys. There was only one set of footprints and he couldn't have worn size six or seven boots. Moreover, he hadn't been the Father Christmas Billy Powis and George Townley had seen. Nor could Harriet have played Santa Claus—she had been miles away when the parcels had been delivered the night before last. So who had?

After twenty minutes, Miss Crindle came to a decision. She made two telephone calls, then put on another cardigan and her coat and went to see Sheila Richards.

"It was all a mistake," Jason said, looking uncomfortable.

P.C. Roberts eyed him stolidly. He was quite sure it hadn't been a mistake, but if Jason was going to maintain it had, there wasn't much he could do.

"The turkeys had been put aside," Jason went on. It would have been obvious to the most obtuse listener that his heart wasn't in it. "They hadn't been stolen at all."

"I see, sir," Roberts said. He was tempted to add something about wasting police time being an offense, but decided against it. "So you don't want us to take any further action?"

"No." Jason almost writhed. Further action was what he wanted above almost everything else, but Sheila had made it all too clear that if he didn't drop the whole business she would leave him. She wasn't given to making idle threats, and Jason had believed her. For all his faults, he loved his wife.

It was Miss Crindle who was responsible. He didn't know what she had told Sheila, but whatever it was it had had a marked effect.

In fact, Miss Crindle had said quite simply that she knew who had taken the turkeys and that she hoped Jason's wife would be able to persuade him to drop the whole matter. She looked down at Sheila's feet. Sheila was nearly six feet tall, and her feet were much larger than her sister-in-law's. "It was Colin, wasn't it?" Sheila said.

Miss Crindle smiled enigmatically.

"But—" Sheila looked distraught "—Jason was sure it was Harry. He said she'd talked about the Renwicks and the Randalls and Josie Gardner a few days ago. She said he ought to give them turkeys."

"It was," Miss Crindle said.

"But it can't have been," Sheila protested. "Harry was staying with Pat the night the parcels were left."

"That wasn't her," Miss Crindle agreed.

"Then who?"

"Colin. It was Harriet's idea. She was very angry with Jason and she thought she'd teach him a lesson and help some people to have a better Christmas at the same time. She suggested it to Colin and he jumped at the idea."

"But they'd fallen out," Sheila objected. "She told me they had a terrible row. I still don't see."

"They took it in turns to cover each other," Miss Crindle told her. "First, while Colin was being towed out of that ditch, Harriet was making sure she was seen in her Santa Claus getup at the other end of the village. They want-ed people to talk about Santa Claus being about."

"It's the sort of daft idea that would appeal to them," Sheila agreed mis-erably. "They've never grown up, either of them."

"We can do with a touch of youthful spirits sometimes," Miss Crindle said. "They didn't look on what they were doing as stealing."

"I tried to phone her that afternoon. Mum said she was out."

Miss Crindle nodded. "She knew Jason didn't lock the shed. She went there that night, took the four smallest turkeys, and carried them across the meadow to Colin, who was waiting in his car. She's a strong girl and it wasn't very far. Colin hid them until the next night, then, while Harriet was safe at the Dellars', he delivered them. *He* couldn't have stolen them, because the foot-prints in the snow were too small, and Harriet couldn't have delivered them because she was miles away. There was only one set of prints in the meadow and only one round the Renwicks'. Nobody was looking for two people work-ing alternately."

Sheila stared at her. "Except you," she said. "Whatever made you think of it?"

"Well—" Miss Crindle hesitated, then she smiled. "First, their quarrel was a little too public. Harriet and Colin may be high-spirited, but they wouldn't want to have a real argument with half the village looking on. It was almost as if it were being staged for other people's benefit. And when I saw Harriet just afterward, she didn't seem upset at all. Then her eyelid started twitching. It did it again when she told me she didn't know anything about the turkeys. I *knew* she was involved then."

"Oh," Sheila said, understanding.

"It's always done that when she's telling fibs, ever since she was a little girl at school," Miss Crindle said. "When you're a teacher as long as I was, you don't forget things like that. Then, the footprints at the Renwicks' aren't the same size as the others—they must be tens, at least. I tackled Harriet just now, and she told me the truth."

"Oh," Sheila said again. Uneasily she added, "I wonder what Jason's going to say."

"I'm sure you can manage him," Miss Crindle told her.

Mrs. Grundy laughed. "Then I'll have to get another one," she said cheerfully. "Really, Mr. Richards, it doesn't matter at all. To be frank, a ten-pound turkey would have been far too big for just my husband and me. I'm sure Mrs. Gardner and her children will enjoy it much more. But I must insist you let me pay you for it."

Jason met her eye, then looked away. "No," he said gruffly. "That's all right, Mrs. Grundy, I've written those four birds off. They're a present from us. After all, it's Christmas. "

Mrs. Grundy nearly fainted.

Anthony Boucher

MYSTERY FOR CHRISTMAS

That was why the Benson jewel robbery was solved—because Aram Melekian was too much for Mr. Quilter's temper.

His almost invisible eyebrows soared, and the scalp of his close-cropped head twitched angrily. "Damme!" said Mr. Quilter, and in that mild and archaic oath there was more compressed fury than in paragraphs of uncensored profanity. "So you, sir, are the untrammeled creative artist, and I am a drudging, hampering hack!"

Aram Melekian tilted his hat a trifle more jauntily. "That's the size of it, brother. And if you hamper this untrammeled opus any more, Metropolis Pictures is going to be suing its youngest genius for breach of contract."

Mr. Quilter rose to his full lean height. "I've seen them come and go," he announced; "and there hasn't been a one of them, sir, who failed to learn something from me. What is so creative about pouring out the full vigor of your young life? The creative task is mine, molding that vigor, shaping it to some end."

"Go play with your blue pencil," Melekian suggested. "I've got a dream coming on."

"Because I have never produced anything myself, you young men jeer at me. You never see that your successful screen plays are more my effort than your inspiration." Mr. Quilter's thin frame was aquiver.

"Then what do you need us for?"

"What—Damme, sir, what indeed? Ha!" said Mr. Quilter loudly. "I'll show you. I'll pick the first man off the street that has life and a story in him. What more do you contribute? And through me he'll turn out a job that will sell. If I do this, sir, then will you consent to the revisions I've asked of you?"

"Go lay an egg," said Aram Melekian. "And I've no doubt you will."

Mr. Quilter stalked out of the studio with high dreams. He saw the horny-handed son of toil out of whom he had coaxed a masterpiece signing a contract with F.X. He saw a discomfited Armenian genius in the background

661

busily devouring his own words. He saw himself freed of his own sense of frustration, proving at last that his was the significant part of writing.

He felt a bumping shock and the squealing of brakes. The next thing he saw was the asphalt paving.

Mr. Quilter rose to his feet undecided whether to curse the driver for knocking him down or bless him for stopping so miraculously short of danger. The young man in the brown suit was so disarmingly concerned that the latter choice was inevitable.

"I'm awfully sorry," the young man blurted. "Are you hurt? It's this bad wing of mine, I guess." His left arm was in a sling.

"Nothing at all, sir. My fault. I was preoccupied . . ."

They stood awkwardly for a moment, each striving for a phrase that was not mere politeness. Then they both spoke at once.

"You came out of that studio," the young man said. "Do you" (his tone was awed) "do you *work* there?"

And Mr. Quilter had spotted a sheaf of eight and a half by eleven paper protruding from the young man's pocket. "Are you a writer, sir? Is that a manuscript?"

The young man shuffled and came near blushing. "Naw. I'm not a writer. I'm a policeman. But I'm going to be a writer. This is a story I was trying to tell about what happened to me— But are you a writer? In *there?*"

Mr. Quilter's eyes were aglow under their invisible brows. "I, sir," he announced proudly, "am what makes writers tick. Are you interested?"

He was also, he might have added, what makes *detectives* tick. But he did not know that yet.

The Christmas trees were lighting up in front yards and in windows as Officer Tom Smith turned his rickety Model A onto the side street where Mr. Quilter lived. Hollywood is full of these quiet streets, where ordinary people live and move and have their being, and are happy or unhappy as chance wills, but both in a normal and unspectacular way. This is really Hollywood— the Hollywood that patronizes the twenty-cent fourth-run houses and crowds the stores on the Boulevard on Dollar Day.

To Mr. Quilter, saturated at the studio with the other Hollywood, this was always a relief. Kids were playing ball in the evening sun, radios were tuning in to Amos and Andy, and from the small houses came either the smell of cooking or the clatter of dish-washing.

And the Christmas trees, he knew, had been decorated not for the benefit of the photographers from the fan magazines, but because the children liked them and they looked warm and friendly from the street.

"Gosh, Mr. Quilter," Tom Smith was saying, "this is sure a swell break for me. You know, I'm a good copper. But to be honest I don't know as I'm very bright. And that's why I want to write, because maybe that way I can train myself to be and then I won't be a plain patrolman all my life. And besides, this writing, it kind of itches-like inside you."

"*Cacoëthes scribendi,*" observed Mr. Quilter, not unkindly. "You see, sir, you have hit, in your fumbling way, on one of the classic expressions for your condition."

"Now that's what I mean. You know what I mean even when I don't say it. Between us, Mr. Quilter . . . "

Mr. Quilter, his long thin legs outdistancing even the policeman's, led the way into his bungalow and on down the hall to a room which at first glance contained nothing but thousands of books. Mr. Quilter waved at them. "Here, sir, is assembled every helpful fact that mortal need know. But I cannot breathe life into these dry bones. Books are not written from books. But I can provide bones, and correctly articulated, for the life which you, sir— But here is a chair. And a reading lamp. Now, sir, let me hear your story."

Tom Smith shifted uncomfortably on the chair. "The trouble is," he confessed, "it hasn't got an ending."

Mr. Quilter beamed. "When I have heard it, I shall demonstrate to you, sir, the one ending it inevitably must have."

"I sure hope you will, because it's got to have and I promised her it would have and— You know Beverly Benson?"

"Why, yes. I entered the industry at the beginning of talkies. She was still somewhat in evidence. But why . . . ?"

"I was only a kid when she made *Sable Sin* and *Orchids at Breakfast* and all the rest, and I thought she was something pretty marvelous. There was a girl in our high school was supposed to look like her, and I used to think, 'Gee, if I could ever see the real Beverly Benson!' And last night I did."

"Hm. And this story, sir, is the result?"

"Yeah. And this too." He smiled wryly and indicated his wounded arm. "But I better read you the story." He cleared his throat loudly. *"The Red and Green Mystery,"* he declaimed. "By Arden Van Arden."

"A pseudonym, sir?"

"Well, I sort of thought . . . Tom Smith—that doesn't sound like a writer."

"Arden Van Arden, sir, doesn't sound like anything. But go on."

And Officer Tom Smith began his narrative:

THE RED AND GREEN MYSTERY

by ARDEN VAN ARDEN

It was a screwy party for the police to bust in on. Not that it was a raid or anything like that. God knows I've run into some bughouse parties that way, but I'm assigned to the jewelry squad now under Lieutenant Michaels, and when this call came in he took three other guys and me and we shot out to the big house in Laurel Canyon.

I wasn't paying much attention to where we were going and I wouldn't have known the place anyway, but I knew *her*, all right. She was standing in the doorway waiting for us. For just a minute it stumped me who she was, but then I knew. It was the eyes mostly. She'd changed a lot since *Sable Sin*, but you still couldn't miss the Beverly Benson eyes. The rest of her had got older (not older exactly either—you might maybe say richer) but the eyes were still the same. She had red hair. They didn't have technicolor when she was in pictures and I hadn't even known what color her hair was. It struck me funny seeing her like that—the way I'd been nuts about her when I was a kid and not even knowing what color her hair was.

She had on a funny dress—a little-girl kind of thing with a short skirt with flounces, I guess you call them. It looked familiar, but I couldn't make it. Not until I saw the mask that was lying in the hall, and then I knew. She was dressed like Minnie Mouse. It turned out later they all were—not like Minnie Mouse, but like all the characters in the cartoons. It was that kind of a party— a Disney Christmas party. There were studio drawings all over the walls, and there were little figures of extinct animals and winged ponies holding the lights on the Christmas tree.

She came right to the point. I could see Michaels liked that; some of these women throw a big act and it's an hour before you know what's been stolen. "It's my emeralds and rubies," she said. "They're gone. There are some other pieces missing too, but I don't so much care about them. The emeralds and the rubies are the important thing. You've got to find them."

"Necklaces?" Michaels asked.

"A necklace."

"Of emeralds *and* rubies?" Michaels knows his jewelry. His old man is in the business and tried to bring him up in it, but he joined the force. He knows a thing or two just the same, and his left eyebrow does tricks when he hears or sees something that isn't kosher. It was doing tricks now.

"I know that may sound strange, Lieutenant, but this is no time for discussing the esthetics of jewelry. It struck me once that it would be exciting to have red and green in one necklace, and I had it made. They're perfectly cut and matched, and it could never be duplicated."

Michaels didn't look happy. "You could drape it on a Christmas tree," he said. But Beverly Benson's Christmas tree was a cold white with the little animals holding blue lights.

Those Benson eyes were generally lovely and melting. Now they flashed. "Lieutenant, I summoned you to find my jewelry, not to criticize my taste. If I wanted a cultural opinion, I should hardly consult the police."

"You could do worse," Michaels said. "Now tell us all about it."

She took us into the library. The other men Michaels sent off to guard the exits, even if there wasn't much chance of the thief still sticking around. The Lieutenant told me once, when we were off duty, "Tom," he said, "you're the most useful man in my detail. Some of the others can think, and some of them can act; but there's not a damned one of them can just stand there and look so much like the Law." He's a little guy himself and kind of on the smooth and dapper side; so he keeps me with him to back him up, just standing there.

There wasn't much to what she told us. Just that she was giving this Disney Christmas party, like I said, and it was going along fine. Then late in the evening, when almost everybody had gone home, they got to talking about jewelry. She didn't know who started the talk that way, but there they were. And she told them about the emeralds and rubies.

"Then Fig—Philip Newton, you know—the photographer who does all those marvelous sand dunes and magnolia blossoms and things—" (her voice went all sort of tender when she mentioned him, and I could see Michaels taking it all in) "Fig said he didn't believe it. He felt the same way you do, Lieutenant, and I'm sure I can't see why. 'It's unworthy of you, darling,' he said. So I laughed and tried to tell him they were really beautiful—for they are, you know—and when he went on scoffing I said, 'All right, then, I'll show you.' So I went into the little dressing room where I keep my jewel box, and they weren't there. And that's all I know."

Then Michaels settled down to questions. When had she last seen the necklace? Was the lock forced? Had there been any prowlers around? What else was missing? And suchlike.

Beverly Benson answered impatiently, like she expected us to just go out there like that and grab the thief and say, "Here you are, lady." She had shown the necklace to another guest early in the party—he'd gone home long ago, but she gave us the name and address to check. No, the lock hadn't been forced. They hadn't seen anything suspicious, either. There were some small things missing, too—a couple of diamond rings, a star sapphire pendant, a pair of pearl earrings—but those didn't worry her so much. It was the emerald and ruby necklace that she wanted.

That left eyebrow went to work while Michaels thought about what she'd said. "If the lock wasn't forced, that lets out a chance prowler. It was somebody who knew you, who'd had a chance to lift your key or take an impression of it. Where'd you keep it?"

"The key? In my handbag usually. Tonight it was in a box on my dressing table."

Michaels sort of groaned. "And women wonder why jewels get stolen! Smith, get Ferguson and have him go over the box for prints. In the meantime, Miss Benson, give me a list of all your guests tonight. We'll take up the servants later. I'm warning you now it's a ten-to-one chance you'll ever see your Christmas tree ornament again unless a fence sings; but we'll do what we can. Then I'll deliver my famous little lecture on safes, and we'll pray for the future."

When I'd seen Ferguson, I waited for Michaels in the room where the guests were. There were only five left, and I didn't know who they were yet. They'd all taken off their masks; but they still had on their cartoon costumes. It felt screwy to sit there among them and think: This is serious, this is a felony, and look at those bright funny costumes.

Donald Duck was sitting by himself, with one hand resting on his long-billed mask while the other made steady grabs for the cigarette box beside him. His face looked familiar; I thought maybe I'd seen him in bits.

Three of them sat in a group: Mickey Mouse, Snow White, and Dopey. Snow White looked about fourteen at first, and it took you a while to realize she was a woman and a swell one at that. She was a little brunette, slender and cool-looking—a simple real kind of person that didn't seem to belong in a Hollywood crowd. Mickey Mouse was a hefty blond guy about as tall as I am and built like a tackle that could hold any line; but his face didn't go with his body. It was shrewd-like, and what they call sensitive. Dopey looked just that—a nice guy and not too bright.

Then over in another corner was a Little Pig. I don't know do they have names, but this was the one that wears a sailor suit and plays the fiddle. He had bushy hair sticking out from under the sailor cap and long skillful-looking hands stretched in front of him. The fiddle was beside him, but he didn't touch it. He was passed out—dead to the world, close as I could judge.

He and Donald were silent, but the group of three talked a little.

"I guess it didn't work," Dopey said.

"You couldn't help that, Harvey." Snow White's voice was just like I expected—not like Snow White's in the picture, but deep and smooth, like a stream that's running in the shade with moss on its banks. "Even an agent can't cast people."

"You're a swell guy, Madison," Mickey Mouse said. "You tried, and thanks. But if it's no go, hell, it's just no go. It's up to her."

"Miss Benson is surely more valuable to your career." The running stream was ice cold.

Now maybe I haven't got anything else that'd make me a good detective, but I do have curiosity, and here's where I saw a way to satisfy it. I spoke to all of them and I said, "I'd better take down some information while we're waiting for the Lieutenant." I started on Donald Duck. "Name?"

"Daniel Wappingham." The voice was English. I could tell that much. I don't have such a good ear for stuff like that, but I thought maybe it wasn't the best English.

"Occupation?"

"Actor."

And I took down the address and the rest of it. Then I turned to the drunk and shook him. He woke up part way but he didn't hear what I was saying. He just threw his head back and said loudly, "Waltzes! Ha!" and went under again. His voice was guttural—some kind of German, I guessed. I let it go at that and went over to the three.

Dopey's name was Harvey Madison; occupation, actor's representative— tenpercenter to you. Mickey Mouse was Philip Newton; occupation, photographer. (That was the guy Beverly Benson mentioned, the one she sounded thataway about.) And Snow White was Jane Newton.

"Any relation?" I asked.

"Yes and no," she said, so soft I could hardly hear her.

"Mrs. Newton," Mickey Mouse stated, "was once my wife." And the silence was so strong you could taste it.

I got it then. The two of them sitting there, remembering all the little things of their life together, being close to each other and yet somehow held apart. And on Christmas, too, when you remember things. There was still something between them even if they didn't admit it themselves. But Beverly Benson seemed to have a piece of the man, and where did Dopey fit in?

It sort of worried me. They looked like swell people—people that belonged together. But it was my job to worry about the necklace and not about people's troubles. I was glad Michaels came in just then.

He was being polite at the moment, explaining to Beverly Benson how Ferguson hadn't got anywhere with the prints and how the jewels were probably miles away by now. "But we'll do what we can," he said. "We'll talk to these people and find out what's possible. I doubt, however, if you'll ever see that necklace again. It was insured, of course, Miss Benson?"

"Of course. So were the other things, and with them I don't mind. But this necklace I couldn't conceivably duplicate, Lieutenant."

Just then Michael's eye lit on Donald Duck, and the eyebrow did tricks worth putting in a cartoon. "We'll take you one by one," he said. "You with the tail-feathers, we'll start with you. Come along, Smith."

Donald Duck grabbed a fresh cigarette, thought a minute, then reached out again for a handful. He whistled off key and followed us into the library.

"I gave all the material to your stooge here, Lieutenant," he began. "Name, Wappingham. Occupation, actor. Address—"

Michaels was getting so polite it had me bothered. "You won't mind, sir," he purred, "if I suggest a few corrections in your statement?"

Donald looked worried. "Don't you think I know my own name?"

"Possibly. But would you mind if I altered the statement to read: Name, Alfred Higgins. Occupation, jewel thief—conceivably reformed?"

The Duck wasn't so bad hit as you might have thought. He let out a pretty fair laugh and said, "So the fat's in the fire at last. But I'm glad you concede the possibility of my having reformed."

"The possibility, yes." Michaels underlined the word. "You admit you're Higgins?"

"Why not? You can't blame me for not telling you right off; it wouldn't look good when somebody had just been up to my old tricks. But now that you know— And by the way, Lieutenant, just how do you know?"

"Some bright boy at Scotland Yard spotted you in an American picture. Sent your description and record out to us just in case you ever took up your career again."

"Considerate of him, wasn't it?"

But Michaels wasn't in a mood for bright chatter any longer. We got down to work. We stripped that duck costume off the actor and left him shivering while we went over it inch by inch. He didn't like it much.

At last Michaels let him get dressed again. "You came in your car?"

"Yes."

"You're going home in a taxi. We could hold you on suspicion, but I'd sooner play it this way."

"Now I understand," Donald said, "what they mean by the high-handed American police procedure." And he went back into the other room with us.

All the same that was a smart move of Michaels'. It meant that Wappingham-Higgins-Duck would either have to give up all hope of the jewels (he certainly didn't have them on him) or lead us straight to them, because of course I knew a tail would follow that taxi and camp on his doorstep all next week if need be.

Donald Duck said goodnight to his hostess and nodded to the other guests. Then he picked up his mask.

"Just a minute," Michaels said. "Let's have a look at that."

"At this?" he asked innocent-like and backed toward the French window. Then he was standing there with an automatic in his hand. It was little but damned nasty-looking. I never thought what a good holster that long bill would make.

"Stay where you are, gentlemen," he said calmly. "I'm leaving undisturbed, *if* you don't mind."

The room was frozen still. Beverly Benson and Snow White let out little

668

gasps of terror. The drunk was still dead to the world. The other two men looked at us and did nothing. It was Donald's round.

Or would've been if I hadn't played football in high school. It was a crazy chance, but I took it. I was the closest to him, only his eyes were on Michaels. It was a good flying tackle and it brought him to the ground in a heap consisting mostly of me. The mask smashed as we rolled over on it and I saw bright glitters pouring out.

Ferguson and O'Hara were there by now. One of them picked up his gun and the other snapped on the handcuffs. I got to my feet and turned to Michaels and Beverly Benson. They began to say things both at once about what a swell thing I'd done and then I keeled over.

When I came to I was on a couch in a little dark room. I learned later it was the dressing room where the necklace had been stolen. Somebody was bathing my arm and sobbing.

I sort of half sat up and said, "Where am I?" I always thought it was just in stories people said that, but it was the first thing popped into my mind.

"You're all right," a cool voice told me. "It's only a flesh wound."

"And I didn't feel a thing. . . . You mean he winged me?"

"I guess that's what you call it. When I told the Lieutenant I was a nurse he said I could fix you up and they wouldn't need the ambulance. You're all right now." Her voice was shaky in the dark, but I knew it was Snow White.

"Well, anyways, that broke the case pretty quick."

"But it didn't." And she explained: Donald had been up to his old tricks, all right; but what he had hidden in his bill was the diamonds and the sapphire and the pearl earrings, only no emerald and ruby necklace. Beverly Benson was wild, and Michaels and our men were combing the house from top to bottom to see where he'd stashed it.

"There," she said. She finished the story and the bandaging at the same time. "Can you stand up all right now?"

I was still kind of punchy. Nothing else could excuse me for what I said next. But she was so sweet and tender and good I wanted to say something nice, so like a dumb jerk I up and said, "You'd make some man a grand wife."

That was what got her. She just went to pieces—dissolved, you might say. I'm not used to tears on the shoulder of my uniform, but what could I do? I didn't try to say anything—just patted her back and let her talk. And I learned all about it.

How she'd married Philip Newton back in '29 when he was a promising young architect and she was an heiress just out of finishing school. How the fortune she was heiress to went fooey like all the others and her father took the quick way out. How the architect business went all to hell with no building going on and just when things were worst she had a baby. And then how

669

Philip started drinking, and finally— Well, anyways, there it was.

They'd both pulled themselves together now. She was making enough as a nurse to keep the kid (she was too proud to take alimony), and Philip was doing fine in this arty photographic line he'd taken up. A Newton photograph was The Thing to Have in the smart Hollywood set. But they couldn't come together again, not while he was such a success. If she went to him, he'd think she was begging; if he came to her, she'd think he was being noble. And Beverly Benson had set her cap for him.

Then this agent Harvey Madison (that's Dopey), who had known them both when, decided to try and fix things. He brought Snow White to this party; neither of them knew the other would be here. And it was a party and it was Christmas, and some of their happiest memories were Christmases together. I guess that's pretty much true of everybody. So she felt everything all over again, only—

"You don't know what it's done for me to tell you this. Please don't feel hurt; but in that uniform and everything you don't seem quite like a person. I can talk and feel free. And this has been hurting me all night and I had to say it."

I wanted to take the two of them and knock their heads together; only first off I had to find that emerald and ruby necklace. It isn't my job to heal broken hearts. I was feeling O.K. now, so we went back to the others.

Only they weren't there. There wasn't anybody in the room but only the drunk. I guessed where Mickey and Dopey were: stripped and being searched.

"Who's that?" I asked Snow White.

She looked at the Little Pig. "Poor fellow. He's been going through torture tonight too. That's Bela Strauss."

"Bella's a woman's name."

"He's part Hungarian." (I guess that might explain anything.) "He comes from Vienna. They brought him out here to write music for pictures because his name is Strauss. But he's a very serious composer—you know, like . . ." and she said some tongue twisters that didn't mean anything to me. "They think because his name is Strauss he can write all sorts of pretty dance tunes, and they won't let him write anything else. It's made him all twisted and unhappy, and he drinks too much."

"I can see that." I walked over and shook him. The sailor cap fell off. He stirred and looked up at me. I think it was the uniform that got him. He sat up sharp and said something in I guess German. Then he thought around a while and found some words in English.

"Why are you here? Why the police?" It came out in little one-syllable lumps, like he had to hunt hard for each sound. I told him. I tried to make it simple, but that wasn't easy. Snow White knew a little German, so she helped.

"Ach!" he sighed. "And I through it all slept!"

"That's one word for it," I said.

But this thief of jewels—him I have seen." It was a sweet job to get it out of him, but it boiled down to this: Where he passed out was on that same couch where they took me—right in the dressing-room. He came to once when he heard somebody in there, and he saw the person take something out of a box. Something red and green.

"Who was it?"

"The face, you understand, I do not see it. But the costume, yes. I see that clear. It was Mikki Maus." It sounded funny to hear something as American as Mickey Mouse in an accent like that.

It took Snow White a couple of seconds to realize who wore the Mickey Mouse outfit. Then she said "Philip" and fainted.

Officer Tom Smith laid down his manuscript. "That's all, Mr. Quilter."

"All, sir?"

"When Michaels came in, I told him. He figured Newton must've got away with the necklace and then the English crook made his try later and got the other stuff. They didn't find the necklace anywhere; but he must've pulled a fast one and stashed it away some place. With direct evidence like that, what can you do? They're holding him."

"And you chose, sir, not to end your story on that note of finality?"

"I couldn't, Mr. Quilter. I . . . I like that girl who was Snow White. I want to see the two of them together again and I'd sooner he was innocent. And besides, when we were leaving, Beverly Benson caught me alone. She said, 'I can't talk to your Lieutenant. He is *not* sympathetic. But you . . .' " Tom Smith almost blushed. "So she went on about how certain she was that Newton was innocent and begged me to help her prove it. So I promised."

"Hm," said Mr. Quilter. "Your problem, sir, is simple. You have good human values there in your story. Now we must round them out properly. And the solution is simple. We have two women in love with the hero, one highly sympathetic and the other less so; for the spectacle of a *passée* actress pursuing a new celebrity is not a pleasant one. This less sympathetic woman, to please the audience, must redeem herself with a gesture of self-immolation to secure the hero's happiness with the heroine. Therefore, sir, let her confess to the robbery."

"Confess to the . . . But Mr. Quilter, that makes a different story out of it. I'm trying to write as close as I can to what happened. And I promised—"

"Damme, sir, it's obvious. She did steal the necklace herself. She hasn't worked for years. She must need money. You mentioned insurance. The necklace was probably pawned long ago, and now she is trying to collect."

"But that won't work. It really was stolen. Somebody saw it earlier in the evening, and the search didn't locate it. And believe me, that squad knows how to search."

"Fiddle-faddle, sir." Mr. Quilter's close-cropped scalp was beginning to twitch. "What was seen must have been a paste imitation. She could dissolve that readily in acid and dispose of it down the plumbing. And Wappingham's presence makes her plot doubly sure; she knew him for what he was, and invited him as a scapegoat."

Tom Smith squirmed. "I'd almost think you were right, Mr. Quilter. Only Bela Strauss did see Newton take the necklace."

Mr. Quilter laughed. "If that is all that perturbs you . . ." He rose to his feet. "Come with me, sir. One of my neighbors is a Viennese writer now acting as a reader in German for Metropolis. He is also new in this country; his cultural background is identical with Strauss's. Come. But first we must step down to the corner drugstore and purchase what I believe is termed a comic book."

Mr. Quilter, his eyes agleam, hardly apologized for their intrusion into the home of the Viennese writer. He simply pointed at a picture in the comic book and demanded, "Tell me, sir. What character is that?"

The bemused Viennese smiled. "Why, that is Mikki Maus."

Mr. Quilter's finger rested on a pert little drawing of Minnie.

Philip Newton sat in the cold jail cell, but he was oblivious of the cold. He was holding his wife's hands through the bars and she was saying, "I could come to you now, dear, where I couldn't before. Then you might have thought it was just because you were successful, but now I can tell you how much I love you and need you—need you even when you're in disgrace. . . ."

They were kissing through the bars when Michaels came with the good news. "She's admitted it, all right. It was just the way Smith reconstructed it. She'd destroyed the paste replica and was trying to use us to pull off an insurance frame. She cracked when we had Strauss point out a picture of what he called 'Mikki Maus.' So you're free again, Newton. How's that for a Christmas present?"

"I've got a better one, officer. We're getting married again."

"You wouldn't need a new wedding ring, would you?" Michaels asked with filial devotion. "Michaels, Fifth between Spring and Broadway—fine stock."

Mr. Quilter laid down the final draft of Tom Smith's story, complete now with ending, and fixed the officer with a reproachful gaze. "You omitted, sir, the explanation of why such a misunderstanding should arise."

Tom Smith shifted uncomfortably. "I'm afraid, Mr. Quilter, I couldn't remember all that straight."

"It is simple. The noun *Maus* in German is of feminine gender. Therefore a *Mikki Maus* is a female. The male, naturally, is a *Mikki Mäserich*. I recall a delightful Viennese song of some seasons ago, which we once employed as background music, wherein the singer declares that he and his beloved will be forever paired, '*wie die Mikki Mikki Mikki Mikki Mikki Maus und der Mikki Mäserich.*' "

"Gosh," said Tom Smith. "You know a lot of things."

Mr. Quilter allowed himself to beam. "Between us, sir, there should be little that we do not know."

"We sure make a swell team as a detective."

The beam faded. "As a detective? Damme, sir, do you think I cared about your robbery? I simply explained the inevitable denouement to this story."

"But she didn't confess and make a gesture. Michaels had to prove it on her."

"All the better, sir. That makes her mysterious and deep. A Bette Davis role. I think we will first try for a magazine sale on this. Studios are more impressed by matter already in print. Then I shall show it to F.X., and we shall watch the squirmings of that genius Aram Melekian."

Tom Smith looked out the window, frowning. They made a team, all right; but which way? He still itched to write, but the promotion Michaels had promised him sounded good, too. Were he and this strange lean old man a team for writing or for detection?

The friendly red and green lights of the neighborhood Christmas trees seemed an equally good omen either way.

Margery Allingham

THE CASE IS ALTERED

$\mathbf{M}$r. Albert Campion, sitting in a first-class smoking compartment, was just reflecting sadly that an atmosphere of stultifying decency could make even Christmas something of a stuffed-owl occasion, when a new hogskin suitcase of distinctive design hit him on the knees. At the same moment a golf bag bruised the shins of the shy young man opposite, an armful of assorted magazines burst over the pretty girl in the far corner, and a blast of icy air swept round the carriage. There was the familiar rattle and lurch which indicates that the train has started at last, a squawk from a receding porter, and Lance Feering arrived before him apparently by rocket.

"Caught it," said the newcomer with the air of one confidently expecting congratulations, but as the train bumped jerkily he teetered back on his heels and collapsed between the two young people on the opposite seat.

"My dear chap, so we noticed," murmured Campion, and he smiled apologetically at the girl, now disentangling herself from the shellburst of newsprint. It was his own disarming my-poor-friend-is-afflicted variety of smile that he privately considered infallible, but on this occasion it let him down.

The girl, who was in the early twenties and was slim and fair, with eyes like licked brandy-balls, as Lance Feering inelegantly put it afterward, regarded him with grave interest. She stacked the magazines into a neat bundle and placed them on the seat opposite before returning to her own book. Even Mr. Feering, who was in one of his more exuberant moods, was aware of that chilly protest. He began to apologize.

Campion had known Feering in his student days, long before he had become one of the foremost designers of stage decors in Europe, and was used to him, but now even he was impressed. Lance's apologies were easy but also abject. He collected his bag, stowed it on a clear space on the rack above the shy young man's head, thrust his golf things under the seat, positively blushed when he claimed his magazines, and regarded the girl with pathetic humility. She glanced at him when he spoke, nodded coolly with just enough graciousness not to be gauche, and turned over a page.

Campion was secretly amused. At the top of his form Lance was reputed to be irresistible. His dark face with the long mournful nose and bright eyes were unhandsome enough to be interesting, and the quick gestures of his short painter's hands made his conversation picturesque. His singular lack of success on this occasion clearly astonished him and he sat back in his corner eyeing the young woman with covert mistrust.

Campion resettled himself to the two hours' rigid silence which etiquette demands from firstclass travelers who, although they are more than probably going to be asked to dance a reel together if not to share a bathroom only a few hours hence, have not yet been introduced.

There was no way of telling if the shy young man and the girl with the brandy-ball eyes knew each other, and whether they too were en route for Underhill, Sir Philip Cookham's Norfolk place. Campion was inclined to regard the coming festivities with a certain amount of lugubrious curiosity. Cookham himself was a magnificent old boy, of course, "one of the more valuable pieces in the Cabinet," as someone had once said of him, but Florence was a different kettle of fish. Born to wealth and breeding, she had grown blasé towards both of them and now took her delight in notabilities, a dangerous affectation in Campion's experience. She was some sort of remote aunt of his.

He glanced again at the young people, caught the boy unaware, and was immediately interested.

The illustrated magazine had dropped from the young man's hand and he was looking out of the window, his mouth drawn down at the corners and a narrow frown between his thick eyebrows. It was not an unattractive face, too young for strong character but decent and open enough in the ordinary way. At that particular moment, however, it wore a revealing expression. There was recklessness in the twist of the mouth and sullenness in the eyes, while the hand which lay upon the inside arm rest was clenched.

Campion was curious. Young people do not usually go away for Christmas in this top-step-at-the-dentist's frame of mind. The girl looked up from her book.

"How far is Underhill from the station?" she inquired.

"Five miles. They'll meet us." The shy young man turned to her so easily and with such obvious affection that any romantic theory Campion might have formed was knocked on the head instantly. The youngster's troubles evidently had nothing to do with love.

Lance had raised his head with bright-eyed interest at the gratuitous information and now a faintly sardonic expression appeared upon his lips. Campion sighed for him. For a man who fell in and out of love with the abandonment of a seal round a pool, Lance Feering was an impossible optimist. Already he was regarding the girl with that shy despair which so many ladies had found too piteous to be allowed to persist. Campion washed his hands of him and turned away just in time to notice a stranger glancing in at them from the corridor. It was a dark and arrogant young face and he recognized it instantly, feeling at the same time a deep wave of sympathy for old Cookham. Florence, he gathered, had done it again.

Young Victor Preen, son of old Preen of the Preen Aero Company, was certainly notable, not to say notorious. He had obtained much publicity in his short life for his sensational flights, but a great deal more for adventures less creditable; and when angry old gentlemen in the armchairs of exclusive clubs let themselves go about the blackguardliness of the younger generation, it was very often of Victor Preen that they were thinking.

He stood now a little to the left of the compartment window, leaning idly against the wall, his chin up and his heavy lids drooping. At first sight he did not appear to be taking any interest in the occupants of the compartment, but when the shy young man looked up, Campion happened to see the swift glance of recognition, and of something else, which passed between them. Presently, still with the same elaborate casualness, the man in the corridor wandered away, leaving the other staring in front of him, the same sullen expression still in his eyes.

The incident passed so quickly that it was impossible to define the exact nature of that second glance, but Campion was never a man to go imagining things, which was why he was surprised when they arrived at Minstree station to hear Henry Boule, Florence's private secretary, introducing the two and to notice that they met as strangers.

It was pouring with rain as they came out of the station, and Boule, who, like all Florence's secretaries, appeared to be suffering from an advanced case of nerves, bundled them all into two big Daimlers, a smaller car, and a shooting-brake. Campion looked round him at Florence's Christmas bag with some dismay. She had surpassed herself. Besides Lance there were at least half a dozen celebrities: a brace of political highlights, an angry looking lady novelist, Madja from the ballet, a startled R. A., and Victor Preen, as well as some twelve or thirteen unfamiliar faces who looked as if they might belong to Art, Money, or even mere Relations.

Campion became separated from Lance and was looking for him anxiously when he saw him at last in one of the cars, with the novelist on one side and the girl with brandy-ball eyes on the other, Victor Preen making up the ill-assorted four.

Since Campion was an unassuming sort of person he was relegated to the brake with Boule himself, the shy young man, and the whole of the luggage. Boule introduced them awkwardly and collapsed into a seat, wiping the beads from off his forehead with a relief which was a little too blatant to be tactful.

Campion, who had learned that the shy young man's name was Peter Groome, made a tentative inquiry of him as they sat jolting shoulder to shoulder in the back of the car. He nodded.

"Yes, it's the same family," he said. "Cookham's sister married a brother of my father's. I'm some sort of relation, I suppose."

The prospect did not seem to fill him with any great enthusiasm and once again Campion's curiosity was piqued. Young Mr. Groome was certainly not in seasonable mood.

In the ordinary way Campion would have dismissed the matter from his mind, but there was something about the youngster which attracted him, something indefinable and of a despairing quality, and moreover, there had been that curious intercepted glance in the train.

They talked in a desultory fashion throughout the uncomfortable journey. Campion learned that young Groome was in his father's firm of solicitors, that he was engaged to be married to the girl with the brandy-ball eyes, who was a Miss Patricia Bullard of an old north country family, and that he thought Christmas was a waste of time.

"I hate it," he said with a sudden passionate intensity which startled even his mild inquisitor. "All this sentimental good-will-to-all-men business is false and sickening. There's no such thing as good will. The world's rotten."

He blushed as soon as he had spoken and turned away.

"I'm sorry," he murmured, "but all this bogus Dickensian stuff makes me writhe."

Campion made no direct comment. Instead he asked with affable inconsequence, "Was that young Victor Preen I saw in the other car?"

Peter Groome turned his head and regarded him with the steady stare of the willfully obtuse.

"I was introduced to someone with a name like that, I think," he said carefully. "He was a little baldish man, wasn't he?"

"No, that's Sir George." The secretary leaned over the luggage to give the information. "Preen is the tall young man, rather handsome, with the very curling hair. He's *the* Preen, you know." He sighed. "It seems very young to be a millionaire, doesn't it?"

"Obscenely so," said Mr. Peter Groome abruptly, and returned to his despairing contemplation of the landscape.

Underhill was *en fête* to receive them. As soon as Campion observed the preparations, his sympathy for young Mr. Groome increased, for to a jaundiced eye Lady Florence's display might well have proved as dispiriting as Preen's bank balance. Florence had "gone all Dickens," as she said herself at the top of her voice, linking her arm through Campion's, clutching the R. A. with her free

677

hand, and capturing Lance with a bright birdlike eye.

The great Jacobean house was festooned with holly. An eighteen-foot tree stood in the great hall. Yule logs blazed on iron dogs in the wide hearths and already the atmosphere was thick with that curious Christmas smell which is part cigar smoke and part roasting food.

Sir Philip Cookham stood receiving his guests with pathetic bewilderment. Every now and again his features broke into a smile of genuine welcome as he saw a face he knew. He was a distinguished-looking old man with a fine head and eyes permanently worried by his country's troubles.

"My dear boy, delighted to see you. Delighted," he said, grasping Campion's hand. "I'm afraid you've been put over in the Dower House. Did Florence tell you? She said you wouldn't mind, but I insisted that Feering went over there with you and also young Peter." He sighed and brushed away the visitor's hasty reassurances. "I don't know why the dear girl never feels she has a party unless the house is so overcrowded that our best friends have to sleep in the annex," he said sadly.

The "dear girl," looking not more than fifty-five of her sixty years, was clinging to the arm of the lady novelist at that particular moment and the two women were emitting mirthless parrot cries at each other. Cookham smiled.

"She's happy, you know," he said indulgently. "She enjoys this sort of thing. Unfortunately I have a certain amount of urgent work to do this weekend, but we'll get in a chat, Campion, some time over the holiday. I want to hear your news. You're a lucky fellow. You can tell your adventures."

The lean man grimaced. "More secret sessions, sir?" he inquired.

The cabinet minister threw up his hands in a comic but expressive little gesture before he turned to greet the next guest.

As he dressed for dinner in his comfortable room in the small Georgian dower house across the park, Campion was inclined to congratulate himself on his quarters. Underhill itself was a little too much of the ancient monument for strict comfort.

He had reached the tie stage when Lance appeared. He came in very elegant indeed and highly pleased with himself. Campion diagnosed the symptoms immediately and remained irritatingly incurious.

Lance sat down before the open fire and stretched his sleek legs.

"It's not even as if I were a goodlooking blighter, you know," he observed invitingly when the silence had become irksome to him. "In fact, Campion, when I consider myself I simply can't understand it. Did I so much as speak to the girl?"

"I don't know," said Campion, concentrating on his dressing. "Did you?"

"No." Lance was passionate in his denial. "Not a word. The hard-faced female with the inky fingers and the walrus mustache was telling me her life story all the way home in the car. This dear little poppet with the eyes was nothing more than a warm bundle at my side. I give you my dying oath on that. And yet—well, it's extraordinary, isn't it?"

Campion did not turn round. He could see the artist quite well through the mirror in front of him. Lance had a sheet of notepaper in his hand and was regarding it with that mixture of feigned amusement and secret delight which was typical of his eternally youthful spirit.

"Extraordinary," he repeated, glancing at Campion's unresponsive back. "She had nice eyes. Like licked brandy-balls."

"Exactly," agreed the lean man by the dressing table. "I thought she seemed 'very taken up with her fiancé, young Master Groome, though," he added tactlessly.

"Well, I noticed that, you know," Lance admitted, forgetting his professions of disinterest. "She hardly recognized my existence in the train. Still, there's absolutely no accounting for women. I've studied 'em all my life and never understood 'em yet. I mean to say, take this case in point. That kid ignored me, avoided me, looked through me. And yet look at this. I found it in my room when I came up to change just now."

Campion took the note with a certain amount of distaste. Lovely women were invariably stooping to folly, it seemed, but even so he could not accustom himself to the spectacle. The message was very brief. He read it at a glance and for the first time that day he was conscious of that old familiar flicker down the spine as his experienced nose smelled trouble. He re-read the three lines.

"There is a sundial on a stone pavement just off the drive. We saw it from the car. I'll wait ten minutes there for you half an hour after the party breaks up tonight."

There was neither signature nor initial, and the summons broke off as baldly as it had begun.

"Amazing, isn't it?" Lance had the grace to look shamefaced.

"Astounding." Campion's tone was flat. "Staggering, old boy. Er—fishy."

"Fishy?"

"Yes, don't you think so?" Campion was turning over the single sheet thoughtfully and there was no amusement in the pale eyes behind his horn-rimmed spectacles. "How did it arrive?"

"In an unaddressed envelope. I don't suppose she caught my name. After all, there must be some people who don't know it yet." Lance was grinning impudently. "She's batty, of course. Not safe out and all the rest of it. But I liked her eyes and she's very young."

Campion perched himself on the edge of the table. He was still very serious.

"It's disturbing, isn't it?" he said. "Not nice. Makes one wonder."

"Oh, I don't know." Lance retrieved his property and tucked it into his pocket. "She's young and foolish, and it's Christmas."

Campion did not appear to have heard him. "I wonder," he said. "I should keep the appointment, I think. It may be unwise to interfere, but yes, I rather think I should."

"You're telling me." Lance was laughing. "I may be wrong, of course," he added defensively, "but I think that's a cry for help. The poor girl evidently saw that I looked a dependable sort of chap and—er—having her back against the wall for some reason or other she turned instinctively to the stranger with the kind face. Isn't that how you read it?"

"Since you press me, no. Not exactly," said Campion, and as they walked over to the house together he remained thoughtful and irritatingly uncommunicative.

Florence Cookham excelled herself that evening. Her guests were exhorted "to be young again," with the inevitable result that Underhill contained a company of irritated and exhausted people long before midnight.

One of her ladyship's more erroneous beliefs was that she was a born organizer, and that the real secret of entertaining people lay in giving everyone something to do. Thus Lance and the R. A.—now even more startled-looking than ever—found themselves superintending the decoration of the great tree, while the girl with the brandy-ball eyes conducted a small informal dance in the drawing room, the lady novelist scowled over the bridge table, and the ballet star refused flatly to arrange amateur theatricals.

Only two people remained exempt from this tyranny. One was Sir Philip himself, who looked in every now and again, ready to plead urgent work awaiting him in his study whenever his wife pounced upon him, and the other was Mr. Campion, who had work to do on his own account and had long mastered the difficult art of self-effacement. Experience had taught him that half the secret of this maneuver was to keep discreetly on the move and he strolled from one part to another, always ready to look as if he belonged to any one of them should his hostess's eye ever come to rest upon him inquiringly.

For once his task was comparatively simple. Florence was in her element as she rushed about surrounded by breathless assistants, and at one period the very air in her vicinity seemed to have become thick with colored paper wrappings, yards of red ribbons, and a colored snowstorm of little address tickets as she directed the packing of the presents for the Tenants' Tree, a second monster which stood in the ornamental barn beyond the kitchens.

Campion left Lance to his fate, which promised to be six or seven hours' hard labor at the most moderate estimate, and continued his purposeful meandering. His lean figure drifted among the company with an apparent aimlessness which was deceptive. There was hidden urgency in his lazy movements and his pale eyes behind his spectacles were inquiring and unhappy.

He found Patricia Bullard dancing with Preen, and paused to watch them as they swung gracefully by him. The man was in a somewhat flamboyant mood, flashing his smile and his noisy witticisms about him after the fashion of his kind, but the girl was not so content. As Campion caught sight of her pale face over her partner's sleek shoulder his eyebrows rose. For an instant he almost believed in Lance's unlikely suggestion. The girl actually did look as though she had her back to the wall. She was watching the doorway nervously and her shiny eyes were afraid.

Campion looked about him for the other young man who should have been present, but Peter Groome was not in the ballroom, nor in the great hall, nor yet among the bridge tables in the drawing room, and half an hour later he had still not put in an appearance.

Campion was in the hall himself when he saw Patricia slip into the anteroom which led to Sir Philip's private study, that holy of holies which even Florence treated with a wholesome awe. Campion had paused for a moment to enjoy the spectacle of Lance, wild eyed and tight lipped, wrestling with the last of the blue glass balls and tinsel streamers on the Guests' Tree, when he caught sight of the flare of her silver skirt disappearing round a familiar doorway under one branch of the huge double staircase.

It was what he had been waiting for, and yet when it came his disappointment was unexpectedly acute, for he too had liked her smile and her brandy-ball eyes. The door was ajar when he reached it, and he pushed it open an inch or so farther, pausing on the threshold to consider the scene within. Patricia was on her knees before the paneled door which led into the inner room and was trying somewhat ineffectually to peer through the keyhole.

Campion stood looking at her regretfully, and when she straightened herself and paused to listen, with every line of her young body taut with the effort of concentration, he did not move.

Sir Philip's voice amid the noisy chatter behind him startled him, however, and he swung round to see the old man talking to a group on the other side of the room. A moment later the girl brushed past him and hurried away.

Campion went quietly into the anteroom. The study door was still closed and he moved over to the enormous period fireplace which stood beside it. This particular fireplace, with its carved and painted front, its wrought iron dogs and deeply recessed inglenooks, was one of the showpieces of Underhill.

At the moment the fire had died down and the interior of the cavern was dark, warm and inviting. Campion stepped inside and sat down on the oak set-tee, where the shadows swallowed him. He had no intention of being unduly officious, but his quick ears had caught a faint sound in the inner room and Sir Philip's private sanctum was no place for furtive movements when its master was out of the way. He had not long to wait.

A few moments later the study door opened very quietly and someone came out. The newcomer moved across the room with a nervous, unsteady tread, and paused abruptly, his back to the quiet figure in the inglenook. Campion recognized Peter Groome and his thin mouth narrowed. He was sorry. He had liked the boy.

The youngster stood irresolute. He had his hands behind him, holding in one of them a flamboyant parcel wrapped in the colored paper and scarlet rib-bon which littered the house. A sound from the hall seemed to fluster him for he spun round, thrust the parcel into the inglenook which was the first hiding place to present itself, and returned to face the new arrival. It was the girl again. She came slowly across the room, her hands outstretched and her face raised to Peter's.

In view of everything, Campion thought it best to stay where he was, nor had he time to do anything else. She was speaking urgently, passionate sinceri-ty in her low voice.

"Peter, I've been looking for you. Darling, there's something I've got to say and if I'm making an idiotic mistake then you've got to forgive me. Look here, you wouldn't go and do anything silly, would you? Would you, Peter? Look at me."

"My dear girl." He was laughing unsteadily and not very convincingly with his arms around her. "What on earth are you talking about?"

She drew back from him and peered earnestly into his face.

"You wouldn't, would you? Not even if it meant an awful lot. Not even if for some reason or other you felt you *had* to. Would you?"

He turned from her helplessly, a great weariness in the lines of his sturdy back, but she drew him round, forcing him to face her.

"Would he what, my dear?"

Florence's arch inquiry from the doorway separated them so hurriedly that she laughed delightedly and came briskly into the room, her gray curls a trifle disheveled and her draperies flowing.

"Too divinely young, I love it!" she said devastatingly. "I must kiss you both. Christmas is the time for love and youth and all the other dear charming things, isn't it? That's why I adore it. But my dears, not here. Not in this silly poky little room. Come along and help me, both of you, and then you can slip away and dance together later on. But don't come in this room. This is Philip's dull part of the house. Come along this minute. Have you seen my precious tree? Too incredibly distinguished, my darlings, with two great artists at work on it. You shall both tie on a candle. Come along."

She swept them away like an avalanche. No protest was possible. Peter shot a single horrified glance towards the fireplace, but Florence was gripping his arm; he was thrust out into the hall and the door closed firmly behind him.

Campion was left in his corner with the parcel less than a dozen feet away from him on the opposite bench. He moved over and picked it up. It was a long flat package wrapped in holly-printed tissue. Moreover, it was unexpectedly heavy and the ends were unbound.

He turned it over once or twice, wrestling with a strong disinclination to interfere, but a vivid recollection of the girl with the brandy-ball eyes, in her silver dress, her small pale face alive with anxiety, made up his mind for him and, sighing, he pulled the ribbon.

The typewritten folder which fell on to his knees surprised him at first, for it was not at all what he had expected, nor was its title, "Report on Messrs. Anderson and Coleridge, Messrs. Saunders, Duval and Berry, and Messrs. Birmingham and Rose," immediately enlightening, and when he opened it at random a column of incomprehensible figures confronted him. It was a scribbled pencil note in a precise hand at the foot of one of the pages which gave him his first clue.

"These figures are estimated by us to be a reliable forecast of this firm's full working capacity,"

he read, and after that he became very serious indeed.

Two hours later it was bitterly cold in the garden and a thin white mist hung over the dark shrubbery which lined the drive when Mr. Campion, picking his way cautiously along the clipped grass verge, came quietly down to the sundial walk. Behind him the gabled roofs of Underhill were shadowy against a frosty sky. There were still a few lights in the upper windows, but below stairs the entire place was in darkness.

Campion hunched his greatcoat about him and plodded on, unwonted severity in the lines of his thin face.

He came upon the sundial walk at last and paused, straining his eyes to see through the mist. He made out the figure standing by the stone column, and heaved a sigh of relief as he recognized the jaunty shoulders of the Christmas tree decorator. Lance's incurable romanticism was going to be useful at last, he reflected with wry amusement.

He did not join his friend but withdrew into the shadows of a great clump of rhododendrons and composed himself to wait. He intensely disliked the situation in which he found himself. Apart from the extreme physical discomfort involved, he had a natural aversion towards the project on hand, but little fairhaired girls with shiny eyes can be very appealing.

It was a freezing vigil. He could hear Lance stamping about in the mist, swearing softly to himself, and even that supremely comic phenomenon had its unsatisfactory side.

They were both shivering and the mist's damp fingers seemed to have stroked their very bones when at last Campion stiffened. He had heard a rustle behind him and presently there was a movement in the wet leaves, followed by the sharp ring of feet on the stones. Lance swung round immediately, only to drop back in astonishment as a tall figure bore down.

"Where is it?"

Neither the words nor the voice came as a complete surprise to Campion, but the unfortunate Lance was taken entirely off his guard.

"Why, hello, Preen," he said involuntarily. "What the devil are you doing here?"

The newcomer had stopped in his tracks, his face a white blur in the uncertain light. For a moment he stood perfectly still and then, turning on his heel, he made off without a word.

"Ah, but I'm afraid it's not quite so simple as that, my dear chap."

Campion stepped out of his friendly shadows and as the younger man passed, slipped an arm through his and swung him round to face the startled Lance, who was coming up at the double.

"You can't clear off like this," he went on, still in the same affable, conversational tone. "You have something to give Peter Groome, haven't you? Something he rather wants?"

"Who the hell are you?" Preen jerked up his arm as he spoke and might have wrenched himself free had it not been for Lance, who had recognized Campion's voice and, although completely in the dark, was yet quick enough to grasp certain essentials.

"That's right, Preen," he said, seizing the man's other arm in a bear's hug. "Hand it over. Don't be a fool. Hand it over."

This line of attack appeared to be inspirational, since they felt the powerful youngster stiffen between them.

"Look here, how many people know about this?"

"The world—" Lance was beginning cheerfully when Campion forestalled him.

"We three and Peter Groome," he said quietly. "At the moment Sir Philip has no idea that Messr. Preen's curiosity concerning the probable placing of government orders for aircraft parts has overstepped the bounds of common sense. You're acting alone, I suppose?"

"Oh, lord, yes, of course." Preen was cracking dangerously. "If my old man gets to hear of this I—oh, well, I might as well go and crash."

"I thought so." Campion sounded content. "Your father has a reputation to consider. So has our young friend Groome. You'd better hand it over."

"What?"

"Since you force me to be vulgar, whatever it was you were attempting to use as blackmail, my precious young friend," he said. "Whatever it may be, in fact, that you hold over young Groome and were trying to use in your attempt to force him to let you have a look at a confidential government report concerning the orders which certain aircraft firms were likely to receive in the next six months. In your position you could have made pretty good use of them, couldn't you? Frankly, I haven't the faintest idea what this incriminating document may be. When I was young, objectionably wealthy youths accepted I. O. U.'s from their poorer companions, but now that's gone out of fashion. What's the modern equivalent? An R. D. check, I suppose?"

Preen said nothing. He put his hand in an inner pocket and drew out an envelope which he handed over without a word. Campion examined the slip of pink paper within by the light of a pencil torch.

"You kept it for quite a time before trying to cash it, didn't you?" he said. "Dear me, that's rather an old trick and it was never admired. Young men who are careless with their accounts have been caught out like that before. It simply wouldn't have looked good to his legal-minded old man, I take it? You two seem to be hampered by your respective papas' integrity. Yes, well, you can go now."

Preen hesitated, opened his mouth to protest, but thought better of it. Lance looked after his retreating figure for some little time before he returned to his friend.

"Who wrote that blinking note?" he demanded.

"He did, of course," said Campion brutally. "He wanted to see the report but was making absolutely sure that young Groome took all the risks of being found with it."

"Preen wrote the note," Lance repeated blankly.

"Well, naturally," said Campion absently. "That was obvious as soon as the report appeared in the picture. He was the only man in the place with the necessary special information to make use of it."

Lance made no comment. He pulled his coat collar more closely about his throat and stuffed his hands into his pockets.

All the same the artist was not quite satisfied, for, later still, when Campion was sitting in his dressing gown writing a note at one of the little escritoires which Florence so thoughtfully provided in her guest bedrooms, he came padding in again and stood warming himself before the fire.

"Why?" he demanded suddenly. "Why did I get the invitation?"

"Oh, that was a question of luggage," Campion spoke over his shoulder.

"That bothered me at first, but as soon as we fixed it onto Preen that little mystery became blindingly clear. Do you remember falling into the carriage this afternoon? Where did you put your elegant piece of gent's natty suitcasing? Over young Groome's head. Preen saw it from the corridor and assumed that the chap was sitting *under his own bag*! He sent his own man over here with the note, told him not to ask for Peter by name but to follow the nice new pigskin suitcase upstairs."

Lance nodded regretfully. "Very likely," he said sadly. "Funny thing. I was sure it was the girl."

After a while he came over to the desk. Campion put down his pen and indicated the written sheet.

"Dear Groome," it ran, "I enclose a little matter that I should burn forthwith. The package you left in the inglenook is still there, right at the back on the left-hand side, cunningly concealed under a pile of logs. It has not been seen by anyone who could possibly understand it. If you nipped over very early this morning you could return it to its appointed place without any trouble. If I may venture a word of advice, it is never worth it."

The author grimaced. "It's a bit avuncular," he admitted awkwardly, "but what else can I do? His light is still on, poor chap. I thought I'd stick it under his door."

Lance was grinning wickedly. "That's fine," he murmured. "The old man does his stuff for reckless youth. There's just the signature now and that ought to be as obvious as everything else has been to you. I'll write it for you. 'Merry Christmas. Love from Santa Claus.' "

"You win," said Mr. Campion.

Thomas Larry Adcock

CHRISTMAS COP

By the second week of December, when they light up the giant fir tree behind the statue of a golden Prometheus overlooking the ice-skating rink at Rockefeller Center, Christmas in New York has got you by the throat.

Close to five hundred street-corner Santas (temporarily sober and none too happy about it) have been ringing bells since the day after Thanksgiving; the support pillars on Macy's main selling floor have been dolled up like candy canes since Hallowe'en; the tipping season arrives in the person of your apartment-house super, all smiles and open-palmed and suddenly available to fix the leaky pipes you've complained about since July; total strangers insist not only that you have a nice day but that you be of good cheer on top of it; and your Con Ed bill says HAPPY HOLIDAYS at the top of the page in a festive red-and-green dot-matrix.

In addition, New York in December is crawling with boosters, dippers, yokers, smash-and-grabbers, bindlestiffs on the mope, aggressive pros offering special holiday rates to guys cruising around at dusk in station wagons with Jersey plates, pigeon droppers and assorted other bunco artists, purveyors of all manner of dubious gift items, and entrepreneurs of the informal branch of the pharmaceutical trade. My job is to try and prevent at least some of these fine upstanding perpetrators from scoring against at least some of their natural Yuletide prey—the seasonal hordes of out-of-towners, big-ticket shoppers along Fifth Avenue, blue-haired Wednesday matinee ladies, and wide-eyed suburban matrons lined up outside Radio City Music Hall with big, snatchable shoulder bags full of credit cards.

I'm your friendly neighborhood plainclothesman. *Very* plain clothes. The guy in the grungy overcoat and watch cap and jeans and beat-up shoes and a week's growth of black beard shambling along the street carrying something in a brown paper bag—that ubiquitous New York bum you hurry past every day while holding your breath—might be me.

687

The name is Neil Hockaday, but everybody calls me Hock, my fellow cops and my snitches alike. And that's no pint of muscatel in my paper bag, it's my point-to-point shortwave radio. I work out of a boroughwide outfit called Street Crimes Unit-Manhattan, which is better known as the befitting S.C.U.M. patrol.

For twelve years, I've been a cop, the last three on S.C.U.M. patrol, which is a prestige assignment despite the way we dress on the job. In three years, I've made exactly twice the collars I did in my first nine riding around in precinct squad cars taking calls from sector dispatch. It's all going to add up nicely when I go for my gold shield someday. Meanwhile, I appreciate being able to work pretty much unsupervised, which tells you I'm at least a half honest cop in a city I figure to be about three-quarters crooked.

Sometimes I do a little bellyaching about the department—and who doesn't complain along about halfway through the second cold one after shift? —but mainly I enjoy the work I do. What I like about it most is how I'm always up against the elements of chance and surprise, one way or another.

That's something you can't say about most careers these days. Not even a cop's, really. Believe it or not, you have plenty of tedium if you're a uniform sealed up in a blue-and-white all day, even in New York. But the way my job plays, I'm out there on the street mostly alone and it's an hour-by-hour proposition: fifty-eight minutes of walking around with my pores open so I don't miss anything and two minutes of surprise.

No matter what, I've got to be ready because surprise comes in several degrees of seriousness. And when it does, it comes out of absolutely nowhere.

On the twenty-fourth of December, I wasn't ready.

To me, it was a day like any other. That was wishful thinking, of course. To a holiday-crazed town, it was Christmas Eve and the big payoff was on deck—everybody out there with kids and wives and roast turkeys and plenty of money was anxious to let the rest of us know how happy they were.

Under the circumstances, it was just as well that I'd pulled duty. I wouldn't have had anyplace to go besides the corner pub, as it happened—or, if I could stand it, the easy chair in front of my old Philco for a day of *Christmas in Connecticut* followed by *Miracle on Thirty-fourth Street* followed by *A Christmas Carol* followed by *March of the Wooden Soldiers* followed by Midnight Mass live from St. Patrick's.

Every year since my divorce five years ago, I'd dropped by my ex-wife's place out in Queens for Christmas Eve. I'd bring champagne, oysters, an expensive gift, and high hopes of spending the night. But this year she'd wrecked my plans. She telephoned around the twentieth to tell me about this new boyfriend of hers—some guy who wasn't a cop and whose name sounded like a respiratory disease, Flummong—and how he was taking her out to some rectangular state in the Middle West to meet his parents, who grow wheat. Swell.

So on the twenty-fourth, I got up at the crack of noon and decided that the only thing that mattered was business. Catching bad guys on the final, frantic shopping day—that was the ticket. I reheated some coffee from the day before, then poured some into a mug after I picked out something small, brown, and dead. I also ate a week-old piece of babka and said, "Bah, humbug!" right out loud.

I put on my quilted longjohns and strapped a lightweight .32 automatic Baretta Puma around my left ankle. Then I pulled on a pair of faded grey corduroys with holes in the knees, a black turtleneck sweater with bleach stains to wear over my beige bulletproof vest and my patrolman's badge on a chain, a New York Knicks navy-blue stocking cap with a red ball on top, and Army-surplus boots. The brown-paper bag for my PTP I'd saved from the past Sunday when I'd gotten bagels down on Essex Street and shaved last.

I strapped on my shoulder holster and packed away the heavy piece, my .44 Charter Arms Bulldog. Then I topped off my ensemble with an olive-drab officer's greatcoat that had seen lots of action in maybe the Korean War. One of the side pockets was slashed open. Moths and bayonet tips had made holes in other places. I dropped a pair of nickel-plated NYPD bracelets into the good pocket.

By half past the hour, I was in the Bleecker Street subway station near where I live in the East Village. I dropped a quarter into a telephone on the platform and told the desk sergeant at Midtown South to be a good guy and check me off for the one o'clock muster. A panhandler with better clothes than mine and a neatly printed plywood sandwich sign hanging around his shoulders caught my eye. The sign read, TRYING TO RAISE $1,000,000 FOR WINE RESEARCH. I gave him a buck and caught the uptown D train.

When I got out at Broadway and Thirty-fourth Street, the weather had turned cold and clammy. The sky had a smudgy grey overcast to it. It would be the kind of afternoon when everything in Manhattan looks like a black-and-white snapshot. It wasn't very Christmaslike, which suited me fine.

Across the way, in a triangle of curbed land that breaks up the Broadway and Sixth Avenue traffic flow at the south end of Herald Square, winos stood around in a circle at the foot of a statue of Horace Greeley. Greeley's limed shoulders were mottled by frozen bird dung and one granite arm was forever pointed toward the westward promise. I thought about my ex and the Flummong guy. The winos coughed, their foul breath hanging in frosted lumps of exhaled air, and awaited a ritual opening of a large economy-sized bottle of Thunderbird. The leader broke the seal and poured a few drops on the ground, which is a gesture of respect to mates recently dead or imprisoned. Then he took a healthy swallow and passed it along.

On the other side of the statue, a couple of dozen more guys carrying the stick (living on the street, that is) reclined on benches or were curled up over heating grates. All were in proper position to protect their stash in the event of sleep: money along one side of their hat brims, one hand below as a sort of pillow. The only way they could be robbed was if someone came along and cut off their hands, which has happened.

Crowds of last-minute shoppers jammed the sidewalks everywhere. Those who had to pass the bums (and me) did so quickly, out of fear and disgust, even at this time of goodwill toward men. It's a curious thing how so many comfortable middle-class folks believe vagrants and derelicts are dangerous, especially when you consider that the only people who have caused them any serious harm have been other comfortable middle-class folks with nice suits and offices and lawyers.

Across Broadway, beyond the bottle gang around the stone Greeley, I recognized a mope I'd busted about a year ago for boosting out of a flash clothes joint on West Fourteenth street. He was a scared kid of sixteen and lucky I'd gotten to him first. The store goons would have broken his thumbs. He was an Irish kid who went by the street name Whiteboy and he had nobody. We have lots of kids like Whiteboy in New York, and other cities, too. But we don't much want to know about them.

Now he leaned against a Florsheim display window, smoking a cigarette and scoping out the straight crowd around Macy's and Gimbels. Whiteboy, so far as I knew, was a moderately successful small-fry shoplifter, purse snatcher, and pickpocket.

I decided to stay put and watch him watch the swarm of possible marks until he got up enough nerve to move on somebody he figured would give him the biggest return for the smallest risk, like any good businessman. I moved back against a wall and stuck out my hand and asked passers-by for spare change. (This is not exactly regulation, but it guarantees that nobody will look at my face and it happens to be how I cover the monthly alimony check.) A smiling young fellow in a camel topcoat, the sort of guy who might be a Jaycee from some town up in Rockland County, pressed paper on me and whispered, "Bless you, brother." I looked down and saw that he'd given me a circular from the Church of Scientology in the size, color, and shape of a dollar bill.

When I looked up again, Whiteboy was crossing Broadway. He tossed his cigarette into the street and concentrated on the ripe prospect of a mink-draped fat lady on the outside of a small mob shoving its way into Gimbels. She had a black patent-leather purse dangling from a rhinestone-studded strap clutched in her hand. Whiteboy could pluck it from her pudgy fingers so fast and gently she'd be in third-floor housewares before she noticed.

I followed after him when he passed me. Then, sure enough, he made the snatch. I started running down the Broadway bus lane toward him. Whiteboy must have lost his touch because the fat lady turned and pointed at him and hollered "Thief!" She stepped right in front of me and I banged into her and she shrieked at me, "Whyn't you sober up and get a job, you bum you?"

Whiteboy whirled around and looked at me full in the face. He made me. Then he started running, too.

He darted through the thicket of yellow taxicabs, cars, and vans and zigzagged his way toward Greeley's statue. There was nothing I could do but chase him on foot. Taking a shot in such a congestion of traffic and pedestrians would get me up on IAD charges just as sure as if I'd stolen the fat lady's purse myself.

Then a funny thing happened.

Just as I closed in on Whiteboy, all those bums lying around on the little curbed triangle suddenly got up and blocked me as neatly as a line of zone defensemen for the Jets. Eight or ten big, groggy guys fell all over me and I lost Whiteboy.

I couldn't have been more frustrated. A second collar on a guy like Whiteboy would have put him away for two years' hard time, minimum. Not to mention how it would get me a nice commendation letter for my personal file. But in this business, you can't spend too much time crying over a job that didn't come off. So I headed east on Thirty-second toward Fifth Avenue.

At mid-block, I stopped to help a young woman in a raggedy coat with four bulging shopping bags and three shivering kids. She set the bags on the damp sidewalk and rubbed her bare hands as I neared her. Two girls and a boy, the oldest maybe seven, huddled around her. "How much farther?" one of the girls asked.

I didn't hear an answer. I walked up and asked the woman, "Where you headed, lady?" She looked away, embarrassed because of the tears in her eyes. She was small and slender, with light-brown skin and black hair pulled straight back from her face and held with a rubber band. A gust of dry wind knifed through the air.

"Could you help me?" she finally asked. "I'm just going up to the hotel at the corner. These bags are cutting my hands."

She meant the Martinique. It's a big dark hulk of a hotel, possibly grand back in the days when Herald Square was nearly glamorous. Now it's peeling and forbidding and full of people who have lost their way for a lot of different reasons—most of them women and children. When welfare families can't pay the rent anymore and haven't any place to go, the city puts them up "temporarily" at the Martinique. It's a stupid deal even by New York's high standards of senselessness. The daily hotel rate amounts to a monthly tab of about two grand for one room and an illegal hotplate, which is maybe ten times the rent on the apartment the family just lost.

"What's your name?" I asked her.

She didn't hesitate, but there was a shyness to her voice. "Frances. What's yours?"

"Hock." I picked up her bags, two in each hand. "Hurry up, it's going to snow," I said. The bags were full of children's clothes, a plastic radio, some storybooks, and canned food. I hoped they wouldn't break from the sidewalk dampness.

Frances and her kids followed me and I suppose we looked like a line of shabby ducks walking along. A teenage girl in one of those second-hand men's tweed overcoats you'd never find at the Goodwill took our picture with a Nikon equipped with a telephoto lens.

I led the way into the hotel and set the bags down at the admitting desk. Frances's three kids ran off to join a bunch of other kids who were watching a couple of old coots with no teeth struggling with a skinny spruce tree at the entry of what used to be the dining room. Now it was dusty and had no tables, just a few graffiti-covered vending machines.

Frances grabbed my arm when I tried to leave her. "It's not much, I know that. But maybe you can use it all the same." She let me go, then put out a hand like she wanted to shake. I slipped off my glove and took hold of her small, bone-chilled fingers. She passed me two dimes. "Thanks, and happy Christmas."

She looked awfully brave and awfully heartsick, too. Most down-and-outers look like that, but people who eat regularly and know where their next dollar will likely come from make the mistake of thinking they're stupid and confused, or maybe shiftless or crazy.

I tried to refuse the tip, but she wouldn't have any of that. Her eyes misted up again. So I went back out to the street, where it was starting to snow.

The few hours I had left until the evening darkness were not productive. Which is not to say there wasn't enough business for me. Anyone who thinks crooks are nabbed sooner or later by us sharp-witted, hard-working cops probably also thinks there's a tooth fairy. Police files everywhere bulge with unfinished business. That's because cops are pretty much like everybody else in a world that's not especially efficient. Some days we're inattentive or lazy or hungover—or in my case on Christmas Eve, preoccupied with the thought that loneliness is all it's cracked up to be.

For about an hour after leaving Frances and the kids at the Martinique, I tailed a mope with a big canvas laundry sack, which is the ideal equipment when you're hauling off valuables from a place where nobody happens to be home. I was practically to the Hudson River before I realized the perp had made me a long time back and was just having fun giving me a walk-around on a raw, snowy day. Perps can be cocky like that sometimes. Even though I was ninety-nine percent sure he had a set of lock picks on him, I didn't have probable cause for a frisk.

I also wasted a couple of hours shadowing a guy in a very uptown cashmere coat and silk muffler. He had a set of California teeth and perfect sandy-blond hair. Most people in New York would figure him for a nice simple TV anchorman or maybe a *GQ* model. I had him pegged for a shoulder-bag bus dipper, which is a minor criminal art that can be learned by anyone who isn't moronic or crippled in a single afternoon. Most of its practitioners seem to be guys who are too handsome. All you have to do is hang around people waiting for buses or getting off buses, quietly reach into their bags, and pick out wallets.

I read this one pretty easily when I noticed how he passed up a half empty Madison Avenue bus opposite B. Altman's in favor of the next one, which was overloaded with chattering Lenox Hill matrons who would never in a thousand years think such a nice young man with nice hair and a dimple in his chin and so well dressed was a thief.

Back and forth I went with this character, clear up to Fifty-ninth Street, then by foot over to Fifth Avenue and back down into the low Forties. When I finally showed him my tin and spread him against the base of one of the cement lions outside the New York Public Library to pat him down, I only found cash on him. This dipper was brighter than he looked. Somewhere along the line, he'd ditched the wallets and pocketed only the bills and I never once saw the slide. I felt fairly brainless right about then and the crowd of onlookers that cheered when I let him go didn't help me any.

So I hid out in the Burger King at Fifth and Thirty-eighth for my dinner hour. There aren't too many places that could be more depressing for a holiday meal. The lighting was so oppressively even that I felt I was inside an ice cube. There was a plastic Christmas tree with plastic ornaments chained to a wall so nobody could steal it, with dummy gifts beneath it. The gifts were strung together with vinyl cord and likewise chained to the wall. I happened to be the only customer in the place, so a kid with a bad complexion and a broom decided to sweep up around my table.

To square my pad for the night, I figured I had to make some sort of bust, even a Mickey Mouse. So after my festive meal (Whopper, fries, Sprite, and a toasted thing with something hot and gummy inside it), I walked down to Thirty-third Street and collared a working girl in a white fake-fox stole, fish-net hose, and a red-leather skirt. She was all alone on stroll, a freelance, and looked like she could use a hot meal and a nice dry cell. So I took her through the drill. The paperwork burned up everything but the last thirty minutes of my tour.

When I left the station house on West Thirty-fifth, the snow had become wet and heavy and most of midtown Manhattan was lost in a quiet white haze. I heard the occasional swish of a car going through a pothole puddle. Plumes of steam hissed here and there, like geysers from the subterranean. Everybody seemed to have vanished and the lights of the city had gone off, save for the gauzy red-and-green beacon at the top of the Empire State Building. It was rounding toward nine o'clock and it was Christmas Eve and New York seemed settled down for a long winter's nap.

There was just one thing wrong with the picture. And that was the sight of Whiteboy. I spotted him on Broadway again, lumbering down the mostly blackened, empty street with a big bag on his back like he was St. Nicholas himself.

I stayed out of sight and tailed him slowly back a few blocks to where I'd lost him in the first place, to the statue of Greeley. I had a clear view of him as he set down his bag on a bench and talked to the same bunch of grey, shapeless winos who'd cut me off the chase. Just as before, they passed a bot-tle. Only this time Whiteboy gave it to them. After everyone had a nice jolt, they talked quickly for a couple of minutes, like they had someplace impor-tant to go.

I hung back in the darkness under some scaffolding. Snow fell between the cracks of planks above me and piled on my shoulders as I stood there try-ing to figure out their act. It didn't take me long.

When they started moving from the statue over to Thirty-second Street, every one of them with a bag slung over his shoulder, I hung back a little. But my crisis of conscience didn't last long. I followed Whiteboy and his unlikely crew of elves—and wasn't much surprised to find the blond shoulder-bag dip-per with the cashmere coat when we got to where we were all going. Which was the Martinique. By now, the spindly little spruce I'd felt sorry for that after-noon was full of bright lights and tinsel and had a star on top. The same old coots I'd seen when I helped Frances and her kids there were standing around playing with about a hundred more hungry-looking kids.

Whiteboy and his helpers went up to the tree and plopped down all the bags. The kids crowded around them. They were quiet about it, though. These were kids who didn't have much experience with Norman Rockwell Christmases, so they didn't know it was an occasion to whoop it up.

Frances saw me standing in the dimly lit doorway. I must have been a sight, covered in snow and tired from walking my post most of eight hours. "Hock!" she called merrily.

And then Whiteboy spun around like he had before and his jaw dropped open. He and the pretty guy stepped away from the crowd of kids and mothers and the few broken-down men and walked quickly over to me. The kids looked like they expected all along that their party would be busted up. Frances knew she'd done something very wrong hailing me like she had, but how could she know I was a cop?

"We're having a little Christmas party here, Hock. Anything illegal about that?" Whiteboy was a cool one. He'd grown tougher and smarter in a year and talked to me like we'd just had a lovely chat the other day. We'd have to make some sort of deal, Whiteboy and me, and we both knew it.

"Who's your partner?" I asked him. I looked at the pretty guy in cashmere who wasn't saying anything just yet.

"Call him Slick."

"I like it," I said. "Where'd you and Slick get all the stuff in the bags?"

"Everything's bought and paid for, Hock. You got nothing to worry about."

"When you're cute, you're irritating, Whiteboy. You know I can't turn around on this empty-handed."

Then Slick spoke up. "What you got on us, anyways? I've just about had my fill of police harassment today, Officer. I was cooperative earlier, but I don't intend to cooperate a second time."

I ignored him and addressed Whiteboy. "Tell your friend Slick how we all appreciate discretion and good manners on both sides of the game."

Whiteboy smiled and Slick's face grew a little red.

"Let's just say for the sake of conversation," Whiteboy suggested, "that Slick and me came by a whole lot of money some way or other we're unwilling to disclose since that would tend to incriminate us. And then let's say we used that money to buy a whole lot of stuff for those kids back of us. And let's say we got cash receipts for everything in the bags. Where's that leave us, Officer Hockaday?"

"It leaves you with one leg up, temporarily. Which can be a very uncomfortable way of standing. Let's just say that I'm likely to be hard on your butts from now on."

"Well, that's about right. Just the way I see it." He lit a cigarette, a Dunhill. Then he turned back a cuff and looked at his wristwatch, the kind of piece that cost him plenty of either nerve or money. Whiteboy was moving up well for himself.

"You're off duty now, aren't you, Hock? And wouldn't you be just about

695

out of overtime allowance for the year?"

"Whiteboy, you better start giving me something besides lip. That is, unless you want forty-eight hours up at Riker's on suspicion. You better believe there isn't a judge in this whole city on straight time or overtime or any kind of time tonight or tomorrow to take any bail application from you."

Whiteboy smiled again. "Yeah, well, I figure the least I owe you is to help you see this thing my way. Think of it like a special tax, you know? Around this time of year, I figure the folks who can spare something ought to be taxed. So maybe that's what happened, see? Just taxation."

"Same scam as the one Robin Hood ran?"

"Yeah, something like that. Only Slick and me ain't about to start living out of town in some forest."

"You owe me something more, Whiteboy."

"What?"

"From now on, you and Slick are my two newest snitches. And I'll be expecting regular news."

There is such a thing as honor among thieves. This is every bit as true as the honor among Congressmen you read about in the newspapers all the time. But when enlightened self-interest rears its ugly head, it's also true that rules of gallantry are off.

"Okay, Hock, why not?" Whiteboy shook my hand. Slick did, too, and when he smiled his chin dimple spread flat. Then the three of us went over to the Christmas tree and everybody there seemed relieved.

We started pulling merchandise out of the bags and handing things over to disbelieving kids and their parents. Everything was the best that money could buy, too. Slick's taste in things was top-drawer. And just like Whiteboy said, there were sales slips for it all, which meant that this would be a time when nobody could take anything away from these people.

I came across a pair of ladies' black-leather gloves from Lord & Taylor, with grey-rabbit-fur lining. These I put aside until all the kids had something, then I gave them to Frances before I went home for the night. She kissed me on the cheek and wished me a happy Christmas again.

Edward D. Hoch

THE THEFT OF THE CHRISTMAS STOCKING

It always seemed more like Christmas with snow in the air, even if there were only fat white flakes that melted as they hit the sidewalk. Walking briskly along Fifth Avenue at noon on Christmas Eve, Nick Velvet was aware of the last-minute crowds clutching red-and-green shopping bags that must have delighted the merchants. When he turned in at the building on the corner of Fifty-fourth Street, he wasn't surprised to see that the pre-Christmas festivities had spread even here, within the confines of one of Manhattan's most exclusive private clubs.

The slender, sour-faced man behind the desk inside the door eyed Nick for an instant and asked, "Are you looking for the Dellon-Simpson Christmas party?"

"Mr. Charles Simpson," Nick confirmed. "I have an appointment with him here."

The guardian of the door consulted his list. "You'd be Mr. Velvet?"

"That's right."

"You'll find Mr. Simpson in the library, straight ahead. He's expecting you."

Nick crossed the marble floor, past a curving staircase that led up to a surprisingly noisy party, and entered the library through tall oak doors that shut out virtually all sound. Inside was a club-room from a hundred years ago, complete with an elderly member dozing in front of the fireplace.

"Mr. Velvet?" a voice asked, and Nick turned and saw a figure rising from the shadow of an oversized wing chair.

"That's correct. You'd be Charles Simpson?"

"I would be." By the flickering firelight, Nick could make out a tall man with a noble face and furry white sideburns. He looked to be a vigorous sixty or so and his handshake was a grip of steel. "Thank you for coming."

"I'm keeping you from your firm's Christmas party."

"Nonsense. Business before pleasure, even on Christmas Eve. I want you to steal something for me, Mr. Velvet."

"That's my business. You understand the conditions? Nothing of value, and my fee—"

"I was told in advance. But it must be done tonight. Is that a problem?"

"No. What's the object?"

Simpson's face crinkled into a tight-lipped smile. "A Christmas stocking. I want you to steal the Christmas stocking hanging from the fireplace at my granddaughter's. Any time after midnight."

"Does it contain something valuable?"

"The gift inside will be valueless, but I want that, too."

"Where does she live?"

"With her mother in a duplex apartment on upper Fifth Avenue." He produced a piece of paper from his pocket. "Here's the address. I warn you, the building has tight security. "

"I'll get in."

"Phone me at this number if you're successful." He walked Nick to the lobby, and as Nick started for the door he said, "Oh, and Mr. Velvet—" ·

Nick turned. "Yes?"

"Merry Christmas. "

After explaining on the·phone to Gloria why he wouldn't be home until well after midnight, Nick journeyed up Fifth Avenue to the address he'd been given. It proved to be a fine old building with a doorman, and a security guard seated behind a bank of television monitors. There would be a TV camera in each of the elevators, at the service entrance, and probably in the stairwell.

Nick walked around the block and thought about it. The most likely way to gain access to the building would be to pose as a delivery man. He could rent a uniform, buy a poinsettia, and walk right past the doorman as if he were delivering it to one of the apartments. It wouldn't work after midnight, of course. He'd have to gain access to the building much earlier and find a hiding place out of range of the TV cameras.

Surprisingly—or not—as Nick again approached the front of the building, a florist's van pulled up in front of the building. A young man got out, walked quickly around to the rear, and opened the doors. He brought out a huge poinsettia that almost hid his face and walked into the lobby with it. Nick stopped on the sidewalk to light a cigarette and pause as if in thought.

The doorman immediately took the plant from the young man, checked the address tag, and sent him on his way. He picked up the house phone and presently one of the building employees appeared to complete the plant's delivery. Through it all, the security man never left his post behind the TV monitors.

Nick sighed and strolled away. A delivery wouldn't gain him access to the apartment, not even on Christmas Eve. It would have to be something else. He glanced again at the note he carried in his pocket: Florence Beaufeld, it read. Apt. 501.

The name was not Simpson, he'd noticed at once. If the child was his granddaughter, that meant the mother she lived with was probably Charles Simpson's daughter, separated, widowed, or divorced. Nick wondered why Simpson couldn't go to the apartment himself on Christmas Day and perform his own stocking theft.

Nick wasn't paid to think too much about the motives of his clients—that had gotten him into trouble enough in the past—but he did feel he should know whether Florence was the mother's or the daughter's name. The phone-book showed only one Beaufeld at that address: Beaufeld, F. It seemed likely that Florence was the child's mother, Florence Simpson Beaufeld.

None of which would help him gain entrance to the apartment after midnight. He crossed Fifth Avenue and tried to get a better view of the building from Central Park. Assuming Apartment 501 was on the fifth floor, it had to face either the side street or the park. The other two sides of the building abutted adjoining buildings on Fifth Avenue and the side street. But the top stories of all three buildings were set back, so there was no access between them across the rooftops. No one could have reached the top of any of the buildings except Santa Claus.

The more Nick thought about it, the more convinced he became that it would have to be Santa Claus.

At eleven-thirty that night, he approached the front door of the building. The padding of the Santa Claus suit was warm and uncomfortable, smelling faintly of scented powder, and the bag of fancily wrapped gifts he'd slung over his shoulder weighed more than he'd expected. The doorman saw him coming and held open the portals for him. That was the first good sign. Santa was expected.

"Ho ho ho!" Nick thundered in the heartiest voice he could manage.

The doorman smiled good-naturedly. "Got a gift for me, Santa?"

"Ho ho ho!" Nick took out one of the gifts he'd bought to fill the top of the sack. "Right here, sonny!"

The doorman smiled and accepted the slim flat box. "Looks like a necktie to me. Thanks a lot, Santa. Which party do you want, the Brewsters or the Trevensons?"

"Brewsters," Nick decided.

"Seventeenth floor."

Nick glanced toward the security guard and saw him looking through the early edition of the following morning's *Times*. He entered the nearest elevator and pressed the button for seventeen. As soon as the door closed and the elevator started to rise, he hit the fifth-floor button, too. The TV camera might spot him getting off at the wrong floor, but it was less of a risk than being seen running down the stairwell with his bag of tricks.

The corridor on the fifth floor was silent and deserted, lit only by an indirect glow from unseen fixtures near the ceiling. There were only three doors, so he knew 501 was going to be a large apartment. He glanced at his watch and saw that it wasn't yet midnight. Then he listened at the door of 501. Hearing nothing, he reached deep into his bag and extracted a leather case of lock picks. It took him just forty-five seconds to unlock the door. He was mildly surprised that the chain lock wasn't latched, but the reason quickly became obvious. The woman of the house, Florence Beaufeld, was preparing to go out.

By the glow of a twelve-foot Christmas tree standing near the spiral staircase in the duplex, he saw a handsome brown-haired woman of around forty adjusting a glistening earring. It was her hair, done in an unusual style that evoked the idea of a layered helmet, that caught his attention. She finished adjusting the earring, straightened the neckline of her red-velvet dress, and picked up a sequined purse.

Nick slipped into the dining area, taking shelter in the shadows behind a china cabinet, as the woman stepped to the foot of the staircase and called out, "I'm going up to the Brewsters' party, Michelle. Go to bed now, it's almost midnight. And don't peek at your gifts!" There was a mumbled reply from upstairs as Mrs. Beaufeld let herself out of the apartment.

Nick waited, sweating in his Santa suit, until he heard a grandfather clock chime midnight. Then he left his hiding place and moved silently across the carpeted floor toward the lighted Christmas tree. A fireplace was beyond the tree, along an inside wall, and above it was an oil portrait of Florence Beaufeld seated with a protective arm around a lovely young girl about eight years old. Below it, taped to the mantel, was a single red Christmas stocking, bulging with an unseen gift.

Carefully setting down the bag, Nick moved to the mantel. He reached out and took the stocking in his hand, carefully pulling the tape away from the wood. As he did, he heard the slightest of sounds behind him and turned to see a young woman in a short nightgown and bare legs standing at the foot of the staircase, a tiny automatic held firmly in her right hand.

"Get your hand off my stocking, Santa," she said, "or I'll send you back to the North Pole in a wooden box . . ."

Nick did as he was told. "Come now," he said gruffly, "you don't want to point that thing at Santa."

She motioned slightly with the pistol. "Take off the hat and beard. I like to see who I'm talking to."

He tossed the red hat on the floor and pulled the sticky beard away from his skin.

"Satisfied now?" he asked in his normal voice.

"Say, you're not bad-looking. Who are you?"

"Do you mind if I take off this coat and padding before we talk? It's really quite uncomfortable."

"Sure, but don't try anything. I've seen all the movies." She watched him while he dropped the coat on the floor with the rest and then pulled the padding from his pants. He'd worn jeans and a black turtleneck under the Santa suit in case he had to shed it to make his escape. With the padding out, the red pants fell by themselves and he stepped out of them.

"Now, what was your question?"

"Who are you?"

She spoke with an educated, private-school voice, even when her words were tough and gritty. Nick guessed Michelle Beaufeld was now in her late teens.

"I'm a friend of your grandfather," he told her.

"Charles Simpson?" The truth seemed to dawn on her. "Oh, no!" She started to laugh. "He wanted you to steal the gift!"

"Well, the stocking the gift is in."

She shook her head. "Santa Claus, the thief! Won't that make a story for the papers? Grandpa Tries To Steal Child's Christmas Gift."

"You're no child," Nick pointed out. "Why don't you put away that gun? I'm not going to hurt you."

She motioned toward the Santa Claus outfit on the floor. "Put your pants back on."

"They're too big for me without the padding."

"That's the idea. If you try to rush me, they'll trip you up."

When he'd done as she ordered, she sat in an easy chair and carefully set the pistol down on an end table by her side. "Now we can talk," she said. "I know Grandpa wouldn't send anyone to harm me, but I can understand his wanting to get his hands on that gift. Let's have a look at it—toss the stocking over here. No funny business now!"

Nick did as he was told, convinced now that she wouldn't think of shooting him any more than he'd think of harming her. The stocking landed on the chair by her side and she picked it up, withdrawing the gift in its holiday wrapping. As she worked at unwrapping it, she reminded Nick of her mother adjusting the earring earlier. She had her mother's high cheekbones and pouting lips, and was well on her way to becoming a great beauty. Putting aside the wrapping, she held up a little plastic pig for Nick to see. It was a gift more suitable for a child of five or six. "There we go! I'll put it with the others."

"What others?"

"Didn't Grandpa tell you? They're gifts from my father. He sends one every Christmas."

"Does he know how old you are?"

"Of course he does. They have a special meaning."

"Oh?"

"*That's* what Grandpa's dying to find out—what their special meaning is."

"Do *you* know?" he asked.

"Well—not yet," she admitted. "It's about something I'm supposed to get when I'm eighteen."

"How old are you now?"

"Seventeen. My birthday's next month."

"Does your father ever come to see you?"

She shook her head. "Not since I was twelve. The only time I hear from him is at Christmas, and then it's just the gift in the stocking. There hasn't been a note since the first time."

"How does he deliver them? I know you don't believe in Santa Claus."

That brought a genuine smile. "I don't know. I suppose Mother must put them there, although she's always denied it."

"What does your grandfather have to do with any of this?"

Her face showed exasperation, then uncertainty. "Why am I telling you my family history when I should be calling the police?"

"Because you wouldn't want to call the police and implicate your grandfather. You told me yourself how funny the headline would look. Besides, I might be able to help you."

"How?"

"It seems to me you've got a real mystery on your hands. If I can solve it for you, there'd be no need for you to keep this little pig, would there?"

"What do you mean?"

"You'd have the answer to your mystery and I'd have the gift to deliver to your grandfather in the stocking."

"He's paying you for this, isn't he?"

"Yes," Nick admitted.

"How much?"

"A great deal. It's how I make my living."

She picked up the automatic and for a split second he thought she was going to shoot him, after all. "Take off those foolish red pants," she said, "and let's have a beer."

*

The kitchen had a sleek contemporary look that clashed with the rest of the apartment. Michelle opened the refrigerator and brought out two bottles of a popular German beer. "Aren't you a bit young to be drinking beer?" Nick asked as she poured two glasses.

"Aren't you a bit old to be a thief?"

"All right," he agreed with a smile, "let's get down to business. Tell me about your father."

"His name is Dan Beaufeld. When I was a child, he ran a charterboat business in Florida. He was away from New York most of the time, especially in the winter when he had a lot of tourist business. Sometimes my mother would take me down to visit him and we'd get to ride on one of his deep-sea-fishing boats. I was twelve the last time I saw him, five years ago. That was when my mother divorced him. At the time I had no idea what it was all about. Somehow I blamed myself, which I guess a lot of kids do. My mother had bought this apartment with her own money, so she stayed here. My father moved to Florida year-round."

"Did you understand what caused the divorce?"

"Not at first. I knew my grandfather had been part of it. I thought he'd poisoned my mother's mind against my father. Once when he found me sobbing in my room, he told me I shouldn't cry over my father because he was a bad man—an evil man."

Charter boats in Florida in the mid-1980s suggested only one thing to Nick. "Could your father have been involved in drug traffic?"

"That's what Grandpa finally told me, just last year. He said he'd made a lot of money using his boats for drug smuggling and that the police were still looking for him. That was why Grandpa forced my mother to divorce him. He was afraid the family would be tainted or something."

"What about these mysterious gifts?"

"They started when I was thirteen. There was a note attached to the first one. It was from my father and he said I was always in his thoughts. He said to keep the gifts, and when I was eighteen they'd make me wealthy. The gifts have appeared in my stocking every Christmas, but there were never any more notes."

"What were the gifts?"

"The first was a little toy bus with a greyhound on the side. Then there was a copy of Poe's poem 'The Raven,' which I loved when I was fourteen. The third year was an apple, and I ate that. Last year there was a snapshot of Mother my father had taken when they were still married. Now there's this plastic pig."

"An odd combination of gifts," Nick admitted. "I can't see—"

"Who the hell are *you*?" a voice asked from the doorway.

703

Nick turned to see Florence Beaufeld standing wide-eyed at the kitchen door, taking in the scene before her.

He stood up, more as a reflex action than from any real fear of attack. "I'm pleased to meet you, Mrs. Beaufeld. My name is Nick Velvet."

"What are you doing here with my daughter?"

"Mother—"

"Were you sent by her father? Are you this year's Christmas gift?"

"He was sent to steal the gift, Mother! I caught him by the fireplace dressed up like Santa Claus."

"And you're sitting here chatting with him? Where are the police?"

"I didn't call them."

"My God, Michelle!"

"I'm perfectly all right, Mother. Please."

"Go upstairs and put on some clothes. I'll attend to Mr. Velvet."

Michelle hesitated and then decided to obey her mother's command. She left the kitchen without a word and went up the staircase, taking the automatic with her. Florence Beaufeld turned back to Nick. "Now tell me the truth. What are you doing here?"

"I was hired by your father, Mrs. Beaufeld."

"I should have guessed as much. Whenever I mentioned those Christmas gifts from Dan it threw him into a frenzy. I vowed not to tell him if there was one this year, but he had to know. He said Dan was planning to give Michelle a large sum of illegal drug money."

"Why would he do that?"

Mrs. Beaufeld shook her head. "Only because he loves her, I suppose, and she's his daughter. He's been hiding out from the police for over five years now, and he's never seen her in all that time."

"What do *you* make of these gifts?"

"I suppose they're a message of some sort, like a child's puzzle, but I haven't been able to read it. Was there another gift tonight?"

"A plastic pig. But perhaps I don't have to tell you that—your daughter suspects you're the one who leaves them for her."

"I swear I'm not! I have no contact with Dan. That stocking was empty earlier this evening. I looked."

"At what time?"

"Shortly before ten, I think."

"Who was in the apartment after that?"

"Only Michelle and me."

"No one else?"

"I have a woman who cooks and cleans for us. She left at about that time. I can't remember whether I looked at the stocking before or after she let herself out."

"Would you give me her name and address?"

"Are you a detective of some sort?"

"Only a professional trying to earn some money. I was hired to bring your father the stocking with the latest gift. Maybe if I solve the riddle for your daughter, she'll let me have it. Then everyone will be happy."

"Well, I'm certain Agnes isn't involved, but you can have her address if you want." She wrote it on a piece of notepaper.

"One other thing. Before I leave, could I see the gifts your daughter received? She told me she ate the apple, but the others?"

She studied him through narrowed eyes. "You have a way with you, Mr. Velvet. For all I know you're nothing but a common thief, yet you charmed my daughter and now you seem to be doing the same with me. Come upstairs. I'll ask Michelle to show you the gifts."

He followed her up the staircase and waited discreetly in the hallway while she checked to see that her daughter was wearing a robe. Then he entered the girl's bedroom. All seventeen years of her life seemed to be crammed haphazardly into it. Michelle led him to a bookcase where a rock star's poster dominated shelves of alphabet books and stuffed toys. There the four objects were lined up, just as she had described them—the toy bus, the Poe poem, the snapshot of Mrs. Beaufeld, and now the pig.

"Michelle will be eighteen next month," Nick said. "It's my understanding the message must be complete, whatever it is, if it's to direct her to a fortune by then."

"But how is he able to get in here to leave these things?"

"I'm hoping Agnes can tell me that," Nick said.

The clock was chiming one as he left the apartment.

Downstairs, a different doorman and security guard were on duty. Nick slipped the doorman a ten-dollar bill. "Merry Christmas."

"Thank you, sir. Are you a resident here?"

"Only a visitor. I was wondering if you've worked here long enough to remember Dan Beaufeld. He was in Apartment 501 before his divorce about five years ago."

"Sorry, I just started last year." He called over to the security guard watching the television monitors. "Larry, were you here five years ago?"

The man shook his head. "Just over four years. The old-timers get the day and evening shifts."

"Thanks anyway," Nick said. He went out into the cold night air and took a cab home. Gloria was waiting up for him, to exchange gifts over a bottle of champagne.

*   *   *

The Beaufeld maid and cook, Agnes Wilson, lived on Fifth Avenue, too, but far uptown in Harlem. It was noon on Christmas Day when Nick visited the housing project where her apartment was located. Her husband eyed him suspiciously and asked, "What do you want with Agnes?"

"I just have a couple of questions. It won't take a minute."

"You a cop?"

"Do I look like one? I'm a friend of the Beaufeld family. "

Agnes Wilson was small and pretty, with deep-brown eyes and a friendly smile. "I never knew Mr. Beaufeld," she said. "They were still married when I started there, but he was always in Florida. I never saw him. "

"Mrs. Wilson, someone left a Christmas toy in Michelle's stocking by the fireplace last night. Do you know anything about it?"

"No."

"You didn't leave it? You weren't paid to leave it?"

"No one paid me to do anything."

"Not Dan Beaufeld?"

"Not him or anyone else."

Nick leaned forward in his chair. "Michelle has received gifts in her stocking for five years now—a toy bus, a poem, an apple, a photograph, and a plastic pig. Do these mean anything to you?"

"No, they don't." She seemed genuinely surprised. "I didn't know about the gifts. A couple of years back I mentioned to Mrs. Beaufeld that I thought Michelle was pretty old to be hanging a stocking on the fireplace Christmas Eve, but she just shrugged it off. It wasn't any of my business, so I shut up. Maybe it wasn't so odd, after all. I worked for a German family once that hung stockings on the fireplace for St. Nicholas every Christmas—all of them, even the parents."

"Did any strangers come to the door this week when Michelle or her mother were out?"

"No strangers get by the doorman in that building. They've got TV cameras in the elevators and everything."

Nick got up to leave, handing her a folded ten-dollar bill. "Thank you for your time, Mrs. Wilson. I hope you and your husband have a Merry Christmas."

Agnes's husband saw him to the door. "You always go calling on Christmas Day?"

"Just like Santa Claus," Nick told him with a smile.

He telephoned Charles Simpson from a pay phone at the corner. "Are you having a good holiday?" he asked.

"Is that you, Velvet? What luck have you had?"

"Fair. I had the stocking in my hands, but I don't have it now."

"What was in it?"

"If I tell you, do I get paid?"

"A partial payment. I won't know if I need the stocking and the gift until I see them."

"All right. I'll try to have them tonight, or tomorrow morning for sure."

He hung up and grabbed a bus heading downtown. Ten minutes later he was back at the Beaufelds' building. The doorman was the same one who'd been on duty the previous day when he'd first scouted the building. Nick asked him if he'd known Dan Beaufeld.

The doorman told him he'd only been there three years.

Nick asked the security guard the same question. "Me? I've been here a year. I know the mother and daughter, not the ex-husband. He never comes around, does he?"

"Not lately," Nick agreed. "Do you have keys to all the apartments?"

"We have one set of master keys, but they never leave this locked desk unless they have to be used in an emergency."

"And there's always someone on duty here?"

"Always," the guard said, beginning to look suspiciously at Nick. "The doorman and I are never away at the same time."

"That certainly speaks well for the security here. No one gets in who isn't expected."

"Including you," the doorman said. "Who are you here to see, anyway?"

"Florence Beaufeld."

The doorman called up on the phone and then sent Nick up on the elevator.

Florence Beaufeld met him at the door with word that they'd be leaving soon to have Christmas dinner with her father. "He'll be picking us up in his car."

"This won't take long. Are you likely to discuss the gift in Michelle's Christmas stocking?"

"No chance of that."

Michelle came down the stairs. "Are *you* back again?" She was wearing a sparkling green party dress with a flared skirt. "Have you solved the riddle yet?"

"I may have. But first I'd like to see a picture of your father. A snapshot, anything."

"I threw them all away after the divorce," Florence said.

"I have one," Michelle told him and went off to get it. She returned with a snapshot of a handsome man with a moustache and a broad grin, squinting into the camera.

Nick studied it for a moment and nodded. "Now I can tell you about the gifts. It's just a theory, but I think it's correct. Here's my proposition. If I'm right, you give me the stocking and the latest gift to deliver to your grandfather."

"All right," Michelle agreed, and her mother nodded, gripping her hands together.

"I had no idea what the five gifts meant until I glimpsed those old alphabet books in your room, Michelle. I imagine your dad used to read to you from those when you were learning the alphabet." Michelle nodded silently. "Those books always use simple objects or animals to stand for the letters. Many of them start out 'A is for Apple.' "

Her mother took it up. "Of course! 'B is for Bus,' 'R is for Raven,' 'A is for Apple'—but then there was the photo of me."

"Mother?" Nick said. " 'M is for Mother,' 'P is for Pig.' "

"Bramp?" Michelle laughed. "What does that mean?"

"That stumped me, too, until I remembered it wasn't just any bus. It had a greyhound on the side. 'G is for Greyhound.' That would give us gramp."

"Gramp," Florence Beaufeld said.

"Gramp!" her daughter repeated. "You mean Grandpa? The money was to come from him?"

"Obviously out of the question," Nick agreed. "He'd never act as a channel for your father's money, not when he opposed the whole thing so vigorously. He even hired me in the hope of learning the location of the money before you found it."

"But gramp certainly means grandfather," Florence pointed out. "It has no other meaning that I know of."

"True enough. But remember that your former husband was limiting himself to a five-letter word by using this system of symbolic Christmas gifts. The word had to be completed by today, a month before Michelle's eighteenth birthday. If gramp stands for grandfather, could the word grandfather itself signify something other than Michelle's flesh-and-blood grandfather?"

He saw the light dawn on Michelle's face first. "The grandfather clock!"

Nick smiled. "Let's take a look."

In the base of the clock, below the window where the pendulum swung, they found the package. Inside were neatly banded packages of hundred-dollar bills.

Florence Beaufeld stood up, breathing hard. "There's close to a half million dollars here."

"He couldn't risk entering this apartment too many times, so he hid the money in advance. If you hadn't found it, he'd probably have found a way to give you a more obvious hint."

"You mean Dan has been in this apartment?"

Nick nodded. "For the last five Christmas Eves."

"But—"

She was interrupted by the buzzer, and the doorman's voice announced the arrival of Mr. Simpson's car.

"Go on," Nick urged them. "I'll catch you up on the rest later. "

It was shortly before midnight when Nick stepped from the shadows near the building and intercepted the man walking quickly toward the entrance. "Larry?"

The night-security man turned to stare at Nick. "You're the fellow who was asking all those questions."

"That's right. I finally got some answers. You're Dan Beaufeld, aren't you?"

"I—"

"There's no point in denying it. I've seen your picture. You shaved off your moustache, but otherwise you look pretty much the same."

"Where did I slip up? Or was it just the photo?" There was a tone of resignation in his voice.

"There were other things. If Dan Beaufeld was leaving those Christmas gifts himself, he had to have a way into the apartment. A building employee seemed likely in view of the tight security, and one of the security men seemed most likely. There are master keys in the security desk and it would have been easy for you to have one duplicated. The gifts were always left shortly before midnight on Christmas Eve, and that implied someone who might start work on the midnight shift. You couldn't leave your post after midnight. Last night as I was leaving, you told me you'd been here just over four years—enough to cover the last five Christmases. You also said old-timers got the day and evening shifts, yet the day security man told me he's only been here a year. That made me wonder if you preferred the midnight shift so you'd be less likely to be seen and recognized by people who might know you. Of course you spent most of your time in Florida, even before the divorce, and without the moustache it was doubtful any of the other employees or residents would recognize you. On those occasions when Michelle or her mother came in after midnight, you could simply hide your face behind a newspaper or bend down behind the TV monitors."

"I had to be close to her," Dan Beaufeld admitted. "I had to watch my daughter growing up, even if it meant risking arrest. I'd see her going off to school or to parties, watching from across the street, and that was enough.

Working here made me feel close to them both. Michelle had a custom of hanging up her Christmas stocking, so I started leaving the gifts every year to let her know I was near and to prepare her for the money she'd get when she turned eighteen.

"I knew the maid let herself out around ten o'clock, and Florence never bothered to relatch the chain lock until bedtime. I entered with my master key, making certain they weren't in the downstairs rooms, and left the gift in the stocking before midnight. Last year I had to come back twice because they were sitting by the fireplace, but usually Florence was out at someone's Christmas party and it was all clear."

"Last night you left the money, too—in the grandfather clock."

Beaufeld grinned. "So they read the clues properly."

"It's drug money, isn't it?"

"Some of it, but I'm out of that now. I used some fake ID to start a new life, a clean life."

"Charles Simpson still wants you in prison."

Dan Beaufeld took a deep breath. "Sometimes I think about turning myself in. Some of the crimes are beyond the statute of limitations now, and a lawyer told me that if I surrendered I'd probably get off with a lenient sentence."

"Why don't you talk it over with Florence and Michelle? They don't want your money, they want you. They're waiting up there for you now."

Dan Beaufeld turned his eyes skyward, toward the lighted windows he must have looked at hundreds of times before. "What are *you* getting out of this?" he asked.

Nick Velvet, who had serious doubts about collecting his fee from Charles Simpson, merely answered, "I don't need to get anything out of this one. It's Christmas."

Herbert Resnicow

THE CHRISTMAS BEAR

"Up there, Grandma," Debbie pointed, all excited, tugging at my skirt, "in the top row. Against the wall. See?" I'm not really her grandma, but at six and a half the idea of a great-grandmother is hard to understand. All her little friends have grandmothers, so she has a grandmother. When she's a little older, I'll tell her the whole story.

The firehouse was crowded this Friday night, not like the usual weekend where the volunteer firemen explain to their wives that they have to polish the old pumper and the second-hand ladder truck. They give the equipment a quick lick-and-a-promise and then sit down to an uninterrupted evening of pinochle. Not that there's all that much to do in Pitman anyway—we're over fifty miles from Pittsburgh, even if anyone could afford to pay city prices for what the big city offers—but still, a man's first thought has to be of his wife and family. Lord knows I've seen too much of the opposite in my own generation and all the pain and trouble it caused, and mine could've given lessons in devotion to this new generation that seems to be interested only in fun. What they call fun.

Still, they weren't all bad. Even Homer Curtis, who was the worst boy of his day, always full of mischief and very disrespectful, didn't turn out all that bad. That was after he got married, of course; not before. He was just voted fire chief and, to give him credit, this whole Rozovski affair was his idea, may God bless him.

Little Petrina Rozovski—she's only four years old and she's always been small for her age—her grandfather was shift foreman over my Jake in the mine while we were courting. We married young in those days because there was no future and you grabbed what happiness you could and that's how I came to be the youngest great-grandmother in the county, only sixty-seven, though that big horse-faced Mildred Ungaric keeps telling everybody I'm over seventy. Poor Petrina has to have a liver transplant, and soon. Real soon. You wouldn't believe what that costs, even if you could find the right liver in the first place. Seventy-five thousand dollars, and it could go to a lot more than that, depending. There isn't that much money in the whole county.

There was talk about going to the government—as if the government's got any way to just give money for things like this or to make somebody give her baby's liver to a poor little girl—or holding a raffle, or something, but none of the ideas was worth a tinker's dam. Then Homer, God bless him, had this inspiration. The volunteer firemen—they do it every year—collect toys for the poor children, which, these days, is half the town, to make sure every child gets *some* present for Christmas. And we all, even if we can't afford it, we all give something. Then one of them dresses up as Santa Claus and they all get on the ladder truck and, on Christmas Eve, they ride through the town giving out the presents. There's a box for everyone, so nobody knows who's getting a present, but the boxes for the families where the father is still working just have a candy bar in them or something like that. And for the littlest kids, they put Santa on top of the ladder and two guys turn the winch and lift him up to the roof as though he's going to go down the chimney and the kids' eyes get all round and everybody feels the way a kid should on Christmas Eve.

We had a town meeting to discuss the matter. "Raffles are no good," Homer declared, "because one person wins and everybody else loses. This year we're going to have an auction where everybody wins. Everybody who can will give a good toy—it can be used, but it's got to be good—in addition to what they give for the poor kids. Then the firemen will auction off those extra toys and the idea of that auction is to pay as *much* as possible instead of as little." That was sort of like the Indian potlatches they used to have around here that my grandfather told me about. Well, you can imagine the opposition to that one. But Homer overrode them all. Skinny as he is, when he stands up and raises his voice—he's the tallest man in town by far—he usually gets his way. Except with his wife, and that's as it should be. "Anyway," he pointed out, "it's a painless way of getting the donations Rozovski needs to get a liver transplant for Petrina."

Shorty Porter, who never backed water for anyone, told Homer, "Your brain ain't getting enough oxygen up there. Even if every family in town bought something for ten dollars on the average, with only twelve hundred families in town, we'd be short at least sixty-three thousand dollars, not to mention what it would cost for Irma Rozovski to stay in a motel near the hospital. And not everybody in town can pay more than what the present he bids on is worth. So you better figure on getting a lot less than twelve thousand, Homer, and what good that'll do, I fail to see." Levi Porter always had a good head for figures. One of these days we ought to make him mayor, if he could take the time off from busting his butt in his little back yard farm which, with his brood, he really can't.

"I never said," Homer replied, "that we were going to raise enough money this way to take care of the operation and everything. The beauty of my plan is . . . I figure we'll raise about four thousand. Right, Shorty?"

"That's about what I figured," Shorty admitted.

712

"We give the money to Hank and Irma and they take Petrina to New York. They take her to a TV station, to one of those news reporters who are always looking for ways to help people. We have a real problem here, a real emergency, and Petrina, with that sweet little face and her big brown eyes, once she appears on TV, her problems are over. If only ten percent of the people in the U.S. send in one cent each, that's all, just one cent, we'd get two hundred fifty thousand dollars. That would cover everything and leave plenty over to set up an office, right here in Pitman, for a clearing house for livers for all the poor little kids in that fix. And the publicity would remind some poor unfortunate mother that her child—children are dying in accidents every day and nobody knows who or where, healthy children—her child's liver could help save the life of a poor little girl."

Even Shorty had to admit it made sense. "And to top it all," Homer added, "if we do get enough money to set up a liver clearing house, we've brought a job to Pitman, for which I'd like to nominate Irma Rozovski, to make up for what she's gone through. And if it works out that way, maybe even two jobs, so Hank can have some work too." Well, that was the clincher. We all agreed and that's how it came about that I was standing in front of the display of the auction presents in the firehouse on the Friday night before Christmas week while Deborah was tugging and pointing at that funny-looking teddy bear, all excited, like I'd never seen her before.

Deborah's a sad little girl. Not that she doesn't have reason, what with her father running off just before the wedding and leaving Caroline in trouble; I never did like that Wesley Sladen in the first place. The Social Security doesn't give enough to support three on, and nobody around here's about to marry a girl going on twenty-nine with another mouth to feed, and I'm too old to earn much money, so Carrie's working as a waitress at the Highway Rest. But thanks to my Jake, we have a roof over our heads and we always will. My father was against my marrying him. I was born a Horvath, and my father wanted me to marry a nice Hungarian boy, not a damn foreigner, but I was of age and my mother was on my side and Jake and I got married in St. Anselm's and I wore a white gown, and I had a right to, not like it is today.

That was in '41 and before the year was out we were in the war. Jake volunteered and, not knowing I was pregnant, I didn't stop him. He was a good man, made sergeant, always sent every penny home. With me working in the factory, I even put a little away. After Marian was born, the foreman was nice enough to give me work to do at home on my sewing machine, so it was all right. Jake had taken out the full G.I. insurance and, when it happened, we got ten thousand dollars, which was a lot of money in those days. I bought the house, which cost almost two thousand dollars, and put the rest away for the bad times.

My daughter grew up to be a beautiful girl and she married a nice boy, John Brodzowski, but when Caroline was born, complications set in and Marian never made it out of the hospital. I took care of John and the baby for six months until John, who had been drinking, hit a tree going seventy. The police said it was an accident. I knew better but I kept my mouth shut because we needed the insurance.

So here we were, quiet little Deborah pulling at me and pointing at that teddy bear, all excited, and smiling for the first time I can remember. "That's what I want, Grandma," she begged. "He's my bear."

"You have a teddy bear," I told her. "We can't afford another one. I just brought you to the firehouse to look at all the nice things."

"He's not a teddy bear, Grandma, and I love him."

"But he's so funny looking," I objected. And he was, too. Black, sort of, but shining blueish when the light hit the right way, with very long hair. Ears bigger than a teddy bear's, and a longer snout. Not cute at all. Some white hairs at the chin and a big crescent-shaped white patch on his chest. And the eyes, not round little buttons, but slanted oval pieces of purple glass. I couldn't imagine what she saw in him. There was a tag, with #273 on it, around his neck. "Besides," I said, "I've only got eighteen dollars for all the presents, for everything. I'm sure they'll want at least ten dollars for him on account of it's for charity."

She began crying, quietly, not making a fuss; Deborah never did. Even at her age she understood, children do understand, that there were certain things that were not for us, but I could see her heart was broken and I didn't know what to do.

Just then the opening ceremonies started. Young Father Casimir, of St. Anselm's, gave the opening benediction, closing with "It is more blessed to give than to receive." I don't know how well that set with Irma Rozovski and the other poor people there, but he'll learn better when he gets older. Then Homer brought up Irma, with Petrina in her arms looking weaker and yellower than ever, to speak. "I just want to thank you all, all my friends and neighbors, for being so kind and . . ." Then she broke down and couldn't talk at all. Petrina didn't cry, she never cried, just looked sad and hung onto her mother. Then Homer came and led Irma away and said a few words I didn't even listen to. I knew what I had to do and I'd do it. Christmas is for the children, to make the children happy, that's the most important part. The children. I'd just explain to Carrie, when she got home, that I didn't get her anything this year and I didn't want her to get me anything. She'd understand.

I got hold of Homer in a corner and told him, "Look, Homer, for some reason Deborah's set on that teddy bear in the top row. Now all I've got is eighteen dollars, and I don't think you'd get anywhere near that much for it at the auction, but I don't want to take a chance on losing it and break Deborah's heart. I'm willing to give it all to you right now, if you'll sell it to me."

"Gee, I'd like to, Miz Sophie," he said, "but I can't. I have to go according to the rules. And if I did that for you, I'd have to do it for everybody, then with everybody picking their favorites, nobody would bid on anything and we couldn't raise the money for Petrina to go to New York."

"Come on, Homer, this ain't the first time you've broken some rules. Besides, I wouldn't tell anyone; I'd just take it off the shelf after everybody's left and no one would know the difference. It's an ugly looking teddy bear anyway."

"I'm real sorry, Mrs. Slowinski," he said, going all formal on me, "but I can't. Besides, there's no way to get it now. Those shelves, they're just boxes piled up with boards across them. You look at them crooked, and the whole thing'll fall down. There's no way to get to the top row until you've taken off the other rows. That's why the numbers start at the bottom."

"You're a damned fool, Homer, and I'm going to get that bear for Deborah anyway. I'm going to get him for a lot less than eighteen dollars too, so your stubbornness has cost the fund a lot of money and you ought to be ashamed of yourself."

We didn't go back to the firehouse until two days before Christmas Eve, Monday, when Carrie was off. Deborah had insisted on showing the bear to her mother to make sure we knew exactly which bear it was she wanted, but when we got there the bear was gone. Poor Deborah started crying, real loud this time, and even Carrie couldn't quiet her down. I picked her up and told her, swore to her, that I would get that bear back for her, but she just kept on sobbing.

I went right up to Homer to tell him off for selling the bear to somebody else instead of to me but before I could open my mouth, he said, "That wasn't right, Mrs. Slowinski, but as long as it's done, I won't make a fuss. Just give me the eighteen dollars and we'll forget about it."

That was like accusing me of stealing, and Milly Ungaric was standing near and she had that nasty smile on her face, so I knew who had stolen the bear. I ignored what Homer said and asked, "Who was on duty last night?" We don't have a fancy alarm system in Pitman; one of the firemen sleeps in the firehouse near the phone.

"Shorty Porter," Homer said, and I went right off.

I got hold of him on the side. "Levi, did you see anyone come in last night?" I asked. "I mean late."

"Only Miz Mildred," he said. "Just before I went to sleep."

Well, I knew it was her, but that wasn't what I meant. "I mean after you went to sleep. Did any noise wake you up?"

"When I sleep, Miz Sophie, only the phone bell wakes me up."

She must have come back later, the doors are never locked, and taken the bear. She's big enough, but how could she reach it? She couldn't climb over the shelves, everything would be knocked over. And she couldn't reach it from the floor. So how did she do it? Maybe it wasn't her, though I would have liked it to be. I went back to Homer. He was tall enough and had arms like a chimpanzee. "Homer," I said, "I'm going to forget what you said if you'll just do one thing. Stand in front of the toys and reach for the top shelf."

He got red, but he didn't blow. After a minute he said, sort of strangled, "I already thought of that. If I can't reach it by four feet, nobody can. Tell you what; give me seventeen dollars and explain how you did it, and I'll pay the other dollar out of my own pocket."

"You always were a stupid, nasty boy, Homer, and you always will be. Well, if you won't help me, I'll have to find out by myself, start at the beginning and trace who'd want to steal a funny-looking bear like that. Who donated the bear?"

"People just put toys in the boxes near the door. We pick out the ones for the auction and the ones for the Santa Claus boxes. No way of knowing who gave what."

I knew he wouldn't be any help, so I got Carrie and Debbie and went to the one man in town who might help me trace the bear, Mr. Wong. He doesn't have just a grocery, a *credit* grocery, thank God; he carries things you wouldn't even find in Pittsburgh. His kids were all grown, all famous scientists and doctors and professors, but he still stayed here, even after Mrs. Wong died. Mrs. Wong never spoke a word of English, but she understood everything. Used to be, her kids all came here for Chinese New Year—that's about a month after ours—and they'd have a big feast and bring the grandchildren. Funny how Mrs. Wong was able to raise six kids in real hard times, but none of her children has more than two. Now, on Chinese New Year, Mr. Wong closes the store for a week and goes to one of his kids. But he always comes back here.

"Look I have for you," he said, and gave Debbie a little snake on a stick, the kind where you turn it and the snake moves like it's real. She was still sniffling, but she smiled a little. The store was chock full of all kinds of Chinese things; little dragons and fat Buddhas with bobbing heads and candied ginger. I knew I was in the right place.

"Did you ever sell anyone a teddy bear?" I asked. "Not a regular teddy bear, but a black one with big purple eyes."

"No sell," he said. "Give."

"Okay." I had struck gold on the first try. "Who'd you give it to?"

"Nobody. Put in box in firehouse."

"You mean for the auction?"

"Petrina nice girl. Like Debbie. Very sick. Must help."

"But . . ." Dead end. I'd have to find another way to trace the bear so I could find out who'd want to steal it. "All right, where'd you get the teddy bear?"

"Grandmother give me. Before I go U.S. Make good luck. Not teddy bear. Blue bear. From Kansu."

"You mean there's a bear that looks like this?"

"Oh yes. Chinese bear. Moon bear. Very danger. Strong. In Kansu."

"Your grandmother *made* it? For you?"

"Not *make*, make. Grandfather big hunter, kill bear. Moon bear very big good luck. Eat bear, get strong, very good. Have good luck in U.S."

"That bear is real bearskin?"

"Oh yes. Grandmother cut little piece for here," he put his hand under his chin, "and for here," he put his hand on his chest. "Make moon." He moved his hand in the crescent shape the bear had on its chest. "Why call moon bear."

"You had that since you were a little boy?" I was touched. "And you gave it for Petrina? Instead of your own grandchildren?"

"Own grandchildren want sportcar, computer, skateboard, not old Chinese bear."

Well, that was typical of all modern kids, not just Chinese, but it didn't get me any closer to finding out who had stolen the teddy bear, the moon bear. Deborah, though, was listening with wide eyes, no longer crying. But what was worse, that romantic story would make it all the harder on her if I didn't get that bear back. She went up to the counter and asked, "Did it come in?"

"Oh yes." He reached down and put a wooden lazy tongs on top of the counter.

"I got it for you, Grandma," Debbie said, "for your arthritis, so you don't have to bend down. I was going to save it for under the tree, but you looked so sad . . ."

God bless you, Deborah, I said in my heart, that's the answer. I put my fingers in the scissor grip and extended the tongs. They were only about three feet long, not long enough, and they were already beginning to bend under their own weight. No way anyone, not even Mildred Ungaric, could use them to steal the moon bear. Then I knew. For sure. I turned around and there it was, hanging on the top shelf. I turned back to Mr. Wong and said, casually, "What do you call that thing grocers use to get cans from the top shelf? The long stickhandle with the grippers at the end?"

"Don't know. In Chinese I say, 'Get can high shelf.' "

"Doesn't matter. Why did you steal the bear back? Decided to sell it to a museum or something?"

"'No. Why I steal? If I want sell, I no give." He was puzzled, not insulted. "Somebody steal moon bear?"

He was right. But so was I. At least I knew *how* it was stolen. You didn't need a "get can high shelf." All the thief needed was a long thing with a hook on the end. Or a noose. Like a broomstick. Or a fishing rod. Anything that would reach from where you were standing to the top of the back row so you could get the bear without knocking over the shelves or the other toys. It had to be Mildred Ungaric; she might be mean, but she wasn't stupid. Any woman had enough long sticks in her kitchen, and enough string and hooks to make a bear-stealer, though she'd look awful funny walking down the street carrying one of those. But it didn't have to be that way. There was something in the firehouse that anyone could use, one of those long poles with the hooks on the end they break your windows with when you have a fire. All you'd have to do is get that hook under the string that held the number tag around the moon bear's neck and do it quietly enough not to wake Levi Porter. Which meant that anyone in town could have stolen the moon bear.

But who would? It would be like stealing from poor little Petrina herself. Mildred was mean, but even she wouldn't do that. Homer was nasty; maybe he accused me to cover up for himself. Mr. Wong might have changed his mind, in spite of what he said; you don't give away a sixty-year-old childhood memory like that without regrets. Levi Porter was in the best position to do it; there was only his word that he slept all through the night and he has eight kids he can hardly feed. Heck, anyone in town could have done it. All I knew was that I didn't.

So who stole the moon bear?

That night I made a special supper for Carrie, and Deborah served. There's nothing a waitress enjoys so much on her time off as being served. I know; there was a time I waitressed myself. After supper, Carrie put Deborah to bed and read to her, watched TV for a while, then got ready to turn in herself. There's really nothing for a young woman to do in Pitman unless she's the kind that runs around with the truckers that stop by, and Carrie wasn't that type. She had made one mistake, trusted one boy, but that could have happened to anybody. And she did what was right and was raising Deborah to be a pride to us all.

I stayed up and sat in my rocker, trying to think of who would steal that bear, but there was no way to find that out. At least it wasn't a kid, a little kid, who had done it; those firemen's poles are heavy. Of course it could have been a teenager, but what would a teenager want with a funny-looking little bear like that? There were plenty of better toys in the lower rows to tempt a teenager, toys that anyone could take in a second with no trouble at all. But none of them had been stolen. No, it wasn't a teenager; I was pretty sure of that.

Finally, I went to sleep. Or to bed, at least. I must have been awake for half the night and didn't come up with anything. But I did know one thing I had to do.

That night being the last night before Christmas Eve, they were going to hold the auction for Petrina in the firehouse. I didn't want to get there too early; no point in making Deborah feel bad seeing all the other presents bought up and knowing she wasn't going to get her moon bear. But I did want her to know it wasn't just idle talk when I promised I'd get her bear back.

Debbie and I waited until the last toy was auctioned off and Porter announced the total. Four thousand, three hundred seventy-two dollars and fifty cents. More than we had expected and more than enough to send the Rozovskis to New York. Then I stood up and said, "I bid eighteen dollars, cash, for the little black bear, Number 273."

Homer looked embarrassed. "Please, Mrs. Slowinski, you know we don't have that bear anymore.

"I just want to make sure, *Mr.* Curtis, that when I find that bear, it's mine. Mine and Deborah's. So you can just add eighteen dollars to your total, *Mr.* Porter, and when that bear turns up, it's mine." Now if anyone was seen with the bear, everybody'd know whose it was. And what's more, if the thief had a guilty conscience, he'd know where to return the bear.

That night I stayed in my rocking chair again, rocking and thinking, thinking and rocking. I was sure I was on the right track. Why would anyone want to take the moon bear? That had to be the way to find the thief; to figure out why anyone would take the bear. But as much as I rocked, much as I thought, I was stuck right there. Finally, after midnight, I gave up. There was no way to figure it out. Maybe if I slept on it . . . Only trouble was, tomorrow was Christmas Eve, and even if I figured out who took the bear, there was no way I could get it back in time to put it under the tree so Debbie would find it when she woke up Christmas morning. For all I knew, the bear was in Pittsburgh by now, or even back in China. Maybe I shouldn't have warned the thief by making such a fuss when I bought the missing bear.

Going to bed didn't help. I lay awake, thinking of everything that had happened, from the time we first stood behind the firetrucks and saw the bear, to the time in Mr. Wong's store when I figured out how the bear had been stolen. Then all of a sudden it was clear. I knew who had stolen the bear. That is I knew *how* it had been stolen and that told me *who* had stolen it which told me how, which . . . What really happened was I knew it all, all at once. Of course, I didn't know *where* the bear was, not exactly, but I'd get to that eventually. One thing I had to remember was not to tell Deborah what I had figured out. Not that I was wrong— I *wasn't* wrong; everything fit too perfectly—but I might not be able to get the bear back. After all, how hard would it be to destroy the bear, to burn it or throw it in the dump, rather than go to jail?

The next morning Deborah woke me. "It's all right, Grandma," she said. "I didn't really want that old moon bear. I really wanted a wetting doll. Or a plain doll. So don't cry." I wasn't aware I was crying, but I guess I was. Whatever else I had done in my life, whatever else Carrie had done, to bring to life, to bring up such a sweet wonderful human being, a girl like this, one to be so proud of, that made up for everything. I only wished Jake could have been here with me to see her. And Wesley Sladen, the fool, to see what he'd missed.

I didn't say anything during breakfast—we always let Carrie sleep late because of her hours but right after we washed up, I dressed Deborah warmly. "We're going for a long walk," I told her. She took my hand and we started out.

I went to the garage where he worked and motioned Levi Porter to come out. He came, wiping his hands on a rag. Without hesitating, I told him what I had to tell him. "You stole the teddy bear. You swiveled the ladder on the ladder truck around, pointing in the right direction, and turned the winch until the ladder extended over the bear. Then you crawled out on the flat ladder and stole the bear. After you put everything back where it was before, you went to sleep."

Well, he didn't bat an eye, just nodded his head. "Yep, that's the way it was," he said, not even saying he was sorry. "I figured you knew something when you bought the missing bear. Nobody throws away eighteen dollars for nothing." Deborah just stared up at him, not understanding how a human being could do such a thing to her. She took my hand for comfort, keeping me between her and Shorty Porter.

"Well, that's *my* bear," I said. "I bought it for Deborah; she had her heart set on it." He wasn't a bit moved. "She loved that bear, Porter. You broke her heart."

"I'm sorry about that, Miz Sophie," he said, "I really didn't want to hurt anybody. I didn't know about Debbie when I stole the bear."

"Well, the least you could do is give it back. If you do, I might consider, just *consider*, not setting the law on you." I didn't really want to put a man with eight children in jail and, up till now, he'd been a pretty good citizen, but I wasn't about to show him that. "So you just go get it, *Mr.* Porter. Right now, and hop to it."

"Okay, Miz Sophie, but it ain't here. We'll have to drive over." He stuck his head in the shop and told Ed Mahaffey that he had to go someplace, be back soon, and we got in his pickup truck.

I wasn't paying attention to where we were going and when he stopped, my heart stopped too. Petrina was lying on the couch in the living room, clutching the moon bear to her skinny little chest. Irma was just standing there wondering what had brought us. "It's about the teddy bear," Levi Porter apologized. "It belongs to Debbie. I have to take it back."

We went over to the couch. "You see," he explained to me, "on opening night, Petrina fell in love with the bear. I wanted to get it for her, but I didn't have any money left. So I took it, figuring it wasn't really stealing; everything there was for Petrina anyway. If I'd knowed about Debbie, I would've worked out something else, maybe."

He leaned over the couch and gently, very gently, took the moon bear out of Petrina's hands. "I'm sorry, honey," he told the thin little girl, "it's really Debbie's. I'll get you a different bear soon." The sad little girl let the bear slip slowly out of her hands, not resisting, but not really letting go either. She said nothing, so used to hurt, so used to disappointment, so used to having everything slip away from her, but her soft dark eyes filled with tears as Shorty took the bear. I could have sworn that the moon bear's purple glass eyes looked full of pain, too.

Shorty put the bear gently into Debbie's arms and she cradled the bear closely to her. She put her face next to the bear's and kissed him and whispered something to him that I didn't catch, my hearing not being what it used to be. Then she went over to the couch and put the bear back into Petrina's hands. "He likes you better," she said. "He wants to stay with you. He loves you."

We stood there for a moment, all of us, silent. Petrina clutched the bear to her, tightly, lovingly, and almost smiled. Irma started crying and I might've too, a little. Shorty picked Deborah up and kissed her like she was his own. "You're blessed," he said to me. "From heaven."

He drove us home, and on the way back I asked Debbie what she said to the bear. "I was just telling him his name," she said innocently, "and he said it was exactly right."

"What is his name?" I asked.

"Oh, that was *my* name for him, Grandma. Petrina told him *her* name; he has a different name now," and that's all she would say about it.

I invited Shorty in but he couldn't stay; had to get back to the garage. If he took too long—well, there were plenty of good mechanics out of work. He promised he'd get Deborah another gift for Christmas, but he couldn't do it in time for tonight. I told him not to worry; I'd work out something.

When we got home, I got started making cookies with chocolate sprinkles, the kind Deborah likes. She helped me. After a while, when the first batch of cookies was baking, her cheeks powdered with flour and her pretty face turned away, she said, quietly, "It's all right not to get a present for Christmas. As long as you know somebody *wanted* to give it to you and spent all her money to get it."

My heart was so full I couldn't say anything for a while. Then I lifted her onto my lap and hugged her to my heart. "Oh, Debbie my love, you'll understand when you're older, but you've just gotten the best Christmas present of all: the chance to make a little child happy."

I held her away and looked into her wise, innocent eyes and wondered if, maybe, she already understood that.

Francis M. Nevins, Jr.

THE SHAPE OF THE NIGHTMARE

Onn the afternoon of the second day before Christmas, just before the terror swept the airport, Loren Mensing was studying the dispirited and weaving line in front of the ticket counter and wishing fervently that he were somewhere else.

He had turned in his exam grades at the law school, said goodbye to the handful of December graduates among his students, and wasted three days moping, with the dread of spending the holidays alone again festering inside him like an untreated wound. The high-rise apartment building he'd lived in for years was being converted to condominiums, dozens of tenants had moved out and dozens more had flown south for the holidays, and the isolation in the building reinforced his sense of being alone in the world.

He had called a travel agent and booked passage on a week-long Caribbean cruise where, if he was lucky, he might find someone as seasonally lonely as he was himself. A *Love Boat* fantasy that he tried desperately to make himself believe. He drove to the airport through swirling snow that froze to ice on the Volkswagen's windshield. He checked his bags, went through security at the lower level, and was lounging near the departure gate for Flight 317, nonstop to Miami, when he heard his name over a microphone.

And learned that he'd been bumped.

"I'm very sorry, Mr. Mensing." The passenger service rep seemed to look bored, solicitous, and in charge all at once. "We have to overbook flights because so many reserved-seat holders don't cancel but don't show up either. Today everyone showed up! You have a right to compensatory cash payment plus a half-fare coupon for the next Miami flight." His racing fingers leafed through the schedule book. "Which departs in just five hours. If you'll take this form to the counter on the upper level they'll write you a fresh ticket."

If he took the next flight he'd miss connections with the excursion ship. He kept his rage under control, detached himself from the horde of travelers at the departure gate, and stalked back upstairs to find a supervisor and demand a seat on the flight he was scheduled to take. When he saw the length of the line at the upper level he almost decided to go home and forget the cruise altogether.

A large metropolitan airport two days before Christmas. Men, women, children, bundled in overcoats and mufflers and down jackets and snowcaps, pushing and jostling and shuffling in the interminable lines that wove and shifted in front of the ticket counters like multicolored snakes. Thousands of voices merging into an earsplitting hum. View through panoramic windows of snow sifting through the gray afternoon, of autos and trucks and taxis crawling to a halt. Honeyed robot voices breaking into the recorded Christmas carols to make flight announcements no one could hear clearly.

Loren was standing apart from the line, trying to decide whether to join it or surrender his fantasy and go home, when it happened.

He heard a voice bellowing something through the wall of noise in the huge terminal. "Bon! Bonreem!" That was what it sounded like in the chaos. It was coming from a man standing to one side of the line like himself. A short sandy-haired man wearing jeans and a down jacket and red ski cap, shouting the syllables in a kind of fury. "Bonreem!"

A man standing in the line turned his head to the right, toward the source of the shout, as if he were hearing something that related to him. A woman in a tan all-weather coat with a rain hood, just behind the man in the line, began to turn her head in the same direction.

The sandy-haired man dropped into a combat crouch, drew a pistol from the pocket of his down jacket, and fired four times at the two who were turning. In the bedlam of the airport the shots sounded no louder than coughs. The next second the face of the man in the line was blown apart. Someone screamed. Then everyone screamed. The man with the shattered face fell to the tiled floor, his fingers still moving, clutching air. The line in front of the ticket counter dissolved into a kaleidoscope of figures running, fainting, shrieking. Instinctively Loren dropped to the floor.

The killer raced for the exit doors, stumbled over Loren's outstretched feet, fell on one knee, hard, cried out in pain, picked himself up, and kept running. John Wilkes Booth flashed through Loren's mind. He saw uniformed figures racing toward them, city and airport police, pistols drawn. Two of them blocked the exit doors. The killer wheeled left, stumbled down the main concourse out of sight, police rushing after him.

In the distance Loren heard more screams, then one final shot.

The public-address system was still playing "White Christmas."

At first they put Loren in with the other witnesses, all of them herded into a large auditorium away from the public areas of the airport. Administrative people brought in doughnuts and urns of coffee on wheeled carts. The witnesses sat or stood in small knots—friends, family groups, total strangers, talking compulsively and pacing and clinging to each other. A few stood or sat alone. Loren was one of them. He was still stunned and he knew no one there to talk to.

After a while he pulled out of shock and looked around the room at the other loners. An old man with a wispy white mustache, probably a widower on his way to visit grandchildren for Christmas. A thin dour man with a cleft chin who blinked continually behind steel-rimmed glasses as if the sun were shining in his eyes. In a folding chair in a corner of the auditorium he saw the woman in the tan hooded coat, her head bowed, eyes indrawn, hugging herself and trying not to shudder. He started to get out of his chair and move toward her.

Another woman flung back the swing doors of the auditorium and stood in the entranceway, a tall fortyish woman in a pantsuit, her hair worn long and straight and liberally streaked with gray. "Loren Mensing?" she called out. Her strong voice cut through the hubbub of helpless little conversations in the vast room. "Is there a Loren Mensing here?"

Loren raised his hand and the woman came over to him. "I'm Gene Holt," she said. "Sergeant Holt, city police, Homicide. You're wanted in the conference room."

He followed her to a room down the hall with a long oak table in the center, flanked by chairs. The air was thick with smoke from cigarettes and a few pipes. He counted at least twenty men in the room—airport police, local police, several in plainclothes. The man at the head of the conference table stood up and beckoned. "Lou Belford," he introduced himself. "Special Agent in charge of the F.B.I. office for the area. The locals just told me you're a sort of detective yourself in an oddball way."

"I used to be deputy legal adviser on police matters for the mayor's office," Loren said. "A part-time position. I teach law for a living."

"And you've helped crack some weird cases, right?"

"I've helped a few times," Loren conceded.

"Well, we've got a weird one here, Professor," Belford grunted. "And you're our star witness. Tell me what you saw."

As Loren told his story Belford scrawled notes on a pad. "It all fits," he said finally. "The guy tripped over your feet and hurt his knee. When he saw he couldn't get out the front exit he headed for the side doors that lead to the underground parking ramps. If he hadn't stumbled over you he could have made it out of the building. Bad luck for him."

"You caught him then? Who was he, and why did he kill that man?"

"We didn't catch him," Belford said. "Cornered him in the gift shop. He saw he was trapped and ate his gun. One shot, right through the mouth. Dead on the spot."

Loren clenched his teeth.

"He wasn't carrying ID," Belford went on, "but we made him a while ago. His name was Frank Wilt. Vietnam vet, unemployed for the last three years. He couldn't hold a job, claimed his head and body were all screwed up from exposure to that Agent Orange stuff they used in the war. The VA couldn't do a thing to help him."

"The man he killed worked for the Veterans Administration?" Loren guessed.

"No, no." Belford shook his head impatiently. "Wilt was obviously desperate for money. It looks as if he took a contract to waste somebody. We just learned he put twenty-five hundred dollars in a bank account Monday. That part of the case is easy. It's the other end we need help with."

"Other end? You mean the victim?" Loren's mind sped to a conclusion from the one fact he knew for certain. "So that's why the F.B.I. are involved! Murder in an airport isn't a Federal crime, and neither is murder by a veteran. So there must be something special about the victim." He leaned forward, elbows on the conference table. "Who was he?"

"The accountant who testified against Lo Scalzo and Pollin in New York last year," Belford said. "John Graham. We gave him and his family new identities under the Witness Relocation Program. They've been living in the city for eighteen months. And now, Professor, we've got an exam for you. Question one: How did the mob find out who and where Graham was? Question two: Why did they hire a broken-down vet to waste him instead of sending in a professional hit man?"

Loren had a sudden memory of one of his own law-school professors who had delighted in posing impossible riddles in class. The recollection made him distinctly uncomfortable.

He stayed with the investigators well into the evening, helping Lieutenant Krauzer of Homicide and Sergeant Holt and the F.B.I. agents interrogate all the actual and possible witnesses. Shortly before midnight, bone-weary and almost numb with the cold, he excused himself, trudged out into the public area of the airport, retrieved his luggage, and grabbed a tasteless snack in the terminal coffee shop. He found his VW in the underground parking garage and drove through hard-packed snow back to his high-rise.

He was unlocking his apartment door when he heard footsteps behind him and whirled, then relaxed. It was the woman, the one in the tan hooded coat who had been standing in the line directly behind John Graham at the time of the murder. "Please let me in, Mr. Mensing," she said. Her voice was soft but filled with desperation, her face taut with tension and fatigue. Loren was afraid she'd collapse at any moment. "Come on in," he nodded. "You need a drink worse than I do."

Ten minutes later they were sitting on the low-backed blue couch, facing the night panorama of the city studded with diamond lights, a pot of coffee, a bottle of brandy, and a plate of cheese and crackers on the cocktail table in front of them. Slowly the warmth, the drinks, and the presence of someone she could trust dissipated the tightness from the woman. Loren guessed that she was about thirty, and that not too long ago she had been lovely.

"Thank you," she said. "I haven't eaten since early this morning, I mean yesterday morning."

"Let me make you a real meal." Loren got up from the couch. "I don't have much in the refrigerator but I think I could manage some scrambled eggs."

"No." She reached out with her hand to stop him. "Maybe later. I'd like to talk now if you don't mind. You may want to kick me out when I'm through." She gave a nervous high-pitched giggle, and Loren sat down again and held her hand, which still felt all but frozen.

"My name is Donna," she began. "Donna Keever. That's my maiden name. I'm married. No, I was married. My husband died just about a year ago. His name was Greene, Charles Greene." Her eyes filled with tears. "It was a year ago last week," she mumbled. "You must have read about it."

Loren groped in the tangle of his memory. Yes, that was it, last year's Christmas heartbreak story in the media. Charles Greene and his six-year-old daughter had been driving home from gift shopping, going west on U.S. 47, when a car traveling east on the same highway hit a rut. The eastbound lane at that point was slightly higher than the westbound because of the shape of a hill on which U.S. 47 was built. The eastbound auto had bounced up into the air, literally flown across the median, and landed nose first on top of Greene's car. Then it had bounced off, flown over the roofs of other passing cars, and landed in the ditch at the side of the highway. Greene, his child, and the other driver, who turned out to be driving on an expired license and with his blood full of alcohol, all died instantly. "I remember," Loren said softly.

"I was ill that day," Donna Greene said, "or I'd have been shopping with Chuck and Cindy. That's the only reason I'm still alive while my family's dead. Isn't life wonderful?"

"It was just chance," Loren told her. "You can't feel guilty about it and ruin the rest of your life."

"No!" Her voice rose to the pitch of a scream. "It wasn't chance. That accident didn't just happen. Someone wanted to kill Chuck or Cindy or me. Or all of us!"

She broke then, and Loren held her while she sobbed. When she could talk again he asked her the obvious question. "Have you told the police what you think?"

"Not the police, not the lawyer who's handling the wrongful death claim for me, not anyone. It was only last week that I knew. A burglar broke into my house a week ago Monday night, came into my bedroom. He was wearing a stocking mask and he—he put his hands on me. I screamed my head off and scared him away. The police said it was just a burglar, but I knew. That man was going to kill me! The police think I'm exaggerating, that I'm still crazy with grief because of the accident."

"How about family? Friends? Have you told them of your suspicions?"

"My parents and Chuck's are all dead. My older brother ran away from home about fifteen years ago, when I was fifteen and he was twenty, and no one's heard from him since. I don't work, I don't have a boyfriend and I just couldn't go to my women friends with something like this."

"What made you come to me?" he asked gently.

"Out at the airport auditorium, when that policewoman or whatever she was paged you, I recognized your name. I've read how you've helped people in trouble. When they let me go I looked up where you live in the phone book and came up here to wait for you."

"Why were you at the airport?"

"I had to get away. If I stayed here I knew that burglar would come back and kill me, if I didn't kill myself first. And I was right! You were there, you saw that man, that gunman standing a few feet from me and he called my name, Donna Greene, and I started to turn and he shot at me and hit the man next to me in the line. Oh, God, somebody, help me!" She broke again, terror and despair poured out of her, and Loren held her and made comforting sounds while his mind raced.

Yes, the two names, John Graham and Donna Greene, sounded just enough alike that in the crowded terminal, with noises assaulting the ears from every side, both of them might have thought their name was being called and turned. To Loren, less than a dozen feet away, the name had sounded like "Bonreem." But which of the two *had* Frank Wilt been paid to kill? If Donna was right, the double-barreled question posed by Agent Belford became meaningless. And if she was the intended victim, what would the person who had hired Wilt do next?

All the time he was soothing Donna Greene he fought with himself. "Don't get involved again," something inside told him. "The last time you saved someone he went out later and killed a bunch of innocent people. This time you're already partly responsible for Wilt's death. And for all you know this woman may be a raving paranoid."

And then all at once he knew what to do, something that would reconcile the conflicting emotions within him and make his Christmas a lot brighter too. He waited until Donna was under control again before he explained.

"I've been thinking," he said. "I don't think I'm qualified to judge whether you're right or wrong about being the target at the airport. But I know someone who is—a woman private detective up in Capital City named Val Tremaine. She's fantastically good at her work. I'm going to ask her to come down and spend a couple of days on your case, getting to know you, talking with you, forming judgments. You'll like her. Her husband died young too and she had to start life over." He disengaged himself gently and rose to his feet. "I'll make the call from my study. You'll be all right?"

"I'm better now. I just needed someone I could open up to who wouldn't treat me like a fool or a lunatic. Look, Mr. Mensing, I'm not a charity case. My lawyer is suing the estate of that other driver for three million dollars. He was rich, his attorneys already offered to settle for three-quarters of a million. I'm not asking you or your detective friend to work for nothing."

"Don't worry about money now," Loren said, and went down the inner hall to the second bedroom that was fixed up as his study, closing the door behind him. He had to check his address book for the number of Val's house, the lovely house nestled on the side of a mountain forty miles from the capital's center, the house she had built as therapy after her husband had died. God, had it been that long since he'd called her? He wondered what had made their relationship taper off, his choice or hers or just the natural drifting of two people who cared deeply for each other but were hundreds of miles apart. He hoped she wouldn't mind his calling in the middle of the night. He hoped very much that she'd be alone.

On the fourth ring she answered, her voice heavy with sleep and bewilderment and a touch of anger.

"Hi, Val, it's me . . . Yes, much too long. I've missed you too. Want to make up for lost time?" He told her about his involvement in the airport murder which she'd heard reported on the evening's TV newscasts, and about the riddle of the intended target which Donna Greene had dropped in his lap. "So if you haven't any other plans for the holidays, why not spend Christmas here? Check her story, be her bodyguard if she needs one, help her start functioning again. Take her to the police with me if you believe she's right." He knew better than to hold out the prospect of a substantial fee. That wasn't the way Val operated.

"You've got yourself a guest," she said. "You know, I was going to invite you up to my place for Christmas but—well, I wasn't sure you'd come."

"I'd have come," he told her softly. If she had invited him he wouldn't have been at the airport this afternoon, and maybe Frank Wilt would be alive and able to tell who had hired him, and maybe Donna Greene would be dead. Chance.

"I'll have to get someone to run the office and I'll need an hour to pack. No way I can get a plane reservation this time of year, so I'll drive. See you around, oh, say eight in the morning if I don't get stuck in the snow."

"I hope you like quiche for breakfast," Loren said.

*   *   *

A soft rapping on the front door jerked him out of a doze on the blue couch. Sullen gray light filling the living room told him it was morning. His watch on the end table read 7:14. "Yes?" he called in the door's direction.

"Me." He recognized Val's voice, undid the deadbolt and the chain lock. The second she was inside with her suitcase he kissed her. It was their first kiss in months and they both made it last. Then they just looked at each other. Val's cheeks were red from the cold and her eyes showed the strain of a long drive through snow-haunted darkness. She was beautiful as ever.

"I missed you," he whispered. "Mrs. Greene's asleep in the bedroom."

They talked quietly in the kitchen while they grated some cheddar, cut a strip of pepper and an onion and ham slices into bits, beat two eggs in cream and melted butter, poured the ingredients into a ready-made pie crust, seasoned them with salt and nutmeg, and popped the quiche into the oven. Loren reported on the murder and Donna's story as the aroma of hot melted cheese filled the kitchen.

"The first step isn't hard to figure," Val said, cutting the quiche into thirds as Loren poured orange juice and coffee. "She'll have to look at pictures of Wilt and tell us if he was her Monday-night burglar. If she identifies him we'll know she was the target at the airport."

"But if she can't identify him," Loren pointed out, "it's not conclusive the other way. Maybe two guys were after her, maybe she didn't get a good look at the burglar . . . We do make a delicious quiche, partner."

"And I'm glad we saved a third of it for our client," Val said, "because the minute she gets up I'm borrowing your bed. I can't take sleepless nights the way I used to."

They left Val asleep and drove downtown through the snow in Loren's VW and entered the office of the homicide detail a little after eleven. Lieutenant Krauzer was in his cubicle, and from his rumpled red-eyed look he'd been working through the night. He was a balding soft-spoken overweight man in his fifties who never seemed to react to anything but, like a human sponge, absorbed whatever came before him.

The lieutenant listened to Loren's story and to Donna Greene's, then picked up his phone handset, and twirled the dial. "Gene, you still have the Wilt photos? Yeah, bring them in, please."

"We've learned a bunch about Frank Wilt since you hung it up last night, Professor," Krauzer said. "He spent most of his time in bars, one joint in particular that's owned by a guy with mob connections. That could explain how he was hired for the hit if the target was John Graham, but it doesn't explain why. Damn

729

it, the mob just doesn't pay washed-up vets to waste a top man on their hit list.

"Your story reads better on that score, Mrs. Greene. An amateur hires Wilt for a private killing. He messes it up at your house last week and runs. He follows you to the airport yesterday, tries again, and messes it up again, because the guy next to you in line happened to have a name that sounds a little like yours, turned faster than you did, and took the bullets meant for you. But, ma'am, you just can't ask me to believe that there's a plot to wipe out your family, because there's no way on earth the freak accident that killed your husband and daughter could have been anything but—"

A knock sounded on the cubicle door and a woman entered. Loren recognized her as Sergeant Holt from last night. She placed a sheaf of photos on Krauzer's desk and left after the lieutenant thanked her. Loren handed the pictures to Donna and watched her face as she squinted and studied the shots with intense deliberation. In the outer office phones were ringing constantly, voices rising and falling, doors slamming, and in the street Loren heard the wail of sirens. Violent crime seemed to thrive on holidays.

There was a hunted look in Donna Greene's eyes when she handed the photos back to Krauzer. "I can't tell," she said in almost a whisper. "I think the burglar was taller but with that stocking mask he wore and in the dark I couldn't see his face well enough to be sure. Oh, I'm sorry!" She began to cry again and Loren reached out for her. Krauzer lifted the phone and a minute later Sergeant Holt came back in, put her arm around the other woman, and led her away.

Leaving Loren alone with Krauzer and free to ask the lieutenant for a large favor.

The Homicide specialist kept shaking his head sadly. "I can't spare the personnel to put a twenty-four-hour watch on her, Professor. Not short-handed the way we are around Christmas. Not without more proof she's really in danger. I like the lady, I think she was totally honest with us, and I know she's scared half to death, but—"

"But she's paranoid?" Loren broke in. "Like all the dissidents in the Sixties and Seventies who thought the government was persecuting them? Look, suppose she's right the way they were right?"

"Then you've got Val Tremaine to protect her," Krauzer said, "and we both know they don't come better." He gave Loren a bleak but knowing smile. "Go on, get out of here with your harem, and have a merry Christmas. Call me if something should happen."

If something should happen . . .

He decided to let Val sleep at the apartment and take Donna shopping so that he and his unexpected guests could have some sort of Christmas. After weaving through downtown streets in a crazy-quilt pattern to throw off any possible followers, he swung the VW onto the Interstate and drove out to the tri-leveled Cherrywood Mall. On the day before Christmas there was more safety among the crowds of frantic last-minute shoppers than behind fortress walls.

The excursion seemed to take Donna out of herself, erase some of the hunted look from her eyes. It was after four and their arms were full of brightly wrapped packages when they slipped into a dark quiet bar on the mall's third level.

"Feeling better?" Loren asked as they sipped Alexanders.

"Much." She smiled hesitantly in the dimness. "Mr. Mensing, these are the happiest few hours I've had since, well, since last year. I can never repay you. You've even made me begin to feel different about everything that's happened to me."

"Different how?"

"I've decided it wasn't just blind chance that I didn't go in the car with Chuck and Cindy that day and that the man next to me was shot and not me. I think I'm meant to live awhile yet. And, oh, God, there's so much I've got to do after the holidays to put my life back in order. The house is a hopeless mess and the tires on my car are getting bald and I need a new will—Chuck and I had mutual wills, we each left everything to the other—and, you know, I may start dating again." She looked into her glass and then into Loren's eyes. "You're, ah, not available, right?"

"I'm honestly not sure," Loren said. "Val and I have been out of touch for months and we've been sort of preoccupied since she got in this morning." He paused, blinked behind his glasses, bewildered as he habitually was by the thought that any young woman could find a bear-bodied, unaggressive, overly learned intellectual in his late thirties even slightly desirable. "But look. However that turns out, I'm your friend. Val and I both are."

"To friendship," she said as they touched glasses. "To a new life."

It was the strangest Christmas Eve he'd ever spent. To an outsider it would have seemed that an exotic fantasy had become real—a man and two lovely women, a high-rise well stocked with food and drink. As night fell and with it fresh snow, Loren made a bowl of hot mulled wine and played the new recording of the Dvorak Piano Quintet No. 5 that he'd bought as his Christmas present to himself. Later he turned on the radio to an FM station and they listened to traditional carols as he gave Val and Donna the gifts he'd purchased at Cherrywood. Their squeals of delight warmed him more than the wine.

Part of him felt relaxed and at peace and part of him stayed alert like an animal in fear of predators. But as midnight approached he found it harder and harder to believe there was danger. Not with the snow outside turning to ice as

731

it fell, not behind the deadbolt and chain lock in a haven twenty stories high.

A little after 12:30 they exchanged good-night kisses and Loren surrendered his bedroom to the women. When they'd closed the door behind them he made a last ritual concession to security by tugging the massive blue couch over against the front door before arranging its cushions on the living-room rug in a makeshift bed.

He was fitting a spare sheet over the couch cushions when Val came back, her blonde hair falling soft and loose over the shoulders of the floor-length caftan he'd given her for Christmas. She smiled and helped him smooth the sheets. "Now you'll sleep better," she said. "I feel like a toad kicking you out of your bed on Christmas Eve."

"Can't be helped. Donna's asleep?"

"Out like a light. You were right to serve decaffeinated coffee." She sat on a sheet-draped cushion. "And thanks to that nap I had before the sergeant dropped by, I'm not tired in the least—"

"Sergeant?" Loren asked. He was suddenly alert.

Her face dropped slightly. "Oh, rats, I wasn't supposed to tell you. Lieutenant Krauzer sent a man over this afternoon just in case Donna was in danger. He came while you were shopping, showed me his ID, looked this place over, and set up a stakeout in 20-B, the vacant apartment across the hall. He said not to tell you and Donna so you'd act natural and not scare any suspects away. But it's good to know Sergeant Holt is standing guard."

Loren leaped to his feet. "Sergeant *who?*" he shouted.

"Gene Holt, Lieutenant Krauzer's assistant. He's been in 20-B since midafternoon. The couple that lives there is in Florida—"

"Describe him." Loren's face was white, and wet fear crawled down his spine.

"A tall man in his middle thirties, thin face, cleft chin. He wears glasses and blinks a lot as if his eyes were weak."

In that moment Loren saw the shape of the nightmare. "That's it," he muttered, and stood there frozen with understanding. He could hear clocks ticking, the night stirrings of the building, the plock-plock of icy snow falling on the outdoor furniture on his balcony. Every sound was magnified now, transformed into menace.

Val shook his shoulders, fear twisting her own face. "Loren, what in God's name is the matter?"

"Sergeant Gene Holt," Loren told her, "is a woman. And now I know who Weak Eyes is too."

"He had a badge and identification!" she protested.

"And if you know the right document forger you can have stuff like that made to order while you wait." He pushed her aside, headed for the phone on a stand in the corner. "I'm calling Krauzer and getting some real cops here."

The phone exploded into sound before he'd crossed the room and he jumped as if shot. A second ring, a third. He picked it up as if it were a cobra, forced it to his ear. Silence. Then a voice, smooth, low, calm. "Unfortunately, Professor, I can't let you call for reinforcements," it said.

Loren slammed the phone down, held it in its cradle for a count of ten, then lifted the handset. He didn't hear a dial tone. He punched the hook furiously. Still no dial tone. He whirled to Val. "Him," he whispered. "He must have planted a bug here while he was pretending to check the place out for security. He heard every word we said all evening and was just waiting for all of us to go to bed. We can't phone outside—he's tying up the line by keeping the phone in 20-B off the hook."

"We can phone for help from one of the other apartments on this floor!"

"We can't. 20-C moved out when the building converted to condo and 20-D's out of town. Besides, he's at the front door of 20-B. If you try to go out in the hall he's got you."

"Let's get out on the balcony and scream for help!"

"Who'd hear us in that storm?"

Val swung around, raced down the inner hall to the bedroom. Loren knew why. To throw on street clothes and get her gun. If she'd brought one with her. Loren hadn't asked.

The phone shrilled again. Loren stared at it as if hypnotized. He let it ring six times, nine. Over the rings he heard Donna's sobs of terror from the bedroom. Oh, God, if only it were Krauzer on the other end, or Belford the F.B.I. man, or anyone in the world except Weak Eyes, anyone Loren could ask to call the police! On the twelfth ring he picked up the receiver.

"Mensing," the low calm voice said, "I have just placed a charge of plastic explosive on the outside of your door. You have two minutes to take down that barricade I heard you put up and send Donna across the hall. Do that and you and Tremaine live."

Loren slammed the phone down. Val in a dark gray jumpsuit ran back into the living room. There was no gun in her hand. Loren almost cried out with frustration. "Donna's in your closet," she whispered. "I pushed the dresser against the door."

Loren nodded, held her close, and spoke feverishly into her ear. Time slipped away into nothingness. Val went down the inner hall, turning off lights, opened the fusebox, and cut the master switch. The apartment was pitch-dark now. Loren found the hall closet, put on rubbers, and his heaviest overcoat. Then he tugged the couch away from the front door, undid the deadbolt and chain, and ran across the room.

He slipped on the couch cushions in the middle of the floor and pain shot through his ankle. He bit down on his lower lip, hobbled the rest of the way across the room, threw open the door leading to his balcony. Sudden cold stunned him, made him shake uncontrollably as he stood outside, behind the curtained balcony door, and watched through the thin elongated crack.

The front door was flung back and Weak Eyes leaped in, using a combat crouch like Wilt at the airport. In his hand there was a gun. His eyes focused on the patch of light across the dark room, the light coming from the balcony. He stalked across the room like a wolf. Loren tensed, waiting. Yes, he was close enough to the balcony now, time for Val to make her move.

There she went, crawling across the wall-to-wall carpet in the dark, all but invisible in her jumpsuit, making the front door and then for the firestairs.

Weak Eyes heard nothing, didn't turn. He kicked the balcony door all the way open, looked down the long balcony. There was nothing to see but a white-painted cast-iron outdoor table and three matching chairs. He took a cautious step out onto the balcony, his eyes trying to pierce the deeper shadows at the far end.

Loren brought the fourth iron chair down hard on the back of the killer's neck. Weak Eyes howled, flung his arms up for balance. The gun flew out of his hand into the slush. He skidded halfway down the balcony, his belly slammed into the outdoor table.

Loren kept hitting him with the chair until Weak Eyes wasn't moving. It was all Loren could do to keep from hurling him over the balcony rail and down twenty stories to the street.

Loren was still standing there, his teeth chattering in the cold, his ankle throbbing, sweat pouring down him, when a few minutes later Val and two uniformed patrolmen rushed out to the balcony.

"What a world," Lieutenant Krauzer grunted eight hours later. "Her own brother."

Weak Eyes was in a cell, Donna had been taken to the hospital under sedation, and they were gathered in Loren's apartment. He sat on the blue couch with his right leg raised on a kitchen chair and the ankle bandaged tightly. Val sat on a hassock at his side, refilling his coffee cup, handing him tissues when he sneezed. Outside, Christmas morning dawned in shades of smoky gray.

"It had to be her brother," Loren said. "Once Val described the fake Gene Holt it all clicked, because I remembered seeing a man of that exact description in the airport auditorium after the Graham murder. And then I remembered three things Donna had mentioned in passing: that she and her late husband had had mutual wills, that she hadn't gotten around to making a new will yet, and that her wrongful-death suit against the driver of the car that killed her family was going to net her a lot of money.

"Now suppose she'd been killed by that burglar, or at the airport? Who would have wound up with that money? Obviously if she died intestate it would go to her next of kin. Who's her next of kin? Her parents are dead, her only child is dead—*but she had a brother who dropped out of sight fifteen years ago.*

"Now the picture clears up," he went on. "Charles and Cindy Greene die in a tragic accident that gets heavy coverage in the media. Wherever he was at the time, Donna's brother hears of it, sees huge financial possibilities, comes to the city quietly, and begins shadowing her. He satisfied himself that the wrongful-death action is going to produce big money and that his sister hasn't made out a new will. He had to get rid of her before she does. He looks around—the forged ID and bugging equipment and plastique show he has underworld connections—and hires Frank Wilt for the hit.

"Wilt breaks into her house a week ago Monday night and bungles the job. Brother gives him another chance. Wilt follows her to the airport, makes his move—and by blind chance a man with a name similar to Donna's is next to her in line, turns faster than she does, and dies instead of her.

"Brother has gone to the airport too, as a backup in case Wilt blew it again. He and Donna are both rounded up as witnesses and taken to the auditorium but either she doesn't see him in the crowd or just doesn't recognize him after fifteen years. When she's let go he follows her to my place and works out a plan to kill her here, doing the job himself this time. He reads the newspaper stories about the airport murder, picks up the name of Sergeant Gene Holt, and uses it as his cover identity but makes the big mistake of assuming from the name that the sergeant is a man."

"And that bit of chauvinism's going to cost him twenty years in the slam." Krauzer yawned and lumbered wearily to his feet. "Well, if you'll excuse me it's Christmas morning and I've got grandkids to play Santy for." He winked broadly at Val. "Remember he's a sick man and needs his rest."

When he had let himself out Val slid off the hassock to sit on the floor. "Funny," Loren said as he ran his hand through her hair. "The way Christmas turned out isn't anything like what I either was afraid of or hoping for. I can't walk, I haven't slept in two nights, I've got the chills, but all in all I feel good. The crazy way this world goes, I'll be damned if I know if it's all chance or if it's meant."

"I'll take the world either way if you're part of it," Val told him softly.

Robert Turner

CHRISTMAS GIFT

There was no snow and the temperature was a mild sixty-eight degrees and in some of the yards nearby the shrubbery was green, along with the palm trees, but still you knew it was Christmas Eve. Doors on the houses along the street held wreaths, some of them lighted. A lot of windows were lighted with red, green, and blue lights. Through some of them you could see the lighted glitter of Christmas trees. Then, of course, there was the music, which you could hear coming from some of the houses, the old familiar songs, "White Christmas," "Ave Maria," "Silent Night."

All of that should have been fine because Christmas in a Florida city is like Christmas anyplace else, a good time, a tender time. Even if you're a cop. Even if you pulled duty Christmas Eve and can't be home with your own wife and kid. But not necessarily if you're a cop on duty with four others and you're going to have to grab an escaped con and send him back, or more probably have to kill him because he was a lifer and just won't *go* back.

In the car with me was McKee, a Third-Grade, only away from a beat a few months. Young, clear-eyed, rosy-cheeked All-American-boy type, and very, very serious about his work. Which was fine; which was the way you should be. We were parked about four houses down from the rented house where Mrs. Bogen and her three children were living.

At the same distance the other side of the house was a sedan in which sat Lieutenant Mortell and Detective First-Grade Thrasher. Mortell was a bitter-mouthed, needle-thin man, middle-aged and with very little human expression left in his eyes. He was in charge. Thrasher was a plumpish, ordinary guy, an ordinary cop.

On the street behind the Bogen house was another precinct car with two other Firsts in it, a couple of guys named Dodey and Fischman. They were back there in case Earl Bogen got away from us and took off through some yards to that other block. I didn't much think he'd get to do that.

After a while McKee said: "I wonder if it's snowing up north. I'll bet the hell it is." He shifted his position. "It don't really seem like Christmas, no snow. Christmas with palm trees, what a deal!"

"That's the way it was with the first one," I reminded him.

He thought about that. Then he said: "Yeah. Yeah. That's right. But I still don't like it."

I started to ask him why he stayed down here, then I remembered about his mother. She needed the climate; it was all that kept her alive.

"Y'know," McKee said then, "sarge, I been thinking; this guy Bogen must be nuts."

"You mean because he's human? Because he wants to see his wife and kids on Christmas?"

"Well, he must know there's a *chance* he'll be caught. If he is, it'll be worse for his wife and kids, won't it? Why the hell couldn't he just have *sent* them presents or something and then called them on the phone? Huh?"

"You're not married, are you, McKee?"

"No."

"And you don't have kids of your own. So I can't answer that question for you."

"I still think he's nuts."

I didn't answer. I was thinking how I could hound the stinking stoolie who had tipped us about Earl Bogen's visit home for Christmas, all next year, without getting into trouble. There was a real rat in my book, a guy who would stool on something like that, I was going to give him a bad time if it broke me.

Then I thought about what Lieutenant Mortell had told me an hour ago. "Tim," he said. "I'm afraid you're not a very good cop. You're too sentimental. You ought to know by now a cop can't be sentimental. Was Bogen sentimental when he crippled for life that manager of the finance company he stuck up on his last hit? Did he worry about *that* guy's wife and kids? Stop being a damned fool, will you, Tim?"

That was the answer I got to my suggestion that we let Earl Bogen get in and see his family and have his Christmas and catch him on the way out. What was there to lose, I'd said. Give the guy a break, I'd said. I'd known, of course, that Mortell wouldn't have any part of that, but I'd had to try anyhow. Even though I knew the lieutenant would think of the same thing I had—that when it came time to go, Bogen might be twice as hard to take.

McKee's bored young voice cut into my thoughts: "You think he'll really be armed? Bogen, I mean."

"I think so."

"I'm glad Mortell told us not to take any chances with him, that if he even makes a move that looks like he's going for a piece, we give it to him. He's a smart old cop, Mortell."

"That's what they say. But did you ever look at his eyes?"

"What's the matter with his eyes?" McKee said.

"Skip it," I said. "A bus has stopped."

We knew Earl Bogen had no car; we doubted he'd rent one or take a cab. He was supposed to be short of dough. A city bus from town stopped up at the corner. When he came he'd be on that, most likely. But he wasn't on this one. A lone woman got off and turned up the avenue. I let out a slight sigh and looked at the radium dial of my watch. Ten fifty. Another hour and ten minutes and we'd be relieved; it wouldn't happen on our tour. I hoped that was the way it would be. It was possible. The stoolie could have been wrong about the whole thing. Or something could have happened to change Bogen's plans, or at least to postpone his visit to the next day. I settled back to wait for the next bus.

McKee said: "Have you ever killed a guy, sarge?"

"No," I said. "I've never had to. But I've been there when someone else did."

"Yeah? What's it like?" McKee's voice took on an edge of excitement. "I mean for the guy who did the shooting? How'd he feel about it?"

"I don't know. I didn't ask him. But I'll tell you how he looked. He looked as though he was going to be sick to his stomach, as though he should've been but couldn't be."

"Oh," McKee said. He sounded disappointed. "How about the guy that was shot? What'd he do? I've never seen a guy shot."

"Him?" I said. "Oh, he screamed."

"Screamed?"

"Yeah. Did you ever hear a child scream when it's had a door slammed on its fingers? That's how he screamed. He got shot in the groin."

"Oh, I see," McKee said, but he didn't sound as though he really did. I thought that McKee was going to be what they called a good cop—a nice, sane, completely insensitive type guy. For the millionth time I told myself that I ought to get out. Not after tonight's tour, not next month, next week, tomorrow, but right now. It would be the best Christmas present in the world I could give myself and my family. And at the same time I knew I never would do that. I didn't know exactly why. Fear of not being able to make a living outside; fear of winding up a burden to everybody in my old age the way my father was— those were some reasons but not the whole thing. If I talk about how after being a cop so long it gets in your blood no matter how you hate it, that sounds phony. And it would sound even worse if I said one reason I stuck was in hopes that I could make up for some of the others, that I could do some good sometimes.

"If I get to shoot Bogen," McKee said, "he won't scream."

"Why not?"

"You know how I shoot. At close range like that, I'll put one right through his eyes."

"Sure, you will," I told him. "Except that you won't have the chance. We'll get him, quietly. We don't want any shooting in a neighborhood like this on Christmas Eve."

Then we saw the lights of the next bus stop up at the corner. A man and a woman got off. The woman turned up the avenue. The man, medium height but very thin, and his arms loaded with packages, started up the street.

"Here he comes," I said. "Get out of the car, McKee. "

We both got out, one on each side. The man walking toward us from the corner couldn't see us. The street was heavily shaded by strings of Australian pine planted along the walk.

"McKee," I said. "You know what the orders are. When we get up to him, Thrasher will reach him first and shove his gun into Bogen's back. Then you grab his hands and get the cuffs on him fast. I'll be back a few steps covering you. Mortell will be behind Thrasher, covering him. You got it?"

"Right," McKee said.

We kept walking, first hurrying a little, then slowing down some, so that we'd come up to Bogen, who was walking toward us, just right, before he reached the house where his family were but not before he'd passed Mortell and Thrasher's car.

When we were only a few yards from Bogen, he passed through an open space, where the thin slice of moon filtered down through tree branches. Bogen wore no hat, just a sport jacket and shirt and slacks. He was carrying about six packages, none of them very large but all of them wrapped with gaudily colored paper, foil, and ribbon. Bogen's hair was crew cut instead of long the way it was in police pictures and he'd grown a mustache; but none of that was much of a disguise.

Just then he saw us and hesitated in his stride. Then he stopped. Thrasher, right behind him, almost bumped into him. I heard Thrasher's bull-froggy voice say: "Drop those packages and put your hands up, Bogen. Right now!"

He dropped the packages. They tumbled about his feet on the sidewalk and two of them split open. A toy racing car was in one of them. It must have been still slightly wound up because when it broke out of the package, the little motor whirred and the tiny toy car spurted across the sidewalk two or three feet. From the other package, a small doll fell and lay on its back on the sidewalk, its big, painted eyes staring upward. It was what they call a picture doll, I think; anyhow, it was dressed like a bride. From one of the other packages a liquid began to trickle out onto the sidewalk and I figured that had been a

739

bottle of Christmas wine for Bogen and his wife.

But when Bogen dropped the packages he didn't raise his hands. He spun around and the sound of his elbow hitting Thrasher's face was a sickening one. Then I heard Thrasher's gun go off as he squeezed the trigger in a reflex action, but the flash from his gun was pointed at the sky.

I raised my own gun just as Bogen reached inside his jacket but I never got to use it. McKee used his. Bogen's head went back as though somebody had jolted him under the chin with the heel of a hand. He staggered backward, twisted, and fell.

I went up to Bogen with my flash. The bullet from McKee's gun had entered Bogen's right eye and there was nothing there now but a horrible hole. I moved the flash beam just for a moment, I couldn't resist it, to McKee's face. The kid looked very white but his eyes were bright with excitement and he didn't look sick at all. He kept licking his lips, nervously. He kept saying: "He's dead. You don't have to be worrying about him, now. He's dead."

Front door lights began to go on then in nearby houses and people began coming out of them. Mortell shouted to them: "Go on back inside. There's nothing to see. Police business. Go on back inside."

Of course, most of them didn't do that. They came and looked, although we didn't let them get near the body. Thrasher radioed back to headquarters. Mortell told me: "Tim, go tell his wife. And tell her she'll have to come down and make final identification for us."

"Me?" I said. "Why don't you send McKee? He's not the sensitive type. Or why don't you go? This whole cute little bit was your idea, anyhow, lieutenant, remember?"

"Are you disobeying an order?"

Then I thought of something. "No," I told him. "It's all right. I'll go."

I left them and went to the house where Bogen's wife and kids lived. When she opened the door, I could see past her into the cheaply, plainly furnished living room that somehow didn't look that way now, in the glow from the decorated tree. I could see the presents placed neatly around the tree. And peering around a corner of a bedroom, I saw the eyes, big with awe, of a little girl about six and a boy about two years older.

Mrs. Bogen saw me standing there and looked a little frightened. "Yes?" she said. "What is it?"

I thought about the newspapers, then. I thought: "What's the use? It'll be in the newspapers tomorrow, anyhow." Then I remembered that it would be Christmas Day; there wouldn't *be* any newspapers published tomorrow, and few people would bother about turning on radios or television sets.

"Don't be alarmed," I told her, then. "I'm just letting the people in the neighborhood know what happened. We surprised a burglar at work, ma'am, and he ran down this street. We caught up with him here and had to shoot him. But it's all over now. We don't want anyone coming out, creating any more disturbance, so just go back to bed, will you please?"

Her mouth and eyes opened very wide. "Who—who was it?" she said in a small, hollow voice.

"Nobody important," I said. "Some young hood."

"Oh," she said then and I could see the relief come over her face and I knew then that my hunch had been right and Bogen hadn't let her know he was coming; he'd wanted to surprise her. Otherwise she would have put two and two together.

I told her good night and turned away and heard her shut the door softly behind me.

When I went back to Mortell I said: "Poor Bogen. He walked into the trap for nothing. His folks aren't even home. I asked one of the neighbors and she said they'd gone to Mrs. Bogen's mother's and wouldn't be back until the day after Christmas."

"Well, I'll be damned," Mortell said, watching the men from the morgue wagon loading Bogen onto a basket.

"Yes," I said. I wondered what Mortell would do to me when he learned what I'd done and he undoubtedly would, eventually. Right then I didn't much care. The big thing was that Mrs. Bogen and those kids were going to have their Christmas as scheduled. Even when I came back and told her what had happened, the day after tomorrow, it wouldn't take away the other.

Maybe it wasn't very much that I'd given them but it was something and I felt a little better. Not much, but a little.

James Powell

SANTA'S WAY

Lieutenant Field parked behind the Animal Protective League van. The night was cold, the stars so bright he could almost taste them. Warmer constellations of tree lights decorated the dark living rooms on both sides of the street. Field turned up his coat collar. Then he followed the footprints in the snow across the lawn and up to the front door of the house where a uniformed officer stood shuffling his feet against the weather.

Captain Fountain was on the telephone in the front hallway and listening so hard he didn't notice Field come in. "Yes, Commissioner," he said. "Yes, sir, Commissioner." Then he laid a hand over the mouthpiece, looked up at a light fixture on the ceiling, and demanded, "Why me, Lord? Why me?" (The department took a dim view of men talking to themselves on duty. So Fountain always addressed furniture or fixtures. He confided much to urinals. They all knew how hard-done-by Fountain was.) Turning to repeat his question to the hatrack he saw Field. "Sorry to bring you out on this of all nights, Roy," he said. He pointed into the living room and added cryptically, "Check out the fireplace, why don't you?" Then he went back to listening.

Field crossed to the cold hearth. There were runs of blood down the sides of the flue. Large, red, star-shaped spatters decorated the ashes.

A woman's muffled voice said, "I heard somebody coming down the chimney." A blonde in her late thirties sitting in a wing chair in the corner, her face buried in a handkerchief. She looked up at Field with red-rimmed eyes. "After I called you people I even shouted up and told him you were on your way. But he kept on coming."

Captain Fountain was off the telephone. From the doorway he said, "So Miss Doreen Moore here stuck her pistol up the flue and fired away."

"Ka-pow, ka-pow, ka-pow," said the woman, making her hand into a pistol and, in Field's opinion, mimicking the recoil quite well. But he didn't quite grasp the situation until men emerged from the darkness on the other side of the picture window and reached up to steady eight tiny reindeer being lowered down from the roof in a large sling.

"Oh, no!" said Field.

"Oh, yes," said Fountain. "Come see for yourself."

Field followed him upstairs to the third-floor attic where the grim-faced Animal Protective League people, their job done, were backing down the ladder from the trap door in the roof.

Field and Fountain stood out on the sloping shingles under the stars. Christmas music came from the radio in the dashboard of the pickle-dish sleigh straddling the ridge of the roof. Close at hand was Santa, both elbows on the lip of the chimney, his body below the armpits and most of his beard out of sight down the hole. He was quite dead. The apples in his cheeks were Granny Smiths, green and hard.

Only the week before Field had watched the PBS documentary "Santa's Way." Its final minutes were still fresh in his mind. Santa in an old tweed jacket sat at his desk at the Toy Works backed by a window that looked right down onto the factory floor busy with elves. Mrs. Claus, her eyes on her knitting, smiled and nodded at his words and rocked nearby. "Starting out all we could afford to leave was a candy cane and an orange," Santa had said. "The elves made the candy canes and it was up to me to beg or borrow the oranges. Well, one day the United Fruit people said, 'Old timer, you make it a Chiquita banana and we'll supply them free and make a sizable donation to the elf scholarship fund.' But commercializing Christmas wasn't Santa's way. So we made do with the orange. And look at us now." He lowered his hairy white head modestly. "The Toy Works is running three shifts making sleds and dolls and your paint boxes with your yellows, blues, and reds. The new cargo dirigible lets us restock the sleigh in flight." Santa gave the camera a sadder look. "Mind you, there's a down side," he acknowledged. "We've strip-mined and deforested the hell out of the North Pole for the sticks and lumps of coal we give our naughty little clients. And our bond rating isn't as good as it used to be. Still, when the bankers say, 'Why not charge a little something, a token payment for each toy?' I always answer, 'That isn't Santa's way.' "

An urgent voice from the sleigh radio intruded on Field's remembering. "We interrupt this program for a news bulletin," it said. "Santa is dead. We repeat, Santa is dead. The jolly old gentleman was shot several times in the chimney earlier this evening. More details when they are available." At that late hour all good little boys and girls were in bed. Otherwise, Field knew, the announcer would've said, "Antasay is eadday," and continued in pig Latin.

Field stood there glumly watching the street below where the A.P.L. people were chasing after a tiny reindeer which had escaped while being loaded into the van. Lights had come on all over the neighborhood and faces were appearing in windows. After a moment, he turned his attention to the corpse.

But Fountain was feeling the cold. "Roy," he said impatiently, "Santa came down the wrong chimney. The woman panicked. Ka-pow, ka-pow, ka-pow! Cut and dried."

Field shook his head. "Rooftops are like fingerprints," he reminded the Captain. "No two are alike. Santa wouldn't make a mistake like—" He frowned, leaned forward, and put his face close to the corpse's.

"It wasn't just the smell of whiskey on his lips, Miss Moore," said Field. "You see, if Santa'd been going down the chimney his beard would've been pushed up over his face. But it was stuck down inside. Miss Moore, when you shot Santa he was on his way up that chimney."

The woman twisted the handkerchief between her fingers. "All right," she snapped. Then in a quieter voice she said, "All right, Nicky and I go back a long way. Right around here is end of the line for his Christmas deliveries. I'll bet you didn't know that."

Field had guessed as much. Last year when his kids wondered why the treat they left on a tray under the tree was never touched he had suggested maybe Santa was milk-and-cookied out by the time he got to their house.

"Anyway," continued Miss Moore, "Nicky'd always drop by afterwards for a drink and some laughs and one thing would lead to another. But I'm not talking one-night stands," she insisted. "We took trips. We spent time together whenever he could get away. He said he loved Mrs. Claus but she was a saint. And I wasn't a saint, he said, and he loved me for that. And I was crazy about him. But tonight he tried to walk out on me. So I shot him."

In the distance Field heard the police helicopter come to take the sleigh on the roof to Impound.

Fountain said, "Better get Miss Moore down to the station before this place is crawling with reporters. I'll wait for the boys with the flue-extractor rig."

Field turned on his car radio to catch any late-breaking developments. "O Tannenbaum, O Tannenbaum, how beautiful your branches!" sang a small choir. They drove without speaking for a while. Then out of nowhere the woman said, "You know that business about Nicky having a belly that shook like a bowl full of jelly? Well, that was just the poet going for a cheap rhyme. Nicky took care of himself. He exercised. He jogged. And he had this twinkle in his eye that'd just knock my socks off."

"I heard about the twinkle," Field admitted.

"But underneath it all there was this deep sadness," she said. "It wasn't just the fund-raising, the making the rounds every year, hat in hand, for money to keep the North Pole going. And it wasn't the elves, although they weren't always that easy to deal with. 'They can be real short, Doreen,' he told me once. 'Hey, I know elves are short, Nicky. Give me credit for some brains,' I said. He said, 'No, Doreen, I mean abrupt.'

"One time I asked him why he got so low and he said, 'Doreen, when I look all those politicians, bankers, lawyers, and captains of industry in the eye do you know who I see staring back at me? Those same naughty little boys and girls I gave the sticks and lumps of coal to. Where did I go wrong, Doreen? How did they end up running the show?'

"Well, a while back Nicky got this great idea how he could walk away from the whole business. Mr. Santa franchises. He'd auction the whole operation off country by country. Mr. Santa U.S.A. gets exclusive rights to give free toys to American kids and so on, country by country. 'And the elves'd take care of Mrs. Claus,' he said. 'They love her. She's a saint. And with the money I'll raise you and me'll buy a boat and sail away. We'll live off my patented Mr. Santa accessories. You know, my wide belt and the metered tape recorder of my laugh at a buck a 'ho!' "

Suddenly a voice on the radio said, "We now take you to New York where Leviathan Cribbage, elf observer to the United Nations, is about to hold a press conference." After the squeal of a microphone being adjusted downward a considerable distance, a high-pitched little voice said, "The High Council of Elves has asked me to issue the following statement: 'Cast down as we are by the murder of our great leader, Santa Claus, we are prepared, as a memorial to the man and his work, to continue to manufacture and distribute toys on the night before Christmas. In return we ask that our leader's murderer, whom we know to be in police custody, be turned over to elf justice. If the murderer is not in our hands within twenty-four hours the Toy Works at the North Pole will be shut down permanently.' " The room erupted into a hubbub of voices.

"Turn me over to elf justice?" said Miss Moore with a shudder. "That doesn't sound so hot."

"It won't happen," Field assured her as he parked the car. "Even a politician couldn't get away with a stunt like that."

Four detectives were crowded around the squad room television set. Field took Miss Moore into his office. Gesturing her into a chair, he sat down at his desk and said, "Now where were we?"

"With a buck a 'ho!' and me waiting there tonight with my bags packed," she said. "And here comes Nicky down the chimney. 'Doreen,' he says. 'I've only got a minute. I've still deliveries to make. Honey, I told Mrs. Claus about us. She's forgiven me, as I knew she would. But I can't see you again.'

" 'What about the Mr. Santa auction?' said I.

" 'Some auction,' he said. 'Everybody wanted America or Germany. Nobody wanted to be the Bangladeshi or the Ethiopian Mr. Santa. Crazy, isn't it? Everybody wants to load up the kids who've already got everything when giving to kids with nothing is the real fun.' Then he looked at me and said, 'It got me thinking about where I went wrong, Doreen. Maybe I should have given my naughty little clients toys, too. Maybe then they wouldn't have grown up into the kinds of people they did. Anyway, I'm going to give it a try. From now on, I'll be Santa of all the children, naughty or nice. Good-bye, Doreen,' he said and turned to go.

"That's when I pulled out the revolver I keep around because I'm alone so much. I was tired of men who put their careers ahead of their women. I swore I'd kill him if he tried to leave. He went 'ho-ho-ho!' and took the gun out of my hand. He knew I couldn't shoot. I burst into tears. He gathered me in his arms and gave me a good-bye kiss. Emptying the bullets onto the rug, he tossed the pistol aside and walked over to the fireplace. 'You're a nice girl, Doreen,' he said with a twinkle in his eye. 'Don't let anybody ever tell you different.' But just before he ducked his head under the mantel I saw the twinkle flicker."

"Flicker?" asked Field.

"Like he was thinking maybe he'd figured me wrong," she explained. "Like maybe I'd reload the gun. Well, up the chimney he went, hauling ass real fast. And suddenly, I was down on my knees pushing those bullets back into that pistol, furious that I'd wasted my whole life just to be there any time that old geezer in his red wool suit with that unfashionably wide belt could slip his collar and be with me, furious that he was dumping me just so he could give toys to naughty little boys and girls. I was trembling with rage. But every bullet I dropped I picked up again. When I'd gotten them all I went over and emptied the pistol up the chimney. Then I called you people."

Field's telephone rang. "Roy," said his wife, "I just heard the news about Santa. Roy, there aren't any presents under our tree. What are we going to do?"

"Lois, I can't talk now," said Field. "Don't worry. I'll think of something." He hung up the phone. Maybe if he worked all night he could cobble together some toys out of that scrap lumber in the basement.

Fountain was signaling from the doorway. He had an efficient-looking young woman with him. Field stepped outside. "Roy, this is Agent Mountain, Federal Witness Protection Program," he said. "I just got off the phone with the Commissioner. We're not bringing charges."

"Captain, we could be talking premeditated murder here," insisted Field, telling the part about her putting the bullets back into the pistol.

Fountain shrugged. "You want a trial? You want all the nice little boys and girls finding out that Santa was murdered and why? No way, Roy. She walks. But we can't let those damn knee-highs get her."

"You mean elves?" asked Field, who had never heard elves referred to in that derogatory way before.

"You got it," said Fountain. "So Agent Mountain's here to relocate her, give her a whole new identity."

Agent Mountain waved through the door at Doreen Moore. "Hi, honey," she said cheerily. "It looks like it's back to being a brunette."

*   *   *

Field put on his overcoat and closed his office door behind him. He stopped for a moment in front of the squad room television set. Somebody from the State Department was saying, "Peter, let's clear up one misconception right now. Elves are not short genetically. Their growth has been stunted by smoking and other acts of depravity associated with a perverse lifestyle. Can we let such twisted creatures hold our children's happiness hostage? I think not. I refer the second part of your question to General Frost."

A large man in white camouflage placed a plan of the Toy Works at the North Pole on an easel. "In case of a military strike against them, the elves intend to destroy the Toy Works with explosive charges set here, here, and here," he said, tapping with a pointer. "As I speak, our airborne forces, combined with crack RCMP dogsled units, have moved to neutralize—"

Field's phone was ringing. He hurried back to his office. "Hey, Lieutenant," said Impound, "we found presents in Santa's sleigh, some with your kids' names on them. Want to come by and pick them up?"

Field came in with the presents trapped between his chin and his forearm, closing the door quietly behind him. His wife was rattling around in the kitchen. He didn't call out to her, not wanting to wake the children. The light from the kitchen would be enough to put the presents under the tree. He was halfway across the living room when the lights came on. His children were staring down at him from the top of the stairs. Zack and Lesley, the eldest, exchanged wise glances. Charlotte was seven. She'd lost her first baby tooth that afternoon and her astonished mouth had a gap in it.

Field smiled up at them. "Santa got held up in traffic," he lied. "So he deputized a bunch of us as Santa's little helpers to deliver his presents." Charlotte received this flimsy nonsense with large, perplexed eyes. It was the first time he had ever told her anything she didn't believe instantly.

Ordering the children back to bed, Field went into the kitchen. Lois was watching a round-table discussion called "Life After Santa" on the little television set. When he told her about the presents from Impound she said, "Thank God." He didn't tell her what had just happened with the kids. Maybe one of these days he'd be able to sit down and give them the straight scoop, how there really had been this nice guy called Santa Claus who went around in a sleigh pulled by reindeer giving kids presents because he loved them, so, of course, we had to shoot him.

He turned on the kettle to make himself a cup of instant coffee and sat down beside his wife. On the screen a celebrated economist was saying, "Of course, we'll have to find an alternate energy source. Our entire industrial base has always depended on Santa's sticks and lumps of coal."

"But what a golden opportunity to end our kids' dependence on free toys," observed a former National Security advisor. "That's always smelled like socialism

747

to me. Kids have to learn there's no free lunch. We should hand the Toy Works over to private enterprise. I hear Von Clausewitz Industries are interested in getting into toys."

"What about distribution?" asked someone else.

"Maybe we could talk the department stores into selling toys for a week or two before Christmas."

"Selling toys?" asked someone in disbelief.

The National Security advisor smiled. "We can hardly expect the Von Clausewitz people to pick up the tab. No, the toys'll have to be sold. But the play of the marketplace will hold prices—"

Field heard a sound. Someone had raised an upstairs window. Footsteps headed down the hall toward the children's rooms. He took the stairs two at a time, reaching the top with his service revolver drawn. Someone was standing in the dark corner by Charlotte's door. Crouching, pistol at the ready, Field snapped on the hall light. "Freeze!" he shouted.

The woman turned and gave him a questioning look. She had immense rose-gossamer wings of a swallow-tail cut sprouting from her shoulder-blades and a gown like white enamel shimmering with jewels. He didn't recognize who it was behind the surgical mask until she tugged at the wrists of her latex gloves, took a shiny quarter from the coin dispenser at her waist and stepped into Charlotte's room.

Field came out of his crouch slowly. Returning his weapon to its holster he went back down to the kitchen. He turned off the kettle, found the whiskey bottle in the cupboard and poured himself a drink with a trembling hand. "Lois," he said, "I almost shot the Tooth Fairy."

"Oh, Roy," she scolded in a tired voice.

On the television screen someone said, "Of course, we'll need a fund to provide toys for the children of the deserving poor."

"Don't you mean 'the deserving children of the poor'?" someone asked.

" 'Deserving children of the deserving poor,' " suggested another.

Lois shook her head. "Store-bought toys, Roy?" she asked. "We've got mortgage payments, car payments, Lesley's orthodontist, and saving for the kids' college. How can we afford store-bought toys?"

It'd been a hard day. He didn't want to talk about next year's toys. "Lois, please—" he started to say a bit snappishly. But here the program broke for a commercial and a voice said, "Hey, Mom, hey, kids, is Dad getting a little short? (And we don't mean abrupt). Why not send him along to see the folks at Tannenbaum Savings and Loan. All our offices have been tastefully decorated for the season. And there's one near you. So remember—" here a choir chimed in "—Owe Tannenbaum, Owe Tannenbaum, how beautiful their branches!"

George Baxt

I SAW MOMMY KILLING
SANTA CLAUS

We buried my mother yesterday, so I feel free to tell the truth. She lived to be ninety-three because, like the sainted, loyal son I chose to be, I didn't blab to the cops. I'm Oscar Leigh and my mother was Desiree Leigh. That's right—Desiree Leigh, inventor of the Desiree face cream that promised eternal youth to the young and rejuvenation to the aged. It was one of the great con games in the cosmetics industry. I suppose once this is published, it'll be the end of the Desiree cosmetics empire, but frankly, my dears, I don't give a damn. Desiree Cosmetics was bought by a Japanese combine four years ago, and my share (more than two billion) is safely salted away. I suppose I inherit Mom's billions, too, but what in heaven's name will I do with it all? Count it, I guess.

Desiree Leigh wasn't her real name. She was born Daisy Ray Letch, and who could go through life with a surname like Letch? For the past fourteen years she's been entertaining Alzheimer's and that was when I began to take an interest in her past. She was always very mysterious about her origins and equally arcane about the identity of my father. She said he was killed in North Africa back in 1943 and that his name was Clarence Kolb. I spent a lot of money tracing Clarence, until one night, in bed watching an old movie, the closing credits rolled and one of the character actors was named Clarence Kolb. I mentioned this to Mother the next morning at breakfast, but she said it was a coincidence and she and my father used to laugh about it.

She had no photos of my father, which I thought was strange. When they married a few months before the war, they settled in Brooklyn, in Coney Island. Surely they must have had their picture taken in one of the Coney Island fun galleries? But no, insisted Mother, they avoided the boardwalk and the amusement parks—they were too poor for such frivolities. How did Father make his living? He was a milkman, she said—his route was in Sheepshead Bay. She said he worked for the Borden Company. Well, let me tell you this; there is no record of a Clarence Kolb ever having been employed by the Borden Milk

Company. It cost an ugly penny tracking that down.

Did Mom work, too, perhaps? "Oh, yes," she told me one night in Cannes where our yacht was berthed for a few days, "I worked right up until the day before you were born."

"What did you do?" We were on deck playing honeymoon bridge in the blazing sunlight so Mom could keep an eye on the first mate, with whom she was either having an affair or planning to have one.

"I worked in a laboratory." She said it so matter of factly while collecting a trick she shouldn't have collected that I didn't believe her. "You don't believe me." (She not only conned, stole, and lied, she was a mind-reader.)

"Sure I believe you." I sounded as convincing as an East Berlin commissar assuring would-be emigrés they'd have their visas to freedom before sundown.*

"It was a privately owned laboratory," she said, sneaking a look at the first mate, who was sneaking a look at the second mate. "It was a couple of blocks from our apartment."

"What kind of a laboratory was it?" I asked, mindful that the second mate was sneaking a look at me.

"It was owned by a man named Desmond Tester. He fooled around with all kinds of formulas."

"Some sort of mad scientist?"

She chuckled as she cheated another trick in her favor. "I guess he *was* kind of mad in a way. He had a very brilliant mind. I learned a great deal from him."

"Is that where you originated the Desiree creams and lotions?"

"The seed was planted there."

"How long were you with this—"

"Desmond Tester. Let me see now. Your daddy went into the Army in February of '42. I didn't know I was pregnant then or he'd never have gone. On the other hand, I suppose if I *had* known, I would have kept it to myself so your dad could go and prove he was a hero and not just a common everyday milkman."

"I don't see anything wrong in delivering milk."

"There's nothing heroic about it, either. Where was I?"

"Taking my king of hearts, which you shouldn't be."

She ignored me and favored the first mate with a seductive smile, and I blushed when the second mate winked at me. "Anyway, I took time off to give birth to you and then I went right back to work for Professor Tester. A nice lady in the neighborhood looked after you. Let me think, what was her name? Oh, yes—Blanche Yurka."

*Ed. note: A joyful note to anachronism—shortly after this story was written.

"Isn't that the name of the actress who played Ma Barker in a gangster movie we saw on the late show?"

"I don't know, is it? That's my ten of clubs you're taking," she said sharply.

"I've captured it fair and square with the queen of clubs," I told her. "How come you never married again?"

"I guess I was too busy being a career woman. I was assisting Professor Tester in marketing some of his creams and lotions by then. I had such a hard time cracking the department stores."

"When did you come up with your own formulas?"

"That was after the professor met with his unfortunate death."

Unfortunate, indeed. I saw her kill him.

It was Christmas of 1950—in fact, it was Christmas Day. Mom was preparing to roast a turkey at the professor's house—our apartment was much too small for entertaining—and I remember almost everyone who was there. It was mostly kids from the neighborhood, the unfortunate ones whose families couldn't afford a proper Christmas dinner. There must have been about ten of them. Mother and the professor were the only adults, although Mom still insists there was a woman there named Laurette with whom the professor was having an affair. Mom says this woman was jealous of her because she thought Mom and the professor were having a little ding-dong of their own. (I've always suspected my mother of doing quite a bit of dinging and donging in the neighborhood when she couldn't meet a grocery bill or a butcher bill or satisfy the landlord or Mr. Kumbog, who owned the liquor store.)

Mom says it was Laurette who shot the professor in the heart and ran away (and was never heard of again, need I tell you?) —but I'm getting ahead of myself. It happened like this: Mom was in the kitchen stuffing the turkey when Professor Tester appeared in the doorway dressed in the Santa Claus suit. He had stuffed his stomach but still looked no more like Santa Claus than Monty Woolley did in *Life Begins at Eight-Thirty*.

"Daisy Ray, I have to talk to you," he said.

"Just let me finish stuffing this turkey and get it in the oven," she told him. "I'd like to feed the kids by around five o'clock when I'm sure they'll be tired of playing Post Office and Spin the Bottle and Doctor." I remember her asking me, "Sonny, have you been playing Doctor?"

"As often as I can," I replied with a smirk. And I still do. Now I'm a specialist.

"Daisy Ray, come with me to the laboratory," Tester insisted.

"Oh, really, Desmond," Mother said, "I don't understand your tone of voice."

"There are a lot of things going on around here that are hard to understand," the professor said ominously. "Daisy Ray!" He sounded uncannily like Captain Bligh summoning Mr. Christian.

I caught a very strange and very scary look on my mother's face. And then she did something I now realize should have made the professor realize that something unexpected and undesirable was about to befall him. She picked up her handbag, which was hanging by its strap on the back of a chair, and followed him out of the room. "Sonny, you stay here." Her voice sounded as though it was coming from that echo chamber I heard on the spooky radio show, *The Witch's Tale*.

"Yes, Mama."

I watched her follow Professor Tester out of the kitchen. I was frightened. I was terribly frightened. I had a premonition that something awful was going to happen, so I disobeyed her orders and tiptoed after them.

The laboratory was in the basement. I waited in the hall until I heard them reach the bottom of the stairs and head for the main testing room, then I tiptoed downstairs, praying the stairs wouldn't squeak and betray me. But I had nothing to worry about. They were having a shouting match that would have drowned out the exploding of an atom bomb.

The door to the testing room was slightly ajar and I could hear everything.

"What have you done with the formula?" he raged.

"I don't know what you're talking about." Mama was quite cool, subtly underplaying him. It was one of those rare occasions when I almost admired her.

"You damn well know what I'm talking about, you thief!"

"How dare you!" What a display of indignation—had she heard it, Norma Shearer would have died of envy.

"You stole the formula for my rejuvenating cream! You've formed a partnership with the Sibonay Group in Mexico!"

"You're hallucinating. You've been taking too many of your own drugs."

"I've got a friend at Sibonay—he's told me everything! I'm going to put you behind bars unless you give me back my formula!"

Although I didn't doubt for one moment that my mother had betrayed him, I still had to put my hand over my mouth to stifle a laugh. I mean, have you ever seen Santa Claus blowing his top? It's a scream in red and white.

"Don't you touch me! Don't you lay a hand on me!" Mother's handbag was open and she was fumbling for something in it. He slapped her hard across the face. Then I heard the *pop* and the professor was clutching at his chest. Through his fingers little streams of blood began to form.

Mom was holding a tiny pearl-handled pistol in her hand, the kind Kay

Francis used to carry around in a beaded bag. My God, I remember saying to myself, I just saw Mommy killing Santa Claus.

I turned tail and ran. I bolted up the stairs and into the front of the house, where the other kids who couldn't possibly have heard what had gone on in the basement were busy choosing up sides for a game called Kill the Hostess. I joined in and there wasn't a peep out of Mom for at least half an hour.

I began to wonder if maybe I had been hallucinating, if maybe I hadn't seen Mom slay the professor. I left the other kids and—out of curiosity and I suppose a little anxiety—I went to the kitchen.

You've got to hand it to Mom (you might as well, she'd take it anyway): the turkey was in the oven, roasting away. She had prepared the salad. Vegetables were simmering, timed to be ready when the turkey was finished roasting. She was topping a sweet-potato pie with little round marshmallows. She looked up when I came in and asked, "Enjoying yourself, Sonny?"

I couldn't resist asking her. "When is Santa Claus coming with his bag of presents for us?"

"Good Lord, when indeed! Now, where could Santa be, do you suppose?"

Dead as a doornail in the testing room, I should have responded, but instead I said, "Shucks, Mom, it beats me."

She thought for a moment and then said brightly, "I'll bet he's downstairs working on a new formula. Go down and tell him it's time he put in his appearance."

Can you top that? Sending her son into the basement to discover the body of the man she'd just assassinated?

Well, I dutifully discovered the body and started yelling my head off, deciding that was the wisest course under the circumstances. Mom and the kids came running. When they saw the body, the kids began shrieking, me shrieking the loudest so that maybe Mom would be proud of me, and Mom hurried and phoned the police.

What ensued after the police arrived was sheer genius on my mother's part. I don't remember the detective's name—by now he must be in that Big Squadroom in the Sky—but I'm sure if he was ever given an I.Q. test he must have ended up owing them about fifty points. Mom was saying hysterically, "Oh, my God, to think there was a murderer in the house while I was in the kitchen preparing our Christmas dinner and the children were in the parlor playing guessing games!" She carried the monologue for about ten minutes until the medical examiner came into the kitchen to tell the detective the professor had been done in by a bullet to the heart.

"Any sign of the weapon?" asked the detective.

"It's not *my* job to look for one," replied the examiner testily.

So others were dispatched to look for a weapon. Knowing Mom, it wouldn't be in her handbag, but where, I wondered, could she have stashed it? I stopped in mid-wonder when I heard her say, "It might have been Laurette."

"Who's she?" asked the detective.

Mom folded her hands, managing to look virtuous and sound scornful. "She was the professor's girl friend, if you know what I mean. He broke it off with her last week and she wasn't about to let him off so easy. She's been phoning and making threats, and this morning he told me she might be coming around to give him his Christmas present." She added darkly, "That Christmas present was called—*death!*"

"Did you see her here today?" the detective asked. Mom said she hadn't. He asked us all if we'd seen a strange lady come into the house. I was tempted to tell him the only strange lady I saw come into the house was my mother, but I thought of that formula and how wealthy we'd become and I became a truly loving son.

"She could have come in by the cellar door," I volunteered.

It was the first time I saw my mother look at me with love and admiration. "It's on the other side of the house, and with all the noise we were making—"

"And I had the radio on in the kitchen, listening to the *Make Believe Ballroom,*" was the fuel Mother added to the fire I had ignited. The arson was successful. The police finally left—without finding the weapon—taking the body with them, and Mom proceeded with Christmas dinner as though killing a man was an everyday occurrence.

The dinner was delicious, although some of us kids noted the turkey had a slightly strange taste to it.

"Turkey can be gamey," Mama trilled—and within the next six months she was on her way to becoming one of the most powerful names in the cosmetics industry.

I remained a bachelor. I worked alongside Mother and her associates and watched as, one by one over the years, she got rid of all of them. She destroyed the Sibonay people in Mexico by proving falsely and at great cost, that they were the front for a dope-running operation. She thought it would be fun if I could become a mayor of New York City, but a psychic told me to forget about it and go into junk bonds—which I did and suffered staggering losses. (The psychic died a mysterious death, which she obviously hadn't foretold herself.)

Year after year, Christmas after Christmas, I was sorely tempted to tell Mama I saw her kill Santa Claus. Year after year, Christmas after Christmas, I was aching to know where she had hidden the weapon.

And then I found out. It was Christmas Day fourteen years ago.

The doctors, after numerous tests, had assured me that Mom was show-ing signs of Alzheimer's. Such as when applying lipstick, she ended up cover-ing her chin with rouge. And wearing three dresses at the same time. And fil-ing her shoes and accessories in the deep freeze. It was sad, really, even for a murderess who deserved no mercy. Yet she insisted on cooking the Christmas dinner herself that year.

"It's going to be just like that Christmas Day when we had that wonder-ful dinner with the neighborhood kiddies," she said. "And Professor Tester dressed up as Santa Claus and brought in that big bag of games and toys. And he gave me the wonderful gift of the exclusive rights to the formula for the Desiree Rejuvenating Lotion."

There were twenty for dinner and, believe it or not, Mother cooked it impeccably. The servants were a bit nervous, but the guests were too drunk to notice. Then, while eating the turkey, Mother asked me across the table, "Does the turkey taste the same way it did way back when, Sonny?"

And then I remembered how the turkey had tasted that day forty years ago when Mama had said something about turkey sometimes tasting gamey. I looked at her and, ill or not, there was mockery in her eyes. It was then that I said to her, not knowing if she would understand what I meant: "Mama, I saw what you did."

There was a small smile on her face. Slowly her head began to bob up and down. "I had a feeling you did," she said. "But you haven't answered me. Does the turkey taste the same way it did then?"

I spoke the truth. "No, Mama, it doesn't. It's very good."

She was laughing like a madwoman. Everyone at the table looked embar-rassed and there was nowhere for me to hide. "Is this a private joke between you and your mother?" the man at my right asked me. But I couldn't answer. Because my mother had reached across the table and shoved her hand into the turkey's cavity, obscenely pulling out gobs of stuffing and flinging it at me.

"Don't you know why the turkey tasted strange? Can't you guess why, Sonny? Can't you guess what I hid in the stuffing so those damn fool cops wouldn't find it? Can't you guess, Sonny? Can't you?"

Peter Lovesey

SUPPER WITH MISS SHIVERS

The door was stuck. Something inside was stopping it from opening, and Fran was numb with cold. School had broken up for Christmas that afternoon—"Lord dismiss us with Thy blessing"—and the jubilant kids had given her a blinding headache. She'd wobbled on her bike through the London traffic, two carriers filled with books suspended from the handlebars. She'd endured exhaust fumes and maniac motorists, and now she couldn't get into her own flat. She cursed, let the bike rest against her hip, and attacked the door with both hands.

"It was quite scary, actually," she told Jim when he got in later. "I mean, the door opened perfectly well when we left this morning. We could have been burgled. Or it could have been a body lying in the hall."

Jim, who worked as a systems analyst, didn't have the kind of imagination that expected bodies behind doors. "So what was it—the doormat?"

"Get knotted. It was a great bundle of Christmas cards wedged under the door. Look at them. I blame you for this, James Palmer."

"Me?"

Now that she was over the headache and warm again, she enjoyed poking gentle fun at Jim. "Putting our address book on your computer and running the envelopes through the printer. This is the result. We're going to be up to our eyeballs in cards. I don't know how many you sent, but we've heard from the plumber, the dentist, the television repairman, and the people who moved us in, apart from family and friends. You must have gone straight through the address book. I won't even ask how many stamps you used."

"What an idiot," Jim admitted. "I forgot to use the sorting function."

"I left some for you to open."

"I bet you've opened all the ones with checks inside," said Jim. "I'd rather eat first."

"I'm slightly mystified by one," said Fran. "Do you remember sending to someone called Miss Shivers?"

"No. I'll check if you like. Curious name."

"It means nothing to me, but she's invited us to a meal."

Fran handed him the card—one of those desolate, old-fashioned snow scenes of someone dragging home a log. Inside, under the printed greetings, was the signature *E. Shivers (Miss)* followed by *Please make my Christmas— come for supper seven next Sunday, 23rd.* In the corner was an address label.

"Never heard of her," said Jim. "Must be a mistake."

"Maybe she sends her cards by computer," said Fran, and added, before he waded in, "I don't think it's a mistake, Jim. She named us on the envelope. I'd like to go."

"For crying out loud—Didmarsh is miles away. Berkshire or somewhere. We're far too busy."

"Thanks to your computer, we've got time in hand," Fran told him with a smile.

The moment she'd seen the invitation, she'd known she would accept. Three or four times in her life she'd felt a similar impulse and each time she had been right. She didn't think of herself as psychic or telepathic, but sometimes she felt guided by some force that couldn't be explained scientifically. A good force, she was certain. It had convinced her that she should marry no one else but Jim, and after three years together she had no doubts. Their love was unshakable. And because he loved her, he would take her to supper with Miss Shivers. He wouldn't understand *why* she was so keen to go, but he would see that she was in earnest, and that would be enough . . .

"By the way, I checked the computer," he told her in front of the destinations board on Paddington Station next Sunday. "We definitely didn't send a card to anyone called Shivers."

"Makes it all the more exciting, doesn't it?" Fran said, squeezing his arm.

Jim was the first man she had trusted. Trust was her top requirement of the opposite sex. It didn't matter that he wasn't particularly tall and that his nose came to a point. He was loyal. And didn't Clint Eastwood have a pointed nose?

She'd learned from her mother's three disastrous marriages to be ultra-wary of men. The first—Fran's father, Harry—had started the rot. He'd died in a train crash just a few days before Fran was born. You'd think he couldn't be blamed for that, but he could. Fran's mother had been admitted to hospital with complications in the eighth month, and Harry, the rat, had found someone else within a week. On the night of the crash he'd been in London with his mistress, buying her expensive clothes. He'd even lied to his pregnant wife, stuck in hospital, about working overtime.

For years Fran's mother had fended off the questions any child asks about a father she has never seen, telling Fran to forget him and love her stepfather instead. Stepfather the First had turned into a violent alcoholic. The divorce had taken nine years to achieve. Stepfather the Second—a Finn called Bengt (Fran called him Bent)—had treated their Wimbledon terraced house as if it were a sauna, insisting on communal baths and parading naked around the place. When Fran was reaching puberty, there were terrible rows because she wanted privacy. Her mother had sided with Bengt until one terrible night when he'd crept into Fran's bedroom and groped her. Bengt walked out of their lives the next day, but, incredibly to Fran, a lot of the blame seemed to be heaped on her, and her relationship with her mother had been damaged forever. At forty-three, her mother, deeply depressed, had taken a fatal overdose.

The hurts and horrors of those years had not disappeared, but marriage to Jim had provided a fresh start. Fran nestled against him in the carriage and he fingered a strand of her dark hair. It was supposed to be an Intercity train, but B.R. were using old rolling-stock for some of the Christmas period and Fran and Jim had this compartment to themselves.

"Did you let this Shivers woman know we're coming?"

She nodded. "I phoned. She's over the moon that I answered. She's going to meet us at the station."

"What's it all about, then?"

"She didn't say, and I didn't ask."

"You didn't? Why not, for God's sake?"

"It's a mystery trip—a Christmas mystery. I'd rather keep it that way."

"Sometimes, Fran, you leave me speechless."

"Kiss me instead, then."

A whistle blew somewhere and the line of taxis beside the platform appeared to be moving forward. Fran saw no more of the illusion because Jim had put his lips to hers.

Somewhere beyond Westbourne Park Station, they noticed how foggy the late afternoon had become. After days of mild, damp weather, a proper December chill had set in. The heating in the carriage was working only in fits and starts and Fran was beginning to wish she'd worn trousers instead of opting decorously for her corduroy skirt and boots.

"Do you think it's warmer farther up the train?"

"Want me to look?"

Jim slid aside the door. Before starting along the corridor, he joked, "If I'm not back in half an hour, send for Miss Marple."

"No need," said Fran. "I'll find you in the bar and mine's a hot cuppa."

She pressed herself into the warm space Jim had left in the corner and rubbed a spy-hole in the condensation. There wasn't anything to spy. She shivered and wondered if she'd been right to trust her hunch and come on this trip. It was more than a hunch, she told herself. It was intuition.

It wasn't long before she heard the door pulled back. She expected to see Jim, or perhaps the man who checked the tickets. Instead, there was a fellow about her own age, twenty-five, with a pink carrier bag containing something about the size of a box file. "Do you mind?" he asked. "The heating's given up altogether next door."

Fran gave a shrug. "I've got my doubts about the whole carriage."

He took the corner seat by the door and placed the bag beside him. Fran took stock of him rapidly, hoping Jim would soon return. She didn't feel threatened, but she wasn't used to these old-fashioned compartments. She rarely used the trains these days except the tube occasionally.

She decided the young man must have kitted himself in an Oxfam shop. He had a dark-blue car coat, black trousers with flares, and crepe-soled ankle boots. Around his neck was one of those striped scarves that college students wore in the sixties, one end slung over his left shoulder. And his thick, dark hair matched the image. Fran guessed he was unemployed. She wondered if he was going to ask her for money.

But he said, "Been up to town for the day?"

"I live there." She added quickly, "With my husband. He'll be back presently."

"I'm married, too," he said, and there was a chink of amusement in his eyes that Fran found reassuring. "I'm up from the country, smelling the wellies and cowdung. Don't care much for London. It's crazy in Bond Street this time of year."

"Bond Street?" repeated Fran. She hadn't got him down as a big spender.

"This once," he explained. "It's special, this Christmas. We're expecting our first, my wife and I."

"Congratulations."

He smiled. A self-conscious smile. "My wife, Pearlie—that's my name for her—Pearlie made all her own maternity clothes, but she's really looking forward to being slim again. She calls herself the frump with a lump. After the baby arrives, I want her to have something glamorous, really special. She deserves it. I've been putting money aside for months. Do you want to see what I got? I found it in Elaine Ducharme."

"I don't know it."

"It's a very posh shop. I found the advert in some fashion magazine." He had already taken the box from the carrier and was unwrapping the pink ribbon.

"You'd better not. It's gift-wrapped."

"Tell me what you think," he insisted, as he raised the lid, parted the tissue, and lifted out the gift for his wife. It was a nightdress, the sort of night-dress, Fran privately reflected, that men misguidedly buy for the women they adore. Pale-blue, in fine silk, styled in the empire line, gathered at the bodice, with masses of lace interwoven with yellow ribbons. Gorgeous to look at and hopelessly impractical to wash and use again. Not even comfortable to sleep in. His wife, she guessed, would wear it once and pack it away with her wedding veil and her love letters.

"It's exquisite."

"I'm glad I showed it to you." He started to replace it clumsily in the box.

"Let me," said Fran, leaning across to take it from him. The silk was irresistible. "I know she'll love it."

"It's not so much the gift," he said as if he sensed her thoughts. "It's what lies behind it. Pearlie would tell you I'm useless at romantic speeches. You should have seen me blushing in that shop. Frilly knickers on every side. The girls there had a right game with me, holding these nighties against themselves and asking what I thought."

Fran felt privileged. She doubted if Pearlie would ever be told of the gauntlet her young husband had run to acquire the nightdress. She warmed to him. He was fun in a way that Jim couldn't be. Not that she felt disloyal to Jim, but this guy was devoted to his Pearlie, and that made him easy to relax with. She talked to him some more, telling him about the teaching and some of the sweet things the kids had said at the end of the term.

"They value you," he said. "They should."

She reddened and said, "It's about time my husband came back." Switching the conversation away from herself, she told the story of the mysterious invitation from Miss Shivers.

"You're doing the right thing," he said. "Believe me, you are."

Suddenly uneasy for no reason she could name, Fran said, "I'd better look for my husband. He said I'd find him in the bar."

"Take care, then."

As she progressed along the corridor, rocked by the speeding train, she debated with herself whether to tell Jim about the young man. It would be difficult without risking upsetting him. Still, there was no cause really.

The next carriage was of the standard Intercity type. Teetering toward her along the center aisle was Jim, bearing two beakers of tea, fortunately capped with lids. He'd queued for ten minutes, he said. And he'd found two spare seats.

They claimed the places and sipped the tea. Fran decided to tell Jim what had happened. "While you were getting these," she began—and then stopped, for the carriage was plunged into darkness.

Often on a long train journey, there are unexplained breaks in the power supply. Normally, Fran wouldn't have been troubled. This time, she had a horrible sense of disaster, a vision of the carriage rearing up, thrusting her sideways. The sides seemed to buckle, shattered glass rained on her, and people were shrieking. Choking fumes. Searing pain in her legs. Dimly, she discerned a pair of legs to her right, dressed in dark trousers. Boots with crepe soles. And blood. A pool of blood.

"You've spilt tea all over your skirt!" Jim said.

The lights came on again, and the carriage was just as it had been. People were reading the evening paper as if nothing at all had occurred. But Fran had crushed the beaker in her hand—no wonder her legs had smarted.

The thickness of the corduroy skirt had prevented her from being badly scalded. She mopped it with a tissue. "I don't know what's wrong with me— I had a nightmare, except that I wasn't asleep. Where are we?"

"We went through Reading twenty minutes ago. I'd say we're almost there. Are you going to be okay?"

Over the public-address system came the announcement that the next station stop would be Didmarsh Halt.

So far as they could tell in the thick mist, they were the only people to leave the train at Didmarsh.

Miss Shivers was in the booking hall, a gaunt-faced, tense woman of about fifty, with cropped silver hair and red-framed glasses. Her hand was cold, but she shook Fran's firmly and lingered before letting it go.

She drove them in an old Maxi Estate to a cottage set back from the road not more than five minutes from the station. Christmas-tree lights were visible through the leaded window. The smell of roast turkey wafted from the door when she opened it. Jim handed across the bottle of wine he had thoughtfully brought.

"We're wondering how you heard of us."

"Yes, I'm sure you are," the woman answered, addressing herself more to Fran than Jim. "My name is Edith. I was your mother's best friend for ten years, but we fell out over a misunderstanding. You see, Fran, I loved your father."

Fran stiffened and turned to Jim. "I don't think we should stay."

"Please," said the woman, and she sounded close to desperation, "we did nothing wrong. I have something on my conscience, but it isn't adultery, whatever you were led to believe."

They consented to stay and eat the meal. Conversation was strained, but the food was superb. And when at last they sat in front of the fire sipping coffee, Edith Shivers explained why she had invited them. "As I said, I loved your father Harry. A crush, we called it in those days when it wasn't mutual. He was kind to me, took me out, kissed me sometimes, but that was all. He really loved your mother. Adored her."

"You've got to be kidding," said Fran grimly.

"No, your mother was mistaken. Tragically mistaken. I know what she believed, and nothing I could say or do would shake her. I tried writing, phoning, calling personally. She shut me out of her life completely."

"That much I can accept," said Fran. "She never mentioned you to me."

"Did she never talk about the train crash—the night your father was killed, just down the line from here?"

"Just once. After that it was a closed book. He betrayed her dreadfully. She was pregnant, expecting me. It was traumatic. She hardly ever mentioned my father after that. She didn't even keep a photograph."

Miss Shivers put out her hand and pressed it over Fran's. "My dear, for both their sakes I want you to know the truth. Thirty-seven people died in that crash, twenty-five years ago this very evening. Your mother was shocked to learn that he was on the train, because he'd said nothing whatsoever to her about it. He'd told her he was working late. She read about the crash without supposing for a moment that Harry was one of the dead. When she was given the news, just a day or two before you were born, the grief was worse because he'd lied to her. Then she learned that I'd been a passenger on the same train, as indeed I had, and escaped unhurt. Fran, that was chance—pure chance. I happened to work in the City. My name was published in the press, and your mother saw it and came to a totally wrong conclusion."

"That my father and you—"

"Yes. And that wasn't all. Some days after the accident, Harry's personal effects were returned to her, and in the pocket of his jacket they found a receipt from a Bond Street shop for a nightdress."

"Elaine Ducharme," said Fran in a flat voice.

"You *know?*"

"Yes."

"The shop was very famous. They went out of business in 1969. You see—"

"He'd bought it for her," said Fran, "as a surprise."

Edith Shivers withdrew her hand from Fran's and put it to her mouth. "Then you know about me?"

"No."

Their hostess drew herself up in her chair. "I must tell you. Quite by chance on that night twenty-five years ago, I saw him getting on the train. I still loved him and he was alone, so I walked along the corridor and joined him. He was carrying a bag containing the nightdress. In the course of the journey he showed it to me, not realizing that it wounded me to see how much he loved her still. He told me how he'd gone into the shop—"

"Yes," said Fran expressionlessly. "And after Reading, the train crashed."

"He was killed instantly. The side of the carriage crushed him. But I was flung clear—bruised, cut in the forehead, but really unhurt. I could see that Harry was dead. Amazingly, the box with the nightdress wasn't damaged." Miss Shivers stared into the fire. "I coveted it. I told myself if I left it, someone would pick it up and steal it. Instead, I did. *I* stole it. And it's been on my conscience ever since."

Fran had listened in a trancelike way, thinking all the time about her meeting in the train.

Miss Shivers was saying, "If you hate me for what I did, I understand. You see, your mother assumed that Harry bought the nightdress for me. Whatever I said to the contrary, she wouldn't have believed me."

"Probably not," said Fran. "What happened to it?"

Miss Shivers got up and crossed the room to a sideboard, opened a drawer, and withdrew a box—the box Fran had handled only an hour or two previously. "I never wore it. It was never meant for me. I want you to have it, Fran. He would have wished that."

Fran's hands trembled as she opened the box and laid aside the tissue. She stroked the silk. She thought of what had happened, how she hadn't for a moment suspected that she had seen a ghost. She refused to think of him as that. She rejoiced in the miracle that she had met her own father, who had died before she was born—met him in the prime of his young life, when he was her own age.

Still holding the box, she got up and kissed Edith Shivers on the forehead. "My parents are at peace now, I'm sure of it. This is a wonderful Christmas present," she said.

Jacqueline Vivelo

APPALACHIAN BLACKMAIL

$\mathbf{M}$y great-aunt Molly Hardison was a wealthy woman. By the standards of the coal mining town that was home to my family, she was fabulously rich. We didn't have any particular claim on her; she had nearer relatives. Still, she never forgot us children—and there were eight of us—at Christmastime. Once in every two or three years, she would come and spend the holiday with us.

Mama said Christmas with us was more like Aunt Molly's own childhood holidays than Christmas at her grand house or with her sons and their snooty wives.

We were poor all the time, and some years we were poorer than others. Nevertheless, at Christmas our house would be filled with evergreen boughs, pine cones, and red ribbons. Mama would keep hot cider simmering on the back of the woodstove so the house always smelled of cinnamon and cloves. No matter how bad things were Papa could take his hunting dog, first Ol' Elsie and then later her son Ol' Ben, and bring in game. He brought home quail by the dozens, deer, wild turkeys.

Sometimes he'd be the only person we knew who had found a turkey, but he'd always get ours for the holiday. I think he was smart in the ways of turkeys. I was his tomboy and counted myself in on his discussions about hunting with my brothers. Papa would follow a goodsized turkey gobbler for weeks, learning its ways and finding its roosts. Turkeys like to move around, which is why they fool so many hunters, and they almost always have more than one roost.

I listened to all my father could tell us about hunting and would have gone with him when he began to take Joe and Cliff, but Mama put her foot down. I had to content myself with taking care of the hunting dog.

"Maybe someday, Betsy," Papa consoled me. "You'd make a fine hunter."

In any case, our house looked and smelled good at Christmas. It was filled with all the food a resourceful country family could provide. In our neck of the woods that was better than most city families, poor or rich, could do.

So, fairly regularly Aunt Molly would come and spend Christmas in our bustling, over-crowded house. Whether she was there or not, she always sent presents. Her sister, our own grandmother, was dead, which made her something of a stand-in. But we children understood that presents for Christmas and our birthdays would be all we could expect from Aunt Molly, except, of course, for my sister Molly.

I don't think any scheming was involved on my mother's part. I think she just liked the name Molly. She named her first daughter for her mother and her second daughter for her aunt. It didn't hurt that both Mollys happened to be green-eyed redheads. Our Molly was the only redhead among the eight of us and the only one with green eyes. We understood, all of us from oldest to youngest, that our Molly was special to Aunt Molly.

Aunt Molly made it clear that something more than seasonal presents would come Molly's way. I was five the Christmas that Aunt Molly first brought her ruby and diamond necklace with her. Molly was twelve that year when our great-aunt put that magnificent necklace on her for the first time.

"It isn't yours yet, but it will be. I'm not having it go to either of my daughters-in-law. It'll be yours."

We were all in awe of those old stones that glowed with fire. Even the boys took a look, rolled their eyes, and murmured, "Wowee."

"When?" my sister Amanda, oldest of all and most practical, asked.

Aunt Molly fairly cackled.

"When? Well, you see, she'll get to keep it when she marries. Marriage," Great-aunt Molly said, "is the only choice open to a girl. It's the only way to live."

From then on, every Christmas that Aunt Molly spent with us included another look at the necklace and another review of what Molly had to do to get it.

When my sister Amanda was nineteen, she married Dr. Harvey Brittaman, a young G.P. who had just taken up practice in our area. Great-aunt Molly gave them a full set of fine dishes, a hundred and two pieces.

Everybody agreed that none of the rest of us girls was likely to do any better than Amanda had. After all, a doctor!

Sister Molly was seventeen that year. I always thought she was the best-looking of all of us, though later on my little sister Cindy turned out to be a beauty, too. Molly had creamy fair skin without freckles and deep dark red hair. She was slim and tall and wore her hair long. She liked nothing in the world better than reading and carried a book with her everywhere. She would sit on a damp hillside and read until someone, usually me, went and told her to come home.

She had lots of admirers in high school, but two were the frontrunners. Malcolm Bodey was a football player, and Jerry Rattagan edited the school newspaper. Malcolm was planning to go into the mines like the rest of his family. Jerry was going on to the state university.

"You wait for the older men," Aunt Molly told sister Molly when she came for Amanda's wedding. "These boys are fine, but someone better will come along."

That wedding started me thinking. I was ten at the time. I thought about losing Amanda. I thought about marrying in general. I thought about me. I tried to picture me marrying one of the boys I knew, and it was an awful thought. I decided to try again to persuade Mama to let Papa teach me to hunt. I figured what I'd really like was to be a woodsman and live alone in a cabin in the woods. In our house I never had any time or any place alone.

Then I thought about Molly, Molly and the ruby and diamond necklace. For the first time I saw that the necklace hadn't been anything but trouble. For one thing, it had turned my sister Amanda bitter. Here she was, the oldest and the first married, but she wasn't getting the necklace. Aunt Molly had given her Royal Doulton china worth a king's ransom, but it didn't take away the sting. Amanda bore the brunt of the sense of rejection, but I suddenly saw that it was there for all of us, boys as well as girls.

A year later Molly graduated from high school and went to work at Lacy's drugstore. She didn't talk to any of us about what she wanted, but it was easy to see she was unhappy. Malcolm was determined to marry her, and it seemed to me she was weakening.

I felt like there was something about Molly I was missing, so out on the hillside one day I just asked her outright, "How do you really feel about that necklace Aunt Molly's going to give you when you get married?"

Well, she told me. I guess nobody had ever asked her that question before. She spilled out her feelings, her hopes, her wishes—everything in one long outburst. "Didn't you know?" she asked. "Didn't you guess? You're the one who's always watching everybody. I thought you didn't miss a thing—not that I expected anybody else to guess. But I thought you would."

I felt pretty stupid. Once she told me, it seemed obvious.

That next Christmas was one that Aunt Molly spent with us. She showed up two days before Christmas, in time to put her presents under the tree and to help with some of the cooking. Her coming brought back all the things I'd been thinking about when Amanda was married. When you're eleven-going-on-twelve, you're plagued by weighty thoughts.

My brother Cliff was my confidant in the family, but he'd picked that moment to have a chest cold or flu of some sort. He had been moved into the little room at the head of the stairs that was used as a sickroom whenever Mama suspected one of us had something contagious. We were only supposed to pass notes to each other, sending them in on the food trays.

I stood my serious thoughts all on my own for as long as I could, then went and knocked on the sickroom door.

"Who is it?" If a toad had a voice, it might sound all croupy like Cliff's that day.

"It's Betsy. I'm coming in."

I went to the far end of the bed and sat by Cliff's feet. He didn't say you shouldn't be here. He just said, "I can't talk so good."

"Well, you can listen." And I told him all the things I had thought about marriage, about the necklace, and about Molly. While I was talking, some things that had never entered my mind before seemed clear. Cliff croaked that since he wasn't the marrying type and I wasn't either, maybe we could both be hunters.

I felt a lot better after that. I wasn't weird after all. I slipped out of his room before Mama showed up with his lunch.

After supper that night we all gathered in the parlor. Cliff, his chest wrapped with flannel cloths that smelled of camphor, was bundled into a chair by the fireplace, Ol' Ben asleep at his feet. Even Amanda was with us. Her husband Harvey was there, too, but the two youngest children didn't know that because Harvey was dressed as Santa Claus and carried a big bag of toys.

He distributed presents, and we all opened them. There would be more in the morning under the tree, but we liked to spread Christmas out as far as we could.

Christmas Eve was always the time Aunt Molly asked Molly to wear the ruby and diamond necklace, "for a while, so I can see it on you, child." Aunt Molly laid it out on the table, and we all saw that it was still as impressive as ever. It seemed to catch the lights of the Christmas tree and the glow of the candles, not only reflecting but matching with light of its own.

Just as Aunt Molly said, "Come here, my dear, and let me put this on you," Cliff had a fit of coughing. Everyone's attention turned from the necklace to Cliff.

Aunt Molly laid the necklace down and stood up to look over the back of Cliff's chair. One younger child climbed on each arm of the chair, Cindy on one side and Tommy on the other. Harvey, who was a doctor first and Santa second, tossed his sack to one side and clumped across the room in oversized shoes. Someone tramped on Ol' Ben's tail in an effort to get to Cliff, and I led the dog, drugged by food and the warmth of the fire, toward the door.

"He's all right. Move back, everyone," Papa said. "Don't open that door," he added to me. "I don't want a draft through here until I get another blanket."

I slapped Ol' Ben on the bottom and sent him off to his box in the kitchen.

The little ones scrambled back to their presents. Aunt Molly, with a hand pressed to her bosom, turned back to the table. Mama picked up a bottle of cough medicine and then almost dropped it as Aunt Molly screamed.

"Who picked up the necklace? Molly, do you have it already?"

Looks of bewilderment met her questions. "Don't go out!" she commanded Santa Claus, who was trying to slip out the door with his empty sack to change back into his identity as Dr. Brittaman. "Don't anyone move out of this room until I find the necklace."

"You can't suspect Santa Claus!" my brother James shouted, which was a cue for a good bit of silly chatter that had a bad effect on Aunt Molly's temper. She was much more thorough and more demanding in her search than she might have been otherwise.

Mama and Papa kept trying to make light of it. Of course the necklace was there. It had to be. None of us would take it. Aunt Molly said she would have granted that an hour earlier but the fact was someone *had*.

Our Santa Claus suggested we quarter the room and search it inch by inch with Aunt Molly supervising each stage of the search until the necklace turned up. That search was classic, something to pass into legend within our family. First, there were twelve people in the room, counting Aunt Molly herself, and someone insisted she should not be exempt from being searched. Santa and his sack were checked. Even Cliff agreed to be searched, his chair, his blankets, his clothes, his flannel wraps, every inch of the space around him.

Every branch of the tree was examined, every present inspected for signs of tampering. Two of them had to be opened and then repackaged because young hands had been scrabbling at them. But neither one contained the necklace. Chairs were overturned. The hanging light fixture was checked. It became a game to suggest new possibilities.

Maybe because he had been caught trying to get out the door, Harvey went to extremes to see that he and his props were cleared of suspicion. He also made sure every suggestion, no matter how unreasonable, was followed up. The windows were tested, even though everyone knew no one had opened a door or window. An icy wind was blowing, and it was snowing outside. Opening up just long enough to toss something out would have let in a blast the rest would have noticed, not to mention that the necklace would have been lost in the snow.

Aunt Molly had never seemed the least bit pitiful to anyone before that night. Now she looked like a broken woman. Her face was blotchy, and her shoulders sagged. I felt truly sorry for her. Like everyone else that night, I wanted to find her necklace and restore it to her, but it just wasn't possible.

Mama put her arm around her and told her she'd walk her up to her room. At the door, Aunt Molly turned and, looking at Molly, said, "I'm sorry, dear."

"We'll find it," Mama told Aunt Molly. "We'll still find it."

Papa, Amanda, and Dr. Brittaman were all shaking their heads behind Mama and Aunt Molly's backs. I knew what they were thinking. That necklace had just plain vanished, and it didn't seem likely it could ever be found. If it wasn't in that room, well, it just wasn't anywhere.

Papa carried Cliff back to his bed. The rest of us also began to get ready to sleep. Somehow no one knew quite what to say to Molly.

We shuffled through nighttime rituals in uneasy silence. This was no way to go to bed on Christmas Eve. Aunt Molly was hurt, and to all appearances, we had a thief in our family. A dull misery settled around my heart.

You wouldn't think a holiday could recover from a disaster like that, but the next day was one of the best Christmases of our lives. Strangely enough, it was all due to Aunt Molly, too. Several times during breakfast I saw her fingering a small piece of folded paper. She opened her presents with the rest of us and sounded sincerely grateful for her box of handkerchiefs, bottle of toilet water, book of poetry, and the handmade gifts from the younger children. If she was grieving, she was doing it bravely. It seemed to me she just looked thoughtful.

In the middle of the afternoon when the younger children were playing and Amanda and Harvey had gone home, Aunt Molly said she had something to say. She gathered Mama and Papa and Molly around the table. I hung around to hear what was going on.

"I've been doing some thinking since last night," she told them. "No, don't interrupt," she cautioned as my mother began to speak. "I think I wanted to arrange for my namesake to have my life all over again, a thing that's not possible, not even reasonable." She stopped and sighed.

"It's all right about the necklace. I mean, it isn't all right that you lost it," Molly told her, "but it's all right that it isn't coming to me."

Aunt Molly ignored her and continued, "I'd like to see this young woman go on with her studies. Toward that end, I want to pay her way to college." At a sign of protest from my father, Aunt Molly said dryly, "Believe me, four years' tuition will be less than the value of that necklace. You will not, of course, get the necklace," she added to Molly.

"Thank you," said Molly, her eyes wet and shining.

Molly walked on air for the rest of the day. Aunt Molly beamed. My parents kept exchanging smiles. The rest of us were infected by their joy, so it felt like Christmas morning all day and half the night.

I worked it out the other day that Aunt Molly on that Christmas was about the age I am now. I, of course, am not old at all, though she seemed old to me then. She just recently died, having lived into her nineties. Her large estate was divided among her children and grandchildren, but her will made provision for a sealed manila envelope to be delivered to me.

When I opened the envelope, I found a correctly folded letter on thick creamy stationery together with a yellowed slip of paper folded into a square. I opened the slip of paper first and read the message:

> You can have you mizerable necklace back if you promise Molly don't haf to git married. She don't want a husban. She wants to go to collige.

I wouldn't have believed the spelling could have been that bad. I unfolded the accompanying letter and read:

> Dear Betsy,
>
> I don't know how many years will pass before you get this back, but I want to return your note to you.
>
> For days I was baffled by the disappearing stunt you pulled. No one had left the room, yet the necklace wasn't in the room, I told myself. Continuing to puzzle over the problem, I repeated that paradox endlessly. Finally I varied it a bit and said, "Not one creature went out of the room." I stopped as I reached that point because I realized a "creature" had left—that smelly old hound. Then I knew my ruby and diamond necklace must have gone out of the room with the dog. He was wearing it there in his box by the kitchen stove all the time we were searching, wasn't he? Of course, I also remembered that you were the one who sent the dog out of the room while Cliff kept the rest of us distracted. What a determined child you must have been to hold out against all that adult energy!
>
> You always were a clever child, Betsy.

Aunt Molly'd gone home that year with her necklace. Late on Christmas afternoon, it showed up without explanation on her bed. She made sure everyone saw it one last time, then after that holiday never mentioned it again.

When the new semester began a few weeks after Christmas, my sister Molly started college.

Margery Allingham

ON CHRISTMAS DAY IN THE MORNING

Sir Leo Persuivant, the Chief Constable, had been sitting in his comfortable study after a magnificent lunch and talking shyly of the sadness of Christmas while his guest, Mr. Albert Campion, most favored of his large house party, had been laughing at him gently.

It was true, the younger man had admitted, his pale eyes sleepy behind his horn-rimmed spectacles, that, however good the organization, the festival was never quite the same after one was middle-aged, but then only dear old Leo would expect it to be, and meanwhile, what a truly remarkable bird that had been!

But at that point the Superintendent had arrived with his grim little story and everything had seemed quite spoiled.

At the moment their visitor sat in a highbacked chair, against a paneled wall festooned with holly and tinsel, his round black eyes hard and preoccupied under his short gray hair. Superintendent Bussy was one of those lean and urgent countrymen who never quite lose their fondness for a genuine wonder. Despite years of experience and disillusion, the thing that simply can't have happened and yet indubitably *has* happened, retains a place in their cosmos. He was holding forth about one now. It had already ruined his Christmas and had kept a great many other people out in the sleet all day; but nothing would induce him to leave it alone even for five minutes. The turkey sandwiches, which Sir Leo had insisted on ordering for him, were disappearing without him noticing them and the glass of scotch and soda stood untasted.

"You can see I had to come at once," he was saying for the third time. "I had to. I don't see what happened and that's a fact. It's a sort of miracle. Besides," he eyed them angrily, "fancy killing a poor old *postman* on Christmas morning! That's inhuman, isn't it? Unnatural."

Sir Leo nodded his white head. "Horrible," he agreed. "Now, let me get this clear. The man appears to have been run down at the Benham-Ashby crossroads . . ."

Bussy took a handful of cigarettes from the box at his side and arranged them in a cross on the table.

"Look," he said. "Here is the Ashby road with a slight bend in it, and here, running at right angles slap through the curve, is the Benham road. As you know as well as I do, Sir Leo, they're both good wide main thoroughfares, as roads go in these parts. This morning the Benham postman, old Fred Noakes, a bachelor thank God and a good chap, came along the Benham Road loaded down with Christmas mail."

"On a bicycle?" asked Campion.

"Naturally. On a bicycle. He called at the last farm before the crossroads and left just about 10 o'clock. We know that because he had a cup of tea there. Then his way led him over the crossing and on towards Benham proper."

He paused and looked up from his cigarettes.

"There was very little traffic early today, terrible weather all the time, and quite a bit of activity later; so we've got no skid marks to help us. Well, to resume: no one seems to have seen old Noakes, poor chap, until close on half an hour later. Then the Benham constable, who lives some 300 yards from the crossing and on the Benham road, came out of his house and walked down to his gate to see if the mail had come. He saw the postman at once, lying in the middle of the road across his machine. He was dead then."

"You suggest he'd been trying to carry on, do you?" put in Sir Leo.

"Yes. He was walking, pushing the bike, and had dropped in his tracks. There was a depressed fracture in the side of his skull where something—say, a car mirror—had struck him. I've got the doctor's report. I'll show you that later. Meanwhile there's something else."

Bussy's finger turned to his other line of cigarettes.

"Also, just about 10, there were a couple of fellows walking here on the *Ashby* road, just before the bend. They report that they were almost run down by a wildly driven car which came up behind them. It missed them and careered off out of their sight round the bend towards the crossing. But a few minutes later, half a mile farther on, on the other side of the crossroads, a police car met and succeeded in stopping the same car. There was a row and the driver, getting the wind up suddenly, started up again, skidded and smashed the car into the nearest telephone pole. The car turned out to be stolen and there were four half-full bottles of gin in the back. The two occupants were both fighting drunk and are now detained."

Mr. Campion took off his spectacles and blinked at the speaker.

"You suggest that there was a connection, do you? —that the postman and the gin drinkers met at the crossroads? Any signs on the car?"

Bussy shrugged his shoulders. "Our chaps are at work on that now," he said. "The second smash has complicated things a bit, but last time I 'phoned they were hopeful."

"But my dear fellow!" Sir Leo was puzzled. "If you can get expert evidence of a collision between the car and the postman, your worries are over. That is, of course, if the medical evidence permits the theory that the unfortunate fellow picked himself up and struggled the 300 yards towards the constable's house."

Bussy hesitated.

"There's the trouble," he admitted. "If that were all we'd be sitting pretty, but it's not and I'll tell you why. In that 300 yards of Benham Road, between the crossing and the spot where old Fred died, there is a stile which leads to a footpath. Down the footpath, the best part of a quarter of a mile over very rough going, there is one small cottage, and at that cottage letters were delivered this morning. The doctor says Noakes might have staggered the 300 yards up the road leaning on his bike, but he puts his foot down and says the other journey, over the stile and so on, would have been absolutely impossible. I've talked to the doctor. He's the best man in the world on the job and we won't shake him on that."

"All of which would argue," observed Mr. Campion brightly, "that the postman was hit by a car *after* he came back from the cottage—between the stile and the constable's house."

"That's what the constable thought." Bussy's black eyes were snapping. "As soon as he'd telephoned for help he slipped down to the cottage to see if Noakes had actually called there. When he found he had, he searched the road. He was mystified though because both he and his missus had been at their window for an hour watching for the mail and they hadn't seen a vehicle of any sort go by either way. If a car did hit the postman where he fell, it must have turned and gone back afterwards."

Leo frowned at him. "What about the other witnesses? Did they see any second car?"

"No." Bussy was getting to the heart of the matter and his face shone with honest wonder. "I made sure of that. Everybody sticks to it that there was no other car or cart about and a good job too, they say, considering the way the smashed-up car was being driven. As I see it, it's a proper mystery, a kind of not very nice miracle, and those two beauties are going to get away with murder on the strength of it. Whatever our fellows find on the car they'll never get past the doctor's testimony."

Mr. Campion got up sadly. The sleet was beating on the windows, and from inside the house came the more cheerful sound of tea cups. He nodded to Sir Leo.

"I fear we shall have to see that footpath before it gets too dark. In this weather, conditions may have changed by tomorrow."

Sir Leo sighed. " 'On Christmas day in the morning!' " he quoted bitterly. "Perhaps you're right."

They stopped their dreary journey at the Benham police station to pick up the constable. He proved to be a pleasant youngster with a face like one of the angel choir and boots like a fairy tale, but he had liked the postman and was anxious to serve as their guide.

They inspected the crossroads and the bend and the spot where the car had come to grief. By the time they reached the stile, the world was gray and freezing, and all trace of Christmas had vanished, leaving only the hopeless winter it had been invented to refute.

Mr. Campion negotiated the stile and Sir Leo followed him with some difficulty. It was an awkward climb, and the path below was narrow and slippery. It wound out into the mist before them, apparently without end.

The procession slid and scrambled on in silence for what seemed a mile, only to encounter a second stile and a plank bridge over a stream, followed by a brief area of what appeared to be simple bog. As he struggled out of it, Bussy pushed back his dripping hat and gazed at the constable.

"You're not having a game with us, I suppose?" he inquired.

"No, sir." The boy was all blush. "The little house is just here. You can't make it out because it's a bit low. There it is, sir. There."

He pointed to a hump in the near distance which they had all taken to be a haystack. Gradually it emerged as the roof of a hovel which squatted with its back towards them in the wet waste.

"Good Heavens!" Sir Leo regarded its desolation with dismay. "Does anybody really live there?"

"Oh, yes, sir. An old widow lady. Mrs. Fyson's the name."

"Alone?" He was aghast. "How old?"

"I don't rightly know, sir. Quite old. Over 75, must be."

Sir Leo stopped in his tracks and a silence fell on the company. The scene was so forlorn, so unutterably quiet in its loneliness, that the world might have died.

It was Campion who broke the spell.

"Definitely no walk for a dying man," he said firmly. "Doctor's evidence completely convincing, don't you think? Now that we're here, perhaps we should drop in and see the householder."

Sir Leo shivered. "We can't *all* get in," he objected. "Perhaps the Superintendent . . ."

"No. You and I will go." Campion was obstinate. "Is that all right with you, Super?"

Bussy waved them on. "If you have to dig for us we shall be just about here," he said cheerfully. "I'm over my ankles now. What a place! Does anybody ever come here *except* the postman, Constable?"

Campion took Sir Leo's arm and led him firmly round to the front of the cottage. There was a yellow light in the single window on the ground floor and, as they slid up a narrow brick path to the very small door, Sir Leo hung back. His repugnance was as apparent as the cold.

"I hate this," he muttered. "Go on. Knock if you must."

Mr. Campion obeyed, stooping so that his head might miss the lintel. There was a movement inside, and at once the door was opened wide, so that he was startled by the rush of warmth from within.

A little old woman stood before him, peering up without astonishment. He was principally aware of bright eyes.

"Oh, dear," she said unexpectedly, and her voice was friendly. "You *are* damp. Come in." And then, looking past him at the skulking Sir Leo, "Two of you! Well, isn't that nice. Mind your poor heads."

The visit became a social occasion before they were well in the room. Her complete lack of surprise, coupled with the extreme lowness of the ceiling, gave her an advantage from which the interview never entirely recovered.

From the first she did her best to put them at ease.

"You'll have to sit down at once," she said, laughing as she waved them to two little chairs, one on either side of the small black stove. "Most people have to. I'm all right, you see, because I'm not tall. This is my chair here. You must undo that," she went on, touching Sir Leo's coat. "Otherwise you may take cold when you go out. It is so very chilly, isn't it? But so seasonable and that's always nice."

Afterwards it was Mr. Campion's belief that neither he nor Sir Leo had a word to say for themselves for the first five minutes. They were certainly seated and looking round the one downstairs room which the house contained before anything approaching a conversation took place.

It was not a sordid room, yet the walls were unpapered, the furniture old without being in any way antique, and the place could hardly have been called neat. But at the moment it was festive. There was holly over the two pictures and on the mantle above the stove, and a crowd of bright Christmas cards.

Their hostess sat between them, near the table. It was set for a small tea party and the oil lamp with the red and white frosted glass shade, which stood in the center of it, shed a comfortable light on her serene face.

She was a short, plump old person whose white hair was brushed tightly to her little round head. Her clothes were all knitted and of an assortment of colors, and with them she wore, most unsuitably, a maltese-silk lace collarette and a heavy gold chain. It was only when they noticed she was blushing that they realized she was shy.

"Oh," she exclaimed at last, making a move which put their dumbness to shame. "I quite forgot to say it before. A Merry Christmas to you! Isn't it wonderful how it keeps coming round? Very quickly, I'm afraid, but it is so nice when it does. It's such a *happy* time, isn't it?"

Sir Leo pulled himself together with an effort which was practically visible.

"I must apologize," he began. "This is an imposition on such a day. I . . ." But she smiled and silenced him again.

"Not at all," she said. "Oh, not at all. Visitors are a great treat. Not everybody braves my footpath in the winter."

"But some people do, of course?" ventured Mr. Campion.

"Of course." She shot him her shy smile. "Certainly every week. They send down from the village every week and only this morning a young man, the policeman to be exact, came all the way over the fields to wish me the compliments of the season and to know if I'd got my post!"

"And you had!" Sir Leo glanced at the array of Christmas cards with relief. He was a kindly, sentimental, family man, with a horror of loneliness.

She nodded at the brave collection with deep affection.

"It's lovely to see them all up there again, it's one of the real joys of Christmas, isn't it? Messages from people you love and who love you and all so *pretty*, too."

"Did you come down bright and early to meet the postman?" Sir Leo's question was disarmingly innocent, but she looked ashamed and dropped her eyes.

"I wasn't up! Wasn't it dreadful? I was late this morning. In fact, I was only just picking the letters off the mat there when the policeman called. He helped me gather them, the nice boy. There were such a lot. I lay lazily in bed this morning thinking of them instead of moving."

"Still, you heard them come." Sir Leo was very satisfied. "And you knew they were there."

"Oh, yes." She sounded content. "I knew they were there. May I offer you a cup of tea? I'm waiting for my party . . . just a woman and her dear little boy; they won't be long. In fact, when I heard your knock I thought they were here already."

Sir Leo excused them, but not with any undue haste. He appeared to be enjoying himself. Meanwhile, Mr. Campion, who had risen to inspect the display on the mantle shelf more closely, helped her to move the kettle so that it should not boil too soon.

The Christmas cards were splendid. There were nearly 30 of them in all, and the envelopes which had contained them were packed in a neat bundle and tucked behind the clock, to add even more color to the whole.

In design, they were mostly conventional. There were wreaths and firesides, saints and angels, with a secondary line of gardens in unseasonable bloom and Scotch terriers in tam-o'shanter caps. One magnificent card was entirely in ivorine, with a cutout disclosing a coach and horses surrounded by roses and for-get-me-nots. The written messages were all warm and personal, all breathing affection and friendliness and the out-spoken joy of the season:

The very best to you, Darling, from all at The Limes.

To dear Auntie from Little Phil.

Love and Memories. Edith and Ted.

There is no wish like the old wish. Warm regards, George.

For dearest Mother.

Cheerio. Lots of love. Just off. Writing. Take care of yourself. Sonny.

For dear little Agnes with love from us all.

Mr. Campion stood before them for a long time but at length he turned away. He had to stoop to avoid the beam and yet he towered over the old woman who stood looking up at him.

Something had happened. It had suddenly become very still in the house. The gentle hissing of the kettle sounded unnaturally loud. The recollection of its lonely remoteness returned to chill the cosy room.

The old lady had lost her smile and there was wariness in her eyes.

"Tell me." Campion spoke very gently. "What do you do? Do you put them all down there on the mat in their envelopes before you go to bed on Christmas Eve?"

While the point of his question and the enormity of it was dawning upon Sir Leo, there was silence. It was breathless and unbearable until old Mrs. Fyson pierced it with a laugh of genuine naughtiness.

"Well," she said, "it does make it more fun!" She glanced back at Sir Leo whose handsome face was growing steadily more and more scarlet.

"Then . . . ?" He was having difficulty with his voice. "Then the postman did *not* call this morning, ma'am?"

She stood looking at him placidly, the flicker of the smile still playing round her mouth.

"The postman never calls here except when he brings something from the Government," she said pleasantly. "Everybody gets letters from the Government nowadays, don't they? But he doesn't call here with *personal* letters because, you see, I'm the last of us." She paused and frowned very faintly. It rippled like a shadow over the smoothness of her quiet, careless brow. "There's been so many wars," she said sadly.

"But, dear lady . . ." Sir Leo was completely overcome. There were tears in his eyes and his voice failed him.

She patted his arm to comfort him.

"My dear man," she said kindly. "Don't be distressed. It's not sad. It's Christmas. We all loved Christmas. They sent me their love at Christmas and you see *I've still got it*. At Christmas I remember them and they remember me . . .

777

wherever they are." Her eyes strayed to the ivorine card with the coach on it. "I do sometimes wonder about poor George," she remarked seriously. "He was my husband's elder brother and he really did have quite a shocking life. But he once sent me that remarkable card and I kept it with the others. After all, we ought to be charitable, oughtn't we? At Christmas time . . ."

As the four men plodded back through the fields, Bussy was jubilant.

"That's done the trick," he said. "Cleared up the mystery and made it all plain sailing. We'll get those two crooks for doing in poor old Noakes. A real bit of luck that Mr. Campion was here," he added generously, as he squelched on through the mud. "The old girl was just cheering herself up and you fell for it, eh, Constable? Oh, don't worry, my boy. There's no harm done, and it's a thing that might have deceived anybody. Just let it be a lesson to you. I know how it happened. You didn't want to worry the old thing with the tale of a death on Christmas morning, so you took the sight of the Christmas cards as evidence and didn't go into it. As it turned out, you were wrong. That's life."

He thrust the young man on ahead of him and came over to Mr. Campion.

"What beats me is how you cottoned to it," he confided. "What gave you the idea?"

"I merely read it, I'm afraid." Mr. Campion sounded apologetic. "All the envelopes were there, sticking out from behind the clock. The top one had a ha'penny stamp on it, so I looked at the postmark. It was 1914."

Bussy laughed "Given to you," he chuckled. "Still, I bet you had a job to believe your eyes."

"Ah." Mr. Campion's voice was thoughtful in the dusk. "That, Super, that was the really difficult bit."

Sir Leo, who had been striding in silence, was the last to climb up onto the road. He glanced anxiously towards the village for a moment or so, and presently touched Campion on the shoulder.

"Look there." A woman was hurrying towards them and at her side, earnest and expectant, trotted a small, plump child. They scurried past and as they paused by the stile, and the woman lifted the boy onto the footpath, Sir Leo expelled a long sighing breath.

"So there was a party," he said simply. "Thank God for that. Do you know, Campion, all the way back here I've been wonderin'."

Rex Stout

SANTA CLAUS BEAT

"Christmas Eve," Art Hipple was thinking to himself, "would be a good time for the murder."

The thought was both timely and characteristic. It was 3 o'clock in the afternoon of December 24, and though the murder would have got an eager welcome from Art Hipple any day at all, his disdainful attitude toward the prolonged hurly-burly of Christmas sentiment and shopping made that the best possible date for it. He did not actually turn up his nose at Christmas, for that would have been un-American; but as a New York cop not yet out of his twenties who had recently been made a precinct dick and had hung his uniform in the back of the closet of his furnished room, it had to be made clear, especially to himself, that he was good and tough. A cynical slant on Christmas was therefore imperative.

His hope of running across a murder had begun back in the days when his assignment had been tagging illegally parked cars, and was merely practical and professional. His biggest ambition was promotion to Homicide, and the shortest cut would have been discovery of a corpse, followed by swift, brilliant, solo detection and capture of the culprit. It had not gone so far as becoming an obsession; as he strode down the sidewalk this December afternoon he was not sniffing for the scent of blood at each dingy entrance he passed; but when he reached the number he had been given and turned to enter, his hand darted inside his jacket to touch his gun.

None of the three people he found in the cluttered and smelly little room one flight up seemed to need shooting. Art identified himself and wrote down their names. The man at the battered old desk, who was twice Art's age and badly needed a shave, was Emil Duross, proprietor of the business conducted in that room—Duross Specialties, a mail-order concern dealing in gimcrack jewelry. The younger man, small, dark and neat, seated on a chair squeezed in between the desk and shelves stacked with cardboard boxes, was II. E. Koenig, adjuster, according to a card he had proffered, for the Apex Insurance

Company. The girl, who had pale watery eyes and a stringy neck, stood backed up to a pile of cartons the height of her shoulder. She had on a dark brown felt hat and a lighter brown woolen coat that had lost a button. Her name was Helen Lauro, and it could have been not rheum in her eyes but the remains of tears.

Because Art Hipple was thorough it took him twenty minutes to get the story to his own satisfaction. Then he returned his notebook to his pocket, looked at Duross, at Koenig, and last at the girl. He wanted to tell her to wipe her eyes, but what if she didn't have a handkerchief?

He spoke to Duross. "Stop me if I'm wrong," he said. "You bought the ring a week ago to give to your wife for Christmas and paid sixty-two dollars for it. You put it there in a desk drawer after showing it to Miss Lauro. Why did you show it to Miss Lauro?"

Duross turned his palms up. "Just a natural thing. She works for me, she's a woman, and it's a beautiful ring."

"Okay. Today you work with her—filling orders, addressing packages, and putting postage on. You send her to the post office with a bag of the packages. Why didn't she take all of them?"

"She did."

"Then what are those?" Art pointed to a pile of little boxes, addressed and stamped, on the end of a table.

"Orders that came in the afternoon mail. I did them while she was gone to the post office."

Art nodded. "And also while she was gone you looked in the drawer to get the ring to take home for Christmas, and it wasn't there. You know it was there this morning because Miss Lauro asked if she could look at it again, and you showed it to her and let her put it on her finger, and then you put it back in the drawer. But this afternoon it was gone, and you couldn't have taken it yourself because you haven't left this room. Miss Lauro went out and got sandwiches for your lunch. So you decided she took the ring, and you phoned the insurance company, and Mr. Koenig came and advised you to call the police, and—"

"Only his stock is insured," Koenig put in. "The ring was not a stock item and is not covered."

"Just a legality," Duross declared scornfully. "Insurance companies can't hide behind legalities. It hurts their reputation."

Koenig smiled politely but noncommittally.

Art turned to the girl. "Why don't you sit down?" he asked her. "There's a chair we men are not using."

"I will never sit down in this room again," she declared in a thin tight voice.

"Okay." Art scowled at her. She was certainly not comely. "If you did take the ring you might—"

"I didn't!"

"Very well. But if you did you might as well tell me where it is because you won't ever dare to wear it or sell it."

"Of course I wouldn't. I knew I wouldn't. That's why I didn't take it."

"Oh? You thought of taking it?"

"Of course I did. It was a beautiful ring." She stopped to swallow. "Maybe my life isn't much, but what it is, I'd give it for a ring like that, and a girl like me, I could live a hundred years and never have one. Of course I thought of taking it—but I knew I couldn't ever wear it."

"You see?" Duross appealed to the law. "She's foxy, that girl. She's slick."

Art downed an impulse to cut it short, get out, return to the station house, and write a report. Nobody here deserved anything, not even justice—especially not justice. Writing a brief report was all it rated, and all, ninety-nine times out of a hundred, it would have got. But instead of breaking it off, Art sat and thought it over through a long silence, with the three pairs of eyes on him. Finally he spoke to Duross:

"Get me the orders that came in the afternoon mail."

Duross was startled. "Why?"

"I want to check them with that pile of boxes you addressed and stamped."

Duross shook his head. "I don't need a cop to check my orders and shipments. Is this a gag?"

"No. Get me the orders."

"I will not!"

"Then I'll have to open all the boxes." Art arose and headed for the table. Duross bounced up and got in front of him and they were chest to chest.

"You don't touch those boxes," Duross told him. "You got no search warrant. You don't touch anything!"

"That's just another legality." Art backed off a foot to avoid contact. "And since I guessed right, what's a little legality? I'm going to open the boxes here and now, but I'll count ten first to give you a chance to pick it out and hand it to me and save both of us a lot of bother. One, two, three—"

"I'll phone the station house!"

"Go ahead. Four, five, six, seven, eight, nine . . ."

Art stopped at nine because Duross had moved to the table and was fingering the boxes. As he drew away with one in his hand Art demanded, "Gimme." Duross hesitated but passed the box over, and after a glance at the address Art ripped the tape off, opened the flap of the box, took out a wad of tissue paper, and then a ring box. From that he removed a ring, yellow gold, with a large greenish stone. Helen Lauro made a noise in her throat. Koenig let out a grunt, evidently meant for applause. Duross made a grab, not for the ring but for the box on which he had put an address, and missed.

"It stuck out as plain as your nose," Art told him, "but of course my going for the boxes was just a good guess. Did you pay sixty-two bucks for this?"

Duross's lips parted, but no words came. Apparently he had none. He nodded, not vigorously.

Art turned to the girl. "Look, Miss Lauro. You say you're through here. You ought to have something to remember it by. You could make some trouble for Mr. Duross for the dirty trick he tried to play on you, and if you lay off I expect he'd like to show his appreciation by giving you this ring. Wouldn't you, Mr. Duross?"

Duross managed to get it out. "Sure I would."

"Shall I give it to her for you?"

"Sure." Duross's jaw worked. "Go ahead."

Art held out the ring and the girl took it, but not looking at it because she was gazing incredulously at him. It was a gaze so intense as to disconcert him, and he covered up by turning to Duross and proffering the box with an address on it.

"Here," he said, "you can have this. Next time you cook up a plan for getting credit with your wife for buying her a ring, and collecting from the insurance company for its cost, and sending the ring to a girl friend—all in one neat little operation—don't do it. And don't forget you gave Miss Lauro that ring before witnesses."

Duross gulped and nodded.

Koenig spoke. "Your name is not Hipple, officer, it's Santa Claus. You have given her the ring she would have given her life for, you have given him an out on a charge of attempted fraud, and you have given me a crossoff on a claim. That's the ticket! That's the old yuletide spirit! Merry Christmas!"

"Nuts," Art said contemptuously, and turned and marched from the room, down the stairs, and out to the sidewalk. As he headed in the direction of the station house he decided that he would tone it down a little in his report. Getting a name for being tough was okay, but not too damn tough. That insurance guy sure was dumb, calling him Santa Claus—him, Art Ripple, feeling as he did about Christmas.

Which reminded him, Christmas Eve would be a swell time for the murder.

Dan Stumpf

WHITE LIKE THE SNOW

Lieutenant Mayhew brought one of the rookies upstairs to the detective bureau last week, I guess to show where he could go in a few years if he kept his pants clean. I did my bit to make an impression by hiding the magazine I was reading under a report I closed out six weeks ago. Not for Nicky-New-Guy, you understand, but more for Mayhew's benefit. Anyway, the kid got to looking at some of the old photos we hang around the place and damn if he didn't spot an old one of Sergeant Sughrue, smiling at the camera like a clean shotgun, and ask who it was.

"Someone before my time." Mayhew's one of the chief's five-year wonders. He looked at the picture closer, then half turned to me. "How 'bout it, Jake? You know this guy?"

Yeah, I knew him; time was when half the folks in town lived in mortal fear of Sergeant "Sugar" Sughrue and the rest of us just worried about him a lot. But nobody remembers him much these days, and the picture'd hung there so long I quit seeing it myself. So I said, "That's just some guy I killed once." The kid hesitated, laughed; Mayhew laughed, then pushed him down the hall and I got back to my magazine.

Not that I actually *did* kill Sughrue; that was just hype. Hell, I been here almost twenty years and never even shot anybody very much. But I was there when Sughrue died, and I maybe had something to do with it, so I guess what I told the kid wasn't too far off the mark at that.

It was Christmas morning, maybe ten years ago, maybe not that long. And it was snowing to beat hell; over a foot since midnight and no end in sight. I was supposed to take care of business in the detective bureau, but there wasn't much, this being Christmas in the suburbs, so I brought in a portable TV to pass the time. I was lugging it into the station and I passed Dibbs on the way out—he has the cubicle next to mine—and we wished each other "Merry Christmas" kind of automatically.

At least it was automatic for me; Dibbs took it serious, though, and stopped to look sorry for me. "Damn, Jake," he said, "nothing worse than working Christmas, is there?"

Well, there's lots of things worse than working Christmas at a suburban police department: young love and getting your foot stuck in a cannon are the two I know most about, but there's bound to be more. Actually, with not much work to do and all the food folks bring in, it's not bad at all. But I looked mournful for Dibbs's sake and went in to goof off for eight hours.

It should have been that simple. I wish it had been, sometimes. I mean, Sughrue was a pain all right, but what I went through was sure a tall price to get rid of him. And on Christmas, too.

I should tell you about Sergeant "Sugar" Sughrue. Lots of folks used to wonder what made him act so mean all the time, but I think he just figured if you got a God-given talent for something, you oughta use it, and he sure as hell had the touch for making folks around him unhappy. If not plain scared. See, Sughrue was big and fast and strong, and he could shoot good. Him and me, we were on the range one time and he put five shots in a playing card fifty feet away while I was still pulling my piece out of the holster and looking for the target. That's how good he was.

He was smart, too, and he liked to show it off. No one I ever saw at the station ever won an argument with Sughrue. Even if they were right. Sughrue'd just talk and argue and beat on them with words till they gave up. You win arguments that way, but you never convince anybody.

Being dangerous and capable like he was, it's no wonder Sughrue made sergeant fast. And it's no wonder he didn't go any farther. Once he got into a spot where he could give orders and chew folks out on a regular basis, the brass could see how much he liked it, which was way too much. And about that time, talk started about him and the crowd at Smokey's, and that was pretty much as far as his careeer ever went.

So that's all you need to know about Sughrue, except he shouldn't even have been in that day; sergeants get holidays off unless we call them in for something, and Sughrue being like he was, the building could burn down, no one would call him. But I hadn't been there more than an hour and in he comes, looking like hell's own hangover. He didn't even stop to rag me; just shuffled into his office and shut the door.

Well, it was good I didn't have to talk to him, but bad, too, because any minute he might come back out, so I couldn't get too laid back. No idea how long he'd be in there or even what he was doing here on Christmas. If Sughrue came out and saw me having fun, or not looking busy enough, or even just not looking miserable, he'd make sure I got that way in a hurry.

I sighed, turned off my TV, and went to the dispatch room to find a magazine I could hide under a report; old tricks are still the best.

It was quiet in there, too. Sometimes phones ring and guys yammer on the radio all the time, but this being Christmas, no one was doing much. Ed Rosemont turned from the radio console when I came in; his big swivel chair groaning under him made the only noise in the room. I gave him a look and jerked my thumb at Sughrue's office. "The hell's he doing here?"

"I will be damned if I know." Rosey's got one of those big, rich, pear-shaped voices, and a body to match—the kind I been working on all my life but never could get just right. Always struck me funny, hearing him swear in that important-sounding voice. "He said he had paperwork to catch up. What do you think?"

"Whoever he's sleeping with sobered up and kicked him out, is my theory," I said. Sughrue always had a reputation for acting nasty, but he never had any trouble getting women. Just keeping them. "Where's he hang his pants lately, anyway?"

Turned out neither me nor Rosey knew who Sughrue was jumping with since his last divorce. But that didn't keep us from tossing ideas around, and that led to a lively discussion about who else might be sleeping with who else, and what with one thing and another, we went on for nearly half an hour. Which is how I came to be there when we got the call. And saw Rosey's face go from polite to serious to scared as he sat upright and started jotting stuff down on the pad.

"Hold on the line," he said finally, and keyed the mike to alert the guys who were probably damn near asleep in their cars by now. "Eighteen and Twenty-Seven." He pushed each word slow and distinct, even for him. "Code Fifty-two—that's Code Five-two—at Smokey's—that's Smokey's—Seventy-seven Village Street. See Bob Gates, standing by in front."

"Damn," I said. "A stiff at Smokey's." It looked like I was going to have to go out in all that weather and act busy; *double damn*. But I didn't know the worst of it yet.

"Wuzzit?" I asked. "Some wino fall asleep in the door?" Smokey's is in a part of town where that happens some, so maybe I wouldn't have to do much besides take pictures.

But my life just ain't that pretty. Rosey looked up at me with no look at all in his eyes and said, "It is Mr. Smollett, Jake. And Bob says he was shot."

That was worth a whistle, and I gave it one. If you believe some folks, Fred "Smokey" Smollett just ran a real busy bar at the edge of town, where we border up on the city. If you believe others, he ran everything out of that bar that would run for money: games, women, drugs, and the occasional bit of stolen property. If you believe still other people, he paid us for the privilege.

Mind you, he never paid me anything. I never got that high up the ladder. Never even got high enough to know for certain he was paying off. But there was lots of talk, and it don't pay not to listen.

"Tell 'em just to hold the scene." If this was what it sounded like, I was going to have to get off my ass and do some detective work. But not much; once the brass learned who it was and what it was, they'd fall all over each other to get to Smokey's. "Call the lieutenant and see if we can get a real photographer out there. See if he'll let us call Dibbs." Dibbs wouldn't much like that after working all night, but he'd been to more evidence schools than me, so he was the man for an important job. And this was one. Talk was, Smollett had his hooks in some pretty major people here in the department, and that would include—

"What's up?" Sergeant Sughrue was leaning on the doorframe, still looking bad hungover but talking casual. Rosey told him and he nodded, still leaning, still talking casual. "Cancel those calls," he said. "Marley and me can take a look and see what has to be done before we go dragging everyone out on Christmas overtime." He turned to me. "Fetch the car, Jake; I'll get the kit." And he slouched off.

Rosey and I traded looks. We both of us knew I was a bad photographer and even worse handling evidence. Any other day of the year, there'd be brass hats enough around the place to make sure a job like this got handled by the best—or carefulest—we had. But this was Merry-dammit-Christmas, the brass was at home, and Sergeant Sughrue had just handed us a direct order. Rosey sure as hell wasn't going to cross him.

And me neither, I guess. I cursed the bones of old Kris Kringle and went out to get the car.

Traffic was light, and a good thing, too, because the streets were godawful. We saw just one snow plow on our way across town, slumping through the snow drifts like a whipped dog. The rest of the way, it was find the road and try to stay on it.

After a while, though, I got into the tracks made by the cruisers already on the scene ahead of us, and I figured this might be my chance. Now that I could drive with one hand, I reached out and got the radio mike.

"I'll just make sure Rosey called the lieutenant—"

That was as far as I got with it before Sughrue's big left hand jerked out and knocked the mike clean from my fingers.

That was a funny moment, right then. I mean, Sughrue had a temper, all right, and he was fast and mean and looked to be hungover bad, but hitting my hand like that was past the edge, even for him. I looked over—real quick because I had to pay attention to the road—and just for a second he was bent over, his face screwed up like he was mad as hell. Then his eyes opened up and locked on mine.

It couldn't have been more than a quarter of a second, that glance, because I had to look right back at the road, but it was long enough for something to pass between us. Something really ugly.

"I'll call him from Smokey's." Sughrue slumped back in the seat, his voice softer than I expected. I thought he was going to say more, and I think he thought so, too, but we were both quiet the rest of the way.

And that thing that passed between us, whatever it was, kept biting my butt.

I wasn't long figuring it out, either. It didn't take a real educated nose to smell the stink around this business pretty quick, and by the time we got to Smokey's, I'd pretty much put it together.

I saw it like this: Smollett, who probably has more dirt on the department in general and Sughrue in particular than was safe for anyone, gets shot dead. And it happens on Christmas, when the senior detectives and the brass hats are all at home with the kiddies. And here's Sughrue, he just comes tripping into work on Christmas morning looking like slime on a shingle and insisting him and me are going to investigate this all by ourselves—him that supposedly Smollett was paying off, and me . . .

Some folks say I became a cop because I'm too lazy to work and not smart enough to steal, but they're only half right. I could see this one coming down Main Street. And I was getting scared, because when Sughrue knocked that mike out of my hand and we looked at each other, I could tell he didn't *want* anyone at that crime scene who'd act like he gave a damn. And maybe in my eyes he saw I'd figured that out. And if he *did* see it, my life wasn't worth dryer lint, because Sughrue was that much faster and stronger and meaner than me that if he got worried about me giving him up, and decided to do something about it, I was damn sure to finish second.

That's what I was thinking when we walked into Smokey's that Christmas day, and it was pretty damn grim, if you ask me. Of course, Sughrue's dead now, and maybe I killed him, and I for sure didn't have it all figured out like I thought I did. But you can understand, maybe, why I was sweating like a crack-head when Sughrue told the uniforms at the scene to secure the area and take a statement from old Bob Gates, who used to sweep up the place, while he and I went into the office where Smollett was laying around dead.

It looked like the office of every bar everywhere. Maybe bigger than some, but with the same battered desk, cheap paneling, and old steel safe you see in all of them. Only here the safe hung open; a dead man sat behind the desk, white like the snow, leaning way back in his chair, with a raunchy cigar still clenched in his teeth; and there was blood all over.

And I mean, There Was Blood All Over; it was on the wall behind

Smollett's body in big splash patterns, it was soaked into the carpet under his chair, it was spritzed across the top of his desk, and it dribbled from his private toilet—a closet-sized deal off to one side—clear to the front of the desk.

"Let's check out the bathroom," Sughrue said, and I followed him quick. It wasn't quite as gross as the rest of the place, but there was plenty of blood on the floor by the sink, and like I said, the trail of drops to the front of the desk.

"This is where it started," Sughrue said when we'd looked around a little. "Smollett got shot here, went to his desk, tried to call for help, then fell back in his chair and bled to death. I'll call the coroner." He took a couple of slow steps back to the office and dialed the dead man's phone.

And if I had any doubts about the smell around this thing, I stopped having them right then. Because we never call the coroner till we're completely through gathering evidence. Last thing we want is those guys coming in with their jumpsuits and body bags, stepping all over everything. But here Sughrue calls them first thing.

I didn't say a word, though. No sense letting on I knew any more than he already thought I did. *Just stay quiet, act dumb, and maybe you'll get out of this better than Smollett did*, I told myself.

So I took pictures, knowing that no better than I am, and in this light, they'd be worthless. I got shots of Smollett in his chair, supposedly showing how he'd sat down, leaned back against the wall where his blood was spattered, and bled to death. I took pictures of the empty safe, thinking whoever shot him also took all the incriminating records *(that's how long ago this was; nowadays there'd be computer disks and backup files and all, but back then, if it wasn't on paper, it wasn't there, period)*, and just as the guys from the coroner's came clomping in, I got pictures of the blood on Smollett's desk and the drips running from his toilet into the office. And like I say, I knew every damn one of them was worthless: The way I handled a camera, no one'd even recognize it was Smollett unless they saw the cigar stuck in his mouth, and the other shots would be too light or too dark, or just not pointed right to show which way the blood was splattered—

So maybe I'm not bright, after all. It took me all the while they were moving Smollett to figure out what that blood was telling me. And to tie it in with how Sughrue was sitting heavy in a spare seat off to one side while the coroner's boys made their haul. But by the time they left, I was almost curious about all this.

"You collect, Marley," Sughrue sighed. "I'll tag. Start in the toilet where it started, and work out to the desk."

The toilet where it started? Well, that was one theory. Of course, it wouldn't explain how so much of Smollett got splattered back against the wall behind his chair, or why there wasn't more of him spilled over the desk he supposedly leaned across. It wouldn't even account for why the blood drops on the carpet were *in front* of the desk, and trailed toward the toilet, not away from it. No, the only story that would explain all that was one where Smollett and whoever killed him got up in each other's face over his desk and one of them pulled a gun but didn't do it quick enough to keep the other one from shooting him. Or shooting him back.

But I had a feeling that wasn't how Sughrue wanted things to look, and they damn well weren't going to look like that when we left. Well, I sure as hell wasn't going to stick my foot in his story just now. I got down on my knees—not much fun for a guy of my build—and started scraping half-dried blood from the floor onto little sterile pieces of paper that went into little sterile envelopes for Sughrue to put labels on.

Sughrue didn't get up. Just sat there with his pen out and wrote down what part of the room each envelope came from before putting it carefully in the kit.

That's another thing shows how long ago this was: Nowadays you can get DNA identification from a blood smear and know whose it was and what he ate last Thursday. But back then, all you could get was blood type. So if Sughrue was fiddling with the envelopes like I thought he was, all the blood that got to the lab would be from behind the desk. The envelopes might say this sample or that sample was from the toilet or the front of the desk, but . . .

Then I thought of one other thing, and it almost got me killed right there. Which shows where thinking will get you. I was picking up blood from behind the desk, and when I got up I sort of routinely opened and closed the desk drawers. There was the usual clutter of coin wrappers, old receipts, and business cards, but "No gun," I said, and then kicked myself for saying it, because Sughrue turned to me real fast—fast like when he'd knocked the mike out of my fingers—and I couldn't see where his right hand was, which scared me so that I tried to cover.

"I mean" —I said it slow and dumb-like— "I was thinking there'd be one. Guess not, though; I never heard of him to pack." Fact is, you could look in a million back-room offices in bars like this and find a gun in every one of them. It's like bar owners think they're supposed to have one, or maybe they come with the liquor license or something. And considering Smollett's reputation, it was damn funny there *wasn't* one here. Maybe it was with the records gone from the safe. But I could see I wasn't going to get much older by saying that in front of Sughrue, so I just stood there looking stupid till he finally untensed and moved his hand out where I could see it empty.

"That's enough," he said. What with pictures and samples and the coroner's boys, we'd been there maybe two hours. "Let's get this to the station and ready for the lab." He got to his feet, slow, wincing a little.

So here I was with a guy who I thought had done the murder we were investigating, a guy who was also maybe roping me in as his accomplice, and who might just put me out of my misery if he thought I'd figured that out. And all I could think was, *I wonder how he plans to keep anyone else from looking over the scene and reading it right.* And I never did find that out.

Funny how your mind works. I mean, I should've been thinking a lot of other stuff, about Smollett and Sughrue, and if my guesses were right—about both of them—and whether Sughrue thought I was going along with whatever his plans were, and what ideas he might have about my future. But what I remember most was worrying about how he was going to keep everyone else from seeing what I saw in the back room there at Smokey's.

So this next part nobody believes. I must've told it a hundred times in the week after it happened and never got anything but funny looks, but it's true just like I'm going to say: We were walking out the back of Smokey's, to the car. And the snow hadn't let up a bit, but it'd been packed down by the uniforms standing around holding the scene for us. So as I followed Sughrue out the back door, onto the little landing there, I stepped onto that smooth-packed snow and my foot slid out from under me, and I lurched up to keep from falling and bumped into Sughrue, and he went down. Hard. Into the snow.

And he yelped.

Like I say, most folks don't think it happened that way. I could see on their faces when I got to that part, they all figured I pushed Sughrue on purpose. But it ain't so; I was there, I seen it, and it was pure luck, good or bad.

Anyway, Sughrue hit the snow and he yelped and laid there. After a second, I reached down to help him up, but he kind of half swung at me so I pulled back.

He rolled over then and got to his feet, but it wasn't like anything I ever saw before. You know how sometimes you get hurt and feel like you're moving in slow motion? Well, now I saw just that. Sughrue moving in slow motion. It was almost like he floated onto his side, holding his coat shut real tight, then got to his knees, then his feet, and I swear I wouldn't have been surprised if he drifted up into the falling snow and vanished in the gray clouds.

He might as well have.

We looked at each other again. We both knew now that he'd got shot last night, and I knew that the guy who'd done it just went to the morgue. And Sughrue knew I knew, and there wasn't a damn thing he could do about it but walk back to the car with me.

And I mean to tell you, that ride back was weird. We had this thing between us now, and we both knew what it was, and neither one of us said a word all the way back to the station. I wasn't worried about Sughrue anymore, I wasn't even thinking what I should do about this sorry mess. I just kept trying to remember a word I read in a book once about something the Greeks call it, when fear turns to pity.

I never did think of that word. I don't think I had one other clear thought in my head all the time I fought the car through the snow-drifted streets. I parked and followed Sughrue across the parking lot to the station, seeing his steps get stiff and lurchy. And slow. I followed him up the stairs to the second floor even slower, hearing his breath get loud and raspy as he pulled himself up the steps one at a time, and I mean, One. At. A. Time.

I never saw his face again. Not while he was alive, anyway. I stood there at the top of the stairs and watched the back of him ooze down the hall to his office and get the door closed. Then I figured it was safe and I told Rosey to call the lieutenant.

Lieutenant Franklin retired a few years back, then died or something. So no one but me remembers pushing open the door to Sughrue's office and seeing him sprawled back in his chair, white like Smollett was, white like the snow, with his coat hanging open and red blood spread all over his shirt and down on the floor. The same blood that was trailed from the front of Smollett's desk into the bathroom where last night he'd gone to stop the bleeding and thought he had till he went down in the snow and opened up the wound again.

But all that was a long time ago, and nobody remembers Sughrue much anymore, and us who were there reported what we had to and covered up the rest and never talked about it after. In a few years it was like it never happened at all. Like I say, I'd even quit seeing Sughrue's picture on the wall till the new kid made a point of it.

And even though I looked at it again on the way out that night, it didn't mean much to me; just some guy I killed once, that's all.

John Mortimer

RUMPOLE AND THE
CHAMBERS PARTY

Christmas comes but once a year. Once a year I receive a gift of socks from She Who Must Be Obeyed; each year I add to her cellar of bottles of lavender water, which she now seems to use mainly for the purpose of "laying down" in the bedroom cupboard (I suspect she has only just started on the 1980 vintage).

Tinseled cards and sprigs of holly appear at the entrance to the cells under the Old Bailey and a constantly repeated tape of "God Rest Ye Merry Gentlemen" adds little zest to my two eggs, bacon, and sausage on a fried slice in the Taste-Ee-Bite, Fleet Street; and once a year the Great Debate takes place at our December meeting. Should we invite solicitors to our Chambers party?

"No doubt at the season of our Savior's birth we should offer hospitality to all sorts and conditions of men," "Soapy" Sam Ballard, q.c., our devout Head of Chambers, opened the proceedings in his usual manner, that of a somewhat backward bishop addressing Synod on the wisdom of offering the rites of baptism to non-practicing, gay Anglican converts of riper years.

"All conditions of men and *women*." Phillida Erskine-Brown, q.c., nee Trant, the Portia of our Chambers, was looking particularly fetching in a well fitting black jacket and an only slightly flippant version of a male collar and tie. As she looked doe-eyed at him, Ballard, who hides a ridiculously susceptible heart beneath his monkish exterior, conceded her point.

"The question before us is, does all sorts and conditions of men, and women, too, of course, include members of the junior branch of the legal profession?"

"I'm against it!" Claude Erskine-Brown had remained an aging junior whilst his wife Phillida fluttered into silk, and he was never in favor of radical change. "The party is very much a family thing for the chaps in Chambers, and the clerk's room, of course. If we ask solicitors, it looks very much as though we're touting for briefs."

"I'm very much in favor of touting for briefs." Up spake the somewhat grey barrister, Hoskins. "Speaking as a man with four daughters to educate. For heaven's sake, let's ask as many solicitors as we know, which, in my case, I'm afraid, is not many."

"Do you have a view, Rumpole?" Ballard felt bound to ask me, just as a formality.

"Well, yes, nothing wrong with a bit of touting, I agree with Hoskins. But I'm in favor of asking the people who really provide us with work."

"You mean solicitors?"

"I mean the criminals of England. Fine conservative fellows who should appeal to you, Ballard. Greatly in favor of free enterprise and against the closed shop. I propose we invite a few of the better-class crooks who have no previous engagements as guests of Her Majesty, and show our gratitude."

A somewhat glazed look came over the assembly at this suggestion and then Mrs. Erskine-Brown broke the silence with: "Claude's really being awfully stuffy and old-fashioned about this. I propose we invite a smattering of solicitors, from the better-class firms."

Our Portia's proposal was carried *nem con*, such was the disarming nature of her sudden smile on everyone, including her husband, who may have had some reason to fear it. Rumpole's suggestion, to nobody's surprise, received no support whatsoever.

Our clerk, Henry, invariably arranged the Chambers party for the night on which his wife put on the Nativity play in the Bexley Heath Comprehensive at which she was a teacher. This gave him more scope for kissing Dianne, our plucky but somewhat hit-and-miss typist, beneath the mistletoe which swung from the dim, religious light in the entrance hall of number three Equity Court.

Paper streamers dangled from the bookcase full of All England Law Reports in Ballard's room and were hooked up to his views of the major English cathedrals. Barristers' wives were invited, and Mrs. Hilda Rumpole, known to me only as She Who Must Be Obeyed, was downing sherry and telling Soapy Sam all about the golden days when her daddy, C. H. Wystan, ran Chambers. There were also six or seven solicitors among those present.

One, however, seemed superior to all the rest, a solicitor of the class we seldom see around Equity Court. He had come in with one hand outstretched to Ballard, saying, "Daintry Naismith, happy Christmas. Awfully kind of you fellows to invite one of the junior branch." Now he stood propped up against the mantelpiece, warming his undoubtedly Savile Row trousers at Ballard's gas fire and receiving the homage of barristers in urgent need of briefs.

He appeared to be in his well preserved fifties, with grey wings of hair above his ears and a clean-shaven, pink, and still single chin poised above what I took to be an old Etonian tie. Whatever he might have on offer, it wouldn't, I was sure, be a charge of nicking a frozen chicken from Safeways. Even his murders, I thought, as he sized us up from over the top of his gold-rimmed half glasses, would take place among the landed gentry.

He accepted a measure of Pommeroy's very ordinary white plonk from Portia and drank it bravely, as though he hadn't been used to sipping Chassagne-Montrachet all his adult life.

"Mrs. Erskine-Brown," he purred at her, "I'm looking for a hard-hitting silk to brief in the Family Division. I suppose you're tremendously booked up."

"The pressure of my work," Phillida said modestly, "is enormous."

"I've got the Geoffrey Twyford divorce coming. Pretty hairy bit of in-fighting over the estate and the custody of young Lord Shiplake. I thought you'd be just right for it."

"Is that the Duke of Twyford?" Claude Erskine-Brown looked suitably awestruck. In spite of his other affectations, Erskine-Brown's snobbery is completely genuine.

"Well, if you have a word with Henry, my clerk"—Mrs. Erskine-Brown gave the solicitor a look of cool availability—"he might find a few spare dates."

"Well, that is good of you. And you, Mr. Erskine-Brown, mainly civil work now, I suppose?"

"Oh, yes. Mainly civil." Erskine-Brown lied cheerfully; he's not above taking on the odd indecent assault when tort gets a little thin on the ground. "I do find crime so sordid."

"Oh, I agree. Look here. I'm stumped for a man to take on our insurance business, but I suppose you'd be far too busy."

"Oh, no. I've got plenty of time." Erskine-Brown lacked his wife's laid-back approach to solicitors. "That is to say, I'm sure I could make time. One gets used to extremely long hours, you know." I thought that the longest hours Erskine-Brown put in were when he sat, in grim earnest, through the *Ring* at Covent Garden, being a man who submits himself to Wagner rather as others enjoy walking from Land's End to John O'Groats.

And then I saw Naismith staring at me and waited for him to announce that the Marquess of Something or Other had stabbed his butler in the library and could I possibly make myself available for the trial. Instead he muttered, "Frightfully good party," and wandered off in the general direction of Soapy Sam Ballard.

"What's the matter with you, Rumpole?" She Who Must Be Obeyed was at my elbow and not sounding best pleased. "Why didn't you push yourself forward?" Erskine-Brown had also moved off by this time to join the throng.

"I don't care for divorce," I told her. "It's too bloodthirsty for me. Now if he'd offered me a nice gentle murder—"

"Go after him, Rumpole," she urged me, "and make yourself known. I'll go and ask Phillida what her plans are for the Harrods sale."

Perhaps it was the mention of the sale which spurred me toward that undoubted source of income, Mr. Daintry Naismith. I found him talking to Ballard in a way which showed, in my view, a gross overestimation of that old darling's forensic powers. "Of course the client would have to understand that the golden tongue of Samuel Ballard, q.c., can't be hired on the cheap," Naismith was saying. I thought that to refer to our Head of Chambers, whose voice in Court could best be compared to a rusty saw, as golden-tongued was a bit of an exaggeration.

"I'll have to think it over." Ballard was flattered but cautious. "One does have certain principles about"—he gulped, rather in the manner of a fish struggling with its conscience—"encouraging the publication of explicitly sexual material."

"Think it over, Mr. Ballard. I'll be in touch with your clerk." And then, as Naismith saw me approach, he said, "Perhaps I'll have a word with him now." So this legal Santa Claus moved away in the general direction of Henry and once more Rumpole was left with nothing in his stocking.

"By the way," I asked Ballard, "did *you* invite that extremely smooth solicitor?"

"No, I think Henry did." Our Head of Chambers spoke as a man whose thoughts are on knottier problems. "Charming chap, though, isn't he?"

Later in the course of the party I found myself next to Henry. "Good work inviting Mr. Daintry Naismith," I said to our clerk. "He seems set on providing briefs for everyone except me."

"I don't really know the gentleman," Henry admitted. "I think he must be a friend of Mr. Ballard's. Of course, we hope to see a lot of him in the future."

Much later, in search of a small cigar, I remembered the box, still in its special Christmas reindeer-patterned wrapping, that I had left in my brief tray. I opened the door of the clerk's room and found the lights off and Henry's desk palely lit by the old gas lamp outside in Equity Court.

There was a dark-suited figure standing beside the desk who seemed to be trying the locked drawers rather in the casual way that suspicious-looking youths test car handles. I switched on the light and found myself staring at our star solicitor guest. And as I looked at him, the years rolled away and I was in Court defending a bent house agent. Beside him in the dock had been an equally curved solicitor's clerk who had joined my client as a guest of Her Majesty.

"Derek Newton," I said, "Inner London Sessions. Raising mortgages on deserted houses that you didn't own. Two years."

"I knew you'd recognize me, Mr. Rumpole. Sooner or later."

"What the hell do you think you are doing?"

"I'm afraid—well, barristers' chambers are about the only place where you can find a bit of petty cash lying about at Christmas." The man seemed resolved to have no secrets from Rumpole.

"You admit it?"

"Things aren't too easy when you're knocking sixty, and the business world's full of wide boys up to all the tricks. You can't get far on one good suit and the Old Etonian tie nowadays. You always defend, don't you, Rumpole? That's what I've heard. Well, I can only appeal to you for leniency."

"But coming to our party," I said, staggered by this most confident of tricksters, "promising briefs to all the learned friends—"

"I always wanted to be admitted as a solicitor." He smiled a little wistfully. "I usually walk through the Temple at Christmastime. Sometimes I drop in to the parties. And I always make a point of offering work. It's a pleasure to see so many grateful faces. This is, after all, Mr. Rumpole, the season of giving."

What could I do? All he had got out of us, after all, was a couple of glasses of Pommeroy's Fleet Street white; that and the five-pound note he "borrowed" from me for his cab fare home. I went back to the party and explained to Ballard that Mr. Daintry Naismith had made a phone call and had to leave on urgent business.

"He's offered me a highly remunerative brief, Rumpole, defending a publisher of dubious books. It's against my principles, but even the greatest sinner has a right to have his case put before the Court."

"And put by your golden tongue, old darling," I flattered him. "If you take my advice, you'll go for it."

It was, after all, the season of goodwill, and I couldn't find it in my heart to spoil Soapy Sam Ballard's Christmas.

Edward D. Hoch

THE SPY AND THE CHRISTMAS CIPHER

It was just a few days before the Christmas recess at the University of Reading when Rand's wife Leila said to him over dinner, "Come and speak to my class on Wednesday, Jeffrey."

"What? Are you serious?" He put down his fork and stared at her. "I know nothing about archaeology."

"You don't have to. I just want you to tell them a Christmas story of some sort. Remember last year? The Canadian writer Robertson Davies was over here on a visit and he told one of his ghost stories."

"I don't know any good ghost stories."

"Then tell them a cipher story from before you retired. Tell them about the time you worked through Christmas Eve trying to crack the St. Ives cipher."

Ivan St. Ives. Rand hadn't thought of him in years.

Yes, he supposed it was a Christmas story of sorts.

It was Christmas Eve morning in 1974, when Rand was still head of Concealed Communications, operating out of the big old building overlooking the Thames. He remembered his superior, Hastings, making the rounds of the offices with an open bottle of sherry and a stack of paper cups, a tradition that no one but Hastings ever looked forward to. A cup of government sherry before noon was not something to warm the heart or put one in the Christmas spirit.

"It promises to be a quiet day," Hastings said, pouring the ritual drink. "You should be able to leave early and finish up your Christmas shopping."

"It's finished. I have no one but Leila to buy for." Rand accepted the cup and took a small sip.

"Sometimes I wish I was as well organized as you, Rand." Hastings seemed almost disappointed as he sat down in the worn leather chair opposite Rand's desk. "I was going to ask you to pick up something for me."

"On the day before Christmas? The stores will be crowded."

Hastings decided to abandon the pretense. "They say Ivan St. Ives is back in town."

"Oh? Surely you weren't planning to send him a Christmas gift?"

St. Ives was a double agent who'd worked for the British, the Russians, and anyone else willing to pay his price. There were too many like him in the modern world of espionage, where national loyalties counted for nothing against the lure of easy money.

"He's back in town and he's not working for us."

"Who, then?" Rand asked. "The Russians?"

"Perkins and Simplex, actually."

"Perkins and Simplex is a department store."

"Exactly. Ivan St. Ives has been employed over the Christmas season as their Father Christmas—red suit, white beard, and all. He holds little children on his knee and asks them what they want for Christmas."

Rand laughed. "Is the spying business in some sort of depression we don't know about? St. Ives could always pick up money from the Irish if nobody else would pay him."

"I just found out about it last evening, almost by accident. I ran into St. Ives's old girlfriend, Daphne Sollis, at the Crown and Piper. There's no love lost between the two of them and she was quite eager to tell me of his hard times."

"It's one of his ruses, Hastings. If Ivan St. Ives is sitting in Perkins and Simplex wearing a red suit and a beard it's part of some much more complex scheme."

"Maybe, maybe not. Anyway, this is his last day on the job. Why don't you drop by and take a look for yourself?"

"Is that what this business about last-minute shopping has been leading up to? What about young Parkinson—isn't this more his sort of errand?"

"Parkinson doesn't know St. Ives. You do."

There was no disputing the logic of that. Rand drank the rest of his sherry and stood up. "Do I have to sit on his lap?"

Hastings sighed. "Just find out what he's up to, Jeff."

The day was unseasonably warm, and as Rand crossed Oxford Street toward the main entrance of Perkins and Simplex he was aware that many in the lunchtime crowd had shed their coats or left them back at the office. The department store itself was a big old building that covered an entire block facing Oxford Street. It dated from Edwardian times, prior to World War I, and was a true relic of its age. Great care had been taken to maintain the exterior just as it had been, though the demands of modern merchandising had taken their toll with the interior. During the previous decade the first two floors had been gutted and transformed into a pseudo-atrium, surrounded by a balcony on which some of the store's regular departments had become little shops. The ceiling was frosted glass, lit from above by fluorescent tubes to give the appearance of daylight.

It was in this main atrium, near the escalators, that Father Christmas had been installed on his throne amidst sparkly white mountains of ersatz snow that was hardly in keeping with the outdoor temperature. The man himself was stout, but not as fat as American Santa Clauses. His white beard and the white-trimmed cowl of his red robe effectively hid his identity. It might have been Ivan St. Ives, but Rand wasn't prepared to swear to it. He had to get much closer if he wanted to be sure.

He watched for a time from the terrace level as a line of parents and tots wound its way up the carpeted ramp to Father Christmas's chair. There he listened carefully to each child's request, sometimes boosting the smallest of them to his knee and patting their heads, handing each one a small brightly wrapped gift box from a pile at his elbow.

After observing this for ten or fifteen minutes, Rand descended to the main floor and found a young mother approaching the end of the line with her little boy. "Pardon me, ma'am," Rand said. "I wonder if I might borrow your son and take him up to see Father Christmas."

She stared at him as if she hadn't heard him correctly. "No, I can take him myself."

Rand showed his identity card. "It's official business."

The woman hesitated, then stood firm. "I'm sorry. Roger would be terrified if I left him."

"Could I come along, then, as your husband?"

She stared at the card again, as if memorizing the name. "I suppose so, if it's official business. No violence or anything, though?"

"I promise."

They stood in line together and Rand took the little boy's hand. Roger stared up at him with his big brown eyes, but his mother was there to give him confidence. "I hate shopping on Christmas Eve," she told Rand. "I always spend too much when I wait until the last minute."

"I think most of us do that." He smiled at the boy. "Are you ready, Roger? We're getting closer to Father Christmas."

In a moment the boy was on the bearded man's knee, having his head patted as he told him what he wanted to find under the tree next day. Then he received his brightly wrapped gift box and they were on their way back down the ramp.

"Thank you," Rand told the woman. "You've been a big help." He went back up to the terrace level and spent the next hour watching Ivan St. Ives, double agent, passing out gifts to a long line of little children.

"It's St. Ives," Rand told Hastings when he returned to the office. "No doubt of it."

"Did he recognize you?"

"I doubt it." He explained how he'd accompanied himself with the woman and child. "If he did, he might have assumed I was with my family."

"So he's just making a little extra Christmas money?"

"I'm afraid it's more than that."

"You spotted something."

"A great deal, but I don't know what it means. I watched him for more than an hour in all. After he listened to each child, he handed them a small gift. I watched one little girl opening hers. It was a clear plastic ball to hang on a Christmas tree, with figures of cartoon characters inside."

"Seems harmless enough."

"I'm sure the store wouldn't be giving out anything that wasn't. The trouble is, while I watched him I noticed a slight deviation from his routine on three different occasions. In these cases, he chose the gift box from a separate pile, and handed it to the parent rather than the child."

"Well, some of the children are quite small, I imagine."

"In those three cases, none of the boxes were opened in the store. They were stowed away in shopping bags by the mother or father. One little boy started crying for his gift, but he didn't get it."

Hastings thought about it.

"Do you think an agent would take a position as a department store Father Christmas to distribute some sort of message to his network?"

"I think we should see one of those boxes, Hastings."

"If there *is* a message, it probably says 'Merry Christmas.' "

"St. Ives has worked for some odd people in the past, including terrorists. When I left the store, there were still seven or eight boxes left on his special pile. If I went back there now with a couple of men—"

"Very well," Hastings said. "But please be discreet, Rand. It's the day before Christmas."

It's not easy to be discreet when seizing a suspected spy in the midst of a crowd of Christmas shoppers. Rand finally decided he wanted one of the free gifts more than he wanted the agents at this point, so he took only Parkinson with him. As they passed through the Oxford Street entrance of Perkins and Simplex, the younger man asked, "Is this case likely to run through the holidays? I was hoping to spend Christmas and Boxing Day with the family."

"I hope there won't even be a case," Rand told him. "Hastings heard Ivan

St. Ives was back in the city, working as Father Christmas for the holidays. I confirmed the fact and that's why we're here."

"To steal a child's gift?"

"Not exactly steal, Parkinson. I have another idea."

They encountered a woman and child about to leave the store with the familiar square box. "Pardon me, but is that a gift from Father Christmas?" Rand asked her.

"Yes, it is."

"Then this is your lucky day. As a special holiday treat, Perkins and Simplex is paying every tenth person ten pounds for their gift." He held up a crisp new bill. "Would you like to exchange yours for a tenner?"

"I sure would!" The woman handed over the opened box and accepted the ten-pound note.

"That was easy," Parkinson commented when the woman and child were gone. "What next?"

"This might be a bit more difficult," Rand admitted. They retreated to a men's room where Rand fastened the festive paper around the gift box once more, resticking the piece of tape that held it together. "There, looks as good as new."

Parkinson got the point. "You're going to substitute this for one of the special ones."

"Exactly. And you're going to help."

They resumed Rand's earlier position on the terrace level, where he observed that the previous stack of boxes had dwindled to three. If he was right, they would be gone shortly, too. "How about that man?" Parkinson pointed out. "The one with the little boy."

"Why him?"

"He doesn't look that fatherly to me. And the boy seems a bit old to believe in Father Christmas."

"You're right," Rand said a moment later. "He's getting one of the special boxes. Come on!"

As the man and the boy came down off the ramp and mingled with the crowd, Rand moved in. The man was clutching the box just as the others had when Rand managed to jostle him. The box didn't come loose, so Rand jostled again with his elbow, this time using his other hand to yank it free. The man, in his twenties with black hair and a vaguely foreign look, muttered something in a language Rand didn't understand. There was a trace of panic in his face as he bent to retrieve the box. Rand pretended to lose his footing then, and came down on top of the man. The crowd of shoppers parted as they tumbled to the floor.

"Terribly sorry," Rand muttered, helping the man to his feet.

At the same moment, Parkinson held out the brightly wrapped package. "I believe you dropped this, sir."

Anyone else might have cursed Rand and made a scene, but this strange man merely grasped the box and hurried away without a word, the small boy trailing along behind. "Good work," Rand said, brushing off his jacket. "Let's get this back to the office."

"Aren't we going to open it?"

"Not here."

Thirty minutes later, Rand was carefully unwrapping the gift on Hastings' desk. Both Parkinson and Hastings were watching apprehensively, as if expecting a snake to spring out like a jack-in-the-box. "My money's on drugs," Parkinson said. "What else could it be?"

"Is the box exactly the same as the others?" Hastings asked.

"Just a bit heavier," Rand decided. "A few ounces."

But inside there seemed to be nothing but the same plastic tree ornament. Rand removed the tissue paper and stared at the bottom of the box.

"Nothing," Parkinson said.

"Wait a minute. Something had to make it heavier." Rand reached in and pried up the bottom piece of cardboard with his fingernails. It was a snugly fitted false bottom. Beneath it was a thin layer of a grey puttylike substance. "Better not touch it," Hastings cautioned.

"That's plastique—plastic explosive."

The man from the bomb squad explained that it was harmless without a detonator of some sort, but they were still relieved when he removed it from the office. "How much damage would that much plastic explosive do?" Rand wanted to know.

"It would make a mess of this room. That's about all."

"What about twelve or fifteen times that much?"

"Molded together into one bomb? It could take out a house or a small building."

They looked at each other glumly. "It's a pretty bizarre method for distributing explosives," Parkinson said.

"It has its advantages," Hastings said. "The bomb is of little use until enough of the explosive is gathered together. If one small box falls into government hands, as this one did, the rest is still safe. No doubt it was delivered to St. Ives only recently, and this served as the perfect method for getting it to his network—certainly better than the mails during the Christmas rush."

"Then you think it's to be reassembled into one bomb?" Rand asked.

"Of course. And it's to be used sometime soon."

"The IRA? Russians? Arabs?"

Hastings shrugged. "Take your pick. St. Ives has worked for all of them."

Rand held the box up to the light, studying the bottom. "This may be some writing, some sort of invisible ink that's beginning to become visible. Get one of the technicians up here to see if we can bring it out."

Heating the bottom of the box to bring out the message proved an easy task, but the letters that appeared were anything but easy to read: MPPMP MBSHG OEXAS-EWHMR AWPGG GBEBH PMBWE ALGHQ.

"A substitution cipher," Parkinson decided at once. "We'll get to work on it."

"Forty letters," Rand observed, "in the usual five-letter groups. There are five Ms, five Ps, and five Gs. Using letter frequencies, one of them could be E, but in such a short message you can't be sure."

"GHQ at the end could stand for General Headquarters," Hastings suggested.

Rand shook his head. "The entire message would be enciphered. Chances are that's just a coincidence."

Parkinson took the message off to the deciphering room and Rand confidently predicted he'd have the answer within an hour.

He didn't.

"It's tougher than it looks," Parkinson told them. "There may not be any Es at all."

"Run it through the computer," Rand suggested. "Use a program that substitutes various frequently used letters for the most frequently used letters in the message. See if you hit on anything."

Hastings glanced at the clock. "It's after six and my niece has invited me for Christmas Eve. Can you manage without me?"

"Of course. Merry Christmas."

After he'd gone, Rand picked up the phone and told Leila he'd be late. She was living in England now, and he'd planned to spend the holiday with her.

"How late?" she asked.

"These things have been known to last all night."

"Oh, Jeffrey. On Christmas Eve?"

"I'll call you later if I can," Rand promised. "It might not take that long."

He went down the hall and stood for a time watching the computer experts work on the message. They seemed to be having no better luck than Parkinson's people. "How long?" he asked one.

"In the worst possible case it could take us until morning to run all the combinations."

Rand nodded. "I'll be back."

They had to know what the message said, but they also had to find Ivan

St. Ives. The employment office at Perkins and Simplex would be closed now. His only chance was that pub where Hastings had spoken with Daphne Sollis. The Crown and Piper.

It was on a corner, as London pubs often are, and the night before Christmas didn't seem to have made much of a dent in the early-evening business. The bar was crowded and all the tables and booths were occupied. Rand let his eyes wander over the faces, seeking out either St. Ives or Daphne, but neither one seemed to be there. He didn't know either of them well, though he thought he would recognize St. Ives out of his Father Christmas garb. He was less certain about recognizing Daphne Sollis.

"Seen Daphne around?" he asked the bartender as he ordered a pint.

"Daphne Jenkins?"

"Daphne Sollis."

"Do I know her?"

"She was in here last night, talking to a grey-haired man wearing rimless glasses. He was probably dressed in a plaid topcoat."

"I don't— Wait a minute, you must mean Rusty. Does she have red hair?"

"Not the last time I knew her, but these things change."

"Well, if it's Rusty she comes in a couple of nights a week, usually alone. Once recently she was with a creepy-looking gent who kept laughing like Father Christmas. I sure wouldn't want *him* bringing gifts to my kids. He'd scare 'em half to death."

"Does she live around here?"

"No idea, mate." He went off to wait on another customer.

So whatever Daphne had told Hastings about her relationship with Ivan St. Ives, they were hardly enemies. He'd been with her recently in the Crown and Piper, apparently since he took on the job as Father Christmas.

Rand thought it unlikely that Daphne would visit the pub two nights in a row, but on the other hand she might stop by if she was lonely on Christmas Eve. He decided to linger over his pint and see if she appeared. Thirty minutes later he was about to give it up and head for Leila's flat when he heard the bartender say, "Hey, Rusty! Fellow here's been askin' after you."

Rand turned and saw Daphne Sollis standing not five feet behind him, unwrapping a scarf to reveal a tousled head of red hair. "Daphne!" She looked puzzled for a moment and he identified himself. "Ivan St. Ives introduced us a year or so back. He did some work for me."

She nodded slowly as it came back to her. "Oh, yes—Mr. Rand. I remember you now. Is this some sort of setup? The other one, Hastings, was here just last night."

"No setup, but I *would* like to talk with you, away from this noise. How about the lobby of the hotel next door?"

"Well—all right."

The hotel lobby was much quieter. They sat beneath a large potted palm and no one disturbed them. "What do you want?" she asked. "What did your friend Hastings want last night?"

"It was only happenstance that he met you, though I'll admit I came to the Crown and Piper looking for you. I need to locate Ivan St. Ives."

"I told Hastings we're on the outs."

"I saw him at Perkins and Simplex earlier today."

"Then you've already located him."

"No," Rand explained. "His Christmas job would have ended today. I need to know where he's living."

"I said we're on the outs."

"You were drinking with him at the Crown and Piper just a week or two ago."

She bit her lip and stared off into space. "I don't know where he's living. He rang me up and we had a drink for old times' sake. That's when he told me about the Christmas job. He talked about getting back together again, but I don't know. He works for a lot of shady people."

"Who's he working for now?"

"Just the store, so far as I know. He said he'd fallen on hard times."

Rand leaned forward. "It could be worth some money if you located him for us, told us who he's palling around with."

She seemed to consider the idea. "I could tell you plenty about who he's palled around with in the past. It wasn't just our side, you know."

"I know."

"But it would have to be after New Year's. I'm going to visit a girlfriend in Hastings, on the coast. Is your friend Hastings from there?"

"From Leeds, actually." Rand was frowning. "I need St. Ives now."

"I'm sorry, I can't help you. Perhaps the store has his address."

"I'll have to ask them." Rand stood up. "Can I buy you a pint back at the pub?"

"I'd better skip it now," she said, glancing at her watch. "I want to get home and change. I'm going to Midnight Mass with some friends."

"If you'll jot down your phone number I'd like to ring you up after New Year's."

"Fine," she agreed.

He'd intended to phone Leila after he left Daphne, but back at the Double-C office, Parkinson was in a state of dejection. "We've run every possible substitution of the letter E and there's still nothing. We're going down the letter-frequency list now, working on T, A, O, and N."

"Forty characters without a single E. Unusual, certainly. "

"Any luck locating St. Ives?"

"Not yet."

Rand worked with them for a time and then dozed on his office couch. It was long after midnight when Parkinson shook him awake. "I think we've got part of it."

"Let me see."

The younger man produced long folds of computer printout. "On this one we concentrated on the first six characters—the repetitive MPPMPM. We got nowhere substituting E, T, or A, but when we tried the next letters on the frequency list, O and N, look what came up."

Rand focused his sleepy eyes and read NOONON. "Noon on?"

"Exactly. And there's another ON combination later in the message."

"Just a simple substitution cipher after all," Rand marveled. "School children make them up all the time."

"And it took us all these hours to get this far."

"St. Ives didn't worry about making the cipher too complex because he was writing it in invisible ink. It was our good luck that the box warmed enough so that some of the message began to appear."

"A terrorist network armed with plastic explosives, and St. Ives is telling them when and where to set off the bomb. Do you think we should phone Hastings?"

Rand glanced at the clock. It was almost dawn on Christmas morning. "Let's wait till we get the rest of it.

He followed Parkinson down the hall to the computer room where the others were at work. Not bothering with the machines, he went straight to the old blackboard at the far end of the room. "Look here, all of you. The group of letters following *noon on* is probably a day of the week, or a date if it's spelled out. If it's a day of the week, three of these letters have to stand for *day.*"

As he worked, he became aware that someone had chalked the most common letter-frequency list down the left side of the board, starting with E, T, A, O, N, and continuing down to Q, X, Z. It was the list from David Kahn's massive 1967 book, *The Codebreakers*, which everyone in the department had on their shelves. He stared at it and noticed that M and P came together about halfway down the list. Together, just like N and O in the regular alphabet. Quickly he chalked the letters A to Z next to the frequency list. "Look here! The key is the standard letter-frequency list. ABCDE is enciphered as ETAON. There are no Ns in the message we found, so there are no Es in the plaintext."

The message became clear at once: NOONO NTHIS DAYCH ARING CROSS STATI ONTRA CKSIX. "Noon on this day, Charing Cross Station, Track six," Rand read.

"Noon on which day?" Parkinson questioned. "It was after noon yesterday before he distributed most of the boxes."

"He must mean today. Christmas Day. A Christmas Day explosion at Charing Cross Station."

"I'll phone Hastings," Parkinson decided. "We can catch them in the act."

Police and Scotland Yard detectives converged on the station shortly after dawn. Staying as unobtrusive as possible, they searched the entire area around track six. No bomb was found.

Noon came and went, and no bomb exploded.

Rand turned up at Leila's flat late that afternoon. "Only twenty-four hours late," she commented drily, holding the door open for him.

"And not in a good mood."

"You mean you didn't crack it after all this time?"

"We cracked it, but that didn't do us much good. We don't have the man who sent it, and we may be unable to prevent a terrorist bombing."

"Here in London?"

"Yes, right here in London." He knew a few police were still at Charing Cross Station, but he also knew it was quite easy to smuggle plastic explosives past the tightest security. They could be molded into any shape, and metal detectors were of no use against them.

He tried to put his mind at ease during dinner with Leila, and later when she asked if he'd be spending the night he readily agreed. But he awakened before dawn and walked restlessly to the window, looking out at the glistening streets where rain had started to fall. It would be colder today, more like winter.

The bomb hadn't gone off at Charing Cross Station yesterday. Either the time or the place was wrong.

But it hadn't gone off anywhere else in London, so he could assume the place was correct. It was the time that was off.

The time, or the day.

This day.

Noon on this day.

He went to Leila's telephone and called Parkinson at home. When he heard his sleepy voice answer, he said, "This is Rand. Meet me at the office in an hour."

"It's only six o'clock," Parkinson muttered. "And a holiday."

"I know. I'm sorry. But I'm calling Hastings, too. It's important."

He leaned over the bed to kiss Leila but left without awakening her.

An hour later, with Hastings and Parkinson seated before him in the office, Rand picked up a piece of chalk. "You see, we assumed the wrong meaning for the word 'this.' If someone wants to indicate 'today,' they say it—they don't say 'this day.' On the other hand, if I write the word 'this' on the desk in front of me—" he did so with the piece of chalk "—what am I referring to?"

"The desk," Parkinson replied.

"Right. If I wrote the word on a box, what would I be referring to?"

"The box."

"When St. Ives's message said, 'this day,' he wasn't referring to Christmas Eve or Christmas Day. He was telling them Boxing Day. Even if they were foreign, they'd know it was the day after Christmas here and a national holiday."

"That's today," Hastings said.

"Exactly. We need to get the men back to Charing Cross Station."

The station was almost deserted. The holiday travelers were at their destinations, and it was too soon for anyone to have started home yet. Rand stood near one of the newsstands looking through a paper while the detectives again searched unobtrusively around track six. It was nearly noon and time was running out.

"No luck," Hastings told him. "They can't find a thing."

"Plastique." Rand shook his head. "It could be molded around a girder and painted most any color. We'd better keep everyone clear from now until after noon." It was six minutes to twelve.

"Are you sure about this, Rand? St. Ives is using a dozen or more people. Perhaps they all didn't understand his message."

"They had to come together to assemble the small portions of explosive into a deadly whole. Most of them would understand the message even if a few didn't. I'm sure St. Ives trained them well."

"It's not a busy day. He's not trying to kill a great many people or he'd have waited until a daily rush hour."

"No," Rand agreed. "I think he's content to—" He froze, staring toward the street entrance to the station. A man and a woman had entered and were walking toward track six. The man was Ivan St. Ives and the woman was Daphne Sollis.

Rand had forgotten that the train to Hastings left from Charing Cross Station.

He ran across the station floor, through the beams of sunlight that had suddenly brightened it from the glass-enclosed roof. "St. Ives!" he shouted.

Ivan St. Ives had just bent to give Daphne a good-bye kiss. He turned suddenly at the sound of his name and saw Rand approaching. "What *is* this?" he asked.

"Get away from him, Daphne!" Rand warned.

"He just came to see me off. I told you I was visiting—"

"Get away from him!" Rand repeated more urgently.

St. Ives met his eyes, and glanced quickly away, as if seeking a safe exit. But already the others were moving in. His eyes came back to Rand, recognizing him. "You were at the store, in line for Father Christmas! I knew I'd seen you before!"

"We broke the cipher, St. Ives. We know everything."

St. Ives turned and ran, not toward the street from where the men were coming but through the gate to track six. A police constable blew his whistle, and the sound merged with the chiming of the station clock. St. Ives had gone about fifty feet when the railway car to his left seemed to come apart with a blinding flash and roar of sound that sent waves of dust and debris billowing back toward Rand and the others. Daphne screamed and covered her face.

When the smoke cleared, Ivan St. Ives was gone. It was some time later before they found his remains among the wreckage that had been blown onto the adjoining track. By then, Rand had explained it to Hastings and Parkinson. "Ivan St. Ives was a truly evil man. When he was hired to plan and carry out a terrorist bombing in London over the Christmas holidays, he decided quite literally to kill two birds with one stone. He planned the bombing for the exact time and place where his old girlfriend Daphne Sollis would be. To make certain she didn't arrive too early or too late, he even escorted her to the station himself. She knew too much about his past associations, and he wanted her out of his life for good. I imagine one of his men must have ridden the train into Charing Cross Station and hidden the bomb on board before he left."

But he didn't tell any of this to Daphne. She only knew that they'd come to arrest St. Ives and he'd been killed by a bomb while trying to flee. A tragic coincidence, nothing more. She never knew St. Ives had tried to kill her.

In a way Rand felt it was a Christmas gift to her.

Jeffry Scott

INSPECTOR TIERCE AND THE CHRISTMAS VISITS

Coppers are only human, Jill Tierce told herself, without much conviction, after Superintendent Haggard's invitation to a quiet drink after work. Actually he'd passed outside the open door of her broom-closet office, making Jill start by booming, "Heads up, girlie! Pub call, I'm buying. Back in five . . ." before bustling away, rubbing his hands.

Taking acceptance for granted was very Lance Haggard, and so was the empty, outward show of bonhomie, but there you were.

Unless forced to behave otherwise, Superintendent Haggard generally did no more than nod to Inspector Tierce in passing. This hadn't broken her heart. He had a reputation: it was whispered that he pulled strokes. Nothing criminal, he wasn't bent, but he had a knack of pilfering credit for ideas or successes, coupled with deft evasive action if his own projects went wrong.

Refusing to waste time on Jill Tierce owed less to sexism than to the fact that she was of no present use to him. Leg mangled on duty, she was recovering slowly. Fighting against being invalided out of the Wessex-Coastal Force, lying like a politician about miracles of surgery and physiotherapy, and disguising her limp by willpower, she had won a partial victory. Restricted to light duties on a part-time basis, she was assigned to review dormant cases —and Lance Haggard, skimming along the fast track, wasn't one to waste time on history.

It wasn't professional, then, and she doubted a pass. Superintendent Haggard was a notoriously faithful husband. Moreover, Inspector Tierce was clearsighted about her looks: too sharp-featured for prettiness, and the sort of pale hair that may deserve the label but escapes being called blonde.

What was he up to? Then she'd glanced out of the smeary window at her elbow and seen strings of colored lights doubly blurred by the glass and another flurry of snow. There was the explanation, Christmas spirit. She smiled wryly. The superintendent probably kept a checklist of seasonal tasks, so many off-duty hours per December week devoted to stroking inferiors who might mature into rivals or allies. She supposed she ought to feel flattered.

A police cadet messenger tapped at the door and placed a file on Jill's desk without leaving the corridor, by leaning in and reaching. He had a lipstick smudge in the lee of one earlobe. Mistletoe had been hung in the canteen at lunchtime, only five days to the twenty-fifth now.

Big deal, she thought sourly.

The new file was depressingly fat. She transferred it from the in tray to the bottom of the pending basket, noting that the covers were quite crisp though the buff cardboard jacket had begun to fade. More than a year old, Inspector Tierce estimated. Then Superintendent Haggard was back, jingling his car keys impatiently.

He drove a mile or so out of town, to a Dickensian pub by the river. The saloon bar evoked a sporting squire's den, Victorian-vintage trophy fish in glass cases on the walls, no jukebox, and just token sprigs of non-plastic holly here and there. "Quiet and a bit classy," Lance Haggard commented. "I stumbled on this place last summer, thought it would suit you."

Sure you did, she jeered, not aloud. Apart from an older man and younger woman murmuring in a snug corner (boss courting a soon-to-be-even-more-personal assistant, Jill surmised cattily) they had the bar to themselves. "Done all your Christmas shopping?" Haggard inquired. "Going anywhere for the break, or spending it with Mum and Dad?"

Satisfied that small-talk obligations were discharged, he continued before she could match banality with banality, "I've had a file passed to you, luv. Before you drown in details, seemed a good idea to talk you through it."

Despite a flick of irritation, Jill Tierce was vaguely relieved. It was upsetting when leopards changed their spots. Superintendent Haggard's were still in place, he wasn't dispensing Christmas cheer but attempting to spread blame; if she reviewed one of his setbacks, she assumed part of the responsibility.

"I'm listening," she said flatly.

To her surprise, Haggard was . . . what? Not hangdog exactly, yet defensive. Obviously shelving a prepared presentation, he said, "Forget so-called perfect crimes—untraceable poisons, trick alibis, some bright spark who's a master of disguise. *Im*perfect crimes are the bastards to deal with. Chap had a brainstorm, lashes out at a total stranger, and runs for his life. Unless he gets collared on the spot, blood still running, we've no chance. Or, say, this respectable housewife is getting messages from Mars, personal relay station in a flying saucer. Eh? Height of the rush hour, she's in a crowd and shoves a child under a bus. Goes on home, like normal. No planning, no sane motive, they don't even try that hard to get away, they just . . . go about their business.

"It gets to me," he admitted needlessly. "Well, this one instance does.

811

Prostitute killed, and what's a streetwalker but somebody in extra danger from crazies? Mitzi Field, twenty-four years old but looked younger. Mitzi was just her working name, mind."

"There's a surprise."

He didn't rise to the sarcasm. "Dorothy Field on the death certificate but we'll stick to Mitzi, that's what she was known as, to the few who did know her.

"She was found in Grand Drive ten days before Christmas three years ago. Dead of repeated blows from something with sharp angles, most likely a brick. I see her getting into some curb crawler's car, and he drove her to where she was attacked. Saw red—wanted what she wouldn't provide, she tried ripping him off, plenty of possible reasons—snatched the nearest weapon, bashed her as she turned to run, kept bashing." The theory was delivered with pointed lack of emotion, Superintendent Haggard back in full control.

"Drove her there . . . the car was seen?" Jill held up a hand. "Sorry, not thinking straight." Mount Wolfe was one of the city's best quarters, Grand Drive its best address.

"Exactly," said Haggard. "Mitzi had started living rough, so she looked tatty. She'd had a mattress in a squat, that old factory on Victoria Quay, but the council demolished it the week before her death. The docks were her beat. She was wearing those big boots, like the movie—"

"Pretty Woman," Jill suggested.

"Those're the jokers, long boots and hot-pants and a ratty leather jacket with her chest hanging out—in December! The boots were borrowed from another girl, too tight, had to be sliced off her feet. Walking two miles from the docks to where she was found would have crippled her. And okay, it was dark, but a feller and a blatantly obvious hooker didn't foot it all the way up the Mount and along to the end of Grand Drive without being noticed. Which they were not, house-to-house checks established that."

Taking another, rationed sip of champagne—the pub sold it by the glass, else Haggard might not have stood for the drink of her choice, she suspected—Inspector Tierce frowned doubtfully.

"Grand Drive's the last place a working girl would pick for business. It's a private road, and they're very territorial round there—sleeping policeman bumps every fifty yards to stop cars using it for a shortcut, and if a non-resident parks in the road, somebody rings us within minutes, wanting him shifted . . ."

"Stresses that the punter was a stranger here," Haggard argued. "Businessman on an overnight, or he tired of motorway driving, detoured into town for a meal and a change of scene. Mitzi wasn't a local, either. Londoner originally, family split up after she was sexually abused. Went on the game after absconding from a council home when she was fifteen. Summer before her death she worked the transport cafes, Reading, Bath, Bristol, drifted far as here and stayed.

"For my money, the punter spotted her at the docks. Then they drove around. She had no crib, did the business in cars or alleys. Maybe this punter was scared of getting mugged if they stuck around the docks. Driving at random, they spot a quiet-looking street, plenty of deep shadow at the far end where the trees are. Must have seemed safe enough, and so it was—for him. Nobody saw them arrive or him leaving. Some pet lover daft enough to walk the dog in a hailstorm found Mitzi's body that night, but she could have lain there till morning otherwise.

"All known curb crawlers were interviewed and cleared. Ditto the Dodgy List." Superintendent Haggard referred to the extensive register of sex offenders whose misdeeds ranged from assaults to stealing underwear off washing lines. "Copybook imperfect crime: guy blew a gasket and got the hell out. Ensuring the perfect result for him."

"Thanks for hyping me up," Inspector Tierce responded dryly. She'd been right, ambitious Haggard wanted to distance himself from defeat. Cutting corners to achieve it; in theory, if not always in practice, the assistant chief decreed what files she studied. Unless she made a stand, final disposition of the Dorothy "Mitzi" Field case would rest with her rather than the superintendent.

"I haven't finished." But he stayed silent for a moment before seeming to digress. "Know the old wives' tale about a murderer having to return to the scene of the crime? Laughable! Only I've got a screwy notion that superstitions have a basis in fact. Anyway, a man has been hanging about in Grand Drive recently. Sitting in his car like he's waiting for somebody . . . right where the kid's body lay. He's a local, which blows my passing stranger stuff out of the water—still, I'm not proud, I am happy to take any loose end offered."

But that's the point, Jill parried mentally, keeping a poker face, you're not taking it. And a helpful colleague giving loose ends a little tug just might end up under the pile of rocks they release.

"This fellow," Superintendent Haggard continued doggedly, "has been haunting Grand Drive. Uniformed branch looked into it after several complaints from residents. They're a bit exclusive up there, not to mention paranoid about burglars, scared the bloke was casing their houses. What jumped out at me was one old girl being pretty certain the same chap, leastways somebody in an identical car, did the same thing at Christmastime last year. She was adamant that he was there for an hour or more every day for a week."

He treated her to a phony's smile. "Got to be interesting. Because whatever this man is, he's no burglar. A pest and a pain in the arse, but no record and a steady job, good references. Uniforms didn't have to trace him, they just waited, and sure enough, he rolled up and parked at the end of Grand Drive. Nowhere near his house, incidentally, and well off the route to it. He gave them a cock-and-bull yarn about birdwatching. They pressed him, and he mouthed off about police harassment, started teaching them the law."

The smile turned into a sneer. "The man is Noel Sarum, you'll have heard of him. Yes, *the* Noel Sarum. Spokesman for the Wessex chapter of Fight for Your Rights, does that disgraceful column in the local paper, born trouble-maker. Very useful cover if he happens to have a down on hookers and let it get the better of him three years ago."

Inspector Tierce set her flute of champagne aside. "You forgot your oven gloves. Ought to have them on, handing me a hot potato."

Lance Haggard spoke a laugh. "You can deal with it. Routine review of the Field case, search for possible witnesses overlooked in the original trawl. Sarum can't object to an approach on those terms—he's always banging on about being ready to do his civic duty without knuckling under to mindless bullying."

"You tell him that, then. It was your case."

"Ah." Superintendent Haggard took a long pull at his draught Guiness. "It wasn't, you see. I've kept myself *au fait*, but . . . no, it's not down to me."

Shifting restively, he went off on another tangent. "My daughter . . . Beth was nearly eighteen back then, but her mental age is nearer six or seven. Lovely girl, couldn't ask for a nicer, but never mind the current jargon, sim-pleminded. You knew about that," he accused edgily.

Jill hadn't, but she nodded and waited.

"Beth used to go to special school, homecraft and so forth. . . . She may have to look after herself when me and the wife have snuffed it. I couldn't give Beth a lift every day. No problem, bus stop outside our house. Nell sees the girl aboard, three stops later, out she gets. But one night a water main burst, and the bus went a different way. Beth was set down two streets from us. It confused her.

"Nell phoned me, frantic, when the girl was an hour overdue. I pulled rank, had the area cars searching. What we hadn't imagined was Beth getting on *another* bus, she thought they all went to our house. This one's terminus was the docks, and the driver made her get out. She was crying but he didn't want to know.

"Of course I shot home, and damned if a taxi didn't pull up behind me, with Nell and a young woman who'd found her: Mitzi Field. I recognized her from court, she was a regular. Cut a long story short, Beth was wandering the docks, running away if any male asked why she was crying; we'd drilled that into her, never talk to strange men. Mitzi twigged she needed help, looked us up in the phonebook, and flagged down a cab."

Haggard fiddled with his empty glass. "Nell made her come in for some grub and a cup of tea. God forgive me, grateful or no, I was pleased to see the back of her, the girl was dirty under the paint and dead cheap. Nell, my wife, isn't practical except round the house. Church on Sunday, says her prayers every night. She wanted to help Mitzi, give her a fresh start, once our girl was in bed and I'd explained what Mitzi was. I told Nell to forget it, the best help to her sort is leaving them alone. She'd still sleep rough and be on the game with a thousand quid in her purse.

"Easy to say when you don't want hassle—and how would it have looked, me taking a common prostitute, a dockside brass, under my wing? A month later she got herself killed."

He put a hand atop Jill Tierce's. "Comes back to me every Christmas, how we owed that girl and . . . we didn't let her down but . . . you follow? It was Len Poole's inquiry, I can't involve myself. You can. Christmas, and I'm asking for a present. Something isn't kosher about Noel Mr. Crusader Bloody Sarum; give him a spin, and help ease my blasted conscience."

Taking his hand back, he blustered, "Any of that personal stuff leaks out, I'll skin you alive." But it was appeal rather than threat. Oh yes, Jill reflected, coppers were human all right—even devoutly ambitious ones.

Noel Sarum lived in one of the Monopoly-board houses of a new estate, Larkspur Crest. For no good reason Inspector Tierce had expected a student-type flat festooned in Death to Tories banners, fragrant with pot fumes and dirty socks.

Like most police officers, she was aware of Sarum. His know-your-rights column in the weekly paper kept sniping at law enforcers. Jill had acknowl-edged that the diatribes were justified in general terms, yet still she felt resent-ful, attacked while denied another right—of defense. Somehow she'd formed a picture of an acrid character with a straggly beard and John Lennon glasses, spitting venom via his word processor. He was a teacher, too, probably indoc-trinating whole generations of copper-baiters. Not that they needed encour-agement.

She was taken aback by the man opening the glossy front door of pin-neat Number 30. Fifty, she judged, but relatively unlined, face open under a shock of silver-gray hair. Track suit and trainers reinforced the youthful, vigor-ous impression. Before she could speak, he beamed and exclaimed, "Why, it's the lame duck!"

Sensitive over her treacherous leg, she bristled, then recognized the face and decoded his remark. It was the Samaritan from that half-marathon in the happy time before she'd been hurt. Talked into running for charity, she'd not

815

realized that the friendly fellow partnering her for the final miles was Sarum, scourge of the police.

Jill had been quite taken with him. He'd struck her as a man appreciating female company for its own sake. If he'd been ten years younger or she a decade older, she might have tried making something of it. As things were, when the event finished he'd wrapped her in a foil blanket and trotted away to help somebody else.

"You're a police, um, person," he said, returning Inspector Tierce's warrant card. "I wondered what you did for a living, never thought of *that*. Come on in."

The living room contrived to be homely and pristine, sealed woodblock floor reflecting carefully tended plants. "Passes inspection, huh? I lost my wife five years ago, but I try to maintain her standards. Must have known you were coming, that's the coffee perking, not my tummy rumbling. Take a pew, I'll get it—black, white, sugar, no sugar?"

He was just as he'd been on the charity run, chatting as if resuming a relationship after minutes instead of years. Some people did it naturally, and in her experience, the majority were as uncomplicated as their manner. He made reasonable coffee, as well . . . "What's the problem? Can't be anything too shattering, but you're a senior rank."

Disingenuous, Jill thought; he must have a shrewd idea what brought her.

"You've been seen in Grand Drive for extended periods over the last two years. Watching, hanging about. Spare me the stuff about a free country; you put the wind up the neighborhood, and no wonder. It's no-hawkers-no-lurkers territory. Storm in a teacup is your comeback, but the snag is a woman was done to death at your favorite haunt three years ago."

"Two and two makes me a murder suspect, is that it?" His tone was even. Sensing that Noel Sarum savored debate, she gained a better understanding of his newspaper column.

"No, you invited suspicion all on your own," she replied calmly. "Gave my uniformed colleagues some guff about wanting to confirm the presence of a rare bird in Grand Drive, a . . . can't read PC Harris's writing, but he told me the name and I remembered it long enough to make a phone call.

"It's your bad luck that a cousin of mine is an ornithologist—the bird you chose hasn't touched England since 1911, and even that sighting was doubted. However, it's something an intelligent amateur might pick to blind the cops with science. According to my expert." And she smiled cheekily.

Noel Sarum's mouth curved up at the corners, too. "Got me." Then his jaw set. "As a matter of fact, that was my *third* Christmas of going to Grand Drive. Breaking no law, causing no nuisance. Which is all you need from me."

"Believe it or not I'd agree if it weren't for Mitzi Field. The dead girl. Worthless girl, some might say, squalid little life, good riddance. But we don't agree, do we. I've got to account for loose ends, and you're flapping about in the wind, Mr. Sarum."

"Noel," he corrected abstractedly. "The kids call me First Noel, this time of year. Every class thinks it's being brilliantly original. . . ." Stubborn streak resurfacing, he grumbled. "After your pals pounced on me, I went to the *Gazaette* office and researched the murder in the back numbers. That winter I was supply-teaching at Peterborough, didn't get back to the city until the week after it happened. The night she was killed, I was chaperoning a Sixth Form dance more than a hundred miles away from Grand Drive."

"Bloody hell," Jill muttered. "What's the matter with you, why not tell the uniforms that?"

Taken aback by her impatience and the subtext of disgust, he shrugged helplessly. "I didn't think of it at the time."

Fair enough, Inspector Tierce granted. People didn't remember their whereabouts a week ago, let alone years later. Though Noel Sarum might be lying. . . .

Guessing the reaction, he brightened. "Hang on, I'm not escaping, just looking in the glory-hole."

She watched him delve in a cupboard under the stairs. Soon he returned, waving a pamphlet. "Here you are, Beacon School newsletter, date at the top of every page."

It was a slim, computer printed magazine. Sarum's finger jabbed at a poorly reproduced photograph in which he was recognizable, arm round the shoulders of a jolly, overweight woman in owl spectacles. " 'First Noel' got the Christmas spirit, Mrs. May got the grope, and the Sixth 'got down' with a vengeance last Thursday night," ran the disrespectful caption.

"Mrs. May's the head teacher, the kids loved that snap," he chuckled. Tuning him out, Jill found the first page of her notebook. Yes, the date was right, Mitzi Field had died at about nine P.M. that faraway Thursday night when Noel Sarum was hugging the head teacher. His tone hardened. "Sorry to disappoint you."

"Oh, drop it," she said crossly. "I liked you on that stupid run, I still like you, though what I'd really like is to shake you till your stupid teeth rattle."

Taken aback, he fiddled with the school magazine.

"You've got a bee in your bonnet about the police, fine. But that's no excuse for wasting two uniformed officers' time, and mine. Heaven knows what it is with you and Grand Drive, I don't care."

She broke off, eyes narrowing. "Hey! I think this was a setup. You have an ironclad alibi, so why not encourage the dim coppers to hassle you? Weeks and weeks of columns to be wrung out of that. Cancel the liking-you bit, you're sick. Feel free to complain about my attitude. I'll be happy to defend it, on the record."

Appalled, Noel Sarum protested. "It's not like that . . . *setup?* It never crossed my mind!" Cracking his knuckles, he glowered at the carpet. "It's strictly personal, can't you people get that through your heads?" After which, perversely (not only coppers are human), he told her the whole story.

Fifteen minutes later, Inspector Tierce said, "Why the heck didn't you press every bell and find her that way? Can't be that many flats in half a dozen houses."

"What would I say when each door opens?" Sarum demanded. "I don't even know if she's married, she was wearing gloves, I couldn't see if she had a wedding ring. Supposing her husband answered, imagine the trouble I could cause."

"I still can't make out how you chatted her up and didn't have the gumption to get her name, even a first name."

Still high-colored from enthusiasm and embarrassment, Sarum sputtered, "I didn't chat her up. It was . . . idyllic, a little miracle. We looked at each other and started talking as if we'd known each other forever. Somehow I couldn't bring myself to ask her name or give mine, it might have broken the spell."

"Yes, you told me," Jill butted in, lips tingling from the strain of keeping a straight line. The copper-bashing demon she had pictured snarling over his columns turned out to be a hopeless, helpless romantic. Noel Sarum, a widower well into middle age, patrolled Grand Drive once a year because he was suffering belated pangs of puppy love.

Having met his ideal woman one Christmas Eve, driven her home, and departed on air, he'd been unable to decide which house in Grand Drive was hers. Similar period and the same architect, and they looked different by daylight.

She could understand why he hadn't confided in a couple of constables patently ready to take him for some kind of weirdo. After all, he was the Know Your Rights fanatic, worried that they'd turn his romantic vigil into a mocking anecdote to belittle him. Inevitably he'd been combative.

It was already dark when Jill Tierce left Larkspur Crest. Fresh snow crunched under the tires. She slowed as her lights picked up a group of children crossing the road, dragging a muffled-up baby on the improvised sledge of a tin tray. At the foot of the hill a Rotary Club float blared canned carols, a squad of executive Santas providing harness-bells sound effects with their collecting tins.

Everything went a little scatty in this season, though nicely so, Inspector

Tierce mused. She'd bought no presents so far, that was scatty, dooming her to Christmas Eve panic.

Not the least of her scattiness, either. She thought: I can't believe I'm doing this, but stayed on course towards Grand Drive.

By six that evening, bad leg nagging savagely—it disapproved of stairs, and she had climbed a number of flights—Jill was showing her warrant card and saying with the glibness of practice, "This may sound odd, but bear with me. . . . Two Christmases ago, if you remember that far back, did you go Christmas Eve shopping at the Hi-Save in City Center?"

"I expect so." The woman's voice was unexpectedly deep and hoarse from such a slim body. "I use Hi-Save for all but deli stuff, it's loads cheaper."

"I mustn't lead you, put ideas in your head, but that Christmas Eve did you have help with your shopping, like your bags carried to the car?"

"I don't take the c— Oh, him, the knight errant!" She opened the door wider and stood aside. "Come in, you look chilled."

Constance—"Connie, please, the other's so prissy"—French remembered Noel Sarum, all right.

"He picked me up in the checkout line that Christmas Eve. Well, I picked him up, had he but known." Brown, almond eyes sparkled wickedly. "It was such a scrum, the line was endless, all the trolleys were taken so I was lugging three or four of those wretched baskets, and he did the polite, offered to share the load while we waited.

"Single men who aren't teenagers are so pathetic, aren't they? And he was kind and clean and cuddly, I really *took* to him." She'd insisted on making them mugs of hot chocolate ("with the teeniest spike of brandy to cheer it up") after Jill Tierce refused a cocktail.

And I could take to a pad like this, Inspector Tierce reflected a shade drowsily. Connie French had two floors of one of Grand Drive's former mansions. Her living room was spacious yet cosy, elegant antique pieces to dress it, costly modern furniture for wallowing.

Ms. French sat a little straighter. "What's this about, dear?"

"I'm glad you asked that." Jill pulled a face. "Officially I'm eliminating a loose end, confirming somebody's reason for . . . never mind, confirming a story. Don't quote me, but I was curious. A witness was terribly impressed by you and . . ."

Connie waited, and Jill said, "It's just that you knocked him for six, he hasn't got over it—and call it the Christmas syndrome, or downright nosiness, but I wondered if you'd felt the same."

"I have thought about him since." Connie smiled weakly, blushing. "A lot, on and off. Look, there is always enough for two when it's a casserole, and a glass of wine can't put you over the limit for driving. Terrible thing to tell a woman, but you look exhausted. Stay for a meal."

They got on famously. A long while later, table cleared, dishwasher loaded, they'd put the world to rights and compared Most Terrible Male Traits (nasal fur, aggressive driving, and pointless untruths topping the painstakingly compiled list).

Inspector Tierce was deciding that she'd better go home by cab and pick her car up tomorrow—should have known she was unable to drink *one* glass of wine—when Connie French became fretful.

"What is it with that chap, Jill? I could tell he fancied me. Oh, not the flared nostrils and ripping the thin silk from my creamy shoulders, he wasn't that sort, but we really hit it off. Greek gods and toy boys are all very well, but what you need is a man who's comfy as old shoes. I've only met two or three, one was my brother and the others were friends' husbands. . . ."

"Tell me his name, I'll ring him." Connie reached for the phonebook on the end table at her side.

"I can't do that, I shouldn't be here anyway, certainly not gossiping. Christmas has a lot to answer for." It struck Jill that they were talking animatedly but with a certain precision over trickier words; perhaps the Beaujolais Villages in easy reach on the coffee table between them was not the first bottle.

"Wouldn't ring him anyway. My late husband, as in divorced, not RIP, said I had no pride but . . . is he gay? My supermarket chap, not the ex."

"Sarum? Certainly not." Frowning at the alliteration as much as the slip, Jill muttered, "I must make tracks."

"Night's young," Connie said on a pleading note. "He drove me home, I nearly asked him up for a drink—but something stopped me. I wanted him to at least introduce himself first, and after all that, he just took himself off."

"You'd stunned him," Jill said.

"Bull," Ms. French countered. But she was thoughtful. "Honest injun?"

"That's the impression I got. The twit's been keeping a vigil out there in the run-up to Christmas, ever since, hoping to pull the fancy-seeing-you-here bit."

Connie went to the bay window. "Typical of my luck, I never saw him."

"He stayed in his car, from up here he'd be an anonymous roof." Joining her, Inspector Tierce asked, "Were you questioned in the house-to-house sweep after Mitzi Field's body was found?"

"I was playing bridge that night, didn't get home till it was all over." Connie hugged herself. "Just as well. I couldn't bear it if I'd been up here watching some silly TV show while . . . ugh!"

"Looks pretty now." Snow crusted high walls and hedges, whiteness and moonlight giving Grand Drive a luminous quality.

"Christmas card," Connie French suggested, making the comment bleak. "I spend hours at this window sometimes, it's like a box seat for the seasonal stuff—carol singers from St. Stephen's in full Dickens costume, crinolines and caped coats and candle-lanterns. Then there are the children returning to the nest, back from boarding school, or a bit older, very proud of The Car and their university scarves.

"My daughter lives in California, she might ring on Christmas Day, probably will before New Year's. . . . Mummy's an afterthought."

To Jill's dismay, Connie French was crying silently, a single, fat tear sliding down the side of her elegant nose.

Inspector Tierce woke the next morning with the mildest of hangovers, little more than a nasty taste in the mouth, and a flinching sensation at the memory of her hostess.

The provoking thing was that she didn't pity Connie French. The sorrow had been alcohol-based and transitory; minutes afterwards they'd played an old Dory Previn album, whooping approval of the bitchy lyrics. Connie might have been briefly maudlin, but she was too sparky for extensive self-pity.

No, this was not about Connie, but something she had said or done kept niggling and scratching in the subconscious. Every time Jill recollected the profile etched against the window, decorated by a crystal tear—and the image was persistent, like that pop tune you cannot stop humming—an alarm went off.

"Think of something else," Inspector Tierce advised out loud, competing against the hair dryer's breathy roar. Nearly too late to post greetings cards, not that she'd bought them yet. She *had* bought some in good time one year. They were in A Safe Place to this day, waiting to be found.

Oh dear, she was better off thinking about the Mitzi Field case. Very well, Noel Sarum was in the clear. He could have printed that school magazine himself, or altered the date, but only in a Golden Age detective story. He'd been far away, and Connie French had confirmed his reason for haunting Grand Drive at a particular time of year. Further, while everyone was a potential lifetaker, Noel Sarum belonged at the safest, last-resort end of the spectrum.

And that revived Superintendent Haggard's imperfect crime. She could picture a man on perhaps his first and last sojourn in the city, stopping at a street woman's signal and unrecognized, very likely unseen, driving away with her. To drive on, soon afterwards, taking care to stay away.

"Hopeless," Jill mumbled and, skipping breakfast, went off to her broom closet, cardboard-flavored coffee, and the case file.

It assured her that everything needful had been done. A fruitless check for witnesses to the crime, an unrewarding search for tire tracks, footprints, any physical evidence apart from Mitzi Field's body. Local and then regional sexual offenders interrogated. Other prostitutes questioned, fellow tenants of her last known address, the demolished squat, traced and interviewed.

Nothing to go on; conscientious Detective-Inspector Poole, exactly the breed of plodder who catches most criminals, had demonstrated that if nothing else. Or had he?

Inspector Tierce stood up awkwardly, massaging scar tissue through her skirt. She hadn't thought the location significant, merely incongruous, when Superintendent Haggard told her of it. Previous reading of the file had left her cold. But now it was different because . . . because of Connie French. Something—*what?*—that she'd said last night.

She'd said so much, that was the snag. Squinting, lips moving silently, Jill talked herself through a lengthy and meandering conversation. Until reaching the point where Connie had lamented an uncaring daughter . . . bingo.

Children coming home for the holidays, of course. That's what families did at Christmas, families and friends of the family. Driven by nostalgia, tradition, the chance to purge year-long offenses during the annual truce, or (if mercenary souls) simply to collect presents, they headed for hearth and home.

She leafed through to a terse section of the dossier, the London end. A few discreet sentences covered Mitzi's life from just before her ninth birthday until she absconded from the council home six years later.

Lots of digging needed. Inspector Tierce felt sorry for Len Poole, and profoundly grateful that she did not have to follow up her idea.

Inspector Poole, a careworn, resigned character, took one look at the name on the file and groaned, "Haggard's got you at it as well, has he? Wish he'd mind his own business."

"Amen to that, but I'm stuck with it. Len, what was that girl doing on Grand Drive? Haggard thinks she took a client to a road full of snobs and busybodies because she didn't know any better. Or the punter was ignorant and Mitzi Field didn't care. Did you buy that?"

"No opinion—I'd need facts to form one, and the only certainty was that she was killed there." He wasn't being awkward, that was how his mind worked. "Long way to go for a quickie in a motor, right enough. Then again, Vice was chasing street prozzies at the time, she might have wanted to get well away from the redlight area."

"Supposing," said Jill, "she wasn't taken to Grand Drive and killed? Supposing she was *leaving* there, heading back to her beat, when it happened?"

"I'm not quite with you."

"She didn't walk all the way, wasn't dressed for it, therefore she went in a car, that's the conventional wisdom. Doesn't follow. A bus runs from dockland to a stop round the corner from Grand Drive every half hour. She could have taken herself there, right? Visited somebody, left again, and either her attacker was waiting, or he was the one she'd called on, and he chased her out of doors."

"Try reading the file," Inspector Poole urged. "No known sex offenders among the residents, remember. We grilled all Les Girls, whether or not they'd associated with Ms. Field, and none of them had a client in Grand Drive; far as they were aware, that is. Down-market hookers don't keep names and addresses. Her mates were sure Mitzi had never been up there before."

"Yes, but it was Christmas, Len. When we all get sudden urges to see Mum and Dad, look up Auntie Flo, send a card to that nice former neighbor who nursed us through whooping cough. Mitzi Field had a family of sorts, once upon a time."

Digesting the implications, Inspector Poole said, "Crumbs." He did not go in for bad language. "You do get 'em, the wild hunches. All right, she was Mitzi Field, but her mother remarried, to a man called, don't tell me . . . Edwardes. The stepfather who supposedly seduced the little girl. The mother died in 1984, Edwardes was never charged, lack of evidence, they just took the child away. He'd dropped off the radar screen by 1990, dead or gone abroad, certainly hasn't paid tax or claimed unemployment benefits for a long time. All in the file, dear. I may be slow but I ain't stupid."

"Perish the thought. But that still leaves Auntie Flo and the kindly neighbor."

"Crumbs," he repeated, even more feelingly, "you don't want much. We're talking ten, fifteen years back, and in London." Inspector Poole took possession of the file. "It's a thought, I can't deny it. More's the pity."

On Christmas Eve afternoon, Len Poole rapped jauntily at Jill's office door. "London doesn't get any better. I've had two days up there, and how those lads in the Met stand the life is beyond me. Noise, pollution, bad manners, homeless beggars everywhere. But I did find a helpful social worker, they do exist even if it's an endangered species, and this chap had a good memory.

"Great idea of yours—but I'm afraid James Edwardes, Mitzi's allegedly wicked stepfather, doesn't live at Grand Drive. He works the fairs in the Republic of Ireland, hasn't been in England for years."

Hitching half his skinny rump onto the corner of the desk, Inspector Poole added innocently, "No trace of Auntie Flo. But I'll tell you who did have a Grand Drive address until recently—Anthony Challis."

Since he had to have worked hard and fast and was full of himself over it, Jill Tierce played along. "Challis?"

"He lodged with Mitzi's family in the eighties. Freelance electrician, good earner, about to get married. But then Mitzi Field, only she was little Dorothy then, accused nice Mr. Challis of doing things to her. Her mother called the police, and then Dorothy admitted it wasn't Challis after all, it was her stepfather who kept raping her." Len Poole grimaced distastefully. "Ugly . . . my tame social worker said he'd never believed Challis had touched her. What it was, they discovered, Edwardes not only abused her, he practically brainwashed the poor kid, said she'd be struck down if she told on him. When it got too much for her, she accused Tony Challis—ironically enough, because he was kind, would never hurt her. She'd just wanted it out in the open, so the grownups would make it stop. Ruining Challis wasn't on her agenda, if she had such a thing, but that was the effect.

"After Dorothy-Mitzi was taken into council care, her mother threw Edwardes out, and Tony Challis went to other digs. No charges were brought in the end—the child was considered unreliable on account of changing her story. Rumors spread, mud stuck, Challis's fiancée told him to get lost, his regular customers followed suit . . ."

"Ugly," Jill agreed.

"Gets worse. Challis is a Wessex man, he talked a lot about this part of the world when he was lodging with Mitzi's folks. Maybe that's why she stuck around, having drifted here. Anyway, Challis took to drink, hit the gutter before he straightened up. Returned to his native heath, as posh books put it, found work as a janitor for Coastal Properties. They own several apartment houses on Grand Drive and gave him a basement flat in the end one on the left. Too dark and cramped for letting, and it gave them a good excuse to pay him peanuts.

"Mitzi Field wasn't looking for Challis—if she'd had a grain of sense she would have kept well clear—but she found him. Once a month he picked up supplies from a discount hardware store on her beat in dockland. He didn't notice her, which is natural; the last time he'd seen Dorothy, she was a child. But she must have seen him going in and out of the hardware place and pumped somebody there, discovered where he worked."

Len Poole sighed and shook his head. "Just as you said, it was Christmas. Tony Challis is watching TV in his basement one night, and suddenly this shabby little tart is at the side door, saying, I'm Dorothy, Mr. Challis, don't you remember me? Wanted to say sorry, hoped he was doing all right now, she hadn't wanted to make trouble for him. And so on.

"Challis says, and I believe him, he was in a daze while she talked to him. 'Noises, she was making noises,' he told me. She was dead when the actual words came back to him. Mitzi left, and for a minute—the chap's a drinker, mark you—he wondered whether he'd been hallucinating. Then he wished he had been. Challis hadn't hated *Dorothy*; he understood she was a victim who dragged him down with her, no malice involved. But she'd become Mitzi . . . ruining him and still ending up like that, that was past bearing.

"Next moment, it seemed to him, he was standing over her in the street, holding one of those little stone lions: half the big houses along the drive had them on either side of the porch. He had the lion by its head, the square base was allover blood.

"He accepted that he must have killed her, but he didn't feel like a murderer. All he felt was scared witless. He slipped back to his basement, washed the lion, and put it back in place. Then he prayed. Been praying ever since.

"From Met Police records and that social worker, I got the names of five people linked to Field when she was a child. Only one was among the residents of Grand Drive at the time she was killed. No problem finding him, he didn't move far, one of those new council flats near the marina. Soon as I said who I was, Challis goes, 'Thank God, now I can tell somebody.' "

Jill Tierce addressed her folded hands, almost inaudibly. "She wanted to make amends for what happened all those years ago, and he killed her for trying?"

Inspector Poole slid off the desk, his expression mixing wonder and compassion over her naivete. "If you can make sense of the why and wherefore, be sure to tell Challis. He can't sort it out. It's people, Jill . . . she was one of them that gets sentimental at Christmas, never considered she'd be opening a wound. As for him, he wasn't the kind man who'd lodged with her mum. Not anymore. She stirred up an embittered semialcoholic, temper overdue to snap."

Len Poole hesitated, cleared his throat. "Nobody's fault, luv, not even his. Though he'll go away for it."

"We got a result, which is all that matters."

"Not what I meant—though there is always that, at the end of the day."

Inspector Tierce's day, apparently over, had a postscript.

She'd wanted to watch the black and white movie of Scrooge for the fifth Christmas Eve in a row but went to bed instead. Her father would be calling "fairly early" to collect her for Christmas lunch, meaning crack of dawn.

The phone woke her. The caller sounded drunk, though on nothing more than girlish high spirits, it emerged.

"We've just got back from midnight Mass, now we can be the first to wish you Merry Christmas."

"Wha'? Who is it?" Jill pulled the alarm clock radio round on the bedside table, sending paperbacks, a bottle of cough mixture, and her pain tablets cascading to the floor. "It's twenty to two!" The voice's identity registered belatedly. "Connie, I'll kill you."

"Don't be like that. I rang him after all, you see. And I'm so *happy*."

"Bully for you. What in the world are you on about?"

"Noel, of course. You let his name slip the other night—"

"Did I, by gum." Fully awake and up on one elbow, Inspector Tierce rolled gummy eyes. "That was very unprofessional."

"Sarum's an unusual surname, only one in the local phonebook, and we talked for hours—" Following squeaks and a rattle, Noel Sarum came on the phone.

"And here I am! Well, I'll be leaving in a minute," he added sheepishly.

Another interlude of cryptic noises and then Connie French trilled, "He's so stuffy, of course he's not leaving at this time of the morning."

She said something aside, answering Noel in the background. "He wants you to know we're engaged and says I'm indiscreet, the idiot. I say, you must come to our wedding, it'll be February or March. You have to, you're the matchmaker."

"Let's talk about it next year. I'm pleased you are pleased, Connie. Tell Noel to go easy on the law in future; he owes me. 'Bye."

Lying back in the darkness, a phrase from the Bible popped into her head, a Sunday school fragment clear as if spoken for her benefit: "Out of the strong came forth sweetness." Something about bees using the remains of a savage lion as their hive. Why think of that? Mitzi Field was battered with a stone lion. Nothing sweet there, that was not the connection.

Connie was gorgeously happy, and Noel worshipped her. It couldn't last, euphoria didn't, yet it was a promising prelude to something better. They might fight eventually, but they would not be lonely.

That was what had triggered the parable of bees and a beast of prey. Out of evil, good can come. "Merry Christmas," Jill Tierce whispered to the pillow.

Martin Werner

CHRISTMAS PARTY

People in the advertising business said the Christmas party at French & Saunders was the social event of the year. For it wasn't your ordinary holiday office party. Not the kind where the staff gets together for a few mild drinks out of paper cups, some sandwiches sent in from the local deli, and a long boring speech by the company president. At F&S it was all very different: just what you'd expect from New York's hottest advertising agency.

The salaries there were the highest in town, the accounts were strictly blue chip, and the awards the agency won over the years filled an entire boardroom. And the people, of course, were the best, brightest, and most creative that money could buy.

With that reputation to uphold, the French & Saunders Christmas party naturally had to be the biggest and splashiest in the entire industry.

Year after year, that's the way it was. Back in the late Seventies, when discos were all the rage, the company took over Numero Uno, the club people actually fought over to get in. Another year, F&S hired half the New York Philharmonic to provide entertainment. And in 1989, the guest bartenders were Mel Gibson, Madonna, and the cast of *L.A. Law*.

There was one serious side to the party. That's when the president reviewed the year's business, announced how much the annual bonus would be, and then named the Board's choices for People of the Year, the five lucky employees who made the most significant contributions to the agency's success during the past twelve months.

The unwritten part to this latter (although everyone knew it, anyway) was that each one of the five would receive a very special individual bonus— some said as high as $50,000 apiece.

Then French & Saunders bought fifteen floors in the tallest, shiniest new office tower on Broadway, the one that had actually been praised by the *N.Y.*

Times architecture critic.

The original plan was to hold the party in the brand-new offices that were to be ready just before Christmas. A foolish idea, as it turned out, because nothing in New York is ever finished when it's promised. The delay meant the agency had to scramble and find a new party site—either that, or make do in the half finished building itself.

Amazingly—cleverly?—enough, that was the game plan the party committee decided to follow. Give the biggest, glitziest party in agency history amid half finished offices in which paneless windows looked out to the open skies, where debris and building supplies stood piled up in every corner, and where doors opened on nothing but a web of steel girders and the sidewalk seventy floors below.

Charlie Evanston, one of the company's senior vice-presidents (he had just reached the ripe old of age of fifty), was chosen to be party chairman. He couldn't have been happier. For Charlie had a deepdown feeling that this was finally going to be his year. After being passed over time and again for one of those five special Christmas bonuses, he just knew he was going to go home a winner.

Poor Charlie.

In mid-November—the plans for the party proceeding on schedule— the agency suddenly lost their multi-million-dollar Daisy Fresh Soap account, no reason given. Charlie had been the supervisor on the account for years, and although he couldn't be held personally responsible for the loss a few people (enemies!) shook their heads and wondered if maybe someone else, someone a little stronger—and younger—couldn't have held on to the business.

Two weeks later, another showpiece account—the prestigious Maximus Computer Systems—left the agency. Unheard of.

The trade papers gave away the reason in the one dreaded word "kick-backs." Two French & Saunders television producers who had worked on the account had been skimming it for years.

Again, Charlie's name came up. Not that he had anything remotely to do with the scandal. The trouble was that he personally had hired both offenders. And people remembered.

There's a superstition that events like these happen in threes, so it was only a question of time before the next blow. And, sure enough, two weeks before Christmas, it happened. A murder, no less. A F&S writer shot his wife, her lover, and himself.

With that, French & Saunders moved from front-page sidelines in the trade papers straight to screaming headlines in every tabloid in town. In less than a month, it had been seriously downgraded from one of New York's proudest enterprises to that most dreaded of advertising fates—an agency "in trouble."

It was now a week before Christmas and every F&S employee was carrying around his or her own personal lump of cold, clammy fear. The telltale signs were everywhere. People making secret telephone calls to headhunters and getting their resumes in order. Bitter jokes about the cold winter and selling apples on street corners told in the elevators and washrooms. Rumors that a buyout was in the making and *nobody* was safe.

And yet, strange as it sounds, there were those who still thought there would be a happy ending. At the Christmas party, perhaps. A last-minute announcement that everything was as before—the agency was in good shape and, just like always, everyone would get that Christmas bonus.

Charlie was one of the most optimistic. He didn't know why. Just a gut feeling that the world was still full of Christmas miracles and, bad times or not, he was going to be one of F&S's five magical People of the Year.

Poor Charlie.

A few days before the party, his phone rang. It was the voice of J. Stewart French, president and chairman of the board.

"Hi, Charlie. Got a minute?"

"Sure."

"I wonder if you'd mind coming up to my office. I've got a couple of things I'd like to talk to you about."

Nothing menacing about that, thought Charlie. J probably wants to discuss the party. The food. The caterers. The security measures that would be needed so that no one would be in any danger in those half finished offices.

Very neatly, very efficiently, Charlie got out his files and headed upstairs. When he arrived in the president's office—it was the only one that had been completely finished (vulgar but expensive, thought Charlie)—J was on the phone, his face pale and drawn, nothing like the way he usually looked, with that twelve-months-a-year suntan he was so proud of. He nodded over the phone. "Sit down, Charlie, sit down."

Charlie sank into one of the comfortable $12,000 chairs beside the desk and waited. After a minute the conversation ended and J turned to give him his full attention. Charlie had known J for fifteen years and had never seen him so nervous and ill at ease.

Then he spoke.

"Charlie, they tell me you've really got the Christmas party all together. Looks like it'll be a smash."

"We're hoping so, J."

"Well, we can certainly use some good times around here. I don't have to tell *you* that. It's been a bad, *bad* year."

"Things'll be better. I know it."

"Do you really think so, Charlie? Do you? I'd like to believe that, too. That's why this party means so much to me. To all of us. Morale—"

"I know."

"Well, you've certainly done your part. More than your part. That's why I called you in."

Here it comes, thought Charlie, here comes my special Christmas bonus! Ahead of time, before anyone else hears about it!

"I wanted you to be one of the first to know. The Board and I have agreed that, even with all our troubles, there'll be something extra in every-body's paycheck again this year. Nothing like before, of course, but it will be something."

"That's wonderful."

"Yeah. Wonderful. We monkeyed around with the budget and found we could come up with a few bucks. The *problem* is, we'll have to make some cuts here and there."

"Cuts?"

"Well, for one thing, I'm afraid there won't be any of those special bonus-es this year, Charlie. And I'll level with you—you were down for one. After all these years, you had really earned it. I can't tell you how sorry—"

Sure, thought Charlie. "It's not the end of the world, J," he said. "Maybe next year."

"No, Charlie, that's not all. With our losses and the cost of moving—I don't know how to tell you this, but we're doing something else. We're cutting back—some of our best people. I've never had to do anything like that in my life."

You bastard, Charlie thought. "Go on, J," he said. "I think I know what you're going to say."

J looked at him miserably. "You're one of the people we'll have to lose, Charlie. Wait a minute, please hear me out—it's nothing personal. I wanted to save you. After all, we've been together fifteen years. I talked and talked, I even threatened to resign myself. But no one wanted to listen."

Sure, Charlie thought.

"They said you hadn't produced anything worthwhile in years. And there was the business of those two crazies you hired. And—"

"Is that it?" Charlie asked.

"Don't get me wrong, Charlie. Please, let's do the Christmas party as we planned, just as if nothing happened. As for leaving, take your time. I got you a year's severance. And you can use your office to make calls, look around, and—"

"No problem, J." Charlie was moving to the door. "I understand. And don't worry about the party. Everything's all taken care of."

Not even a handshake.

Many people at some time or other have fantasized about killing the boss. In Charlie's case, it was different. From the minute he heard the bad news from J, he became a changed man. Not outwardly, of course. He wasn't about to become an overnight monster, buy a gun, make a bomb, sharpen an axe. No, he would be the same Charlie Evanston. Friendly. Smiling. Efficient. But now that he knew the worst, he began piling up all the long-suppressed injustices he had collected from J for fifteen years. The conversations that stopped abruptly when he entered an executive meeting. The intimate dinners at J's that he and his wife were never invited to. The countless other little slights. And, finally, this.

December 20. Party time! Everyone agreed it was the best bash French & Saunders had ever thrown.

The day was fair and warm. The milling crowds that drifted from the well stocked bars and refreshment tables didn't even notice there wasn't a heating system. The lack of carpets, the wide-open window spaces, the empty offices—it all added to the fun.

Carefully groomed waiters in white gloves and hard hats pressed their way from room to room, carrying silver trays laden with drinks and hors d'oeuvres. A heavy metal band blared somewhere. A troupe of strolling violinists pressed in and out. From the happy faces, laughter, and noise, you'd never know the agency had a care in the world.

But Charlie Evanston knew. He pushed his way over to a small crowd pressing around J. All of them were drunk, or on the way, and J, drink in hand, was swaying slightly. His laugh was louder than anybody's whenever one of the clients told a funny story. He spotted Charlie and shouted to him. "Charlie, c'mere a minute! Folks, you all know my old pal Charlie Evanston. We've been together since this place opened its doors. He's the guy who put this whole great party together."

There were murmurs of approval as J drew Charlie into his embrace.

"J," Charlie said, "I just came to ask you to come over here and let me show you something."

"Oh, Charlie, always business. Can't it wait till next week? After the holidays?"

"No, I think it's important. Please come over here. Let me show you."

"Oh, for Chrissakes, Charlie. What *is* it?"

"Just follow me. Won't take long."

J pulled away from the group with a back-in-a-minute wave of his hand and followed Charlie down a narrow hall to a room that would one day become the heart of the agency's computer operation.

It was empty. Even the floors hadn't been finished. Just some wooden planks, a few steel beams—and the sidewalk below. J glanced around the room and turned to Charlie. "So? What's the problem?"

"Don't you get it, J? There isn't a single Keep Out sign on that outside door. The workmen even forgot to lock it. Someone could walk in here and fall straight down to Broadway!"

"Oh, come on, Charlie, this place is off the beaten path—no one's going to be coming this way. Stop worrying."

"Yes, but—"

"No buts, Charlie. Just tell one of the security guards. My God, you drag me all the way out here just to see this. Jesus Christ, I'll bet I could even *walk* across one of these steel beams. The workmen do it every day."

It was uncanny. Charlie knew that was exactly what J would say. It was part of the macho, daredevil reputation he had cultivated so carefully. "Hey, wait a minute, J," he said.

"No. Serious. Watch me walk across this beam right here. It can't be more than twenty feet long. And I'll do it with a drink in each hand."

"Come on, J, don't be crazy."

But J had already taken his first tentative step on the beam—with Charlie directly behind him.

It was all so simple. Now all Charlie had to do was give J the tiniest of shoves in the back, watch him stagger and plunge over the side, and it would be all over.

As J continued to move along the beam, he seemed to grow more confident. Charlie continued to follow a few steps behind, his right arm outstretched. It was now or never. Suddenly he made his move. But J moved a couple of quick steps faster and Charlie missed J's back by an inch. Instead, he felt himself slipping over the side. He gasped. Then all he remembered was falling.

The hospital room was so quiet you could barely hear a murmur from the corridor outside.

On the single bed there lay what looked like a dead body. Every inch was covered in a rubbery casing and yards and yards of white gauze. All you could see of what was underneath was a little round hole where the mouth was supposed to be and another opening where a blood-shot blue eye stared up at the ceiling. Charlie Evanston.

The door opened slightly, admitting J, followed by one of Charlie's doctors.

J shuddered. He always did, every time he'd visited over the past six months. He turned to the doctor. "How's he doing today?"

"About the same. He tries to talk a little now and then."

"Can he hear me yet? Can he understand?"

"We think so. But don't try and get anything out of him."

"Yes. I know." He bent over the bed. "Charlie. Charlie. It's me, J. I just wanted you to know I'm here. And I want to thank you again—I guess I'll be thanking you for the rest of my life—for reaching out and trying to save me at that damn Christmas party."

The blue eye blinked. A tear began to tremble on the edge.

"I was a fool. Only a fool would have tried to do what I did. And you tried to stop me. I felt you grab my jacket and try to hold me back. Then you took the fall for me."

The blue eye stared.

"So what I came to say—what I hope you can understand—is that no matter how long it takes you're going to get the best care we can find. Just get well. Everything's going to be okay."

The blue eye continued to look at J without blinking.

"And, Charlie, here's the best news of all. The agency's just picked up three big accounts. Over a hundred million."

A light breeze blew the curtains from the window.

"So today the Board asked me to come up here and give you a special bonus. Not a Christmas bonus—more like Purple Heart. You deserve it, Charlie. You saved the old man's life, you bastard!"

Charlie tried to nod, but it was impossible.

"And just wait till you come back," J said enthusiastically. "You're a hero, Charlie! We've got all kinds of great things waiting for you. All kinds of plans. It's going to be a whole new ballgame, Charlie! Imagine!"

Yeah, thought Charlie. Imagine.

Sir Arthur Conan Doyle

THE ADVENTURE OF THE BLUE CARBUNCLE

I had called upon my friend Sherlock Holmes upon the second morning after Christmas, with the intention of wishing him the compliments of the season. He was lounging upon the sofa in a purple dressing-gown, a pipe-rack within his reach upon the right, and a pile of crumpled morning papers, evidently newly studied, near at hand. Beside the couch was a wooden chair, and on the angle of the back hung a very seedy and disreputable hard-felt hat, much the worse for wear, and cracked in several places. A lens and a forceps lying upon the seat of the chair suggested that the hat had been suspended in this manner for the purpose of examination.

"You are engaged," said I; "perhaps I interrupt you."

"Not at all. I am glad to have a friend with whom I can discuss my results. The matter is a perfectly trivial one"—he jerked his thumb in the direction of the old hat—"but there are points in connection with it which are not entirely devoid of interest and even of instruction."

I seated myself in his armchair and warmed my hands before his crackling fire, for a sharp frost had set in, and the windows were thick with the ice crystals. "I suppose," I remarked, "that, homely as it looks, this thing has some deadly story linked on to it—that it is the clue which will guide you in the solution of some mystery and the punishment of some crime."

"No, no. No crime," said Sherlock Holmes, laughing. "Only one of those whimsical little incidents which will happen when you have four million human beings all jostling each other within the space of a few square miles. Amid the action and reaction of so dense a swarm of humanity, every possible combination of events may be expected to take place, and many a little problem will be presented which may be striking and bizarre without being criminal. We have already had experience of such."

"So much so," I remarked, "that of the last six cases which I have added to my notes, three have been entirely free of any legal crime."

"Precisely. You allude to my attempt to recover the Irene Adler papers,

834

to the singular case of Miss Mary Sutherland, and to the adventure of the man with the twisted lip. Well, I have no doubt that this small matter will fall into the same innocent category. You know Peterson, the commissionaire?"

"Yes."

"It is to him that this trophy belongs."

"It is his hat."

"No, no; he found it. Its owner is unknown. I beg that you will look upon it not as a battered billycock but as an intellectual problem. And, first, as to how it came here. It arrived upon Christmas morning, in company with a good fat goose, which is, I have no doubt, roasting at this moment in front of Peterson's fire. The facts are these: about four o'clock on Christmas morning, Peterson, who, as you know, is a very honest fellow, was returning from some small jollification and was making his way homeward down Tottenham Court Road. In front of him he saw, in the gaslight, a tallish man, walking with a slight stagger, and carrying a white goose slung over his shoulder. As he reached the corner of Goodge Street, a row broke out between this stranger and a little knot of roughs. One of the latter knocked off the man's hat, on which he raised his stick to defend himself, and swinging it over his head, smashed the shop window behind him. Peterson had rushed forward to protect the stranger from his assailants; but the man, shocked at having broken the window, and seeing an official-looking person in uniform rushing towards him, dropped his goose, took to his heels, and vanished amid the labyrinth of small streets which lie at the back of Tottenham Court Road. The roughs had also fled at the appearance of Peterson, so that he was left in possession of the field of battle, and also of the spoils of victory in the shape of this battered hat and a most unimpeachable Christmas goose."

"Which surely he restored to their owner?"

"My dear fellow, there lies the problem. It is true that 'For Mrs. Henry Baker' was printed upon a small card which was tied to the bird's left leg, and it is also true that the initials 'H.B.' are legible upon the lining of this hat; but as there are some thousands of Bakers, and some hundreds of Henry Bakers in this city of ours, it is not easy to restore lost property to any of them."

"What, then, did Peterson do?"

"He brought round both hat and goose to me on Christmas morning, knowing that even the smallest problems are of interest to me. The goose we retained until this morning, when there were signs that, in spite of the slight frost, it would be well that it should be eaten without unnecessary delay. Its finder has carried it off, therefore, to fulfil the ultimate destiny of a goose, while I continue to retain the hat of the unknown gentleman who lost his Christmas dinner."

"Did he not advertise?"

"No."

"Then, what clue could you have as to his identity?"

"Only as much as we can deduce."

"From his hat?"

"Precisely."

"But you are joking. What can you gather from this old battered felt?"

"Here is my lens. You know my methods. What can you gather yourself as to the individuality of the man who has worn this article?"

I took the tattered object in my hands and turned it over rather ruefully. It was a very ordinary black hat of the usual round shape, hard and much the worse for wear. The lining had been of red silk, but was a good deal discoloured. There was no maker's name; but, as Holmes had remarked, the initials "H.B." were scrawled upon one side. It was pierced in the brim for a hat-securer, but the elastic was missing. For the rest, it was cracked, exceedingly dusty, and spotted in several places, although there seemed to have been some attempt to hide the discoloured patches by smearing them with ink.

"I can see nothing," said I, handing it back to my friend.

"On the contrary, Watson, you can see everything. You fail, however, to reason from what you see. You are too timid in drawing your inferences."

"Then, pray tell me what it is that you can infer from this hat?"

He picked it up and gazed at it in the peculiar introspective fashion which was characteristic of him. "It is perhaps less suggestive than it might have been," he remarked, "and yet there are a few inferences which are very distinct, and a few others which represent at least a strong balance of probability. That the man was highly intellectual is of course obvious upon the face of it, and also that he was fairly well-to-do within the last three years, although he has now fallen upon evil days. He had foresight, but has less now than formerly, pointing to a moral retrogression, which, when taken with the decline of his fortunes, seems to indicate some evil influence, probably drink, at work upon him. This may account also for the obvious fact that his wife has ceased to love him."

"My dear Holmes!"

"He has, however, retained some degree of self-respect," he continued, disregarding my remonstrance. "He is a man who leads a sedentary life, goes out little, is out of training entirely, is middle-aged, has grizzled hair which he has had cut within the last few days, and which he anoints with lime-cream. These are the more patent facts which are to be deduced from his hat. Also, by the way, that it is extremely improbable that he has gas laid on in his house."

"You are certainly joking, Holmes."

"Not in the least. Is it possible that even now, when I give you these results, you are unable to see how they are attained?"

"I have no doubt that I am very stupid, but I must confess that I am unable to follow you. For example, how did you deduce that this man was intellectual?"

For answer Holmes clapped the hat upon his head. It came right over the forehead and settled upon the bridge of his nose. "It is a question of cubic capacity," said he; "a man with so large a brain must have something in it."

"The decline of his fortunes, then?"

"This hat is three years old. These flat brims curled at the edge came in then. It is a hat of the very best quality. Look at the band of ribbed silk and the excellent lining. If this man could afford to buy so expensive a hat three years ago, and has had no hat since, then he has assuredly gone down in the world."

"Well, that is clear enough, certainly. But how about the foresight and the moral retrogression?"

Sherlock Holmes laughed. "Here is the foresight," said he, putting his finger upon the little disc and loop of the hat-securer. "They are never sold upon hats. If this man ordered one, it is a sign of a certain amount of foresight, since he went out of his way to take this precaution against the wind. But since we see that he has broken the elastic and has not troubled to replace it, it is obvious that he has less foresight now than formerly, which is a distinct proof of a weakening nature. On the other hand, he has endeavored to conceal some of these stains upon the felt by daubing them with ink, which is a sign that he has not entirely lost his self-respect."

"Your reasoning is certainly plausible."

"The further points, that he is middle-aged, that his hair is grizzled, that it has been recently cut, and that he uses lime-cream, are all to be gathered from a close examination of the lower part of the lining. The lens discloses a large number of hair-ends, clean cut by the scissors of the barber. They all appear to be adhesive, and there is a distinct odour of lime-cream. This dust, you will observe, is not the gritty, gray dust of the street but the fluffy brown dust of the house, showing that it has been hung up indoors most of the time; while the marks of moisture upon the inside are proof positive that the wearer perspired very freely, and could therefore, hardly be in the best of training."

"But his wife—you said that she had ceased to love him."

"This hat has not been brushed for weeks. When I see you, my dear Watson, with a week's accumulation of dust upon your hat, and when your wife allows you to go out in such a state, I shall fear that you also have been unfortunate enough to lose your wife's affection."

"But he might be a bachelor."

"Nay, he was bringing home the goose as a peace-offering to his wife.

Remember the card upon the bird's leg."

"You have an answer to everything. But how on earth do you deduce that the gas is not laid on in his house?"

"One tallow stain, or even two, might come by chance; but when I see no less than five, I think that there can be little doubt that the individual must be brought into frequent contact with burning tallow—walks upstairs at night probably with his hat in one hand and a guttering candle in the other. Anyhow, he never got tallow-stains from a gas-jet. Are you satisfied?"

"Well, it is very ingenious," said I, laughing; "but since, as you said just now, there has been no crime committed, and no harm done save the loss of a goose, all this seems to be rather a waste of energy."

Sherlock Holmes had opened his mouth to reply, when the door flew open, and Peterson, the commissionaire, rushed into the apartment with flushed cheeks and the face of a man who is dazed with astonishment.

"The goose, Mr. Holmes! The goose, sir!" he gasped.

"Eh? What of it, then? Has it returned to life and flapped off through the kitchen window?" Holmes twisted himself round upon the sofa to get a fairer view of the man's excited face.

"See here, sir! See what my wife found in its crop!" He held out his hand and displayed upon the center of the palm a brilliantly scintillating blue stone, rather smaller than a bean in size, but of such purity and radiance that it twinkled like an electric point in the dark hollow of his hand.

Sherlock Holmes sat up with a whistle. "By Jove, Peterson!" said he, "this is treasure trove indeed. I suppose you know what you have got?"

"A diamond, sir? A precious stone. It cuts into glass as though it were putty."

"It's more than a precious stone. It is *the* precious stone."

"Not the Countess of Morcar's blue carbuncle!" I ejaculated.

"Precisely so. I ought to know its size and shape, seeing that I have read the advertisement about it in *The Times* every day lately. It is absolutely unique, and its value can only be conjectured, but the reward offered of one thousand pounds is certainly not within a twentieth part of the market price."

"A thousand pounds! Great Lord of mercy!" The commissionaire plumped down into a chair and stared from one to the other of us.

"That is the reward, and I have reason to know that there are sentimental considerations in the background which would induce the Countess to part with half her fortune if she could but recover the gem."

"It was lost, if I remember aright, at the Hotel Cosmopolitan," I remarked.

"Precisely so, on December 22nd, just five days ago. John Horner, a plumber, was accused of having abstracted it from the lady's jewel-case. The evidence against him was so strong that the case has been referred to the Assizes. I have some account of the matter here, I believe." He rummaged amid his newspapers, glancing over the dates, until at last he smoothed one out, doubled it over, and read the following paragraph:

"Hotel Cosmopolitan Jewel Robbery. John Horner, 26, plumber, was brought up upon the charge of having upon the 22d inst., abstracted from the jewel-case of the Countess of Morcar the valuable gem known as the blue carbuncle. James Ryder, upper-attendant at the hotel, gave his evidence to the effect that he had shown Horner up to the dressing-room of the Countess of Morcar upon the day of the robbery in order that he might solder the second bar of the grate, which was loose. He had remained with Horner some little time, but had finally been called away. On returning, he found that Horner had disappeared, that the bureau had been forced open, and that the small morocco casket in which, as it afterwards transpired, the Countess was accustomed to keep her jewel, was lying empty upon the dressing-table. Ryder instantly gave the alarm, and Horner was arrested the same evening; but the stone could not be found either upon his person or in his rooms. Catherine Cusack, maid to the Countess, deposed to having heard Ryder's cry of dismay on discovering the robbery, and to having rushed into the room, where she found matters as described by the last witness. Inspector Bradstreet, B division, gave evidence as to the arrest of Horner, who struggled frantically, and protested his innocence in the strongest terms. Evidence of a previous conviction for robbery having been given against the prisoner, the magistrate refused to deal summarily with the offence, but referred it to the Assizes. Horner, who had shown signs of intense emotion during the proceedings, fainted away at the conclusion and was carried out of the court.

"Hum! So much for the police-court," said Holmes thoughtfully, tossing aside the paper. "The question for us now to solve is the sequence of events leading from a rifled jewel-case at one end to the crop of a goose in Tottenham Court Road at the other. You see, Watson, our little deductions have suddenly assumed a much more important and less innocent aspect. Here is the stone; the stone came from the goose, and the goose came from Mr. Henry Baker, the gentleman with the bad hat and all the other characteristics with which I have bored you. So now we must set ourselves very seriously to finding this gentleman and ascertaining what part he has played in this little mystery. To do this, we must try the simplest means first, and these lie undoubtedly in an advertisement in all the evening papers. If this fails, I shall have recourse to other methods."

"What will you say?"

"Give me a pencil and that slip of paper. Now, then:

"Found at the corner of Goodge Street, a goose and a black felt hat. Mr. Henry Baker can have the same by applying at 6:30 this evening at 221B Baker Street.

That is clear and concise."

"Very. But will he see it?"

"Well, he is sure to keep an eye on the papers, since, to a poor man, the loss was a heavy one. He was clearly so scared by his mischance in breaking the window and by the approach of Peterson that he thought of nothing but flight, but since then he must have bitterly regretted the impulse which caused him to drop his bird. Then, again, the introduction of his name will cause him to see it, for everyone who knows him will direct his attention to it. Here you are, Peterson, run down to the advertising agency and have this put in the evening papers."

"In which, sir?"

"Oh, in the *Globe, Star, Pall Mall, St. James's, Evening News Standard, Echo,* and any others that occur to you."

"Very well, sir. And this stone?"

"Ah, yes, I shall keep the stone. Thank you. And, I say, Peterson, just buy a goose on your way back and leave it here with me, for we must have one to give to this gentleman in place of the one which your family is now devouring."

When the commissionaire had gone, Holmes took up the stone and held it against the light. "It's a bonny thing," said he. "Just see how it glints and sparkles. Of course it is a nucleus and focus of crime. Every good stone is. They are the devil's pet baits. In the larger and older jewels every facet may stand for a bloody deed. This stone is not yet twenty years old. It was found in the banks of the Amoy River in southern China and is remarkable in having every characteristic of the carbuncle, save that it is blue in shade instead of ruby red. In spite of its youth, it has already a sinister history. There have been two murders, a vitriol-throwing, a suicide, and several robberies brought about for the sake of this forty-grain weight of crystallized charcoal. Who would think that so pretty a toy would be a purveyor to the gallows and the prison? I'll lock it up in my strong box now and drop a line to the Countess to say that we have it."

"Do you think that this man Horner is innocent?"

"I cannot tell."

"Well, then, do you imagine that this other one, Henry Baker, had anything to do with the matter?"

"It is, I think, much more likely that Henry Baker is an absolutely innocent man, who had no idea that the bird which he was carrying was of considerably more value than if it were made of solid gold. That, however, I shall determine by a very simple test if we have an answer to our advertisement."

"And you can do nothing until then?"

"Nothing."

"In that case I shall continue my professional round. But I shall come back in the evening at the hour you have mentioned, for I should like to see the solution of so tangled a business."

"Very glad to see you. I dine at seven. There is a woodcock, I believe. By the way, in view of recent occurrences, perhaps I ought to ask Mrs. Hudson to examine its crop."

I had been delayed at a case, and it was a little after half-past six when I found myself in Baker Street once more. As I approached the house I saw a tall man in a Scotch bonnet with a coat which was buttoned up to his chin waiting outside in the bright semicircle which was thrown from the fanlight. Just as I arrived the door was opened, and we were shown up together to Holmes's room.

"Mr. Henry Baker, I believe," said he, rising from his armchair and greeting his visitor with the easy air of geniality which he could so readily assume. "Pray take this chair by the fire, Mr. Baker. It is a cold night, and I observe that your circulation is more adapted for summer than for winter. Ah, Watson, you have just come at the right time. Is that your hat, Mr. Baker?"

"Yes, sir, that is undoubtedly my hat."

He was a large man with rounded shoulders, a massive head, and a broad, intelligent face, sloping down to a pointed beard of grizzled brown. A touch of red in nose and cheeks, with a slight tremor of his extended hand, recalled Holmes's surmise as to his habits. His rusty black frock-coat was buttoned right up in front, with the collar turned up, and his lank wrists protruded from his sleeves without a sign of cuff or shirt. He spoke in a slow staccato fashion, choosing his words with care, and gave the impression generally of a man of learning and letters who had had ill-usage at the hands of fortune.

"We have retained these things for some days," said Holmes, "because we expected to see an advertisement from you giving your address. I am at a loss to know now why you did not advertise."

Our visitor gave a rather shamefaced laugh. "Shillings have not been plentiful with me as they once were," he remarked. "I had no doubt that the gang of roughs who assaulted me had carried off both my hat and the bird. I did not care to spend more money in a hopeless attempt at recovering them."

"Very naturally. By the way, about the bird, we were compelled to eat it."

"To eat it!" Our visitor half rose from his chair in his excitement.

"Yes, it would have been of no use to anyone had we not done so. But I presume that this other goose upon the sideboard, which is about the same weight and perfectly fresh, will answer your purpose equally well?"

"Oh, certainly, certainly," answered Mr. Baker with a sigh of relief.

"Of course, we still have the feathers, legs, crop, and so on of your own bird, so if you wish—"

The man burst into a hearty laugh. "They might be useful to me as relics of my adventure," said he, "but beyond that I can hardly see what use the *disjecta membra* of my late acquaintance are going to be to me. No, sir, I think that, with your permission, I will confine my attentions to the excellent bird which I perceive upon the sideboard."

Sherlock Holmes glanced sharply across at me with a slight shrug of his shoulders.

"There is your hat, then, and there your bird," said he. "By the way, would it bore you to tell me where you got the other one from? I am somewhat of a fowl fancier, and I have seldom seen a better grown goose."

"Certainly, sir," said Baker, who had risen and tucked his newly gained property under his arm. "There are a few of us who frequent the Alpha Inn, near the Museum—we are to be found in the Museum itself during the day, you understand. This year our good host, Windigate by name, instituted a goose club, by which, on consideration for some few pence every week, we were each to receive a bird at Christmas. My pence were duly paid, and the rest is familiar to you. I am much indebted to you, sir, for a Scotch bonnet is fitted neither to my years nor my gravity." With a comical pomposity of manner he bowed solemnly to both of us and strode off upon his way.

"So much for Mr. Henry Baker," said Holmes when he had closed the door behind him. "It is quite certain that he knows nothing whatever about the matter. Are you hungry, Watson?"

"Not particularly."

"Then I suggest that we turn our dinner into a supper and follow up this clue while it is still hot."

"By all means."

It was a bitter night, so we drew on our ulsters and wrapped cravats about our throats. Outside, the stars were shining coldly in a cloudless sky, and the breath of the passers-by blew out into smoke like so many pistol shots. Our footfalls rang out crisply and loudly as we swung through the doctors' quarter, Wimpole Street, Harley Street and so through Wigmore Street into Oxford Street. In a quarter of an hour we were in Bloomsbury at the Alpha

Inn, which is a small public-house at the corner of one of the streets which runs down into Holborn. Holmes pushed open the door of the private bar and ordered two glasses of beer from the ruddy-faced, white-aproned landlord.

"Your beer should be excellent if it is as good as your geese," said he.

"My geese!" The man seemed surprised.

"Yes. I was speaking only half an hour ago to Mr. Henry Baker, who was a member of your goose club."

"Ah! yes, I see. But you see, sir, them's not *our* geese."

"Indeed! Whose, then?"

"Well, I got the two dozen from a salesman in Covent Garden."

"Indeed? I know some of them. Which was it?"

"Breckinridge is his name."

"Ah! I don't know him. Well, here's your good health, landlord, and prosperity to your house. Good-night.

"Now for Mr. Breckinridge," he continued, buttoning up his coat as we came out into the frosty air. "Remember, Watson, that though we have so homely a thing as a goose at one end of this chain, we have at the other a man who will certainly get seven years' penal servitude unless we can establish his innocence. It is possible that our inquiry may but confirm his guilt; but, in any case, we have a line of investigation which has been missed by the police, and which a singular chance has placed in our hands. Let us follow it out to the bitter end. Faces to the south, then, and quick march!"

We passed across Holborn, down Endell Street, and so through a zigzag of slums to Covent Garden Market. One of the largest stalls bore the name of Breckinridge upon it, and the proprietor, a horsy-looking man, with a sharp face and trim side-whiskers, was helping a boy to put up the shutters.

"Good-evening. It's a cold night," said Holmes.

The salesman nodded and shot a questioning glance at my companion.

"Sold out of geese, I see," continued Holmes, pointing at the bare slabs of marble.

"Let you have five hundred to-morrow morning."

"That's no good."

"Well, there are some on the stall with the gas-flare."

"Ah, but I was recommended to you."

"Who by?"

"The landlord of the Alpha."

"Oh, yes; I sent him a couple of dozen."

"Fine birds they were, too. Now where did you get them from?"

To my surprise the question provoked a burst of anger from the salesman.

"Now, then, mister," said he, with his head cocked and his arms akimbo, "what are you driving at? Let's have it straight, now."

"It is straight enough. I should like to know who sold you the geese which you supplied to the Alpha."

"Well, then, I shan't tell you. So now!"

"Oh, it is a matter of no importance; but I don't know why you should be so warm over such a trifle."

"Warm! You'd be as warm, maybe, if you were as pestered as I am. When I pay good money for a good article there should be an end of the business; but it's 'Where are the geese?' and 'Who did you sell the geese to?' and 'What will you take for the geese?' One would think they were the only geese in the world, to hear the fuss that is made over them."

"Well, I have no connection with any other people who have been making inquiries," said Holmes carelessly. "If you won't tell us the bet is off, that is all. But I'm always ready to back my opinion on a matter of fowls, and I have a fiver on it that the bird I ate is country bred."

"Well, then, you've lost your fiver, for it's town bred," snapped the salesman.

"It's nothing of the kind."

"I say it is."

"I don't believe it."

"D'you think you know more about fowls than I, who have handled them ever since I was a nipper? I tell you, all those birds that went to the Alpha were town bred."

"You'll never persuade me to believe that."

"Will you bet, then?"

"It's merely taking your money, for I know that I am right. But I'll have a sovereign on with you, just to teach you not to be obstinate."

The salesman chuckled grimly. "Bring me the books, Bill," said he.

The small boy brought round a small thin volume and a great greasy-backed one, laying them out together beneath the hanging lamp.

"Now then, Mr. Cocksure," said the salesman, "I thought that I was out of geese, but before I finish you'll find that there is still one left in my shop. You see this little book?"

"Well?"

"That's the list of the folk from whom I buy. D'you see? Well, then, here on this page are the country folk, and the numbers after their names are where their accounts are in the big ledger. Now, then! You see this other page in red ink? Well, that is a list of my town suppliers. Now, look at that third name. Just read it out to me."

" 'Mrs. Oakshott, 117, Brixton Road—249,' " read Holmes.

"Quite so. Now turn that up in the ledger."

Holmes turned to the page indicated. "Here you are, 'Mrs. Oakshott, 117 Brixton Road, egg and poultry supplier.' "

"Now, then, what's the last entry?"

" 'December 22d. Twenty-four geese at 7s. 6d.' "

"Quite so. There you are. And underneath?"

" 'Sold to Mr. Windigate of the Alpha, at 12s.' "

"What have you to say now?"

Sherlock Holmes looked deeply chagrined. He drew a sovereign from his pocket and threw it down upon the slab, turning away with the air of a man whose disgust is too deep for words. A few yards off he stopped under a lamp-post and laughed in the hearty, noiseless fashion which was peculiar to him.

"When you see a man with whiskers of that cut and the 'Pink 'un' protruding out of his pocket, you can always draw him by a bet," said he. "I daresay that if I had put £100 down in front of him, that man would not have given me such complete information as was drawn from him by the idea that he was doing me on a wager. Well, Watson, we are, I fancy, nearing the end of our quest, and the only point which remains to be determined is whether we should go on to this Mrs. Oakshott tonight, or whether we should reserve it for tomorrow. It is clear from what that surly fellow said that there are others besides ourselves who are anxious about the matter, and I should—"

His remarks were suddenly cut short by a loud hubbub which broke out from the stall which we had just left. Turning round we saw a little rat-faced fellow standing in the centre of the circle of yellow light which was thrown by the swinging lamp, while Breckinridge, the salesman, framed in the door of his stall, was shaking his fists fiercely at the cringing figure.

"I've had enough of you and your geese," he shouted. "I wish you were all at the devil together. If you come pestering me any more with your silly talk I'll set the dog at you. You bring Mrs. Oakshott here and I'll answer her, but what have you to do with it? Did I buy the geese off you?"

"No; but one of them was mine all the same," whined the little man.

"Well, then, ask Mrs. Oakshott for it."

"She told me to ask you."

"Well, you can ask the King of Proosia, for all I care. I've had enough of it. Get out of this!" He rushed fiercely forward, and the inquirer flitted away into the darkness.

"Ha! this may save us a visit to Brixton Road," whispered Holmes. "Come with me, and we will see what is to be made of this fellow." Striding through the scattered knots of people who lounged round the flaring stalls, my companion speedily overtook the little man and touched him upon the shoulder. He sprang round, and I could see in the gas-light that every vestige of colour had been driven from his face.

"Who are you, then? What do you want?" he asked in a quavering voice.

"You will excuse me," said Holmes blandly, "but I could not help overhearing the questions which you put to the salesman just now. I think that I could be of assistance to you."

"You? Who are you? How could you know anything of the matter?"

"My name is Sherlock Holmes. It is my business to know what other people don't know."

"But you can know nothing of this?"

"Excuse me, I know everything of it. You are endeavoring to trace some geese which were sold by Mrs. Oakshott, of Brixton Road, to a salesman named Breckinridge, by him in turn to Mr. Windigate, of the Alpha, and by him to his club, of which Mr. Henry Baker is a member."

"Oh, sir, you are the very man whom I have longed to meet," cried the little fellow with outstretched hands and quivering fingers. "I can hardly explain to you how interested I am in this matter."

Sherlock Holmes hailed a four-wheeler which was passing. "In that case we had better discuss it in a cosy room rather than in this wind-swept marketplace," said he. "But pray tell me, before we go further, who it is that I have the pleasure of assisting."

The man hesitated for an instant. "My name is John Robinson," he answered with a sidelong glance.

"No, no; the real name," said Holmes sweetly. "It is always awkward doing business with an alias."

A flush sprang to the white cheeks of the stranger. "Well, then," said he, "my real name is James Ryder."

"Precisely so. Head attendant at the Hotel Cosmopolitan. Pray step into the cab, and I shall soon be able to tell you everything which you would wish to know."

The little man stood glancing from one to the other of us with half-frightened, half-hopeful eyes, as one who is not sure whether he is on the verge of a windfall or of a catastrophe. Then he stepped into the cab, and in half an hour we were back in the sitting-room at Baker Street. Nothing had been said during our drive, but the high, thin breathing of our new companion, and the claspings and unclaspings of his hands, spoke of the nervous tension within him.

"Here we are!" said Holmes cheerily as we filed into the room. "The fire looks very seasonable in this weather. You look cold, Mr. Ryder. Pray take the basketchair. I will just put on my slippers before we settle this little matter of yours. Now, then! You want to know what became of those geese?"

"Yes, sir."

"Or rather, I fancy, of that goose. It was one bird, I imagine, in which you were interested—white, with a black bar across the tail."

Ryder quivered with emotion. "Oh, sir," he cried, "can you tell me where it went to?"

"It came here."

"Here?"

"Yes, and a most remarkable bird it proved. I don't wonder that you should take an interest in it. It laid an egg after it was dead—the bonniest, brightest little blue egg that ever was seen. I have it here in my museum."

Our visitor staggered to his feet and clutched the mantelpiece with his right hand. Holmes unlocked his strongbox and held up the blue carbuncle, which shone out like a star, with a cold, brilliant, many-pointed radiance. Ryder stood glaring with a drawn face, uncertain whether to claim or to disown it.

"The game's up, Ryder," said Holmes quietly. "Hold up, man, or you'll be into the fire! Give him an arm back into his chair, Watson. He's not got blood enough to go in for felony with impunity. Give him a dash of brandy. So! Now he looks a little more human. What a shrimp it is, to be sure!"

For a moment he had staggered and nearly fallen, but the brandy brought a tinge of colour into his cheeks, and he sat staring with frightened eyes at his accuser.

"I have almost every link in my hands, and all the proofs which I could possibly need, so there is little which you need tell me. Still, that little may as well be cleared up to make the case complete. You had heard, Ryder, of this blue stone of the Countess of Morcar's?"

"It was Catherine Cusack who told me of it," said he in a crackling voice.

"I see—her ladyship's waiting-maid. Well, the temptation of sudden wealth so easily acquired was too much for you, as it has been for better men before you; but you were not very scrupulous in the means you used. It seems to me, Ryder, that there is the making of a very pretty villain in you. You knew that this man Horner, the plumber, had been concerned in some such matter before, and that suspicion would rest the more readily upon him. What did you do, then? You made some small job in my lady's room—you and your confederate Cusack—and you managed that he should be the man sent for. Then, when he had left, you rifled the jewel-case, raised the alarm, and had this unfortunate man arrested. You then—"

Ryder threw himself down suddenly upon the rug and clutched at my companion's knee. "For God's sake, have mercy!" he shrieked. "Think of my father! of my mother! It would break their hearts! I never went wrong before! I never will again. I swear it. I'll swear it on a Bible. Oh, don't bring it into court! For Christ's sake, don't!"

"Get back into your chair!" said Holmes sternly. "It is very well to cringe and crawl now, but you thought little enough of this poor Horner in the dock for a crime of which he knew nothing."

"I will fly, Mr. Holmes. I will leave the country, sir. Then the charge against him will break down."

"Hum! We will talk about that. And now let us hear a true account of the next act. How came the stone into the goose, and how came the goose into the open market? Tell us the truth, for there lies your only hope of safety."

Ryder passed his tongue over his parched lips. "I will tell you it just as it happened, sir," said he. "When Horner had been arrested, it seemed to me that it would be best for me to get away with the stone at once, for I did not know at what moment the police might not take it into their heads to search me and my room. There was no place about the hotel where it would be safe. I went out, as if on some commission, and I made for my sister's house. She had married a man named Oakshott, and lived in Brixton Road, where she fattened fowls for the market. All the way there every man I met seemed to me to be a policeman or a detective; and, for all that it was a cold night, the sweat was pouring down my face before I came to the Brixton Road. My sister asked me what was the matter, and why I was so pale; but I told her that I had been upset by the jewel robbery at the hotel. Then I went into the back yard and smoked a pipe, and wondered what it would be best to do.

"I had a friend once called Maudsley, who went to the bad, and has just been serving his time in Pentonville. One day he had met me, and fell into talk about the ways of thieves, and how they could get rid of what they stole. I knew that he would be true to me, for I knew one or two things about him; so I made up my mind to go right on to Kilburn, where he lived, and take him into my confidence. He would show me how to turn the stone into money. But how to get to him in safety? I thought of the agonies I had gone through in coming from the hotel. I might at any moment be seized and searched, and there would be the stone in my waistcoat pocket. I was leaning against the wall at the time and looking at the geese which were waddling about round my feet, and suddenly an idea came into my head which showed me how I could beat the best detective that ever lived.

"My sister had told me some weeks before that I might have the pick of her geese for a Christmas present, and I knew that she was always as good as her word. I would take my goose now, and in it I would carry my stone to Kilburn. There was a little shed in the yard, and behind this I drove one of the birds—a fine big one, white, with a barred tail. I caught it, and, prying its bill open, I thrust the stone down its throat as far as my finger could reach. The bird gave a gulp, and I felt the stone pass along its gullet and down into its crop. But the creature flapped and struggled, and out came my sister to know what was the matter. As I turned to speak to her the brute broke loose and fluttered off among the others.

" 'Whatever were you doing with that bird, Jem?' says she.

" 'Well,' said I, 'you said you'd give me one for Christmas, and I was feeling which was the fattest.'

" 'Oh,' says she, 'we've set yours aside for you—Jem's bird, we call it. It's the big white one over yonder. There's twenty-six of them, which makes one for you, and one for us, and two dozen for the market.'

" 'Thank you, Maggie,' says I; 'but if it is all the same to you, I'd rather have that one I was handling just now.'

" 'The other is a good three pound heavier,' said she, 'and we fattened it expressly for you.'

" 'Never mind. I'll have the other, and I'll take it now,' said I.

" 'Oh, just as you like,' said she, a little huffed. 'Which is it you want, then?'

" 'That white one with the barred tail, right in the middle of the flock.'

" 'Oh, very well. Kill it and take it with you.'

"Well, I did what she said, Mr. Holmes, and I carried the bird all the way to Kilburn. I told my pal what I had done, for he was a man that it was easy to tell a thing like that to. He laughed until he choked, and we got a knife and opened the goose. My heart turned to water, for there was no sign of the stone, and I knew that some terrible mistake had occurred. I left the bird, rushed back to my sister's, and hurried into the back yard. There was not a bird to be seen there.

" 'Where are they all, Maggie?' I cried.

" 'Gone to the dealer's, Jem.'

" 'Which dealer's?'

" 'Breckinridge, of Covent Garden.'

" 'But was there another with a barred tail?' I asked, 'the same as the one I chose?'

" 'Yes, Jem; there were two barred-tailed ones, and I could never tell them apart.'

"Well, then, of course I saw it all, and I ran off as hard as my feet would carry me to this man Breckinridge; but he had sold the lot at once, and not one word would he tell me as to where they had gone. You heard him yourselves tonight. Well, he has always answered me like that. My sister thinks that I am going mad. Sometimes I think that I am myself. And now—and now I am myself a branded thief, without ever having touched the wealth for which I sold my character. God help me! God help me!" He burst into convulsive sobbing, with his face buried in his hands.

There was a long silence, broken only by his heavy breathing, and by the measured tapping of Sherlock Holmes's finger-tips upon the edge of the table. Then my friend rose and threw open the door.

"Get out!" said he.

"What, sir! Oh, Heaven bless you!"

"No more words. Get out!"

And no more words were needed. There was a rush, a clatter upon the stairs, the bang of a door, and the crisp rattle of running footfalls from the street.

"After all, Watson," said Holmes, reaching up his hand for his clay pipe, "I am not retained by the police to supply their deficiencies. If Horner were in danger it would be another thing; but this fellow will not appear against him, and the case must collapse. I suppose that I am commuting a felony, but it is just possible that I am saving a soul. This fellow will not go wrong again; he is too terribly frightened. Send him to jail now, and you make him a jail-bird for life. Besides, it is the season of forgiveness. Chance has put in our way a most singular and whimsical problem, and its solution is its own reward. If you will have the goodness to touch the bell, Doctor, we will begin another investigation, in which, also, a bird will be the chief feature."

Ennis Duling

THE EMBEZZLER'S CHRISTMAS PRESENT

Entire mornings could pass at the First National Bank without anyone speaking to Herb Cubbey about anything that wasn't business. Checks were cashed, and money was entered in personal accounts at the window where Herb worked. Customers were rewarded with a nod and a barely audible thank you. At the end of the day his records were always in perfect order.

Twenty-five-year-old Sue Rigney, who worked two windows away, thought that Herb moved around the bank as if he were a frightened herbivore (she liked the pun) in a jungle of meateaters. He might have blended into a paneled wall, his brown bow tie and the pattern of his remaining hair serving as protective coloration. Like a mouse at the cat's water dish, he poured water for tea, allowed it to steep weakly, and then darted away, leaving only the spore of the tea bag. Sue noticed that he used a tea bag more than once.

Sue had heard the other tellers and the secretaries discussing Herb's personal life. He spent his evenings at home with his widowed mother, and that was the sum of his life. Probably he kept a goldfish, watched the same television shows each week, and made his mother breakfast in bed on Sundays.

The secretaries made occasional jokes about Herb's saintly mother, but he was such little game that they usually found other targets such as the newly appointed assistant manager, Edward Bridgewright, who at thirty-three was exactly Herb's age. In fact, they had both entered the bank's employ at the same time, and while Herb remained at his original position, Bridgewright had risen to better things.

One morning before opening, a group of secretaries and tellers gathered near the coffee machine and talked about the Christmas presents they were giving their boyfriends and husbands. When Herb appeared, Sue, who at the moment had no boyfriend and wanted to keep the fact a secret, said, "What are you giving your mother for Christmas, Herb?"

Herb squeezed his tea bag between two spoons. "I really shouldn't say."

"Aw, come on, Herb," Dot Levin said. After twenty years at the bank, she liked to play mother to the younger employees. "Your mother is such a wonderful woman." Sue wished she hadn't said anything.

"I know I shouldn't tell you this," Herb said, "but I'm giving her ten thousand dollars." The water in his cup had turned a light amber. "Merry Christmas to you all." He looked down at his cup as he balanced it in retreat.

"Did he say ten thousand?" Dot asked.

"Where would the little man get that kind of money?" said Jan Washington, a strikingly beautiful black woman.

At that moment Mr. Bridgewright stepped out of the elevator and marched toward the conversation. "Girls, girls, girls, this is no time to stand around and talk. Back to work!"

"This is my break time, Mr. Bridgewright," Sue said.

He gave her one of his sincere smiles, the type she always saw before he asked her for a date.

"And Herb Cubbey has lots of money," Paula Kimble said.

"No, he doesn't. Work!"

Sue slipped away with the rest of them.

In the parking lot after closing, Herb's money was again the topic of conversation. "Maybe the man lied," Jan suggested.

"No!" Sue insisted. She thought that Herb deserved his privacy as much as anyone. She hated it when the others started to pry into her life.

"Herbert has never told a lie since he was born," Paula said. "He's afraid his mommy might slap his hand."

"Then he inherited it," Sue said.

John Franks from the trust department said, "I drove him home two years ago during the bus strike. He lives over in Bultman Village. You know those little bungalows built back in the Roaring Twenties. They looked better then, I imagine. He asked me in, and the old lady served me tea and biscuits. She looked like she was posing for a painting with her knitting. She kept telling me how hard it was to make ends meet and how her husband had been a wonderful man but didn't have a head for money. No, Herb didn't have any money then."

"A rich uncle," Sue said.

"A man like that with no idea in the world of how to spend money would be lucky enough to have an uncle leave him a bundle," Dot said.

"Worry not, ladies," John said. "I see Herb coming now. I'll just ask him."

As Herb walked by, he touched his hat. John said, "Sorry to hear about your relative dying like that, Mr. Cubbey. Your uncle, wasn't it?"

Herb glanced down. "You must be mistaken, Mr. Franks. My family has excellent health, except for my father, of course, and that was years ago. Good night all."

John watched him until he was out of sight and then he said, "He's a sly one. If he inherited the money, he's not telling."

"He seems to be a very private sort of person," Sue said.

"He has responsibilities," Jan said.

"He's not shy; he's just a Scrooge," Paula said.

"Goes home and counts it at night," Jan agreed. "Won't let anyone get any use out of it except his mother and what's she need with the cash?"

"Maybe he just saved that much and decided to give it to his mother," Sue suggested.

The next morning John steered Sue into Mr. Bridgewright's office. "Ed, I just want you to know how poorly trained your employee is," he said grinning.

"What?" Mr. Bridgewright gave his supervisor's frown.

"I was trying to explain to Susie here that Herb Cubbey could no more save up enough money to give his mom ten thousand dollars than I could convince the trust department to play the ponies. Now I don't want you giving away any state secrets, but let us put down a round figure for Herb's salary." He switched on a calculator and pushed Sue in front. "Look about right, Ed? Now let's subtract food and clothing for two, house maintenance, and taxes. We can multiply the small remainder by fifty-two weeks in a year. He could save that much, but the canary would have to go hungry. Women just don't have a head for money. That's one of the things that's so charming about them."

She twisted out of John's grasp and hurried to the door. "Maybe he made it on Wall Street!"

There was a long silence. "Maybe he did," Mr. Bridgewright said.

"Several hundred thousand," John added with awe in his voice.

At the coffee machine that noon Paula touched Herb's arm. "Would you be willing to give a poor girl like me a little advice, Herb?"

"I beg your pardon?"

"Advice. You know—good ideas from your storehouse of wisdom."

"Certainly," he said doubtfully.

"What percent of a portfolio should a small investor have in stocks?"

Herb backed away as if she had been making demands on him in a foreign language. "I don't understand."

By Christmas Eve most people had concluded that there had been a misunderstanding. Dot said that Herb was probably giving his mother "ten towels and a dollar."

"Weird present!" Jan said.

"But he can afford it," Dot said.

But Paula, who wouldn't let go, cornered him by the drinking fountain. "Is your mother's present all ready, Herb?" she said.

"All but the signature."

"Won't she be surprised by such a large sum of money?"

"Oh, I don't think so. She's used to it." And then Herb smiled. Nobody had seen him really smile before, but they were sure it made him look roguish.

So as Christmas passed, Sue noticed that people's attitude toward Herb had begun to change. His fearful movements around the bank were clear signs of the secretiveness that had made him his money. His near baldness reminded them of the complete baldness of a TV star. His bow tie was like that of a famous lawyer who had been in the news. His tea drinking was a sign of international tastes.

"How are you doing today, Herb honey?" Paula said each morning.

Jan put forward the theory that Herb was a gambler. "He couldn't admit to it and still work in a bank, could he?"

Once Sue met Herb by the candy machine in the basement. "I'm sorry for how the others are treating you," she said. "I feel like I started all this."

"I don't mind really, Sue, although I don't understand a lot that they say to me. John asked me today what I thought of a copper kettle in the third. I don't know anything about kettles."

"I wish I could make it up to you in some way," she said. "Maybe dinner. How about New Year's?" Then she realized that she was doing exactly what she was apologizing for.

"I appreciate the offer, but I'll have to check with my mother. She usually has some friends over, and she might need me." He had a surprised, cornered look on his face.

Sue wasn't sure she wanted to go out with Herb—she was certain she wasn't going to mention the possibility to anyone—but he was kind and polite, characteristics that made him a good deal more attractive than John Franks or Mr. Bridgewright.

Instead of the gambler's image fading, it grew, along with that of the Wizard of Wall Street and the fortunate heir. Only Mr. Bridgewright scoffed at the entire question. Later Sue figured that he would have continued to pay no attention if it hadn't been for her.

"I just want to give you one last opportunity to go out with me on New Year's, Susie," he said after calling her into his office.

"No, thank you. I have a date already." And then before she could clamp her mouth shut, she said, "With Herb!"

The word got around the bank fast. Paula said that Herb might not be much to look at and that his mother might be a millstone, but money made up for a lot of faults.

"We never took you for the greedy type," Dot teased.

"I'm not going out with him for his money."

"With a man like him, what else is there?" Paula said.

"I kind of feel sorry for him."

"You'll feel sorry for him all right when he starts giving you diamonds."

For the next two days, Sue noticed Mr. Bridgewright standing at the door to his office watching Herb. When Herb left his window for the men's room, Bridgewright would make a mark in a notebook. Jan noticed, too. "The man goes to the john more than anyone I've ever seen."

John whispered the conclusion first: "Embezzlement!"

"What an awful thing to say," Sue said.

"First thing you know he'll figure out a way to steal thousands at once, and he'll be off to South America," Paula said.

John laughed. "I can just picture him in a hotel room in Rio wishing he could understand what they were saying on TV."

"Are you serious?" Sue demanded.

"Bridgewright is," John said.

"He can't be."

"I expect the examiners to swoop down at any moment."

The next afternoon, December 31st, Bridgewright stepped over to Herb's cash drawer at the end of the day. "We're going to have someone else check your drawer tonight, Mr. Cubbey," he said. A grim-faced young man in a gray suit stood at his elbow.

"Certainly," Herb said in a voice filled with surprise.

"And Mr. Hamilton wants to see you in his office immediately." Mr. Hamilton was the bank president.

"Yes, sir." Herb walked a few steps away and stood looking out the plate glass window at the bustle on Main Street. Sue could see his shoulders slump in defeat.

Mr. Bridgewright came over to her. "Well, Miss Rigney, we're going to be at the bottom of the Herbert Cubbey case soon enough. Mr. Hamilton has been informed. We've played games far too long."

"I don't think Herb even knows what game we're playing," Sue said.

She went to where Herb stood and squeezed his arm. "Whatever happens, Herb, I know you're innocent."

"Am I in some sort of trouble?" He seemed terribly afraid, and she wanted to mother him.

"They say you stole the money."

"What money?"

"The ten thousand dollars you gave your mother for Christmas."

He swallowed hard. "You didn't really think I had all that money?"

"You said you did."

"If I did have that much, I'd take you out on New Year's to the best restaurant in town. You'd have flowers, and we'd drink champagne and dance all night."

"It doesn't take that much money to have a good time," Sue said. "I already lied and told Mr. Bridgewright we were going out."

"All right then," he said, straightening his shoulders. "We'll make some plans when we get back from talking to Mr. Hamilton. Will you come along with me?"

Sue followed him to the elevator.

"Could I have the opportunity to explain?" Herb said to President Hamilton.

"I expect you'd like one, Cubbey," Hamilton said. He was a short, heavy man with bushy eyebrows. "You should anyway! I'm an old man, so I don't need to be subtle. No time for it. So let's hear it. Bridgewright tells me you've been giving away thousands of dollars and the only explanation is you've got your hand in the till."

"I've honestly accounted for every cent that I've handled."

"Thought so. What about the gift?"

"I wrote my mother a check for ten thousand dollars at Christmas. I never should have told anyone."

"How's that again?"

"We haven't had much since my father passed away, so we pretend. Every year we write each other large checks. This year she gave me a check for two thousand. The year before I wrote one for five thousand, and she gave me one for eight thousand. *Checks* that is. We sit around and talk about what we'd like to buy until midnight, and then we burn the checks in the fireplace. We've always had a good time doing it. It must sound strange to outsiders."

Mr. Hamilton chuckled. "It's unusual, that's for sure, but not a bad idea. You get the pleasure of the money without the cost, which is not bad management at all. Not bad at all. Shows a good deal more sense than Mr. Bridgewright just exhibited."

"Do you have any further questions, sir?"

"Why hasn't an honest, imaginative young man like you received a promotion recently? Who's running this bank anyway? That's what I'd like to know."

Ron Goulart

BELIEVING IN SANTA

As it turned out, he didn't get a chance to murder anybody. He did make an impressive comeback, revitalizing his faltering career and saying goodbye to most of his financial worries. But in spite of all that, there are times when Oscar Sayler feels sad about not having been able to knock off his former wife.

Twenty-five years ago Oscar had been loved by millions of children. Well, actually, they adored his dummy, Screwy Santa, but they tolerated Oscar. For several seasons his early morning kid show was the most popular in the country, outpulling Captain Kangaroo and all the other competition. Multitudes of kids, and their parents, doted on Oscar's comic version of Santa Claus and tried to live by the show's perennial closing line—"Gang, try to act like it was Christmas every day!"

For the past decade and more, though, Oscar hadn't been doing all that well. In early December of last year, when he got the fateful phone call from the New York talent agency, he was scraping by on the $25,000 a year he earned from the one commercial voice job he'd been able to come up with lately. Oscar lived alone in a one-bedroom condo in a never-finished complex in New Beckford, Connecticut. He was fifty-five—well, fifty-seven actually—and he didn't look all that awful.

Since he'd given up drinking, his face was no longer especially puffy and it had lost that lobsterish tinge. His hair, which was nearly all his own, still had a nice luster to it. There was, really, no reason why he couldn't appear on television again.

When the agent called him at a few minutes after four P.M. on a bleak, chill Monday afternoon, Oscar was flat on his back in his small tan living room. He'd vowed to complete two dozen situps every day.

He crawled over to the phone on the coffee table. "Hello?"

"Is your son there?"

Oscar pulled himself up onto the sofa arm, resting the phone on his knees. "Don't have a son. My daughter, however, is the noted television actress Tish Sale, who stars in the *Intensive Care* soap opera, and hasn't set foot across dear old Dad's threshold for three, possibly four—"

"Spare me," requested the youthful, nasal voice. "You must be Oscar Sayler then. You sounded so old that I mistook you for your father."

"Nope, my dad sounded like this—'How about a little nip after dinner, my boy?' Much more throaty and with a quaver. Who the hell are you, by the way?"

"Vince Mxyzptlk. I'm with Mimi Warnicker & Associates, the crackerjack talent agency."

"Oops." Oscar sat on a cushion and straightened up. "That's a powerful outfit."

"You bet your ass it is," agreed the young agent. "You're not represented at the moment, are you?"

"No, because I find I can get all the acting jobs I want without—"

"C'mon, Oscar, old buddy, you ain't exactly rolling in work right now," cut in Vince disdainfully. "In fact, your only gig is doing the voice of the infected toe in those godawful Dr. Frankel's Foot Balm radio spots." He made a scornful noise.

"I do a very convincing itching toe, Vince. Fact is, there's talk of—"

"Listen, I can get you tons of work. Talk shows, commercials, lectures, TV parts, eventually some plum movie work. But first you—"

"How exactly are—"

"But first you have got to win your way back into the hearts and minds of the public."

"Just how do I accomplish that, Vince?"

"You just have to sit there with that lamebrained dummy on your knee."

"Screwy Santa? Hell, nobody's been interested in him for years."

"Let me do the talking for a bit, okay? Here's what's under way," continued the agent. *"Have a Good Day, USA!*, which has just become the top morning talk and news show, is planning a six-minute nostalgia segment for this Friday. The theme is 'Whatever happened to our favorite kids' shows?' Something they calculate'll have a tremendous appeal for the Boomers and Busters who make up their pea-brained audience. So far they've signed that old duffer who used to be Captain Buckeroo and—"

"Kangaroo."

"Oscar, are you more interested in heckling me than in making an impressive comeback? Would you prefer to go on living in squalor in that rural crackerbox, to voice tripe for Dr. Frankel throughout the few remaining years of your shabby life?"

"Okay, but his name is Captain Kangaroo, not—"

"Attend to me, Oscar. I assured Liz, who's putting this segment together, that I'd dig you up, wipe off the cobwebs, and have you there bright and early Friday. Can you drag yourself into Manhattan and meet me at the Consolidated Broadcasting headquarters building on Fifty-third no later than six A.M.?"

"Sure, that's no problem."

"Most importantly, can you bring that dimwitted dummy?"

Without more than a fraction of a second of hesitation Oscar answered, "Of course, yeah, absolutely." It didn't seem the right time to tell Mxyzptlk that his former wife, who currently loathed him and had ousted him eleven long years ago from the mansion they once shared, had retained custody of the only existing Screwy Santa dummy in the world. "We'll both see you on Friday, Vince."

It commenced snowing at dusk, a paltry, low-budget snow that didn't look as though it was up to blanketing the condo-complex grounds and masking its raw ugliness.

Glancing at his wristwatch once more, Oscar punched out his daughter's New York City number.

After four rings there came a twanging noise. "Merry Christmas," said Tish in her sexiest voice. "I'm not able to come to the phone right now, but if you'll leave your name and number, I'll get back to you real soon."

Oscar had been working all afternoon on the voice he was going to use. A mixture of paternal warmth and serious illness. "Patricia, my dear," he began, getting the quaver just about perfect, "this is your dad. Something quite serious has come up and I'd like very much to speak to you, my only child, in the hope that—"

"Holy Jesus," observed his daughter, coming onto the line. "What was that old television show you used to tell me about when I was little? Where they gave the contestants the gong for a rotten perf—"

"*The Amateur Hour.* Now, kid, I need—"

"Consider yourself gonged, Pop."

"Okay, all right, I overdid it a mite," he admitted. "Yet I do have a serious problem."

"My time is sort of limited, Dad. I'm getting ready for a date. You should've phoned me earlier."

"I assumed you were taping *Intensive Care.*"

She sighed. "Didn't you tell me you watched my soap faithfully?"

"I do, kid. It's on my must-see list every day."

"I've been in a coma for two weeks. So I don't have to show up at—"

"Sorry to hear that. Anything serious?"

"Near-fatal car crash. We killed that asshole, Walt Truett, thank God."

"But you'll survive?"

"Sure, with only a touch of amnesia."

Oscar asked, "When are you due to come out of your stupor?"

"Next Thursday."

"I'll start watching, I swear," he promised his daughter. "Now, as to the purpose of this call."

"It's Mom, isn't it?"

"Well, not exactly, kid." He filled her in about the offer from the talent agency and the upcoming appearance on *Have a Good Day, USA!* "This will revive my career."

"You think so? A couple of early morning minutes with a pack of over-the-hill doofers?"

"It's a shot. The only snag is—well, kid, they insist that I bring Screwy along."

"Obviously. You guys are a team."

"And your dear mother has custody of him."

Tish said, "She's not going to loan him to you."

"She might, if you were to—"

"Nope, she won't. A few months ago, when I noticed him up on a shelf in the mud room, I suggested that—"

"She keeps the most beloved dummy in America in the mud room?"

"In a shoe box," she answered. "And, Dad, Screwy Santa hasn't been beloved for a couple of decades now. "

"I know, neither have I," he said ruefully. "But, damn it, he helped pay for that mansion."

"Her romantic novels are paying for things now. Did you notice that *Kiss Me, My Pirate* was number two on the *Times*—"

"I extract the book section from the Sunday paper with surgical gloves and toss it immediately into the trash unopened. To make certain I never see so much as a mention of that slop she cranks out or, worse, a publicity photo of her mottled countenance."

"Let's get back to the point. I suggested to her back then that she return Screwy Santa to you."

"And?"

"You don't want to hear what she said," his daughter assured him. "It had, among other things, to do with Hell freezing over. But can't you dig up another dummy by Friday?"

"Impossible, that's the only one extant. We lost the backup copy during that ill-fated nostalgia tour through the Midwest years ago."

"Couldn't you carve another, since you built the others?"

"Kid, I may've fudged the truth a bit when I used to recount Screwy's history to you," he said. "In reality, the dummies were built by a prop man at the old WWAG-TV studios. And he, alas, is long in his grave."

"This is very disillusioning," Tish complained. "One of the few things I still admired about you, Dad, was your woodcarving ability."

"Listen, couldn't you call Mitzi and tell her that I'm expiring, that I want to be reunited with my dummy for one last time before I go on to glory?"

"She'd burst out laughing if I told her you were about to kick off, Dad. And probably dance a little jig."

"Okay, suppose we make a business deal with her? Offer the old shrew, say, fifteen percent of the take. "

"What take? *Have a Good Day, USA!* pays scale. I know, I did one last year to plug my abortion on *Intensive Care*."

"You looked terrific on that broadcast."

"You didn't even see it."

"Didn't I?"

"No, and you admitted as much at the time."

"Well, back to my immediate problem."

"Why don't you use one of the old Screwy Santa dolls? They look a lot like the dummy."

"Except they don't have movable mouths."

"It'd be better than nothing. I can loan you mine," she offered. "It's stuffed away in a closet."

"No, kid, I really have to have the real dummy."

"Afraid there's nothing I can do. I mean, if I so much as mention that you need Screwy Santa, Mom's liable to take an axe to him."

"Well, thanks anyway for listening to an old man's woes and—"

"Here comes the gong again," his daughter said. "Anyhow, I have to go put on some clothes. Bye."

After hanging up, he stayed on the sofa and brooded. After about ten minutes he said aloud, "I'll have to outwit Mitzi."

The snow improved the next morning, giving a Christmas-card gloss to the usually dismal view from his small living room window.

At ten A.M. he put the first phase of his latest plan into operation. He phoned his former wife's mansion over in Westport.

"Residence of Mitzi Sunsett Sayler," answered a crisp female voice.

"Yes, how are you?" inquired Oscar in a drawling, slightly British accent. "Ogden Brokenshire here."

"Yes?"

"Ogden Brokenshire of the Broadcasting Hall of Fame. Have I the honor of addressing the esteemed novelist Mitzi Sunsett Sayler herself?"

"Of course not, Mr. Brokenshire: I'm Clarissa Dempster, Mrs. Sayler's secretary."

"I see, my dear. Well, perhaps I can explain my mission to you, child, and you can explain the situation to your employer."

"That depends on—"

"We would like to enshrine Screwy Santa."

"Enshrine whom?"

"The ingenious dummy that Mrs. Sayler's one-time husband used in the days when he brought joy and gladness to the hearts of—"

"Oh, that thing," said the secretary. "My parents, wisely, never allowed me to watch that dreadful show when I was a child."

"Nonetheless, dear child, our board has voted, unanimously I might add, to place Screwy Santa on permanent display in the museum."

"Hold on a moment. I'll speak to Mrs. Sayler." The secretary went away.

In less than two minutes Mitzi started talking. "Who is this ?"

"Good morning, I'm Ogden Brokenshire. As I was explaining to your able secretary, my dear Mrs. Sayler, I'm an executive with the Broadcasting Hall of—"

"You haven't improved at all, you no-talent cheesehead."

"I beg your pardon, madam?"

"Oscar, love, you never could do a believable Brit."

"I don't happen to be British, dear lady. The fact that I was educated in Boston sometimes gives people that impression."

"Forget it, Oscar," advised his erstwhile wife. "I don't know why you want to get your clammy hands on that wooden dornick, but you'll never have him. And, dear heart, if you ever try to communicate with me again—in whatever wretched voice—I'll sic the law on you." She, rather gently, hung up on him.

"Looks like," decided Oscar, "I'm going to need a new plan."

He kept working on plans for nearly an hour, pacing his small living room, muttering, pausing now and then to gaze out at the falling snow.

Then the phone rang.

"Yeah?"

"We have hit a slight snag," announced Vince Mxyzptlk.

"Don't they want me?"

"Sure they want you, old buddy. Hell, they're prowling the lofty corridors at Consolidated crying out for you," said the youthful agent. "In fact, they can't wait until Friday."

"What do you mean—do they want me to do a separate segment on my own?"

862

"Not exactly. But Liz, *and* her boss, are very anxious to see you tomorrow."

Frowning, Oscar nodded. "An audition, huh?"

"Sort of, yeah," admitted the agent. "It has nothing, really, to do with you. But when one of their scouts unearthed the clunk who used to be Mr. Slimjim on that *Mr. Slimjim & Baby Gumdrop* turkey, he turned out to weigh three hundred pounds now and possess not a single tooth. So, as you can understand, Oscar, they want to see and hear all these wonderful stars of yesteryear in advance."

"Tomorrow?"

"At three P.M. Is that a problem for you?"

"Not exactly, but I—"

"I'm getting a lot of interest in you. Once you do well on Friday, the jobs will start rolling in."

"I understand, it's only—"

"I needn't remind you, Oscar, that a lot of talents in your present position would kill for this opportunity."

"You're absolutely right," he agreed. "See you tomorrow ."

He had a great new plan worked out by three that afternoon. But he had to wait until after dark to get going on it.

Dressed in dark clothes, Oscar slipped quietly out of his apartment and into the lean-to that passed for a garage. As usual, none of the roads in the sparsely inhabited complex had been plowed. The snow was soft, though, and not too high, and Oscar was able to drive down to the plowed lanes and byways of New Beckford without any serious delays.

He drove over to nearby Westport and parked in the lot behind Borneo's. There were only a few spaces left and he could see that the restaurant-bar was packed with people. The food and drink at Borneo's was just passable, but it sat only a half mile over the hill from Mitzi's mansion.

As he was crossing the lot a fire engine went hooting by, headed downhill.

Borneo himself was behind the bar. "Evening, Oscar."

He managed to elbow his way up to a narrow spot at the ebony bar. "The usual."

Borneo scratched at his stomach through the fabric of his bright tropical shirt. "Refresh my memory."

"Club soda, alas."

"Coming up."

Outside in the snowy night another fire engine went roaring by, followed by what sounded like a couple of police cars.

Oscar hoped all this activity wouldn't foul up his plan. So far everything was going well. People were seeing him, he was establishing an alibi. In another ten or fifteen minutes he'd go back to the john. Then he'd slip out the side door.

Once in the open, he'd make his way down to the mansion. Being careful, of course, that no one noticed him sneaking off.

Mitzi, being a skinflint, and in spite of her great wealth, had never bothered to put in a new alarm system. The original setup was still in place, and he knew how to disarm that.

Okay, once he got inside, after making certain that she was alone, he'd . . . well, he'd use the length of pipe he dug up in the garage this afternoon.

Once Mitzi was dead and done for, he'd gather up enough jewels and valuables to make it look like the usual burglary. Then he'd rescue Screwy Santa from the mud room and get the hell away.

Back here at the parking lot he'd stash the loot in his car, slip unobtrusively back into the place, and tell Borneo he'd had a sudden touch of stomach flu and had to stay back in the bathroom a few minutes.

It wasn't exactly foolproof, but it ought to work. He'd own Screwy again and Mitzi would be gone from his life.

He chuckled at the thought. Yeah, the idea of killing her off had come to him this afternoon and he'd taken to it immediately.

Tish might be a little suspicious about how he came by the dummy. He'd tell her something along the lines that he'd found the heirs of the old defunct prop man at the last minute and, gosh, they had a spare Screwy Santa. He'd always been a gifted liar and conning his daughter wouldn't be all that difficult.

"Don't worry about that now," he told himself.

"How's that?" inquired Borneo, setting a glass of sparkling water down in front of him.

"Nothing, I was just—"

"That must be some fire." Borneo paused to listen as yet another truck went howling by out in the night.

Oscar sipped the club soda, drumming the fingers of his free hand on the dark bar top. He'd make his move in about five minutes.

The phone behind the bar rang and Borneo caught it up. "Borneo's. Huh? Channel eight? Okay." Hanging up, he switched channels on the large television set mounted above the mirror.

And there was Mitzi, glowering out of the screen. Wearing a fuzzy bathrobe and not enough makeup, she was being interviewed by a slim black newswoman and gesturing at the mansion that was blazing behind her up across the wide night lawn.

"Good God," muttered Oscar.

"That's just downhill from us," observed Borneo.

"Yeah, I know."

The entire sprawling house was going up in flames.

"What exactly happened, Mrs. Sayler?" the reporter asked her.

"It was that goddamn cheesehead."

"Which cheesehead would that be?"

"Screwy Santa, that abominable dummy."

"I'm not certain that I quite under—"

"Aw, you're too damn young. Everybody is these days. I always knew that dornick would do me in eventually."

"You mean this was arson?"

"I mean, dear heart, that I decided to cremate that loathsome lump of wood. I took him and his shoebox, carried them into the living room, and tossed him into the fireplace."

Oscar pressed both hands to his chest. "There goes my comeback."

Mitzi continued, "Then . . . I don't know. His stupid beard seemed to explode . . . flames came shooting out of the fireplace. They hit the drapes and those caught fire . . . then the damn furniture started to go." She shook her head angrily. "Now the whole shebang is ablaze." Looking directly into the camera, she added, "If you're out there watching, Oscar . . ." She gave him the finger.

Borneo raised his shaggy eyebrows high. "Hey, is she talking to you, Oscar?"

"I'm not in the mood for conversation just now." Abandoning his club soda, he walked out into the night.

His daughter phoned a few minutes shy of midnight. "I didn't want you to worry."

"I'm way beyond worry, kid."

"When I caught the report about Mom's mansion on the news, I figured you'd assume that Screwy Santa was gone."

"Certainly I assumed that. There was Mitzi, fatter than ever, hollering for all the world to hear that my poor hapless creation was the cause of the whole blinking conflagration."

"It was a ringer, Dad."

"Eh?"

"I dropped by to visit Mom this afternoon and when she went away to yell at Clarissa, I substituted my old Screwy Santa doll for your dummy," explained Tish. "In a way, I may be responsible for that dreadful fire. The doll's a lot more flammable than—"

"No, there was some parent flap at the time, but we proved beyond a doubt that the dolls were perfectly safe if—"

"I have your dummy here in my apartment."

"You've really got Screwy?"

"Yes, he's sitting on my bed right this minute," she assured her father. "It's lucky I went out there when I did and saved him before Mom got going on her plan to destroy the little guy. Why did you go and telephone her and make it crystal clear that you were in desperate need of him? That was dippy, since it inspired her to destroy him."

"I didn't call her as myself. But somehow she penetrated my—"

"That's because, trust me, you do a terrible British voice. When do you need him?"

"Tomorrow."

"I thought you weren't doing the show until Friday."

"Well, and keep this to yourself, kid, there's a possibility they'll devote a separate seg all to me."

"That would be great."

"So can I pick him up tomorrow?"

"Sure, come by around one and I'll take you to lunch."

"Can't make lunch, because I have some people to see while I'm in the Apple. But I'll pop in, give you a paternal hug, and grab Screwy Santa," he said. "Thanks. You're a perfect daughter."

"Perfect for you, I guess. Bye."

Everything worked out well for Oscar. He did, in fact, do a segment of his own, which ran nearly four minutes, on *Have a Good Day, USA!* And Vince Mxyzptlk was able to get him an impressive batch of other jobs. At the moment there's also the possibility of a new kid show for Oscar and Screwy Santa on cable.

Oscar was able to leave his forlorn condo for a three-bedroom colonial in Brimstone, Connecticut, last month.

While he was packing, he came across the length of pipe he'd intended to use on Mitzi. He slapped it across the palm of his hand a few times, and, sighing, tossed it into a carton.

Peter Lovesey

PASS THE PARCEL

The roads were treacherous on Christmas Day and Andy and Gemma took longer than they expected to drive the twenty-five miles to Stowmarket. While Gemma concentrated on keeping the car from skidding, Andy complained about the party in prospect. "You and I must be crazy doing this. I mean, what are we putting our lives at risk for? Infantile games that your sister insists on playing simply because in her tiny mind that's the only permissible way of celebrating. The food isn't anything special. If Pauline produces those enormous cheese straws with red streaks like varicose veins, I'll throw up. I promise you. All over the chocolate log."

Gemma said, "We're not going for the food."

"The games?"

"The family."

"Your brother Reg, you mean? The insufferable Reg? I can't wait to applaud his latest stunt. What's he planning for this year, would you say? A stripogram? Or a police raid? He's a real bunch of laughs, is Reg."

Gemma negotiated a sharp bend and said, "Will you shut up about Reg? There are others in my family."

"Of course. There's Geoff. He'll be sitting in the most comfortable chair and speaking to nobody."

"Give it a rest, will you?" Gemma said through her teeth.

"I'd like to. They're showing *Apocalypse Now* on BBC2. I'd like to be giving it a rest in front of the telly with a large brandy in my fist."

Andy's grumbling may have been badly timed, but it was not unreasonable. Any fair-minded person would have viewed Christmas with this particular set of in-laws as an infliction. There were four in the current generation of Weavers, all in their thirties now, the sisters Gemma and Pauline and the brothers Reg and Geoff. Pauline, the hostess, eight years Gemma's junior, was divorced. She would have been devastated if the family had spent Christmas anywhere else but in Chestnut Lodge, the mansion she had occupied with her former husband and kept as her share of the settlement. No one risked devastating Pauline. As the youngest, she demanded and received everybody's cooperation.

"I could endure the food if it wasn't for the games," Andy started up again. "Why do we put up with them? Why not something intelligent instead of charades and—God help us—pass the parcel? I know, you're going to tell me it's a tradition in the family, but we don't have to be lumbered with traditions forevermore just because sweet little Pauline likes playing the games she did when she was a kid. She's thirty-one now, for Christ's sake. Does she sleep with a teddy bear?"

When they reached Stowmarket and swung left, Andy decently dipped into his reserve of bonhomie. "They probably dread it as much as we do, poor sods. Let's do our best to be convivial. You did bring the brandy?"

"On the backseat with the presents," said Gemma.

Chestnut Lodge had been built about 1840 for a surgeon. Not much had been done to the exterior since. The stonework wanted cleaning and there were weeds growing through the gravel drive.

Someone had left a parcel the size of a shoebox on the doorstep. Andy picked it up and carried it in with their presents.

"So sorry, darling," Gemma told Pauline. "The roads were like a rink in places. Are we the last?"

"No, Reg isn't here yet."

"Wanting to make the usual grand entrance?"

"Probably."

"You're wearing your pearls. And what a gorgeous dress."

Pauline always wore something in pink or yellow with layers of net. She was in competition with the fairy on the tree, according to Andy.

She smiled her thanks for the compliment. "Not very practical for the time of year, but I couldn't resist it. Let's take your coats. And Happy Christmas."

"First I'll park these under the tree," said Andy. "The brown paper one isn't from us, by the way. We found it on your doorstep. Doesn't feel heavy enough for booze, more's the pity."

"I do like surprises," said Pauline.

"A secret admirer?" said Gemma.

"At my age?"

"Oh, come on, what does that say for me, pushing forty?"

"You've got your admirer."

Gemma rolled her eyes upwards and said nothing.

"Come and say hello to Geoff." Pauline cupped her hand to her mouth as she added, "Hasn't had any work for three months, he told me."

"Oh, no."

Their accountant brother, short and fat, with half-glasses, greeted Gemma. "Merry Christmas" was likely to be the extent of his conversation for the day unless someone asked him about his garden.

Pauline brought in a tray of tea things.

Andy said, "Not for me, I'll help myself to a brandy, if you don't mind. Want one, Geoff?"

Geoff shook his head.

"Any trouble getting here?"

Geoff gave a shrug.

"Roads okay your way, then?"

Geoff thought about it and gave another shrug.

Pauline said, "It's nearly four. Reg ought to be here. It's not as if he has far to come. Geoff has a longer trip and he was here by three-thirty."

"Knowing Reg of old, he could be planning one of his stunts," said Andy. "Remember the year of the ghost in the bathroom, Pauline?"

"Don't!" she said. "Will I ever forget it? It was so real, and he *knew* I was scared of living here alone."

Between them, they recalled Reg's party tricks in recent years: the time he arrived with his friend masquerading as an African bishop; the year the Queen's voice came out of the cocktail cabinet; and the live turkey in Geoff's car.

"You've got to give him full marks for trying," said Andy. "It would be a dull old Christmas without him."

"I'd rather have it dull," said Pauline.

"Me, too," said Gemma. "I may be his flesh and blood, but I don't share his sense of humor."

"Only because it could be your turn this time," said Andy. "Poor old Geoff got it last year. The sight of that turkey pecking your hand when you opened the door, Geoff, I'll never forget."

Geoff stared back without smiling.

Ten minutes later, Pauline said, "I've had the cocktail sausages warming for over an hour. They'll be burnt to a cinder. And we haven't even opened a single present."

"Want me to phone him, see if he's left?" Andy offered.

"Of course he's left," said Gemma. "He must have."

Pauline started to say, "I hope nothing's—"

Gemma said quickly, "He's all right. He wants to keep us in suspense. We're playing into his hands. I think we should get on with the party without him. Why don't we open some presents?"

"I think we ought to wait for Reg."

"You could open the one we found on the doorstep," Andy suggested to Pauline.

"Unless it *is* something personal," said Gemma.

That induced a change of mind from Pauline. "I've got nothing to hide from any of you."

Andy retrieved the parcel from under the tree, turned it over, and examined the brown paper wrapping. "There's nothing written on it. Maybe it isn't meant for Pauline after all."

"If it was left on her doorstep, it's hers," said Gemma.

Pauline sat in a chair with the parcel deep in the froth of her skirt and picked at the Sellotape. She was too fastidious to tear the paper.

"You want scissors," said Andy.

"I can manage." She eased open the brown paper. "It's gift-wrapped inside."

"Where's the tag?" said Gemma. "Who's it from?"

"There isn't one." Pauline examined the tinsel-tied parcel in its shiny red wrapper.

"Open it, then."

She worked at one edge of the paper with one of her long, lacquered fingernails. "Look, there's more wrapping inside."

"Just like pass the parcel," said Gemma.

Andy gave his wife a murderous look.

The paper yielded to Pauline's gentle probing. Underneath was yet another wrapping, with a design of holly and Christmas roses. She said, "I think you're right. This is meant for a game."

Andy swore under his breath.

"Let's all play, then," said Gemma with an amused glance at her husband's reaction.

"After tea."

"No, now. While we're waiting for Reg. Pull up a chair everyone and sit in a circle. I'll look after the music."

"Just three of us?" said Andy.

Gemma mocked him with a look. "You know how Pauline adores this game."

Andy and Pauline positioned themselves close to where Geoff was already seated, while Gemma selected a CD and placed it on the deck of the music center.

"What is it—'The Teddy Bears' Picnic'?" said Andy.

Pauline was impervious to sarcasm. " 'Destiny,' " she said as the sound of strings filled the room.

"That's an old one."

"Start passing it, then," said Gemma. "I'm not playing this for my amusement."

Pauline handed the parcel to Andy, who held it to his chest. "No cheating," said Pauline.

He passed it to Geoff and the music stopped. Geoff unwrapped a piece of pink paper and revealed a silver layer beneath.

"Tough," said Andy. "Play on, maestro."

As the game resumed, Pauline told her sister, "You're supposed to have your back to us. It isn't fair if you can see who the parcel has reached."

"She likes playing God," said Andy. "Whoops." The music had stopped and the parcel was on his lap. He ripped it open; no finer feelings. "Too bad. Give it another whirl, Gem."

Geoff was the next to remove a layer. He did it in silence as usual.

"More music?" said Gemma.

"You got it," said Andy.

Three more wrappings came off before Pauline got a turn. The parcel was appreciably smaller.

"This could be it," said Andy. "You can see the shape."

"But of what?" said Pauline "It looks like a box to me." She was pink in the face as she peeled back the paper, but it was clear that another burst of music would be necessary.

When Andy received the parcel he held it to his ear and gave it a shake. Nothing rattled.

"Come on, pass it," said Pauline, drumming her shoes on the carpet.

Geoff fumbled and dropped the parcel as the music stopped. Pauline snatched it up.

"Not so fast," said Andy. "Geoff hadn't passed it to you."

But she had already unfolded the tissue paper from around a matchbox, one of the jumbo size capable of holding two hundred and fifty matches.

"One more round, apparently," said Gemma, and she turned up the music again. To sustain the suspense, a longer stretch of "Destiny" was wanted.

"What could it be?" said Pauline.

"Matches," said Andy.

"A silk scarf would be nice," said Pauline.

"Game on," said Andy.

The matchbox was sent on its way around the three players.

"No looking," Andy reminded his wife. "We're down to the wire now. This has to be impartial."

"Faster," said Pauline.

"She's a goer, your sister," said Andy.

The matchbox fairly raced from lap to lap.

"Do you mind? I didn't know you cared," said Andy when Pauline's impetuous hand clasped his thigh.

Even Geoff was leaning forward, absorbed in the climax of the game. The music stopped just as he was passing the box to Pauline. They both had their hands on it.

"Mine," she said.

Geoff apparently knew better than to thwart his younger sister.

"I suppose it's only justice that you get the prize, as it was left on your doorstep," said Andy. "Let's see what you've got."

Unable to contain her curiosity, Gemma came over to see.

Pauline slid the box half-open, dropped it into her lap, and said in horror, "Oh, I don't believe it!"

"It's a joke, said Gemma. "It must be a joke."

"It isn't," said Pauline in a thin, strained voice. "That's somebody's thumb. Ugh!" She hooked the box off her skirt as if it were alive and dropped it on the coffee table.

Large and pale, the offending digit lay on a bed of cotton wool.

"No it isn't," said Andy. "It's too big for a thumb. It's a big toe."

"A toe?"

"Yes, it's too fleshy for a thumb."

"It must be out of a joke shop," said Gemma. "If Reg is responsible for this, I'll strangle him."

"Typical of his humor," said Andy.

Then Geoff spoke. "I think it's real."

"It *can't* be," said Gemma.

"Open it right out," said Andy.

"I'm not touching it," said Pauline.

Andy lifted the box and opened it, separating the drawer from its casing.

"I can't bear to look," said Pauline. "Keep it away from me."

"It's the real thing," said Andy. "You can see where it was—"

"God in Heaven—we don't wish to see," said Gemma. "Put it somewhere out of sight and give Pauline some of that brandy we brought."

"What a vile trick," said Pauline.

Andy reunited the two sections of the matchbox and placed it on a bookshelf before going to the brandy bottle. "Anybody else want some Dutch courage?"

Geoff gave a nod.

Andy's hand shook as he poured. Everyone was in a state of shock.

"He's gone too far this time," said Gemma. "He's ruined Christmas for all of us. I shall tell him. Are you all right, love?"

Pauline took a gulp of brandy and gave a nod.

"It's ghoulish," said Gemma.

"Sick," said Andy. "You all right, Geoff? You've gone very pale."

"I'm okay," Geoff managed to say.

"Drink some brandy, mate."

Gemma said, "Andy, would you take it right out of the room and get rid of it? It's upsetting us all."

Andy picked the matchbox off the bookshelf and left the room. Gemma collected the discarded sheets of wrapping paper and joined him in the kitchen. "Where would Reg have got such a ghoulish thing?" she whispered.

Andy shrugged. "Who knows? I don't imagine a branch manager at the Midland Bank comes across many severed toes."

"What are we going to do? Pauline's nerves are shattered and Geoff looks ready to faint."

"A fresh cup of tea is supposed to be good for shock. What am I going to do with this?"

"I don't know. Bury it in the garden."

"Pauline is sure to ask where it went."

"Then we'd better take it with us when we go. We can dump it some-where on the way home."

"Why should we have to deal with it?" said Andy. "I'll give it back to bloody Reg. He can get rid of it."

"If he has the gall to show his face here. Just keep it out of everyone's sight in the meantime."

To satisfy himself that the toe really was of human origin, Andy slid open the matchbox again. This time he noticed a folded piece of paper tucked into one end. "Hey, there's something inside. I think it's a note." After reading the typed message, he handed it to Gemma. "What do you make of that?"

She stared at the paper. "It can't be true. It's got to be a hoax."

They joined Pauline and Geoff in the living room. "We thought you might appreciate some tea," said Gemma.

"You're marvellous," said Pauline. "I should have thought of that."

"Getting over the shock?"

"I think so."

"You too, Geoff?"

Geoff gave a nod.

Andy cleared his throat. "I found this note in the matchbox."

"A note?" said Pauline. "From Reg?"

"Apparently not. It says, 'If you want the rest of your brother—' "

"Oh, no!" said Pauline.

" 'If you want the rest of your brother, bring ten thousand pounds or equivalent to the telephone box at Chilton Leys at five-thirty. Just one of you.

If you don't, or if you call the police, you can find the bits all over Suffolk.' "

"Andy, I think she's going to faint."

"I'm all right," said Pauline. "If this is true, that toe . . ."

"But it isn't true," said Andy, spacing the words. "It's Reg having us on, as he does every year."

"Are you sure?"

"He'll turn up presently grinning all over his fat face. The best thing we can do is get on with the party."

There was little enthusiasm for unwrapping presents or eating over-cooked sausage, so they turned on the television and watched for a while.

"How could we possibly put our hands on ten thousand pounds on Christmas Day?" said Pauline during the commercial break.

"That's the giveaway," said Andy. "A professional kidnapper would know better."

"You've got three hundred in notes in your back pocket," said Gemma. "You know you have. You said we needed it over the holiday in case of emergencies."

"Three hundred is peanuts compared to ten grand."

"I've got about a hundred and twenty in my bag," said Gemma.

Geoff took out his wallet and counted the edges of his bank notes.

"Doesn't look as if Geoff can chip in much," said Andy.

Gemma said on a note of reproach, "Andy."

Andy said, "No offence, mate."

Geoff put his wallet away.

"Well, that's it. We couldn't afford to pay the kidnappers if they existed," Andy summed up. "How much do you have in the house, Pauline?"

"In cash? About two hundred."

"Less than eight hundred between us."

"But I've got a thousand in travellers' cheques for my holiday in Florida."

"Still a long way short," said Andy.

"Good thing it's only a hoax," said Gemma.

"There are my pearls," said Pauline, fingering them. "They cost over a thousand. And I have some valuable rings upstairs."

"If we're talking jewellery, Gemma's ruby necklace is the real thing," said Andy.

"So is your Rolex watch," Gemma countered. "And the gold ingot you wear under your shirt."

"I notice you haven't offered your earrings. They cost a bomb, if I remember right."

"Oh, shut up."

"Where the hell is Chilton Leys anyway?"

"Not far," said Pauline.

"I passed it on my way here," said Geoff.

They were silent for an interval. Then Andy said, "Well, has anyone spoken to Reg on the phone in the past twenty-four hours?"

"It must be a week since we spoke," said Pauline.

"What time is it?" said Gemma.

"Five past five."

"He would have been here by now," said Pauline. "Or if he had trouble with the car he would have phoned."

"Anyone care for another drink?" asked Andy.

"How many is that you've had already?" said Gemma.

"I want to say something," said Pauline.

"Feel free," said Andy, with the bottle in his hand.

She smoothed her skirt. "I'm not saying you're wrong, but if it wasn't a hoax and Reg really had been kidnapped, we could never forgive ourselves if these people murdered him because we did nothing about it."

"Come off it," said Andy.

"I mean, why are we refusing to respond to the note? Is it because we're afraid of making fools of ourselves? Is that all it is?"

"We don't believe it, that's why," said Gemma.

"You mean you don't want to run the risk of Reg having the last laugh? It's all about self-esteem, isn't it? How typical of our family—all inflated egos. We'd rather run the risk of Reg being murdered than lay ourselves open to ridicule."

"That isn't the point," said Andy. "We're calling his bluff."

"So you say. And if by some freak of circumstances you're mistaken, how will any of us live with it for the rest of our lives? I'm telling you, Andy, I'm frightened. I know what you're thinking. I can see it in your eyes. I'm gullible, a stupid, immature female. Well I don't mind admitting I'm bloody frightened. If none of you wants to take this seriously that's up to you. I do. I'm going to put all the money I have into a bag and take it to that phone box. If nobody comes, what have I lost? Some dignity, that's all. You can laugh at me every Christmas from now on. But I mean it." She stood up.

"Hold on," said Andy. "We've heard what you think. What about the rest of us?"

"It isn't quite the same for you, is it?" said Pauline. "He's my brother."

"He's Gemma's brother, too. And Geoff's."

Andy switched to his wife. "What do *you* want to do about it?"

Gemma hesitated.

"Or Geoff," said Andy. "Do you have an opinion, Geoff?"

Geoff's hand went to his collar as if it had tightened suddenly.

Gemma said, "Pauline is right. Ten to one it's Reg having us on, but we can't take the risk. We've got to do something."

Geoff nodded. He backed his sisters.

Pauline said, "I'm going upstairs to collect my jewellery, such as it is. We pool everything we have, right?"

"Right," said Gemma, unfixing her gold earrings and turning to Andy. "Do you want to be part of this, or not?"

Andy slapped his wad of bank notes on the table. "I don't believe in these kidnappers anyway."

"Let's have your watch, then," said Gemma. "And the ingot."

Geoff took out his wallet and emptied it.

The heap of money and valuables markedly increased when Pauline returned. She'd found some family heirlooms, including their grandmother's diamond-studded choker, worth several thousand alone. With her own pieces and the travellers' cheques, the collection must have come close to the value demanded in the note. She scooped everything into a denim bag with bamboo handles and said, "I'll get my coat."

Gemma told her, "Not you, sweetie. That's a job for one of the men."

Andy said, "Give the bag to me."

"You're not going anywhere," said Gemma. "You're way over the limit with all the brandy you've had. Besides, you don't know the way."

They turned to look at Geoff. He knew the way. He had said so.

"I'll go," he said, rising quite positively from the armchair. He looked a trifle unsteady in the upright position, but he'd been seated a long time. Maybe the brandy hadn't gone to his head. He had certainly drunk less than Andy.

Gemma still felt it necessary to ask, "Will you be all right?"

Geoff nodded. He had spoken. There was no need for more words.

Pauline asked, "Would you like me to come?"

Andy said, "The instruction was clear. If you believe it, Geoff's got to go alone."

In the hall, Pauline helped Geoff on with his padded jacket. "If you see anyone, don't take them on, will you? We just want you and Reg safely back."

Geoff looked incapable of taking anyone on as he shuffled across the gravel to his old Cortina, watched from the door by the others. He placed the bag on the passenger seat and got in.

"Is he sober?" Gemma asked.

"He only had a couple," said Andy.

"He looked just the same when he arrived," said Pauline. "He's had a hard time lately. So many businesses going bust. They don't need accountants."

Gemma said, "If anything happened to him just because Reg is acting the fool, I'd commit murder, I don't mind saying."

They heard the car start up and watched it trundle up the drive.

When the front door closed again, Gemma asked, "What time is it?"

"Twenty past," said Pauline. "He should just about make it."

Andy said, "I don't know why you two are taking this seriously. If I believed for a moment it was a genuine ransom demand I wouldn't have part-ed with three hundred pounds and a Rolex, I assure you."

"So what would you have done, cleverclogs?" said Gemma.

This wrongfooted Andy. He spread his hands wide as if the answer were too obvious to go into.

"Let's hear it," said Gemma. "Would you have called the police and put my brother's life at risk?"

"Certainly I'd have called them," said Andy, recovering his poise. "They have procedures for this sort of emergency. They'd know how to handle it without putting anyone's life at risk."

"For example?"

"Well, they'd observe the pickup from a distance. Probably they'd attach some tiny bugging device to the goods being handed over. They might coat some of the banknotes with a dye that responds to ultraviolet light."

Gemma turned to Pauline. "I'm wondering if we should call them."

Andy said, "It's too late. The police would have no option but to come down like a ton of bricks. Someone would get hurt."

Pauline said, "Oh God, no. Let's wait and see what happens."

"We won't have long to wait. That's one thing," said Andy. "You don't mind if I switch on the telly, Pauline?"

They sat in silence watching a cartoon film about a snowman.

Before it finished, Pauline went to the window and pulled back the cur-tain to look along the drive.

"See anything?" asked Gemma.

"No."

"How long has he been gone?"

"Twenty-five minutes. Chilton Leys is only ten minutes from here, if that. He ought to be back by now."

"Stop fussing, you two," said Andy. "You give me the creeps."

Just after six, Pauline announced, "A car's coming. I can see the head-lights."

"Okay," said Andy from his armchair. "What are we going to do about Reg when he pisses himself laughing and says it was a hoax?"

Pauline ran to the front door and opened it. Gemma was at her side.

"That isn't Geoff's Cortina," said Gemma. "It's a bigger car."

Without appearing to hurry, Andy joined them at the door. "That's Reg's

Volvo. Didn't I tell you he was all right?"

The car drew up beside Andy's and Reg got out, smiling. He was alone. "Where's the red carpet, then?" he called out. "Merry Christmas, everyone. Wait a mo. I've got some prezzies in the back." He dipped into his car again.

"You'd think nothing had happened," muttered Gemma.

Laden with presents, Reg strutted towards them. "Who gets to kiss me first, then?" He appeared unfazed, his well-known ebullient self.

Andy remarked. "He's walking normally. We've been suckered."

Gemma said, "You bastard, Reg. Don't come near me, you sadist."

Pauline shouted, "Dickhead."

Reg's face was a study in bewilderment.

Andy said, "Where's Geoff?"

"How would I know?" answered Reg. "Hey, what is this? What am I supposed to have done?"

"Pull the other one, matey," said Andy.

"You've ruined Christmas for all of us," said Pauline, succumbing to tears.

"I wish I knew what you were on about," said Reg. "Shall we go inside and find out?"

"You're not welcome," Pauline whimpered.

"Okay, okay," said Reg. "It's a fair cop and I deserve it after all the stunts I pulled. Who thought of unloading all this on me? Andy, I bet."

Suddenly Gemma said in a hollow voice, "Andy, I don't think he knows what this is about."

"What?"

"I know my own brother. He isn't bluffing. He didn't expect this. Listen, Reg did anyone kidnap you?"

"Kidnap me?"

"We'd better go inside, all of us," said Gemma.

"Kidnap me?" repeated Reg, when they were in Pauline's living room. "I'm gobsmacked."

Pauline said, "Andy found this parcel on my doorstep and—"

"Shut up a minute," said Andy. "You're playing into his hands. Let's hear his story before we tell him what happened here. You've got some answering to do, Reg. For a start, you're a couple of hours late."

Reg frowned. "You haven't been here all afternoon?"

"Of course we have. We were here by four o'clock."

"You didn't get the message, then?"

"What message?"

"I've been had then. Geoff phoned at lunchtime to say that Pauline's heating was off. A problem with the boiler. He said the party had been relocated to his place at five."

Pauline said, "There's nothing wrong with my boiler."

"Shut up and listen," said Gemma.

Reg continued, "I turned up at Geoff's house and there was a note for me attached to the door. Hold on—I should have it here." He felt in his pocket. "Yes, here it is." He handed Gemma an envelope with his name written on it.

She took out the note and read to the others, " 'Caught YOU this year. Now go to Pauline's and see what reception you get.' It's Geoff's handwriting."

"He's a slyboots," said Reg, "but I deserve it. He was pretty annoyed by the turkey episode last year."

"You're not the only victim," said Gemma.

"Were you sent on a wild-goose chase?"

"No. But I think he may have tricked us. He *must* have. He led us to believe you were kidnapped. That's why he went to this trouble to keep you away."

"Crafty old devil."

"He took ten grand off us," said Andy.

"What?"

"He persuaded us to put up a ransom for you."

"Now who are you kidding?"

"It's true," said Gemma. "We put together everything we had, cash, jewellery, family heirlooms, and Geoff went off to deliver it to the kidnappers."

"Strike me pink!"

"And he isn't back yet," said Andy.

Pauline said, "Geoff wouldn't rob his own family."

"Don't count on it," said Reg. "He doesn't give a toss for any of us."

"Geoff?"

"Did you know he's emigrating?"

"No."

"It's true," said Reg. "He's off to Australia any day now. I picked this up on the grapevine through a colleague in the bank. I think the accident made him reconsider his plan, so to speak."

"What accident?"

"There you are, you see. I only heard about that from the same source. Old Geoff was in hospital for over a week at the end of September and the last thing he wanted was a visit from any of us."

"A road accident?"

"No, he did it himself. You know how keen he is on the garden. He's got this turfed area sloping down to the pond. He ran the mower over his foot and severed his big toe."

Edward D. Hoch

THE THEFT OF
SANTA'S BEARD

The New York stores had closed at nine that evening, disgorging gift-laden Christmas shoppers by the hundreds. Most were too busy shifting the weight of their parcels and shopping bags to bother digging for coins as they passed the bell-ringing Santa on the corner. He was a bit thin and scraggly compared to the overstuffed Santas who worked the department stores and bounced tiny children on their knees while asking for their Christmas lists. His job was only to ring a little hand-held bell and accept donations in a chimney-shaped container.

This Santa's name was Russell Bajon and he'd come to the city expecting better things. After working at a variety of minimum-wage jobs and landing a couple of short-lived acting roles off Broadway, he'd taken the Santa Claus job for the holidays. There was no pay, but they supplied his meals and a place to sleep at night. And there were good fringe benefits, enough to keep him going till he was back on his feet with a part in a decent play.

After another fifteen minutes the crowd from the stores had pretty well scattered. There were still people on the dark streets, as there would be for most of the night, but those remaining hurried by his chimney without even a glance. He waited a few more minutes and then decided to pack up. The truck would be coming by shortly to collect the chimney and give him a ride back to the men's dorm where he slept.

He was bending over the chimney with its collection basket when someone bumped him from behind. He straightened and tried to turn, but by that time the thin copper wire was cutting into his throat.

By the time the second Santa Claus had been strangled to death, the tabloids had the story on page one. No Clues to Claus Killer, one of them trumpeted, while another proclaimed, Santa Strangler Strikes Again. Nick Velvet glanced over the articles with passing interest, but at that point they were nothing to directly affect him.

"Where was the latest killing?" Gloria asked as she prepared breakfast.

"In the subway. An elderly Santa on his way to work."

She shook her head. "What's this world coming to when somebody starts strangling Santa Clauses?"

The next morning Nick found out. He was seated in the office of the Intercontinental Protection Service, across the desk from a man named Grady Culhane. The office was small and somewhat plain, not what Nick had expected from the pretentious name. Culhane himself was young, barely past thirty, with black hair, thick eyebrows, and an Irish smile. He spread his hands flat on the uncluttered desktop and said, "I understand you steal things of little or no value."

"That's correct," Nick replied. "My standard fee is twenty-five thousand dollars, unless it's something especially hazardous."

"This should be simple enough. I want you to steal the beard from a department store Santa Claus. It's the Santa at Kliman's main store, and it must be done tomorrow before noon. Santa's hours there are noon to four and five to eight."

"What makes it so valuable to you?"

"Nothing. It's worth no more than any other false white beard. I just need it tomorrow."

"I usually get half the money down and the other half after the job," Nick said. "Is that agreeable?"

"Sure. It'll have to be a check. I don't have that much cash on hand."

"So long as I can cash it at your bank."

He made out the check and handed it over. "Here's a sketch map I drew of Kliman's fourth floor. This is the dressing room Santa uses."

"So the beard is probably there before noon. Why don't you just walk in and steal it?" Nick wondered. "Why do you need me?"

"You ever been in Kliman's? They've got security cameras all over the store, including hidden ones in the dressing rooms. This is only Santa's room during the Christmas season. The rest of the year it's used by the public, and the camera is probably still operational. I can't afford to be seen stealing the beard or anything else."

"What about me?"

"That's your job. That's what I'm paying you for."

"Fair enough," Nick agreed, folding the check once and slipping it into his pocket. "I'll be back here tomorrow with the beard."

Nothing had been said about the two Santa Claus killings, but somehow, as Nick Velvet left the building, he had the feeling he was becoming involved in something a lot more complex than a simple robbery.

The Santa Claus killings were still big news the following morning, and

Nick read the speculations about possible motives as he traveled into midtown on the subway. The second man to die, Larry Averly, was a retired plumber who'd been earning some spare cash as a holiday Santa Claus. The first victim, Bajon, had died on Monday evening, the fourteenth, while the second death came the following morning. Nick had the feeling the press was almost disappointed that another killing had not followed on Wednesday. Now it was Thursday, eight days before Christmas, and the street before Kliman's block-long department store was crowded with shoppers.

He entered the store with the first wave of customers when the doors opened at ten, making his way up the escalator to the fourth floor. After a half-hour of lingering in the furniture department, he wandered over to the dressing-room door that Grady Culhane had indicated on his map. When no one was looking, he slipped inside.

His first task was to locate the closed-circuit television camera. He found it without difficulty—a circular lens embedded in the very center of a round wall clock. Not wanting to blot out the view entirely and arouse the suspicion of possible observers, Nick moved a coat rack in front of the clock, blocking most of the little room. Then he quickly opened a pair of lockers. But there was no Santa Claus costume, no beard, in either one. He'd been hoping that the store's Santa changed into his costume on the premises, but it looked as if he might come to work already dressed, like the street Santa who'd been strangled in the subway.

If that was the case, however, Culhane wouldn't have told him to come to this room. It was already nearly eleven and Nick decided to wait till noon to see what happened. He positioned himself behind the clothes rack, but at the far end, away from the television camera. Exactly at eleven-thirty, the door opened and someone came in. He could see a tall, fairly broad-shouldered person carrying a large canvas tote bag. There was a flash of red as a Santa Claus suit came into view.

Nick Velvet breathed a sigh of relief. The white beard came out of the bag and he saw the prize within his grasp. He stepped from his hiding place, ready to deliver a knockout blow if necessary. "Keep quiet and give me the beard," he said.

The figure turned and Nick froze in his tracks. Santa was a woman.

She was probably in her late thirties, large boned but not unattractive, with dark brown hair that was already partly covered by the Santa Claus wig and cap. Nick's sudden appearance seemed not to have frightened her but only angered her as any unexpected interruption might. "You just made the mistake of your life, mister," she told him in a flat tone of voice.

"I don't want to hurt you. Give me that beard."

"I have a transmitter in my pocket. I've already called for help."

He realized suddenly that she thought he was the Santa strangler. "I'm not here to hurt you," he tried to assure her. .

But it was too late for assurances. The dressing-room door burst open and Nick faced two men with drawn revolvers. "Freeze!" the first man ordered, crouching in a shooter's stance. "Police!"

"Look, this is all a mistake."

"And you made it, mister!" The second man moved behind Nick to frisk him.

Nick decided it was time for a bit of his own electronic technology. He brought his left arm down enough to hit the small transmitter in his breast pocket. Immediately there was a sharp crack from the direction of the furniture department, and billowing smoke could be seen through the open dressing-room door. The first man turned his head and Nick kicked the gun from his hand, poking his elbow back simultaneously to catch the second detective in the ribs. As he went out the door he made a grab for the white beard the lady Santa was holding in her hand, but he missed by several inches.

"Stop or I'll shoot!" one of the detectives yelled, but Nick knew he wouldn't. The floor was crowded with shoppers, and the cloud from Nick's well-placed smoke bomb was already enveloping everyone.

Five minutes later he was out of the store and safely away, but without the beard he'd been hired to steal.

Later that afternoon Nick returned to the office of the Intercontinental Protection Service. Grady Culhane was not in a pleasant mood. "That was you at the store this morning, wasn't it?" he asked pointedly. "The radio says someone set off a smoke bomb and two shoppers were slightly injured in the panic."

"I'm sorry if anyone was hurt. You didn't tell me Santa Claus was a woman. That threw off my timing and enabled a couple of detectives to get the drop on me."

"What about the beard?"

"I didn't get it."

Culhane cursed. "That means Santa will be back in place as soon as they get the smoke cleared out and things back to normal."

Nick was beginning to see at least a portion of the scheme. "You wanted the beard stolen so Santa couldn't appear."

"Sure. It was easier than stealing the whole costume, except that you bungled it."

"They could have found another beard quickly enough," Nick argued.

Grady Culhane shook his head. "They don't sell them in the store. I checked. The delay would have been an hour or two, and that was all I needed."

"For what?"

He eyed Nick uncertainly for a moment before deciding to yield. "All right, I'll tell you about it. But I want something in return. I want that beard tomorrow, and no slip-ups this time!"

"You'll have it, so long as you play square with me. What's this all about? Does it involve the Santa Claus killings?"

The dark-haired young man reached into a desk drawer and extracted a sheet of paper which he passed across the desk to Nick. It was a copy of a crudely printed extortion letter addressed to the president of Kliman's department store: "Tuesday, December 15—I have just come from killing my second Santa Claus of the Christmas season. The deaths of Bajon and Averly were meant as a demonstration. A third Santa Claus will die in your store, in full view of the children, unless you are prepared to pay me one million dollars in cash within forty-eight hours, by noon Thursday." There was no signature.

"Sounds like a crackpot," Nick decided, returning the letter. "He doesn't even give directions for paying the money."

"This letter was hand-delivered by a messenger service Tuesday afternoon. A second letter came yesterday, with instructions. They haven't shown me that one."

"You've been hired by Kliman's store?"

Culhane nodded. "Frankly, it's the first major client I've had. Even though the police have been called in, the store is paying me as a personal bodyguard for Santa."

"Or Mrs. Santa."

He smiled. "She's an unemployed actress named Vivian Delmos. I just met her yesterday after I talked with you. There are some female Santas around. They're good with children. If their voices are deep enough and the suit is padded enough, no one knows the difference. I didn't know the cops would be guarding her too."

"How much are they paying you?" Nick asked.

"That's proprietary information," the young man answered stiffly.

"I figure fifty thousand, at least, if you can afford to pay me twenty-five."

"I don't get a thing if the Santa strangler kills her."

"You thought he'd strike right at noon, so you needed me to keep her from going out there then. That means they decided not to pay."

"It's not just them. There are other stores involved. The killer is trying to shake down the largest stores in New York."

"The police must have a description from the messenger company that delivered this note."

Grady Culhane shook his head. "They deny any knowledge of it. One of their messengers was probably stopped in the street and paid to deliver it.

Naturally he won't admit it now and risk losing his job."

"What happens after the smoke is cleared out?"

"The Delmos woman puts on her beard and goes back out there. I'll probably have to be standing next to her, and I'm too big for those elves' costumes."

"Don't worry," Nick promised. "This time I'll get the beard."

On his second visit to the store Nick Velvet wore a grey wig and a matching false moustache. He was taking no chances on coming face-to-face with one
of those detectives again. In the atrium at the center of the main floor where
Santa's throne was in place, a sign announced that he would not return until
noon the following day due to the illness of one of his reindeer. Nick found a
pay telephone and called Culhane at his office.

"You're off the hook until tomorrow," he said.

"I just heard from the store."

"Do you still want the beard?"

"Of course—unless the police come up with the extortionist by then."

Nick hung up and decided he should know more than he did about the
Santa Claus killings. He went down to the subway newsstand and bought all the
local papers. It wasn't the lead item anymore but the unsolved killings still filled
several columns inside each paper. The first victim, Russell Bajon, was a young
homeless man—a would-be actor—who'd been staying at the men's dorm maintained by a charitable organization. He'd been collecting money for the charity at
one of their Christmas chimneys when he'd been strangled. One of the other
Santas, a man named Chris Stover, had come by in a van a few minutes later to
find a crowd gathering around the fallen man. No one admitted to having seen
the actual killing.

The second victim had followed less than twelve hours later, on Tuesday
morning. Larry Averly lived in a rundown hotel on the fringes of Greenwich
Village, a place where Nick had grown up. His Christmas job as a Santa Claus for
a local radio station's holiday promotion involved coming to work in costume
that day, since they were doing a remote broadcast from the Central Park skating rink. He'd been heading for a subway exit near the park when the killer
struck. This time two people saw the attack and scared him off, but not in time
to save the victim. The killer was described as a white man of uncertain age wearing a bulky coat. Averly hadn't been carrying any identification in his shabby wallet and it had taken police most of the day to trace his room key to the hotel
where he'd been staying. The radio station had hired him through an employment agency and didn't even know his name. They'd finally learned it just in time
for the six o'clock news.

The papers, of course, carried nothing about the extortion plot. That would
have been enough to get the story back on page one. Nick read them all and

then tossed them aside. He had his own problem to consider. Stealing Santa's beard the following day would be next to impossible in Kliman's store, but the alternatives were equally impossible. He knew Vivian Delmos carried her costume to work in a large canvas bag, but he wasn't about to mug her on the way to work. Still . . .

Culhane had mentioned that the lady Santa Claus was an unemployed actress. Nick phoned Actors' Equity and had her address within minutes. Vivian Delmos resided on East Forty-ninth Street. He called her number and got the expected answering machine. Next he phoned Gloria to say that he wouldn't be home till late.

The address on Forty-ninth was past Third Avenue, in an apartment building across the street from the Turtle Bay block. The Delmos woman must have been successful at some stage of her career to afford the moderately high rents in the neighborhood. There was no answer to Nick's ring so he took up a position down the block on the other side of the street. Within twenty minutes he saw Vivian Delmos appear, walking briskly and carrying her canvas bag. He crossed the street to intercept her at her door, but she was a bit faster than he'd realized. She was halfway through the door by the time he reached it.

Blocking its closing with his hand, he began, "Miss Delmos—"

She turned, recognized him instantly, and acted without a word, yanking on his wrist and pulling him inside but off balance. He felt himself falling forward as she twisted his arm behind him. Then he was on the floor, his cheek pressed against the hall carpeting, while she pulled painfully on the arm. Her foot was on his neck.

"Mister, you just made your second big mistake. I hope you don't mind a broken arm."

"Wait a minute! I just want to talk!"

"How'd you find me? Did you follow me home?"

"Through Equity."

"Got a job for me?" She gave his arm a painful wrench. "I'm real good in action parts."

"I don't doubt it! Please let me up."

"Nice and slow," she warned, relaxing the pressure on his arm. "We're going upstairs while I call the police."

"All right."

She led him ahead of her up the stairs, keeping a grip on his arm. They paused outside a door at the top while she put down the canvas bag and got out her key. "Inside!"

The apartment was large but plainly furnished, as if in some sort of limbo while awaiting its permanent decor. "I'm not trying to kill you," Nick assured her. "When you saw me earlier I was only trying to steal your beard."

"My what?"

"The beard from your Santa Claus outfit."

She released his arm and gave him a shove toward the sofa. "What's your name?"

"Nick Velvet. I steal things." He decided to stay on the sofa for the moment. Facing her now, he had a chance to confirm his earlier impressions. She was into early middle age but still had a good figure. By the strength she'd shown in overpowering him, he guessed that she worked out regularly. It had been an unlucky day from the start.

"I'm Vivian Delmos, but I guess you know that. You called me by name." She walked to the phone without taking her eyes off him.

"I was hired to steal your beard," he told her. "You have nothing to fear from me."

"The people at Kliman's weren't too happy when you set off that smoke bomb."

"I only did it to escape. If I hadn't needed it I'd have returned later and removed it."

"What does all this have to do with the Santa strangler?"

"The killings are part of an extortion plot against the big department stores. My job was to keep you from being the next victim."

"By stealing my beard?" She gave a snort of disbelief. "Kliman's wanted to replace me with a cop but I wouldn't let them. I finally convinced everyone I could take care of myself, but they still made me carry that beeper. And this noon after you tried to attack me—"

"Steal your beard," Nick corrected.

"—steal my beard, they canceled Santa's appearances for the rest of the day. I lost a day's pay because of you!"

"Give me the beard and stay home tomorrow, too. I'll pay you a thousand dollars for it."

"Are you whacky or something?"

"Just a good businessman. I'm getting too old to be tossed around by a woman who works out at the gym every day."

"Three times a week," she corrected. "I'm an actress and I find it a good way to keep fit."

Nick worked his shoulder a bit, getting the kinks out. "It sure doesn't keep me fit. How about it? A thousand dollars?"

"They'll find another beard for me, or use the cop after all." She'd moved away from the phone at least, and Nick was thankful for that.

"It's the easiest money you'll ever make. Far easier than doing some off-Broadway play eight times a week."

"How'd you know I was off-Broadway?" she asked, immediately suspicious.

"I guessed. What difference does it make?"

"You didn't—" she began and then cut herself short. "Look, I'll agree to your condition if you do one thing for me."

"What's that?"

"I want you to go down to the men's dorm at the Outreach Center and pick up Russell Bajon's belongings."

"Bajon? The first victim?"

"That's right."

"Did you know him?"

"Slightly. We appeared in a play together."

Nick shook his head. "I don't understand any of this. What right do you have to his belongings?"

"As much right as anyone. The paper says he left no family."

"But why would you want his things?"

"Just to remember him by. He was a nice guy."

"Why can't you get them yourself?"

"I don't want people to see me there."

It was a weak reason, and her whole story was weak, but Nick was into it now. Unless he wanted to risk seriously injuring her, it seemed the only way to get the beard. "All right. I'll go down there now and then I'll be back for the beard."

Outside it had started to snow a little, but somehow it didn't seem much like the week before Christmas.

The Outreach Center was a sort of nondenominational mission located on the West Side near the river. Some of their operating expenses came from the city, but much of the money was from private donors. The Center gave homeless people a safe place to sleep if they were afraid of the city shelters, but certain rules applied. Drugs, alcohol, and weapons were forbidden, and guests of the Center were expected to earn their keep. In December that often meant dressing up in a Santa Claus suit and manning one of the Center's plywood chimneys with a donation bag inside.

The first person Nick saw as he entered the front door of the Outreach Center was a young man in sweater and jeans seated at an unpretentious card table. "I've come to pick up Russell Bajon's belongings," Nick told him. "The family sent me."

The young man seemed indifferent to the request. Apparently people who stayed at the men's dorm weren't expected to have anything worth stealing. "I'll get Chris."

Nick waited in the bare hallway until the young man returned with an older worker with thinning hair, wearing a faded Giants sweatshirt. "I'm Chris Stover. What can I do for you?"

"Russell Bajon's family sent me for his belongings."

The man frowned. "Didn't know he had a family. There sure wasn't much in the way of belongings. We were going to throw them out."

"Could I see them?"

Stover hesitated and then led him down the corridor to a storage room. For all its drabness, the dormitory building seemed to be well fitted for its clients, with a metal railing along the wall and smoke alarms in the ceiling. Nick stood by the door as Stover pulled out some boxes from one shelf in the storage room. "If I'd been five minutes earlier, Russ might be alive today," he said.

"I think I saw your name in the paper—"

"Sure! I placed him there and I was picking him up. When I rounded the corner I saw a crowd of people gathering. He was dead by the time I got to him."

"Nobody saw anything?"

"I guess not. Who pays attention in New York? I swear once I was driving by Radio City Music Hall about six in the morning, when they were having their Christmas show. Some guy was walking two camels around the block for their morning exercise and hardly anyone even noticed." He slit open the tape on one of the boxes and peered inside. "Nothing but clothing in here."

"I'll just take it along anyway."

When he opened the second box he frowned a bit. "Well, there are some letters in this one, and a couple of books." He looked up at Nick. "Maybe I should have some sort of authorization to release these."

"I can give you his sister's phone number." He'd worked that out with Vivian in advance. "You can check with her."

"Never heard about a sister," the man muttered. Then, "Our director is away today. I better wait till he gets back. Come back tomorrow."

"Sure thing." Nick turned to leave, his hand unobtrusively on the door's latchbolt. Stover shut the door and they walked back down the corridor together.

"See you later," the man told him and disappeared into a little office.

Immediately Nick turned and vaulted onto the handrail that ran along the wall, steadying himself with one hand against the ceiling, With his other hand he reached toward one of the smoke alarms. This model had a plastic button in the center of the unit for testing the battery, and he shoved a thin dime between the button and the casing, keeping it depressed. Immediately a loud blaring noise filled the hall. He jumped down to the floor as people began to look out of the rooms.

Some headed immediately for the exits while others stood around looking for some sign of smoke. Nick slipped into the storeroom just as Chris Stover emerged from his office to join the others. There was little chance of getting out with two boxes so Nick settled for the one containing the letters and books. He peeked down the hall and saw that Stover had gotten a ladder from somewhere to examine the blaring alarm. Perhaps he had noticed the edge of the dime holding the button in.

Nick went out the storeroom window as the smoke alarm was suddenly silenced.

Vivian Delmos seemed just a bit surprised to see him back so soon. "I thought you were going to get me Russell Bajon's things."

"I did. They're in this box. There was another box with a few pants and shirts, but I figured this was what you wanted."

"I'll know soon enough."

She opened the box and began looking through the objects, setting aside a worn pair of shoes and some socks and handkerchiefs. When she came to the books she examined them more carefully. One was a paperback edition of some of Shakespeare's tragedies, the others were a small dictionary and a book on acting. But she soon tossed these aside too, and turned only briefly to the letters, shaking the envelopes to make certain nothing small was hidden in them.

"You got the wrong box," she grumbled.

"I'm sorry."

She seemed to relent then. "No, what I'm looking for probably wasn't in the other box either. Somebody told me Bajon was involved with a shoplifting ring, stealing watches and jewelry from fancy stores during the Christmas season. I thought if he had anything in his belongings—"

"—that you'd take it?"

She flushed a bit at Nick's words. "I'm no thief. When Russell and I were in the play together I loaned him a few hundred dollars. I could use that money now. I figured anything I found among his belongings would pay the debt."

"Any jewelry or valuables he had were probably removed by whoever went through his clothes." As he spoke he was looking down at one of the envelopes that had been in the box. It was addressed to Russell Bajon at the Outreach Center. The return address bore only the surname of the sender: *Averly*.

It took him a few seconds to realize the significance of the name. The Santa strangler's second victim had been named Larry Averly. Nick slipped the letter out of the envelope and read the few lines quickly: "Russ—I was happy to do you the favor. No need to send me any more money. Keep some of the pie for yourself. Merry Christmas! Larry." The note was undated, but the envelope had been postmarked December second.

Nick returned the letter to its envelope and slipped it into his pocket. It told him nothing, except that the two victims might have known each other.

Maybe Bajon had replaced Averly as one of the Santas.

"Thanks for your efforts anyway," Vivian Delmos said.

"I did what I could."

When he didn't move, she asked, "Are you waiting for something more?"

"Yes."

"What's that?"

"Your beard."

That evening Nick returned to Grady Culhane's little office off Times Square. The young security man seemed uneasy as soon as he walked in the door. "I was hoping you wouldn't come here," he said.

Nick opened the paper bag he was carrying. "Why's that? I've brought you the beard."

"The beard was yesterday. Things have moved beyond that now. The cops are all over the place."

"What do you mean?"

"The extortion payoff. The money was left exactly as instructed, on the upper deck of the ferry that left Staten Island at three o'clock, before the evening rush hour. The police had it covered from every angle, even if he'd tossed the package overboard to a waiting boat."

"What happened?"

"Nothing. When the ferry docked in Manhattan some little old lady picked up the package and turned it in to lost and found."

"She got to it before the extortionist."

"Maybe," Culhane answered gloomily.

"What's the matter?"

"The Outreach Center reported that someone was snooping around the first victim's things this afternoon, and stole a box."

"That was me."

"I was afraid it might be. That means the cops are after you."

"How come?"

"They figure the killer was at the Outreach Center and that's why he couldn't pick up the extortion money from the three o'clock ferry."

"I certainly don't go around strangling Santas!" Nick objected. "You didn't even hire me till after the killings."

"I know, but try to tell them that! They need a fall guy, right away, or the city could lose millions in Christmas sales this final week. Who wants to bring the kids to see Santa Claus if he might be dead?"

A thought suddenly struck Nick. "You seemed nervous when I came in. Are they watching this office?"

"I had to tell them you were the one who set off the smoke bomb in the store yesterday. They were spending too much time on that angle and I tried to show them it was a dead end by admitting my part in it. Instead they got to thinking you were involved somehow."

"Just give me the rest of my money and I'm out of here."

"I don't have it right now."

Nick decided he'd overstayed his welcome. "I'll be in touch," he promised as he headed for the door.

They were waiting in the hall. A tall black man with a badge in one hand and a gun in the other barked, "Police! Up against the wall!"

His name was Sergeant Rynor and he was no more friendly within the confines of the precinct station. "You deny you were at the Outreach Center between three and four this afternoon, Mr. Velvet?"

"I told you I want a lawyer," Nick answered.

"He'll be here soon enough. And when he arrives we're going to run a lineup. Then we'll talk about the Santa Claus killings."

Ralph Aarons was a dapper Manhattan attorney whom Nick had used on rare occasions. He wasn't in the habit of getting in legal jams, especially in the New York area. Aarons made a good appearance, but he was hardly the sort to defend an accused serial Santa strangler.

"They've got a witness named Stover," the lawyer told him. "If he can place you at the Outreach Center, it may be trouble."

"We'll see," Nick said. He'd been thinking hard while he waited for Aarons to arrive.

Sergeant Rynor appeared in the doorway. "We're ready for you, Velvet. Up here on stage, please."

There were five other men, and Nick took the third position. The others were about his age and size but with different coloring and appearance. He guessed at least two of them were probably detectives. Chris Stover was brought in and escorted into a booth with a one-way glass. Over a loudspeaker, each of them was asked to step forward in turn. Then it was over. Apparently it had taken only a moment for Stover to identify him.

As Nick was being led away, Chris Stover and the other detectives came out of the booth. Nick paused ten feet from him and pointed dramatically. "That's the man!" his voice thundered like the wrath of God. "He's the one who killed the Santas and I can prove it!"

Nick couldn't prove it, and Chris Stover should have snorted and kept on walking. But he was taken off guard, startled into a foolish action. Perhaps in that unthinking instant he imagined the whole lineup had been merely a trick to unmask him. He gave one terrified glance at Nick and then tried to run, shoving two detectives out of the way in his dash for freedom.

It was Sergeant Rynor who finally grabbed him, before he even got close to the door.

"We're holding him," the black detective told Nick Velvet ten minutes later in the interrogation room, "but you'd better have a good story. Are you trying to tell us that Chris Stover is the extortionist who's been threatening the city's department stores for the past several days?"

"I don't think there was ever a real extortion plot. It was a matter of a big threat being used as a smokescreen to hide a smaller but no less deadly crime— the murders of Russell Bajon and Larry Averly."

"You'd better explain that."

Nick leaned back in the chair and collected his thoughts. "Grady Culhane told me about the extortion threats and even showed me a copy of the first letter. It was delivered to Kliman's president on Tuesday afternoon, shortly after the second strangling of a Santa Claus. Those two killings were meant to appear to be random acts against two random Santas, committed as a demonstration that the extortionist meant business. But the note mentioned the names of the two victims—Bajon and Averly. You didn't identify the second victim until later that day, and the killer had no chance to steal identification from his victim. The strangler knew the names of Bajon and Averly because these killings weren't random at all. He deliberately selected these victims, not as part of an extortion plot but for another motive altogether."

Rynor was making notes now, along with taping Nick's interrogation. Ralph Aarons, perhaps sensing things were going well for Nick, made no attempt to interrupt. "What other motive?" the detective asked.

"I learned earlier today that Bajon might have been involved in a shoplifting ring. And I also have a letter here that the second victim sent to Bajon two weeks ago. Not only did they know each other, but Averly had arranged for Bajon to take over some money-making enterprise from him. I think you'll find that Averly used to act as a Santa Claus for the Outreach Center. This year he passed the job on to Bajon, who became involved with the shoplifting."

"You're telling me that a man dressed in a bulky and highly visible Santa Claus costume was shoplifting?"

"No, I'm telling you that Santa stood on the corner with his collection chimney and the shoplifters came out of the stores with watches, rings, and other jewelry, and dropped them in the chimney. If the man was caught, there was no evidence on him, and the store detectives never considered Santa as an accessory."

"It's just wild enough to be true. But why would Stover kill them?"

"Bajon must have been skimming off the loot, or threatening to blackmail Stover. Once he decided to kill Bajon, he knew he had to kill Averly too, because the older man knew what was going on. When I guessed about Santa's chimney

893

being used for shoplifting loot, Chris Stover became the most likely brains behind the operation. After all, he was the one who picked up the Santas and chimneys each night. He was the one who told them where to stand. Only Monday night he parked the van in the next block and walked up and strangled Bajon, then hurried back to the van and acted like he was just driving up."

"Maybe," Sergeant Rynor said thoughtfully. "It could have been like that. The extortion letter was just a red herring to cover the real motive. He never had any intention of going after that money on the Staten Island ferry."

"Can you prove all this?" Aarons asked, his legal mind in gear.

"We'll get a search warrant for Stover's office and room at the Center. If we find any shoplifted items there, I think he'll be ready to talk, and name the rest of the gang."

Nick knew he wasn't off the hook unless they found what they were looking for, but he came up lucky. The police uncovered dozens of jewelry items, along with a spool of wire that matched the wire used to kill the two Santas. After that, Chris Stover ceased his denials.

The way things turned out, Nick never did collect the balance of his fee from Grady Culhane. Some people just didn't have any Christmas spirit.

Georges Simenon

A MATTER OF LIFE
AND DEATH

"At home we always used to go to Midnight Mass. I can't remember a Christmas when we missed it, though it meant a good half hour's drive from the farm to the village."

The speaker, Sommer, was making some coffee on a little electric stove.

"There were five of us," he went on. "Five boys, that is. The winters were colder in those days. Sometimes we had to go by sledge."

Lecœur, on the switchboard, had taken off his earphones to listen. "In what part of the country was that?"

"Lorraine."

"The winters in Lorraine were no colder thirty or forty years ago than they are now—only, of course, in those days the peasant had no cars. How many times did you go to Midnight Mass by sledge?"

"Couldn't say, exactly."

"Three times? Twice? Perhaps no more than once. Only it made a great impression on you, as you were a child."

"Anyhow, when we got back, we'd all have black pudding, and I'm not exaggerating when I tell you I've never had anything like it since. I don't know what my mother used to put in them, but her *boudins* were quite different from anyone else's. My wife's tried, but it wasn't the same thing, though she had the exact recipe from my eldest sister—at least, my sister swore it was."

He walked over to one of the huge, uncurtained windows, through which was nothing but blackness, and scratched the pane with a fingernail.

"Hallo, there's frost forming. That again reminds me of when I was little. The water used to freeze in our rooms and we'd have to break the ice in the morning when we wanted to wash."

"People didn't have central heating in those days," answered Lecœur coolly.

There were three of them on night duty. *Les nuiteux*, they were called. They had been in that vast room since eleven o'clock, and now, at six on that

Christmas morning, all three were looking a bit jaded. Three or four empty bottles were lying about, with the remains of the sandwiches they had brought with them.

A lamp no bigger than an aspirin tablet lit up on one of the walls. Its position told Lecœur at once where the call came from.

"Thirteenth Arrondissement, Croulebarbe," he murmured, replacing his earphones. He seized a plug and pushed it into a hole.

"Croulebarbe? Your car's been called out—what for?"

"A call from the Boulevard Masséna. Two drunks fighting."

Lecœur carefully made a little cross in one of the columns of his notebook.

"How are you getting on down your way?"

"There are only four of us here. Two are playing dominoes."

"Had any *boudin* tonight?"

"No. Why?"

"Never mind. I must ring off now. There's a call from the Sixteenth."

A gigantic map of Paris was drawn on the wall in front of him and on it each police station was represented by a little lamp. As soon as anything happened anywhere, a lamp would light up and Lecœur would plug into the appropriate socket.

"Chaillot? Hallo! Your car's out?"

In front of each police station throughout the twenty arrondissements of Paris, one or more cars stood waiting, ready to dash off the moment an alarm was raised.

"What with?"

"Veronal."

That would be a woman. It was the third suicide that night, the second in the smart district of Passy.

Another little cross was entered in the appropriate column of Lecœur's notebook. Mambret, the third member of the watch, was sitting at a desk filling out forms.

"Hallo! Odéon? What's going on? Oh, a car stolen."

That was for Mambret, who took down the particulars, then phoned them through to Piedbœuf in the room above. Piedbœuf, the teleprinter operator, had such a resounding voice that the others could hear it through the ceiling. This was the forty-eighth car whose details he had circulated that night.

An ordinary night, in fact—for them. Not so for the world outside. For this was the great night, *la nuit de Noël*. Not only was there the Midnight Mass, but all the theaters and cinemas were crammed, and at the big stores, which stayed open till twelve, a crowd of people jostled each other in a last-minute scramble to finish off their Christmas shopping.

Indoors were family gatherings feasting on roast turkey and perhaps also on *boudins* made, like the ones Sommer had been talking about, from a secret recipe handed down from mother to daughter.

There were children sleeping restlessly while their parents crept about playing the part of Santa Claus, arranging the presents they would find on waking.

At the restaurants and cabarets every table had been booked at least a week in advance. In the Salvation Army barge on the Seine, tramps and paupers queued up for an extra special.

Sommer had a wife and five children. Piedbœuf, the teleprinter operator upstairs, was a father of one week's standing. Without the frost on the windowpanes, they wouldn't have known it was freezing outside. In that vast, dingy room they were in a world apart, surrounded on all sides by the empty offices of the Préfecture de Police, which stood facing the Palais de Justice. It wasn't till the following day that those offices would once again be teeming with people in search of passport visas, driving licenses, and permits of every description.

In the courtyard below, cars stood waiting for emergency calls, the men of the flying squad dozing on the seats. Nothing, however, had happened that night of sufficient importance to justify their being called out. You could see that from the little crosses in Lecœur's notebook. He didn't bother to count them, but he could tell at a glance that there were something like two hundred in the drunks' column.

No doubt there'd have been a lot more if it hadn't been that this was a night for indulgence. In most cases the police were able to persuade those who had had too much to go home and keep out of trouble. Those arrested were the ones in whom drink raised the devil, those who smashed windows or molested other people.

Two hundred of that sort—a handful of women among them—were now out of harm's way, sleeping heavily on the wooden benches in the lockups.

There'd been five knifings. Two near the Porte d'Italie. Three in the remoter part of Montmartre, not in the Montmartre of the Moulin Rouge and the Lapin Agile but in the Zone, beyond where the Fortifs used to be, whose population included over 100,000 Arabs living in huts made of old packing cases and roofing-felt.

A few children had been lost in the exodus from the churches, but they were soon returned to their anxious parents.

"Hallo! Chaillot? How's your veronal case getting on?"

She wasn't dead. Of course not! Few went as far as that. Suicide is all very well as a gesture—indeed, it can be a very effective one. But there's no need to go and kill yourself!

"Talking of *boudin*," said Mambret, who was smoking an enormous meerschaum pipe, "that reminds me of—"

They were never to know what he was reminded of. There were steps in the corridor, then the handle of the door was turned. All three looked round at once, wondering who could be coming to see them at ten past six in the morning.

"*Salut!*" said the man who entered, throwing his hat down on a chair.

"Whatever brings you here, Janvier?"

It was a detective of the Brigade des Homicides, who walked straight to the stove to warm his hands.

"I got pretty bored sitting all by myself and I thought I might as well come over here. After all, if the killer's going to do his stuff I'd hear about it quicker here than anywhere."

He, too, had been on duty all night, but round the corner, in the Police Judiciaire.

"You don't mind, do you?" he asked, picking up the coffeepot. "There's a bitter wind blowing."

It had made his ears red.

"I don't suppose we'll hear till eight, probably later," said Lecœur.

For the last fifteen years, he had spent his nights in that room, sitting at the switchboard, keeping an eye on the big map with the little lamps. He knew half the police in Paris by name, or, at any rate, those who did night duty. Of many he knew even their private affairs, as, when things were quiet, he would have long chats with them over the telephone to pass the time away. "Oh, it's you, Dumas. How are things at home?"

But though there were many whose voices were familiar, there were hardly any of them he knew by sight.

Nor was his acquaintance confined to the police. He was on equally familiar terms with many of the hospitals.

"Hallo! Bichat? What about the chap who was brought in half an hour ago? Is he dead yet?"

He was dead, and another little cross went into the notebook. The latter was, in its unpretentious way, quite a mine of information. If you asked Lecœur how many murders in the last twelve months had been done for the sake of money, he'd give the answer in a moment—sixty-seven.

"How many murders committed by foreigners?"

"Forty-two. "

You could go on like that for hours without being able to trip him up. And yet he trotted out his figures without a trace of swank. It was his hobby, that was all.

For he wasn't obliged to make those crosses. It was his own idea. Like the chats over the telephone lines, they helped to pass the time away, and the result gave him much the same satisfaction that others derive from a collection of stamps.

He was unmarried. Few knew where he lived or what sort of a life he led outside that room. It was difficult to picture him anywhere else, even to think of him walking along the street like an ordinary person. He turned to Janvier to say: "For your cases, we generally have to wait till people are up and about. It's when a concierge goes up with the post or when a maid takes her mistress's breakfast into the bedroom that things like that come to light."

He claimed no special merit in knowing a thing like that. It was just a fact. A bit earlier in summer, of course, and later in winter. On Christmas Day probably later still, as a considerable part of the population hadn't gotten to bed until two or even later, to say nothing of their having to sleep off a good many glasses of champagne.

Before then, still more water would have gone under the bridge—a few more stolen cars, a few belated drunks.

"Hallo! Saint-Gervais?"

His Paris was not the one known to the rest of us—the Eiffel Tower, the Louvre, the Opéra—but one of somber, massive buildings with a police car waiting under the blue lamp and the bicycles of the *agents cyclistes* leaning against the wall.

"The chief is convinced the chap'll have another go tonight," said Janvier. "It's just the night for people of that sort. Seems to excite them."

No name was mentioned, for none was known. Nor could he be described as the man in the fawn raincoat or the man in the grey hat, since no one had ever seen him. For a while the papers had referred to him as Monsieur Dimanche, as his first three murders had been on Sunday, but since then five others had been on weekdays, at the rate of about one a week, though not quite regularly.

"It's because of him you've been on all night, is it?" asked Mambret.

Janvier wasn't the only one. All over Paris extra men were on duty, watching or waiting.

"You'll see," put in Sommer, "when you do get him you'll find he's only a loony."

"Loony or not, he's killed eight people," sighed Janvier, sipping his coffee. "Look, Lecœur—there's one of your lamps burning."

"Hallo! Your car's out? What's that? Just a moment."

They could see Lecœur hesitate, not knowing in which column to put a cross. There was one for hangings, one for those who jumped out of the window, another for—

"Here, listen to this. On the Pont d'Austerlitz, a chap climbed up onto the parapet. He had his legs tied together and a cord round his neck with the end made fast to a lamppost, and as he threw himself over he fired a shot into his head!"

"Taking no risks, what? And which column does that one go into?"

"There's one for neurasthenics. We may as well call it that."

Those who hadn't been to Midnight Mass were now on their way to early service. With hands thrust deep in their pockets and drops on the ends of their noses, they walked bent forward into the cutting wind, which seemed to blow up a fine, icy dust from the pavements. It would soon be time for the children to be waking up, jumping out of bed, and gathering barefoot around lighted Christmas trees.

"But it's not at all sure the fellow's mad. In fact, the experts say that if he was he'd always do it the same way. If it was a knife, then it would always be a knife."

"What did he use this time?"

"A hammer."

"And the time before?"

"A dagger."

"What makes you think it's the same chap?"

"First of all, the fact that there've been eight murders in quick succession. You don't get eight new murderers cropping up in Paris all at once." Belonging to the Police Judiciaire, Janvier had, of course, heard the subject discussed at length. "Besides, there's a sort of family likeness between them all. The victims are invariably solitary people, people who live alone, without any family or friends."

Sommer looked at Lecœur, whom he could never forgive for not being a family man. Not only had he five children himself, but a sixth was already on the way. "You'd better look out, Lecœur—you see the kind of thing it leads to!"

"Then, not one of the crimes has been committed in one of the wealthier districts."

"Yet he steals, doesn't he?"

"He does, but not much. The little hoards hidden under the mattress— that's his mark. He doesn't break in. In fact, apart from the murder and the money missing, he leaves no trace at all."

Another lamp burning. A stolen car found abandoned in a little side street near the Place des Ternes.

"All the same, I can't help laughing over the people who had to walk home."

Another hour or more and they would be relieved, except Lecœur, who had promised to do the first day shift as well so that his opposite number could join in a family Christmas party somewhere near Rouen.

It was a thing he often did, so much so that he had come to be regarded as an ever-ready substitute for anybody who wanted a day off.

"I say, Lecœur, do you think you could look out for me on Friday?"

At first the request was proffered with a suitable excuse—a sick mother, a funeral, or a First Communion, and he was generally rewarded with a bottle of wine. But now it was taken for granted and treated quite casually.

To tell the truth, had it been possible, Lecœur would have been only too glad to spend his whole life in that room, snatching a few hours' sleep on a camp bed and picnicking as best he could with the aid of the little electric stove. It was a funny thing—although he was as careful as any of the others about his personal appearance, and much more so than Sommer, who always looked a bit tousled, there was something a bit drab about him which betrayed the bachelor.

He wore strong glasses, which gave him big, globular eyes, and it came as a surprise to everyone when he took them off to wipe them with the bit of chamois leather he always carried about to see the transformation. Without them, his eyes were gentle, rather shy, and inclined to look away quickly when anyone looked his way.

"Hallo! Javel?"

Another lamp. One near the Quai de Javel in the 15th Arrondissement, a district full of factories.

"*Votre car est sorti?*"

"We don't know yet what it is. Someone's broken the glass of the alarm in the Rue Leblanc."

"Wasn't there a message?"

"No. We've sent our car to investigate. I'll ring you again later."

Scattered here and there all over Paris are red-painted telephone pillars standing by the curb, and you have only to break the glass to be in direct telephone communication with the nearest police station. Had a passerby broken the glass accidentally? It looked like it, for a couple of minutes later Javel rang up again.

"Hallo! Central? Our car's just got back. Nobody about. The whole district seems quiet as the grave. All the same, we've sent out a patrol."

How was Lecœur to classify that one? Unwilling to admit defeat, he put a little cross in the column on the extreme right headed "Miscellaneous."

"Is there any coffee left?" he asked.

"I'll make some more."

The same lamp lit up again, barely ten minutes after the first call.

"Javel? What's it this time?"

"Same again. Another glass broken."

"Nothing said?"

"Not a word. Must be some practical joker. Thinks it funny to keep us on the hop. When we catch him he'll find out whether it's funny or not!"

"Which one was it?"

"The one on the Pont Mirabeau."

"Seems to walk pretty quickly, your practical joker!"

There was indeed quite a good stretch between the two pillars.

So far, nobody was taking it very seriously. False alarms were not uncommon. Some people took advantage of these handy instruments to express their feelings about the police. *"Mort aux flics!"* was the favorite phrase.

With his feet on a radiator, Janvier was just dozing off when he heard Lecœur telephoning again. He half opened his eyes, saw which lamp was on, and muttered sleepily, "There he is again."

He was right. A glass broken at the top of the Avenue de Versailles.

"Silly ass," he grunted, settling down again.

It wouldn't be really light until half past seven or even eight. Sometimes they could hear a vague sound of church bells, but that was in another world. The wretched men of the flying squad waiting in the cars below must be half frozen.

"Talking of *boudin*—"

"What *boudin*?" murmured Janvier, whose cheeks were flushed with sleep.

"The one my mother used to—"

"Hallo! What? You're not going to tell me someone's smashed the glass of one of your telephone pillars? Really? It must be the same chap. We've already had two reported from the Fifteenth. Yes, they tried to nab him but couldn't find a soul about. Gets about pretty fast, doesn't he? He crossed the river by the Pont Mirabeau. Seems to be heading in this direction. Yes, you may as well have a try."

Another little cross. By half past seven, with only half an hour of the night watch to go, there were five crosses in the Miscellaneous column.

Mad or sane, the person was a good walker. Perhaps the cold wind had something to do with it. It wasn't the weather for sauntering along.

For a time it had looked as though he was keeping to the right bank of the Seine, then he had sheered off into the wealthy Auteuil district, breaking a glass in the Rue la Fontaine.

"He's only five minutes' walk from the Bois de Boulogne," Lecœur had said. "If he once gets there, they'll never pick him up."

But the fellow had turned round and made for the quays again, breaking a glass in the Rue Berton, just around the corner from the Quai de Passy.

The first calls had come from the poorer quarters of Grenelle, but the man had only to cross the river to find himself in entirely different surroundings—quiet, spacious, and deserted streets, where his footfalls must have rung out clearly on the frosty pavements.

Sixth call. Skirting the Place du Trocadéro, he was in the Rue de Longchamp.

"The chap seems to think he's on a paper chase," remarked Mambret. "Only he uses broken glass instead of paper."

Other calls came in in quick succession. Another stolen car, a revolver-shot in the Rue de Flandres, whose victim swore he didn't know who fired it, though he'd been seen all through the night drinking in company with another man.

"Hallo! Here's Javel again. Hallo! Javel? It can't be your practical joker this time: he must be somewhere near the Champs Elysées by now. Oh, yes. He's still at it. Well, what's your trouble? What? Spell it, will you? Rue Michat. Yes, I've got it. Between the Rue Lecourbe and the Boulevard Felix Faure. By the viaduct—yes, I know. Number 17. Who reported it? The concierge? She's just been up, I suppose. Oh, shut up, will you! No, I wasn't speaking to you. It's Sommer here, who can't stop talking about a *boudin* he ate thirty years ago!"

Sommer broke off and listened to the man on the switchboard.

"What were you saying? A shabby seven-story block of flats. Yes—"

There were plenty of buildings like that in the district, buildings that weren't really old, but of such poor construction that they were already dilapidated. Buildings that as often as not thrust themselves up bleakly in the middle of a bit of wasteland, towering over the little shacks and hovels around them, their blind walls plastered with advertisements.

"You say she heard someone running downstairs and then a door slam. The door of the house, I suppose. On which floor is the flat? The *entresol*. Which way does it face? Onto an inner courtyard— Just a moment, there's a call coming in from the Eighth. That must be our friend of the telephone pillars."

Lecœur asked the new caller to wait, then came back to Javel.

"An old woman, you say. Madame Fayet. Worked as charwoman. Dead? A blunt instrument. Is the doctor there? You're sure she's dead? What about her money? I suppose she had some tucked away somewhere. Right. Call me back. Or I'll ring you."

He turned to the detective, who was now sleeping soundly.

"Janvier! Hey, Janvier! This is for you."

"What? What is it?"

"The killer."

"Where?"

"Near the Rue Lecourbe. Here's the address. This time he's done in an old charwoman, a Madame Fayet."

Janvier put on his overcoat, looked round for his hat, and gulped down the remains of the coffee in his cup.

"Who's dealing with it?"

"Gonesse, of the Fifteenth."

"Ring up the P.J., will you, and tell them I've gone there."

A minute or two later, Lecœur was able to add another little cross to the six that were already in the column. Someone had smashed the glass of the pillar in the Avenue d'Iéna only one hundred and fifty yards from the Arc de Triomphe.

"Among the broken glass they found a handkerchief flecked with blood. It was a child's handkerchief."

"Has it got initials?"

"No. It's a blue-check handkerchief, rather dirty. The chap must have wrapped it round his knuckles for breaking the glass."

There were steps in the corridor. The day shift coming to take over. They looked very clean and close-shaven and the cold wind had whipped the blood into their cheeks.

"Happy Christmas!"

Sommer closed the tin in which he brought his sandwiches. Mambret knocked out his pipe. Only Lecœur remained in his seat, since there was no relief for him.

The fat Godin had been the first to arrive, promptly changing his jacket for the grey-linen coat in which he always worked, then putting some water on to boil for his grog. All through the winter he suffered from one never-ending cold which he combated, or perhaps nourished, by one hot grog after another.

"Hallo! Yes, I'm still here. I'm doing a shift for Potier, who's gone down to his family in Normandy. Yes. I want to hear all about it. Most particularly. Janvier's gone, but I'll pass it on to the P.J. An invalid, you say? What invalid?"

One had to be patient on that job, as people always talked about their cases as though everyone else was in the picture.

"A low building behind, right. Not in the Rue Michat, then? Rue Vasco de Gamma. Yes, yes. I know. The little house with a garden behind some railings. Only I didn't know he was an invalid. Right. He doesn't sleep much. Saw a young boy climbing up a drainpipe? How old? He couldn't say? Of course not, in the dark. How did he know it was a boy, then? Listen, ring me up again, will you? Oh, you're going off. Who's relieving you? Jules? Right. Well, ask him to keep me informed."

"What's going on?" asked Godin.

"An old woman who's been done in. Down by the Rue Lecourbe."

"Who did it?"

"There's an invalid opposite who says he saw a small boy climbing up a drainpipe and along the top of a wall."

"You mean to say it was a boy who killed the old woman?"

"We don't know yet."

No one was very interested. After all, murders were an everyday matter to these people. The lights were still on in the room, as it was still only a bleak, dull daylight that found its way through the frosty window panes. One of the new watch went and scratched a bit of the frost away. It was instinctive. A childish memory perhaps, like Sommer's *boudin*.

The latter had gone home. So had Mambret. The newcomers settled down to their work, turning over the papers on their desks.

A car stolen from the Square la Bruyère.

Lecœur looked pensively at his seven crosses. Then, with a sigh, he got up and stood gazing at the immense street plan on the wall.

"Brushing up on your Paris?"

"I think I know it pretty well already. Something's just struck me. There's a chap wandering about smashing the glass of telephone pillars. Seven in the last hour and a half. He hasn't been going in a straight line but zigzagging— first this way, then that."

"Perhaps he doesn't know Paris."

"Or knows it only too well! Not once has he ventured within sight of a police station. If he'd gone straight, he'd have passed two or three. What's more, he's skirted all the main crossroads where there'd be likely to be a man on duty." Lecœur pointed them out. "The only risk he took was in crossing the Pont Mirabeau, but if he wanted to cross the river he'd have run that risk at any of the bridges."

"I expect he's drunk," said Godin, sipping his rum.

"What I want to know is why he's stopped."

"Perhaps he's got home."

"A man who's down by the Quai de Javel at half past six in the morning isn't likely to live near the Etoile."

"Seems to interest you a lot."

"It's got me scared!"

"Go on."

It was strange to see the worried expression on Lecœur's face. He was notorious for his calmness and his most dramatic nights were coolly summarized by the little crosses in his notebook.

"Hallo! Javel? Is that Jules? Lecœur speaking. Look here, Jules, behind the flats in the Rue Michat is the little house where the invalid lives. Well, now, on one side of it is an apartment house, a red-brick building with a grocer's shop on the ground floor. You know it?

"Good. Has anything happened there? Nothing reported. No, we've heard nothing here. All the same, I can't explain why, but I think you ought to inquire."

He was hot all at once. He stubbed out a half finished cigarette.

"Hallo! Ternes? Any alarms gone off in your neighborhood? Nothing? Only drunks? Is the *patrouille cycliste* out? Just leaving? Ask them to keep their eyes open for a young boy looking tired and very likely bleeding from the right hand. Lost? Not exactly that. I can't explain now."

His eyes went back to the street plan on the wall, in which no light went on for a good ten minutes, and then only for an accidental death in the Eighteenth Arrondissement, right up at the top of Montmartre, caused by an escape of gas.

Outside, in the cold streets of Paris, dark figures were hurrying home from the churches . . .

One of the sharpest impressions Andre Lecœur retained of his infancy was one of immobility. His world at that period was a large kitchen in Orleans, on the outskirts of the town. He must have spent his winters there, too, but he remembered it best flooded with sunlight, with the door wide open onto a little garden where hens clucked incessantly and rabbits nibbled lettuce leaves behind the wire netting of their hutches. But, if the door was open, its passage was barred to him by a little gate which his father had made one Sunday for that express purpose.

On weekdays, at half past eight, his father went off on his bicycle to the gas works at the other end of the town. His mother did the housework, doing the same things in the same order every day. Before making the beds, she put the bedclothes over the windowsill for an hour to air.

At ten o'clock, a little bell would ring in the street. That was the greengrocer, with his barrow, passing on his daily round. Twice a week at eleven, a bearded doctor came to see his little brother, who was constantly ill. Andre hardly ever saw the latter, as he wasn't allowed into his room.

That was all, or so it seemed in retrospect. He had just time to play a bit and drink his milk, and there was his father home again for the midday meal.

If nothing had happened at home, lots had happened to him. He had been to read the meters in any number of houses and chatted with all sorts of people, about whom he would talk during dinner.

As for the afternoon, it slipped away quicker still, perhaps because he was made to sleep during the first part of it.

For his mother, apparently, the time passed just as quickly. Often had he heard her say with a sigh: "There, I've no sooner washed up after one meal than it's time to start making another!"

Perhaps it wasn't so very different now. Here in the Préfecture de Police the nights seemed long enough at the time, but at the end they seemed to have slipped by in no time, with nothing to show for them except for these columns of the little crosses in his notebook.

A few more lamps lit up. A few more incidents reported, including a collision between a car and a bus in the Rue de Clignancourt, and then once again it was Javel on the line.

It wasn't Jules, however, but Gonesse, the detective who'd been to the scene of the crime. While there he had received Lecœur's message suggesting something might have happened in the other house in the Rue Vasco de Gama. He had been to see.

"Is that you, Lecœur?" There was a queer note in his voice. Either irritation or suspicion.

"Look here, what made you think of that house? Do you know the old woman, Madame Fayet?"

"I've never seen her, but I know all about her."

What had finally come to pass that Christmas morning was something that Andre Lecœur had foreseen and perhaps dreaded for more than ten years. Again and again, as he stared at the huge plan of Paris, with its little lamps, he had said to himself, "It's only a question of time. Sooner or later, it'll be something that's happened to someone I know."

There'd been many a near miss, an accident in his own street or a crime in a house nearby. But, like thunder, it had approached only to recede once again into the distance.

This time it was a direct hit.

"Have you seen the concierge?" he asked. He could imagine the puzzled look on the detective's face as he went on: "Is the boy at home?"

And Gonesse muttered, "Oh? So you know him, too?"

"He's my nephew. Weren't you told his name was Lecœur?"

"Yes, but—"

"Never mind about that. Tell me what's happened."

"The boy's not there."

"What about his father?"

"He got home just after seven."

"As usual. He does night work, too."

"The concierge heard him go up to his flat—on the third floor at the back of the house."

"I know it."

"He came running down a minute or two later in a great state. To use her expression, he seemed out of his wits."

"The boy had disappeared?"

"Yes. His father wanted to know if she'd seen him leave the house. She hadn't. Then he asked if a telegram had been delivered."

"Was there a telegram?"

"No. Can you make head or tail of it? Since you're one of the family, you might be able to help us. Could you get someone to relieve you and come round here?"

"It wouldn't do any good. Where's Janvier?"

"In the old woman's room. The men of the Identité Judiciaire have already got to work. The first thing they found were some child's fingerprints on the handle of the door. Come on—jump into a taxi and come round."

"No. In any case, there's no one to take my place."

That was true enough up to a point. All the same, if he'd really got to work on the telephone he'd have found someone all right. The truth was he didn't want to go and didn't think it would do any good if he did.

"Listen, Gonesse, I've got to find that boy, and I can do it better from here than anywhere. You understand, don't you? Tell Janvier I'm staying here. And tell him old Madame Fayet had plenty of money, probably hidden away somewhere in the room."

A little feverish, Lecœur stuck his plug into one socket after another, calling up the various police stations of the Eighth Arrondissement.

"Keep a lookout for a boy of ten, rather poorly dressed. Keep all telephone pillars under observation."

His two fellow-watchkeepers looked at him with curiosity.

"Do you think it was the boy who did the job?"

Lecœur didn't bother to answer. The next moment he was through to the teleprinter room, where they also dealt with radio messages.

"Justin? Oh, you're on, are you? Here's something special. Will you send out a call to all cars on patrol anywhere near the Etoile to keep a lookout for—"

Once again the description of the boy, Francois Lecœur.

"No. I've no idea in which direction he'll be making. All I can tell you is that he seems to keep well clear of police stations, and as far as possible from any place where there's likely to be anyone on traffic duty."

He knew his brother's flat in the Rue Vasco de Gama. Two rather dark rooms and a tiny kitchen. The boy slept there alone while his father was at work. From the windows you could see the back of the house in the Rue Michat, across a courtyard generally hung with washing. On some of the windowsills were pots of geraniums, and through the windows, many of which were uncurtained, you could catch glimpses of a miscellaneous assortment of humanity.

As a matter of fact, there, too, the windowpanes ought to be covered with frost. He stored that idea up in a corner of his mind. It might be important.

"You think it's a boy who's been smashing the alarm glasses?"

"It was a child's handkerchief they found," said Lecœur curtly. He didn't want to be drawn into a discussion. He sat mutely at the switchboard, wondering what to do next.

In the Rue Michat, things seemed to be moving fast. The next time he got through it was to learn that a doctor was there as well as an examining magistrate who had most likely been dragged from his bed.

What help could Lecœur have given them? But if he wasn't there, he could see the place almost as clearly as those that were, the dismal houses and the grimy viaduct of the Métro which cut right across the landscape.

Nothing but poor people in that neighborhood. The younger generation's one hope was to escape from it. The middle-aged already doubted whether they ever would, while the old ones had already accepted their fate and tried to make the best of it.

He rang Javel once again.

"Is Gonesse still there?"

"He's writing up his report. Shall I call him?"

"Yes, please. Hallo, Gonesse, Lecœur speaking. Sorry to bother you, but did you go up to my brother's flat? Had the boy's bed been slept in? It had? Good. That makes it look a bit better. Another thing: were there any parcels there? Yes, parcels, Christmas presents. What? A small square radio. Hadn't been unpacked. Naturally. Anything else? A chicken, a *boudin*, a Saint-Honoré. I suppose Janvier's not with you? Still on the spot. Right. Has he rung-up the P.J.? Good."

He was surprised to see it was already half past nine. It was no use now expecting anything from the neighborhood of the Etoile. If the boy had gone on walking as he had been earlier, he could be pretty well anywhere by this time.

"Hallo! Police Judiciaire? Is Inspector Saillard there?"

He was another whom the murder had dragged from his fireside. How many people were there whose Christmas was going to be spoiled by it?

"Excuse my troubling you, Monsieur le Commissaire. It's about that young boy, Francois Lecœur."

"Do you know anything? Is he a relation of yours?"

"He's my brother's son. And it looks as if he may well be the person who's been smashing the glasses of the telephone pillars. Seven of them. I don't know whether they've had time to tell you about that. What I wanted to ask was whether I might put out a general call?"

"Could you nip over to see me?"

"There's no one here to take my place."

"Right. I'll come over myself. Meanwhile you can send out the call."

Lecœur kept calm, though his hand shook slightly as he plugged in once again to the room above.

"Justin? Lecœur again. Appel General. Yes. It's the same boy. Francois Lecœur. Ten and a half, rather tall for his age, thin. I don't know what he's wearing, probably a khaki jumper made from American battle-dress. No, no cap. He's always bare-headed, with plenty of hair flopping over his forehead. Perhaps it would be as well to send out a description of his father, too. That's not so easy. You know me, don't you? Well, Olivier Lecœur is rather like a paler version of me. He has a timid look about him and physically he's not robust. The sort that's never in the middle of the pavement but always dodging out of other people's way. He walks a bit queerly, owing to a wound he got in the first war. No, I haven't the least idea where they might be going, only I don't think they're together. To my mind, the boy is probably in danger. I can't explain why—it would take too long. Get the descriptions out as quickly as possible, will you? And let me know if there's any response."

By the time Lecœur had finished telephoning, Inspector Saillard was there, having only had to come round the corner from the Quai des Orfèvres. He was an imposing figure of a man, particularly in his bulky overcoat. With a comprehensive wave of the hand, he greeted the three men on watch, then, seizing a chair as though it were a wisp of straw, he swung it round towards him and sat down heavily. "The boy?" he inquired, looking keenly at Lecœur.

"I can't understand why he's stopped calling us up."

"Calling us up?"

"Attracting our attention, anyway."

"But why should he attract our attention and then not say anything?"

"Supposing he was followed. Or was following someone."

"I see what you mean. Look here, Lecœur, is your brother in financial straits?"

"He's a poor man, yes."

"Is that all?"

"He lost his job three months ago."

"What job?"

"He was linotype operator at *La Presse* in the Rue du Croissant. He was on the night shift. He always did night work. Runs in the family."

"How did he come to lose his job?"

"I suppose he fell out with somebody."

"Is that a failing of his?"

They were interrupted by an incoming call from the Eighteenth to say that a boy selling branches of holly had been picked up in the Rue Lepic. It turned out, however, to be a little Pole who couldn't speak any French.

"You were asking if my brother was in the habit of quarreling with people. I hardly know what to answer. He was never strong. Pretty well all his childhood he was ill on and off. He hardly ever went to school. But he read a great deal alone in his room."

"Is he married?"

"His wife died two years after they were married, leaving him with a baby ten months old."

"Did he bring it up himself?"

"Entirely. I can see him now bathing the little chap, changing his diapers, and warming the milk for his bottle."

"That doesn't explain why he quarrels with people."

Admittedly. But it was difficult to put it into words.

"Soured?"

"Not exactly. The thing is—"

"What?"

"That he's never lived like other people. Perhaps Olivier isn't really very intelligent. Perhaps, from reading so much, he knows too much about some things and too little about others."

"Do you think him capable of killing the old woman?"

The Inspector puffed at his pipe. They could hear the people in the room above walking about. The two other men fiddled with their papers, pretending not to listen.

"She was his mother-in-law," sighed Lecœur. "You'd have found it out anyhow, sooner or later."

"They didn't hit it off?"

"She hated him."

"Why?"

"She considered him responsible for her daughter's death. It seems she could have been saved if the operation had been done in time. It wasn't my brother's fault. The people at the hospital refused to take her in. Some silly question of her papers not being in order. All the same, Madame Fayet held to it that Olivier was to blame."

"Did they see each other?"

"Not unless they passed each other in the street, and then they never spoke."

"Did the boy know?"

"That she was his grandmother? I don't think so."

"You think his father never told him?"

* * *

Never for more than a second or two did Lecœur's eyes leave the plan of Paris, but, besides being Christmas, it was the quiet time of the day, and the little lamps lit up rarely. Two or three street accidents, a lady's handbag snatched in the Métro, a suitcase pinched at the Gare de l'Est.

No sign of the boy. It was surprising considering how few people were about. In the poor quarters a few little children played on the pavements with their new toys, but on the whole the day was lived indoors. Nearly all the shops were shuttered and the cafes and the little bars were almost empty.

For a moment, the town came to life a bit when the church bells started pealing and families in their Sunday best hurried to High Mass. But soon the streets were quiet again, though haunted here and there by the vague rumble of an organ or a sudden gust of singing.

The thought of churches gave Lecœur an idea. Might not the boy have tucked himself away in one of them? Would the police think of looking there? He spoke to Inspector Saillard about it and then got through to Justin for the third time.

"The churches. Ask them to have a look at the congregations. They'll be doing the stations, of course—that's most important."

He took off his glasses for a moment, showing eyelids that were red, probably from lack of sleep.

"Hallo! Yes. The Inspector's here. Hold on."

He held the receiver to Saillard. "It's Janvier."

The bitter wind was still driving through the streets. The light was harsh and bleak, though here and there among the closely packed clouds was a yellowy streak which could be taken as a faint promise of sunshine to come.

When the Inspector put down the receiver, he muttered, "Dr. Paul says the crime was committed between five and half past six this morning. The old woman wasn't killed by the first blow. Apparently she was in bed when she heard a noise and got up and faced the intruder. Indeed, it looks as though she tried to defend herself with the only weapon that came to hand—a shoe."

"Have they found the weapon she was killed with?"

"No. It might have been a hammer. More likely a bit of lead piping or something of that sort."

"Have they found her money?"

"Only her purse, with some small change in it and her identity card. Tell me, Lecœur, did you know she was a money-lender?"

"Yes. I knew."

"And didn't you tell me your brother's been out of work for three months?"

"He has."

"The concierge didn't know. "

"Neither did the boy. It was for his sake he kept it dark."

The Inspector crossed and uncrossed his legs. He was uncomfortable. He glanced at the other two men who couldn't help hearing everything, then turned with a puzzled look to stare at Lecœur.

"Do you realize what all this is pointing to?"

"I do."

"You've thought of it yourself?"

"No."

"Because he's your brother?"

"No."

"How long is it that this killer's been at work? Nine weeks, isn't it?"

Without haste, Lecœur studied the columns of his notebook.

"Yes. Just over nine weeks. The first was on the twentieth of October, in the Epinettes district."

"You say your brother didn't tell his son he was out of a job. Do you mean to say he went on leaving home in the evening just as though he was going to work?"

"Yes. He couldn't face the idea of telling him. You see—it's difficult to explain. He was completely wrapped up in the boy. He was all he had to live for. He cooked and scrubbed for him, tucked him up in bed before going off, and woke him up in the morning."

"That doesn't explain why he couldn't tell him."

"He couldn't bear the thought of appearing to the kid as a failure, a man nobody wanted and who had doors slammed in his face."

"But what did he do with himself all night?"

"Odd jobs. When he could get them. For a fortnight, he was employed as night watchman in a factory in Billancourt, but that was only while the regular man was ill. Often he got a few hours' work washing down cars in one of the big garages. When that failed, he'd sometimes lend a hand at the market unloading vegetables. When he had one of his bouts—"

"Bouts of what?"

"Asthma. He had them from time to time. Then he'd lie down in a station waiting room. Once he spent a whole night here, chatting with me."

"Suppose the boy woke up early this morning and saw his father at Madame Fayet's?"

"There was frost on the windows."

"There wouldn't be if the window was open. Lots of people sleep with their windows open even in the coldest weather."

"It wasn't the case with my brother. He was always a chilly person. And

913

he was much too poor to waste warmth."

"As far as his window was concerned, the boy had only to scratch away the frost with his fingernail. When I was a boy—

"Yes. So did I. The thing is to find out whether the old woman's window was open."

"It was, and the light was switched on."

"I wonder where Francois can have got to."

"The boy?"

It was surprising and a little disconcerting the way he kept all the time reverting to him. The situation was certainly embarrassing, and somehow made all the more so by the calm way in which Andre Lecœur gave the Inspector the most damaging details about his brother.

"When he came in this morning," began Saillard again, "he was carrying a number of parcels. You realize—"

"It's Christmas."

"Yes. But he'd have needed quite a bit of money to buy a chicken, a cake, and that new radio. Has he borrowed any from you lately?"

"Not for a month. I haven't seen him for a month. I wish I had. I'd have told him that I was getting a radio for Francois myself. I've got it here. Downstairs, that is, in the cloakroom. I was going to take it straight round as soon as I was relieved."

"Would Madame Fayet have consented to lend him money?"

"It's unlikely. She was a queer lot. She must have had quite enough money to live on, yet she still went out to work, charring from morning to evening. Often she lent money to the people she worked for. At exorbitant interest, of course. All the neighborhood knew about it, and people always came to her when they needed something to tide them over till the end of the month."

Still embarrassed, the Inspector rose to his feet. "I'm going to have a look," he said.

"At Madame Fayet's?"

"There and in the Rue Vasco de Gama. If you get any news, let me know, will you?"

"You won't find any telephone there, but I can get a message to you through the Javel police station."

The Inspector's footsteps had hardly died away before the telephone bell rang. No lamp had lit up on the wall. This was an outside call, coming from the Gare d'Austerlitz.

"Lecœur? Station police speaking. We've got him."

"Who?"

"The man whose description was circulated. Lecœur. Same as you. Olivier

Lecœur. No doubt about it, I've seen his identity card."

"Hold on, will you?"

Lecœur dashed out of the room and down the stairs just in time to catch the Inspector as he was getting into one of the cars belonging to the Préfecture.

"Inspector! The Gare d'Austerlitz is on the phone. They've found my brother."

Saillard was a stout man and he went up the stairs puffing and blowing. He took the receiver himself.

"Hallo! Yes. Where was he? What was he doing? What? No, there's no point in your questioning him now. You're sure he didn't know? Right. Go on looking out. It's quite possible. As for him, send him here straightaway. At the Préfecture, yes."

He hesitated for a second and glanced at Lecœur before saying finally, "Yes. Send someone with him. We can't take any risks."

The Inspector filled his pipe and lit it before explaining, and when he spoke he looked at nobody in particular.

"He was picked up after he'd been wandering about the station for over an hour. He seemed very jumpy. Said he was waiting there to meet his son, from whom he'd received a message."

"Did they tell him about the murder?"

"Yes. He appeared to be staggered by the news and terrified. I asked them to bring him along." Rather diffidently he added: "I asked them to bring him here. Considering your relationship, I didn't want you to think—"

Lecœur had been in that room since eleven o'clock the night before. It was rather like his early years when he spent his days in his mother's kitchen. Around him was an unchanging world. There were the little lamps, of course, that kept going on and off, but that's what they always did. They were part and parcel of the immutability of the place. Time flowed by without anyone noticing it.

Yet, outside, Paris was celebrating Christmas. Thousands of people had been to Midnight Mass, thousands more had spent the night roistering, and those who hadn't known where to draw the line had sobered down in the police station and were now being called upon to explain things they couldn't remember doing.

What had his brother Olivier been doing all through the night? An old woman had been found dead. A boy had started before dawn on a breathless race through the streets, breaking the glass of the telephone pillars as he passed them, having wrapped his handkerchief round his fist.

And what was Olivier waiting for at the Gare d'Austerlitz, sometimes in the overheated waiting rooms, sometimes on the windswept platforms, too nervous to settle down in any one place for long?

Less than ten minutes elapsed, just time enough for Godin, whose nose really was running, to make himself another glass of hot grog.

"Can I offer you one, Monsieur le Commissaire?"

"No, thanks."

Looking more embarrassed than ever, Saillard leaned over towards Lecœur to say in an undertone, "Would you like us to question him in another room?"

No. Lecœur wasn't going to leave his post for anything. He wanted to stay there, with his little lamps and his switchboard. Was it that he was thinking more of the boy than of his brother?

Olivier came in with a detective on either side, but they had spared him the handcuffs. He looked dreadful, like a bad photograph faded with age. At once he turned to Andre. "Where's Francois?"

"We don't know. We're hunting for him."

"Where?"

Andre Lecœur pointed to his plan of Paris and his switchboard of a thousand lines. "Everywhere."

The two detectives had already been sent away.

"Sit down," said the Inspector. "I believe you've been told of Madame Fayet's death."

Olivier didn't wear spectacles, but he had the same pale and rather fugitive eyes as his brother had when he took his glasses off. He glanced at the Inspector, by whom he didn't seem the least overawed, then turned back to Andre. "He left a note for me," he said, delving into one of the pockets of his grubby mackintosh. "Here. See if you can understand."

He held out a bit of paper torn out of a schoolboy's exercise book. The writing wasn't any too good. It didn't look as though Francois was the best of pupils. He had used an indelible pencil, wetting the end in his mouth, so that his lips were very likely stained with it.

"Uncle Gedeon arrives this morning Gare d'Austerlitz. Come as soon as you can and meet us there. Love. Bib."

Without a word, Andre Lecœur passed it on to the Inspector, who turned it over and over with his thick fingers. "What's Bib stand for?"

"It's his nickname. A baby name. I never use it when other people are about. It comes from *biberon*. When I used to give him his bottle—" He spoke in a toneless voice. He seemed to be in a fog and was probably only dimly conscious of where he was.

"Who's Uncle Gedeon?"

"There isn't any such person."

Did he realize he was talking to the head of the Brigade des Homicides, who was at the moment investigating a murder?

It was his brother who came to the rescue, explaining, "As a matter of fact, we had an Uncle Gedeon but he's been dead for some years. He was one of my mother's brothers who emigrated to America as a young man."

Olivier looked at his brother as much as to say: What's the point of going into that?

"We got into the habit, in the family, of speaking—jocularly, of course—of our rich American uncle and of the fortune he'd leave us one day."

"Was he rich?"

"We didn't know. We never heard from him except for a postcard once a year, signed Gedeon. Wishing us a happy New Year."

"He died?"

"When Francois was four."

"Really, Andre, do you think it's any use—"

"Let me go on. The Inspector wants to know everything. My brother carried on the family tradition, talking to his son about our Uncle Gedeon, who had become by now quite a legendary figure. He provided a theme for bedtime stories, and all sorts of adventures were attributed to him. Naturally he was fabulously rich, and when one day he came back to France—"

"I understand. He died out there?"

"In a hospital in Cleveland. It was then we found out he had been really a porter in a restaurant. It would have been too cruel to tell the boy that, so the legend went on."

"Did he believe in it?"

It was Olivier who answered. "My brother thought he didn't, that he'd guessed the truth but wasn't going to spoil the game. But I always maintained the contrary and I'm still practically certain he took it all in. He was like that. Long after his schoolfellows had stopped believing in Father Christmas, he still went on."

Talking about his son brought him back to life, transfigured him.

"But as for this note he left, I don't know what to make of it. I asked the concierge if a telegram had come. For a moment I thought Andre might have played us a practical joke, but I soon dismissed the idea. It isn't much of a joke to get a boy dashing off to a station on a freezing night. Naturally I dashed off to the Gare d'Austerlitz as fast as I could. There I hunted high and low, then wandered about, waiting anxiously for him to turn up. Andre, you're sure he hasn't been—"

He looked at the street plan on the wall and at the switchboard. He knew very well that every accident was reported.

"He hasn't been run over," said Andre. "At about eight o'clock he was near the Etoile, but we've completely lost track of him since then."

"Near the Etoile? How do you know?"

"It's rather a long story, but it boils down to this—that a whole series of alarms were set off by someone smashing the glass. They followed a circuitous route from your place to the Arc de Triomphe. At the foot of the last one, they found a blue-check handerchief, a boy's handkerchief, among the broken glass."

"He has handkerchiefs like that."

"From eight o'clock onward, not a sign of him."

"Then I'd better get back to the station. He's certain to go there, if he told me to meet him there."

He was surprised at the sudden silence with which his last words were greeted. He looked from one to the other, perplexed, then anxious.

"What is it?"

His brother looked down at the floor. Inspector Saillard cleared his throat, hesitated, then asked, "Did you go to see your mother-in-law last night?"

Perhaps, as his brother had suggested, Olivier was rather lacking in intelligence. It took a long time for the words to sink in. You could follow their progress in his features.

He had been gazing rather blankly at the Inspector. Suddenly he swung around on his brother, his cheeks red, his eyes flashing. "Andre, you dare to suggest that I—"

Without the slightest transition, his indignation faded away. He leaned forward in his chair, took his head in his two hands, and burst into a fit of raucous weeping.

Ill at ease, Inspector Saillard looked at Andre Lecœur, surprised at the latter's calmness, and a little shocked, perhaps, by what he may well have taken for heartlessness. Perhaps Saillard had never had a brother of his own. Andre had known his since childhood. It wasn't the first time he had seen Olivier break down. Not by any means. And this time he was almost pleased, as it might have been a great deal worse. What he had dreaded was the moment of indignation, and he was relieved that it had passed so quickly. Had he continued on that tack, he'd have ended by putting everyone's back up, which would have done him no good at all.

Wasn't that how he'd lost one job after another? For weeks, for months, he would go meekly about his work, toeing the line and swallowing what he felt to be humiliations, till all at once he could hold no more, and for some trifle—a chance word, a smile, a harmless contradiction—he would flare up unexpectedly and make a nuisance of himself to everybody.

What do we do now? The Inspector's eyes were asking.

Andre Lecœur's eyes answered, Wait.

*

918

It didn't last very long. The emotional crisis waned, started again, then petered out altogether. Olivier shot a sulky look at the Inspector, then hid his face again.

Finally, with an air of bitter resignation, he sat up, and with even a touch of pride said: "Fire away. I'll answer."

"At what time last night did you go to Madame Fayet's? Wait a moment. First of all, when did you leave your flat?"

"At eight o'clock, as usual, after Francois was in bed."

"Nothing exceptional happened?"

"No. We'd had supper together. Then he'd helped me to wash up."

"Did you talk about Christmas?"

"Yes. I told him he'd be getting a surprise."

"The table radio. Was he expecting one?"

"He'd been longing for one for some time. You see, he doesn't play with the other boys in the street. Practically all his free time he spends at home."

"Did it ever occur to you that the boy might know you'd lost your job at the *Presse*? Did he ever ring you up there?"

"Never. When I'm at work, he's asleep."

"Could anyone have told him?"

"No one knew. Not in the neighborhood, that is."

"Is he observant?"

"Very. He notices everything."

"You saw him safely in bed and then you went off. Do you take anything with you—anything to eat, I mean?"

The Inspector suddenly thought of that, seeing Godin produce a ham sandwich. Olivier looked blankly at his empty hands.

"My tin."

"The tin in which you took your sandwiches?"

"Yes. I had it with me when I left. I'm sure of that. I can't think where I could have left it, unless it was at—"

"At Madame Fayet's?"

"Yes."

"Just a moment. Lecœur, get me Javel on the phone, will you? Hallo! Who's speaking? Is Janvier there? Good, ask him to speak to me. Hallo! Is that you, Janvier? Have you come across a tin box containing some sandwiches? Nothing of the sort. Really? All the same, I'd like you to make sure. Ring me back. It's important."

And, turning again to Olivier: "Was Francois actually sleeping when you left?"

"No. But he'd snuggled down in bed and soon would be. Outside, I wandered about for a bit. I walked down to the Seine and waited on the embankment."

"Waited? What for?"

"For Francois to be fast asleep. From his room you can see Madame Fayet's windows."

"So you'd made up your mind to go and see her."

"It was the only way. I hadn't a bean left."

"What about your brother?"

Olivier and Andre looked at each other.

"He'd already given me so much. I felt I couldn't ask him again."

"You rang at the house door, I suppose. At what time?"

"A little after nine. The concierge saw me. I made no attempt to hide— except from Francois."

"Had your mother-in-law gone to bed?"

"No. She was fully dressed when she opened her door. She said, 'Oh, it's you, you wretch!' "

"After that beginning, did you still think she'd lend you money?"

"I was sure of it."

"Why?"

"It was her business. Perhaps also for the pleasure of squeezing me if I didn't pay her back. She lent me ten thousand francs, but made me sign an I.O.U. for twenty thousand."

"How soon had you to pay her back?"

"In a fortnight's time."

"How could you hope to?"

"I don't know. Somehow. The thing that mattered was for the boy to have a good Christmas."

Andre Lecœur was tempted to butt in to explain to the puzzled Inspector, "You see! He's always been like that!"

"Did you get the money easily?"

"Oh, no. We were at it for a long time."

"How long?"

"Half an hour, I daresay, and during most of that time she was calling me names, telling me I was no good to anyone and had ruined her daughter's life before I finally killed her. I didn't answer her back. I wanted the money too badly."

"You didn't threaten her?"

Olivier reddened. "Not exactly. I said if she didn't let me have it I'd kill myself."

"Would you have done it?"

"I don't think so. At least, I don't know. I was fed up, worn out."

"And when you got the money?"

"I walked to the nearest Métro station, Lourmel, and took the underground to Palais Royal. There I went into the Grands Magasins du Louvre. The place was crowded, with queues at many of the counters."

"What time was it?"

"It was after eleven before I left the place. I was in no hurry. I had a good look around. I stood a long time watching a toy electric train."

Andre couldn't help smiling at the Inspector. "You didn't miss your sandwich tin?"

"No. I was thinking about Francois and his present."

"And with money in your pocket you banished all your cares!"

The Inspector hadn't known Olivier Lecœur since childhood, but he had sized him up all right. He had hit the nail on the head. When things were black, Olivier would go about with drooping shoulders and a hangdog air, but no sooner had he a thousand-franc note in his pocket than he'd feel on top of the world.

"To come back to Madame Fayet, you say you gave her a receipt. What did she do with it?"

"She slipped it into an old wallet she always carried about with her in a pocket somewhere under her skirt."

"So you knew about the wallet?"

"Yes. Everybody did. "

The Inspector turned towards Andre.

"It hasn't been found!"

Then to Olivier: "You bought some things. In the Louvre?"

"No. I bought the little radio in the Rue Montmartre."

"In which shop?"

"I don't know the name. It's next door to a shoe shop."

"And the other things?"

"A little farther on. "

"What time was it when you'd finished shopping?"

"Close on midnight. People were coming out of the theaters and movies and crowding into the restaurants. Some of them were rather noisy."

His brother at that time was already here at his switchboard.

"What did you do during the rest of the night?"

"At the corner of the Boulevard des Italiens, there's a movie that stays open all night."

"You'd been there before?"

Avoiding his brother's eye, Olivier answered rather sheepishly: "Two or three times. After all, it costs no more than going into a cafe and you can stay there as long as you like. It's nice and warm. Some people go there regularly to sleep."

"When was it you decided to go to the movies?"

"As soon as I left Madame Fayet's."

Andre Lecœur was tempted to intervene once again to say to the Inspector: "You see, these people who are down and out are not so utterly miserable after all. If they were, they'd never stick it out. They've got a world of their own, in odd corners of which they can take refuge and even amuse themselves."

It was all so like Olivier! With a few notes in his pocket—and Heaven only knew how he was ever going to pay them back—with a few notes in his pocket, his trials were forgotten. He had only one thought: to give his boy a good Christmas. With that secured, he was ready to stand himself a little treat.

So while other families were gathered at table or knelt at Midnight Mass, Olivier went to the movies all by himself. It was the best he could do.

"When did you leave the movie?"

"A little before six."

"What was the film?"

"*Cœurs Ardents*. With a documentary on Eskimos."

"How many times did you see the program?"

"Twice right through, except for the news, which was just coming on again when I left."

Andre Lecœur knew that all this was going to be verified, if only as a matter of routine. It wasn't necessary, however. Diving into his pockets, Olivier produced the torn-off half of a movie ticket, then another ticket—a pink one. "Look at that. It's the Métro ticket I had coming home."

It bore the name of the station—Opéra—together with the date and the time.

Olivier had been telling the truth. He couldn't have been in Madame Fayet's flat any time between five and six-thirty.

There was a little spark of triumph in his eye, mixed with a touch of disdain. He seemed to be saying to them all, including his brother Andre: "Because I'm poor and unlucky I come under suspicion. I know—that's the way things are. I don't blame you."

And, funnily enough, it seemed as though all at once the room had grown colder. That was probably because, with Olivier Lecœur cleared of suspicion, everyone's thoughts reverted to the child. As though moved by one impulse, all eyes turned instinctively toward the huge plan on the wall.

Some time had elapsed since any of the lamps had lit up. Certainly it was a quiet morning. On any ordinary day there would be a street accident coming in every few minutes, particularly old women knocked down in the crowded thoroughfares of Montmartre and other overpopulated quarters.

Today the streets were almost empty—emptier than in August, when half Paris is away on holiday.

Half past eleven. For three and a half hours there'd been no sign of Francois Lecœur.

"Hallo! Yes, Saillard speaking. Is that Janvier? You say you couldn't find a tin anywhere? Except in her kitchen, of course. Now, look here, was it you who went through the old girl's clothes? Oh, Gonesse had already done it. There should have been an old wallet in a pocket under her skirt. You're sure there wasn't anything of that sort? That's what Gonesse told you, is it? What's that about the concierge? She saw someone go up a little after nine last night. I know. I know who it was. There were people coming in and out the best part of the night? Of course. I'd like you to go back to the house in the Rue Vasco de Gama. See what you can find out about the comings and goings there, particularly on the third floor. Yes. I'll still be here."

He turned back to the boy's father, who was now sitting humbly in his chair, looking as intimidated as a patient in a doctor's waiting room.

"You understand why I asked that, don't you? Does Francois often wake up in the course of the night?"

"He's been known to get up in his sleep."

"Does he walk about?"

"No. Generally he doesn't even get right out of bed—just sits up and calls out. It's always the same thing. He thinks the house is on fire. His eyes are open, but I don't think he sees anything. Then, little by little, he calms down and with a deep sigh lies down again. The next day he doesn't remember a thing."

"Is he always asleep when you get back in the morning?"

"Not always. But if he isn't, he always pretends to be so that I can wake him up as usual with a hug."

"The people in the house were probably making more noise than usual last night. Who have you got in the next flat?"

"A Czech who works at Renault's."

"Is he married?"

"I really don't know. There are so many people in the house and they change so often we don't know much about them. All I can tell you is that on Sundays other Czechs come there and they sing a lot of their own songs."

"Janvier will tell us whether there was a party there last night. If there was, they may well have awakened the boy. Besides, children are apt to sleep more lightly when they're excited about a present they're expecting. If he got out of bed, he might easily have looked out of the window, in which case he might have seen you at Madame Fayet's. He didn't know she was his grandmother, did he?"

"No. He didn't like her. He sometimes passed her in the street and he used to say she smelled like a squashed bug."

The boy would probably know what he was talking about. A house like his was no doubt infested with vermin.

"He'd have been surprised to see you with her?"

"Certainly."

"Did he know she lent money?"

"Everyone knew."

"Would there be anybody working at the *Presse* on a day like this?"

"There's always somebody there."

The Inspector asked Andre to ring them up.

"See if anyone's ever been round to ask for your brother."

Olivier looked uncomfortable, but when his brother reached for the telephone directory, he gave him the number. Both he and the Inspector stared at Andre while he got through.

"It's very important, Mademoiselle. It may even be a matter of life and death. Yes, please. See if you can find out. Ask everybody who's in the building now. What? Yes, I know it's Christmas Day. It's Christmas Day here, too, but we have to carry on just the same."

Between his teeth he muttered, "Silly little bitch!"

He could hear the linotypes clicking as he held the line, waiting for her answer.

"Yes. What? Three weeks ago. A young boy—"

Olivier went pale in the face. His eyes dropped, and during the rest of the conversation he stared obstinately at his hands.

"He didn't telephone? Came round himself. At what time? On a Thursday, you say. What did he want? Asked if Olivier Lecœur worked there? What? What was he told?"

Looking up, Olivier saw a flush spread over his brother's face before he banged down the receiver.

"Francois went there one Thursday afternoon. He must have suspected something. They told him you hadn't been working there for some time."

There was no point in repeating what he had heard. What they'd said to the boy was: "We chucked the old fool out weeks ago."

Perhaps not out of cruelty. They may not have thought it was the man's son they were speaking to.

"Do you begin to understand, Olivier?"

Did he realize that the situation was the reverse of what he had imagined? He had been going off at night, armed with his little box of sandwiches, keeping up an elaborate pretense. And in the end he had been the one to be taken in!

924

The boy had found him out. And wasn't it only fair to suppose that he had seen through the Uncle Gedeon story, too?

He hadn't said a word. He had simply fallen in with the game.

No one dared say anything for fear of saying too much, for fear of evoking images that would be heartrending.

A father and a son each lying to avoid hurting the other.

They had to look at it through the eyes of the child, with all childhood's tragic earnestness. His father kisses him good night and goes off to the job that doesn't really exist, saying: "Sleep well. There'll be a surprise for you in the morning."

A radio. It could only be that. And didn't he know that his father's pockets were empty? Did he try to go to sleep? Or did he get up as soon as his father had gone, to sit miserably staring out of the window obsessed by one thought? *His father had no money—yet he was going to buy him a radio!*

To the accompaniment, in all probability, of a full-throated Czech choir singing their national songs on the other side of the thin wall!

The Inspector sighed and knocked out his pipe on his heel.

"It looks as though he saw you at Madame Fayet's."

Olivier nodded.

"We'll check up on this, but it seems likely that, looking down from his window, he wouldn't see very far into the room."

"That's quite right."

"Could he have seen you leave the room?"

"No. The door's on the opposite side from the window."

"Do you remember going near the window?"

"At one time I was sitting on the windowsill."

"Was the window open then? We know it was later."

"It was open a few inches. I'm sure of that, because I moved away from it, as I felt an icy draught on my back. She lived with us for a while, just after our marriage, and I know she couldn't bear not to have her window open all the year round. You see, she'd been brought up in the country."

"So there'd be no frost on the panes. He'd certainly have seen you if he was looking."

A call. Lecœur thrust his contact plug into one of the sockets.

"Yes. What's that? A boy?"

The other two held their breath.

"Yes. Yes. What? Yes. Send out the *agents cyclistes*. Comb the whole neighborhood. I'll see about the station. How long ago was it? Half an hour? Couldn't he have let us know sooner?"

Without losing time over explanations, Lecœur plugged in to the Gare du

Nord.

"Hallo! Gare du Nord! Who's speaking? Ah, Lambert. Listen, this is urgent. Have the station searched from end to end. Ask everybody if they've seen a boy of ten wandering about. What? Alone? He may be. Or he may be accompanied. We don't know. Let me know what you find out. Yes, of course. Grab him at once if you set eyes on him."

"Did you say accompanied?" asked Olivier anxiously.

"Why not? It's possible. Anything's possible. Of course, it may not be him. If it is, we're half an hour late. It was a small grocer in the Rue de Maubeuge whose shopfront is open onto the street. He saw a boy snatch a couple of oranges and make off. He didn't run after him. Only later, when a policeman passed, he thought he might as well mention it."

"Had your son any money?" asked the Inspector.

"Not a sou."

"Hasn't he got a money-box?"

"Yes. But I borrowed what was in it two days ago, saying that I didn't want to change a banknote."

A pathetic little confession, but what did things like that matter now?

"Don't you think it would be better if I went to the Gare du Nord myself?"

"I doubt if it would help, and we may need you here."

They were almost prisoners in that room. With its direct links with every nerve center of Paris, that was the place where any news would first arrive. Even in his room in the Police Judiciaire, the Inspector would be less well placed. He had thought of going back there, but now at last took off his overcoat, deciding to see the job through where he was.

"If he had no money, he couldn't take a bus or the Métro. Nor could he go into a cafe or use a public telephone. He probably hasn't had anything to eat since his supper last night."

"But what can he be doing?" exclaimed Olivier, becoming more and more nervous. "And why should he have sent me to the Gare d'Austerlitz?"

"Perhaps to help you get away," grunted Saillard.

"Get away? Me?"

"Listen. The boy knows you're down and out. Yet you're going to buy him a little radio. I'm not reproaching you. I'm just looking at the facts. He leans on the windowsill and sees you with the old woman he knows to be a money-lender. What does he conclude?"

"I see."

"That you've gone to her to borrow money. He may be touched by it, he may be saddened—we don't know. He goes back to bed and to sleep."

"You think so?"

"I'm pretty sure of it. Anyhow, we've no reason to think he left the house then."

"No. Of course not."

"Let's say he goes back to sleep, then. But he wakes up early, as children mostly do on Christmas Day. And the first thing he notices is the frost on the window. The first frost this winter, don't forget that. He wants to look at it, to touch it."

A faint smile flickered across Andre Lecœur's face. This massive Inspector hadn't forgotten what it was like to be a boy.

"He scratches a bit of it away with his nails. It won't be difficult to get confirmation, for once the frost is tampered with it can't form again in quite the same pattern. What does he notice then? That in the buildings opposite one window is lit up, and one only—the window of the room in which a few hours before he had seen his father. It's guesswork, of course, but I don't mind betting he saw the body, or part of it. If he'd merely seen a foot it would have been enough to startle him."

"You mean to say—" began Olivier, wide-eyed.

"That he thought you'd killed her. As I did myself—for a moment. And very likely not her only. Just think for a minute. The man who's been committing all these murders is a man, like you, who wanders about at night. His victims live in the poorer quarters of Paris, like Madame Fayet in the Rue Michat. Does the boy know anything of how you've been spending your nights since you lost your job? No. All that he has to go on is that he has seen you in the murdered woman's room. Would it be surprising if his imagination got to work?"

"You said just now that you sat on the windowsill. Might it be there that you put down your box of sandwiches?"

"Now I come to think of it, yes. I'm practically sure."

"Then he saw it. And he's quite old enough to know what the police would think when they saw it lying there. Is your name on it?"

"Yes. Scratched on the lid."

"You see! He thought you'd be coming home as usual between seven and eight. The thing was to get you as quickly as possible out of the danger zone."

"You mean—by writing me that note?"

"Yes. He didn't know what to say. He couldn't refer to the murder without compromising you. Then he thought of Uncle Gedeon. Whether he believed in his existence or not doesn't matter. He knew you'd go to the Gare d'Austerlitz."

"But he's not yet eleven!"

"Boys of that age know a lot more than you think. Doesn't he read detective stories?"

"Yes."

"Of course he does. They all do. If they don't read them, they get them on the radio. Perhaps that's why he wanted a set of his own so badly."

"It's true."

"He couldn't stay in the flat to wait for you, for he had something more important to do. He had to get hold of that box. I suppose he knew the courtyard well. He'd played there, hadn't he?"

"At one time, yes. With the concierge's little girl."

"So he'd know about the rainwater pipes, may even have climbed up them for sport."

"Very well," said Olivier, suddenly calm, "let's say he gets into the room and takes the box. He wouldn't need to climb down the way he'd come. He could simply walk out of the flat and out of the house. You can open the house door from inside without knocking up the concierge. You say it was at about six o'clock, don't you?"

"I see what you're driving at," grunted the Inspector. "Even at a leisurely pace, it would hardly have taken him two hours to walk to the Gare d'Austerlitz. Yet he wasn't there."

Leaving them to thrash it out, Lecœur was busy telephoning.

"No news yet?"

And the man at the Gare du Nord answered, "Nothing so far. We've pounced on any number of boys, but none of them was Francois Lecœur."

Admittedly, any street boy could have pinched a couple of oranges and taken to his heels. The same couldn't be said for the broken glass of the telephone pillars, however. Andre Lecœur looked once again at the column with the seven crosses, as though some clue might suddenly emerge from them. He had never thought himself much cleverer than his brother. Where he scored was in patience and perseverance.

"If the box of sandwiches is ever found, it'll be at the bottom of the Seine near the Pont Mirabeau," he said.

Steps in the corridor. On an ordinary day they would not have been noticed, but in the stillness of a Christmas morning everyone listened.

It was an *agent cycliste*, who produced a bloodstained blue-check handkerchief, the one that had been found among the glass splinters at the seventh telephone pillar.

"That's his, all right," said the boy's father.

"He must have been followed," said the Inspector. "If he'd had time, he wouldn't merely have broken the glass. He'd have said something."

"Who by?" asked Olivier, who was the only one not to understand. "Who'd want to follow him?" he asked. "And why should he call the police?"

They hesitated to put him wise. In the end it was his brother who explained:

"When he went to the old woman's he thought you were the murderer. When he came away, he knew you weren't. He knew—"

"Knew what?"

"He knew who was. Do you understand now? He found out something, though we don't know what. He wants to tell us about it, but someone's stopping him."

"You mean?"

"I mean that Francois is after the murderer or the murderer is after him. One is following, one is followed—we don't know which. By the way, Inspector, is there a reward offered?"

"A handsome reward was offered after the third murder and it was doubled last week. It's been in all the papers."

"Then my guess," said Andre Lecœur, "is that it's the kid who's doing the following. Only in that case—"

It was twelve o'clock, four hours since they'd lost track of him. Unless, of course, it was he who had snaffled the oranges in the Rue Maubeuge.

Might not this be his great moment? Andre Lecœur had read somewhere that even to the dullest and most uneventful lives such a moment comes sooner or later.

He had never had a particularly high opinion of himself or of his abilities. When people asked him why he'd chosen so dreary and monotonous a job rather than one in, say, the Brigade des Homicides, he would answer: "I suppose I'm lazy."

Sometimes he would add:

"I'm scared of being knocked about."

As a matter of fact, he was neither lazy nor a coward. If he lacked anything it was brains.

He knew it. All he had learned at school had cost him a great effort. The police exams that others took so easily in their stride, he had only passed by dint of perseverance.

Was it a consciousness of his own shortcomings that had kept him single? Possibly. It seemed to him that the sort of woman he would want to marry would be his superior, and he didn't relish the idea of playing second fiddle in the home.

But he wasn't thinking of all this now. Indeed, if this was his moment of greatness, it was stealing upon him unawares.

Another team arrived, those of the second day shift looking very fresh and well groomed in their Sunday clothes. They had been celebrating Christmas with their families, and they brought in with them, as it were, a whiff of good viands and liqueurs.

Old Bedeau had taken his place at the switchboard, but Lecœur made no move to go.

"I'll stay on a bit," he said simply.

Inspector Saillard had gone for a quick lunch at the Brasserie Dauphine just around the corner, leaving strict injunctions that he was to be fetched at once if anything happened. Janvier was back at the Quai des Orfèvres, writing up his report.

If Lecœur was tired, he didn't notice it. He certainly wasn't sleepy and couldn't bear the thought of going home to bed. He had plenty of stamina. Once, when there were riots in the Place de la Concorde, he had done thirty-six hours nonstop, and on another occasion, during a general strike, they had all camped in the room for four days and nights.

His brother showed the strain more. He was getting jumpy again.

"I'm going," he announced suddenly.

"Where to?"

"To find Bib."

"Where?"

"I don't know exactly. I'll start round the Gare du Nord."

"How do you know it was Bib who stole the oranges? He may be at the other end of Paris. We might get news at any minute. You'd better stay."

"I can't stand this waiting."

He was nevertheless persuaded to. He was given a chair in a corner. He refused to lie down. His eyes were red with anxiety and fatigue. He sat fidgeting, looking rather as, when a boy, he had been put in the corner.

With more self-control, Andre forced himself to take some rest. Next to the big room was a little one with a wash-basin, where they hung their coats and which was provided with a couple of camp beds on which the *nuiteux* could lie down during a quiet hour.

He shut his eyes, but only for a moment. Then his hand felt for the little notebook with never left him, and lying on his back he began to turn over the pages.

There were nothing but crosses, columns and columns of tiny little crosses which, month after month, year after year, he had accumulated, Heaven knows why. Just to satisfy something inside him. After all, other people keep a diary—or the most meticulous household accounts, even when they don't need to economize at all.

Those crosses told the story of the night life of Paris.

"Some coffee, Lecœur?"

"Thanks."

Feeling rather out of touch where he was, he dragged his camp bed into the big room, placing it in a position from which he could see the wall-plan. There he sipped his coffee, after which he stretched himself out again, sometimes studying his notebook, sometimes lying with his eyes shut. Now and again he stole a glance at his brother, who sat hunched in his chair with drooping shoulders, the twitching of his long white fingers being the only sign of the torture he was enduring.

There were hundreds of men now, not only in Paris but in the suburbs, keeping their eyes skinned for the boy whose description had been circulated. Sometimes false hopes were raised, only to be dashed when the exact particulars were given.

Lecœur shut his eyes again, but opened them suddenly next moment, as though he had actually dozed off. He glanced at the clock, then looked round for the Inspector.

"Hasn't Saillard got back yet?" he asked, getting to his feet.

"I expect he's looked in at the Quai des Orfèvres."

Olivier stared at his brother, surprised to see him pacing up and down the room. The latter was so absorbed in his thoughts that he hardly noticed that the sun had broken through the clouds, bathing Paris on that Christmas afternoon in a glow of light more like that of spring.

While thinking, he listened, and it wasn't long before he heard Inspector Saillard's heavy tread outside.

"You'd better go and get some sandwiches," he said to his brother. "Get some for me, too."

"What kind?"

"Ham. Anything. Whatever you find."

Olivier went out, after a parting glance at the map, relieved, in spite of his anxiety, to be doing something.

The men of the afternoon shift knew little of what was afoot, except that the killer had done another job the previous night and that there was a general hunt for a small boy. For them, the case couldn't have the flavor it had for those who were involved. At the switchboard, Bedeau was doing a crossword with his earphones on his head, breaking off from time to time for the classic: "Hallo! Austerlitz. Your car's out."

A body fished out of the Seine. You couldn't have a Christmas without that!

"Could I have a word with you, Inspector?"

The camp bed was back in the cloakroom. It was there that Lecœur led the chief of the homicide squad.

"I hope you won't mind my butting in. I know it isn't for me to make suggestions. But, about the killer—"

He had his little notebook in his hand. He must have known its contents almost by heart.

"I've been doing a lot of thinking since this morning and—"

A little while ago, while he was lying down, it had seemed so clear, but now that he had to explain things, it was difficult to put them in logical order.

"It's like this. First of all, I noticed that all the murders were committed after two in the morning, most of them after three."

He could see by the look on the Inspector's face that he hadn't exactly scored a hit, and he hurried on:

"I've been looking up the time of other murders over the past three years. They were nearly always between ten in the evening and two in the morning."

Neither did that observation seem to make much impression. Why not take the bull by the horns and say straight out what was on his mind?

"Just now, looking at my brother, it occurred to me that the man you're looking for might be a man like him. As a matter of fact, I, too, for a moment wondered whether it wasn't him. Wait a moment—"

That was better. The look of polite boredom had gone from Saillard's face.

"If I'd had more experience in this sort of work I'd be able to explain myself better. But you'll see in a moment. A man who's killed eight people one after the other is, if not a madman, at any rate a man who's been thrown off his balance. He might have had a sudden shock. Take my brother, for instance. When he lost his job it upset him so much that he preferred to live in a tissue of lies rather than let his son—"

No. Put into words, it all sounded very clumsy.

"When a man suddenly loses everything he has in life—"

"He doesn't necessarily go mad."

"I'm not saying he's actually mad. But imagine a person so full of resentment that he considers himself justified in revenging himself on his fellow-men. I don't need to point out to you, Inspector, that other murderers always kill in much the same way. This one has used a hammer, a knife, a spanner, and one woman he strangled. And he's never been seen, never left a clue. Wherever he lives in Paris, he must have walked miles and miles at night when there was no transport available, sometimes, when the alarm had been given, with the police on the lookout, questioning everybody they found in the streets. How is it he avoided them?"

He was certain he was on the right track. If only Saillard would hear him out.

The Inspector sat on one of the camp beds. The cloakroom was small, and as Lecœur paced up and down in front of him he could do no more than three paces each way.

"This morning, for instance, assuming he was with the boy, he went halfway across Paris, keeping out of sight of every police station and every traffic point where there'd be a man on duty."

"You mean he knows the Fifteenth and Sixteenth Arrondissements by heart?"

"And not those only. At least two there, the Twelfth and the Twentieth, as he showed on previous occasions. He didn't choose his victims haphazardly. He knew they lived alone and could be done in without any great risk."

What a nuisance! There was his brother, saying: "Here are the sandwiches, Andre."

"Thanks. Go ahead, will you? Don't wait for me. I'll be with you in a moment."

He bundled Olivier back into his corner and returned to the cloakroom. He didn't want him to hear.

"If he's used a different weapon each time, it's because he knows it will puzzle us. He knows that murderers generally have their own way and stick to it."

The Inspector had risen to his feet and was staring at Andre with a faraway look, as though he was following a train of thought of his own.

"You mean that he's—"

"That he's one of us—or has been. I can't get the idea out of my head."

He lowered his voice.

"Someone who's been up against it in the same sort of way as my brother. A discharged fireman might take to arson. It's happened two or three times. A policeman—"

"But why should he steal?"

"Wasn't my brother in need of money? This other chap may be like him in more ways than one. Supposing he, too, was a night worker and goes on pretending he's still in a job. That would explain why the crimes are committed so late. He has to be out all night. The first part of it is easy enough—the cafes and bars are open. Afterward, he's all alone with himself."

As though to himself, Saillard muttered: "There wouldn't be anybody in the personnel department on a day like this."

"Perhaps you could ring up the director at his home. He might remember . . ."

"Hallo! Can I speak to Monsieur Guillaume, please? He's not in? Where could I reach him? At his daughter's in Ateuil? Have you got the number?"

"Hallo! Monsieur Guillaume? Saillard speaking. I hope I'm not disturbing you too much. Oh, you'd finished, had you? Good. It's about the killer. Yes, there's been another one. No. Nothing definite. Only we have an idea that needs checking, and it's urgent. Don't be too surprised at my question.

"Has any member of the Paris police been sacked recently—say two or three months ago? I beg your pardon? Not a single one this year? I see."

Lecœur felt a sudden constriction around his heart, as though overwhelmed by a catastrophe, and threw a pathetic, despairing look at the wall-map. He had already given up and was surprised to hear his chief go on:

"As a matter of fact, it doesn't need to be as recent as all that. It would be someone who had worked in various parts of Paris, including the Fifteenth and Sixteenth. Probably also the Twelfth and Twentieth. Seems to have done a good deal of night work. Also to have been embittered by his dismissal. What?"

The way Saillard pronounced that last word gave Lecœur renewed hope.

"Sergeant Loubet? Yes, I remember the name, though I never actually came across him. Three years ago! You wouldn't know where he lived, I suppose? Somewhere near Les Halles?"

Three years ago. No, it wouldn't do, and Lecœur's heart sank again. You could hardly expect a man to bottle up his resentments for three years and then suddenly start hitting back.

"Have you any idea what became of him? No, of course not. And it's not a good day for finding out."

He hung up and looked thoughtfully at Lecœur. When he spoke, it was as though he was addressing an equal.

"Did you hear? Sergeant Loubet. He was constantly getting into trouble and was shifted three or four times before being finally dismissed. Drink. That was his trouble. He took his dismissal very hard. Guillaume can't say for certain what has become of him, but he thinks he joined a private detective agency. If you'd like to have a try—"

Lecœur set to work. He had little hope of succeeding, but it was better to do something than sit watching for the little lamps in the street-plan. He began with the agencies of the most doubtful reputation, refusing to believe that a person such as Loubet would readily find a job with a reputable firm. Most of the offices were shut, and he had to ring up their proprietors at home.

"Don't know him. You'd better try Tisserand in the Boulevard Saint-Martin. He's the one who takes all the riffraff."

But Tisserand, a firm that specialized in shadowings, was no good, either.

"Don't speak to me of that good-for-nothing. It's a good two months or more since I chucked him out, in spite of his threatening to blackmail me. If he ever shows up at my office again, I'll throw him down the stairs."

"What sort of job did he have?"

"Night work. Watching blocks of flats."

"Did he drink much?"

"He wasn't often sober. I don't know how he managed it, but he always knew where to get free drinks. Blackmail again, I suppose."

"Can you give me his address?"

"Twenty-seven bis, Rue du Pas-de-la-Mule."

"Does he have a telephone?"

"Maybe. I don't know. I've never had the slightest desire to ring him up. Is that all? Can I go back to my game of bridge?"

The Inspector had already snatched up the telephone directory and was looking for Loubet's number. He rang up himself. There was now a tacit understanding between him and Lecœur. They shared the same hope, the same trembling eagerness, while Olivier, realizing that something important was going on, came and stood near them.

Without being invited, Andre did something he wouldn't have dreamed of doing that morning. He picked up the second earphone to listen in. The bell rang in the flat in the Rue du Pas-de-la-Mule. It rang for a long time, as though the place was deserted, and his anxiety was becoming acute when at last it stopped and a voice answered.

Thank Heaven! It was a woman's voice, an elderly one. "Is that you at last? Where are you?"

"Hallo! This isn't your husband here, Madame."

"Has he met with an accident?"

From the hopefulness of her tone, it sounded as though she had long been expecting one and wouldn't be sorry when it happened.

"It is Madame Loubet I'm speaking to, isn't it?"

"Who else would it be?"

"Your husband's not at home?"

"First of all, who are you?"

"Inspector Saillard."

"What do you want him for?"

The Inspector put his hand over the mouthpiece to say to Lecœur: "Get through to Janvier. Tell him to dash round there as quick as he can."

"Didn't your husband come home this morning?"

"You ought to know! I thought the police knew everything!"

"Does it often happen?"

"That's his business, isn't it?"

No doubt she hated her drunkard of a husband, but now that he was threatened she was ready to stand up for him.

"I suppose you know he no longer belongs to the police force."

"Perhaps he found a cleaner job."

"When did he stop working for the Agence Argus?"

"What's that? What are you getting at?"

"I assure you, Madame, your husband was dismissed from the Agence

Argus over two months ago."

"You're lying."

"Which means that for these last two months he's been going off to work every evening."

"Where else would he be going? To the Folies Bergère?"

"Have you any idea why he hasn't come back today? He hasn't telephoned, has he?"

She must have been afraid of saying the wrong thing, for she rang off without another word.

When the Inspector put his receiver down, he turned round to see Lecœur standing behind him, looking away. In a shaky voice, the latter said:

"Janvier's on his way now."

He was treated as an equal. He knew it wouldn't last, that tomorrow, sitting at his switchboard, he would be once more but a small cog in the huge wheel.

The others simply didn't count—not even his brother, whose timid eyes darted from one to the other uncomprehendingly, wondering why, if his boy's life was in danger, they talked so much instead of doing something.

Twice he had to pluck at Andre's sleeve to get a word in edgewise.

"Let me go and look for him myself," he begged.

What could he do? The hunt had widened now. A description of ex-Sergeant Loubet had been passed to all police stations and patrols.

It was no longer only a boy of ten who was being looked for, but also a man of fifty-eight, probably the worse for drink, dressed in a black overcoat with a velvet collar and an old grey-felt hat, a man who knew his Paris like the palm of his hand, and who was acquainted with the police.

Janvier had returned, looking fresher than the men there in spite of his night's vigil.

"She tried to slam the door in my face, but I'd taken the precaution of sticking my foot in. She doesn't know anything. She says he's been handing over his pay every month."

"That's why he had to steal. He didn't need big sums. In fact, he wouldn't have known what to do with them. What's she like?"

"Small and dark, with piercing eyes. Her hair's dyed a sort of blue. She must have eczema or something of the sort—she wears mittens."

"Did you get a photo of him?"

"There was one on the dining-room sideboard. She wouldn't give it to me, so I just took it."

A heavy-built, florid man, with bulging eyes, who in his youth had probably been the village beau and had conserved an air of stupid arrogance. The photograph was some years old. No doubt he looked quite different now.

"She didn't give you any idea where he was likely to be, did she?"

"As far as I could make out, except at night, when he was supposed to be at work, she kept him pretty well tied to her apron strings. I talked to the concierge, who told me he was scared stiff of his wife. Often she's seen him stagger home in the morning, then suddenly pull himself together when he went upstairs. He goes out shopping with his wife. In fact, he never goes out alone in the daytime. If she goes out when he's in bed, she locks him in."

"What do you think, Lecœur?"

"I'm wondering whether my nephew and he aren't together."

"What do you mean?"

"They weren't together at the beginning, or Loubet would have stopped the boy giving the alarm. There must have been some distance between them. One was following the other."

"Which way round?"

"When the kid climbed up the drainpipe, he thought his father was guilty. Otherwise, why should he have sent him off to the Gare d'Austerlitz, where no doubt he intended to join him after getting rid of the sandwich tin?"

"It looks like it."

"No, Andre. Francois could never have thought—"

"Leave this alone. You don't understand. At that time the crime had certainly been committed. Francois wouldn't have dreamed of burgling someone's flat for a tin box if it hadn't been that he'd seen the body."

"From his window," put in Janvier, "he could see most of the legs."

"What we don't know is whether the murderer was still there."

"I can't believe he was," said Saillard. "If he had been, he'd have kept out of sight, let the boy get into the room, and then done the same to him as he'd done to the old woman."

"Look here, Olivier. When you got home this morning, was the light on?"

"Yes."

"In the boy's room?"

"Yes. It was the first thing I noticed. It gave me a shock. I thought perhaps he was ill."

"So the murderer very likely saw it and feared his crime had had a witness. He certainly wouldn't have expected anyone to climb up the drainpipe. He must have rushed straight out of the house."

"And waited outside to see what would happen."

Guesswork! Yes. But that was all they could do. The important thing was to guess right. For that you had to put yourself in the other chap's place and think as he had thought. The rest was a matter of patrols, of the hundreds of policemen scattered all over Paris, and, lastly, of luck.

937

"Rather than go down the way he'd come, the boy must have left the house by the entrance in the Rue Michat."

"Just a moment, Inspector. By that time he probably knew that his father wasn't the murderer."

"Why?"

"Janvier said just now that Madame Fayet lost a lot of blood. If it had been his father, the blood would have had time to dry up more or less. It was some nine hours since Francois had seen him in the room. It was on leaving the house that he found out who had done it, whether it was Loubet or not. The latter wouldn't know whether the boy had seen him up in the room. Francois would have been scared and taken to his heels."

This time it was the boy's father who interrupted. "No. Not if he knew there was a big reward offered. Not if he knew I'd lost my job. Not if he'd seen me go to the old woman to borrow some money."

The Inspector and Andre Lecœur exchanged glances. They had to admit Olivier was right, and it made them afraid.

No, it had to be pictured otherwise. A dark, deserted street in an outlying quarter of Paris two hours before dawn.

On the other hand, the ex-policeman, obsessed by his sense of grievance, who had just committed his ninth murder to revenge himself on the society that had spurned him, and perhaps still more to prove to himself he was still a man by defying the whole police force—indeed, the whole world.

Was he drunk again? On a night like that, when the bars were open long after their usual closing time, he had no doubt had more than ever. And in that dark, silent street, what did he see with his bulging drink-inflamed eyes? A young boy, the first person who had found him out, and who would now—

"I'd like to know whether he's got a gun on him," sighed the Inspector.

Janvier answered at once:

"I asked his wife. It seems he always carries one about. An automatic pistol, but it's not loaded."

"How can she know that?"

"Once or twice, when he was more than usually drunk, he rounded on her, threatening her with the gun. After that, she got hold of his ammunition and locked it up, telling him an unloaded pistol was quite enough to frighten people without his having to fire it."

Had those two really stalked each other through the streets of Paris? A strange sort of duel in which the man had the strength and the boy the speed?

The boy may well have been scared, but the man stood for something precious enough to push fear into the background: a fortune and the end of his father's worries and humiliations.

*

Having got so far, there wasn't a lot more to be said by the little group of people waiting in the Préfecture de Police. They sat gazing at the street-plan with a picture in their minds of a boy following a man, the boy no doubt keeping his distance. Everyone else was sleeping. There was no one in the streets who could be a help to the one or a menace to the other. Had Loubet produced his gun in an attempt to frighten the boy away?

When people woke up and began coming out into the streets, what would the boy do then? Would he rush up to the first person he met and start screaming "Murder"?

"Yes. It was Loubet who walked in front," said Saillard slowly.

"And it was I," put in Andre Lecœur, "who told the boy all about the pillar telephone system."

The little crosses came to life. What had at first been mysterious was now almost simple. But it was tragic.

The child was risking his skin to save his father. Tears were slowly trickling down the latter's face. He made no attempt to hide them.

He was in a strange place, surrounded by outlandish objects, and by people who talked to him as though he wasn't there, as though he was someone else. And his brother was among these people, a brother he could hardly recognize and whom he regarded with instinctive respect.

Even when they did speak, it wasn't necessary to say much. They understood each other. A word sufficed.

"Loubet couldn't go home, of course."

Andre Lecœur smiled suddenly as a thought struck him.

"It didn't occur to him that Francois hadn't a centime in his pocket. He could have escaped by diving into the Métro."

No. That wouldn't hold water. The boy had seen him and would give his description.

Place du Trocadéro, the Etoile. The time was passing. It was practically broad daylight. People were up and about. Why hadn't Francois called for help? Anyhow, with people in the streets it was no longer possible for Loubet to kill him.

The Inspector was deep in thought.

"For one reason or another," he murmured, "I think they're going about together now."

At the same moment, a lamp lit up on the wall. As though he knew it would be for him, Lecœur answered in place of Bedeau.

"Yes. I thought as much."

"It's about the two oranges. They found an Arab boy asleep in the third-class waiting room at the Gare du Nord. He still had the oranges in his pockets. He'd run away from home because his father had beaten him."

"Do you think Bib's dead?"

"If he was dead, Loubet would have gone home, as he would no longer have anything to fear."

So the struggle was still going on somewhere in this now sunny Paris in which families were sauntering along the boulevards taking the air.

It would be the fear of losing him in the crowd that had brought Francois close to his quarry. Why didn't he call for help? No doubt because Loubet had threatened him with his gun. "One word from you, my lad, and I'll empty this into your guts."

So each was pursuing his own goal: for the one to shake off the boy somehow, for the other to watch for the moment when the murderer was off his guard and give the alarm before he had time to shoot.

It was a matter of life and death.

"Loubet isn't likely to be in the center of the town, where policemen are too plentiful for his liking, to say nothing of the fact that many of them know him by sight."

Their most likely direction from the Etoile was towards Montmartre—not to the amusement quarter, but to the remoter and quieter parts.

It was half past two. Had they had anything to eat? Had Loubet, with his mind set on escape, been able to resist the temptation to drink?

"Monsieur le Commissaire—"

Andre Lecœur couldn't speak with the assurance he would have liked. He couldn't get rid of the feeling that he was an upstart, if not a usurper.

"I know there are thousands of little bars in Paris. But if we chose the more likely districts and put plenty of men on the job—"

Not only were all the men there roped in, but Saillard got through to the Police Judiciaire, where there were six men on duty, and set every one of them to work on six different telephone lines.

"Hallo! Is that the Bar des Amis? In the course of the day have you seen a middle-aged man accompanied by a boy of ten? The man's wearing a black overcoat and a—"

Again Lecœur made little crosses, not in his notebook this time, but in the telephone directory. There were ten pages of bars, some of them with the weirdest names.

A plan of Paris was spread out on a table all ready and it was in a little alley of ill-repute behind the Place Clichy that the Inspector was able to make the first mark in red chalk.

"Yes, there was a man of that description here about twelve o'clock. He drank three glasses of Calvados and ordered a glass of white wine for the boy.

The boy didn't want to drink at first, but he did in the end and he wolfed a couple of eggs."

By the way Olivier Lecœur's face lit up, you might have thought he heard his boy's voice.

"You don't know which way they went?"

"Towards the Boulevard des Batignolles, I think. The man looked as though he'd already had one or two before he came in."

"Hallo! Zanzi-Bar? Have you at any time seen a—"

It became a refrain. As soon as one man had finished, the same words, or practically the same, were repeated by his neighbor.

Rue Damrémont. Montmartre again, only farther out this time. One-thirty. Loubet had broken a glass, his movements by this time being somewhat clumsy. The boy got up and made off in the direction of the lavatory, but when the man followed, he thought better of it and went back to his seat.

"Yes. The boy did look a bit frightened. As for the man, he was laughing and smirking as though he was enjoying a huge joke."

"Do you hear that, Olivier? Bib was still there at one-forty."

Andre Lecœur dared not say what was in his mind. The struggle was nearing its climax. Now that Loubet had really started drinking if was just a question of time. The only thing was: would the boy wait long enough?

It was all very well for Madame Loubet to say the gun wasn't loaded. The butt of an automatic was quite hard enough to crack a boy's skull.

His eyes wandered to his brother, and he had a vision of what Olivier might well have come to if his asthma hadn't prevented him drinking.

"Hallo! Yes. Where? Boulevard Ney?"

They had reached the outskirts of Paris. The ex-Sergeant seemed still to have his wits about him. Little by little, in easy stages, he was leading the boy to one of those outlying districts where there were still empty building sites and desolate spaces.

Three police cars were promptly switched to that neighborhood, as well as every available *agent cycliste* within reach. Even Janvier dashed off, taking the Inspector's little car, and it was all they could do to prevent Olivier from running after him.

"I tell you, you'd much better stay here. He may easily go off on a false trail, and then you won't know anything."

Nobody had time for making coffee. The men of the second day shift had not thoroughly warmed to the case. Everyone was strung up.

"Hallo! Yes. Orient Bar. What is it?"

It was Andre Lecœur who took the call. With the receiver to his ear, he rose to his feet, making queer signs that brought the whole room to a hush.

"What? Don't speak so close to the mouthpiece."

In the silence, the others could hear a high-pitched voice.

"It's for the police! Tell the police I've got him! The killer! Hallo? What? Is that Uncle Andre?"

The voice was lowered a tone to say shakily: "I tell you, I'll shoot, Uncle Andre."

Lecœur hardly knew to whom he handed the receiver. He dashed out of the room and up the stairs, almost breaking down the door of the room.

"Quick, all cars to the Orient Bar, Porte Clignancourt."

And without waiting to hear the message go out, he dashed back as fast as he'd come. At the door he stopped dead, struck by the calm that had suddenly descended on the room.

It was Saillard who held the receiver into which, in the thickest of Parisian dialects, a voice was saying:

"It's all right. Don't worry. I gave the chap a crack on the head with a bottle. Laid him out properly. God knows what he wanted to do to the kid. What's that? You want to speak to him? Here, little one, come here. And give me your popgun. I don't like those toys. Why, it isn't loaded."

Another voice. "Is that Uncle Andre?"

The Inspector looked round, and it was not to Andre but to Olivier that he handed the receiver.

"Uncle Andre. I got him."

"Bib! It's me."

"What are you doing there, Dad?"

"Nothing. Waiting to hear from you. It's been—"

"You can't think how bucked I am. Wait a moment, here's the police. They're just arriving."

Confused sounds. Voices, the shuffling of feet, the clink of glasses. Olivier Lecœur listened, standing there awkwardly, gazing at the wall-map which he did not see, his thoughts far away at the northern extremity of Paris, in a windswept boulevard.

"They're taking me with them."

Another voice. "Is that you, Chief? Janvier here."

One might have thought it was Olivier Lecœur who had been knocked on the head with a bottle by the way he held the receiver out, staring blankly in front of him.

"He's out, right out, Chief. They're lugging him away now. When the boy heard the telephone ringing, he decided it was his chance. He grabbed Loubet's gun from his pocket and made a dash for the phone. The proprietor here's a pretty tough nut. If it hadn't been for—"

A little lamp lit up in the plan of Paris.

"Hallo! Your car's gone out?"

"Someone's smashed the glass of the pillar telephone in the Place Clignancourt. Says there's a row going on in a bar. I'll ring up again when we know what's going on."

It wouldn't be necessary.

Nor was it necessary for Andre Lecœur to put a cross in his notebook under Miscellaneous.

—translated by Geoffrey Sainsbury

Margery Allingham

MURDER UNDER THE MISTLETOE

$\mathbf{M}$urder under the mistletoe—and the man who must have done it couldn't have done it. That's my Christmas and I don't feel merry thank you very much all the same." Superintendent Stanislaus Oates favored his old friend Mr. Albert Campion with a pained smile and sat down in the chair indicated.

It was the afternoon of Christmas Day and Mr. Campion, only a trifle more owlish than usual behind his horn rims, had been fetched down from the children's party which he was attending at his brother-in-law's house in Knightsbridge to meet the Superintendent, who had moved heaven and earth to find him.

"What do you want?" Mr. Campion inquired facetiously. "A little armchair miracle?"

"I don't care if you do it swinging from a trapeze. I just want a reasonable explanation." Oates was rattled. His dyspeptic face with the perpetually sad expression was slightly flushed and not with festivity. He plunged into his story.

"About eleven last night a crook called Sampson was found shot dead in the back of a car in a garage under a small drinking club in Alcatraz Mews—the club is named The Humdinger. A large bunch of mistletoe which had been lying on the front seat ready to be driven home had been placed on top of the body partially hiding it—which was why it hadn't been found before. The gun, fitted with a silencer, but wiped of prints, was found under the front seat. The dead man was recognized at once by the owner of the car who is also the owner of the club. He was the owner's current boyfriend. She is quite a well-known West End character called 'Girlski.' What did you say?"

"I said, 'Oo-er'," murmured Mr. Campion. "One of the Eumenides, no doubt?"

"No." Oates spoke innocently. "She's not a Greek. Don't worry about her. Just keep your mind on the facts. She knows, as we do, that the only person who wanted to kill Sampson is a nasty little snake called Kroll. He has been out of circulation for the best of reasons. Sampson turned Queen's evidence against him in a matter concerning a conspiracy to rob Her Majesty's mails and when he was released last Tuesday Kroll came out breathing retribution."

"Not the Christmas spirit," said Mr. Campion inanely.

"That is exactly what *we* thought," Oates agreed. "So about five o'clock yesterday afternoon two of our chaps, hearing that Kroll was at The Humdinger, where he might have been expected to make trouble, dropped along there and brought him in for questioning and he's been in custody ever since.

"Well, now. We have at least a dozen reasonably sober witnesses to prove that Kroll did not meet Sampson at the Club. Sampson had been there earlier in the afternoon but he left about a quarter to four saying he'd got to do some Christmas shopping but promising to return. Fifteen minutes or so later Kroll came in and stayed there in full view of Girlski and the customers until our men turned up and collected him. *Now* what do you say?"

"Too easy!" Mr. Campion was suspicious. "Kroll killed Sampson just before he came in himself. The two met in the dusk outside the club. Kroll forced Sampson into the garage and possibly into the car and shot him. With the way the traffic has been lately, he'd hardly have attracted attention had he used a mortar, let alone a gun with a silencer. He wiped the weapon, chucked it in the car, threw the mistletoe over the corpse, and went up to Girlski to renew old acquaintance and establish an alibi. Your chaps, arriving when they did, must have appeared welcome."

Oates nodded. "We thought that. *That is what happened.* That is why this morning's development has set me gibbering. We now have two unimpeachable witnesses who swear that the dead man was in Chipperwood West at six last evening delivering some Christmas purchases he had made on behalf of a neighbor. That is *a whole hour* after Kroll was pulled in.

"The assumption is that Sampson returned to Alcatraz Mews sometime later in the evening and was killed by someone else—which we know is not true. Unfortunately, the Chipperwood West witnesses are not the kind of people we are going to shake. One of them is a friend of yours. She asked our Inspector if he knew you because you were 'so good at crime and all that nonsense'."

"Good Heavens!" Mr. Campion spoke piously as the explanation of the Superintendent's unlikely visitation was made plain to him. "I don't think I know Chipperwood West."

"It's a suburb which is becoming fashionable. Have you ever heard of Lady Larradine?"

"Old Lady 'ell?" Mr. Campion let the joke of his salad days escape without its being noticed by either of them. "I don't believe it. She must be dead by this time!"

"There's a type of woman who never dies before you do," said Oates with apparent sincerity. "She's quite a dragon, I understand from our Inspector. However, she isn't the actual witness. There are two of them. Brigadier Brose is one. Ever heard of *him?*"

"I don't think I have."

"My information is that you'd remember him if you'd met him. Well, we'll find out. I'm taking you with me, Campion. I hope you don't mind?"

"My sister will hate it. I'm due to be Santa Claus in about an hour."

"I can't help that." Oates was adamant. "If a bunch of silly crooks want to get spiteful at the festive season, someone must do the homework. Come and play Santa Claus with me. It's your last chance. I'm retiring this summer."

Oates continued in the same vein as he and Mr. Campion sat in the back of a police car threading their way through the deserted Christmas streets where the lamps were growing bright in the dusk.

"I've had bad luck lately," the Superintendent said seriously. "Too much. It won't help my memoirs if I go out in a blaze of no-enthusiasm."

"You're thinking of the Phaeton Robbery," Mr. Campion suggested. "What are you calling your memoirs? *Man-Eaters of the Yard?*"

Oates's mild old eyes brightened, but not greatly.

"Something of the kind," he admitted. "But no one could be blamed for not solving that blessed Phaeton business. Everyone concerned was bonkers. A silly old musical star, for thirty years the widow of an eccentric Duke, steps out into her London garden one autumn morning leaving the street door wide open and all her most valuable jewelry collected from strong-rooms all over the country lying in a brown paper parcel on her bureau in the first room off the hall. Her excuse was that she was just going to take it to the Bond Street auctioneers and was carrying it herself for safety! The thief was equally mental to lift it."

"It wasn't saleable?"

"Saleable? It couldn't even be broken up. The stuff is just about as well-known as the Crown Jewels. Great big enamels which the old Duke had collected at great expense. No fence would stay in the same room with them, yet, of course, they are worth the Earth as every newspaper has told us at length ever since they were pinched!"

"He didn't get anything else either, did he?"

"He was a madman." Oates dismissed him with contempt. "All he gained was the old lady's housekeeping money for a couple of months which was in her handbag—about a hundred and fifty quid—and the other two items which were on the same shelf, a soapstone monkey and a plated paperknife. He simply wandered in, took the first things he happened to see and wandered out again. Any sneak thief, tramp, or casual snapper-upper could have done it and who gets blamed? *Me!*"

He looked so woebegone that Mr. Campion hastily changed the subject. "Where are we going?" he inquired. "To call on her ladyship? Do I understand that at the age of one hundred and forty-six or whatever it is she is cohabiting with a Brig? Which war?"

"I can't tell you." Oates was literal as usual. "It could be the South African. They're all in a nice residential hotel—the sort of place that is very popular with the older members of the landed gentry just now."

"When you say landed, you mean as in Fish?"

"Roughly, yes. Elderly people living on capital. About forty of them. This place used to be called *The Haven* and has now been taken over by two ex-society widows and renamed *The Ccraven*—with two Cs. It's a select hotel-cum-Old Ducks' Home for Mother's Friends. You know the sort of place?"

"I can envisage it. Don't say your murdered chum from The Humdinger lived there too?"

"No, he lived in a more modest place whose garden backs on the CCraven's grounds. The Brigadier and one of the other residents, a Mr. Charlie Taunton, who has become a bosom friend of his, were in the habit of talking to Sampson over the wall. Taunton is a lazy man who seldom goes out and has little money but he very much wanted to get some gifts for his fellow guests—something in the nature of little jokes from the chain stores, I understand; but he dreaded the exertion of shopping for them and Sampson appears to have offered to get him some little items wholesale and to deliver them by six o'clock on Christmas Eve—in time for him to package them up and hand them to Lady Larradine who was dressing the tree at seven."

"And did you say Sampson actually did this?" Mr. Campion sounded bewildered.

"Both old gentlemen—the Brigadier and Taunton—swear to it. They insist they went down to the wall at six and Sampson handed the parcel over as arranged. My Inspector is an experienced man and he doesn't think we'll be able to shake either of them."

"That leaves Kroll with a complete alibi. How did these Chipperwood witnesses hear of Sampson's death?"

"Routine. The local police called at Sampson's home address this morning to report the death, only to discover the place closed. The landlady and her family are away for the holiday and Sampson himself was due to spend it with Girlski. The police stamped about a bit, making sure of all this, and in the course of their investigations they were seen and hailed by the two old boys in the adjoining garden. The two were shocked to hear that their kind acquaintance was dead and volunteered the information that he had been with them at six."

Mr. Campion looked blank. "Perhaps they don't keep the same hours as anybody else," he suggested. "Old people can be highly eccentric."

Oates shook his head. "We thought of that. My Inspector, who came down the moment the local police reported, insists that they are perfectly normal and quite positive. Moreover, they had the purchases. He saw the packages already on the tree. Lady Larradine pointed them out to him when she asked after you. She'll be delighted to see you, Campion."

"I can hardly wait!"

"You don't have to," said Oates grimly as they pulled up before a huge Edwardian villa. "It's all yours."

"My dear Boy! You haven't aged any more than I have!"

Lady Larradine's tremendous voice—one of her chief terrors, Mr. Campion recollected—echoed over the crowded first-floor room where she received them. There she stood in an outmoded but glittering evening gown looking, as always, exactly like a spray-flecked seal.

"I *knew* you'd come," she bellowed. "As soon as you got my oblique little S.O.S. How do you like our little hideout? Isn't it *fun*! Moira Spryg-Fysher and Janice Poole-Poole wanted something to do, so we all put our pennies in it and here we are!"

"Almost too marvelous," murmured Mr. Campion in all sincerity. "We really want a word with Brigadier Brose and Mr. Taunton."

"Of course you do and so you shall! We're all waiting for the Christmas tree. Everybody will be there for that in about ten minutes in the drawing room. My dear, when *we* came they were calling it the Residents' Lounge!"

Superintendent Oates remained grave. He was startled to discover that the dragon was not only fierce but also wily. The news that her apparently casual mention of Mr. Campion to the Inspector had been a ruse to get hold of him shocked the innocent Superintendent. He retaliated by insisting that he must see the witnesses at once.

Lady Larradine silenced him with a friendly roar. "My dear man, you can't! They've gone for a walk. I always turn men out of the house after Christmas luncheon. They'll soon be back. The Brigadier won't miss his Tree! Ah. Here's Fiona. This is Janice Poole-Poole's daughter, Albert. Isn't she a pretty girl?"

Mr. Campion saw Miss Poole-Poole with relief, knowing of old that Oates was susceptible to the type. The newcomer was young and lovely and even her beehive hair and the fact that she appeared to have painted herself with two black eyes failed to spoil the exquisite smile she bestowed on the helpless officer.

"Fabulous to have you really here," she said and sounded as if she meant it. While he was still recovering, Lady Larradine led Oates to the window.

"You can't see it because it's pitch-dark," she said, "but out there, down in the garden, there's a wall and it was over it that the Brigadier and Mr. Taunton spoke to Mr. Sampson at six o'clock last night. No one liked the man Sampson—

I think Mr. Taunton was almost afraid of him. Certainly he seems to have died very untidily!"

"But he *did* buy Mr. Taunton's Christmas gifts for him?"

The dragon lifted a webby eyelid. "You have already been told that. At six last night Mr. Taunton and the Brigadier went to meet him to get the box. I got them into their mufflers so I know! I had the packing paper ready, too, for Mr. Taunton to take up to his room . . . Rather a small one on the third floor."

She lowered her voice to reduce it to the volume of distant traffic. "Not many pennies, but a dear little man!"

"Did you *see* these presents, Ma'am?"

"Not before they were wrapped! That would have spoiled the surprise!"

"I shall have to see them." There was a mulish note in the Superintendent's voice which the lady was too experienced to ignore.

"I've thought how to do that without upsetting anybody," she said briskly. "The Brigadier and I will cut the presents from the Tree and Fiona will be handing them round. All Mr. Taunton's little gifts are in the very distinctive black and gold paper I bought from Millie's Boutique and so, Fiona, you must give every package in black and gold not to the person to whom it is addressed but to the Superintendent. Can you do that, dear?"

Miss Poole-Poole seemed to feel the task difficult but not impossible and the trusting smile she gave Oates cut short his objection like the sun melting frost.

"Splendid!" The dragon's roar was hearty. "Give me your arm, Superintendent. You shall take me down."

As the procession reached the hall, it ran into the Brigadier himself. He was a large, pink man, affable enough, but of a martial type and he bristled at the Superintendent. "Extraordinary time to do your business—middle of Christmas Day!" he said after acknowledging the introductions.

Oates inquired if he had enjoyed his walk.

"Talk?" said the Brigadier. "I've not been talking. I've been asleep in the card room. Where's old Taunton?"

"He went for a walk, Athole dear," bellowed the dragon gaily.

"So he did. You sent him! Poor feller."

As the old soldier led the way to the open door of the drawing room, it occurred to both the Superintendent and Mr. Campion that the secret of Lady Larradine's undoubted attraction for the Brigadier lay in the fact that he could hear *her* if no one else. The discovery cast a new light altogether on the story of the encounter with Sampson in the garden.

Meanwhile, they had entered the drawing room and the party had begun. As Mr. Campion glanced at the company, ranged in a full circle round a magnificent tree loaded with gifts and sparkling like a waterfall, he saw face after familiar face. They were elder acquaintances of the dizzy 1930s whom he had mourned as gone forever, when he thought of them at all. Yet here they all were, not only alive but released by great age from many of the restraints of convention.

He noticed that every type of headgear from night-cap to tiara was being sported with fine individualistic enthusiasm. But Lady Larradine gave him little time to look about. She proceeded with her task immediately.

Each guest had been provided with a small invalid table beside his armchair, and Oates, reluctant but wax in Fiona's hands, was no exception. The Superintendent found himself seated between a mountain in flannel and a wraith in mauve mink, waiting his turn with the same beady-eyed avidity.

Christmas Tree procedure at the CCraven proved to be well organized. The dragon did little work herself. Armed with a swagger stick, she merely prodded parcel after parcel hanging amid the boughs while the task of detaching them was performed by the Brigadier who handed them to Fiona. Either to add to the excitement or perhaps to muffle any unfortunate comment on gifts received by the uninhibited company, jolly Christmas music was played throughout, and under cover of the noise Mr. Campion was able to tackle his hostess.

"Where is Taunton?" he whispered.

"Such a nice little man. Most presentable, but just a little teeny-weeny bit dishonest."

Lady Larradine ignored the question in his eyes and continued to put him in the picture at great speed, while supervising the Tree at the same time. "Fifty-seven convictions, I believe, but only small ones. I only got it all out of him last week. Shattering! He'd been so *useful*, amusing the Brigadier. When he came, he looked like a lost soul with no luggage, but after no time at all he settled in perfectly."

She paused and stabbed at a ball of colored cellophane with her stick before returning to her startled guest.

"Albert, I am terribly afraid that it was poor Mr. Taunton who took that dreadful jewelry of Maisie Phaeton's. It appears to have been entirely her fault. He was merely wandering past her house, feeling in need of care and attention. The door was wide open and Mr. Taunton suddenly found himself inside, picking up a few odds and ends. When he discovered from all that fuss in the newspapers what he had got hold of—how well-known it was, I mean—he was quite horrified and had to hide. And where better place than here with us where he never had to go out?"

"Where indeed!" Mr. Campion dared not glance across the room at the Superintendent unwrapping his black and gold parcels. "Where is he now? Poor Mr. Taunton, I mean."

"Of course I hadn't the faintest idea what was worrying the man until he

950

confessed," the dragon went on stonily. "Then I realized that something would have to be done at once to protect everybody. The wretch had hidden all that frightful stuff in our toolshed for three months, not daring to keep it in the house; and to make matters worse, the impossible person at the end of the garden, Mr. Sampson, had recognized him and *would* keep speaking. Apparently people in the—er—underworld all know each other just like those of us in—er—other closed circles do."

Mr. Campion, whose hair was standing on end, had a moment of inspiration. "This absurd rigmarole about Taunton getting Sampson to buy him some Christmas gifts wholesale was *your* idea!" he said accusingly.

The dragon stared. "It seemed the best way of getting Maisie's jewelry back to her without any *one* person being involved," she said frankly. "I knew we should all recognize the things the moment we saw them and I was certain that after a lot of argument we should decide to pack them up and send them round to her. But, if there *were* any repercussions, we should *all* be in it—quite a formidable array, dear Boy—and the blame could be traced to Mr. Sampson if absolutely necessary. You see, the Brigadier is convinced that Sampson *was* there last night. Mr. Taunton very cleverly left him on the lawn and went behind the tool shed and came back with the box."

"How completely immoral!" Mr. Campion couldn't restrain himself.

The dragon had the grace to look embarrassed.

"I don't think the Sampson angle would ever have arisen," she said. "But if it had, Sampson was quite a terrible person. Almost a blackmailer. Utterly dishonest and inconsiderate. Think how he has spoiled everything and endangered us all by getting himself killed on the *one* afternoon when we said he was here, so that the police were brought in. Just the *one* thing I was trying to avoid. When the Inspector appeared this morning I was so upset I thought of you!"

In his not unnatural alarm Mr. Campion so far forgot himself as to touch her sleeve. "Where is Taunton now?"

The dragon threshed her train. "Really, Boy! What a fidget you are! If you must know, I gave him his Christmas present—every penny I had in cash for he was broke again, he told me—and sent him for a nice long walk after lunch. Having seen the Inspector here this morning he was glad to go."

She paused and a granite gleam came into her hooded eyes. "If that Superintendent friend of yours has the stupidity to try to find him once Maisie has her monstrosities back, none of us will be able to identify him, I'm afraid. And there's another thing. If the Brigadier should be *forced* to give evidence, I am sure he will stick to his guns about Mr. Sampson being down in the garden here at six o'clock last night. That would mean that the man Kroll would have to go unpunished for his revenge murder, wouldn't it? Sampson was a terrible person—but *no one* should have killed him."

Mr. Campion was silenced. He glanced fearfully across the room.

The Superintendent was seated at his table wearing the strained yet slap-happy expression of a man with concussion. On his left was a pile of black and gold wrappings, on his right a rajah's ransom in somewhat specialized form.

From where he stood, Mr. Campion could see two examples amid the rest—a breastplate in gold, pearl, and enamel in the shape of a unicorn and an item which looked like a plover's egg in tourmaline encased in a ducal coronet. There was also a soapstone monkey and a solid-silver paperknife.

Much later that evening Mr. Campion and the Superintendent drove quietly back to headquarters. Oates had a large cardboard box on his knee. He clasped it tenderly.

He had been silent for a long time when a thought occurred to him. "Why did they take him into the house in the first place?" he said. "An elderly crook looking lost! And no luggage!"

Mr. Campion's pale eyes flickered behind his spectacles.

"Don't forget the Duchess' housekeeping money," he murmured. "I should think he offered one of the widows who really run that place the first three months' payment in cash, wouldn't you? That must be an impressive phenomenon in that sort of business, I fancy."

Oates caught his breath and fell silent once more. Presently he burst out again.

"Those people! That woman!" he exploded. "When they were younger they led me a pretty dance—losing things or getting themselves swindled. But now they're old they take the blessed biscuit! Do you see how she's tied my hands, Campion?"

Mr. Campion tried not to grin.

"Snapdragons are just permissible at Christmas," he said. "Handled with extreme caution they burn very few fingers, it seems to me."

Mr. Campion tapped the cardboard box. "And some of them provide a few plums for retiring coppers, don't they, Superintendent?"

Patricia Moyes

WHO KILLED FATHER CHRISTMAS?

"Good morning, Mr. Borrowdale. Nippy out, isn't it? You're in early, I see." Little Miss MacArthur spoke with her usual brisk brightness, which failed to conceal both envy and dislike. She was unpacking a consignment of stout Teddy bears in the stockroom behind the toy department at Barnum and Thrums, the London store. "Smart as ever, Mr. Borrowdale," she added, jealously.

I laid down my curly-brimmed bowler hat and cane and took off my British warm overcoat. I don't mind admitting that I do take pains to dress as well as I can, and for some reason it seems to infuriate the Miss MacArthurs of the world.

She prattled on. "Nice looking, these Teddies, don't you think? Very reasonable, too. Made in Hong Kong, that'll be why. I think I'll take one for my sister's youngest."

The toy department at Barnum's has little to recommend it to anyone over the age of twelve, and normally it is tranquil and little populated. However, at Christmastime it briefly becomes the bustling heart of the great shop, and also provides useful vacation jobs for chaps like me who wish to earn some money during the weeks before the university term begins in January. Gone, I fear, are the days when undergraduates were the gilded youth of England. We all have to work our passages these days, and sometimes it means selling toys.

One advantage of the job is that employees—even temporaries like me—are allowed to buy goods at a considerable discount, which helps with the Christmas gift problem. As a matter of fact, I had already decided to buy a Teddy bear for one of my nephews, and I mentioned as much.

"Well, you'd better take it right away," remarked Miss MacArthur, "because I heard Mr. Harrington say he was taking two, and I think Disaster has her eye on one." Disaster was the unfortunate but inevitable nickname of Miss Aster, who had been with the store for thirty-one years but still made mistakes with her stockbook. I felt sorry for the old girl. I had overheard a conversation between Mr. Harrington, the department manager, and Mr. Andrews, the deputy store manager, and so I knew—but Disaster didn't—that she would be getting the sack as soon as the Christmas rush was over.

Meanwhile, Miss MacArthur was arranging the bears on a shelf. They sat there in grinning rows, brown and woolly, with boot-button eyes and red ribbons round their necks.

It was then that Father Christmas came in. He'd been in the cloakroom changing into his costume—white beard, red nose, and all. His name was Bert Denman. He was a cheery soul who got on well with the kids, and he'd had the Father Christmas job at Barnum's each of the three years I'd been selling there. Now he was carrying his sack, which he filled every morning from the cheap items in the stockroom. A visit to Father Christmas cost 50 pence, so naturally the gift that was fished out of the sack couldn't be worth more than 20 pence. However, to my surprise, he went straight over to the row of Teddy bears and picked one off the shelf. For some reason, he chose the only one with a blue instead of a red ribbon.

Miss MacArthur was on to him in an instant. "What d'you think you're doing, Mr. Denman? Those Teddies aren't in your line at all—much too dear. One pound ninety, they are."

Father Christmas did not answer, and suddenly I realized that it was not Bert Denman under the red robe. "Wait a minute," I said. "Who are you? You're not our Father Christmas."

He turned to face me, the Teddy bear in his hand. "That's all right," he said. "Charlie Burrows is my name. I live in the same lodging house with Bert Denman. He was taken poorly last night, and I'm standing in for him."

"*Well*," said Miss MacArthur. "How very odd. Does Mr. Harrington know?"

"Of course he does," said Father Christmas.

As if on cue, Mr. Harrington himself came hurrying into the stockroom. He always hurried everywhere, preceded by his small black mustache. He said, "Ah, there you are, Burrows. Fill up your sack, and I'll explain the job to you. Denman told you about the Teddy bear, did he?"

"Yes, Mr. Harrington."

"Father Christmas can't give away an expensive bear like that, Mr. Harrington," Miss MacArthur objected.

"Now, now, Miss MacArthur, it's all arranged," said Harrington fussily. "A customer came in yesterday and made a special request that Father Christmas should give his small daughter a Teddy bear this morning. I knew this consignment was due on the shelves, so I promised him one. It's been paid for. The important thing, Burrows, is to remember the child's name. It's . . . er . . . I have it written down somewhere."

"Annabel Whitworth," said Father Christmas. "Four years old, fair hair, will be brought in by her mother."

"I see that Denman briefed you well," said Mr. Harrington, with an icy smile. "Well, now, I'll collect two bears for myself—one for my son and one for my neighbor's boy—and then I'll show you the booth."

Miss Aster arrived just then. She and Miss MacArthur finished uncrating the bears and took one out to put on display next to a female doll that, among other endearing traits, actually wet its diaper. Mr. Harrington led our surrogate Father Christmas to his small canvas booth, and the rest of us busied and braced ourselves for the moment when the great glass doors opened and the floodtide was let in. The toy department of a big store on December 23 is no place for weaklings.

It is curious that even such an apparently random stream of humanity as Christmas shoppers displays a pattern of behavior. The earliest arrivals in the toy department are office workers on their way to their jobs. The actual toddlers, bent on an interview with Father Christmas, do not appear until their mothers have had time to wash up breakfast, have a bit of a go around the house, and catch the bus from Kensington or the tube from Uxbridge.

On that particular morning it was just twenty-eight minutes past ten when I saw Disaster, who was sitting in a decorated cash desk labeled "The Elfin Grove," take 50 pence from the first parent to usher her child into Santa's booth. For about two minutes the mother waited, chatting quietly with Disaster. Then a loudly wailing infant emerged from the booth.

The mother snatched her up, and—with that sixth sense that mothers everywhere seem to develop—interpreted the incoherent screams. "She says that Father Christmas won't talk to her. She says he's asleep."

It was clearly an emergency, even if a minor one, and Disaster was already showing signs of panic. I excused myself from my customer—a middle-aged gentleman who was playing with an electric train set—and went over to see what I could do. By then, the mother was indignant.

"Fifty pence and the old man sound asleep and drunk as like as not, and at half-past ten in the morning. Disgraceful, I call it. And here's poor little Poppy what had been looking forward to—"

I rushed into Father Christmas's booth. The man who called himself Charlie Burrows was slumped forward in his chair, looking for all the world as if he were asleep; but when I shook him, his head lolled horribly, and it was obvious that he was more than sleeping. The red robe concealed the blood until it made my hand sticky. Father Christmas had been stabbed in the back, and he was certainly dead.

I acted as fast as I could. First of all, I told Disaster to put up the CLOSED sign outside Santa's booth. Then I smoothed down Poppy's mother by leading her to a counter where I told her she could select any toy up to one pound and have it free. Under pretext of keeping records, I got her name and address. Finally I cornered Mr. Harrington in his office and told him the news.

I thought he was going to faint. "Dead? Murdered? Are you sure, Mr. Borrowdale?"

"Quite sure, I'm afraid. You'd better telephone the police, Mr. Harrington."

"The police! In Barnum's! What a terrible thing! I'll telephone the deputy store manager first and *then* the police."

As a matter of fact, the police were surprisingly quick and discreet. A plainclothes detective superintendent and his sergeant, a photographer, and the police doctor arrived, not in a posse, but as individuals, unnoticed among the crowd. They assembled in the booth, where the deputy manager—Mr. Andrews—and Mr. Harrington and I were waiting for them.

The superintendent introduced himself—his name was Armitage—and inspected the body with an expression of cold fury on his face that I couldn't quite understand, although the reason became clear later. He said very little. After some tedious formalities Armitage indicated that the body might be removed.

"What's the least conspicuous way to do it?" he asked.

"You can take him out through the back of the booth," I said. "The canvas overlaps right behind Santa's chair. The door to the staff quarters and the stockroom is just opposite, and from there you can take the service lift to the goods entrance in the mews."

The doctor and the photographer between them carried off their grim burden on a collapsible stretcher, and Superintendent Armitage began asking questions about the arrangements in the Father Christmas booth. I did the explaining, since Mr. Harrington seemed to be verging on hysteria.

Customers paid their 50 pence to Disaster in the Elfin Grove, and then the child—usually alone—was propelled through the door of the booth and into the presence of Father Christmas, who sat in his canvas-backed director's chair on a small dais facing the entrance, with his sack of toys beside him. The child climbed onto his knee, whispered its Christmas wishes, and was rewarded with a few friendly words and a small gift from Santa's sack.

What was not obvious to the clientele was the back entrance to the booth, which enabled Father Christmas to slip in and out unobserved. He usually had his coffee break at about 11:15, unless there was a very heavy rush of business. Disaster would pick a moment when custom seemed slow, put up the CLOSED notice, and inform Bert that he could take a few minutes off. When he returned, he pressed a button by his chair that rang a buzzer in the cashier's booth. Down would come the notice, and Santa was in business again.

Before Superintendent Armitage could comment on my remarks, Mr. Harrington broke into a sort of despairing wait, "It must have been one of the customers!" he cried.

"I don't think so, sir," said Armitage. "This is an inside job. He was stabbed in the back with a long thin blade of some sort. The murderer must have opened the back flap and stabbed him clean through the canvas back of his chair. That must have been someone who knew the exact arrangements. The murderer then used the back way to enter the booth—"

"I don't see how you can say that!" Harrington's voice was rising dangerously. "If the man was stabbed from outside, what makes you think anybody came into the booth?"

"I'll explain that in a minute, sir."

Ignoring Armitage, Harrington went on. "In any case, he wasn't our regular Father Christmas! None of us had ever seen him before. Why on earth would anybody kill a man that nobody knew?"

Armitage and the deputy manager exchanged glances. Then Armitage said, "*I* knew him, sir. Very well. Charlie Burrows was one of our finest plain-clothes narcotics officers."

Mr. Harrington had gone green. "You mean—he was a policeman?"

"Exactly, sir. I'd better explain. A little time ago we got a tipoff from an informer that an important consignment of high-grade heroin was to be smuggled in from Hong Kong in a consignment of Christmas toys. Teddy bears, in fact. The drug was to be in the Barnum and Thrums carton, hidden inside a particular Teddy bear, which would be distinguished by having a blue ribbon around its neck instead of a red one."

"Surely," I said, "you couldn't get what you call an important consignment inside one Teddy bear, even a big one."

Armitage sighed. "Shows you aren't familiar with the drug scene, sir," he said. "Why, half a pound of pure high-grade heroin is worth a fortune on the streets."

With a show of bluster Harrington said, "If you knew this, Superintendent, why didn't you simply intercept the consignment and confiscate the drug? Look at the trouble that's been—"

Armitage interrupted him. "If you'd just hear me out, sir. What I've told you was the sum total of our information. We didn't know who in Barnum's was going to pick up the heroin, or how or where it was to be disposed of. We're more interested in getting the people—the pushers—than confiscating the cargo. So I had a word with Mr. Andrews here, and he kindly agreed to let Charlie take on the Father Christmas job. And Charlie set a little trap. Unfortunately, he paid for it with his life." There was an awkward silence.

He went on. "Mr. Andrews told us that the consignment had arrived and was to be unpacked today. We know that staff get first pick, as it were, at new stock, and we were naturally interested to see who would select the bear with the blue ribbon. It was Charlie's own idea to concoct a story about a special present for a little girl—"

"You mean, that wasn't true?" Harrington was outraged. "But I spoke to the customer myself!"

"Yes, sir. That's to say, you spoke to another of our people, who was posing as the little girl's father."

"You're very thorough," Harrington said.

"Yes, sir. Thank you, sir. Well, as I was saying, Charlie made a point of selecting the bear with the blue ribbon and taking it off in his sack. He knew that whoever was picking up the drop would have to come and get it—or try to. You see, if we'd just allowed one of the staff to select it, that person could simply have said that it was pure coincidence—blue was such a pretty color. Difficult to prove criminal knowledge. You understand?"

Nobody said anything. With quite a sense of dramatic effect Armitage reached down into Santa's sack and pulled out a Teddy bear. It had a blue ribbon round its neck.

In a voice tense with strain Mr. Andrews said, "So the murderer didn't get away with the heroin. I thought you said—"

Superintendent Armitage produced a knife from his pocket. "We'll see," he said. "With your permission, I'm going to open this bear."

"Of course."

The knife ripped through the nobbly brown fabric, and a lot of stuffing fell out. Nothing else. Armitage made a good job of it. By the time he had finished, the bear was in shreds: and nothing had emerged from its interior except kapok.

Armitage surveyed the wreckage with a sort of bleak satisfaction. Suddenly brisk, he said, "Now. Which staff members took bears from the stockroom this morning?"

"I did," I said at once.

"Anybody else?"

There was a silence. I said, "I believe you took two, didn't you, Mr. Harrington?"

"I . . . em . . . yes, now that you mention it."

"Miss MacArthur took one," I said. "It was she who unpacked the carton. She said that Dis—Miss Aster—was going to take one."

"I see." Armitage was making notes. "I presume you each signed for your purchases, and that the bears are now with your things in the staff cloakroom." Without waiting for an answer he turned to me. "How many of these people saw Burrows select the bear with the blue ribbon?"

"All of us," I said. "Isn't that so, Mr. Harrington?"

Harrington just nodded. He looked sick.

"Well, then," said Armitage, "I shall have to inspect all the bears that you people removed from the stockroom."

There was an element of black humor in the parade of the Teddies, with their inane grins and knowing, beady eyes: but as one after the other was dismembered, nothing more sensational was revealed than a growing pile of kapok. The next step was to check the stockbook numbers—and sure enough, one bear was missing.

It was actually Armitage's Sergeant who found it. It had been ripped open and shoved behind a pile of boxes in the stockroom in a hasty attempt at concealment. There was no ribbon round its neck, and it was constructed very differently from the others. The kapok merely served as a thin layer of stuffing between the fabric skin and a spherical womb of pink plastic in the toy's center. This plastic had been cut open and was empty. It was abundantly clear what it must have contained.

"Well," said the Superintendent, "it's obvious what happened. The murderer stabbed Burrows, slipped into the booth, and substituted an innocent Teddy bear for the loaded one, at the same time changing the neck ribbon, But he—or she—didn't dare try walking out of the store with the bear, not after a murder. So, before Charlie's body was found, the murderer dismembered the bear, took out the heroin, and hid it." He sighed again. "I'm afraid this means a body search. I'll call the Yard for a police matron for the ladies."

It was all highly undignified and tedious, and poor old Disaster nearly had a seizure, despite the fact that the police matron seemed a thoroughly nice and kind woman. When it was all over, however, and our persons and clothing had been practically turned inside out, still nothing had been found. The four of us were required to wait in the staff restroom while exhaustive searches were made for both the heroin and the weapon.

Disaster was in tears, Miss MacArthur was loudly indignant and threatened to sue the police for false arrest, and Mr. Harrington developed what he called a nervous stomach, on account, he said, of the way the toy department was being left understaffed and unsupervised on one of the busiest days of the year.

At long last Superintendent Armitage came in. He said, "Nothing. Abso-bloody-lutely nothing. Well, I can't keep you people here indefinitely. I suggest you all go out and get yourselves some lunch." He sounded very tired and cross and almost human.

With considerable relief we prepared to leave the staffroom. Only Mr. Harrington announced that he felt too ill to eat anything, and that he would remain in the department. The Misses MacArthur and Aster left together. I put on my coat and took the escalator down to the ground floor, among the burdened, chattering crowd.

I was out in the brisk air of the street when I heard Armitage's voice behind me.

"Just one moment, if you please, Mr. Borrowdale."

I turned. "Yes, Superintendent. Can I help you?"

"You're up at the university, aren't you, sir? Just taken a temporary job at Barnum's for the vacation?"

"That's right."

"Do quite a bit of fencing, don't you?"

He had my cane out of my hand before I knew what was happening. The sergeant, an extraordinarily tough and unattractive character, showed surprising dexterity and speed in getting an arm grip on me. Armitage had unscrewed the top of the cane, and was whistling in a quiet, appreciative manner. "Very nice. Very nice little sword stick. Something like a stilletto. I don't suppose Charlie felt a thing."

"Now, look here," I said. "You can't make insinuations like that. Just because I'm known as a bit of dandy, and carry a sword stick, that's no reason—"

"A dandy, eh?" said Armitage thoughtfully. He looked me up and down in a curious manner, as if he thought something was missing.

It was at that moment that Miss MacArthur suddenly appeared round the corner of the building.

"Oh, Mr. Borrowdale, look what I found! Lying down in the mews by the goods entrance! It must have fallen out of the staffroom window! Lucky I've got sharp eyes—it was behind a rubbish bin, I might easily have missed it!" And she handed me my bowler hat.

That is to say, she would have done if Armitage hadn't intercepted it. It didn't take him more than five seconds to find the packages of white powder hidden between the hard shell of the hat and the oiled-silk lining.

Armitage said, "So you were going to peddle this stuff to young men and women at the university, were you? Charming, I must say. Now you can come back to the Yard and tell us all about your employers—if you want a chance at saving your own neck, that is."

Miss MacArthur was goggling at me. "Oh, Mr. Borrowdale!" she squeaked. "Have I gone and done something wrong?"

I never did like Miss MacArthur.

ACKNOWLEDGMENTS

"A Matter of Life and Death" by Georges Simenon, copyright © 1952 by Georges Simenon, reprinted by permission of the Author's Estate; "A Winter's Tale" by Ann Cleeves, copyright © 1994 by Ann Cleeves, reprinted by permission of Murray Pollinger Literary Agency; "As Dark as Christmas Gets" by Lawrence Block, copyright © 1997 by Lawrence Block, used by permission of the author; "Believing in Santa" by Ron Goulart, copyright © 1994 by Ron Goulart, reprinted by permission of the author; "Christmas Cop" by Thomas Adcock, copyright © 1986 by Davis Publications, Inc., reprinted by permission of the author; "Christmas Party" by Martin Werner, copyright © 1991 by Davis Publications, Inc., reprinted by permission of the author; "Dead on Christmas Street" by John D. MacDonald, copyright © Dorothy P. MacDonald Trust, reprinted by permission of Diskant Associates; "Grist for the Mills of Christmas" by James Powell, copyright © 1994 by James Powell, reprinted by permission of the author; "I Saw Mommy Killing Santa Claus" by George Baxt, copyright © 1990 by Davis Publications, Inc., reprinted by permission of the author; "Miss Crindle and Father Christmas" by Malcom Gray, copyright © 1990 by Davis Publications, Inc., reprinted by permission of Curtis Brown, Ltd.; "Murder Under the Mistletoe" by Margery Allingham, copyright © 1962 by Margery Allingham, © renewed, reprinted by permission of P. & M. Youngman Carter, Ltd.; "Mystery for Christmas" by Anthony Boucher, copyright © 1942 by Anthony Boucher, reprinted by permission of Curtis Brown, Ltd.; "On Christmas Day in the Morning" by Margery Allingham, copyright © 1952 by P. & M. Youngman Carter, Ltd., reprinted by permission of the Estate; "Pass the Parcel" by Peter Lovesey, copyright © 1994 by Peter Lovesey, reprinted by permission of Gelfman Schneider Literary Agents; "Rumpole and the Chambers Party" by John Mortimer, copyright © 1988 by Advanpress, Ltd., reprinted by permission of Sterling